William Fraser

**The Chiefs of Colquhoun and Their Country**

Volume 1

William Fraser

**The Chiefs of Colquhoun and Their Country**
*Volume 1*

ISBN/EAN: 9783337235413

Printed in Europe, USA, Canada, Australia, Japan

Cover: Foto ©Andreas Hilbeck / pixelio.de

More available books at **www.hansebooks.com**

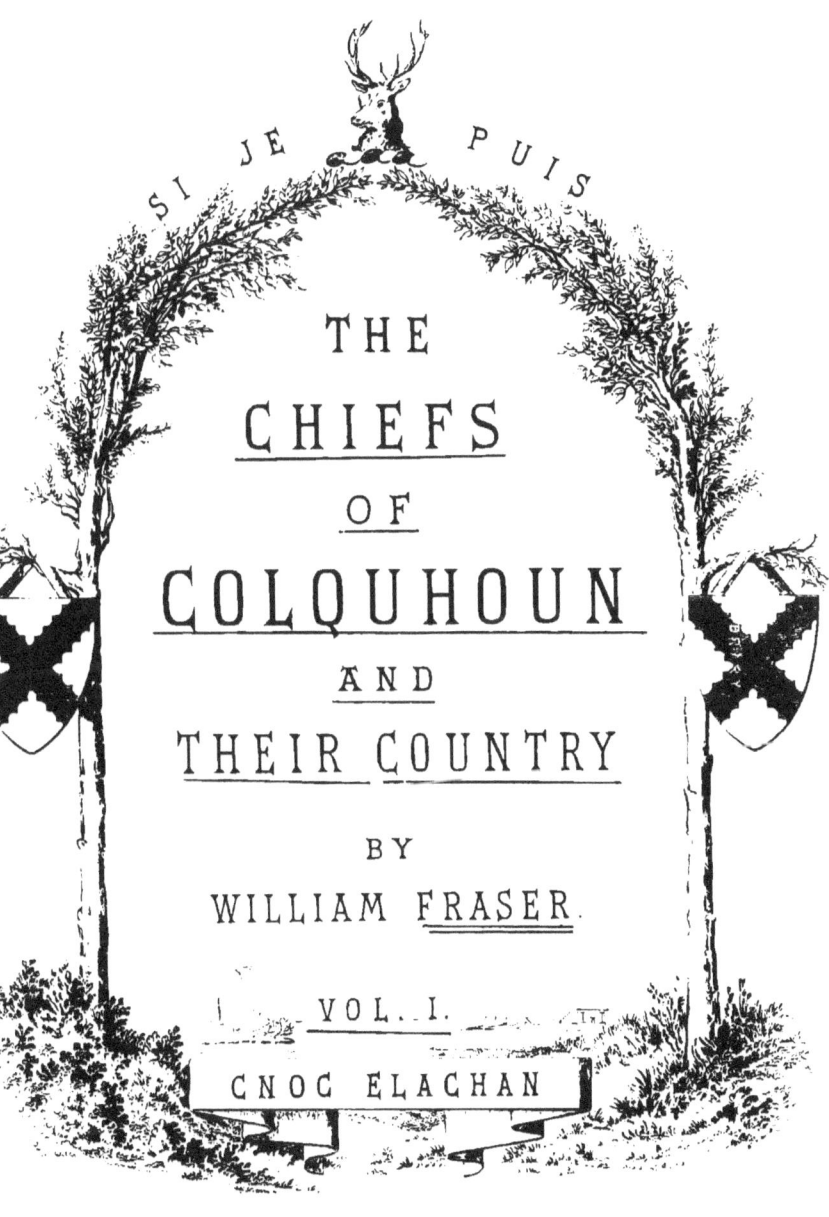

SI JE PUIS

THE
CHIEFS
OF
COLQUHOUN
AND
THEIR COUNTRY

BY

WILLIAM FRASER

VOL. I.

CNOC ELACHAN

# THE CHIEFS OF COLQUHOUN
## AND THEIR COUNTRY.

*Impression : One Hundred and Fifty Copies,*
*In Two Volumes.*

*PRINTED FOR SIR JAMES COLQUHOUN OF COLQUHOUN*
*AND LUSS, BARONET.*

No. *62*

*Presented to*

*The Lady Charlotte Fletcher, of Satton*
*from James Colquhoun*

# PREFACE.

AMONG the baronial families of Scotland, the chiefs of the Clan Colquhoun occupy a prominent place from their ancient lineage, their matrimonial alliances, historical associations, and the extent of their territories in the Western Highlands. These territories now include a great portion of the county of Dumbarton.

Upwards of seven centuries have elapsed since Maldoucu of Luss obtained from Alwyn Earl of Lennox a grant of the lands of Luss; and it is upwards of six hundred years since another Earl of Lennox granted the lands of Colquhoun to Humphrey of Kilpatrick, who afterwards assumed the name of Colquhoun.

The lands and barony of Luss have never been alienated since the early grant of Alwyn Earl of Lennox. For six generations these lands were inherited by the family of Luss in the male line; and in the seventh they became the inheritance of the daughter of Godfrey of Luss, commonly designated "The Fair Maid of Luss," and, as the heiress of these lands, she vested them by her marriage, about the year 1385, in her husband, Sir Robert Colquhoun of Colquhoun. The descendant from that marriage, and the representative of the families of Colquhoun and Luss, is the present baronet, Sir James Colquhoun.

The lands and barony of Colquhoun also descended in the male line of the family of Colquhoun for nearly five centuries; and although the greater part of them has been sold, portions still belong to the present representative of the family. No other family in Dumbartonshire has possessed lands in that county so long as that of Colquhoun.

Considering the vicissitudes which have attended other baronial families, their early neighbours in the Lennox, the long continuance of the Colquhouns in their territories is not a little remarkable. The great Earls of Lennox, from whom the Colquhouns originally derived their chief baronies, came to an early and ignominious end —forfeiting at the same time their lands and their lives. The Stuart Earls of Lennox were scarcely less unfortunate than the original race. Mathew, the second Stuart Earl, who was the brother-in-law of Sir John Colquhoun, fell at Flodden. His son and successor was treacherously killed by Sir James Hamilton of Finnart, at the battle fought near Linlithgow in 1526. This Earl deserved a better fate; for, according to the eulogium of the Chief of the Hamiltons, he was the wisest man, the stoutest man, and the hardiest man ever born in Scotland. His son, the Regent Lennox, also fell in an insurrection against his own authority as Regent; while the tragic fate of the Regent's son, the unhappy Darnley, who also bore, as Regent, the title of Earl of Lennox, is well known. The very name of Lennox seems then to have been ominous of evil to its possessors. The title descended to King James the Sixth, but whether from his natural timidity or from his State policy, he resigned it successively to his nearest collateral kinsmen of the Stuart race. But misfortune still followed this title in the cruel fate of the Lady Arabella Stuart, who was the only daughter of Charles Earl of Lennox, the younger brother of Darnley.

Subsequent holders of the title seldom enjoyed it long or successfully, and the great Lennox estates were ultimately sold to strangers.

The Colquhouns, besides their proximity to the ancient Earls
of Lennox, who were their early neighbours and contemporaries,
were surrounded by several clans, the principal of whom were the
Buchanans of that Ilk, the Macfarlanes of Arrochar, and the Macaulays of Ardincaple.

For many centuries these three clans held territories bounding
with those of the Colquhouns, and during that period those family
feuds, then common to all clans, were of frequent occurrence in the
Western Highlands. In the seventeenth century the Buchanans
ceased to hold their ancient inheritance on Lochlomond, and in it
they were succeeded by the "gallant Grahams," who proved good
neighbours and friends to the Colquhouns. As the Buchanans
lost their hereditary domain of Buchanan, so the Macfarlanes and
Macaulays also ceased to be the owners of Arrochar and Ardincaple: and these baronies were acquired by the Colquhouns, who
added them to their ancient barony of Luss. Thus, of all the
principal clans connected with the county of Dumbarton, the
Colquhouns alone have been able not only to retain their own,
but to acquire the territories of their ancient rivals, who, it is to
be regretted, derived no benefit from the liberal and even extrava-
gant considerations paid by the Colquhouns, owing to intermediate
parties having purchased those territories at comparatively small
prices. The late Mr. Ferguson of Raith, on the re-sale of the
barony of Arrochar to the late Sir James Colquhoun, realized a
profit of about fifty thousand pounds, or nearly double the price

which his father had paid to the Macfarlanes. This large profit, had it been realized by the Macfarlanes, would have rendered them comparatively wealthy.

Although the three clans now mentioned—the Buchanans, the Macfarlanes, and the Macaulays—were all involved in those clan feuds, which were so little calculated for the advancement of civilisation, each of them has the honour to boast of distinguished names. The Buchanans at an early period gave to learning an unrivalled scholar. The Macfarlanes had chiefs renowned for great bravery, and one of them, in the last century, was the most accomplished antiquary of his age. The Macaulays, in still later times, could boast of their noble orator and historian.

Another clan, the Macgregors, although unconnected by territory with the Colquhouns, frequently came into hostile collision with them. After many minor engagements, the feuds between the Colquhouns and the Macgregors culminated in the sanguinary battle of Glenfruin, in which the latter were victorious, although their triumph was dearly bought, their very name being from that time proscribed. From the materials in the Colquhoun Charter-chest, we have been able to give a very complete account of that engagement.

Besides the long-continued possession of their extensive territories, several of the chiefs of the Colquhouns held high offices of State,—such as those of Comptroller of the Exchequer, Great Chamberlain of Scotland, Sheriff-Principal and hereditary Coroner of the county of Dumbarton, and also Governor of the Castle of Dumbarton.

The FIRST VOLUME contains the personal history of the chiefs of Colquhoun and Luss, from Maldouen of Luss in the year 1150, to his descendant and representative, Sir James Colquhoun, the present Baronet of Colquhoun and Luss. As the history of the family extends over so many centuries, it is often connected with events of a highly stirring character in the history of our country, which are not unfrequently noticed in the Memoirs; and in some instances it will be found that new light is thrown upon those events. Full details are given of the state of the Western Highlands at different periods, particularly of the practical operation of the system of clanship, and of the feuds to which it constantly gave rise. From the great extent of territory which the Colquhouns possessed in Dumbartonshire, and from the part which, from their position in that territory as constituting the debatable land between the High lands and the Lowlands in the west, they were often called to act in their native county, their history is to a great extent the history of Dumbartonshire, and the history of Dumbartonshire forms an important part of the history of Scotland.

After having given, in the First Volume, a detailed account of the successive chiefs of the Clan Colquhoun, it seemed desirable to describe the territories, interesting in themselves, with which the Colquhouns for so many centuries have been associated. This description has been attempted in the SECOND VOLUME. This territorial survey comprehends a large proportion of the county of Dumbarton. The lands and barony of Colquhoun, embracing the estates of Auchentorlie, Dumbuck, Barnhill, and Overtown of Col quhoun, and the Castle of Dunglas on the Clyde, formerly the chief

mansion of the Barony of Colquhoun, are first noticed, as having
formed the original possessions of the Colquhouns. Then follow
accounts of the Barony of Luss, the Castle of Rossdhu, the Churches
and Chapels of Luss, and the Sanctuary round the Church of Luss,
the Castle of Bannachra, and the Barony of Arrochar, with its
mountains, lochs, rivulets, and castles ; likewise the ancient Castle
and Chapel of Faslane, and other territories, all now forming the
COLQUHOUN COUNTRY.

Lochlomond and its Islands, so far as these are connected with
the Baronies of Luss and Arrochar, are also fully described. The
Correspondence of Lord Jeffrey in reference to Lochlomond, where
for many years he passed his summer holidays, is now printed for
the first time, and will be found interesting, like all the correspondence of that distinguished man.

As an instance of the imperfect histories of the county of
Dumbarton, including even that of the accurate and well-informed
author of *Caledonia*, it may be noticed that the grant by King
Robert the Bruce, to his faithful adherent, the Earl of Lennox, of
the right of Gyrth or Sanctuary for three miles around the Church
of Luss, has never been mentioned in any county, family, parish,
or other history. This interesting document in the history of Luss
and the Lennox certainly deserves particular notice, and it is now,
for the first time, brought to light, printed and lithographed from
the original, preserved among the Lennox muniments at Buchanan
Castle.

Many of the places described are associated with important
historical events. The ancient Castle of Faslane recalls the memory

of Sir William Wallace, who, when a visitor there on one of his hazardous exploits, met with a cordial reception from his compatriot, Malcolm fifth Earl of Lennox. The woods of Colquhoun and the mountains of Arrochar are intermingled with deeply interesting scenes in the history of Robert the Bruce. The Castle of Bannachra is memorable for the tragic death of Sir Humphrey Colquhoun of Luss, in a conflict with the Macfarlanes.

The Second Volume includes Memoirs of some of the Branches or Cadets of the Colquhouns of Luss—the Colquhouns of Tillyquhoun, and the Colquhouns of Camstradden, with Pedigrees of other Colquhoun families, including those of Glennis and Kenmure, Garscadden and Killermont, Kilmardinny and Barnhill.

The Second Volume further includes a large selection of the Colquhoun and Luss Charters, of which an Abstract is given, to facilitate reference. The feudal muniments of the family have been carefully preserved, while their epistolary correspondence has been nearly as carefully destroyed. Only a very few letters now exist. The interesting letter from Lady Helen Colquhoun on measures connected with the Rebellion of 1745 was accidentally discovered in another repository, after the memoir of herself and her husband had been printed off. The letter has been carefully lithographed for this work.

The materials for these volumes have been derived mainly from the family muniments at Rossdhu. The information thus acquired is of undoubted authenticity, and becomes especially valuable when it delineates and records transactions of remote times. But while these family muniments are the principal authority for the Memoirs, other sources have been drawn on for the history of the Clan Colquhoun. In particular, this work is indebted to His Grace the Duke of Montrose, who has on this, and on so many other occasions, made accessible, in the most liberal and unrestricted manner, his invaluable family muniments. From the frequent references to these, it will be seen how much these Memoirs are indebted to his liberality.

Other proprietors in the Lennox have also afforded the use of their muniments. Sir Robert Gilmour Colquhoun, K.C.B., now of Fincastle, the representative of the family of Camstradden, whose branch forms a prominent section of the Second Volume, kindly communicated the ancient muniments of Camstradden.

To him who is most interested in this work, the Chief and representative of the ancient race which it records, these Volumes are indebted for much important information, which could only be supplied from his accurate knowledge of the history of his CLAN and THEIR COUNTRY.

WILLIAM FRASER.

32 CASTLE STREET, EDINBURGH,
    *December* 1869.

# CONTENTS OF VOLUME FIRST.

## ORIGIN OF THE FAMILY OF COLQUHOUN.

# FAMILY OF LUSS OF LUSS.

XIV. (1.)—SIR HUMPHREY COLQUHOUN, Knight, Fourteenth of Colquhoun and Sixteenth of Luss [1574-1592], married, first, Lady Jean Cunningham (Glencairn) ; and second, Dame Jean Hamilton.

## XVII.—SIR JAMES COLQUHOUN, THIRD BARONET [1676-1680].

c

# INDEX PEDIGREE OF THE FAMILY OF COLQUHOUN OF COLQUHOUN AND LUSS.

(*The Pages refer to those of the Text.*)

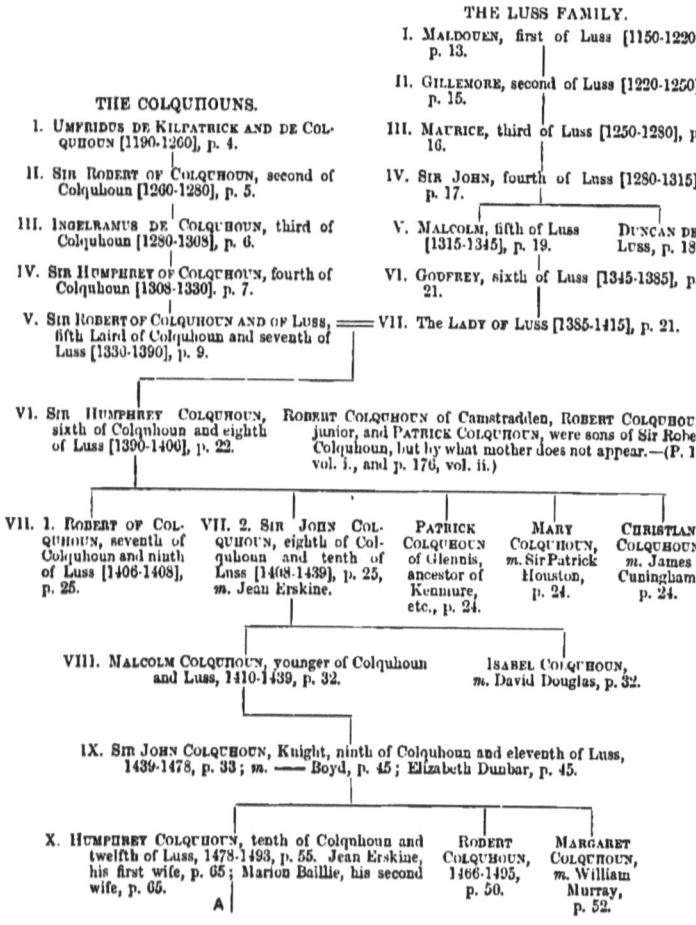

A

A |

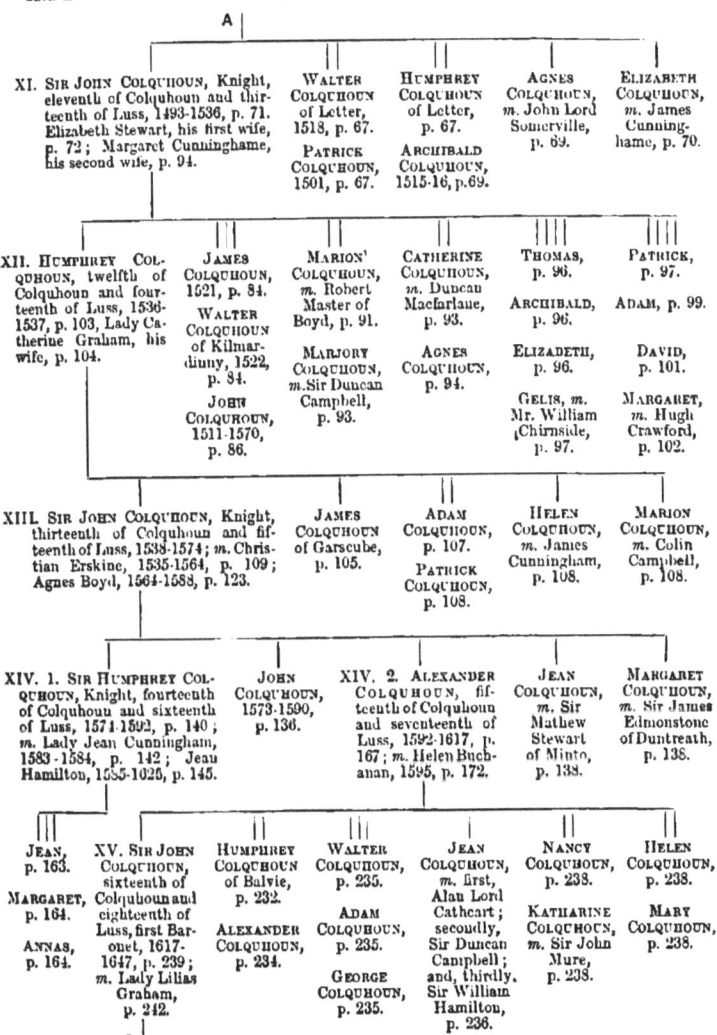

XI. SIR JOHN COLQUHOUN, Knight, eleventh of Colquhoun and thirteenth of Luss, 1493-1536, p. 71. Elizabeth Stewart, his first wife, p. 72; Margaret Cunninghame, his second wife, p. 94.

WALTER COLQUHOUN of Letter, 1518, p. 67.

PATRICK COLQUHOUN, 1501, p. 67.

HUMPHREY COLQUHOUN of Letter, p. 67.

ARCHIBALD COLQUHOUN, 1515-16, p. 69.

AGNES COLQUHOUN, m. John Lord Somerville, p. 69.

ELIZABETH COLQUHOUN, m. James Cunninghame, p. 70.

XII. HUMPHREY COLQUHOUN, twelfth of Colquhoun and fourteenth of Luss, 1536-1537, p. 103, Lady Catherine Graham, his wife, p. 104.

JAMES COLQUHOUN, 1521, p. 84.

WALTER COLQUHOUN of Kilmardinny, 1522, p. 84.

JOHN COLQUHOUN, 1511-1570, p. 86.

MARION COLQUHOUN, m. Robert Master of Boyd, p. 91.

MARJORY COLQUHOUN, m. Sir Duncan Campbell, p. 93.

CATHERINE COLQUHOUN, m. Duncan Macfarlane, p. 93.

AGNES COLQUHOUN, p. 94.

THOMAS, p. 96.

ARCHIBALD, p. 96.

ELIZABETH, p. 96.

GELIS, m. Mr. William Chirnside, p. 97.

PATRICK, p. 97.

ADAM, p. 99.

DAVID, p. 101.

MARGARET, m. Hugh Crawford, p. 102.

XIII. SIR JOHN COLQUHOUN, Knight, thirteenth of Colquhoun and fifteenth of Luss, 1538-1574; m. Christian Erskine, 1535-1564, p. 109; Agnes Boyd, 1564-1588, p. 123.

JAMES COLQUHOUN of Garscube, p. 105.

ADAM COLQUHOUN, p. 107.

PATRICK COLQUHOUN, p. 108.

HELEN COLQUHOUN, m. James Cunningham, p. 108.

MARION COLQUHOUN, m. Colin Campbell, p. 108.

XIV. 1. SIR HUMPHREY COLQUHOUN, Knight, fourteenth of Colquhoun and sixteenth of Luss, 1574-1592, p. 140; m. Lady Jean Cunningham, 1583-1584, p. 142; Jean Hamilton, 1585-1625, p. 145.

JOHN COLQUHOUN, 1573-1590, p. 136.

XIV. 2. ALEXANDER COLQUHOUN, fifteenth of Colquhoun and seventeenth of Luss, 1592-1617, p. 167; m. Helen Buchanan, 1595, p. 172.

JEAN COLQUHOUN, m. Sir Mathew Stewart of Minto, p. 138.

MARGARET COLQUHOUN, m. Sir James Edmonstone of Duntreath, p. 138.

JEAN, p. 163.

MARGARET, p. 164.

ANNAS, p. 164.

XV. SIR JOHN COLQUHOUN, sixteenth of Colquhoun and eighteenth of Luss, first Baronet, 1617-1647, p. 239; m. Lady Lilias Graham, p. 242.

HUMPHREY COLQUHOUN of Balvie, p. 232.

ALEXANDER COLQUHOUN, p. 234.

WALTER COLQUHOUN, p. 235.

ADAM COLQUHOUN, p. 235.

GEORGE COLQUHOUN, p. 235.

JEAN COLQUHOUN, m. first, Alan Lord Cathcart; secondly, Sir Duncan Campbell; and, thirdly, Sir William Hamilton, p. 236.

NANCY COLQUHOUN, p. 238.

KATHARINE COLQUHOUN, m. Sir John Mure, p. 238.

HELEN COLQUHOUN, p. 238.

MARY COLQUHOUN, p. 238.

B |

B

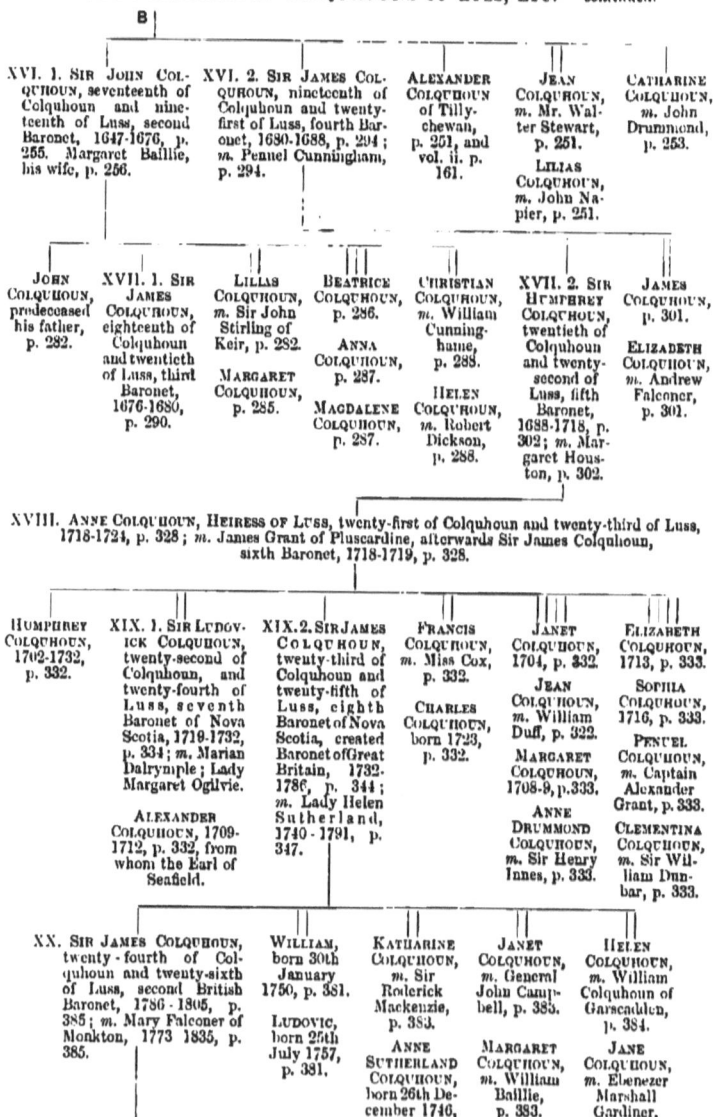

XVI. 1. SIR JOHN COL-QUHOUN, seventeenth of Colquhoun and nineteenth of Luss, second Baronet, 1647-1676, p. 255. Margaret Baillie, his wife, p. 256.

XVI. 2. SIR JAMES COL-QUHOUN, nineteenth of Colquhoun and twenty-first of Luss, fourth Baronet, 1680-1688, p. 294 ; *m.* Pennel Cunningham, p. 294.

ALEXANDER COLQUHOUN of Tilly-chewan, p. 251, and vol. ii. p. 161.

JEAN COLQUHOUN, *m.* Mr. Walter Stewart, p. 251.

LILIAS COLQUHOUN, *m.* John Napier, p. 251.

CATHARINE COLQUHOUN, *m.* John Drummond, p. 253.

JOHN COLQUHOUN, predeceased his father, p. 282.

XVII. 1. SIR JAMES COLQUHOUN, eighteenth of Colquhoun and twentieth of Luss, third Baronet, 1676-1680, p. 290.

LILIAS COLQUHOUN, *m.* Sir John Stirling of Keir, p. 282.

MARGARET COLQUHOUN, p. 285.

BEATRICE COLQUHOUN, p. 286.

ANNA COLQUHOUN, p. 287.

MAGDALENE COLQUHOUN, p. 287.

CHRISTIAN COLQUHOUN, *m.* William Cunninghame, p. 288.

HELEN COLQUHOUN, *m.* Robert Dickson, p. 288.

XVII. 2. SIR HUMPHREY COLQUHOUN, twentieth of Colquhoun and twenty-second of Luss, fifth Baronet, 1688-1718, p. 302; *m.* Margaret Houston, p. 302.

JAMES COLQUHOUN, p. 301.

ELIZABETH COLQUHOUN, *m.* Andrew Falconer, p. 301.

XVIII. ANNE COLQUHOUN, HEIRESS OF LUSS, twenty-first of Colquhoun and twenty-third of Luss, 1718-1724, p. 328 ; *m.* James Grant of Pluscardine, afterwards Sir James Colquhoun, sixth Baronet, 1718-1719, p. 328.

HUMPHREY COLQUHOUN, 1702-1732, p. 332.

XIX. 1. SIR LUDOVICK COLQUHOUN, twenty-second of Colquhoun, and twenty-fourth of Luss, seventh Baronet of Nova Scotia, 1719-1732, p. 334; *m.* Marian Dalrymple ; Lady Margaret Ogilvie.

ALEXANDER COLQUHOUN, 1709-1712, p. 332, from whom the Earl of Seafield.

XIX. 2. SIR JAMES COLQUHOUN, twenty-third of Colquhoun and twenty-fifth of Luss, eighth Baronet of Nova Scotia, created Baronet of Great Britain, 1732-1786, p. 344 ; *m.* Lady Helen Sutherland, 1740-1791, p. 347.

FRANCIS COLQUHOUN, *m.* Miss Cox, p. 332.

CHARLES COLQUHOUN, born 1723, p. 332.

JANET COLQUHOUN, 1704, p. 332.

JEAN COLQUHOUN, *m.* William Duff, p. 322.

MARGARET COLQUHOUN, 1708-9, p. 333.

ANNE DRUMMOND COLQUHOUN, *m.* Sir Henry Innes, p. 333.

ELIZABETH COLQUHOUN, 1713, p. 333.

SOPHIA COLQUHOUN, 1716, p. 333.

PENUEL COLQUHOUN, *m.* Captain Alexander Grant, p. 333.

CLEMENTINA COLQUHOUN, *m.* Sir William Dunbar, p. 333.

XX. SIR JAMES COLQUHOUN, twenty-fourth of Colquhoun and twenty-sixth of Luss, second British Baronet, 1786-1805, p. 385 ; *m.* Mary Falconer of Monkton, 1773-1835, p. 385.

WILLIAM, born 30th January 1750, p. 381.

LUDOVIC, born 25th July 1757, p. 381.

KATHARINE COLQUHOUN, *m.* Sir Roderick Mackenzie, p. 383.

ANNE SUTHERLAND COLQUHOUN, born 26th December 1746, p. 383.

JANET COLQUHOUN, *m.* General John Campbell, p. 383.

MARGARET COLQUHOUN, *m.* William Baillie, p. 383.

HELEN COLQUHOUN, *m.* William Colquhoun of Garscadden, p. 384.

JANE COLQUHOUN, *m.* Ebenezer Marshall Gardiner, p. 384.

C

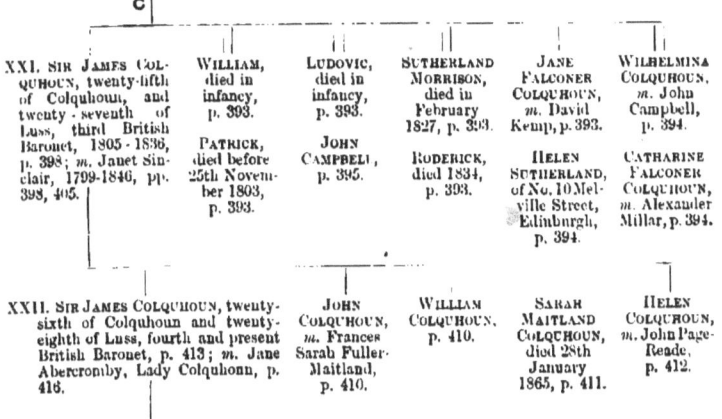

C

XXI. SIR JAMES COL-
QUHOUN, twenty-fifth
of Colquhoun, and
twenty - seventh of
Luss, third British
Baronet, 1805 - 1836,
p. 398; *m.* Janet Sin-
clair, 1799-1846, pp.
398, 405.

WILLIAM,
died in
infancy,
p. 393.

PATRICK,
died before
25th Novem-
ber 1803,
p. 393.

LUDOVIC,
died in
infancy,
p. 393.

JOHN
CAMPBELL,
p. 395.

SUTHERLAND
MORRISON,
died in
February
1827, p. 393.

RODERICK,
died 1834,
p. 393.

JANE
FALCONER
COLQUHOUN,
*m.* David
Kemp, p. 393.

HELEN
SUTHERLAND,
of No. 10 Mel-
ville Street,
Edinburgh,
p. 394.

WILHELMINA
COLQUHOUN,
*m.* John
Campbell,
p. 394.

CATHARINE
FALCONER
COLQUHOUN,
*m.* Alexander
Millar, p. 394.

XXII. SIR JAMES COLQUHOUN, twenty-
sixth of Colquhoun and twenty-
eighth of Luss, fourth and present
British Baronet, p. 413; *m.* Jane
Abercromby, Lady Colquhoun, p.
416.

JOHN
COLQUHOUN,
*m.* Frances
Sarah Fuller-
Maitland,
p. 410.

WILLIAM
COLQUHOUN,
p. 410.

SARAH
MAITLAND
COLQUHOUN,
died 28th
January
1865, p. 411.

HELEN
COLQUHOUN,
*m.* John Page-
Reade,
p. 412.

XXIII. JAMES COLQUHOUN, younger
of Colquhoun and Luss, p. 416.

# ILLUSTRATIONS IN VOLUME FIRST.

# THE CLAN COLQUHOUN OF COLQUHOUN AND LUSS.

## ORIGIN OF COLQUHOUN.

In tracing the history of the family of Colquhoun of Colquhoun and Luss, the origin and remote ancestry of two distinct families—Colquhoun of Colquhoun and Luss of Luss—require to be investigated. Both these families are of high antiquity, and they merged into one in the reign of King David the Second, by the intermarriage of Sir Robert Colquhoun, who was the fifth Laird of Colquhoun, with the daughter of Godfrey of Luss, the sixth Laird of Luss. That lady was heiress of the estate of Luss, and she was commonly called " the Fair Maid of Luss."

The earliest surname under which the family of Colquhoun is traced is that of Kilpatrick. In the reign of King Alexander the Second, which was from the year 1214 to 1249, Umfridus de Kilpatrick obtained from Maldouen third Earl of Lennox a charter of the lands of Colquhoun, situated in the parish of Old or West Kilpatrick, within the earldom of Lennox and shire of Dumbarton. On acquiring the lands of Colquhoun, Umfridus dropped his original surname of Kilpatrick, and adopted that of Colquhoun. The adoption of surnames from lands successively acquired was a common practice in the time of King Alexander the Second, when surnames were less fixed than they came to be in later times. Umfridus is thus the earliest ancestor of the Colquhoun family who is vouched by the testimony of an authentic charter.

Not content, however, with such a satisfactory foundation, several writers on the family of Colquhoun have attempted to find their origin in the younger son of Conoch, a king of Ireland, who, it is said, came to Scotland in the reign of Gregory the Great, King of Scotland, that is,

2    ORIGIN OF THE FAMILY OF COLQUHOUN.

between the years 882 and 893, and obtained from King Gregory a grant of
lands in the shire of Dumbarton, to which he gave the name of Conochan;
a name which gradually became corrupted into Cochon, which afterwards
became Colquhoun.[1]  But it is easy to show that such a theory is utterly
fabulous.  It has often been the mischance of ancient families to have
their early history perversely shrouded in fable and romance, and the story
which represents the younger son of the Irish King Conoch as the founder
of the family of Colquhoun is a fair specimen of the straining after
similarities of names, in the absence of authentic memorials, to account
for the origin of families.  The inventors of this theory overlook the fact
that the earliest surname of the Colquhouns was Kilpatrick, which has
no similarity to Conoch or Conochan.  To prove its probability they
would require to show that the progenitors of Umfridus de Kilpatrick
were Conochs or Conochans or Colquhouns; but of this there is not the
slightest evidence.

The origin of the family of Colquhoun is traced by another theory to
a younger son of one of the ancient earls of Lennox.[2]  The only evidence
on which this theory rests is the similarity of the armorial ensigns borne
by the family of Colquhoun to those of the earls of Lennox, the saltier
being charged upon the shields of both families.  But this heraldic evidence,
standing alone, is insufficient to establish the descent of the Colquhoun
family from that of Lennox.  In early times it was common for families
who held lands from powerful earls to adopt the principal armorial ensigns
of their lord superior.  This was the practice in the earldom of Lennox, as
well as in other earldoms.  In Moray, the holders of lands under the earls
of that name adopted their well-known cognizance of the stars.  In Strathearn, the cheverons of the earls of Strathearn were frequently adopted by
the families holding lands under them, while in Annandale the families
who held lands under the Bruces, as lords of Annandale, very generally
adopted their armorial bearings, and these are adopted at the present day

[1] Nisbet's Heraldry, edition of 1804, vol.
i. p. 133.  Buchanan of Auchmar's Scottish
Surnames, Glasgow, 1723, p. 90.  Baronage
of Scotland, by Sir Robert Douglas, 1764,

p. 23.  Also Histories of the Families of Colquhoun and Luss, in MS. at Rossdhu.

[2] Sir George Mackenzie's Heraldry, MS.

by the families of Maxwell, Johnstone, Jardine, and others, all of whom
have, with some variations, the well-known saltier of the Bruce. Armorial bearings thus adopted were called arms of patronage. Although
the similarity of arms shows in many cases a common descent in families
from remote times, such as the Angus lion, which is borne by the family
of Ogilvy, in virtue of their descent from the ancient earls of Angus,
who carried that cognizance, yet mere heraldic evidence requires corrobo-
ration.

The terms of the charter by Maldouen Earl of Lennox to Umfridus
de Kilpatrick do not indicate any relationship between them. Had any
relationship existed, the probability is that it would have been stated
in the charter by the Earl styling Umfridus as his cousin or other relative.
The absence of any acknowledgment of relationship between them in the
charter leads to the inference that none existed. This negative evidence
seems to outweigh any positive testimony that might be afforded by the
similarity of charges on their shields.

The great apostle of Ireland, St. Patrick, was closely connected with the
parish of Kilpatrick in the Lennox, which is appropriately named after
him, because, according to tradition, he was born at Kilpatrick. But the
fame of the great saint was far from being local. Other churches and
other districts of lands were named after him in different forms. In the
stewartry of Kirkcudbright there are the churches of Kirkpatrick-Durham
and Kirkpatrick-Irongray, and in Annandale there are the parishes of Kirk-
patrick-Juxta and Kirkpatrick-Fleming, and the lands of Rampatrick and
Kirkpatrick. These lands of Kirkpatrick can be traced under that name as
early as the twelfth century. They appear also to have given a surname to
a family of considerable note—the Kirkpatricks of Closeburn in Nithsdale.
They are better known by that designation than as Kirkpatricks of Kirkpatrick. Although the lands of Kirkpatrick furnished them with a surname, they appear to have retained them but for a short period, and to have
acquired the lands of Closeburn, which became their territorial designation.
That family obtained from Robert de Bruce, Lord of Annandale, grants
of various lands and fishings in that district. By a charter without date,
Robert de Bruis granted to Ivo and his heirs the fishing of Blawad and

of Hesther, to be held of the granter, for payment to him annually of one
pound of pepper or six pennies.[1]

Ivo, the grantee in this charter, was the progenitor of the family of
Kirkpatrick. He was then without a surname, as he apparently had not
yet acquired the lands of Kirkpatrick. The charter, although undated,
must have been granted between the year 1124, soon after which Robert
of Bruce acquired the Lordship of Annandale, and the year 1141 when he
died. The grant of the lands of Kirkpatrick to Ivo or his successors has
not been discovered. But it must have been made before the end of
the same century, as in another charter by Robert of Bruce to Roger
Crispin of the lands of Cnoculeran, one of the witnesses is Roger of
Kirkepatric.[2] No connection can be traced between Ivo, the progenitor of
the Kirkpatrick family, and Umfridus de Kilpatrick or Colquhoun.

# I.—UMFRIDUS DE KILPATRICK AND DE COLQUHOUN,
### First of Colquhoun [1190-1260].

UMFRIDUS DE KILPATRICK obtained a charter from Maldouen, third
Earl of Lennox, of the lands of Colquhoun, to be held for rendering to
the Earl, his superior, the third-part of the service of one knight. The
charter is undated, but it must have been granted before, or not later than,
the year 1246, as the Earl's father-in-law, Walter, the High Steward of
Scotland, who was one of the witnesses to the charter, died in that year.[3]
This is the earliest charter extant bearing on the history of the family of
Colquhoun, and it may be translated from the Latin as follows :—

To all his friends, and men present and to come, Maldouen Earl of Lennox,
greeting: Let all men present and to come know, that I have given, granted,
and by this present charter have confirmed to Umfridus de Kilpatrick the whole
land of Colquhoun, by its right divisions, with all its just pertinents, to be held
by him and his heirs of me and my heirs in feu and heritage, freely, quietly,
fully and honourably, in wood and plain, in meadows and pastures, in pools and

---

[1] Original Charter at Drumlaurig.

[2] Original Charter, ibid.

[3] Cartularium Comitatus de Levenax, p.

25 ; Crawfurd's Officers of State, p. 318 ;
Crawfurd's General Description of the Shire
of Renfrew, etc., Robertson's edition, p. 437.

mills, in fishings, and in all other easements belonging to the foresaid lands ; he and his heirs rendering therefrom to me and my heirs the third part of the service of one knight for every service and exaction ; before these witnesses, Sir Walter, Steward of our Lord the King, Malcolm my son, Gillaspee Galbraith, Hamelyn, Malcolm, Duncan, my brothers, Malcolm Beg, Doven my chamberlain, Fergus Makcomyng, and many others.

It may be assumed, therefore, that Umfridus was born towards the close of the twelfth or in the beginning of the thirteenth century, that he flourished during part of the reign of King William the Lion and during the whole reign of Alexander the Second, and that he died in the early part of the reign of Alexander the Third. After obtaining this grant, Umfridus, according to a custom common at that time, dropped the surname of Kilpatrick and assumed that of Colquhoun from his lands of Colquhoun.

Umfridus de Kilpatrick was witness to a charter granted in the year 1250 by Maldouen Earl of Lennox, confirming to the monks of the monastery of Paisley some pasture land in Lennox.[1]

The lands of Colquhoun acquired by Umfridus de Kilpatrick, at a period so early, formed a part of the parish of Kilpatrick, the charter probably conveying to him the whole country from the burn to the possessions of the Church of Kilpatrick. The lands of Colquhoun continued to be the property of his descendants for many generations, and the superiority of part of them still belongs to his lineal representative, the present Sir James Colquhoun of Colquhoun and Luss, Baronet. Some of the vassals pay a year's rental for their entry, and in other cases merely a nominal sum, and in one case it is a pound of pepper.

## II.—Sir ROBERT OF COLQUHOUN,
### Second of Colquhoun [1260-1280].

Sir Robert of Culchon (Colquhoun) appears to have been the next representative of this family, and may be presumed to have been the son of Umfridus de Colquhoun, though no legal evidence to that effect has been

[1] Registrum Monasterii de Passelet, p. 172.

preserved. In 1271 he acted on an inquest, the members of which were appointed to inquire whether Maria, wife of John of Wardrobe, and Elena, wife of Bernard of Erth, and Forveleth, wife of Norrin of Monorgund, daughters of the deceased Finlay of Camsy, were the true and lawful heirs of the deceased Dufgallus, brother of Maldouen Earl of Lennox, and who found that they were so, having been descended from Malcolm, who was the brother of Dufgallus and their grandfather, and that Dufgallus had never married.[1] This Laird of Colquhoun was probably born towards the close of the reign of King William the Lion, flourished during the whole reign of Alexander the Second, and died in the end of the reign of Alexander the Third. After the year 1271 his name does not appear in any record of the period which we have met with.

## III.—INGELRAMUS DE COLQUHOUN,
### Third of Colquhoun [1280-1308].

INGELRAMUS DE COLQUHOUN, who also lived in the reign of Alexander the Third, appears to have succeeded Sir Robert; and although the link of filiation is again wanting, we may venture to regard him as the son of Sir Robert. The first, and indeed almost the only notice of him extant is between the years 1292 and 1333, when he was witness to a charter by Malcolm Earl of Lennox, confirming a charter to Gillemore, son of Maldouen, made on the donation of Maldouen, late Earl of Lennox, to Malcolm of Luss, son and heir of Sir John of Luss, of the lands of Luss. The charter is undated, but from the names of the witnesses and others mentioned therein it may be concluded with certainty that it must have been granted between the years specified.[2]    Ingelramus received from King Robert the Bruce a charter of Salakhill [Sauchie], in Stirlingshire, that part of it formerly given to Osbert, son of Forsyth, amounting to 100s., for the service of two bowmen and three suits of court, being reserved. The charter is without date, but it could not have been granted before the 25th of

---

[1] Registrum Monasterii de Passelet, p. 191.    [2] Cartularium de Levenax, p. 24.

March 1306, when Robert the Bruce began to reign.[1] Ingelramus lived during an exciting period in the history of Scotland—during the reigns of Alexander the Third, of Margaret, Alexander's grand-daughter, of John Balliol, and the interregnum between 1296 and 1306, when the kingdom was divided by powerful factions, and prostrated by the power of Edward the First of England, the period when Sir William Wallace distinguished himself by his heroic exploits for the independence of his country, and the beginning of the reign of Robert the Bruce.

## IV.—Sir HUMPHREY OF COLQUHOUN,
### Fourth of Colquhoun [1308-1330].

HUMPHREY OF COLQUHOUN, who flourished in the reign of Robert the Bruce, succeeded Ingelramus about the year 1308, and may be presumed to have been his son. He received a charter of the barony of Luss from King Robert the Bruce in 1308, for his special service, and for never having deserted Bruce's interest. On the 26th April 1309 he was witness to a charter by King Robert the Bruce, which confirmed to Robert Wischart, Bishop of Glasgow, all the churches, lands, rents, possessions, and goods pertaining to that bishop.[2] In this charter he is designated " Vmfredus de Culchoun, miles."

This charter, dated at Arbroath, to which Humphrey of Colquhoun, knight, was a witness, is worthy of special notice, from its connection with the history of the times in which he lived, and with events in regard to which he doubtless took a deep interest. Robert Wischart, Bishop of Glasgow, in whose favour it was made, was a strenuous defender of the independence of Scotland. When overpowered by circumstances, he, indeed, repeatedly swore fealty to Edward the First of England; but he, as often as circumstances favoured, took part against that hostile invader of his country, against whom he vehemently incited the people to fight. He was amongst the first to join Wallace when he erected the standard against Edward the First; and he equally supported Robert the Bruce when he raised the old

---

[1] Harleian MSS., 4628, 2, British Museum.
[2] Registrum Episcopatus Glasguensis, vol. i. p. 220.

war-cry of Scotland against English domination. He absolved Bruce from
the anathema of the Church for the slaughter of Comyn in the Church of
Dumfries, and took an active part in the preparations made for his coronation. Wischart, however, was taken prisoner by the English in the Castle
of Cupar, which he held against them in 1306. One of the charges brought
against him was that he had used the timber which Edward the First of
England had allowed him for building a steeple to his cathedral, in con-
structing engines of war against that King's castles, and especially the
Castle of Kirkintolach.[1]

At the time when the above charter was made in his favour the bishop
was still in prison; and in the charter King Robert expresses, in affecting
terms, his feelings of commiseration towards him under his long and weari-
some imprisonment. "Since," says he, "it would be a pernicious example,
and dissonant to reason, to render evil for good, much more since it is a
laudable demonstration of gratitude to show favour to those who have
deserved well by a suitable recompense, we, deeply pondering, as we are
bound, the imprisonment and chains, the persecutions and wearinesses
which the venerable father, Lord Robert, by the grace of God, Bishop of
Glasgow, has hitherto constantly endured, and still patiently endures, for
the rights of the Church and of our Kingdom of Scotland, we have freely
granted to the said Lord Bishop all his churches, lands, rents, possessions,
and goods." The bishop, it may be added, was not released till after the
battle of Bannockburn, fought on 24th June 1314, when Bruce's wife, his
sister Christian, his daughter Marjory, the young Earl of Mar, his nephew,
and the Bishop of Glasgow, were exchanged for the Earl of Hereford, who,
on the capitulation of Bothwell Castle by the English into the hands of the
Scots, immediately after that battle, became their prisoner.[2] The bishop
had grown blind in prison. He survived his liberation only two years,
having died in November 1316.

Humphrey of Colquhoun was in the army of Bruce at Bannockburn; and
the valour and skill he then displayed attracted the special notice of his
sovereign, who granted him a charter of Sauchy, in Stirlingshire, for his
good service performed at that battle.

[1] Reg. Episc. Glasguensis, vol. i. p. xxxvi.    [2] Tytler's Hist. of Scotland, vol. i. p. 292.

Sir Humphrey of Colquhoun was also witness to a charter by Malcolm Earl of Lennox to John of Luss, granting him certain privileges and immunities within the bounds of his lands of Luss. This charter is undated, but it was confirmed by King Robert on 6th March 1316, from which it may be presumed that it was granted shortly before that date.[1]

There is a Malcolm Culchone who received from King David the Second (1329-1371) a charter of the lands of Gask, and of 13s. 4d. out of the lands of Balmelyu, in the shire of Aberdeen;[2] but whether he was related to Sir Humphrey of Colquhoun we are unable to determine. In 1329 Malcolme of Culchone, who received annually ten pounds from the royal exchequer till he should be otherwise provided for, was paid by the chamberlain, during the last term of his account for that year, the sum of one hundred shillings.[3] In the year 1357 there was paid by Sir Robert of Pebles, the Chamberlain of Scotland, to Malcolme of Culwone, who is probably the same person as in the preceding account, the sum of £6, 13s. 4d. for the King's use.[4]

# V.—SIR ROBERT OF COLQUHOUN AND OF LUSS,
Fifth Laird of Colquhoun and Seventh of Luss [1330-1390].

### THE HEIRESS OF LUSS.

SIR ROBERT OF COLQUHOUN, Knight, is the next representative of this ancient family that appears on record. We do not find him anywhere called son of Humphrey, though from the time at which he flourished, and the fact that he succeeded him in the lands of Colquhoun, it may be inferred that he was so. " Robert of Colquhoun, knight," was a witness to a relaxation granted by Malcolm fifth Earl of Lennox to Arthur Galbraith of all the suits which, according to the tenour of his charters, he was bound to make to the Earl for the lands of Bannachra, Keangerloch, and others. He was also a witness to a charter granted by the same Earl to Arthur Galbraith of the lands of Buchmonyn and of Gilgirinane; to

[1] Cartularium Comitatus de Levenax, p. 22.    Scotland, printed at Edinburgh, 1836, vol. i.
[2] Robertson's Index, p. 61, No. 5.        p. 94.
[3] Accounts of the Great Chamberlains of    [4] Ibid. vol. i. p. 351.

B

another granted by the same Earl to Sir Patrick of Grame of the lands of Auchencloich and Strablane; and to a relaxation of captions on the lands of the said Sir Patrick by the same Earl.[1] All these transactions must have taken place between the years 1292 and 1333, the period during which that Earl held the earldom.

Sir Robert married, in or previous to the year 1368, the daughter of Godfridus, sixth laird of Luss, his only child and heiress. By this marriage he added greatly to his paternal estates, having by it acquired the extensive property of Luss. From this property he afterwards took his designation, and his descendants, who continue in possession of the lands to the present day, retain it.

The commonly received account of the marriage of Sir Robert with the heiress of Luss is, that in the reign of King David the Second he married the daughter and sole heiress of Humphrey of Luss, with whom he acquired the lands of Luss. As, however, no Humphrey of Luss appears on record, and as Godfridus is the last of the Lusses of whom we have any notice, it is probable that Umfridus has by mistake been written for Godfridus, and that it was the daughter and heiress of the latter whom Sir Robert married. No direct evidence of the marriage indeed exists, but the uniform tradition of the family, and the possession of the estates of Luss, leave no doubt on the subject.

After his marriage to the heiress of Luss, Sir Robert took the designation " de Luss" in addition to that of Colquhoun, though her father, Godfridus, was still alive. "Robert of Colfune (Colquhoun), Laird of Luss," was a witness to an obligation by Malcolm Fleming, Lord of Biggar, in favour of Robert Lord Erskine, warranting the lands of Dalnotar, and others, dated 8th January 1368.[2] In a charter, dated in the same year, he is designated "Robertus dominus de Colquhoun et de Luss," Lord of Colquhoun and of Luss;[3] and in a charter by Isabella Fleeming of Dalnotar to Sir Robert Erskine, knight, of the lands of Achintorlie, in the Lennox, he is similarly

[1] Cartularium Comitatus de Levenax, pp. 29, 30, 38, 40.
[2] Original Obligation in Cumbernauld Charter-chest.
[3] Original Charter in Luss Charter-chest.

This designation which Sir Robert takes in this charter clearly proves that Buchanan of Anchmar is incorrect in asserting that it was Humphrey, Sir Robert's son, who married the heiress of Luss.

designated.[1]  To this latter charter John Lyle, son and heir of Sir John Lyle
of Duchal, knight, was also a witness, which shows that it must have been
granted about the year 1370.[2]  Sir Robert was also a witness under the
simple designation "Robertus de Colquhoun," to a charter, dated 20th
August 1373, by Walter of Fosselane, Lord of Lennox, to Walter Lord of
Buchanan, of the lands of Auchmar, in Stirlingshire, which belonged to
William Boyd.[3]  Sir Robert of Colquhoun and of Luss was dead in 1391,
when his lands of Mykilsalchy (Meikle Sauchy) were in the hands of the
King, the heir not having up to that time obtained infeftment.[4]

By the heiress of Luss, Sir Robert Colquhoun had four sons—

1. Humphrey Colquhoun, who succeeded him.

2. Robert Colquhoun, who obtained from his brother, Sir Humphrey,
   a grant of the lands of Camstradden, part of the estate of Luss.  If
   there was any previous grant of these lands by Sir Robert, the
   father, no trace of it can now be found.

3. Robert, junior, to whom, in the grant of the lands of Camstradden
   quoted below, the lands were destined, failing heirs-male of Robert,
   to whom the charter was granted.  He is designed in the charter
   "frater junior."

4. Patrick, to whom in the same charter the same lands were destined,
   failing heirs-male of Robert, junior.

The charter grant of the lands of Camstradden now mentioned is written
in Latin, and may be thus translated :—

To all who shall see or hear this charter, Humphrey of Colquhoun, Lord
of Luss, everlasting salvation in the Lord : Know ye that I have given, granted,
and by this present charter have confirmed to my beloved and special brother,
Robert of Colquhoun, for his homage and service rendered, and to be rendered
to me, my whole lands of Camysradoch and Achigahane, with the pertinents,
lying in my lordship of Luss, within the earldom of Levenax ; to be held and
had, my said lands of Camysradoch and Achigahane, with the pertinents, by the
said Robert, my brother, and his heirs-male lawfully begotten, or to be begotten,
of his body ; whom perhaps failing, by Robert of Colquhoun, my younger

[1] Crawford's Officers of State, p. 318.       [4] Accounts of the Great Chamberlains of
[2] Vide Douglas's Peerage, under Lyle, Lord.    Scotland, ut supra, vol. ii. p. 185.
[3] Cartularium Comitatus de Levenax, p. 59.

brother, and his heirs-male, in the manner before written ; whom perhaps failing,
by Patrick of Colquhoun, my brother, and his heirs-male, as is before mentioned ; whom also perhaps failing, by me and my lawful heirs whomsoever, in
feu and heritage for ever, of me and my heirs, freely, quietly, wholly, fully, and
peaceably, in wood and plain, in meadows, pastures and pasturages, in roads
and paths, in waters and pools, in aviaries and fishings, in fowlings and hunt-
ings, in pleas and suits, and in their issues, with escheats, merchets and blud-
wyts, and with all other liberties, commodities, easements, and just pertinents
whatsoever, as well not named as named, as well under the earth as above the
earth, belonging to, or that may hereafter in any way belong to, the same lands ;
for rendering therefrom the said Robert, Robert and Patrick, my brothers, and
their heirs, as before mentioned, to me and my heirs, for the common army of our
Lord the King, two cheeses from every house in which cheese is made in the said
lands of Camysradok and Achigahane, and for rendering for the common assistance of our Lord the King as much as belongs to so much land within the
Lordship of Luss for every other service, exaction, or demand.   In testimony
of which thing, my seal is appended to my present charter at Luss, on the
fourth day of the month of July, in the year of our Lord one thousand three
hundred and ninety-five, before these witnesses, Sir Nigel of Balnory and Sir
Robert Lang, chaplains, William Bukroy, Donald Macroger, and John Balnory,
with many others.

This grant of the lands of Camstradden is narrated in a charter of confirmation by Duncan Earl of Lennox, dated at Inchmurrin, 4th July 1395.[1]

The lands of Luss, which Sir Robert acquired by marriage, had for a
long time previous been the property of a family of the name of Luss, their
surname having been derived from the name of their lands.

As by the marriage of Sir Robert with the heiress of Luss the family
of that name became merged with that of Colquhoun, it is proper in this
place to give some account of the family of Luss from its earliest representative, so far as now known, to the heiress of Luss whose property Sir
Robert inherited, and whose family name he also assumed.

---

[1] Cartularium Comitatus de Levenax, p. 77.

# THE FAMILY OF LUSS OF LUSS.

THE family of Luss is of high antiquity, but its origin, like that of other ancient families, is involved in obscurity and uncertainty, although their most ancient Christian names would seem to point to a Celtic extraction. Tradition has here also attempted to supply the place of well-attested history by attributing to the family of Luss a descent from the Saxon blood of the Earls of Lennox. But of such a lineage the earliest charters of that house give no indication. The saltier belonging to the armorial ensigns of the houses of Colquhoun and Lennox, which has been adduced to prove that these families have a common ancestry, has been also used, as already shown, as an argument to prove that the family of Luss originated in the same stock. But in the latter case the argument is even of less force than in the former; for that bearing has not been traced to the family of Luss before it merged in that of Colquhoun. The arms of the Colquhouns, it may be presumed, are those of Umfridus, the first of that name, rather than those of the house of Luss. It is, indeed, possible that they may have been those of Luss, as Sir Robert Colquhoun may have adopted them on his marrying the heiress of that house; but it is nothing more than a possibility; for had he adopted her arms, he would probably have quartered them with his own; nor would he have adopted them while he left her name to sink entirely.

The earliest period at which the family of Luss can be traced from authentic records is about the year 1150.

## I.—MALDOUEN, FIRST OF LUSS [1150-1220].

MALDOUEN, Dean of Levenax,[1] is the first of those ancient lords of Luss that appears on record. He received from Alwyn second Earl of Lennox a charter of the three lower quarters of Luss, viz., Achadhtullech, Dunfin, and Inverlaueran, and another quarter on the west side of Luss.

[1] In the Cartulary of Lennox, p. 12, he is called Dean of Levenax, and at p. 97 he is called Dean of Luss, probably because his church was at Luss.

The charter itself, of the date of which we are ignorant, but which must
have been in or before the year 1224,—the Earl who granted it having
died before 1225,—is not included in the "Cartularium de Levenax," nor
is it known to be now in existence. But that such a charter was given
is certain, from the charter of confirmation or recognition granted by Maldouen third Earl of Lennox to Maldouen, Dean of Luss, and to his son,
Gillemore. Maldouen had been illegally kept from possessing these lands
by Maldouen third Earl of Lennox, who, after his father's death, held possession of them for some time, but how long is not stated. At last Earl Maldouen, prompted, as he himself affirms, by penitence for having detained
them from the rightful owners, reconveyed to Maldouen, who is designated
"formerly Dean of Luss," and Gillemore, his son, by charter the foresaid lands,
with the right of the patronage of the church of Luss, and with all the pleas,
prison dues, escheats, etc., of the said lands. These lands are described in the
writ as contained within these boundaries, namely, from Ald Suidheadhi and
from the Laueran to Lower Duneglas, as Duneglas falls from the mountain
into Lochlomond, on the one side, and from the head of the Laueran, across
by the summit of the mountains, to the lower just boundary between the land
of Luss and the land of Nemhedh (Roseneath), as it descends into Lochlong
on the other side; and thence to the burn called Ald Bealech Nascamche
as it descends into Lochlong; and from the head of that rivulet right across
to the river Duneglas, as it falls into Lochlomond, as said is, and Frechelan
and Elan Rosduue, and Ines Domhnoch. A special reservation is made
in favour of the granter of the lands contained between Cledhebh and
Banbrath (Banry or Bandry), with the islands pertaining thereto.

    These lands thus described were to be held of the Earl of Lennox for
rendering to him and his heirs, for the common army of the King, two
cheeses from every house in the said lands in which cheese was made, for
all other services, forinsic as well as intrinsic, customs, exactions, and
demands, and giving as much common assistance to the King as belonged
to two arrochars of land in the earldom of Levenax.[1]

    The leading boundaries described in that charter still form the bound-
aries of the Luss estates, although from the revolution of names that has

taken place since the date of the above charter, it is difficult to identify with perfect accuracy all the names of the boundaries mentioned in the charter.

The reddendo of cheeses for the King's host stipulated in the grant, as well as in charters of other lands in Luss, would seem to lead to the conclusion that the valleys of Luss, amidst the extensive forest of the Levenax, were famed in those early days for more pasturage, and a more abundant dairy produce, than the present aspect of the country, with so much arable land under tillage, would lead us to suppose. The charter made by Alwyn second Earl of Lennox in favour of Maldouen, seems to have been the first grant of Luss to that family. Soon after this grant was made to them, they were accustomed to take the designation " de Luss;" the territorial name thus supplying their surname. The lands of Luss continued to be possessed by the family till, by the marriage of the heiress of Luss with the Laird of Colquhoun, as already stated, they passed into another family, in which they have continued down to the present day. Some have supposed that this Maldouen was a son of Earl Alwyn ; but this is clearly a mistake, as both Maldouen, his son, and Maldouen, Dean of Lennox, were witnesses to the Earl's charter of the lands of Cochnach to the church of Kilpatrick.[1] Dean Maldouen, however, though not a son, may have been a near kinsman of Earl Alwyn.

## II.—GILLEMORE, Second of Luss [1220-1250].

GILLEMORE succeeded his father, Maldouen, in the lands of Luss. He obtained from Maldouen third Earl of Lennox two charters of these lands. In these charters, the boundaries, rights, and reddendo of the lands are described as in the charter of them already quoted, granted to his father by the said Earl.[2] Gillemakessoc, son of Gillemore, is a witness to one of these charters, made in favour of his father ; but he does not himself seem to have ever possessed the lands of Luss. These charters are undated, but they must have been granted between the years 1225 and 1270, the period during which Maldouen was Earl of Lennox.

<hr>

[1] Cartularium Comitatus de Levenax, p. 97.          [2] *Ibid.* pp. 19, 96, 97.

## III.—MAURICE, Third of Luss [1250-1280].

Maurice is the next laird of Luss that appears on record. " Mauritius de Luss" was witness to a charter by Maldouen Earl of Lennox to Maurice, son of Galbraith, and the heirs of his marriage with Katharine, daughter of Colpatrick, of a carucate of the land of Cartonvenach ; and to another charter by the same Earl in favour of the said Maurice, and Arthur his son, of a fourth part of land in Auchincloich, in exchange for other lands.[1] He was a witness to a charter by the same Earl, in 1250, granting to the monastery of Paisley in pure, free, and perpetual alms, one pasture of land of Levenax, and to the monks thereof the right to hold and possess all other their lands in the earldom of Levenax, as they held them at the time of this grant, or before.[2]    He was also a witness to a charter by Engus, son of Duncan, confirming to the monks of Paisley the church of Kyllinan, dated 5th March 1270.[3]   He appears again as a witness to a charter by Gille-michell, son of Edolf, to Malcolm his son, of the lands of Gartchonerane, and to two confirmations of that charter, one by Duncan, son of Gille-michel Makedolf, and the other, which is dated 17th November 1274, by Malcolm Earl of Lennox.[4]

On 17th August 1277, Maurice, as Laird of Luss, for a certain sum of money, made a charter, granting to God and the blessed St. Mungo and the church of Glasgow the right of cutting and preparing out of any parts of his woods of Luss whatever should be necessary for the woodwork of the steeple and treasury, which the chapter of the Cathedral of Glasgow, in consequence of its growing wealth and importance, was then in the course of erecting, with free access thereto and egress therefrom, and liberty of pasturage for the horses, oxen, and other animals which should be employed in carrying the wood required.[5]   In that age privileges of this description were generally granted gratuitously to the church by the proprietors of the soil from their devotion or their fears ; but on the part

[1] Cartularium Comitatus de Levenax, p. 27.
[2] Registrum Monasterii de Passelet, p. 172.
[3] Ibid. p. 134.

[4] Cartularium Comitatus de Levenax, pp. 84-86.
[5] Registrum Episcopatus Glasguensis, vol. i. p. 191.

of this Celtic laird, it was a purely mercantile transaction. In granting
this privilege he does not even affect to have been governed by a higher
motive than the reception of its value in money; though, in conformity
with the language of the time, the charter is said to be granted "to God
and the blessed St. Mungo, and the Church of Glasgow."

Maurice of Luss is said to have had issue—

1. John, who succeeded him.
2. William of Luss, designed vicar in a document dated 1313, may
   have been his son.[1]

## IV.—SIR JOHN, FOURTH OF LUSS [1280-1315].

SIR JOHN OF LUSS, Knight, succeeded Maurice, and seems to have been
his son. He was high in favour with Malcolm fifth Earl of Lennox, in
whose house he bore the office of Usher (Bacularius). From that Earl
he obtained grants of several remarkable privileges made by a charter,
which is without date, but which was confirmed by King Robert the
Bruce on the 6th of March 1315. By this charter Earl Malcolm, " for
the reverence and honour of our patron, the most holy man, the blessed
Kessog,"[2] renounced in favour of Sir John of Luss, " our beloved and
faithful bacularius," and his heirs, all right which belonged to the earls
of Lennox, as superiors of the estate of Luss, of services, captions, or
services of carriage within these lands. He further exempted Sir John
and his vassals within or without the bounds of the said lands from
being called upon by the bailies or servants of the King's Justiciary,
or by the bailies or servants of the earls of Lennox, to appear and
give testimony as witnesses either in the courts of the King, or in
those of the earldom of Lennox, engaging that he himself and his heirs
should be always prepared to find sufficient witnesses from other men of
his earldom, as often as it should be necessary, that the service of the King
might not seem to miscarry from any defect on their part in producing

[1] Registrum Monasterii de Passelet, p. 376.
[2] St. Kessog, the patron saint of the parish of Luss.

C

witnesses.[1]   Earl Malcolm also granted to Sir John the homage and service, forinsic and intrinsic, due to the earl from the lands of Banwrith
[Banry or Bandry, which is opposite the islands mentioned], together with
the islands of Innesconogaig and Elanclew, as possessed by Maldofen
Macgillemychelmore and his heirs, and Gilchrist Maccristyne and his heirs,
to be held by the said Sir John for rendering for the King's common army
two cheeses, and for the assistance of the King as much service as belongs
to such an extent of land.[2]

On 6th March 1316 the charter granted by Maldouen third Earl
of Lennox to Gillemore, son of Maldouen, Dean of Luss, already men-
tioned, was confirmed by King Robert the Bruce in favour of Sir John of
Luss.[3]   Sir John is mentioned in several charters granted during his life-
time to his son Malcolm by Malcolm fifth Earl of Lennox.[4]   He was
witness to a charter by Malcolm Earl of Lennox to Christian and Margaret
Drummond, daughters of John Drummond, of the lands of Ardeureane and
Ardenalochreth.   He was a witness to another charter by Thomas de
Cremmenane to Murechanich, son of Kork, of a quarter of the land of
Croyne, and to a confirmation of that charter by Malcolm fifth Earl of
Lennox.   In all these charters he is designated "Johannes de Luss,
miles."[5]

Sir John had issue, apparently two sons,—

1. Malcolm, who succeeded him.

2. Duncan.   Duncan of Luss is usually mentioned as the sixth Laird
   of this family, as if he had been the son of Malcolm and grandson of
   Sir John.   There is, however, no evidence of his filiation, and he was
   more probably a younger son of Sir John, or if he was the eldest son
   he must have predeceased his father.   The generations would otherwise be too numerous.   Besides, the only lands which we know of his
   possessing were those of Kilfassane and Ballindalqch, in the earldom
   of Lennox, and those of Auchmar, in the shire of Dumbarton.[6]   He was
   a witness to a charter by Malcolm Earl of Lennox to Patrick Galbraith

[1] Cartularium Comitatus de Levenax, pp. 21, 22.          [2] Ibid. p. 20.
[3] Ibid. p. 98.          [4] Ibid. pp. 23, 24.          [5] Ibid. pp. 47, 80, 81.
[6] Ibid. p. 67 ; Robertson's Index, p. 68, No. 7.

of a half-quarter of the lands of Camkell, and to another by the same
Earl to Gillemore, son of Maliscus Banc, of the lands of Blarechos, in
Strablane.[1] In both these charters he is designated " Duncanus de
Luss." The charters are without date, but they could not have been
later than the year 1333, the granter having fallen in the battle of
Halidonhill, fought 19th July that year. Duncan was forfeited in the
reign of King David the Second, but for what reason does not appear.
His lands of Kilfassane and Ballindalach were granted by a charter,
in which they are said to have formerly belonged to " Duncan of
Luss," by Malcolm Fleming, first Earl of Wygtone, to Andrew of
Cunninghame.[2] The charter is without date, but it must have been
granted between the 9th November 1342, when Sir Malcolm Fleming was created Earl of Wigton, and 1362, when he died. And,
in the year 1366, the lands of Auchmar, in the shire of Dumbarton, which had belonged to Duncan of Luss, and which, on
account of his forfeiture, had fallen into the hands of the Crown,
were granted by a charter by King David the Second to William
Boyd.[3]

## V.—MALCOLM, Fifth of Luss [1315-1345].

MALCOLM OF LUSS succeeded his father, Sir John. He received from
Malcolm fifth Earl of Lennox a charter confirming to him the lands of
Luss as they had been granted to Gillemore by Maldouen third Earl of
Lennox.[4] The charter is without date, but it must have been made
between the year 1292, when Malcolm fifth Earl of Lennox is supposed to
have succeeded his father, and the year 1333, when he fell at Halidonhill.

As usual in charters of that date, it is in Latin, and may be translated
as follows :—

To all who shall see or hear this writing, Malcolm Earl of Levenax, son and
heir of the deceased Lord Malcolm Earl of Levenax, everlasting salvation in the
Lord : Know ye all that we have inspected and diligently listened to a charter

---

[1] Cartularium Comitatus de Levenax,
pp. 32, 48.
[2] Ibid. p. 67.
[3] Robertson's Index, p. 68, No. 7, and
p. 83, No. 182.
[4] Cartularium Comitatus de Levenax, p. 23.

of Gilmore, son of Maldonen, made upon a donation and grant of Lord Maldouen, late Earl of Levenax, of his lands of Luss, with their pertinents, not
obliterated, not cancelled, nor vitiated in any part; which charter we, for us and
our heirs, as freely, fully, quietly, and honourably, as the said charter in itself
by all and in all points testifies and bears, confirm, and for us and our heirs
ratify for ever: which charter does not contain or specify any homage in it, but
for the sake of respect to us and our heirs, we will and concede to Malcolm of
Luss, son and heir of Sir John of Luss, and his heirs, all his foresaid lands of
Luss, with their pertinents, for simple homage only, he and his heirs rendering
it thence only to us and our heirs; and for that service which is contained in
the said charter made to the said Gilmore, son of Maldouen, late Lord of
Luss, by the said Lord Maldouen, late Earl of Levenax, namely, for two cheeses
for the common army of our Lord the King, when occasion requires, from every
house in the said lands of Luss in which cheese is made. Moreover we will,
for us and our heirs, that the said Malcolm and his heirs shall be for ever free
and relieved of wards, reliefs, maritages, and suits of Court, and from all and
whatsoever other secular services, as well forinsic as intrinsic, customs, exactions, and demands, which may ever possibly be exacted or required by us
or our heirs of the said Malcolm or his heirs from his forenamed lands of Luss:
In testimony of which thing we have put our seal to this writing, before these
witnesses, Malcolm Flemyng, Sheriff of Dunbretane, Richard of Culneath, and
Hugh Flemyng, Knights, Sir Nicholas, rector of the church of Luss, Gilbert
of Drummond, Ingeram of Colquhoune, Duncan, son of Murechach, and many
others.

Malcolm of Luss, apparently about the same time that he received the
charter now mentioned, obtained from the same Earl a charter of a carucate
of land and a half-quarter of land in the exterior part of Glyne, lying
between the land and marches of Syf and Lekych, to be held for rendering
forinsic service in the King's common army as much as belonged to such
an extent of land in the earldom of Levenax, and three suits yearly at the
three head courts of Levenax, for every other secular service, exaction, and
demand.[1]

In the year 1326 or 1327 Malcolm of Luss had a royal gift of part
of his teinds out of the estate of Luss,[2] as appears from the account of
Sir Malcolm, Vicar of Dumbarton, commencing 18th February 1326,

[1] Cartularium Comitatus de Levenax,
p. 24.

[2] Accounts of the Great Chamberlains of
Scotland, vol. i. p. 160.

and rendered in the year 1329. He was witness to a charter by Earl
Malcolm to Patrick Galbraith of the lands of Balecarrage, and to a
charter by the same Earl to Gilbert of Carric of the lands of Cronverne
and Buchmonyne.[1] He was also a witness to a charter by Donald sixth
Earl of Levenax to William of Galbraith of the lands of Achrefmoltoune ;
to another by the same Earl to Patrick of Lindsay of the lands of Buchnwl ;
to a third by the same Earl to Robert of Dunbretane of the lands of
Bullul ; and to another by the same Earl to Walter of Foslen of half a
carucate of the lands of Laterwwald [Letrualt].[2] These charters by Donald
sixth Earl of Lennox are without date, but they must have been granted
in or between the years 1333 and 1364, the period during which that Earl
enjoyed the earldom. Malcolm seems to have been the father of Godfrey.
who succeeded him as the sixth Laird of Luss.

## VI.—GODFREY, SIXTH OF LUSS [1345-1385].

GODFREY OF LUSS is the sixth of the family of Luss that appears on
record. He was a witness to a charter by Duncan eighth Earl of Lennox,
who did not become Earl till 1381 or 1382,[3] and who was executed at
Stirling in 1425. He had an only daughter, who succeeded him,[4] and
who was commonly called "The Fair Maid of Luss."

## VII.—THE FAIR MAID OF LUSS [1385-1415].

THE Christian name of this lady, who succeeded her father as the
seventh inheritor of the estate, is not known. She married Sir Robert of
Colquhoun ; and the four sons of that marriage have been already stated
under the notice of their father.[5] As these sons all took the surname of
Colquhoun, the family of Luss, as already observed, was thus merged in
that of Colquhoun.

[1] Cartularium Comitatus de Levenax,
pp. 33, 44.

[2] *Ibid.* pp. 34, 52, 69, 95.

[3] *Ibid.* p. 76.

[4] Some make this lady not the daughter,
but the sister of Godfrey, who, they affirm,
had no child ; but the evidence is in favour
of her being a daughter.

[5] P. 14.

## VI.—SIR HUMPHREY COLQUHOUN,
Sixth of Colquhoun and Eighth of Luss [1390-1406].

SIR HUMPHREY, son of Sir Robert Colquhoun by the Fair Maid of Luss, succeeded his father about the year 1390. Being heir and representative of the families of Colquhoun and of Luss, he and his successors used one, or both, of these designations indiscriminately. On the 28th October 1393, "Humphrey Colquhoun, Lord of that Ilk," was witness to a charter by Duncan eighth Earl of Lennox to John Kennedy of the lands of Buchmonyn, in the earldom of Lennox and shire of Stirling; and under the same designation, he was witness to a charter by the same Earl to Walter Buchanan of the lands of Ladlewn, on the 21st January 1394.[1] On the 6th of May of that year, under the designation of Umfridus de Col-quhoune, Lord of Luss, he was witness to the confirmation by the same Earl of a charter by John Hamilton of Buthernok, of his lands of Buthernok, in the county of Stirling, to Margaret Fraser, in prospect of the marriage to be contracted between him and her.[2] And on the 10th of June, in the year following, under the same designation, he was witness to a charter by the same Earl to Duncan Macfarlane of some lands between the rivers Dywach and Aldanchwlyn on the one side, and the rivers Hernane [Arnan], Hinys [Innis], and Trostane on the other side, with the islands Elanvow, Elan-vanow, Elandowglas, and Elaig, in the earldom of Lennox.[3]

As Lord of Luss, Sir Humphrey, in July 1395, gave to his brother Robert, the elder of that name, a charter of the lands of Camysradoch, afterwards Camstradden, and Achigahane [Auchengaven], in the lord-ship of Luss and earldom of Lennox, whom failing, to his younger brother Robert, whom failing, to his brother Patrick, as appears from the terms of the charter already given.[4] On the 10th of May 1398, under the same designation, he was witness to a charter by Duncan Earl of Lennox to Malisens Carrach of the land of Blarechos, in Strath-blane;[5] and he appears to be the person who, under the name of Umfridus de Colquhoun, was witness to the charter of Robert Earl

---

[1] Cartularium Comitatus de Levenax, pp. 45, 60.   [2] Ibid. p. 73.   [3] Ibid. p. 65.   [4] Vide supra, pp. 11, 12.   [5] Cartularium Comitatus de Levenax, p. 74.

of Fife to Duncan Earl of Lennox of the office of Coronator of the
Earldom of Lennox, dated 6th March 1400.[1] On the 18th of December following, Sir Humphrey, under the designation of "Vmfray of
Culquhune, Lord of that Ilk," was party as a witness, along with four
other "nobyl men and mychty," to a remarkable indenture, the original of
which is written in the vernacular, between Sir John Maxwell, Knight,
Lord of Pollok, and Sir John Maxwell, Knight, and Robert Maxwell, his
eldest and second sons, concerning the division and destination of the lands
of Pollok and Calderwood ;[2] and for the greater security of the part of the
indenture remaining with Sir John Maxwell, the son, the seal of Humphrey
of Colquhoun, Lord of that Ilk, was procured, through
Sir John Maxwell, the father, and Robert, his son, and
set to the indenture at Dumbarton.  This seal is still
appended to the original indenture, although part of
it has accidentally been broken.  Annexed is a wood-
cut impression of the remains of this seal.

Sir Humphrey Colquhoun, under the designation
of "Vmfary of Colqwhone, Lord of Luss," and " Robart
of Colqwhoun," were witnesses to another indenture,
dated at the Balacht, on 18th of October 1405, between Sir Duncan, Earl of the Lennox, on the one part,
and Sir William of Coningham of Kilmawris and
Sir Robert of Maxwell of Calderwood, with consent
of their spouses, Margaret and Elizabeth, daughters
of Sir Robert Danielstoun, on the other part, concerning the lands of Ach-
yuclock, Orrachy-more, Inchecallach, Inchefad, and others.[3]

In a bond of manrent, dated Inchmoryne, 5th April 1406, by Arthure
of Ardenagappil to Duncan seventh Earl of Lennox, the granter, as he
had no seal of his own, procured " the sele of ane nobil mane and a
michti, Wmfray of Culqwone, Lord of Luse," " to set to thir presentis
letteris." " On this seal," it is added, " was engraved a shield, and in

[1] Cartularium Comitatus de Levenax, p. 95.
[2] " Memoirs of the Maxwells of Pollok,"
by William Fraser, Edinburgh, 1863, vol. i.
p. 139.
[3] " Memoirs of the Maxwells of Pollok,"
by William Fraser, Edinburgh, 1863, vol. i.
p. 146 ; Original Indenture at Buchanan.

the middle of the shield was engraved the likeness of a cross, and in the top of the shield was engraved the likeness of a helmet, and to it was annexed above the form of the head of a stag, and in the circumference of the seal was written Vmfridus de Culqwone."[1] No subsequent notice of Sir Humphrey has been discovered, and his death probably occurred soon after. He had three sons and two daughters.

1. Robert, who succeeded him.

2. John, who succeeded his brother.

3. Patrick, the ancestor of the Colquhouns of Glennis, in the county of Stirling.

The two daughters of Sir Humphrey Colquhoun were—

4. Mary, who married Sir Patrick Houstoun of that Ilk, in the county of Renfrew. Sir Patrick died in the year 1450, and Mary in 1456.[2] Both of them were buried in the chapel of Houstoun, where a monument, which recorded simply their names and the time of their death, was erected to their memory. They had a son, Sir John, who succeeded his father, and who married Agnes Campbell, and had issue ; but he did not long survive his father, having died in the same year in which his mother died. Sir Peter, the son and heir of Sir John, was at the battle of Flodden, fought on the 9th September 1513, and he fell with his sovereign, King James the Fourth, and the flower of the nobility and gentry of Scotland, in that fatal engagement.[3]

5. Christian, who married James Cunningham of Glengarnock, in the county of Ayr.

Sir Humphrey Colquhoun was succeeded in his estates of Colquhoun and Luss by his eldest son—

---

[1] The words in the original are:—In quo quidem sigillo sculptum fuerat quoddam scutum, et in medio scuti sculptum fuit ad modum et similitudinem crucis, et in summitate scuti sculptum fuit ad similitudines galic, et ei superauexum ad modum cuiusdam capitis cervi, et in dicti sigilli circumferencia scribebatur " Vmfridus de Culqwone." —[Original Bond at Buchanan.]

[2] Crawfurd's Renfrewshire, p. 103, Semple's edition, 1782. She is called Anne, and her husband, Sir John, by Crawfurd, in his Officers of State, p. 318. But this is clearly a mistake, as the names on their monument in the chapel of Houstoun are Mary and Sir Patrick.

[3] Crawfurd's Renfrewshire, p. 100.

## VII.—(1.) ROBERT OF COLQUHOUN,
Seventh of Colquhoun and Ninth of Luss [1406-1408].

ON the 30th of June 1407, " Robert of Colqwhoue, Lord of Lus," received from William Wallace, Lord of Cragy, a confirmation of all the lands held of the granter, reserving to him his serfs according to law. The following is the confirmation :—

" Be it kent tyl al men throw thir presentes lettres, me, William Wallas, Lord of Cragy, til haffe approfit, ratifiit, and confirmit, and be thir presentis lettres ratifiis and confermis, al euidences, condicionis, gyffyng, sellying, or wadsettyng, that Marion Wallas hase made tyl Robert of Culqwhone, Lord of Lus, of al the landis haldyn of vs, eftir the tenor of the euideucis of the said Marion tyl the saide Robert tharapon made, in all fourme, tenor, and effect, as thai purport, and beris wytues, suffand tyl vs oure serfis, acht and custumit of law. In the wytnes of the qwhilk thyng, I, William Wallas, hes set til mi seele at Perth, the last day of Junii, the yher of oure Lorde thousand foure hundreth and sefyn." [1]

Robert of Colquhoun did not long enjoy his estate, having died in or about the year 1408. He was succeeded by his younger brother, John.

## VII.—(2.) SIR JOHN COLQUHOUN,
Eighth of Colquhoun and Tenth of Luss [1408-1439].

JEAN ERSKINE, his wife.

SIR JOHN COLQUHOUN succeeded his brother Robert in or about the year 1408. He bound himself, between the 25th July 1392 and the 23d April 1411, by letters patent, sealed with his seal, and ratified by his oath, to Duncan seventh Earl of Lennox, that he would marry Margaret, daughter of that Earl, within the term of two years, provided the Earl would discharge him of his maritage according to the form of law within that period. That lady was at that time a widow. She was previously the

---

[1] Original Confirmation at Rossdhu. The seal of this writ is lost. A facsimile of this grant is here given.

wife of Robert Menteith of Rusky, in Menteith, who had infefted her in
some of his lands, 25th July 1392, and to whom she had a son, Murdoch
Menteith of Rusky, who married, and had issue a son and two daughters.
Her father, Duncan Earl of Lennox, publicly required Sir John Colquhoun
of Luss, in presence of a notary public, on 23d April 1411, to fulfil his
engagements to marry her, as appears from a notarial instrument in the
Latin, which narrates the facts, and may be thus translated :—

In the name of God, amen : By the present public instrument let it be
manifestly known to all that, in the year of our Lord one thousand four hundred
and eleven, in the fourth indiction, on the twenty-third day of the month of
April, in the seventeenth year of the Pontificate of the most Holy Father in Christ
and our Lord, Lord Benedict the Thirteenth, by Divine Providence Pope, in
presence of me, notary public, and of the witnesses underwritten, personally
constituted, a noble and potent lord, Lord Duncan Earl of Levenax, addressed
John Colquhoun, Lord of Luss, in regard to some obligations, promises, and
certain agreements, agreed upon, entered into, and contracted between that
Lord Earl and the same John by the said John's obligatory letters-patent, sealed
with his seal, and confirmed by his oath in this manner, namely, that the same
Lord Earl, among other things, wished and asserted that the foresaid John,
being formally bound to that Lord Earl that if it should happen that he should
marry Margaret, lawful daughter of the said Lord Earl, within the term of two
years, as is more fully contained in the obligations themselves made thereupon,
if the same Lord Earl should make the foresaid John free of his maritage according to the form of reason or of law, within the above said term of two years,
which the said Lord Earl offered to do according to the before-mentioned form
of law by the security of obligations or good and sufficient pledges ; which
obligatory letters with effect the same Lord Earl requested to be observed
to him in their form and force in like manner and in effect by the same
John in all things ; and that the said Lord Earl should observe and fulfil
to the same John without delay, the obligations, promises, and agreements,
of this nature so entered into, contracted and agreed upon, in so far as
it was in his power, in form and effect, in all points, articles, and circumstances, as is more fully and effectually contained in the same obligatory
letters : And that the said Lord Earl would make the said John of Colquhoun
thus firm, safe, and secure, and would warrant the said John, as he is better
and more effectually bound to the same John in the foresaid obligatory letters,
against all mortals, according to form of law : And if it should happen that

any should attempt or wish to molest and disturb the foresaid John of Colquhoun in any points contained in the said letters, against the form of law, the
same Lord Earl offered to act in his defence against molestation or disturbance
of this sort, as he would act in a cause touching his own proper person, in any
manner in which he could suitably do so according to the foresaid form : Upon
all which, and sundry premises, the same Lord Earl asked me, notary-public
underwritten, to make to him a public instrument. These things were done
near the burial-ground of the parochial church of St. Patrick, in the diocese of
Glasgow, year, day, month, indiction and pontificate as above, there being present these noble men, John Stewart, Lord of Darnley, Sir John of Hamilton, Lord
of Bardwe, Alexander of Logan, Lord of Catconwell, knights, Hugh of Aldy-
ston, and Sir Robert Lang, rector of Innyschallach, of the diocese of Glasgow,
and other witnesses to the premises specially called and asked.[1]

Then follows, in the usual form, the docquet of the notary, Celestine
Macgillemichael, clerk of the diocese of Argyll.

Whether Sir John implemented these engagements does not appear
from any record that has come under our notice.

The life of this laird was contemporaneous with the reign of King
James the First, to whom, during his long imprisonment in England, he
was a faithful and devoted subject, and whom he so much resembled in
his tragical death. That monarch, as is well known, was made a prisoner
by the English when on his way to France in the year 1406, and was
detained in England by the Government of Henry the Fourth for eighteen
years. The Estates of Scotland, after their King had been long a
prisoner, having assembled at Perth, and held a consultation, agreed to
send an embassy to the English Court to procure his release. Some
nobles were chosen and despatched as ambassadors, and on their arrival
they found the English Court more inclined to the object of their mission than they had expected. The Duke of Gloucester, who administered
the Government, was disposed, from various political considerations, to
permit the return of King James to Scotland, and he had no difficulty
in persuading the English Council to follow this policy. Besides other
advantages, Gloucester hoped not only that he would secure the friendship
of the Scottish monarch, but that he would keep him under the power and

---

[1] Original Instrument at Buchanan.

influence of England by marrying him to Joan, daughter of the Earl of Somerset, who was considered the most beautiful woman of her time, and by whom James had been greatly captivated. The King of Scots being set at liberty, and further conciliated by his marriage with this attractive lady, Gloucester persuaded himself that he would easily manage to get the existing league between Scotland and France broken; and that the Scots being secured as allies, the English would be delivered from hostilities on the part of their immediate neighbours, and would be left free to avenge themselves on France for past injuries, or to prosecute future wars with the greater vigour and success.

But while by powerfully urging on the Council of England these and other advantages that would result from the liberation of the King of Scots, Gloucester succeeded in gaining them over to the approval of his proposal, there were some difficulties to be overcome. One of the most formidable of these was the settlement of the ransom price of the King of Scots. The English Council demanded a greater sum of money for his ransom than the Scots were either inclined or able to pay. A compromise was, however, made; the dowry of his wife was to be retained as the one-half, and the sons of some of the principal Scotch families were to be given in hostage for the payment of the other half. This having been agreed upon, James was set at liberty in the year 1423.

Having distinguished himself by his fidelity to his sovereign during his protracted imprisonment, and being a man of ability, with much influence in the country, Sir John Colquhoun was appointed, during the reign of King James the First, to the office of Governor of Dumbarton Castle. This office he held in 1424, the year after the release of the King. In the account of the customs of the burgh of Linlithgow, rendered on 15th May 1425, from 23d July 1424 to the day of the account, under the head of expenditure, are mentioned " the payment made by command of our Lord the King to John of Colquhone, Keeper of the Castle of Dunbrettane, from the term of the blessed Martin, bypast, as appears by the said John's letters of receipt shown on the account, £26, 13s. 4d.; and the payment made to the said John for the keeping of the said castle, of the term of Pentecost next to come, Sir John Forster (Chamberlain) testifying the receipt upon the account, £13, 6s. 8d."[1]   Sir John Colquhoun held the same office during the minority of King James the Second.

On the 3d of January 1429, "John of Colquhoun, Lord of that Ilk," was one of the assize at the settlement by Sir John Forster, Knight, of Corstorphin, Chamberlain of Scotland, of the dispute between the burghs of Dumbarton and Renfrew, regarding certain rights of fishing.[2] And on the 7th February of the same year, John Macroger of Glen Mackerne [Glenmakuru], resigned in the open head court of the Lord of Luss into the hands of his lord superior, John of Colquhoun, Lord of Luss, all his lands of Gleane Mackehirne, Bannories, Inchgonagane, and Elanchleyff. Among the witnesses are Robert of Colquhoun, Lord of Camstrodane, and Malcolm of Culquhoun.[3]

Sir John of Colquhoun was patron of the parish church of Luss, and about the year 1430, he consented to the annexation of that parish church as a prebendary to the cathedral church of Glasgow. It was then so annexed by John Cameron, Bishop of Glasgow, who, at the same time, erected other parochial churches of the diocese of Glasgow into prebendaries of that cathedral. The patrons, however, were still to retain the right of presentation of vicars to the churches when vacant.[4]

But Sir John Colquhoun had soon after an opportunity of taking a more prominent part in the management of the affairs of his country. He sat as a Member of Parliament in the year 1437—the commencement of the reign of King James the Second.[5]

It was now a dark period in Scottish history. James the First, who was a wise and good prince, remarkable for excellence of genius and cultivation of mind, actively endeavoured to promote the welfare of his subjects, of which the many salutary laws enacted during his reign, which benefited not only his own age, but posterity, are lasting monuments. But his days were prematurely cut short. He was assassinated on the 20th of February

[1] Accounts of the Great Chamberlains of Scotland, etc., vol. iii. pp. 152, 153.

[2] Extract Decreet at Rossdhu.

[3] Original Procuratory of Resignation at Rossdhu. The Bannories here mentioned were probably High and Low Baury (now Baudry) and the hill above Rossdhu, called the Bandry wood.

[4] Registrum Episcopatus Glasguensis, p. 340.

[5] M'Kenzie, MS. Coll.

1437, in the Convent of the Dominicans, at Perth, whilst he sat with the Queen at supper, attended only by a few domestics, in the forty-fourth year of his age and the thirty-first of his reign, by a conspiracy, of which Walter Earl of Athole was the author. Not less than twenty-eight wounds were inflicted on his person by the conspirators, and his Queen, whilst endeavouring to defend him, was wounded in two places. He was succeeded by his only son, James the Second, who was then a child of only seven years of age, and who was crowned, at Holyrood House, on the 27th of March that year. Alexander Livingstone was chosen Regent and William Crichton Chancellor for the Administration of the Government during the King's minority. But these ministers, each being un-happily impelled by ambition, did not work together harmoniously either for the good of the King or of the kingdom. The supreme power in the State was contested by them ; their mutual jealousies produced mutual recriminations ; and these again were followed by the adjustment of their differences. Rival factions were formed, and many powerful families were at feud. The slaughters committed among them were frequent, and these were followed by robberies, burnings, and murders, perpetrated by the friends and vassals of the one party upon the friends and vassals of the other. In this disorganized state of the kingdom, when justice was but feebly administered, the multiplication of acts of violence, especially in the remote parts of the country, and bordering on the Highlands, was to be ex-pected. Taking advantage of such a state of things, a body of the Western Islanders, headed by the principal men of the Isles, Lachlan Maclean or Macleod and Murdoch Gibson, who were two noted robbers, made a descent upon the western coast for the purposes of plunder. Sir John Colquhoun of Luss signalized himself by his promptitude and courage in resisting their incursions, for which he had collected a considerable number of men. He unhappily lost his life in this patriotic enterprise.

The circumstances attending his death have been differently related by our historians. Boece says that, overpowered by the numbers of the enemy, he was slain, with many of his people, when fighting bravely.[1] Buchanan gives a somewhat different version. The chiefs of the party, Lachlan

[1] Boetius, f. 360.

Maclean and Murdoch Gibson, sent a message to Sir John Colquhoun, requesting that he would honour them with a friendly conference, with the view of endeavouring to effect a reconciliation, and they pledged their faith for his personal safety. Not suspecting any hostile or treacherous intention, he left his garrison and went to meet them, attended only by a few of his friends. Whilst he was treating with them, under an assurance of personal safety, these ruthless savages put him and his attendants to death, with circumstances of barbarous cruelty. This tragic scene took place in the Island of Inchmurrin, in Lochlomond, on the 24th of September 1439.[1] The tradition of the district reports that a party of the Western Islesmen made a descent upon the coast, and having pursued some of the inhabitants to the Island of Inchmurrin, put to the sword the Laird of Luss and several others.

These and similar slaughters and robberies, which were committed in most parts of the kingdom, threatening the complete destruction of all order and government, created universal alarm. All felt that it was necessary that something should be done. A Parliament was summoned to meet, for the purpose of devising and adopting such measures as were urgently required in so calamitous a conjuncture, and it was opened on the 2d of August 1440. One of the measures which was adopted was the appointment of justice aires or Circuit Courts, to be held twice in the year, both on the south and on the north sides of the Forth. This was not the first appointment of these courts, for the Act expressly asserts that they were to be held " as auld use and custom is." But they had not, it is probable, been for some time held so regularly, in the distracted condition of the kingdom, as the preservation of the public tranquillity required, and as it was now determined should be done. The Act ordained that lords of regalities within their regalities, and the King's bailies of his regalities, and that the King himself should be in each town where the aire should be held, or near thereby, where his Council thought it necessary.[2] By the same Parliament, for the remedy and punishment of divers crimes, it

[1] Buchanan's History, Aikman's edit., vol. ii. p. 124; Auchinleck Chronicle; Lindsay of Pitscottie's History of Scotland, p. 16; Abercromby's Martial Achievements of the     Scots Nation, vol. ii. p. 324.
[2] Acts of the Parliaments of Scotland, vol. ii. p. 32.

was concluded "that our sovereign Lord the King ride through all the realm incontinent after there be sent to his Council, where any rebellion, slaughter, burning, reife, forfalt, or theft happens; and there to call the Sheriff of the shire where the thing beis done before him, and or (ere) the King depart out of that shire, to set remedy of such harms done, or if any such shall happen to be done, whether the default be in the officers or in the doers, to be punished by the King. The which conclusion and ordinance all the Barons, of common assent and consent, are obliged to assist, both with their power in bodies and goods, as oft as shall be seen speedful, by advice of the Council, for the good and avail of the realm, and the common profit."[1]

Sir John Colquhoun married Jean, daughter of Robert Lord Erskine, who was a co-heir with Lyle of Duchal of the ancient Earls of Mar, by whom he had one son and one daughter,—

1. Malcolm, who predeceased his father.

2. Isabel, who married David Douglas of Mains, after 1440.

## VIII.—MALCOLM COLQUHOUN,
### Younger of Colquhoun and Luss, 1410-1439.

THIS Malcolm Colquhoun was the heir-apparent of his father, Sir John, and is stated by genealogists to have been a young man of high promise.

The only evidence which we have found of him is in a charter by Sir James Scrimzeour, constable of Dundee, dated 13th November 1433, in which he is designed " Malcolm Colquhoun, son and heir-apparent of Sir John Colquhoun of Luss."[2] He died before the year 1439, in the lifetime of his father, leaving by his wife, whose name has not been ascertained, a son, John, who succeeded his grandfather in the estates of Colquhoun and Luss.

---

[1] Acts of the Parliament of Scotland, vol. ii. pp. 32, 33.

[2] Craufurd in his Officers of State and Douglas in his Baronage state that this Malcolm Colquhoun was one of the hostages appointed to proceed to England in security for the payment of the ransom of King James the First on his liberation by the English. This, however, is a mistake. The hostages were twenty-one in number, and their names are given in Rymer's Fœdera (vol. x. p. 307), but the name of Malcolm Colquhoun does not appear in the list.

# IX.—Sir JOHN COLQUHOUN, Knight,

Ninth of Colquhoun and Eleventh of Luss, 1439-1478.

———— Boyd, his first wife.

Elizabeth Dunbar, Countess of Murray, his second wife.

Sir John Colquhoun, son of Malcolm, succeeded his grandfather, Sir John, about the close of the year 1439. He was a man of distinguished abilities, and in every position he acquitted himself in a manner which gained him much credit and honour. He was in high favour both with King James the Second and King James the Third. Between the years 1457 and 1478 he received numerous royal and other charters, which prove the extent of his territorial possessions. During the same period he held successively several important offices of State, which no less clearly indicates the eminence which he had attained as a statesman; and for the services rendered by him to his sovereign and his country, the honour of knight-hood was conferred upon him. It thus appears that in him the family of Colquhoun rose to great wealth and distinction.

On the 22d of February 1457, King James the Second granted him a charter of the lands of Luss, Colquhoun, and Gartscube, in the shire of Dumbarton, and of the lands of Glyn and Sawchie, in the shire of Stirling. The charter, in which he is designated John Colquhoun of that Ilk, proceeds on his own resignation, and by it these lands were united and incorporated into a free barony, to be called the Barony of Luss, to be held, by him and his heirs, of the Crown, for rendering the services therein specified. On the 20th of March 1458, his Majesty also granted him a charter erecting into a Free Forest the lands of Park of Rossdhu, and the lands of Glen-muckeruc, in the shire of Dumbarton, which heritably belonged to Sir John, and had been resigned by him into the hands of the King.[1]

Soon after, Sir John acquired the lands of Saline, in the shire of Fife, which had previously been the property of John de Haliburton. On 26th April 1465, in the presence of a notary-public and of various witnesses, he

---

[1] Original Charters at Rossdhu.

E

delivered to John de Haliburton of Sawling a letter of presentation from the King; and, after it was read, he requested that he might be infefted in the lands of Bordeland of Sawling, according to the tenor of that letter. John de Haliburton declined in the meantime to do so, and retained in his possession the letter of presentation;[1] but on 16th January 1465-6, he resigned all his right and title to the two Sawlings, namely, Black Sawling and Little Sawling, in favour of Sir John.[2] On 10th November in the same year, Sir John, for his counsel, assistance, and favour rendered in many ways to the granter, received from David de Haliburton, son of John de Haliburton, a charter to himself and his heirs, in feu and heritage for ever, of an annual rent of £6, 13s. 4d. Scots, from the lands of Uchtirstoune and Burnhouse, in the shire of Berwick.[3]

On the 24th of March 1465-6, he received from King James the Third a charter, in which he is designed John de Colquhoun of that Ilk, Knight, Comptroller of the Exchequer (*computorum rotulator*), of the half of the lands of Kilmerdoning, in the shire of Dumbarton, and on the confines of Stirlingshire to the east of the church, on the resignation of them by their former proprietor, Alexander de Auchinros, to be held of the Crown, for rendering the services due and wont.[4] On 7th August 1469, he acquired, for payment of a certain sum of money, from John Haliburton, a charter of the four merk land of Nisbet, in East Lothian.[5] On 29th November 1473, he obtained a charter of the lands of Roseneath, in the county of Dumbarton; and on the 8th of October 1474, he further received from King James the Third a charter of the lands of Strone, Kilmone, Invercapill, and Cayveland, in Argyleshire, which formerly belonged to James Scrimgeour of Dudhope, by whom they were resigned into the hands of the King.[6]

From George second Earl of Huntly he obtained an assignation of the lands of Tulycchil, in the Stewartry of Stratherne. But a right to occupy these lands to his exclusion was claimed by Humphrey Murray of Aber-

[1] Original Notarial Instrument at Rossdhu.
[2] Original Instrument of Resignation, ibid.
[3] Original Charter, ibid.

[4] Original Charter at Rossdhu.
[5] Original Charter, ibid.
[6] Original Charters, ibid.  Reg. Mag. Sig. Lib. vii. Nos. 73, 308.

136378?

carny, who had received an assignation of them from another party.
Sir John, therefore, pursued an action against him for the wrongous occupation of them, for the wrongous spoliation of their mails, and for the
wrongous uplifting from them of fourteen bolls of bere.   On 9th July 1476,
when the case was brought before the Lords Auditors, Sir John produced a
letter of assignation of these lands from the Earl of Huntly, and Humphrey
Murray produced a similar letter of assignation from William of Stirling,
who, he alleged, had to them a prior right.  Both parties having been at
length heard, the Lords Auditors assigned to Humphrey Murray, the 2d of
October next, to prove that William of Stirling had power from the Earl
of Huntly to assign or to let the lands to the said Humphrey, and failing
in the proof, to devoid them to Sir John, and to pay to him the mails
thereof from the time of the lease made to Sir John, with the said bolls of
bere, as far as Sir John should prove that the defender had taken them
up.[1]  The final decision of the Lords Auditors is not recorded.

In 1477 and 1478, Sir John acquired various tenements of land and
houses in the burgh of the Canongate, Edinburgh.[2]  All these properties were
to be held of the Lord Abbot and Convent of the Monastery of the Holy
Cross of Edinburgh.  In a notarial instrument relating to these properties, dated 21st October 1478, it is narrated that Humphrey, " son and
apparent heir of Sir John Colquhoun," took instruments in name and
behalf of his father ; a statement which shows that his father was then
alive, and consequently that Bishop Lesley and others are mistaken in
saying that the death of Sir John took place on 1st May 1478.

Sir John also obtained the lands of Kirkton and Inchberry, in the
county of Dumbarton, from Huchou Thomson, son of the deceased Walter
Thomson.  He pursued an action against Hew Lord Fraser for the wrongous occupation of these lands, and for the taking up of their mails for

---

[1] Acta Dominorum Auditorum, p. 46.

[2] On 9th July 1477, he received a charter of a piece of waste ground, six perches
and five yards in length, and eight and a
half yards in breadth, in that burgh.  On
11th September following, he obtained a
charter and sasine of a piece of ground situated therein.  On 4th June 1478, a disposition, and, on the day after, a charter, was
made in his favour of an annual rent of six
shillings, which the granter derived from the
land of Sir John, lying in the same burgh.
—Original Charters and Sasine, and Copy
Disposition at Rossdhu.

three years previous. The case came before the Lords of Council on 19th October 1478, when their Lordships decreed that Lord Fraser should cease from the occupation of these lands in time to come, and that he should pay to Sir John the sum of £30, being the mails thereof, which he had taken up for the three years past, as was proved before the Lords.[1]

Some other lands Sir John acquired at different times, as appears from the references made to them, in the Acts of the Lords of Council in the year 1480. Among these were the lands of Over-Glenny, in the shire of Perth, of which he granted a charter and infeftment to James Menteith of Raduoch, with clause of warrandice;[2] the lands of Westirdenlethir, in the same shire, of which he gave a charter and infeftment to Malcolm M'Rure;[3] and the lands of Galmore and the Middlequarter of Dunfawy, in the same shire, of which he obtained a charter from David Wardlaw, made in his own favour only, and not extending to his heirs.[4]

Sir John was a witness to several charters, relating both to the civil and ecclesiastical transactions of his time. He was witness to an indenture between Robert Lord Fleming and Gilbert Lord Kennedy, concerning the lands of Easter and Wester Mains, and others, in the barony of Lenze and shire of Dumbarton, dated 10th February 1465. In the indenture he is designated Sir John Colquhoun of that Ilk.[5] He was witness to a charter granted by King James the Third, at Edinburgh, 26th February 1471, with consent of the Three Estates of Parliament, to William Lord Monypenny, of the lands of Kirkandris, in the Stewartry of Kirkcudbright, which lands had been resigned by James Lord Hamilton, to whom they belonged heritably, into the hands of the King, in exchange for his Majesty's forty merk lands of Esterbermukkis, Westerbermukkis, and others, in the lordship of Bothwell.[6]

Sir John was also witness to a charter of King James the Third, dated Edinburgh, 14th October 1475, granting to the Cathedral Church of Glasgow, for his singular devotion towards the blessed St. Kentigern, and that

[1] Acta Dominorum Concilii, p. 15.
[2] Ibid. pp. 50, 51.
[3] Ibid. p. 51.
[4] Ibid. p. 68.

[5] Original Indenture in Cumbernauld Charter-Chest.
[6] Acts of the Parliament of Scotland, vol. ii. p. 188.

Saint's mother St. Tenew, and towards the said cathedral, three stones
of wax, in which it had stood infefted from ancient time, to be raised
annually from the lands of Udingston, in the lordship of Bothwell and
shire of Lanark, before these lands had been appropriated to the Crown,
but which had been detained by their possessors for some years past, for
the lights of St. Kentigern and St. Tenew, his mother.  Two and a half
stones were to be distributed for the lights of the first-mentioned saint in
that Cathedral Church, upon his sepulchre; and half a stone was to be
distributed upon the sepulchre of St. Tenew, in the chapel where her
bones reposed.[1]  Another ecclesiastical charter to which Sir John was
a witness, was one by the same monarch to the Bishops of Glasgow,
dated at Edinburgh, 15th July 1476, whereby his Majesty granted and
confirmed anew, with the authority and consent of Parliament, to John
Bishop of Glasgow and his successors, bishops of Glasgow, the right formerly given to them by his Majesty's predecessors, with advice of Parliament, to hold the city of Glasgow, the barony of Glasgow, and the lands
of Bishopforest, for a free regality and barony.  This right included the
power of constituting within the said city a provost, bailies, servants, and
other officers for the government thereof, and of appointing one sergeant,
who should bear a baton or silver rod with the royal arms and the arms of
the Bishop of the said church, for making arrestments and executing the
mandates of that prelate within the said regality, and through all other
lands and possessions belonging to him within his diocese.[2]  This charter
his Majesty granted for his singular devotion towards the blessed confessor,
St. Kentigern, patron of the Cathedral Church of Glasgow, and for his
special favour and love towards the reverend father in Christ, John, Bishop
of that church, his heartily beloved counsellor, for his merits and gratuitous and faithful services rendered to his progenitors and to him.  Sir
John, again, was witness to a charter of confirmation by King James
the Third, dated 15th June 1478, confirming a charter of John Bishop of
Glasgow, by which he gave a tenement at Edinburgh to the Cathedral
Church of Glasgow.[3]

[1] Registrum Episcopatus Glasguensis, tom.
ii. pp. 426-428.

[2] Reg. Episc. Glasg. tom. ii. pp. 430-433.
[3] Ibid. tom. ii. p. 437.

In many of the political transactions of his time, Sir John took an active part; and, while holding the various honourable public offices which, by the patronage of his friends, and from his acknowledged abilities, he obtained, he on several occasions rendered important services to his country, both at home and at the Court of England.

His sovereign, James the Second, by whom he had been much esteemed, fell, in the prime of life, by the sudden explosion of a cannon, when encouraging his troops at the siege of Roxburgh Castle, in August 1460.[1] After this melancholy event, a Parliament was held at Edinburgh, on the 23d of February 1460-1, by which the custody of the deceased King's son, James the Third, who was a minor of only eight years of age, and of his two brothers, and sisters, was committed to the Queen Mother, whilst it was determined that the administration of affairs should be divided among a select few of the nobility. Sir John Colquhoun of Luss, if not a member of the Government at first chosen, was soon after appointed Comptroller of the Exchequer. The other officers of state with whom he was associated were James Kennedy, Bishop of St. Andrews, to whom the chief management of affairs was intrusted; Andrew Stewart, Lord Evandale (natural son of Sir James Stewart, and grandson of Murdoch Duke of Albany), who was Chancellor; Robert Lord Boyd, to whom Sir John was related by marriage, who was Justiciar of Scotland; James Lindsay, Provost of Lincluden, who was Keeper of the Privy Seal; and James Lord Livingston, who was Chamberlain.[2]

Sir John was frequently a member of Parliament, and sat as one of the Barons. His name first appears in the list of members in the Parliament of King James the Third, held at Edinburgh in October 1466, and he was appointed by it one of the Lords Auditors of Complaints.[3] He is designated Sir John Colquhoun of that Ilk, Knight. He was again a member of the Parliament held at Edinburgh in October 1467, and was put on a commission to which it committed power to advise and conclude upon various matters in an adjourned meeting to take place at Stirling, on

[1] Tytler's History of Scotland, vol. i. p. 306.
[2] Crawford's Officers of State, pp. 37, 313; Rymer's Fœdera, tom. xi. p. 476.
[3] Acts of the Parliament of Scotland, vol. ii. p. 85; Acta Dominorum Auditorum. p. 3.

12th January 1467. Among the matters treated upon by that com
mission was the marriage of King James the Third. It was unani-
mously resolved that an embassy should be sent with all haste, before
the month of March or April following, to Denmark and other places
considered expedient, with full power to advise and conclude upon the
marriage of their sovereign Lord, with a suitable person of noble blood,
and to marry and bring home a queen, and that in the said embassy
there should be a prelate, a lord, a knight, or a clerk, to be chosen by
the King, and forty honourable and worshipful persons, or fewer, with
them.[1] According to this ordinance of Parliament, Andrew Muirhead,
Bishop of Glasgow ; William Tulloch, Bishop of Orkney ; Andrew Lord
Evandale, Chancellor; Thomas Boyd, Earl of Arran ; and Mr. Martin
Vans, Grand Almoner and Confessor to the King, were sent ambassadors
to the Court of Denmark to negotiate a marriage between King James
the Third and the Princess Margaret, the only daughter of Christian the
First, King of Denmark and Norway. This they had the good fortune
to bring to a successful termination. The youthful bride landed in
Scotland on 6th July 1468, accompanied by a brilliant train of lords and
ladies, and the marriage was celebrated with much pomp and solemnity on
the 10th of that month, in the Abbey Church of Holyrood House.[2]

In the years 1469, 1471, 1476, and 1478, Sir John was also a member
of Parliament.[3]

He appears on record as occupying the office of Comptroller of the
Exchequer till 1469, when Adam Wallace of Craigie was appointed in his
place.[4]

After the downfall of his friend, Robert Lord Boyd, who was indicted
for high treason before the Parliament, and condemned to be beheaded,
in 1469, though he saved his life by making his escape into England,
where he died at an advanced age, at Alnwick, in the following year, Sir
John, by his loyalty and prudence, preserved his interest at the Court of

[1] Acts of the Parliament of Scotland,
vol. ii. pp. 89, 90.

[2] Balfour's Annals, vol. i. p. 194.

[3] Acts of the Parliament of Scotland,
vol. ii. pp. 93, 98, 102, 121, 188, 191.

[4] Crawfurd's Officers of State, vol. i.
p. 318.

King James the Third.[1]   So high did he stand in the royal favour, that he
continued to receive from his Majesty honourable preferments, and was
employed as before in some of the most important affairs of State.   In
1471, he was appointed Principal Sheriff of Dumbartonshire, and he was
also one of the sheriffs of the shire of Linlithgow.[2]

In 1474, Sir John was still more highly promoted, having been raised
to the position of Great Chamberlain of Scotland.   This was one of the
most ancient offices of State in Scotland.   It existed in the reign of King
Malcolm the Second, and in his time it was, under the Crown, the third
highest office in the commonwealth, ranking next to those of Chancellor
and Justiciar, and taking precedence of those of Steward, Constable, and
Marischall.   In Sir John Colquhoun's time it was still one of the most
honourable, responsible, and lucrative offices of State.   This it is necessary
to bear in mind in considering his position as a statesman, as the office of
that name is now merely a situation in the household establishment of the
Sovereign, having no connexion with the administration of public affairs.

The Great Chamberlain anciently collected the revenues of the Crown
before the appointment of a treasurer, of which there is no trace till the
restoration of King James the First, in 1425, and he disbursed the money
required for the maintenance of the King's household.   The rolls of the royal
receipts and expenditure, which were kept by the Chamberlain, still exist,
affording curious illustrations of the state of the Court, of the condition of
Scotland, its agriculture, commerce, manufactures, and of the customs and
manners of its inhabitants in those early times.[3]   But the Great Chamberlain

[1] In testimony of his duty and affection
to his sovereign, Sir John sent to him a
present of two hounds.   In the Lord High
Treasurer of Scotland's books, connected
with Dumbartonshire, under 3d November
1473, is the following entry :— " Item, to
a man that come fra the lairde of Luss
witht ij grew hundis to the King, xs."

[2] Acta Dominorum Auditorum, p. 54.

[3] The Accounts of the Great Chamberlain
of Scotland, and some other officers of the
Crown, rendered at the Exchequer, extend-

ing from 1263, in the reign of Alexander
the Third, to 1453, in the reign of James
the Second, have been published in three
large volumes, under the editorship of the
late Mr. Thomson, Deputy-Clerk Register.
This is a most important work to the student
of the history and antiquities of Scotland.
as, from the minuteness of its details, it
supplies much important authentic information on his favourite subject not elsewhere
to be obtained.   The original Rolls are
deposited in her Majesty's General Register
House, Edinburgh.

of Scotland was, besides, invested with the power of judging of crimes committed within burghs, and, like the Justiciar, he had his aires or circuit courts through the country annually, or as often as the adequate administration of justice required. His sentences were to be put in execution by the bailies of the burghs. In the third Parliament of King James the Third, held at Edinburgh in November 1469, it was enacted, in reference to chamberlain aires as well as Parliament and Justiciary aires, " that the Court of Parliament, Justice Are, Chawmerlane Are, or sic like courtis, that has continuatione, nede nocht to be continuit fra day to day, but that thai may be of sic strinth and fors as thai had bene continuit fra day to day, vnto the tyme that thai be dissolnit : the Parliament be the King ; the Justice Are be the justice ; the chawmerlane Are be the chawmer lane." [1] In the third Parliament of King James the Fourth, held at Edinburgh in May 1491, it was ordained that inquiry should be made in the Chamberlain aire how the common goods of burghs were spent. [2]

The commission from the Crown, conferring on Sir John Colquhonn of Luss the office of Great Chamberlain of Scotland, has not been preserved ; but an idea of the nature and extent of the jurisdiction of the office to which he was now elevated, may be formed from the commission of Chamberlainry granted by Queen Mary under the Great Seal, 12th November 1553, to James Lord Fleming. From that commission, which invested him with all the rights and powers which his father or any of his predecessors, Great Chamberlains, possessed from her Majesty, or her most noble progenitors, kings of Scotland, we learn that the Chamberlain had full power by himself, or by his deputies whom he might constitute, to appoint and hold circuit courts, as often as it seemed necessary or expedient to him, in the accustomed places in burgh or land within the kingdom, and to continue them ; to cause suits to be called, to fine the absent, to punish delinquents accord-

[1] Acts of the Parliament of Scotland, vol. ii. p. 97.

[2] Ibid. vol. ii. p. 227. It thus appears that it is a mistake to suppose, as Mr. Tytler seems to do in his History (vol. ii. p. 152), that the office of Chamberlain belonged exclusively " to the personal estate of the Sovereign," and that the nature of the office is fully described by simply saying that " those who held it enjoyed the supreme authority in the management of the King's household, and in the regulation of the royal revenue."

ing to the laws and custom of the kingdom, and the number and quality of their crimes, to appoint clerks, sergeants, judges, and all other officers necessary thereto, to cause parties to be sworn, and generally to do what-ever was held to belong to the said office.[1]

In the capacity of Great Chamberlain of Scotland, Sir John Colquhoun, along with Thomas Spence, Bishop of Aberdeen, James Schaw of Sauchie, and the Lyon King-at-Arms, were in July 1474 sent to the Court of England with plenipotentiary power to treat of a marriage between the Prince of Scot-land, who was then only in the third year of his age, and the Princess Cæcilia, daughter of Edward the Fourth, King of England, who was only in her fourth year. So successful were Sir John and his colleagues in this important and delicate mission, that all the preliminaries were agreed upon, and they returned to Edinburgh in the beginning of October, accom-panied or followed by the Bishop of Durham, Lord Scroop, Mr. John Russel, Keeper of the Privy Seal, and Mr. Robert Booth, Doctor of Laws, whom King Edward commissioned to proceed to Scotland to complete what had been so auspiciously begun in England. New commissioners, consist-ing of John, Bishop of Glasgow, William, Bishop of Orkney, Colin Earl of Argyle, David Earl of Crawford, the Abbot of Holyrood House, and the Archdean of St. Andrews, were appointed by King James to treat with those whom King Edward had sent to Scotland, and to arrange the terms of a treaty in reference to the contemplated marriage, which promised so greatly "to contribute to the wealth, peace, honour, and interest of this noble isle, called Great Britain." [2]

On the 26th of October, the treaty or contract of marriage between

---

[1] Crawfurd's Officers of State, vol. i. pp. 251, 464. The office of Chamberlain, in the course of time, lost much of its importance. The Chamberlain aires, from their malad-ministration, became very unpopular in the burghs, which regarded them as instruments of oppression rather than courts of justice. The Lords concerned in the raid of Ruthven, in August 1582, from their hostility to the Duke of Lennox, then heritable Chamber-lain, discharged, by a proclamation issued in the King's name, the keeping of Cham berlain aires. The rights and privileges of the office gradually ceased to be exercised, and at last, in 1703, the Duke of Lennox re-signed it into the hands of Queen Anne, *ad perpetuam remanentiam*. Since that time no Chamberlain has been appointed.—Scot of Scotstarvet's Staggering State of Scots Statesmen, p. xx.

[2] Rymer's Fœdera, tom. xi. p. 821.

the Prince and Princess was agreed to, and signed by the commissioners of both kingdoms.  To render it as secure as possible, the formalities characteristic of feudal times were carefully observed.  On the same day, David Earl of Crawford, as procurator for the King of Scotland, and Lord Scroop, Knight of the Garter, as procurator for the King of England, appeared in the Low Greyfriars' Church at Edinburgh, in presence of the English and Scottish Commissioners and others assembled, and went through the ceremony of betrothment.  Each of these noblemen having declared the character in which he appeared, and demanded that his letters of procuratory should be read, the letters were publicly read accordingly.  Then the Earl of Crawford, taking Lord Scroop by the right hand, solemnly promised for and in name of his master, the King of Scotland, that his Majesty would bestow Prince James, his son, in marriage, upon the Princess Cæcilia, the daughter of Edward King of England, when the Prince and Princess had arrived at the age prescribed by the Canons.  Lord Scroop, having next taken the Earl of Crawford by the right hand, made a like solemn engagement for and in name of his master, King Edward of England.  Upon which two notaries, one for the King of Scotland and the other for the King of England, took instruments before witnesses.  Sir John Colquhoun of Luss was present on this occasion, and he was one of the witnesses to the notarial instrument.[1]

By the treaty, the King of England was to give with his daughter a dowry of 20,000 merks, English money, of which 2000 were to be paid every year at Edinburgh, in the parish church of St. Giles, the first payment to be made on the 2d of February following, and the other instalments on the same day every successive year till complete payment of the whole should be made.  Both Kings were also to assist one another, as often as required, against their respective rebels.  For some state reasons this marriage was, after all, never completed.  But in the meantime King James reaped considerable advantage from the alliance.  He received punctual payment of a portion of the dowry which Edward promised to give with his daughter.  He had now leisure to settle the revenue of his own kingdom, and strengthened by the promise of assistance from the King

[1] Rymer's Fœdera, tom. xi. p. 821.

of England, he could bring such of his subjects as had disturbed the tranquillity of the state, during his minority, to account for their actions.[1]

It was probably as a reward for the services rendered by Sir John, on
the occasion of his mission to the Court of England, that he was soon after
appointed Governor of the Castle of Dumbarton for life, with all the
emoluments pertaining to the office, which included the lands of Cardross,
Cumray, an annual rent from the lands of Cadzow, with the corn-mill of
Paisley, commonly called le Uache Mele (the walk mill). His commission as Governor empowered him to name and appoint all other necessary
officers. It passed the Great Seal, at Edinburgh, on 7th September 1477.[2]

Sir John did not, however, long enjoy this new appointment. A brave
and skilful soldier, as well as an able statesman, he in the following year
joined the army raised by King James the Third for the defence of himself
and his government, against his brother, Alexander Duke of Albany, who
had engaged in an unnatural rebellion against him. The army hastened to
besiege the Castle of Dunbar, which the Duke of Albany had garrisoned
and held against the King and Government. The siege was successful;
for the garrison, after an intrepid defence of some months, were compelled,
from want of provisions, to evacuate, and escaping during the night preceding the day on which the besiegers entered the Castle, sought refuge
in England or France. But Sir John Colquhoun did not live to see the
triumph of the King's cause. The cannon mounted on the ramparts of the
castle by the besieged for their defence, were used with fatal effect against
the besiegers. On the second day of the siege a single cannon-ball killed
three of the most valiant knights in the royal army,—Sir John Colquhoun
of Luss, Sir Andrew Wallace of Craigie, and Sir James Shaw of Sauchie.[3]
The exact time when the siege commenced not being known, the precise
date of the death of Sir John is uncertain. It must, however, have
happened between the 21st of October 1478, when he is referred to in a
notarial instrument as then living, as already observed, and the 14th of

[1] Lesley's History, p. 304 ; Rymer's Fœdera, tom. xi. pp. 814, 815, 821, 822, 824,
etc. ; Abercromby's Martial Achievements
of the Scottish Nation, vol. ii. pp. 424,
425.

[2] Charter in Pub. Arch. quoted in Crawfurd's Officers of State, p. 319.

[3] Balfour's Annals of Scotland, vol. i. p.
202; Lesley's History, p 43 ; Tytler's History of Scotland, vol. iii. p. 375.

June 1479, when his son Humphrey was infefted as heir to his deceased father in certain properties.[1] In a decreet of the Lords of Council, 22d January 1479-80, he is designed "the vmquhile Schir Johne of Culquhone of that Ilk, vschare in the tyme of oure Soucrane Lordis Chawmer durre."[2]

Before his death Sir John Colquhoun made a testament, containing various provisions in favour of his second wife, who survived him. He constituted Mr. Robert Houstoun, parson of Luss, and Patrick Houstoun, his executors. In the year 1484, an action was pursued in the Supreme Civil Court by Mr. Robert Houstoun, parson of Luss, and Patrick Houstoun, executors to the deceased Sir John Colquhoun of the Luss, Knight, against Sir William of Murray of Tullibardine, Knight, John of Murray, his son and heir, and Robert Balmaclone for the wrongous spoliation of certain corn out of the lands of Inverpeffre and Gorte, belonging to the late Sir John. This action the Lords Auditors, on 22d October that year, continued to the 14th of January following.[3]

Sir John married, first, ——— Boyd, a lady of the family of Lord Boyd, by whom he had a son, Humphrey, and a daughter, Margaret. Lady Luss predeceased her husband, who married, secondly, Lady Elizabeth Dunbar, second daughter of James Dunbar, fifth Earl of Murray. This lady was the relict of Archibald Douglas, second son of James seventh Earl of Douglas, who obtained with her the earldom of Murray, having been the sixth Earl of that name. Her elder sister, Janet, with whom she was co-heiress of the earldom of Murray, had, by reason of her seniority, a preferable right, and indeed actually assumed the dignity. But Archibald Douglas, after his marriage with Elizabeth, succeeded, from the almost unlimited power which his family wielded in the affairs of State, in securing that earldom to himself.[4]

[1] Original Instrument of Sasine at Rossdhu.
[2] Acta Dominorum Concilii, p. 49.
[3] Acta Dominorum Auditorum, p. 150*.
[4] In 1454 Janet had assumed the dignity. On 8th November that year, an original grant was made by "Janet of Dunbar, Countess of Murray, and Lady of Fren-

dracht and of Crechton," to her cousin, Walter Ogilvy of Bewfort. To this "her seal of arms is appended, containing four quarters—the first, the arms of Murray, as usual, with the double tressure ; the second, a lion rampant for Crichton, the arms of James Lord Crichton, her husband, also in

The marriage of Archibald Douglas and Elizabeth Dunbar appears to have taken place in the year 1442. They obtained a royal charter of the lands of Kintore, in the bailiery of Kintore, which belonged to Janet and Elizabeth Dunbar, daughters of the deceased James Dunbar, Earl of Murray, heritably, and which the said Janet and Elizabeth resigned into the hands of the Crown in their pure and simple virginity, to be held by Archibald, second son of James Earl of Douglas and the said Elizabeth, and the longest liver of them, and the heirs-male to be lawfully procreated betwixt them ; failing whom, the other heirs therein mentioned. On 26th April 1442, a precept of sasine was addressed by King James the Second to the Sheriff and his bailies of Aberdeen, commanding them, in terms of the charter, to give sasine of the lands of Kintore to the said Archibald and Elizabeth.[1] Soon after obtaining sasine, Archibald Douglas assumed the title of Earl of Murray, which he held for about thirteen years. Having engaged in the rebellion of his twin brother, James ninth Earl of Douglas, against King James the Second, the Earl of Murray was slain in the battle with the King's troops, which was fought on the 1st of May 1455, at the small river Sark, in Arkinholm, in the county of Dumfries.[2] His head was cut off, and carried to the King, who was then at Abercorn. In the following month of June, all the lands, rents, possessions, superiorities, and offices of "Archibald pretended earl of Murray," were declared to be forfeited to the Crown,[3] and the title of Earl of Murray was soon after conferred by the King on his youngest son, Prince David. Elizabeth Dunbar had by Archibald Douglas a son, James, and a daughter, Janet, as we learn from a document to be immediately quoted. Of the history of these children we have no information ; but they were probably involved in the calamities

her right, Earl of Murray, or it may be for Dunbar (the seal being partly defaced), and Janet being a cadet of the Dunbars, Earls of March ; the third exhibits Annandale, indicative also of the latter descent ; and the fourth, a fess cheque between three *frais*, or strawberry blossoms, for Fraser of Frendraught. This branch of the Frasers, who merged in Murray, had married the heiress of the Stewarts of Frendraught, an

ancient stock of the Stewarts, who can be traced as far back as the time of Robert Bruce."—Riddell's Tracts, Legal and Historical, p. 214.

[1] Original Precept in the Charter-Chest of Lord Forbes.

[2] Pinkerton's History of Scotland, vol. i. p. 231.

[3] Acts of the Parliaments of Scotland, vol. ii. p. 76.

which befel their relatives of the house of Douglas, when that powerful house was stript of its great power and proscribed by the Government.[1]

After the death of Archibald Earl of Murray, his relict, Elizabeth Dunbar, married George Lord Gordon, afterwards second Earl of Huntly. She lost no time in arranging this second matrimonial alliance, as the contract for the marriage between her and Lord Gordon is dated at Forres, 20th May 1455, only nineteen days after the death of her first husband. The substance of the contract may here be quoted. The parties to the indenture are designed "Alexander Earl of Huntlie, lord of Gordoun, . . . his spouse, Elizabeth Countass of Huntelie, etc., and George Master of Huntelie, Knight, [son] and appearand heir to the said lord and lady, . . . upon the ta part, and an noble Lady, Elizabeth Countass of Murray, Nicolas of Sutherland, captain of Ternway, Sir Richard of Holland, Channtor of Murray,[2] James of Dunbar, Alexander Flemyng, Huchone of Douglas, and William Inglis, men to the said lady, upon the tother part." It is agreed "that the said George sall marry and have to wife the said Elizabeth Countas of Murray, and nane others indurand her life, and make the dispensation of the authority of our haly fader the Pape be obtained, in all gudely haste, in the sickerest fourme, of all impediments that appears or may appear betwixt them, sua that they may lauchfully complete the said marriage; and in the meantime he sall not constrenzie the said lady to carnal copulation but of her free will. Alsua the said lady's men, now being in Ternway, sall be keepers

---

[1] The fact that, in 1494, Malcolm Colquhoun, grandson of Elizabeth Dunbar, comes forward as her heir, claiming certain lands in her right, seems to afford some foundation for the statement in the text.—Riddell's Tracts, Legal and Historical, p. 87.

[2] Sir Richard of Holland, Channter of Murray, who here appears in the retinue of Elizabeth of Dunbar, Countess of Murray, was the author of the poem entitled the "Howlat," which is dated at Tarnaway, the seat of the Earls of Murray, and which was probably written before the battle in which Archibald Douglas, Earl

of Murray, was slain in 1455. In this poem the author commemorates his honourable patroness : —

" Thus for ane dow of Dunbar drew I this dyte,
  Dowit with ane Dowglas, and boith war thai dowis."

Holland was in England in 1481, and was regarded as a traitor, having, it may be supposed, been obliged to seek shelter in that kingdom in consequence of his connexion with the Douglases. From his name, which is not Scotch, but English, it is supposed that he was a native of England, or was of English descent.

of that house, mony or few, as liks to the said lady, unto the tyme of
the fullfilling of the said marriage lauchfully, quhilk being done be dispensation, the said Castell sall be delivred freely to the said George and
his said spouse" .... "Alsua the said lady and her men sall do all their
gudlie power and diligence, so that the said lord Earl of Huntly have de-
livrance of the Castell of Louchindores." James, the son and heir of the
Countess, being "received be his lady moder, sall be in keeping with her,
or with her advice, quhair she best liks, till his lauchful age withouten bodily
harm till his life." Further, the Earl and his son shall not "constrenzie
. . . the said lady Countass of Murra to mak resignation nor alienation of
the earldom of Murra with the pertinents fra hir heirs gottin, but at her
awin fre will, in the quhilk earldom the said lord, his spouse, and appearand
heire sall defend the said lady, Countass of Murra, at all thair gudely power,
and mak hir sicker at his power of our sovrain lord the King, to be un-
distroblit in the posyession of hir earldome." There is also a guarantee
that "the said lady's men" shall enjoy the lands granted to them by the
deceased Archibald Earl of Murray, her former husband, with her consent,
or by herself in her widowhood, and mention is made of her daughter Janet.[1]

Motives of family aggrandizement led, it may be supposed, to this marriage of the heir of the House of Huntly with the heiress of the earldom
of Murray, the House of Huntly having always coveted the possession of
that earldom. The Master of Huntly, however, afterwards obtained a
divorce from her, not necessarily because she had been guilty of any violation of the marriage vow, for the most frivolous pretences were often in
those times made the ground of divorces when one of the parties had become alienated from the other, or when personal interest or passion
impelled to separation in order to make way for a new matrimonial
alliance, more advantageous or more attractive. She and the Master of
Huntly, it would seem, were within the prohibited degrees of consanguinity,
which rendered a papal dispensation necessary, in order to the legality of
this marriage; and this dispensation, from neglect or otherwise, not having
been obtained, as was agreed to in the marriage-contract, a ready pretext
could be found at any time for its dissolution.

[1] The Miscellany of the Spalding Club, vol. iv. p. 128.

The fact of her having been deprived, by the forfeiture of her late husband, of the earldom of Murray, it is not improbable, may have been the main reason why Elizabeth Dunbar was repudiated by Lord Gordon. That she was deprived of the earldom is evident from an entry in an Exchequer roll of the Account of the earldom of Mar, between 31st July 1455 and 12th October 1456, to the effect that the thanedom of Kintore was in the hands of the King, "by the forfeiture of Elizabeth of Dunbar, formerly Countess of Murray."[1]

The divorce of Elizabeth Dunbar from Lord Gordon, Master of Huntly, must have taken place before the 10th of March 1459, when Annabella, daughter of King James the First, appears in a charter as his wife.[2] That Princess also was solemnly divorced from him on the 24th of July 1471; and it is from her divorce that we learn the fact that he had obtained a divorce from Elizabeth of Dunbar. Annabella was divorced from him, not because of any misconduct on her part, but merely because she and the Master of Huntly were held to be related to each other in the third and fourth degrees of consanguinity, in consequence of Annabella's having been related in the like third and fourth degrees of consanguinity to Elizabeth Dunbar, the Master of Huntly's former wife, from whom, as the deed

---

[1] That the forfeited title of Earl of Murray was conferred by King James the Second upon one of his sons, there seems to be no doubt. In an Exchequer roll, the Account of Strathern, from 16th July 1454 to 18th October 1456, there is a charge for the expenses of "Lord David Earl of Murray." This Prince, of whom no notice is taken in any of our peerage books, was probably the youngest son of James the Second. He died soon after; for in another Account in the same record, brought down to 18th July 1457, the term "quondam" is prefixed to his name.—[Exchequer Rolls, in H.M. General Register House, Edinburgh.]

After the forfeiture of the earldom of Murray to the Crown, the Castle of Tarnaway often became the scene of the carousals of the sovereigns of Scotland, and in its exten-

sive and beautiful grounds they indulged in the pleasures of the chase. In an Exchequer roll in the year 1463, there is an item of expenditure for making and polishing a large number of tables in the forest of Tarnaway. In 1501, King James the Fourth granted to Jane Kennedy, Lady Bothwell, the Castle of Tarnaway, as long as she remained without a husband, or any other man, and dwelt in that castle, which in the writ is designated Dernway, with the King's son and hers, James Stewart—[Privy Seal Records, vol. ii. p. 73]. This celebrated lady, of whom the King was so passionately enamoured, was the daughter of John Lord Kennedy; and James Stewart, here mentioned, her son by the King, was afterwards created Earl of Murray.

[2] Registrum Magni Sigilli, Lib. v. No. 91.

G

states, he "had been lawfully divorced and separated by the judgment of the church." On this ground the marriage of the Princess with the Master of Huntly was pronounced to be illegal.[1]

The exact date of the marriage of Elizabeth Dunbar with Sir John Colquhoun of Luss has not been discovered. But it took place prior to 26th July 1463. The following extract from the Account of Bothkennar, etc., from 6th August 1462 to 26th July 1463, establishes this point, and also proves that a pension had been granted her by the Crown : " Ex penses, etc. By payment made to Elizabeth Dunbar formerly Countess of Murray, of the farms of the lands of Duchra, for her support, in part of payment of 100 merks granted to her by the charter of our lord the King under the Great Seal, John of Colquhoun of Luss, knight, her spouse, confessing the receipt."[2] In the year 1472, Sir John Colquhoun and Elizabeth Dunbar, his spouse, were infefted in a house in Stirling.[3] Sir John's children by his first wife were—

1. Humphrey, who succeeded him.

2. Robert, who was a clergyman, and became Bishop of Argyll. Robert Colquhoun was rector of Luss and of Kippen in 1466. Under that designation he was incorporated a member of the University of Glasgow on 27th October that year.[4]

---

[1] Gordon Charter-Chest. Within less than a month after this divorce was pronounced, namely, on the 18th of August 1471, the banns of the marriage of Lord Gordon with Elizabeth Hay, daughter of William first Earl of Errol, were proclaimed in the church of Fyvie. But the past having proved how slippery Lord Gordon was as a husband, and doubts being entertained as to the legality of the Princess Annabella's divorce, Nicholas, second Earl of Errol, the lady's brother, adopted some precautions for the protection of his sister. In a contract between him and George Lord Gordon, dated 12th May 1476, the latter binds himself that "I sal never presume til hafe actual delen wyt the said Elizabet, nether be slight nor myght, nor any other manner, on to the tyme it be

sene to the said lord Nichol, and her other tender friends, that I may hafe the saide Elizabeth to my wife lauchfully, and this before thir witnesses," etc. This he swears upon the Bible. — [Errol Charter-Chest, quoted in Riddell's Tracts, Legal and Histo-rical, p. 85.] The marriage was not consummated till after the 12th of May 1476, when, by the death of Annabella, the difficulties arising from the doubts entertained as to the legality of her divorce, were removed.

[2] Exchequer Rolls, in H.M. General Register House, Edinburgh.

[3] Original Instrument of Sasine at Ross-dhu.

[4] Munimenta Universitatis Glasguensis, tom. ii. p. 72.

The churches of Luss and Kippen, of which he was first rector, were in the diocese of Dunblane, of which the bishop at that time was John Hepburn.  Having, as rector of these churches, claimed the right of patronage to the vicarage of the church of Kippen, Robert Colquhoun became involved, in consequence, in a contest with that bishop.  On 3d February 1471, in the Chapter House of Dunblane, he publicly presented kneeling to the reverend father in Christ, John Bishop of Dunblane, a chaplain, Sir Robert Colquhoun, together with a presentation to the vicarage of the parochial church of Kippen, which was at that time vacant by the death of Sir James Lauder, the last vicar.  But the bishop refused to receive the presentation, on the ground that he had previously given that vicarage to another person.  On the same day, in the Cathedral Church of Dunblane, the bishop, with the consent of the said rector, deferred the case, till the meeting of the Synod of Dunblane, when it would be brought under the review of the bishop and his presbyters, the rights of the parties concerned not to suffer in the meantime any prejudice.[1]  How the question was decided we have not discovered.

Other notices of Robert Colquhoun occur in the ecclesiastical transactions of the time.  As rector of the churches of St. Kessog of Luss[2] and Kippen, he, on 5th February 1471, deposed a chaplain named Adam from the curacy of Kippen ; but the reasons for which this ecclesiastical sentence was pronounced are not recorded.[3]

In the year 1473, Robert Colquhoun was consecrated Bishop of Argyll, and in this See he continued upwards of twenty years.  As Bishop of Argyll he was present as a member of the Parliament held at Edinburgh, in February 1471, and joined with the other bishops in urging King James the Third, from the great love they had to his person, to remain at home, and not to carry out the intention he had announced to the Parliament of proceeding out of the kingdom at the head of a force for recovering his right to Brittany in France ; a step

[1] Notarial Protocols, Dumbartonshire, in Dennistoun's MSS., vol. viii., Advocates' Library, Edinburgh.

[2] The kirk of Luss was so designated from its patron saint, St. Kessog.

[3] Notarial Protocols, ut supra.

which they conceived would be fraught with peril to the realm, considering his tender age, and that he had no succession or issue.[1]  To
this enterprise King James had been persuaded by Louis the
Eleventh, King of France, who had despatched an ambassador to
his court with the object of persuading him to invade and take
possession of Brittany, promising that he would annex it to the
Crown of Scotland.  Orders had been given for the immediate levy
of 6000 men, whom the King himself, intoxicated by these flattering
persuasions, was to conduct in person on the expedition, whilst the
Parliament had agreed to contribute £6000 to meet the expenses.[2]
But circumstances arose which prevented that expedition.  Robert
Colquhoun, Bishop of Argyll, was also present as a member of the
Parliament held in the year 1476, and was a witness to the charter
granted by King James the Third, whereby John Earl of Ross, who,
for rebellion, had, by the Parliament in November 1475, been
forfeited, was, upon his submission, restored to the title of Lord of
the Isles, and to the possessions thereof, though he was still to remain deprived of the Earldom of Ross.  He was again present as a
member of the Parliaments held in 1478, 1482, and 1485.[3]  His
name appears in writs of the period as bishop of the diocese of
Argyll in 1495 ; but he probably died before 1499, when a bishop
of another name appears as the occupant of that bishopric.[4]

3. Margaret.  She married William Murray, seventh Baron of Tullibardine, who succeeded his father in 1446.  William Murray took
an active and prominent part in public affairs.  He was Sheriff of
Perthshire ; and also one of the Lords Justices who were named to
be of the King's daily council.  When, in compliance with a desire
expressed by Henry the Sixth, King of England, it was resolved
by King James the Second, who had always cultivated friendly
relations with that monarch, that the truce between Scotland and

[1] Acts of the Parliament of Scotland,
vol. ii. pp. 102, 103.

[2] Tytler's History, vol. iii. p. 358.

[3] Acts of the Parliament of Scotland,
vol. ii. pp. 120, 145, 168, 190.

[4] Keith's Historical Catalogue of the Scottish Bishops, p. 288.

England, which would terminate on 6th July 1459, should be renewed, William Murray of Tullibardine was one of the Commissioners who were sent to Newcastle in the character of plenipotentiaries in July that year, to conduct the negotiations for the prolongation of the truce.[1]  The other Commissioners were Ninian, Bishop of Galloway, George Shoreswood, Bishop of Brechin, who was also Chancellor of the Kingdom, William Sinclair, Earl of Orkney and Caithness, the Abbots of Melrose and Holyrood, the Lords Graham, Boyd, and Borthwick, John Arous, Archdean of Glasgow, and Secretary of State, and Nicholas Otterburn, Clerk Register.  William Murray of Tullibardine was knighted by King James the Third.  He greatly enlarged the collegiate church of Tullibardine, which had been founded and largely endowed by his father, Sir David, and which was the burial-place of his family for many generations.  Of the marriage of Sir William Murray and Margaret Colquhoun it is said that there were seventeen sons, and that they all lived to be men.

Tradition relates that Sir William and his seventeen sons, each attended by one servant, and the father by two, all dressed in full Highland costume, armed, and accompanied with pipers to enliven the scene, came to pay a visit of respectful loyalty to their sovereign—but whether it was King James the Second or King James the Third, is uncertain—on the occasion of a temporary sojourn he made at Perth.  His Majesty not having been previously apprised of their coming, some of the royal household, on hearing the sound of the bagpipe, and observing a body of armed men at a little distance advancing towards the residence of the King, were apprehensive, from their number and warlike appearance, that it was some hostile clan or faction who intended to do violence to the person of the monarch—an alarm which was not unnatural, when it is remembered that King James the First had been murdered at Perth so recently as February 1436-7—and the drawbridge was secured and the gates closed with the utmost haste.  But the alarm soon sub-

[1] Rymer's Fœdera, tom. xi. pp. 423, 426, 427; Abercromby's Martial Achievements of the Scots Nation, vol. ii. p. 374.

sided. A messenger having been sent to inquire who the party were, and what was their object, it was found that they were the Baron of Tullibardine and his seventeen sons coming to testify their devotion to their sovereign. They were at once admitted, and honoured with a most gracious reception. The Baron, with pride and pleasure, explained that he was the father of these seventeen young men, who, with himself, had come to cast themselves at the feet of his Majesty, and to pledge themselves to defend his person and government. The King declared himself highly gratified with the expressions of their devoted loyalty, and especially congratulated Sir William on his felicity in having so numerous and so promising a family of sons.[1] The eldest of Sir William's sons was ancestor of the Dukes of Athole and Earls of Tullibardine ; and from several of the other sons various distinguished families of the name of Murray are descended. The second son was killed on entering Ochtertyre House, as he was making his escape from the Drummonds, with whom his family were at feud, he being single, and several of them pursuing him. Another son married a daughter of the Earl of Gowrie, who leapt 'the maiden leap' at Huntingtower, and was buried in the church of Tibbermure, over against the pulpit, on the inside of the wall of the kirk, where, in 1710, her and her husband's names were to be seen.[2]

[1] Tradition in the family of Colquhoun of Luss. The essential parts of this story are confirmed by a tradition preserved in the Tullibardine family. There are at Blair Castle some bed-curtains (of Murray tartan) which have been handed down from generation to generation as the curtains of a bed in which the seventeen brothers slept. It is supposed that the bed must have been in the shape of a bell tent, and that the brothers all lay with their feet to the centre pole ; only the curtains are no longer in the original shape, as at some period they were used for an ordinary bed.

[2] The declaration of George Halley in Ochterarlair, aged sixty-four years, what he can say of the family of Tullibardine, at Tullibardine, 25th April 1710.

# X.—HUMPHREY COLQUHOUN,

Tenth of Colquhoun and Twelfth of Luss, 1478-1493.

JEAN ERSKINE, daughter of Lord Erskine, his first wife.

MARION BAILLIE, Dowager Lady Somerville, his second wife.

DURING his father's lifetime, Humphrey Colquhoun rented the lands of
Kirkmichael, in the shire of Dumbarton, of which he had a lease from John
Sempill of Fulwood, who, on 18th March 1476, bound himself to observe
inviolate the lease of these lands given to " Humphrey Colquhoun, son and
heir-apparent of the Laird of Luss," as contained in an indenture made
between them.[1]

Humphrey succeeded his father, Sir John, in the year 1478. As the
son and heir of his father, he was, on 14th June 1479, upon a precept
from Archibald, Abbot of the Monastery of the Holy Cross of Edinburgh,
infefted in the lands and tenements in the Canongate already mentioned.[2]
On 13th October in the same year he was constituted, by Colin first Earl of
Argyll, the Earl's assignee to his lands of the Lordland of Sauline, in the
barony of Sauline and county of Fife, until they should be secured to him
by charter and sasine, which the Earl bound himself to grant on consulting
with John Earl of Mar, youngest brother of King James the Third, the
Lord Superior;[3] and, on 27th January following, he received from the Earl
of Argyll a charter of these lands.[4] Four days after, namely, on 31st
January 1479-80, he was, upon a precept of sasine from the Earl of Mar,
infefted, as heir of his deceased father, in the lands of Meikle and Little
Sauline, and in the mill thereof.[5]

The fate of John Earl of Mar, Humphrey's superior, during the course of
the year in which these transactions took place, was tragical. He had incurred the deep resentment of the parasites by whom his brother King James
the Third was surrounded, and their thirst for vengeance could be appeased

[1] Notarial Protocols, Dumbartonshire, ut
supra.
[2] Vide p. 35. Orig. Inst. of Sasine at Rossdhu.
[3] Original Assignation at Rossdhu.
[4] Original Charter, ibid.
[5] Original Instrument of Sasine, ibid.

only by his death. He was suddenly arrested during night and carried prisoner to Craigmillar Castle, near Edinburgh. Shortly after, he was accused of conspiring with sorcerers and witches against the life of the King, and was sentenced to be burned—the doom of witchcraft; but being allowed the choice of the kind of death he should die, he chose to have a vein in his leg opened and to bleed to death in a bath. This fate he underwent, it is said, in the Canongate of Edinburgh. Such is the account of our early historians.[1] But, according to a later historian, the Earl, having been seized with a violent fever, was brought to a house in the Canongate, and the physician having opened a vein in his arm and temple to mitigate the fever, the royal patient, in the frenzy of his disease, tore off the bandages, and died from the loss of blood.[2]

Humphrey Colquhoun's right to the lands of Sauline was contested by David Haliburton, who procured a brief of inquest from his Majesty's Chancery, in order to his being infefted in the lands of the Fordland of Sauline, and in the mill thereof. This brief of inquest was served before Thomas Simson, Sheriff of Forfar, or his deputes; and, upon the retour of that inquest, Haliburton was infefted in the said lands. Colin Earl of Argyll and Humphrey Colquhoun of Luss, however, on 14th March 1482, obtained a decreet of reduction of that brief from the Lords Auditors.[3]

On 21st June 1479, Humphrey was retoured, by a special retour of service, as heir of his father, in the lands of Garshake, in the territory of Dumbarton, and in a tenement in that burgh,[4] etc.

From King James the Third, Humphrey obtained a gift of the third of the ward lands of Granton and Stanehouse, in the county of Fife. This portion of these lands Henry Melville of Carnebee, who had received from the King a gift of two parts of them, claimed as his property, and to establish his claim he brought an action against Humphrey Colquhoun of Luss before the Lords of Council. But, on 15th October 1479, the Lords decreed that he had right only to two parts of these lands, and that Humphrey

[1] Lesley's History, pp. 43, 44; Buchanan's History, Aikman's edit. vol. ii. p. 203; Balfour's Annals, vol. i. p. 203.
[2] Drummond of Hawthornden's History of the Jameses, p. 48. Drummond says that he derived this account from the papers of Bishop Elphinstone, a contemporary.
[3] Extract Decreet at Rossdhu.
[4] Original Retour, ibid.

Colquhoun had right to the third part, as was shown by the letters of gift in their favour.[1]

In the year 1480, Humphrey received from the Crown a remission for the relief-duties of his lands, in consequence of his father, Sir John, having fallen at the siege of Dunbar Castle. These duties were £40 for Colquhoun, £10 for Salquhy [Salachy], and £10 for Galeu [Glinns], and four cheeses by duplication of bleuch-farm of the barony of Luss, due to the King.[2]

Humphrey's father, as has been already stated, had granted to James Menteith of Radnoch a charter and infeftment of the lands of Over-Glenny, in the shire of Perth, and to Malcolm M'Rure a charter and infeftment of the lands of Westirdeulettir in the same shire. Colin first Earl of Argyll having claimed these lands as belonging to him in heritage, Menteith and M'Rure pursued each an action against him for the wrongous occupation of them, and against Humphrey Colquhoun of that ilk for the warrandice of them by reason of his father's charter, which contained a clause to that effect. On 13th June 1480, the Lords of Council decreed that the Earl of Argyll did no wrong in occupying these lands, and that, as they had been legally recovered by him from James Menteith, Humphrey should give in warrandice a corresponding amount of land equally good.[3]

The lands of Galmore and the Middlequarter of Dunfawy, in the county of Perth, had been granted by David Wardlaw by charter to Sir Humphrey's father, but not to extend to his heirs. Overlooking the limitation of the grant, Humphrey, on his father's death, claimed these lands as his property. David Wardlaw and Janet, his spouse, contested this claim, and brought before the Lords of Council an action against Humphrey, and Robert Scot and John of Burn, the tenants, for withholding from them the mails of these lands. On 1st July 1480, the Lords of Council decreed that the tenants should pay the mails, for all terms since the decease of Sir John Colquhoun, to Wardlaw and his wife; and ordained that Humphrey should not intromit with the lands in time to come, because the gift of them made to his father was only in favour of him-

<hr />

[1] Acta Dominorum Concilii, p. 32.

[2] Extract from Account of Andrew Lord Evandale, Chancellor of Scotland, Sheriff of Dumbarton, rendered by his Deputy at Edinburgh, 21st June 1480, at Rossdhu.

[3] Acta Dominorum Concilii, p. 51.

self, and for his help, furtherance, and supply. With respect to the mill
of Dunfawy, as Janet, the wife of Wardlaw, had constituted the late Sir
John Colquhoun her assignee to redeem it, and as Humphrey Colquhoun
affirmed that his father had redeemed it before his death, the Lords
assigned him the 2d of October, with continuation of days, to prove that
this had been done.[1]

The Lords of Council afterwards pronounced a decreet in favour of
Humphrey in reference to the mill of Dunfawy; but, notwithstanding this
decreet, David Wardlaw and Janet of Lundy, his spouse, wrongously put
forth Malcolm Gibson, Humphrey's tenant, from that mill, occupied it, and
took up the profits thereof. Humphrey, therefore, pursued an action against
them.   On 11th October 1484, the Lords Auditors decreed that Wardlaw
and his wife had done wrong in occupying the mill of Dunfawy, and in
ejecting from it Humphrey Colquhoun and his tenants, and ordained that
they should desist from all intromitting therewith in future, and that the
mill should be possessed by the said Humphrey in time to come, conformably to the decreet of the Lords of Council previously given.[2]

On 31st May 1481, Humphrey, on a precept from the Chancery of
King James the Third, was infefted as heir of his father in the superiority
of the half of the lands of Kilmardinny, which was held of the King in
chief.[3]  In the following year he reacquired certain lands of Kilmardinny,
which his father had sold to Robert Scot under reversion, by paying to
Walter Scot, son of Robert, who was then dead, the sum of £93, 6s. 8d.[4]

Humphrey and his stepmother, Elizabeth of Dunbar, Countess of Murray, do not appear to have lived on very harmonious terms. Disputes often
arose between them respecting pecuniary matters, and there seems to have
been on neither side a disposition to yield or to compromise their differences.  Each displayed a remarkable activity of zeal in defending his or
her supposed rights.  From the numerous law-suits in which Humphrey
was involved, one is disposed to think that he had a peculiar propensity
for this species of warfare; and his stepmother met him with a spirit and

[1] Acta Dominorum Concilii, p. 68.
[2] Acta Dominorum Auditorum, p. 144*.
[3] Original Instrument of Sasine at Rossdhu.

[4] Original Notarial Instrument of Redemption, dated 28th June 1482.

decision not less energetic than his own. The Lords Auditors of Causes and Complaints, and the Lords of Council, before whom their disputes frequently came, did their best to judge impartially between them. Sometimes the one, and sometimes the other, gained the action. When one question in controversy was settled, the contest between them was renewed on a different point. By these altercations before the Courts of law they certainly contrived to keep each other in hot water, at least for some time.

An action was pursued against Humphrey by his stepmother, Elizabeth Dunbar, Lady of Luss, for wrongously withholding from her £20 of the remainder of the sum paid by David Haliburton for redeeming the lands of Sauline, and 16 merks of her terce of the mails of the land of the Canongate for two years past, and also 46s. 6d., her terce of the mails of the lands of Garshake. Both parties having personally, and by their pro curators, appeared before the Lords Auditors on 10th December 1482, and their allegations having been heard, their Lordships decreed that the Lady of Luss had no right to the £20 claimed by her, because the lands of Sauline were heritage at the time of her husband's decease, and that she was entitled only to the third of the silver, which she granted had been paid to her. With respect to the other sums of 16 merks and 46s. 6d., claimed by her, as it was denied by Humphrey's procurators that he had uplifted them from the lands mentioned, their Lordships assigned to her the 11th day of January following, with continuation of days, to prove that he had taken up these sums.[1]

The Dowager Lady of Luss again pursued an action against her step-son, Humphrey, as heir of his father, for wrongously uptaking and withholding from her 12 merks of her half of the ward of the lands of Stanehouse, and £15 of her part of the lands of Tuliketle, as she alleged. Both parties having been present personally, and by their procurators, before the Lords Auditors, 18th February 1483, and their reasons having been heard, their Lordships decreed that Humphrey should pay to her these sums.[2]

Humphrey, as heir of his father, was again prosecuted by the same indefatigable assertor of her rights for the wrongous detention from her

---

[1] Acta Dominorum Auditorum, p. 104.          [2] Ibid. p. *129.

of four bolls of wheat, four bolls of bear, and ten bolls of oats, pertaining to her of the half of the ward of the lands of Stauehouse, £4 of
silver of the half of the ward of the lands of Tuliketle, and £10 by
reason of an obligation of Simon Logan. When the case was brought
before the Lords Auditors, Humphrey alleged that the debts which his
father owed at the time of his decease exceeded the quantity and avail
of his moveable goods, and of the debts that were owing to him. The
Lords therefore, on 4th July 1483, continued the action, giving him to the
12th of October following, with continuation of days, for the production
of his proof of this allegation.[1] On the 12th of October following, the
Lords Auditors, in presence of Lady Luss and of Humphrey's procurators,
decreed that as Humphrey had failed to prove, as he had offered, that
the debts of his deceased father exceeded the quantity and avail of his
moveable goods, he should make the above payments to Lady Luss.[2]

In reference to another action by Humphrey's stepmother against him,
the Lords Auditors, on 19th October 1484, decreed that he, as heir of his
father, should pay to her the sum of £5, 10s., because he granted in presence
of the Lords that he had recovered the sum of £11 from John Oliphant of
the Drou, by reason of an obligation made to his deceased father ; and with
regard to the half of the sum of 55 merks which she claimed from him, by
reason of another obligation which she alleged had been made by the said
John Oliphant to her deceased husband, Sir John, but which Humphrey
affirmed had been made to himself as his proper debt, and not to his father,
the Lords assigned to her the 14th day of January following, with continuation of days, to prove that the obligation of 55 merks had been made to
her deceased husband, and not to Humphrey.[3]

Humphrey next appears as the prosecutor of his stepmother. He pur
sued an action against her for being relieved from the payment of the half
of the debts contained in his deceased father's testament. On 21st October
1484, when the action came before the Lords Auditors, she alleged that she
ought to have the half of the moveable goods of her deceased husband, Sir
John, according to the decreet of the Lords of Council given before, and
also that he had more moveable goods than were contained in his testa-

ment. Humphrey, on the other hand, affirmed that she had got the half of the goods, and ought to relieve him of the half of the debts. The Lords, therefore, assigned to Humphrey the 14th day of January next, with continuation of days, to prove that she had got the half of Sir John's moveable goods, and also assigned to her the same day to prove what moveable goods Sir John had, besides what were contained in his testament.[1]

Another action was pursued by Humphrey against his stepmother, touching the reparation and upholding of certain tenements in the Canongate of Edinburgh, the burghs of Stirling and Dumbarton, and the destruction of his place and orchard of Dunglas, belonging to him in heritage, and to her in liferent, by reason of conjunct infeftment and terce. The case having been brought before the Lords of Council on 25th October 1484, their Lordships decreed that she should uphold the said lands and tenements, place, and orchard yearly, during her lifetime, in a state of as good repair as they were in when she received them after the death of her husband, and, if necessary, that she should be annually compelled to do so, or else to give them over to Humphrey, as heir, to be built at his own pleasure.[2]

On 24th January 1484-5, the Lords referred the action betwixt Elizabeth Dunbar and Humphrey Colquhoun of the Luss, her step-son, with regard to the goods of the deceased Sir John that were not put in his testament, and also with regard to the payment of his debts, and the party by whom they should be paid, to be determined before the "spirituale Juge ordinar," who had power to make executors-dative.[3]

This is the last entry in the Acts of the Lords Auditors and Lords of Council respecting the differences between Humphrey and his step-mother. We may therefore conclude that this decreet would result in the termination of their disputes concerning their civil rights, and that henceforth they lived on amicable terms.

The lands of the barony of Sauline, in the shire of Fife, having been redeemed from Humphrey Colquhoun, to whose father they had been sold by David Haliburton, by charter and sasine under reversion, the Lords Auditors, on 14th October 1484, decreed that Humphrey Colquhoun, who

[1] Acta Dom. Audit., p. 149*.    [2] Acta Dom. Concilii, p. 89*.    [3] Ibid. p. 95*.

had granted that he had received the sum to be paid according to the
letter of reversion, should constitute procurators, and make a letter of
procuratory under his seal, to resign into the King's hands these lands in
favour of David Haliburton.[1]

A dispute arose betwixt Humphrey Colquhoun and Gabriel of Towris
on the one part, and Alexander Hepburn of Whitesome on the other, with
respect to the mails and duties of the third part of the lands of Granton for
the past nine years, and as to other matters. The litigating parties agreed
in choosing arbiters, who might settle their differences; and, on 1st March
1489, their procurators, having appeared before the Lords of Council, became bound, the holy evangels touched, to stand by the sentence of the
arbiters concerning all actions and controversies betwixt the said parties.
The arbiters were to deliver their sentence betwixt that date and Pasche
following.[2]

During the time of Humphrey Colquhoun, Mr. Robert Erskine was
parson of Luss. A misunderstanding took place between this ecclesiastic
and the proprietor of Luss, who, it appears, would not permit him to uplift
the fruits and teinds of the kirk of Luss. Mr. Erskine accordingly summoned Humphrey to appear before the Lords of Council to answer for
wrongously disturbing him in taking up the teinds, fruits, and duties of
that kirk, and also for causing the Bishop of Argyll, Humphrey's brother,
to intromit with the fruits thereof. On 9th July 1489, Mr. Erskine being
personally present, and Humphrey lawfully summoned and ofttimes called,
and not compearing, the former produced an instrument, signed by Sir
Cuthbert Muligane, public notary, showing that Humphrey would not suffer
him to intromit with the said fruits and teinds. The Lords therefore
ordained that letters should be written charging Humphrey and his brother,
the Bishop of Argyll, to desist from all vexation of Mr. Erskine in future
in the parsonage of Luss, and in the reception of the teinds and fruits
thereof; and that the bishop should restore to him the teinds and fruits of
that kirk, in so far as he had intromitted therewith.[3]

It had been enacted by King James the First that all barons and lords
having lands and lordships near the sea, on the west parts, and especially

[1] Acta Dom. Audit., p. 146*.　　　[2] Acta Dom. Concilii, p. 133.　　　[3] Ibid. p. 122.

opposite the Isles, should have galleys, and should maintain them. In obedience to this enactment, the lairds of Luss had provided themselves with this means of self-defence.[1]

When King James the Fourth, after the suppression of the rebellion raised against him by the Earl of Lennox and others, and the surrender to him of the Castle of Dumbarton, made Dumbarton one of the west coast stations for the navy, which he sedulously employed himself in collecting and strengthening, mention is made of a ship which he purchased from the Laird of Luss, and which was repaired and equipped in Dumbarton. In the Accounts of the Lord High Treasurer of Scotland connected with Dumbartonshire is the following entry :—"1489, December 3. To the Larde of Laucht [Luss] for the schip boycht fra him to the Kingis vsc, iᶜxxxˡⁱ."

A lease of the lands of Furlinbrek and Finnard, in the county of Dumbarton, was granted to Humphrey Colquhoun of Luss by James Douglas of Lethcamrach. After the death of the granter, the Lords Auditors, on the 11th February 1489, decreed that William of Douglas of Lethcamrach, as heir to the deceased James of Douglas, his father, should warrant and keep to Humphrey Colquhoun of Luss the lease of these lands for all the terms to come, contained in the letter of lease produced before the Lords, and admitted by the said William.[2] But these lands neither James Douglas, nor his son William, it appears, had a right to lease. They had been occupied and manured for six years past by Walter Buchanan of that Ilk, who had received a lease of them from Simon Makclere of Fin nard. A litigation arose in consequence between the parties whose claims were conflicting. Humphrey Colquhoun pursued an action before the Lords of Council against Walter Buchanan of that Ilk and the said William of Douglas, for the wrongous occupation and manuring of the lands of Finnard and Furlinbrek by the former for seven years past. When this action was brought before the Lords of Council, on 11th March 1490, Walter Buchanan

---

[1] In the Instructions by Edward IV., King of England, to his Ambassador in Scotland, in the British Museum (Vesp. Caligula, xvi. folio 118, as quoted by Pinkerton, under the year 1475), redress was ordered to be given for a ship belonging to "the Lard of Lus," which had been captured by Lord Grey of England.—[Pinkerton's History of Scotland, vol. i. p. 284.]

[2] Acta Dominorum Auditorum, p. 132.

claimed the lands as belonging to him by reason of a lease from Simon Makclere of Finnard, and produced a letter of lease, dated 15th March 1482, for the term of nineteen years. Humphrey produced another lease of the same lands for the terms of seven years, granted to him by James Douglas of Lethcamrach, dated 8th November 1483.[1] The case remained suspended for several years. But, on 1st March 1491, the Lords of Council decided in favour of Walter Buchanan of that Ilk, and ordained that William Douglas of Lethcamrach should warrant and defend to Humphrey Colquhoun of Luss the lease of the lands of Finnard and Furlinbrek by granting to him the lease of as much and as good and profitable land, in as competent a place, for such terms and mails as were contained in the lease made to him by the late James Douglas of Lethcamrach.[2]

Humphrey Colquhoun was a member of the Parliament of Scotland which, soon after the accession of King James the Fourth, assembled at Edinburgh in October 1488. That King, while Prince of Scotland, and yet in his minority, became involved in the conspiracy entered into by a faction of the nobles and barons against his father, King James the Third, and the issue of which was that the King was killed, 11th June 1488, at Sawchie, after a battle fought between him and the conspirators.[3] The more effectually to secure themselves from the consequences of this conspiracy, King James the Fourth and the nobles and barons implicated were anxious to obtain an acquittal from Parliament, and they procured without difficulty a vote to the effect that the death of the late King was to be imputed solely to himself and to his evil counsellors, and that the new Sovereign and his adherents, who had borne arms against him, were to be held free from all blame on that account.[4] King James the Fourth was quite young when these occurrences took place. In his riper years he is said to have shown much remorse on account of the part he was made to play against his father; and by way of penance he wore an iron girdle about his body.

A charter was granted by Humphrey Colquhoun, 4th June 1489, of his

[1] Acta Dominorum Concilii, p. 179.

[2] Ibid. p. 217.

[3] This battle is sometimes called the field of Stirling, and sometimes the battle of Bannockburn. It was fought on St. Barna-

bas day, according to the references to it in contemporary documents.

[4] Acts of the Parliament of Scotland, vol. ii. pp. 210, 211; Balfour's Annals, vol. i. p. 215.

one merk land of Corechenaghane, in the county of Dumbarton and barony of Luss, to Dugall Makcoul, son of the deceased Duncan Makcoul. These lands belonged heritably to Malcolm Makcoul, Dugall's brother, and Katharine Colquhoun, Malcolm's spouse, and were by them resigned into the hands of Humphrey, to be held by the said Dugall of the granter.[1]

After having been Laird of Colquhoun for fifteen years, Humphrey died on or about the 19th of August 1493, as appears from the retour, by which his son John was served heir to him, dated 19th November in that year, and which narrates that the true heir had failed to prosecute his right for three months or thereby.[2] It does not appear that the honour of knight-hood was ever conferred upon this laird of Luss.

Humphrey was twice married. His first wife was Jean, daughter of Thomas Lord Erskine,[3] by whom he had five sons and two daughters. He married, secondly, Marion, daughter of William Baillie of Lamington, and relict of John third Lord Somerville. This lady was married to Lord Somerville in March 1456, being his second wife, and to him she had a son, Sir John Somerville of Quothquan, the first baron of Cambusnethan, who had the reputation of being "a complete gentleman," and who afterwards fell at Flodden, in 1513, and a daughter, Mary, who married Sir Stephen Lockhart of Cleghorne. Lord Somerville's children by his first wife, dame Helen Hepburn, daughter of Lord Hailes, were a son, William Somerville of Carnwath, and Helen, who married Sir John Jardine of Aplegirth.[4] Marion Baillie figured on the occasion of her son Sir John's bringing home his bride, Elizabeth Carmichael, half-sister to Archibald fifth Earl of Angus, commonly called "Bell-the-cat,"[5] to Cowthally Castle. The infare[6] was to be honoured by King James the Fourth, then in the eighteenth year of his age, and he was met near Inglestoun Bridges by Sir John Somerville of Quothquan, with some fifty gentlemen of his own name, and his father's vassals,

---

[1] Original Charter at Rossdhu.

[2] Original Retour, ibid.

[3] Writs of the Colquhoun family, quoted by Sir Robert Douglas in his Baronage, p. 24.

[4] Memorie of the Somervilles, pp. 211, 268.

[5] This lady was the daughter of a younger brother of Captain Craufurd, by his wife Elizabeth, daughter of Sir Andrew Sibbald of Balgonie, in the county of Fife, some time Treasurer of Scotland, and relict of George fourth Earl of Angus.

[6] The entertainment made for the reception of a bride in the bridegroom's house.

I

who conducted him to the castle. When distant from it nearly a quarter of
a mile, his Majesty and his whole retinue alighted and walked on foot.
"At the outter gate of the castle," says the author of Memorie of the
Somervilles, "Dame Marie[1] Baillzie, then Lady Somervill, being at this tyme
not above the fortieth and sexth year of her age,[2] with her daughter-in-law,
Elizabeth Carmichaell, Sir John of Quathquan's lady, the Lady Aplegirth, the
Lady Cleghorne, the Lady Carmichaell, and the Captaine Craufuird's lady,
with a great many others, that both by affinitie and consanguinitie wer related to the house of Cowthally, with severall other ladyes, wer ther present
to wellcome his Majestie to the infare, and make the intertainement more
splendid." "What ther fare was," adds the same author, "needs not to be
discoursed upon ; it is enough to know it was in Cowthally house, where
three of his Majestie's predecessores had been intertained before, and his
successor King James the Fyfth often. How long his Majestie continued
in Cowthally I cannot be positive, but by the chamberlane's and steward's
accompts I find ther was noe fewer beastes killed then fyftieth kyne, two
hundered sheep, fourtieth bolles of malt, and of meall sexteinth, of butter
twentieth stone, spent at this infare, besyde fishes, tame and wilde foull, in
such abundance, that both the King and the nobilitie declared they had not
seen the lyke in any house within the kingdome."[3]   Marion Baillie became a widow in the year 1491, John Lord Somerville having died in
November that year.

The date of her marriage with Humphrey Colquhoun of Luss is uncertain.   To him she had no issue, and she soon became a widow a second
time.

Marion Baillie appears to have been a lady of much good sense and
warm affections.   Solicitous to do her duty in every circumstance in which
she was placed, she did not allow her affection to her own children to sway

[1] Her name was Marion, as appears from
the Acta Dominorum Auditorum, p. 165.

[2] Somewhat older, we should say. If at
this time she was only forty-six years old, she
would be born about 1443 ; and that would
make her at the time of her marriage with

John Lord Somerville, in March 1456, only
about thirteen years of age.

[3] Memorie of the Somervilles, vol. i, pp.
297-299. The lavish hospitality for which
Cowthally Castle was famed gave rise to a
pun on the name—Cow-daily, as if a cow
had been killed every day of the week.

her to do anything unjust towards the children of her first husband by his
first wife, and by them she was respected and beloved. After the death
of her step-son, William Somerville, Baron of Carnwath, in the year 1488,
she evinced a motherly interest and tenderness in his infant children, John,
afterwards fourth Lord Somerville, who had not completed his fourth year,
and Hugh, afterwards fifth Lord Somerville, who was scarcely two years
of age. The author of Memorie of the Somervilles relates that, in 1510,
" Hugh being at Edinburgh with his step-grandmother, who was the second
tyme a widow, by the death of her second husband, the Laird of Lusse,
was resolved to goe abroad, but could obtain non of his freinds' consent ;
particularly his step-grandmother, who was very kynde to him, even in
oppositione to her owne sone, Sir John of Quathquan,[1] diswaded him from
that resolutione."[2]

The sons of Humphrey Colquhoun by his first wife were—

1. John, who succeeded him.

2. Walter Colquhoun of Letter, in the county of Dumbarton.   In
   1518, Walter Colquhoun of Letter, Sir John Colquhoun of Luss, his
   brother, and Walter, a son of Sir John's, were witnesses to a protest
   of a person named M'Farlane.   In 1519 Walter Colquhoun pursued
   James Noble of Ferme for assedation of the lands of Murroch and
   Gooseholm, in the shire of Dumbarton.[3]

3. Patrick.   On 20th June 1501, Patrick Colquhoun, brother-german
   of John Colquhoun of Luss, acted as one of the bailies of William
   Douglas of Ladcamroch.[4]

4. Humphrey of Letter.   He became clerk of the parish church of
   Luss.   From his brother Sir John, he received in liferent a charter,
   dated 30th July 1505, of the lands commonly called the Letter and
   the Strone, with the houses, mansion, gardens, etc., in the barony of
   Luss and shire of Dumbarton.   The charter bears that Sir John
   granted these lands to his beloved brother-german, Humphrey, for

[1] Sir John Somerville of Quothquan was
sole tutor of his nephews, John fourth Lord
Somerville and Hugh, his brother, and is said
to have aggrandized himself at the expense
of their estate.

[2] Memorie of the Somervilles, vol. i. p.
319.

[3] Records of Dumbarton.

[4] Original Instrument of Sasine. narrating Precept of Sasine, ibid.

the singular fraternal affection which he bore towards him; and
he reserved to himself and his heirs his houses of the said lands of
Strone between the lands of Spittal and the church of Luss.[1]

In 1510 a dispute arose between this Humphrey Colquhoun and
Sir George Fallusdall, chaplain of the perpetual altar and service of
the Blessed Virgin Mary, situated within the parochial church of
Luss, respecting the marches of the lands of Strone, which belonged
to Humphrey, and the lands of Cragynthoye, which belonged to "our
Lady's service in Luss." The contending parties, with consent of
Sir John Colquhoun of Luss, agreed to refer their differences to
certain persons, and to abide by their decision. The arbiters gave
in their decreet on 21st June 1510.[2]

On 31st January 1518-19, Humphrey Colquhoun of Letter, brother
of the Laird of Luss, pursued before the burgh court of Dumbarton
Andrew Cunningham of Drumquhassil, as tutor of James Noble of
Ferme, for assedation of the lands of Murroch and Goosecholm, of
which he affirmed the said Andrew had faithfully promised to him a
lease, similar to what he had from Janet M'Farlane, relict of the father
of the said James Noble, as contained in a letter by her to that
effect. Drumquhassil agreed that Humphrey Colquhoun should have
assedation of these lands, provided he obtained the consent of the
Laird of Luss.[3] On 7th May 1520, Humphrey Colquhoun, under the
designation of "Clerk of the parish church of Luss," compeared before
a notary and witnesses, and revoked the agreement made between
him and his brother, Sir John, regarding the clerkship of that church.[4]
On 9th June 1524, "Humphrey Colquhoun of Lettyr" affirmed that
Sir John Colquhoun of Luss was willing to abide by the decreet
which he (Humphrey) had given concerning the actions moved
between his said brother and Peter Colquhoun.[5] On 7th September
1525, Humphrey, under the same designation, was witness to the
delivery of a letter of wadset by Elison Campbell.[6]

Humphrey Colquhoun married, in 1528, Elizabeth Napier, relict of

---

[1] Original Charters at Rossdhu.          [3] Dumbarton Sasine Records.
[2] Original Notarial Instrument, ibid.    [4] Ibid.   [5] Ibid.   [6] Ibid.

Robert Dennistoun of Colgrain, by whom he had issue. This lady was daughter of John Napier of Merchiston, by Elizabeth, daughter of Patrick de Menteth of Rusky, and grand-daughter of lady Margaret, daughter and co-heiress of Duncan Earl of Lennox. On 19th August 1528, it was agreed between Humphrey Colquhoun of Letter and Elizabeth Napier, that they should marry each other within the space of a year. In this agreement Elizabeth constitutes Humphrey her only cessioner to all her lands and goods, he pay ing for the ward of her lands and also all her debts.[1] In December 1535, he was witness to a precept by his brother, Sir John, for in-fefting his son David in the lands of Kilbride.[2] This is the last notice which has been found of Humphrey Colquhoun of Letter.

5. Archibald. As son of the Laird of Luss, on 20th February 1515-16, he protested and took instruments that the delivery of the stoup[3] by William Lindsay to John Buntyn should not hurt him in his right to the clerkship of the church of Rosneath.

The daughters of Humphrey Colquhoun of Luss by Jean Erskine were—

1. Agnes. She married John fourth Lord Somerville, the eldest son of William Somerville of Carnwath, Master of Somerville, who was the son of John third Lord Somerville, and who, as already stated, died in the year 1488.[4] He succeeded his grandfather, John third Lord Somerville, who died in November 1491.[5] The baronial mansion in

[1] Dumbarton Sasine Records.
[2] Original Instrument of Sasine at Ross-dhu.
[3] This was probably one of the sacred vessels used for holding the wine offered in the celebration of the mass. The giving of this vessel seems to have been a form sometimes adopted in giving sasine to, or in confirmation of, particular ecclesiastical offices.
[4] Memorie of the Somervilles, vol. i. p. 274.
[5] John fourth Lord Somerville was weak in intellect, and unfit to manage his own affairs. His younger brother Hugh, in 1515, endeavoured to obtain a brief of inquest for declar-

ing him an idiot. In this he did not succeed ; but he was empowered to intromit with the whole rents belonging to the lord-ship, the Mains of Cowthally and Lampts being appointed for his brother's mainte-nance, and the title and entry of vassals were reserved to him during his life. It was also ordained that trusty servants should be placed with Lord John, both for the care of his person, and the bringing in of the rents of these lands for the use of his house, which he kept at Cowthally so long as he lived. —Memorie of the Somervilles, vol. i. pp. 274, 322-331.

which he and Agnes Colquhoun resided, was Cowthally Castle.
This castle stood within a morass, surrounded by two ditches of
stagnant water, and was approachable only by a narrow causeway
or tongue of land,—a situation less pleasant and convenient than
many other places which might have been selected for building
within the barony of Carnwath, but well adapted in old times for
the purposes of defence.[1]

John fourth Lord Somerville and Agnes Colquhoun had no
children. He died in the year 1524, and was succeeded by his
brother Hugh. In the year 1525, Dame Agnes Colquhoun, relict of
John Lord Somerville, bound herself to add 40 merks to the tocher
which George Abernethy, burgess of Dumbarton, was to receive from
her brothers, Polmaise[2] and Luss, with Janet Cunningham.[3]    On
28th December 1528, Humphrey Colquhoun of Letter offered himself
ready to give a discharge in name of Dame Agnes Colquhoun, Lady
Somerville, to Lord Somerville of £30.[4]    Sir Robert Douglas, in his
Baronage, referring to writs of the family of Luss, says that Agnes
Colquhoun married James Galbraith of Culcreuch,[5] in Stirlingshire.

2. Elizabeth, who married James Cunningham of Polmaise, in the
county of Stirling, by whom she had issue.

[1] Memorie of the Somervilles, vol. i. pp. 354-357.

[2] James Cunningham of Polmaise, Dame Agnes's brother-in-law.

[3] Dumbarton Sasine Records.

[4] *Ibid.*

[5] Might not this be her first or second husband ?

## XI. Sir JOHN COLQUHOUN, Knight,

Eleventh of Colquhoun and Thirteenth of Luss, 1493-1536.

Lady Elizabeth Stewart (of Lennox), his first wife.

Margaret Cunningham (of Craigends), his second wife.

Sir John Colquhoun succeeded his father Humphrey in the year 1493. On the 30th of September that year, he was served heir to him in the lands of Garshake, within the territory and liberty of the burgh of Dumbarton.[1] On the 19th of November following, he was also served heir to him in the half of the lands of Kilmardinny, in the earldom of Lennox and shire of Stirling. In the retour the lands are said to be worth at that time eight merks, and in time of peace forty shillings,[2] and to be in the hands of the Earl of Lennox, the superior, by reason of the death of the late Humphrey Colquhoun, the true heir having failed to prosecute his right for three months or thereby.[3] On the 31st of December thereafter, Sir John was, on a precept of sasine from the Chancery of King James the Fourth, infefted, as heir of his father, in the lands of Inverlieple and Cayveland, in the shire of Argyll.[4] A precept of clare constat, without date, by Cuthbert Earl of Glencairn and others, his Majesty's bailies, was granted for infefting him, as heir of his father, in the lands of Bordland of Kilmaronock, in the shire of Dumbarton.[5]

In the same year he paid of relief duties four cheeses, for the King's common army, upon the ground of the lands of the barony of Luss, by duplication of the blench-farm of the same; £40 for the lands of Colquhoun; £9 for Garscube; £10 for Salquhy [Salachy]; and £10 for Glinns.[6]

As heir of his father, Sir John was, on 23d May 1494, also infefted in the half of the lands of Kilmardinny;[7] on 1st July in the same year, in

[1] Original Retour at Rossdhu.

[2] The words of this retour imply that the peace of the country was then disturbed, and the reference probably is to the internal commotions caused by the insurrection of Sir John Ross of the Isles.—[Tytler's History, vol. iii. p. 473.]

[3] Original Retour at Rossdhu.

[4] Original Precept, ibid.

[5] Ibid.

[6] Extracts from the Lord Treasurer's Books, at Rossdhu.

[7] Instrument of Sasine, ibid.

a tenement of land, an annual rent of 16s., and a piece of waste land, all
in the Canongate, Edinburgh;[1] and on 28th April 1496, in the mill of
Sauline.[2]

After his father's death, Sir John was involved in a litigation with
David Haliburton about a part of the barony of Sauline, in the shire of
Fife, namely, the lands and mill of Bordland. They had been wadset by
his grandfather, Sir John, and redeemed from his father by David Haliburton, who now claimed them, and who had obtained from Andrew Ayton,
Sheriff-depute of Fife, an inquest for declaring him heir of these lands and
the mill thereof. But this claim Sir John contested; and on 22d October
1493, by his procurator, he solemnly protested in the Sheriff-Court, held
at Cupar in Fife by that Sheriff-depute, that what had been done by that
inquest should not be prejudicial to his rights to the lands and mill of the
Bordland, inasmuch as the letters of inquest obtained by him from the
Royal Chancery had been proclaimed and served in the head Court after
the Feast of the Nativity of our Lord, before the Sheriff of Fife, or his
deputes, and also because his father, Humphrey Colquhoun, died vested
and seised in the said lands and mill; and farther, because he himself and
his father had peaceably possessed them for the space of twenty-five years.[3]
Sir John obtained, in 1495, a reduction of the retour of David Haliburton.[4]

On 6th October 1494, Sir John Colquhoun let to James Abercrombie,
burgess of Stirling, a tenement of land, with the garden and croft there, for
rendering yearly to the Crown the ferm due and wont; to the granter,
£3, 13s. 4d. Scots; to the chaplain of the altar of the Holy Cross in the
parish church of Stirling, 6s. 8d. Scots; and to the chaplain of the altar
of the Blessed Virgin, situated in the same church, 6s. 8d. Scots.[5]

Sir John married, about the year 1480, Elizabeth Stewart, daughter
(apparently the youngest) of John Lord Darnley, afterwards first Earl
of Lennox, of the name of Stewart, by his spouse Margaret, daughter of
Alexander second Lord Montgomerie, ancestor of the Earls of Eglinton;
a matrimonial alliance by which he was enabled to make valuable addi-

[1] Instrument of Sasine at Rossdhu.
[2] Ibid.
[3] Notarial Instrument of Protestation at
Rossdhu.

[4] Denniston's MSS. in Advocates' Library,
Edinburgh, vol. viii.
[5] Original Lease in Mar Charter-chest.

tions to his estate of Luss. From Matthew second Earl of Lennox, his wife's brother, Sir John Colquhoun received a charter, dated 17th April 1496, of the lands of Auchingache, Larg of Glenfruin, Auchenvennel, Stuckiedlow, and Blairhangane, all in the earldom of Lennox and shire of Dumbarton, in liferent, as the dowry of his spouse, Elizabeth Stewart.[1]  On the 6th of April 1498, Sir John Colquhoun and Elizabeth Stewart, his spouse, obtained from King James the Fourth a charter of the ten pound lands of Garscube, with the mill thereof, in the same earldom and shire.[2] Sir John, on the 6th of June 1498, was, on a precept of sasine by Matthew second Earl of Lennox, infefted in the six merk and a half land of Baller-nick-mor, in the same earldom; which the Earl had sold to him.[3]

On 7th December 1497, Archibald second Earl of Argyll, who is designated "master of the household to our sovereign lord," King James the Fourth, renounced and overgave to John Colquhoun of Luss and his heirs the right of conjunct infeftment of the lands of the Bordland of Sauline, which belonged to Elizabeth Countess of Argyll, the Earl's mother, and to himself by her donation. In the writ Sir John is designed "fear" of these lands.[4]  On the 20th of February 1498-9 he had a charter from John Porterfield of that Ilk of an annual rent of sixteen merks from the lands of Cors-ragal,[5] Chapeltoun, and the Schelis, in Lanarkshire, for a certain sum of money paid to the granter.[6]  In 1500 he obtained from Matthew second Earl of Lennox a charter of the lands of Letterwald-mor and Stuck-induff, in the earldom of Lennox and shire of Dumbarton.[7]  Some two years after, he purchased from Patrick Macgregor of Ardinconnal the middle third of the lands of Ardinconnal;[8] and from William Douglas of Ladcanroch the lands of Finnard, Portincaple, and Forlingbrek, all in the earldom of Lennox and shire of Dumbarton.[9]

[1] Original Charter at Rossdhu; Reg. Mag. Sig. Lib. xii. No. 283.
[2] Original Charter at Rossdhu.
[3] Original Instrument of Sasine, ibid.
[4] Original Gift, ibid.
[5] He also acquired from Robert Douglas of Lochleven an annual rent of 14 merks from the lands of Corsragale, etc. Original Precept of Sasine, dated 18th February 1506.

[6] Original Charter at Rossdhu.
[7] The Precept of Sasine is dated 4th May 1500. Original, ibid.
[8] Original Charter, dated 20th February 1501, and Original Instrument of Sasine, dated 18th April 1502, at Rossdhu.
[9] Original Instrument of Sasine, dated 18th April 1502. ibid.

Sir John's grandfather, Sir John, had acquired, in 1465, the half of the lands of Kilmardinny. The other half was acquired about 1440 by Donald Lennox of Ballincoroch. But this half of these lands now became the property of Sir John. He paid to John Lennox of Ballincoroch the sum of 100 merks and £3 Scots for the reversing and giving over of the half of the lands in Kilmardinny, as appears from the discharge by John Lennox, dated 23d February 1505.[1] On 6th April 1506, he was, upon a precept of sasine by Matthew second Earl of Lennox, infefted in these lands.[2] Thus did Sir John become proprietor of the whole of the five pound lands of Kilmardinny, which, as we shall afterwards see, he gave as a portion to one of his sons. He acquired in the same year four perches of land in the burgh of Dumbarton;[3] and in the year following he was infefted in the mill of Auldemyll, in Letterwald, in the earldom of Lennox and shire of Dumbarton.[4]

Some years after, Sir John purchased from Alexander second Earl of Menteith the lands of the two Carucates, extending annually to ten pounds of lands of old extent, and the lands of Cragwihte, extending annually to five pounds of lands of old extent, in the earldom of Menteith and shire of Perth; of which a charter was granted to him by that Earl, dated 13th July 1512.[5]

Sir John Colquhoun's name appears in the sederunt of the Privy Council, at Edinburgh, 24th September 1512, when the action pursued by Robert Lord Crichtoun against William Douglas of Drumlanrig, for being art and part in the slaughter and murder of the deceased Robert Crichtoun of Kirkpatrick, who was killed on 30th July 1508, on the sands of Dumfries, in the fight between the Maxwells and Crichtouns, came before the Lords of Council. The Lords, in presence of the King, decreed that the accused should be put to the knowledge of an assize before the King or his justice, criminally; and they also found that the said Robert was the King's rebel, and at the horn at the time of his

---

[1] Original Discharge at Rossdhu.

[2] Original Precept and Instrument, ibid.

[3] Charter under the Great Seal, dated 4th December 1506. Reg. Mag. Sig. Lib. xiv. No. 288.

[4] Instrument of Sasine, dated 7th January 1507, in original Notarial Transumpt of Protocols, dated 30th August 1540, at Rossdhu.

[5] Original Charter at Rossdhu.

slaughter. Both the prosecutor and the prosecuted were willing that the Lords of Council should be upon the assize. Sir John was not, however, present when the assize, on the 30th of September, delivered their verdict acquitting William Douglas, because it was found that Robert Crichtoun at the time he was slain was his Majesty's rebel, and at his horn.[1]

The Campbells of Argyll, Glenurchy, and Breadalbane had been long at feud with the Macgregors ; and, towards the close of the 15th century, and in the beginning of the 16th, so far had they carried their hostility against them, that they had succeeded in reducing, and even in almost extirpating many of the best families of that name. But at the very time that the hatred between the Campbells and the Macgregors was most intense, the Colquhouns and the Macgregors, it would appear, were on the best of terms. Patrick Macgregor of Ardinconnal was a tenant of Sir John Colquhoun's ; and in a bond granted to him for forty merks, 3d May 1513, he styles him his "dearest master."[2] But if this is to be taken as indicating the existence of a good understanding between the Colquhouns and the Macgregors at the beginning of the sixteenth century, these friendly relations, to whatever extent they went, did not, as we shall afterwards see, long continue.

In the year 1513, Sir John Colquhoun obtained from Angus Campbell of Ardoch Campbell a charter of an annual rent of five merks from the lands of Ardoch Campbell, in the earldom of Lennox and shire of Dumbarton, dated 8th May in that year;[3] and he was infefted therein on the 5th of July following.[4] In the same year he purchased from Robert Nore of Tarbart the two merk lands of old extent of Tullichintaull, in the earldom of Lennox and shire of Dumbarton.[5] He also received from Matthew second Earl of Lennox a charter of the lands of Forlingcareche, and of the lands of Blairwardane, in the said earldom and shire, and was infefted in them on the 12th of the same month.[6]

This was the last transaction which has been traced between Sir John

[1] Pitcairn's Criminal Trials, vol. i. pp. 77*, 78*.

[2] Original Bond at Rossdhu.

[3] Original Charter, ibid.

[4] Original Instrument of Sasine, ibid.

[5] Original Charter, dated 7th August 1513, at Rossdhu.

[6] Original Notarial Transumpt of Protocols, dated 30th August 1540, and original Precept of Sasine, dated 3d August 1513, ibid.

Colquhoun and his brother-in-law, Matthew Earl of Lennox. Shortly after, namely on 9th September 1513, was fought the fatal battle of Flodden, to which that Earl had accompanied King James the Fourth, with whom he was in great favour, and at which, with many other nobles, he was slain with his sovereign.

On 25th August 1515, Sir John Colquhoun entered into an agreement with Christian Douglas, the widow of Henry Thomson, sometime Lyon-King of Arms,[1] with respect to an annual rent of five merks, which was due to him as heir of his father, from the lands of Kellor, Menslesmure, and Farnyslaw, in the barony of Dirlton and shire of Edinburgh. He agreed, provided payment of that annual rent, of which he had received nothing since the entry of Henry Thomson and Christian Douglas, his spouse, to the said lands, was made to him in time to come, to remit to Christian, to whom these lands now belonged, by reason of conjunct infeftment, through the decease of her husband, all annuals owing to him for the terms bygone, and she bound herself to make payment thereof.[2] An annual rent, in which Sir John was infefted on 8th February 1515-16, consisting of ten merks Scots, to be raised from a tenement of land in the town of Leith, on the south side of the Water of Leith, in the barony of Restalrig, and shire of Edinburgh, is worthy of special notice, from the parties by whom the precept was given. These were the celebrated historian, "Hector Boece, Principal of the College of the University of Aberdeen, the pre- bendaries and bursars of the same, lords superior of the lands and annual rents of the house of St. Germains, in Lothian, of the Order of the Jerusalem Crossbearers." It is addressed to their bailies, among whom is Malcolm Colquhoun, but not designed.[3]

In the year 1516, Sir John Colquhoun purchased from Richard Lekky of that Ilk his five merk land of Letterbeg, in the earldom of Lennox and shire of Dumbarton, and obtained from him a charter of these lands, dated 5th September that year.[4] In the following year, he obtained from John third Earl of Lennox a charter of the lands of Strone, at the head of

[1] Henry Thomson is the third of the ascertained Lyon Kings of Arms.—[Mr. Seton's Scottish Heraldry, p. 478.]

[2] Original Contract at Rossdhu.
[3] Original Instrument of Sasine, ibid.
[4] Original Charter, ibid.

Glenfruin, in the same earldom and shire.[1] On 24th January 1518, he was, on a precept of sasine from the same Earl, infefted in the lands of Mamore and Mambeg, also in the earldom of Lennox.[2] In the same year, he purchased from John Makcauslan of Kilbride his two merk lands of Easter Kilbride, and his one merk land of Middle Kilbride;[3] and from Richard Lekky of that Ilk, in that year, the lands of Little Drumfad;[4] and in 1519 the lands of Rachane and Altermony, all in the earldom of Lennox and shire of Dumbarton.[5]

On the death of King James the Fourth at Flodden, his son and successor, King James the Fifth, being a child of little more than one year old, the Queen Mother, Margaret daughter of King Henry the Seventh of England, was declared Regent of the realm. At the same time John Duke of of Albany was summoned from France to Scotland, and chosen governor and protector of the infant Prince and kingdom, by a Convention of the Estates.[6] During the delay of the arrival of the Duke of Albany, the Earl of Arran assumed the office of Regent. In this assumption he was supported, among others, by John third Earl of Lennox, the Master of Glencairn, and Sir John Colquhoun of Luss, whose wife was the paternal aunt of the Earl of Lennox.

Sir John Colquhoun joined these noblemen in a successful attempt to seize the castle of Dumbarton. During a stormy night in January 1514, they found their way into the castle, and expelled from it Lord Erskine, by whom it was held for the Queen Mother's party; and though the Earl of Arran was frustrated in his usurpation of the regency by the arrival of the Duke of Albany in Scotland, they continued to hold the castle of Dumbarton until it was surrendered by the Earl of Lennox, who, having fallen into the hands of his opponents, and having been imprisoned in the castle of Edinburgh, could obtain his liberation only on condition of his surrendering it.

After the departure of the Duke of Albany for France in 1524, King

---

[1] Original Precept of Sasine, dated 13th May 1517, at Rossdhu.

[2] Original Instrument of Sasine, *ibid.*

[3] Charter dated 5th May 1518, and original Instrument of Sasine, dated 23d of the same month.

[4] Original Charter, dated 23d November 1518, and original Instrument of Sasine, dated 17th December thereafter, at Rossdhu.

[5] Original Precept of Sasine, dated 21st September 1519, *ibid.*

[6] Balfour's Annals, vol. i. pp. 237-39.

James the Fifth, who was then only thirteen years of age, was invested with
the supreme authority, but the government was in reality in the hands of
the Earls of Arran, Lennox, and Morton. A pardon was therefore now easily
obtained for Sir John Colquhoun of Luss and others, who had taken part
in the capture of the castle of Dumbarton. On the 11th of July 1526, a
"respite was granted to Sir John Colquhon of Luce, Knight, Patrick
Colquhon, John Logan of Balvey, Walter and Robert his sons, George
Buchquhanan of that Ilk," and twenty-nine others, for "their tressonabill
asseging, taking, and withhalding of our souerane lordis castle and fortalice
of Dumbertene fra his servandis, keparis thairof." On the 16th of July
following, a respite "was granted to Glencairn and others." [1]

   The fate of Sir John's relative, the Earl of Lennox, may be briefly
told : He had formerly been the firm ally of the Earl of Angus, but
the ambition and excesses of that nobleman having roused his indig-
nation, he separated from him, and determined to rescue the King from
the power of Angus, who held him almost a prisoner. In furtherance of
this determination, he fortified in 1526 the castle of Dumbarton and other
places of strength. He next raised an army of nearly 10,000 men, intending to enter the capital and to rescue his sovereign. He was met by the
forces of the Earl of Angus at the river Aven, near Linlithgow ; and the
Earl of Arran, now the opponent of Lennox, who held a prominent place
in Angus's army, having seized the bridge over that river, about a mile to
the west of the town, Lennox's troops, in attempting to cross a difficult
ford on the river, were thrown into disorder, and exposed to a severe fire.
They, notwithstanding, effected the passage, and on the opposite bank
they attacked the enemy with great gallantry; but not having recovered
from the confusion into which they had been thrown, they were completely
routed. Lennox was among the slain ; and it is said that he was killed,
after he had been made prisoner, or had surrendered, by Sir James Hamilton of Finnart, natural son of the Earl of Arran. Arran did himself credit
by the humanity and generosity which, on this occasion, he displayed.
Covering the body of the Earl, who was his uncle, with his cloak, he

---

[1] Register of the Privy Seal of Scotland, quoted in Pitcairn's Criminal Trials, vol. i.
p. 236*.

kneeled over it and touchingly exclaimed, that the wisest and bravest knight in Scotland had been slain that day.[1]

In those rude times, when men were peculiarly prone to violence and rapine, and when, law and order being but imperfectly maintained, this propensity, especially where inveterate enmities existed between families, often burst forth in lawless and even sanguinary deeds, men's properties and lives were much less secure than in the happier days in which we live. This state of insecurity gave rise to the adoption of a means of defence then quite common,—the formation of bonds of friendship or manrent, in which vassals and their chiefs pledged their honour and fidelity to each other; the former to take part in the lawful quarrels of the latter in all causes and against all persons, the sovereign excepted, and the latter to protect the former. In the year 1527, a bond of this description was made between Sir John Colquhoun and his son and apparent heir, Humphrey Colquhoun, and Andrew Lord Evandale, as having the ward of the lands of the earldom of Lennox, the heir of which, Matthew fourth Earl of Lennox, who had succeeded on the death of his father, which has just now been related, being a minor. The bond is in the following terms :—

"2 November 1527.—The quhilk day Johne Napar of Kilmahew and Patrick Culquhoune, paris clerk of Erskyne, haffand credens of ane noble mane, Schir Johne Culquhoun of Luss, Knycht, in writ, etc., tuk vpone thaim at the said Schir Johne, and Vmphra Culquhoue, sone and apperand air to the said Schir Johne of Luss, sal mak ane band of kyndis to tak part wytht ane noble and mychty Lord, Andrew Lord Awendale, and dow for the said Lord, wytht kying and fryndis, in all honest and leful actiones and quereles, for the tyme of the ward of the landis of the Leuenex, befor ony vtheris personis, excepand the our Souerand Lord the Kingis grace. And, siclyk, the forsaid Lord Awendale dowand for the saidis Schir John Culquhoue and Vmphra Culquhoue his sone and apperand air, induryng the tyme of the said ward in all actions and quereles as is aboue expremit, and all the barnis of the said Schir Johne, at hes the ward landis of the said Lord, [shall] cum, and his men and seruandis, for the tyme of the said ward,

excepand the Kingis grace, and efter the tyme of the said ward dowand
seruice to the said Lord before ony vther, excepand the Kingis grace, and
my Lord of Leuenex, the said Lord of Awendale defendand thaim aganis
all vtheris personis, excepand the Kingis grace and my Lord of Lenenex.
Facta fuerunt hec," etc.[1]

In the same year Sir John Colquhoun and his sons, Archibald and
David, purchased the eight merk land of Finnard, Portincaple, and For-
lingbrck, and the forty shilling land of Little Drumfad, in the carldom of
Lennox and shire of Dumbarton, from Andrew Lord Evandale, who had
from the Crown the ward lands and non-entries thereof. Sir John and
his sons, Archibald and David, were to be secured and defended by Lord
Evandale in the peaceable possession of the said ward lands and non-
entries thereof, with their mails and duties, during the period included
in the contract of purchase, that is to say, during the time of the ward
and non-entries of these lands, until the heir or heirs should be lawfully
entered thereto. They obtained from him, 18th November 1527, a bond
to this effect.[2]

On 10th September 1528, Sir John received from King James the Fifth,
for the good, true, and thankful service done to his Majesty, a gift of all
bygone rents of the twenty merks worth of land of the Bordland of Sauline,
that had been in the King's hands, or in the hands of his predecessors
through non-entry of the rightful heir.[3] On 30th October 1531, he obtained
from George Buchanan of that Ilk a charter of the lands of Kirkmichael-
Buchanan, in the carldom of Lennox and shire of Dumbarton.[4]

In order perhaps to concentrate his property in the upper part of the
Lennox, and thus to strengthen his clan, Sir John, in 1533, sold to Laurence Craufurd of Kilbirny a considerable part of the lordship of Colquhoun,
viz., Chapelton, Middleton, Milton, and the half of the mains of Colquhoun.
In these lands, Laurence Craufurd was infefted on the 26th of September
in that year, upon a precept of sasine from Sir John.[5]

Not long after, Sir John purchased from Sir William Cunningham,

[1] Notarial Protocols, Dumbartonshire, in
Dennistoun's MSS.

[2] Original Obligation at Rossdhu.

[3] Original Gift at Rossdhu.

[4] Original Charter, ibid.

[5] Original Instrument of Sasine, ibid.

Knight, son and heir-apparent of Cuthbert Earl of Glencairn, the half of his lands of Borland, in the barony of Kilmaronock and shire of Dumbarton, of which he received a charter, dated 13th January 1534-5.[1]

The details now given, which spread over a period of nearly half a century, relate chiefly to the acquisition or purchase of lands, and show how extensively this Laird of Luss was engaged in family and property transactions. To these more private affairs he seems to have mainly devoted himself, apparently more ambitious to enlarge his possessions than to excel either as a statesman, a courtier, or a soldier. His name, however, repeatedly appears in connexion with the public transactions of his time. He was a member of the Parliament of King James the Fourth, held at Edinburgh in the year 1503, and of the Parliament of King James the Fifth, held at Edinburgh in the year 1525.[2] He is ranked among the barons. His name appears in the sederunt of the Privy Council in 1512.[3] He actively co-operated with John third Earl of Lennox in supporting the claims of the Earl of Arran to the regency during the minority of King James the Fifth, and in seizing the castle of Dumbarton. In the management of his affairs he acted with no common energy and shrewdness, and these qualities, directed to the enlargement of his estate, were certainly crowned with great success. His shrewdness he was indeed blamed for carrying so far as to deceive even those who, it might be supposed, would not have been easily overreached. In a notarial instrument, dated 1st November 1518, regarding a deposition to that effect, it is said : " On which day Donald Campbell, son of the deceased Colin Campbell, affirmed as follows :—The manneris and wais of the Laird of Luss begylit the Zerle of Ergill and the Zerle of Lennox baith. And upon this Sir George Fallusdale, chaplain, sought instruments," etc.[4] From this deposition, without founding upon it anything discreditable to Sir John, it may yet be inferred that in business transactions he was a match, or more than a match, for those who had the reputation of being endowed in no common degree with the attributes of self-interested caution and discretion.

Sir John was occasionally involved, both as a sufferer and as an aggressor, in those family feuds, and in the consequent spoliation of property by

[1] Original Charter at Rossdhu.

[2] Acts of the Parliament of Scotland, vol. ii. pp. 239, 292.

[3] Pitcairn's Criminal Trials, vol. i. p. 78*.

[4] Notarial Protocols, Dumbartonshire.

retaliation, which in his time, and for many generations after, were very frequent. Having been the victim of one of these feuds, he raised, in February 1514, a summons of spulzie against Robert Dennistoun of Colgrain, for having "harried" the mains of Luss and the mailing of Dumfyn of a number of cows, horses, and sheep belonging to him. At a later period he was proceeded against as the offending party in an affair of this description and had to make reparation. In 1531 he made composition before the Circuit Court of Justiciary in Dumbarton for being art and part in the rapine and oppression committed in 1527 upon John M'Kinlay, by taking several cows, oxen, and a horse from his lands of Ballinreich, which had in consequence lain waste and unlaboured ever since.[1]

Sir John Colquhoun always maintained his loyalty as a subject, taking no part with those who formed intrigues and levied war against his sovereign. In the year 1529 he sent a present of venison and veal to King James the Fifth, for which ten shillings is entered in the Treasurer's books as given to a servant of the Laird of Luss, by whom it was brought.[2]

During the time of this laird the ecclesiastical livings of the parish of Luss were held by relatives of the house of Colquhoun. The rector of that parish, from 1513 till at least 1554, was Mr. James Colquhoun, who was a brother of John Colquhoun of Kilmardinny.[3] He used the arms of Colquhoun of Luss, with a fleur-de-lis in base for difference.[4] During his incumbency, Mr. Humphrey Colquhoun was parish clerk from 1520 to 1535, and Mr. Robert Colquhoun was vicar in 1524.

The only instance in which we have found the name of Sir John connected with ecclesiastical matters is in a letter which he wrote in Latin

[1] Dennistoun's MSS., vol. iv. p. 24.

[2] Accounts of the Lord High Treasurer of Scotland.

[3] Mr. James Colquhoun, rector of Luss, is so designated in a notarial instrument, dated 10th April 1554, relating to an arrangement made for the "help and supply" of John Colquhoun, his son.—[Original Notarial Instrument at Rossdhu.]

[4] In a charter dated 13th June 1530, from John Blair of Fynwik, etc., to Sir John Colquhoun of Luss, granting him an annual rent of £3 Scots, to be raised from the lands of Fynwik, in the earldom of Lennox and shire of Dumbarton; among the witnesses are Mr. Robert Colquhoun, rector of Dumbarton, and Mr. James Colquhoun, rector of Luss. And in a precept, dated 21st August 1531, for infefting Sir John in that annual rent, among the witnesses are Mr. Robert Colquhoun, rector of Dumbarton, and Mr. Adam Colquhoun, his brother-german, and Patrick Colquhoun of Ardincounal.—[Original Charter and Precept of Sasine at Rossdhu.]

to Gavin Dunbar, Archbishop of Glasgow, soliciting, on behalf of a clerk in whom he had taken a friendly interest, the patronage of the Archbishop. The following is a translation of the letter :—

"To the most reverend father in Christ our Lord, Lord Gavin, by the grace of God, and of the Apostolic Seat, Archbishop of Glasgow, or to any other Catholic bishop whomsoever, His humble and devoted son, John Colquhoun of Luss, Knight, All reverence and honour,—Reverend Father, since it is pious and meritorious to increase sacred ministers for the sacred mysteries, that the worship of Almighty God may be the more effectually performed, I, for this end, by this letter, present James Laing, clerk, the bearer hereof, born in your diocese, imbued with letters, graced with good manners, legitimate by birth, and free from all vice or canonical impedi ment, and who may be gradually and lawfully promoted to all sacred orders, with a right to £10, to be raised and received annually from my lands of Colquhoun, in the earldom of Lennox and shire of Dumbarton, until God from your paternity shall provide him with a richer benefice, supplicating your paternity, that from love and at my prayers you would graciously vouchsafe to promote the foresaid James, by the imposition of your sacred hands, to all orders not yet received by him, according to the exigency of the times. In testimony whereof my seal is appended to the presents, together with my manual subscription, at Rosdow, on the 30th of August 1534, before these witnesses, Master Adam Colquhoun, David Colquhoun, my carnal sons, Robert Galbraith, and Sir Malcolm Stewinsone, chaplain, with divers others.

The last purchase of lands which was made by Sir John was that of the lands of Letterpeyne, Peywinauthir, Cloudnocht, and Auchinadde, in

¹ Original Letter at Rossdhu.   The seal is not now attached to it.

the earldom of Carrick and shire of Ayr, from Alexander Kennedy of Bargany. But he died before he was put in possession of these lands, and his son and heir, Humphrey, was, upon a precept of sasine from the seller, dated 22d August 1536, infefted in them on the 30th of that month.[1] In the precept of sasine he is designated "quondam Johannes Colquhoun de Luss miles." He died shortly before the date of that precept. He was alive on the 4th of August 1535, but was then indisposed in health. This we learn from a notarial instrument, which narrates that on that day Thomas Charteris went into the personal presence of Sir John, within the place of Rossdhu, and showed him that, in prejudice of the properties and rights of them both, James Erskine of Little Sawchie had put an angular arch upon the aqueduct of the loch of Cultour; and that Sir John denied that this had been done with his permission; and that he consented that cognition should be taken in regard to the placing of that arch before the Sheriff of Stirling,— though, on account of divers impediments, he could not make the journey for the cognition to be taken,— on the understanding that thereby no prejudice should be done to his right to the lands of Sawchie, the fishings of the said lake of Cultour, and the aqueduct thereof.[2]

Sir John was twice married. He married first, as has been seen before, Lady Elizabeth Stewart, fourth daughter of John first Earl of Lennox, of the house of Darnley. By this lady he had four sons and four daughters. The sons were—

1. Humphrey, who succeeded him.

2. James. "James Colquhoun, son of the Laird of Luss," studied at the University of Glasgow, and received the degree of Master of Arts on 27th November 1499. Under the same designation, James Colquhoun was incorporated a member of that University, 26th October 1521.[3]

3. Walter, from whom the Colquhouns of KILMARDINNY, CRAIGTON, etc., are descended. On 5th July 1522, "Walter Colquhoun of Kilmardinny" had from Robert Grahame of Knoxdoliane a lease of his

---

[1] Original Instrument of Sasine at Rossdhu.
[2] Original Instrument, ibid.
[3] Munimenta Universitatis Glasguensis, vol. ii. pp. 139, 274, 275.

five-pound land of Wallaston, in the earldom of Lennox and shire of
Dumbarton, for three years, for the annual rent of sixteen merks
Scots. To this lease among the witnesses were John Colquhoun,
canon of Glasgow, and John Colquhoun, not designed.[1]  Walter's
name is connected with various transactions in which he acted for
"his father, the Laird of Luss." When, on 1st November 1527,
Andrew Lord Evandale faithfully promised to warrant "four skoir
of merkland and aucht of auld extent" to Sir John Colquhoun of
Luss, Knight, Walter Colquhoun asked an instrument, to the effect
that he had obtained the ward of the twelve merk land of old extent
of Ardincomnal from Lord Evandale.[2]  On 2d November 1527, the
said Walter, by his procurator, Patrick M'Gregor, younger, freely
gave over into Lord Evandale's hands all right that the said lord had
given him in the lands of Ardinconnal.  He afterwards purchased
from Gilbert Grahame of Knoxdoliane, the lands of Wallaston and
Ardochimor, in the county of Dumbarton, as appears from an assig
nation dated 28th March 1531, in which the said Gilbert Graham
constituted Alexander Graham, son to William Earl of Montrose,
Janet Countess of Montrose, mother to the said Alexander, and
others, his assignees, for the redemption of the lands of Wallaston
and Ardochimor, which he had sold to Walter Colquhoun, under
reversion, for the sum of 278 merks Scots.[3]  Walter's father, for the
affection he had towards him, granted a charter, duly sealed and
subscribed with his hand, dated at Rossdhu 24th May 1535, to him
and the lawful heirs-male of his body, of the lands of Auchingaich
with the Large, the lands of Auchenvennel-mor, the lands of
Stuckiedow and Blairhangane, in the earldom of Lennox and shire of
Dumbarton, to be held blench, for payment of two pennies yearly.[4]
He died before the 26th of October 1541, as appears from an
instrument of sasine of that date recording the infeftment of John
Colquhoun of Luss in the lands of Kilmardinny.  In that instru-

[1] Original Lease at Rossdhu.

[2] Notarial Protocols, Dumbartonshire,
Dennistoun's MSS.

[3] Original Assignation at Rossdhu.

[4] Original Charter, ibid.

ment among the witnesses is "John Colquhoun, son and heir of the deceased Walter Colquhoun of Kilmardinny."[1]  On the 24th of September 1512, John, son and heir of Walter Colquhoun, was infefted *propriis manibus* by John Colquhoun of Luss as lord superior in the lands of Auchenvennel and Stuckiedow.  Among the witnesses were David Colquhoun of Drumfad and Malcolm Colquhoun.[2]

4.  John.  On 1st April 1511, Sir John Colquhoun gave a precept, following on a charter, for infefting his son John in the lands of Mulichane, in the barony of Mugdok and shire of Stirling.[3]  On 25th October 1513, " John, son of the Laird of Luss, student," was incorporated a member of the University of Glasgow, under the rectorship of Mr. Patrick Graham, brother-german of the Earl of Montrose, canon of Glasgow.[4]  John became a canon of Glasgow, and rector of Stobo. As " canon of the metropolitan church of Glasgow," he was a witness to an instrument upon the oath and promise of obedience and reverence, made by Henry Bishop of Galloway, for himself, and the people and clergy of his diocese, to Gavin Archbishop of Glasgow, his immediate metropolitan, and to his successors canonically entering.  This instrument is dated at Edinburgh, 7th February 1530.[5] In the charter granted by Sir John to his son Thomas Colquhoun, 22d August 1532, of the lands of Finnard, Portincaple, and others, it was provided that if the heirs of Thomas failed, these lands should be inherited by his brother John Colquhoun and his heirs.

Gavin Dunbar, Archbishop of Glasgow, who died in April 1547, among other legacies to various parties enumerated in his testament (which was confirmed 30th May 1548), left to Mr. John Colquhoun, rector of Stobo, a scarlet gown lined with satin.[6]

[1] Original Instrument of Sasine at Rossdhu.

[2] Original Instrument of Sasine, *ibid.*

[3] Original Precept of Sasine, *ibid.*

[4] Munimenta Universitatis Glasguensis, vol. ii. p. 128.

[5] Registrum Episcopatus Glasguensis, tom. ii, p. 542.  The See of Glasgow, through the importunity of King James the Fourth, who was one of the canons of the chapter of Glasgow, was declared metropolitan, or erected into an archbishopric, by a bull of Pope Innocent VIII., dated 9th January 1491.  The bishops of Dunkeld, Dunblane, Galloway, and Argyll, were its suffragans.

[6] Register of Confirmed Testaments in the Commissariot of Glasgow.

On the death of that archbishop, John Colquhoun, as canon of
the Metropolitan Church of Glasgow, joined with the dean and
other canons in a petition to Pope Julius III., requesting that his
Holiness would appoint James Betoun, then Abbot of Arbroath, to
the vacant archbishopric. The petition, translated from the Latin,
is as follows : —

" To the most holy and most blessed father of fathers in Christ
and our Lord, high and mighty Pontiff of the sacred Roman and of
the whole universal Catholic Church, the most humble and devoted
sons of your Holiness, Gavin Hamiltoun, dean, James Balfoure,
treasurer, John Colquhoun, John Steward, Walter Betoun, James
Cottis, Thomas Hay, David Gibson, Robert Creichtoun, David
Crysteson, Archibald Craufurd, William Ker, James Colquhoun,
John Spreulle, and Archibald Dunbar, canons of the Metropolitan Church of Glasgow, in Scotland, [prostrate] themselves with
all humility, subjection, and reverence for the most devout
kisses of your feet: The most blessed father, Gavin Dunbar, our
late lord and last archbishop of Glasgow, of happy memory, being
dead, and his body with reverence delivered up to ecclesiastical
sepulture, We, dean and canons beforesaid, assembling in the
chapter-house of the said Church of Glasgow at the usual hour of
the meeting of the chapter at the ringing of the bell, according to
custom, for the asking of a new pastor and archbishop, having first
of all invoked the grace of the Holy Spirit, and fully observed all
the ceremonies and solemnities customary in such circumstances,
have with one voice and one spirit asked, as by the tenor of these
presents we ask for our and the Church of Glasgow's pastor and
archbishop, the venerable and excellent man, Master James Betoun,
born of a noble family, but a man more noble by his manners,
skilled, moreover, in letters, commended in many ways by his deport-
ment and virtuous actions, wise and circumspect in spiritual and
temporal things, and abundantly adorned with the various gifts of
the virtues with which the Most High has distinguished him, and
presented to us on the day of the date of these presents, by the

hands of the illustrious prince and lord, James Earl of Arran, Lord
Hamilton, tutor to our most serene Lady Mary, by the grace of God
Queen of the Scots, and protector and governor of the same kingdom,
who was present with us for the time in the chapter of the said
Church of Glasgow : Wherefore, most blessed father, we, as devoutly
as humbly, supplicate your Holiness, that, from the most benignant
liberality of your piety and holiness, you would mercifully vouchsafe to approve of our request concerning the said Master James,
thus made, as is premised, and to promote him to the foresaid
church of Glasgow, and to provide him with it, that, by the blessing
of God, he may, as a fit pastor, usefully preside over us, and the
foresaid church, and the flock committed to him." [1]

This petition was not immediately successful. Alexander Gordon,
brother to the Earl of Huntly, was appointed successor to Archbishop Gavin Dunbar. He, however, resigned the office in 1551,
and was succeeded by James Betoun. Being then only in his
twenty-seventh year, Betoun was not of sufficient age, according to
the canons of the Church, for holding the dignity of archbishop ;
but he received from Pope Julius III. a dispensation, and was consecrated at Rome in 1552.[2]

On 4th February 1552-3, Mr. John Colquhoun, parson of Stobo,
gave a letter of reversion of an annual rent of ten merks Scots, to be
uplifted from the lands of Letterwald-mor and Ballernick-mor, to
his brother-german, Mr. Adam Colquhoun of Blairvaddoch (who
had sold to him and his assignees by charter the said annual rent),
to take effect on the payment of 100 merks.[3]

On 25th October 1553, the feast of Crispin and Crispinian, he
was elected rector of the University of Glasgow, in the chapter-
house of the Metropolitan Church of Glasgow.[4] He was elected
rector in the following year, and also in the years 1556 and 1559.

---

[1] Registrum Episcopatus Glasguensis,
tom. ii. p. 562.

[2] Ibid. tom. ii. pp. 566, 567.

[3] Original Letter of Reversion at Rossdhu. This letter determines the relationship of Mr. John Colquhoun, pastor of Stobo.

[4] Munimenta Universitatis Glasguensis.
tom. ii. p. 173.

His name appears at various documents relating to the transactions
of the University. As its rector, he gave his consent to a charter
of feu-farm, dated 28th November 1553, granted by the chaplain
of the chapel of St. Michael the Archangel, of which chapel the
University of Glasgow was undoubted patron, to William Chalmers, citizen of Glasgow, of a tenement in the Rotton Row, for the
yearly rent of 36 shillings.[1]

In February 1555-6, while he held the office of rector of the
University, a letter was granted, under the signet of Queen Mary
and her mother, the Queen Regent, exempting the rector of the
University, the Dean of Faculty, and one of the principal regents,
being beneficed clerks in the diocese of Glasgow, from contributing
any part of the tax of £10,000 granted by the clergy of the realm.
The letter is in the following terms :—

" We and oure decrest moder, Mary, Quene Drowrear and regent
of oure realme, vnderstanding that the Vniuersite of Glasgw, and
membris thairof, haisbene fre and exemit fra all payment of taxtis
and contributionis to ony oure maist nobill progenitouris of gude
mynd sen the first erectione thairof : And beyng myndit rather to
augment nor hurt thare priuilegis, for the zele and favoure we beir
thairto, and commoue wele of our realme : Dischargis, exoneris, and
quietoclamis Maister Johne Colquhoue, person of Stobo, Rector for
the tyme of the said Vniuersite, Maister Johne Layng, person of Luss,
Dene of Facultye, and Maister Johne Houstone, vicar of Glasgu,
regent in the Pedagog tharof, for thair partis of the taxtt and contri
butioun of ten thousand pund grantit to ws and oure said derrest
moder be the clergy of Scotland in the moneth of Januare, the yeir
of God J<sup>m</sup> V<sup>c</sup> fiftyfoure yeiris or tharby : And attore dischargis ane
reuereud fader in God, and oure traist counsaloure, Williame bischop
of Dunblane, collectour generall of the said taxtt, oure familiar
clerk and counsaloure Maister Henry Synclare, dene of Glasgw [and
all] vtheris quhome it efferis, of all asking, cravyng, monyssing, and
ledyng of process quhatsumever aganis the saidis personis for thare

[1] Munimenta Universitatis Glasguensis, tom. i. p. 58.

M

partis of the said taxt of thare foirsaidis beneficis of Stobo, Luss, and vicarage of Glasgu, be the tenore heirof. Gevin vnder oure signett, and subscrivit be oure said derrest moder, Marie, Quene Drowriar, and regent of our realme, at Edinburght, the viij day of Februar, the yeir of God J$^m$ V$^c$ fiftyfive yeris, and of our regime the xiiij yeir," etc.[1]

When, on 25th October 1557, Mr. James Balfour, treasurer of the church of Glasgow, was elected rector of the University of that city, Mr. John Colquhoun, rector of Stobo, was one of the four deputies then chosen to assist the rector in deciding causes brought before him.[2] In the year 1559, as rector of the University, he again gave his consent to a charter of feu-farm granted by Mr. John Davidson, principal regent of the University, and chaplain of the chapel of St. Michael the Archangel, to William Wilson, in Stockwell, citizen of Glasgow, of a tenement and garden lying on the east side of Stock-wellgate, for the yearly rent of eighteen shillings.[3]

Being a canon of the Chapter of the Metropolitan Church of Glasgow, which held its meetings in the chapter-house of the Cathedral, Mr. John Colquhoun took an active part in its transactions; and his name frequently appears at the deeds or proceedings of that body, which had then acquired such high reputation as to draw to the Archbishop of Glasgow's court a great proportion of civil business. He subscribed his name to a confirmation by James, Archbishop of Glasgow, dated 10th October 1556, of the union made by the Dean and Chapter, of the perpetual vicarage of Daliell, with the common table of the vicars of the quire, that at one common table and board they might as fellow-commoners live in better condition, the vicar's pension of £10, with toft, croft, gardens, and mansion being reserved, provided that the two chaplains of the Archbishop, and the two chaplains of the Dean and Sub-Dean, should partake of the fruits of the same, along with the vicars of the quire.[4] As a member of

[1] Munimenta Universitatis Glasguensis, tom. i. p. 59.

[2] Ibid. tom. ii. p. 177.

[3] Munimenta Universitatis Glasguensis, tom. i. p. 65.

[4] Registrum Episcopatus Glasguensis, tom. ii. p. 581.

the Chapter, he gave his consent to the annexation by James, Arch-bishop of Glasgow, 24th January 1557-8, of the perpetual vicarage of Colmonell to the University of his city of Glasgow, for augmenta-tion of the annual rental to be made to the University, and to the Masters and Regents dwelling in it.[1] He again, as one of the Chap-ter, subscribed an assedation of the vicarage of Colmonell, dated 6th May 1570, by Mr. John Davidson, vicar thereof, with consent of the Dean, or President and Chapter of Glasgow, undoubted patrons of the said vicarage, to Mr. Gilbert Kennedy, father brother to Thomas Kennedy of Bargany, for nineteen years.[2]

The daughters of Sir John Colquhoun of Luss by Lady Elizabeth Stewart were—

1. Marion. She married, first, Robert, Master of Boyd, eldest son of Robert, fourth Lord Boyd. He died before his father, and to him she had no issue. She married, secondly, Captain Thomas Crawfurd of Jordanhill, a younger son of Laurence Crawfurd of Kilbirny. Captain Thomas Crawfurd was a man distinguished for his military abilities and bravery. He was at the sanguinary battle of Pinkie, fought on 10th September 1547 between the Scots, under the com-mand of James Earl of Arran, Regent, and the English, under the command of Edward Duke of Somerset, where 8000 of our brave countrymen fell, and where, with many others, he was taken pri-soner by the English. On regaining his liberty he went to France, where he had the honour of being made one of the guard of Scots-men who waited on the person of King Francis the Second, husband of Mary Queen of Scots. He returned to Scotland with the Queen in 1561. In 1562, upon the dissolution of the religious houses, he acquired the lands of Jordanhill from Sir Bartholomew Mont-gomery, chaplain of the chapel of Drumray, to which these lands had been originally mortified, and which his father, about the year 1516, had richly endowed. He remained the loyal subject of Queen Mary till the murder of King Henry, when he associated himself with

---

[1] Munimenta Universitatis Glasguensis, tom. i. p. 62.  [2] Munimenta Universitatis Glasguensis, tom. i. p. 82.

Regent Murray and others to avenge that murder. In March 1571, he especially distinguished himself by the capture of the Castle of Dumbarton, which was held against the King's authority by John Hamilton, Archbishop of St. Andrews, and Lord Fleming, who commanded it. This enterprise he executed by providing his soldiers with ropes and ladders, by means of which they climbed up the highest and most precipitous part of the rock on which the Castle was built---that part being the least guarded; and such was his success that he did not lose a single man, while only four of the enemy were killed, and that more by accident than design.[1] For his gallant exploits and faithful services, he received from King James the Sixth the lands of Bishop's Meadow, Blackstoun Barns, and Mills of Partick, with a pension of £200 yearly payable out of the Priory of St. Andrews. Of these lands he obtained from King James a charter confirming a former charter granted by James Boyd, Arch-bishop of Glasgow, dated the 10th of March 1573.

King James, when only in the ninth year of his age, in token of his youthful admiration of Crawfurd's gallant services, particularly in the taking of the Castle of Dumbarton from the partisans of the Queen, wrote to him the following letter:—

"CAPTEN CRAUFURD,—I haue hard sic report of your gud seruice done to me from the beginning of the weiris agains my onfreindis, as I sall sum day remember the same, God willing, to your greit contentment : In the main quhyle be of gud comfort, and reserue you to that tyme with patience, being assurit of my fauour.—Fare weil. Your gud freind,                      JAMES R.

"15 September, 1575."

"To my speciall gud seruant, Capten Craufurd of Jordanhill."[2]

---

[1] Buchanan's Hist., Aikman's edit., vol. ii. pp. 595-598; Balfour's Annals, vol. i. p. 354; Tytler's History, vol. vi. p. 153.

[2] Annexed to this letter are two holograph ratifications thereof by his Majesty, dated respectively at Falkland, 5th September 1584, and at Linlithgow, 23d March 1591. Original in the Montrose Charter-chest at Buchanan.

To Captain Thomas Crawfurd, Marion Colquhoun had only one daughter, Marion, who became the wife of Sir Robert Fairly of that Ilk, in the shire of Ayr. She predeceased her husband, who married, secondly, Janet Ker, eldest daughter and heiress of Robert Ker of Kersland.[1]

2. Marjory, who married Sir Duncan Campbell, fourth Laird of Glenurchy. They had one son, who died in his minority. The following is the notice of Sir Duncan in the history of the Lairds of Glenurchy, who were the ancestors of the Earls of Breadalbane :—
" Duncan Campbell, eldast and lauchfull sone to the foirsaid Sir Colene, succedit fourt laird of Glenvrquhay. The said Duncane marcit Mariory Colquhoun, dochtir to the Laird of Lus, on quhome he begatt ane sone, quha deit in his minoritie. The foirsaid Duncane levit Laird be the space of threttene yeiris, keping all thingis left to him be his worthy predicessouris. He departed this lylle in the Castell of Glenurquhay, the 5th September 1536, and was honorablie bureit in the Chapel foirsaid of Finlarg."[2] In that work there is a portrait of Sir Duncan Campbell in the fiftieth year of his age. He is represented at full length as a valiant knight in armour, with a long broad-sword in his left hand, and his plumed helmet at his left side. This was one of the sixteen pictures which the celebrated Scottish portrait-painter, George Jamesone, undertook to paint for Sir Colin Campbell between July and September 1635. The portrait of Duncan was painted exactly a century after his death. The likeness must be fanciful.

It is said that Marjory Colquhoun had, by Sir Duncan Campbell, besides the son already mentioned, a daughter, Margaret, who was married to John Macdougall of Raray, in Lorn.[3]

3. Catharine, who married Duncan Macfarlane of that Ilk and of Arrochar, being his second wife. On 17th July 1543, Duncan Macfarlane and Catharine Colquhoun, his spouse, were infefted in

[1] Crawfurd's History of the Shire of Renfrew, Robertson's edition, 1818, pp. 68-71.

[2] The Black Book of Taymouth, p. 18.
[3] Douglas's Peerage, by Wood, vol. i. p. 235.

liferent in the lands of Arrochar, in the earldom of Lennox and
shire of Dumbarton, which heritably belonged to the said Duncan,
and which he had resigned into the hands of Matthew Earl of Lennox,
the superior, for new infeftment.[1]  He was at the battle of Pinkie in
1547, and fell when fighting bravely against the English.  To him
she had a son, Andrew, who succeeded his father, and who was an
ardent supporter of Regent Murray in the measures he adopted
against Queen Mary.  To him and his clan it was mainly owing
that the Regent so quickly and so completely defeated the Queen's
forces at the battle of Langside, fought 13th May 1568, by which her
cause was hopelessly lost.  "In this battle," says Holinshed, "the
valiance of an Highland gentleman, named Macfarlane, stood the
Regent's part in great stead ; for in the hottest brunt of the fight he
came in with two hundred of his friends and countrymen, and so
manfully gave in upon the flank of the Queen's people, that he was
a great cause of disordering them."[2]  In reward for a service so
signal and so opportune, the Regent added to this Highland chieftain's coat-of-arms the crest of a naked man grasping in his right
hand a sheaf of arrows, and pointing with his left to an imperial
crown, and the motto, "This I'll defend," which the family have
ever since borne.[3]  Andrew Macfarlane married Agnes, daughter of
Sir Patrick Maxwell of Newark, by whom he had issue.

4. Agnes, who died unmarried.

Sir John Colquhoun married, secondly, Margaret, daughter of William
Cunningham of Craigends.  This lady survived him.

---

[1] Original Instrument of Sasine at Rossdhu.

[2] Holinshed's Chronicle, vol. v. p. 633.

[3] Nisbet's Heraldry, vol. i. p. 133. Tradition gives a different explanation of the
origin of the Macfarlane crest. The chief
of the Macfarlanes, it is said, being attacked
by some hostile party or clan, and hard
pressed, swam to a rock situated in Loch
Sloy, where he stood and called out "This

I'll defend," which he did successfully, setting his enemies at defiance. From this
circumstance, it is added, the Macfarlanes
derived their arms. The rock where this
incident occurred is still shown, and the
story related by the Arrochar people. The
words "Loch Sloy," with the motto, "This
I'll defend," would seem to favour the tradition ; while the introduction of a crown
is perhaps favourable to the version given
in the text.

In the books of Adjournal of the High Court of Justiciary, there is the following entry regarding the waylaying of Lady Colquhoun :—"16th August 1536.—Walter Macfarlan found John Naper of Kilmahew and John Buntyne of Ardoche, as cautioners for his entry at the next Justice-aire of Dunbertane, to underly the law for art and part of convocation of the lieges in great numbers, in warlike manner, and besetting the way to Margaret Cunynhame, relict of vmquhile Sir John Culquhoune of Luss, knycht, and David Farnely of Colmistoune, being for the tyme in her company, for their slaughter, and for other crimes."[1] How this matter terminated is not known, as the records of the proceedings of the Justice-aires of Dumbarton at that period have not been preserved.

As the relict of Sir John Colquhoun of Luss, Margaret Cunningham was infefted, 16th September 1557, in an annual rent of forty shillings out of the barony of Colquhoun.[2] She married, secondly, Adam Colquhoun of Blairvaddoch. She died on 15th June 1573. The testament testamentar and inventar of the goods, geir, sums of money and debts pertaining to her at the time of her decease, were faithfully made and given up by herself on the 22d day of February 1571, and after her death by Thomas and Mr. Archibald Colquhouns, her sons, whom she had nominated her executors-testamentars. Under the head of the debts which she owed are mentioned —" In the first the said vmquhile Margaret grantit hir to be awand to Thomas Colquhoun for his bairns part of guid and proffett of his lands tane up be hir during his minoritie, £266, 13s. 4d. Item, to Mr. Archibald Colquhoun hir son for the same caus, £266, 13s. 4d. Item, to Bessie Colquhoun hir dochtir for the same caus, £133, 6s. 8d. Item, to Gelis Colquhoun hir dochtir, £133, 6s. 8d."

The will is in the following terms :—

" I, dame Margaret Colquhoun, Lady Luss, haill in spirit and febill in body, subject to seikness and infirmities, makis my testament in manner and form as eftir follows :—Committis my saule to God Almightie, my body to be buriet in the kirk of Glasgow, in the sepulchre of vmquhile my brodir, Mr. James Cunynghame, befoir all hallow altare, and makis and constitutis my executouris, my sons Thomas Colquhoun and Mr. Archibald

[1] Pitcairn's Criminal Trials, vol. i. p. 178*.     [2] Dumbarton Sasine Records.

Colquhoun, and my cousing Mr. Archibald Crawfurd, oversman, and they
to dispone upon my guids conform to my lattir will as thai will answer
thairupon before God. . . . . . (Small legacies). Item, to my cousing the
person of Eglischem j" merkis, and ordanis the rest of my guids and geir to
be disponit among my bairns—Thomas, Mr. Archibald, Bessie, and Gelis, at
the sycht, discretion, and consideration of my said cousing, the parson, oversman : Dated 17th February 1571, before witnesses, Sir Robert Watson, vicar
of Gleschart, Mr. Archibald Crawford, person of Egleschem, and William
Fowlare."[1]

From this deed we learn that Sir John Colquhoun of Luss had by Margaret Cunningham two sons and two daughters. The sons were—

1. Thomas. Sir John, for his affection and favour to his beloved son,
   Thomas Colquhoun, and for the manifold services rendered to him
   by that son, granted him, on 22d August 1532, a charter of the lands
   of Finnard and Portincaple and Forlingbrek, and the lands of Ballernick-mor, in the earldom of Lennox and shire of Dumbarton.

2. Mr. Archibald. "Archibald Colquhoun, son of the deceased Sir John
   Colquhoun, Knight," was incorporated a member of the University
   of Glasgow 26th June 1550, under the rectorship of Mr. William
   Betoun, Canon of Glasgow and St. Andrews, and Archdeacon of
   Lothian.[2] He was designated "of Sallochquhy" [Salachy]. Archibald Colquhoun of Sallochquhy, lawful son of the deceased John
   Colquhoun of Luss, sold his third part of the lands of Kirkmichael-
   Buchanan, in the earldom of Lennox and shire of Dumbarton, to
   Robert Stewart, lawful son of James Stewart of Cardonald, and his
   heirs and assignees whomsoever, heritably, for a certain sum of
   money paid to him "in his great, known and urgent necessity," and
   granted him a charter of these lands, dated at Edinburgh 3d March
   1562.[3]

The daughters were—

1. Elizabeth. The only trace of her is what appears in her mother's

¹ Register of Confirmed Testaments in        ² Munimenta Universitatis Glasguensis,
Commissariot of Edinburgh.                       vol. ii. p. 70.
                                                 ³ Original Charter at Rossdhu.

testament, above quoted, in which she is named as her daughter Bessie.

2. Giles, who became the wife of Mr. William Chirnside, parson of Luss. Dame Margaret Cunninghame, Lady Luss, and her daughter Giles, spouse of Mr. William Chirnside, parson of Luss, had an annual rent of £10 out of Cameron Denzelstoun from Robert Denzel stoun of Colgrain in 1573.[1]

Besides these children, Sir John had three sons, Patrick, Adam, and David, and a daughter, Margaret, who were probably illegitimate, as the term "carnalis" is applied to all of them. From their apparent ages, it may be concluded that they were born before the first marriage of Sir John.

1. Patrick Colquhoun. On 24th August 1523, Patrick Colquhoun, who is designated "carnal son" of Sir John Colquhoun of Luss, Knight, was, on a precept of sasine by Sir John, infefted in the lands of Tullichintaull, in the earldom of Lennox and shire of Dumbarton. Among the witnesses was Patrick Colquhoun of Bannachra.[2] By a letter of bailiery by Sir Thomas Watson, chaplain of the rud altar[3] within the parish kirk of Dumbarton, dated 15th June 1528, Sir John Colquhoun of Luss, knight, and Patrick Colquhoun, his carnal son, were constituted bailies and procurators of the lands of Auchindonane, pertaining to the said chaplainry of Sir Thomas, situated in the earldom of Lennox and shire of Dumbarton, with full power to hold the courts of the said lands and bounds thereof, to pursue thieves and trespassers, to uplift fines and escheats, and to distrain for them if necessary, to choose and swear assizes, and to do whatever was known to belong to the said office of bailiery by law or custom. Having no seal of his own, the granter procured the seal of a worshipful man, Walter Colquhoun of Kilmardinny, which he appended to the letter.[4] Sir John Colquhoun

---

[1] Notarial Protocols, Dumbartonshire, in Dennistoun's MSS.

[2] Protocol of Instrument of Sasine in Notarial Transumpt (Original), dated 23d April 1577, obtained from the Sheriff of Dumbar-

ton by Humphrey Colquhoun of Tullichintaull, son and heir of the deceased Patrick Colquhoun of Tullichintaull, at Rossdhu.

[3] "Rud altar," altar of the cross.

[4] Original Letter of Bailiery at Rossdhu.

of Luss, Knight, "for the paternal affection which he bore towards
his beloved son Patrick," and for the multiplied services rendered to
him by that son, granted a charter, dated 29th August 1526, of the
lands of Tullichintaull and Gortane, to him and the lawful heirs-
male of his body; whom failing, to Adam and David, his brothers,
and the lawful heirs-male of their bodies respectively; whom failing, to return to Sir John and his heirs whomsoever.[1]

Patrick Colquhoun of Tullichintaull married Isabel M'Aulay,
who was apparently of the family of M'Aulay of Ardincaple.

In 1528, Aulay M'Aulay of Ardincaple bound himself not to convey
or sell to Patrick Colquhoun, son of Sir John of Luss, the lands of
Ardincaple.[2] Patrick Colquhoun purchased from George Buchanan
of that Ilk the lands of Kirkmichael-Buchanan, extending yearly
to 40s. land of old extent, in the earldom of Lennox and shire of
Dumbarton. He and his spouse, Isabel M'Aulay, in a backbond to
George Buchanan of that Ilk, dated at Rossdhu 6th February 1528,
bound themselves, that though the said George Buchanan had
sold to them these lands, they should not take up more than eight
merks in the year, and that they should not set, or otherwise interfere with these lands, except in default of the payment of the foresaid eight merks. Among the witnesses were Mr. Robert Colquhoun,
parson of Dumbarton; Mr. James Colquhoun, parson of Luss; and
Archibald Colquhoun of Mamore.[3] Patrick and his wife, Isabel
M'Aulay, obtained a charter of the above-mentioned lands, dated
25th February in the same year, and they were infefted in them
on the 6th of March following.[4] In the precept of sasine he is designated Patrick Colquhoun of Ardinconnal.

In 1535, Patrick and his brother Adam were proceeded against
for intercommuning with Humphrey Galbraith and his accomplices,
who were at the horn for the murder in that year of William
Stirling of Glorat, deputy-keeper of Dumbarton Castle. In the

[1] Original Charter at Rossdhu.
[2] Notarial Protocols, Dumbartonshire, Dennistoun's MSS., vol. viii.
[3] Lennox Charters.
[4] Original Charter and Instrument of Sasine at Rossdhu.

Books of Adjournal of the High Court of Justiciary is the following entry:—"July 20 [1535].—Patrick Colquhoun and Adam
Colquhoun, sons of Sir John Colquhoun of Luss, knight, and
twenty-five others, found surety to underly the law at the next
justice-aire of Dumbarton, for resetting, supplying, intercommuning,
and assisting Humphrey Galbrayth and his accomplices, rebels,
and at the horn, for the cruel slaughter of William Strincling of
Glorat. . . . Sir John Colquhoune of Luss and Donald M'manys
were proved to be sick; and Humphrey Colquhoune, parish clerk of
Luss; Mr. Adam Colquhoune, pensioner of Luss; and David Col
quhoune, clerk, were replegiated by the Archbishop of Glasgow."[1]
Whether or not the parties appeared before the justice-aire of Dun
barton, and what was the result, cannot be ascertained, as the
records of the proceedings of that Court are not now extant.

At Rossdhu, 17th January 1559, John M'Gregor passed to the
presence of John Colquhoun of Luss, Patrick Colquhoun of Ardinconnal, and Humphrey Colquhoun, son and apparent heir to the
said Patrick, and warned them to compear at the parish kirk of
Dumbarton, to receive 500 merks for the redemption of the eight
merk land of Ardinconnal.[2]

Patrick Colquhoun was still living in the year 1565. On 5th June
that year, in presence of Patrick Colquhoun of Ardinconnal and
others, Robert Colquhoun in Glenbog, and James Colquhoun in
Moss, became bound to warrant the said Patrick, at the hands of
Gawyne M'Lelan and others, as to the sum of £20 Scots.[3]

2. Mr. Adam Colquhoun. He obtained from his father, Sir John Colquhoun of Luss, a charter of the lands of Blairwardane, Stuckinduff,
and Meikle Letterwald, in the earldom of Lennox and shire of
Dumbarton; and he was infefted therein on 5th September 1520.[4]
He studied at the University of Glasgow, and was incorporated a
member of that University on the 25th of October 1526, under the

[1] Pitcairn's Criminal Trials, vol. i. p. 170*.  [4] Original Instrument of Sasine at
[2] Dumbarton Sasine Records.      Rossdhu.
[3] Ibid.

rectorship of Mr. John Reid, vicar of the church of Mearns, near
Glasgow, and prebendary of Bothwell.[1]  In 1543 Adam Colquhoun
was clerk of the parish of Kilpatrick.  He purchased from his relative,
Matthew fourth Earl of Lennox, the lands of Faslane and Ballernick-mor, in the lordship of Lennox and shire of Dumbarton, of
which he received a charter in November 1543, and was infefted
therein on the 3d of that month.[2]  The lands of Faslane had long
formed part of the inheritance of the earldom of Lennox.  The old
castle, " the site of which may still be traced at the junction of two
deep glens, whose steep banks must have rendered the fortress almost
impregnable in those days of rude warfare," is associated with the
memory of Sir William Wallace.[3]

Mr. Adam Colquhoun also received from his father, Sir John,
the lands of Blairvaddoch, in the same earldom and shire.

Mr. Adam Colquhoun of Blairvaddoch sold to Patrick M'Causlane
of Caldenocht, and Marjory Colquhoun, his spouse, an annual rent
of ten merks Scots, from the lands of Letterwald-mor; and on 20th
February 1543 they granted him letters of reversion, engaging, on his
payment of one hundred merks Scots, to renounce this annual rent in
his favour.  He also sold an annual rent of eight merks Scots from his
lands of Letterwald-mor to James Colquhoun, carnal son of the deceased Malcolm Colquhoun of Dunfin and Elizabeth Colquhoun, who
granted him letters of reversion, dated 8th June 1551, engaging, on
his payment of 100 merks Scots, to renounce in his favour the said
annual rent.  On 11th July 1554 he infefted *propriis manibus* John
Colquhoun, rector of Stobo, in liferent, and Margaret Colquhoun,
her heirs and assignees, in an annual rent of ten merks, to be raised
from the lands of Letterwald-mor and Ballernick-mor; and on 10th
August 1554 the said John Colquhoun, parson of Stobo, and Margaret
Colquhoun, granted to him letters of reversion of that annual rent,
engaging to resign it in his favour on his payment of 100 merks Scots.[4]

[1] Original Charter at Rossdhu.                    [3] Dennistoun's MSS., Advocates' Library.
[2] Original Charter and Instrument of           [4] Original Instrument of Sasine and
Sasine, *ibid.*                                                     Letters of Reversion at Rossdhu.

The name of Mr. Adam Colquhoun appears in records of the
period as rector of Kilpatrick in 1555 and 1558. He died in the
year last mentioned. In a notarial instrument, dated 29th July
1558, it is narrated that David Colquhoun of Stronratan was served
as the true, lawful, and undoubted heir of the deceased Mr. Adam
Colquhoun, his brother-german, in the lands of Blairvaddoch, Stuckinduff, Letterwald-mor, and Ballernick-mor.[1]

3. David Colquhoun of Stronratan and Drumfad. His father, Sir John,
granted "to his beloved son, David Colquhoun," a charter of the
lands of Little Drumfad, Durling, and Strone, in the earldom of
Lennox and shire of Dumbarton, and David was infefted in them
on 28th September 1520.[2] In 1522 David and his brother Adam
were substituted to a grant which their father had made to their
elder brother Patrick. On 30th December 1535 he was infefted, on
a precept from his father, in the lands of Easter and Middle Kilbride. The witnesses to the precept, which is dated the 10th of
that month, were Humphrey Colquhoun of Letter, brother-german
of the granter; Mr. Robert Colquhoun, rector of Dumbarton;
Mr. James Colquhoun, prebendary of Luss; Mr. Adam Colquhoun,
and Patrick Colquhoun, of Ardinconnal, sons of Sir John the
granter.[3] In 1543 this son is designated of "Drumfad," and in
1558 of "Stronratan," and also of Strone. In that year David,
as already stated, was served heir to his brother Adam in the
lands of Blairvaddoch, Stuckinduff, Letterwald-mor, and Ballernick-mor. On the 24th April that year a precept was given by
Sir John Colquhoun of Luss for infefting David Colquhoun of
Strone, his uncle, as heir to Mr. Adam Colquhoun, his brother, in
these lands; and on 29th July David was infefted in them. On
the same day he resigned them into the hands of Sir John Colquhoun
of Luss as into the hands of his lord superior, that they should
remain for ever with the said John, his heirs and assignees. This
was done in the garden without the mansion of Blairvaddoch, at

[1] Notarial Instrument at Rossdhu.  
[2] Original Instrument of Sasine, ibid.  
[3] Original Instrument of Sasine at Rossdhu.

three o'clock in the afternoon. Among the witnesses was James Colquhoun, brother-german of the said John Colquhoun of Luss.[1] On the same 29th of July David Colquhoun of Stronratan was infefted in the lands of Ballernick-mor by the hands of John Colquhoun of Luss.[2] David died soon after. In a notarial instrument, dated 6th September 1568, on the redemption by John Fleming, burgess of the city of Glasgow, from Sir John Niven, canon of the metropolitan church of Glasgow, and prebendary of Ashkirk, of an annual rent of 8 merks Scots, from the four merk lands of Durlye, in the barony of Luss and shire of Dumbarton, by the payment of £40 Scots, it is said that these lands belonged to the deceased David Colquhoun of Drumfad.[3]

4. Margaret. She married Hugh Crawfurd, eldest son and heir of Lawrence Crawfurd of Kilbirnie, and ancestor of the Viscounts Garnock. On 26th November 1533 "Margaret Colquhoun, carnal (carnalis) daughter of Sir John Colquhoun of Luss, knight," was, on a precept of sasine from Laurence Crawfurd of Kilbirny, dated at Rossdhu 14th May that year, infefted in the lands of the Huckstoun, Hoill, and Smedeland, the lands of Grystoun, and a part of the merk lands of the Threipzardes, in the earldom of Lennox and shire of Dumbarton, according to the tenor of her charter of life-rent.[4] Hugh Crawfurd succeeded his father in 1547. He was a zealous and steadfast supporter of Queen Mary; and after her escape from Lochleven Castle, on 2d May 1568, he joined with those lords who made an unsuccessful effort on her behalf at the battle of Langside, fought on the 13th of that month, for which he was under the necessity of taking a pardon from Regent Murray. To him Margaret Colquhoun had a son, Malcolm, who succeeded his father in 1576.

[1] Original Precept of Sasine and Notarial Instrument of Resignation at Rossdhu.
[2] Original Instrument of Sasine, ibid.
[3] Original Notarial Instrument at Rossdhu.
[4] Original Instrument of Sasine, ibid.

# XII. HUMPHREY COLQUHOUN,

Twelfth of Colquhoun and Fourteenth of Luss, 1536-7.

LADY CATHERINE GRAHAM (of Montrose), his wife.

HUMPHREY COLQUHOUN was an active man of business for a good many years before his accession to the family estates. On 4th October 1524, as son and apparent heir of Sir John Colquhoun of Luss, he compeared before John Napier of Kilmahew, Mr. Robert Colquhoun, vicar of the Kirk of Luss, Patrick Colquhoun, and others, judges-arbiters, and protested, that whatever they did should not prejudice him in time coming with regard to his lands of Correch Kenckan.[1]

On 18th March 1525, Robert Colquhoun of Camstradden, and Patrick Colquhoun his brother, were bound and sworn to fulfil the decreet of Humphrey Colquhoun, son and apparent heir of Sir John Colquhoun of Luss, Knight, Walter Colquhoun, also son to the said Laird of Luss, and others, respecting all actions and debates. Among the witnesses were John Colquhoun, Humphrey Colquhoun, and Adam Colquhoun (*scriba*), writer.[2]

Humphrey Colquhoun succeeded his father, Sir John, in 1536. As already observed, he was, on the 22d of August that year, infefted, as heir of his father, in the lands of Letterpeyne, Peywinauthir, Cloudnocht, and Auchinaddo, in the earldom of Carrick and shire of Ayr.

On 6th August a precept was granted by George Buchanan of that Ilk for infefting Humphrey Colquhoun as heir of his deceased father, Sir John, in the lands of Salachy and Kirkmichael-Buchanan, in the earldom of Lennox and shire of Dumbarton ; and he was infefted in these lands on 27th October following.[3] Humphrey sold to Janet Galbraith, sister of the deceased Andrew Galbraith, his lands of Garshake, in the shire of Dumbarton, under reversion, on payment of one hundred merks Scots. Her letter of reversion, in which she designates him "ane nobill man my traist freind," is dated at Rossdhu, 16th August 1536.[4]

---

[1] Dumbarton Sasine Records.

[2] *Ibid.*

[3] Original Instrument of Sasine at Rossdhu.

[4] Original Letter of Reversion, *ibid.*

On 24th August 1536, Humphrey Colquhoun of Luss, as lord superior, granted to Robert Boyd, afterwards fourth Lord Boyd, and Margaret Colquhoun, daughter and heiress of John Colquhoun of Glinns, his spouse, a charter of the lands of Glinns, in Stirlingshire.[1]

On 17th November 1537, a mandate was given by George fourth Earl of Rothes, Sheriff of Fife, to his bailie and officers of the said shire, conformably to a precept of sasine from the Chancery of King James the Fifth, to infeft Humphrey Colquhoun, as nearest and lawful heir of his father, the deceased Sir John Colquhoun of Luss, in the mill of Sauline, in the barony of Sauline and shire of Fife; and on 19th November Humphrey was infefted therein.[2]

This is the last notice which has been found of Humphrey Colquhoun. He died about the end of January 1537-8, as appears from the retour of his son John, as heir to him, which is dated 30th April 1538, and which narrates that his father, Humphrey, died about three months previous to that date. It does not appear that he ever received the honour of knighthood, the designation of *miles* being never annexed to his name in any of the family writs. Having enjoyed the family inheritance only about a year and a half, he had not, at the time of his death, been served heir to, or completed his title to all his father's extensive estates, as appears from his son Sir John having been served heir in many cases not to his father, but to his grandfather.

Humphrey Colquhoun married Lady Catherine Graham, daughter of William first Earl of Montrose, who fell at the battle of Flodden, on 9th September 1513. In his testament, which bears that he was slain apud Northumberland sub vexillo Regis, the earl acknowledged that he owed the Laird of Luss, on account of his daughter's dowry, . . . . , and the Laird of Luss younger, xx l.[3] Of the marriage of Humphrey Colquhoun and Lady Catherine Graham there were four sons and two daughters. The sons were—

1. John, who succeeded him.

[1] Original Charter at Rossdhu.
[2] Original Precept of Sasine and Instrument of Sasine at Rossdhu. The Instrument of Sasine reads 9th November, which is evidently a mistake.

[3] Note made by George Crawford of the Original Testament in Lord Elphinstone's Charter-chest : Spalding Club Miscellany, Vol. v. pp. 319, 320.

2. James, who is designated of Garscube, and who was ancestor of the branch of the COLQUHOUNS OF GARSCUBE. James Colquhoun, brother of John Colquhoun of Luss, was witness, 28th July 1549, to a charter in favour of Robert Dennistoun of Colgrain. He married, on the 28th of October 1558, Christian, daughter of John Campbell of Glenurchy ; and they obtained from his brother John, whose heir-presumptive he then was, the lands of Garscube in liferent.[1] He afterwards acquired the lands of Easter Tullychewen, in the earldom of Lennox and shire of Dumbarton ; and, on 4th May 1568, he and Christian Campbell, his wife, were infefted in these lands in liferent in conjunct infeft ment, on a precept of sasine by Archibald fifth Earl of Argyll, addressed to his bailie, Robert Colquhoun of Camstradden.[2]

In 1580, James Colquhoun of Garscube purchased from James Lindsay in Stukroger an annual rent of five merks from the dominical lands of Bullule, now Bonhill-Lindsay, in the earldom of Lennox and shire of Dumbarton, of which he obtained a charter from the said James Lindsay dated 30th October that year. Among the witnesses were Adam Colquhoun in Hill; Patrick Colquhoun, natural son of the said James ; John Colquhoun, eldest son of the late John Colquhoun in Dunglas; and Adam Colquhoun in Milton.[3] On 12th November, same year, James Colquhoun of Garscube, tutor of Luss, and Christian Campbell, his spouse, received from Robert Sempill, fiar of Fulwood, with consent of his father, John Sempill of Fulwood, a charter of an annual rent of twenty merks from the lands of Kirkmichael-Sempill, for a certain sum of money paid to the granter in his great, urgent, and known necessity; and they were infefted therein on the following day.[4]

On 10th November 1581, James Colquhoun, tutor of Alexander Colquhoun, son liberal of the late Sir John Colquhoun of Luss, knight, confessed that an annual rent of 50 merks Scots, from

[1] Dumbarton Sasine Records.

[2] Protocol of Instrument of Sasine contained in a Notarial Transumpt, dated 7th February 1575-6. Original at Rossdhu.

[3] Original Charter at Rossdhu.

[4] Original Charter and Instrument of Sasine, ibid.

the barony of Fynlayston, would be lawfully redeemed for 500 merks.[1]

James Colquhoun of Garscube and Christian Campbell, his spouse, had an annual rent of twenty stones of cheese yearly, to be uplifted from the lands of Auchingawan, in the parish of Luss, conformably to a charter made by Robert Colquhoun of Camstradden, and an instrument of sasine thereof. On 8th June 1587 a contract was entered into between them and certain tenants of Robert Dennistoun of Colgrain, whereby the latter, to relieve the said Robert Dennistoun, who was bound to redeem the said annual rent, bound themselves to pay to the said James Colquhoun and his spouse, in consideration of their having resigned the above annual rent, forty bolls of bear or malt.[2] James Colquhoun obtained from Peter Napier of Kilmahew a charter, dated 10th April 1588, of an annual rent of ten merks, to be raised from the lands of Barris, in the dukedom of Lennox and shire of Dumbarton.[3]

Having no issue by his wife, James Colquhoun settled his lands of Easter Tullychewen on his "natural son Patrick," as he is designated in the writ quoted, reserving the liferent of them to his said wife. Patrick was infefted in these lands on 3d September 1577. The precept of sasine, dated 28th June preceding, and addressed to Humphrey Colquhoun of Tullichintaull, is thus subscribed by the granter: "I, James Colquhoun of Garscube, with my hand tuching the pen of Maister Villeame Houstoun, notar subscribar for me at my command, because I can nocht wreit my self."[4]

Patrick Colquhoun married first, in 1574, Janet, sister of John Murray of Strowan; and secondly, Isabella Buchanan, whose parentage is not recorded in any of the family writs which we have examined. He obtained, on 31st December 1577, a legitimation from the Crown.[5] On 14th November that year, his father, in a contract between them, engaged to infeft him and the heirs male lawfully begotten

[1] Dumbarton Sasine Records, fol. 98.
[2] Original Contract at Rossdhu.
[3] Original Charter, ibid.

[4] Original Instrument of Sasine at Rossdhu.
[5] Registrum Magni Sigilli, Lib. xxxiv. No. 604.

betwixt him and the deceased Janet Murray, his late spouse; whom failing, the heirs-male lawfully begotten betwixt him and Isabella Buchanan, his present spouse; whom failing, Alexander Colquhoun of Luss and his heirs-male whomsoever, in the lands of Easter Tullychewen, *alias* Tullychewen Semple, under reversion, the liferent of the said lands being reserved to the granter. And for this Patrick discharged his father of 100 merks owing to him, and also of £100 which had been promised by the deceased Christian Campbell, his father's spouse, to the deceased Jean Murray, the first wife of Patrick.[1] On 14th November 1596, Patrick, on his resignation of the lands of Easter Tullychewen, *alias* Tullychewen Semple, was similarly infefted in these lands by the hands of his father.[2]

James Colquhoun of Garscube died in July 1604.[3]

3. Adam. He became clerk of the parish kirk of Kilpatrick. He is mentioned under this designation in a contract dated 5th August 1559, between him and his brother, John Colquhoun of Luss, on the one part, and John Colquhoun of Kilmardinny on the other.[4] On 10th September 1561, in presence of James Colquhoun of Garscube, Robert Colquhoun of Camstradden, Adam Colquhoun, junior, and others, Adam Colquhoun, clerk of the parish kirk of Kilpatrick, resigned into the hands of John Colquhoun of Luss, his brother, the lands of Craigintowe.[5] On the same day the said John Colquhoun promised to hold the said Adam, his brother, skaithless of the duties of the said lands.[6]

[1] Original Contract at Rossdhu.

[2] Instrument of Sasine, *ibid.*

[3] This fact is stated in a retour of Alexander Colquhoun of Luss as heir to his brother John, dated 11th February 1607. Original at Rossdhu.

[4] Original Contract at Rossdhu.

[5] Notarial Protocols, Dumbartonshire. The rector of Kilpatrick-Juxta, in the diocese of Glasgow, in the preceding year was Humphrey Colquhoun. By letters of procuratory, dated 20th July 1560, he constituted procurators for resigning in his name the rectory of Kilpatrick into the hands of James Archbishop of Glasgow, in favour of Sir James Laing, chaplain of the diocese of Glasgow. Among the witnesses were John Colquhoun of Luss, James Colquhoun of Garscube, Patrick Colquhoun of Ardincon-nal, and Andrew Macfarlane of Arrochar.—[Original Letters of Procuratory at Rossdhu.]

[6] *Ibid.*

4. Patrick.   On 23d January 1547-8, Patrick Colquhoun, brother-german of John Colquhoun of Luss, and acting as his attorney, was, upon a precept of sasine by Archibald Earl of Argyll, infefted in the lands of Glenloing, in the earldom of Lennox and shire of Dumbarton.[1]

Sir Humphrey's daughters by Lady Catharine Graham were :—

1. Helen, who married James Cunningham of Aiket, and had issue.

2. Marion, who married Colin Campbell of Ardkinlas, and had no issue.

Besides these children, Sir Humphrey had a natural daughter, Elizabeth, who married Ewer Campbell, son and heir of Arthur Campbell of Ardgartan.  A charter, dated at Rossdhu, 22d April 1539, was granted by Arthur Campbell of Ardgartan to his beloved son and heir-apparent, Ewer Campbell and Elizabeth Colquhoun, his spouse, in conjunct fee, and to the heirs-male lawfully begotten, or to be begotten betwixt them; whom failing, to the lawful and nearest heirs of the said Ewer whomsoever, of the lands of Ard-callze, Thomenoskar, Dall, and Ewirtonnans, in the barony of Glen-fallocht, in the shire of Perth.  The precept for infefting them in these lands is dated on the same day as the charter.[2]  On 17th February 1539-40, Bessie Colquhoun, carnal daughter of the deceased Humphrey Colquhoun of Luss, and her spouse, Ewer Campbell, son of Arthur Campbell of Strachur, were infefted by the said Arthur in the lands of Forleynmoir, at the head of Loch-long, in the shire of Argyll.[3]

[1] Original Instrument of Sasine at Ross-dhu.

[2] Original Charter and Precept of Sasine, at Rossdhu.

[3] Original Instrument of Sasine, *ibid.*

## XIII.—Sir JOHN COLQUHOUN, Knight,

Thirteenth of Colquhoun and Fifteenth of Luss, 1538-1574

Christian Erskine, his first wife, 1535-1564.

Agnes Boyd, his second wife, 1564-1588.

This laird of Luss had been married only about two years previous to
his accession to the family estates on the death of his father.   The lady
whom he espoused was Christian Erskine, daughter of Robert Lord Erskine,
who was killed at Flodden in the year 1513, by his wife, Dame Elizabeth Campbell, Lady Erskine.   The contract of marriage between John
Colquhoun, younger of Luss, and Christian Erskine, is dated 25th January
1535, and the marriage was to be solemnized in the face of the holy kirk
within twenty days thereafter.   By the contract, Humphrey Colquhoun
of Luss became bound to infeft his son John, and Christian Erskine his
wife, in as much of the lands of Luss as would yield yearly 140 merks
to them in liferent, and to the heirs-male of their marriage ; and Lady
Erskine became bound to pay to Humphrey Colquhoun 2000 merks of
tocher with her daughter Christian.[1]

Dame Elizabeth Campbell, designated "the relict of umquhil Robert
Lord Erskine," in a contract between her and Robert Master of Erskine,
her grandson, dated 2d November 1535, assigned to him certain customs
of Aberdeen, and rents of Garioch and Buchan, etc., extending in all to
100 merks yearly, until the sum of 600 merks which he had bound himself to cause to be paid to John Colquhoun of Luss, in name of tocher,
should be fully paid out of them ; and she resigned to her said grandson her moveable goods for his relief of that sum should she die before it
was fully paid to him.[2]

John Colquhoun was served heir to his father Humphrey in the mill
of Sauline, on 30th April 1538 ; and the retour, as has been before observed, records that the death of his father had taken place about three

---

[1] Original Contract of Marriage at Rossdhu.
[2] Original Contract in Mar Charter-chest.

months previous to that date. He received, on 30th June 1540, a gift of the nonentry duties of the lands and barony of Luss; and on 10th October 1541, he was, by a precept from the Chancery of King James the Fifth, infefted as heir of his paternal grandfather, Sir John, in the lands and barony of Luss, including the lands of Luss, Colquhoun, Garscube, Salachy, and Glen.[1]   On the 15th of the same month, a precept of *clare constat* was given by Mathew fourth Earl of Lennox, for infefting John Colquhoun as heir of his paternal grandfather in the lands of Achingaiche, with the Larg, Auchenvennel, Stuckiedow, and Blairhangane, in the earldom of Lennox and shire of Dumbarton.[2]   On the 26th of the same month, he was, on a precept of sasine by the same earl, infefted in the lands of Kilmardinny. Among the witnesses were John Colquhoun, son and heir of the deceased Walter Colquhoun of Kilmardinny, and Patrick Colquhoun in Kilmardinny.[3]

The first trace of that enmity between the Macgregors and the Colquhouns, which at length became so inveterate, to be found in the Luss family writs, occurs in a document dated in the year 1541. So far back as the year 1527, one of the Macgregor clan, Patrick Macgregor of Laggarie, had despoiled the father of the then laird of Luss of a considerable number of oxen and cows. To obtain redress for this theft committed on his father's property, John Colquhoun of Luss summoned him, on 27th December 1540, to appear before the Lords of the Privy Council, to hear their decreet, ordaining him, in terms of the summons, to restore to the pursuer eight oxen and twelve milk cows, or the price of them, with the profits of the same since the year 1527, when he had stolen them from the lands of Stronc, in Glenfruin.[4]   And on 30th May 1541, Patrick Macgregor of Laggarie was, at the instance of John Colquhoun of Luss, inhibited from selling any of his lands or heritages until he had satisfied John for the spoil which he had reft from him.[5]   These proceedings we may not be entitled to consider as evidence of the existence of a formed feud between the Macgregors and the Colquhouns; but they are symptomatic of growing bad feelings between them, and they explain some of the causes which contributed to produce

[1] Original Instrument of Sasine at Rossdhu.
[2] Original Precept of Sasine, *ibid.*
[3] Original Instrument of Sasine, *ibid.*

[4] Original Summons at Rossdhu.
[5] Original Inhibition, *ibid.*

and to intensify the hatred which afterwards proved so disastrous to both. In the present instance the Macgregors were clearly the aggressors.

On 3d November 1541, John Colquhoun of Luss was again, as heir of his paternal grandfather, infefted in the lands of Ballernick-mor, Kilmardinny, and others,[1] all in the earldom of Lennox and shire of Dumbarton, and held in chief of Matthew Earl of Lennox as the lord superior. The witnesses include Mr. Adam Colquhoun, John Colquhoun of Kilmardinny, John Colquhoun of Milton, Patrick Colquhoun of Ardincoual, and David Colquhoun of Drumfad.[2]

On 6th January 1541, the Laird of Luss obtained a charter of the lands and barony of Luss, with the castle of Rossdhu, the islands of Lochlomond, Inchelmocht, Incheconquhane, and Inchefreithillane, with the fishings in Lochlomond, the advowson of the church, and other pertinents of the barony of Colquhoun, with the manor of Dunglas, on the water of Clyde, and the lands of Garscube.[3]

The Laird of Luss was superior of the lands of Barnhill, from which the name of a branch of the family of Colquhoun is taken. On 31st March 1543, John Colquhoun, in Milton of Colquhoun, and Janet Laing, his spouse, obtained from John Colquhoun of Luss a charter of the two-merk lands of the west half of the lands of Barnhill, in the lordship of Colquhoun and shire of Dumbarton. The limitation in this charter is to the grantees and the heirs-male of their bodies, whom failing, to the heirs-male of the granter. On a precept by John Colquhoun of Luss, dated 28th April 1555, Janet Laing and Walter Colquhoun, her son, were on the following day infefted in the lands in liferent and in fee, respectively.[4] John Colquhoun,

---

[1] The other lands were Mamore, Mamleg, Furlingkarre, Blairvaddan, Letterwald-mor, Stuckinduff, Durling, Glenloyng, Stukintebert, Stroneratan, Ardincounal, Tullichiutaull, and the mill of Auldmill.

[2] Original Instrument of Sasine at Rossdhu.

[3] Registrum Magni Sigilli, Lib. xxviii. No. 241.

[4] Original Charter and Instrument of Sasine in Barnhill Charter-chest. This

Walter Colquhoun granted a charter, dated at Dumbarton, 14th December 1582, to John, his son and apparent heir, and the heirs-male of his marriage with Margaret M'Kie, daughter of John M'Kie, in Chapelton of Colquhoun, of the half of the lands of Barnhill.—(Original Charter in Barnhill Charter-chest.) Walter, when advanced in years, and his eldest son John were slain at the raid of Glenfruin, in 1603, when fighting under the standard of Alexander Colquhoun

in Milton, was in possession of the west half of the lands of Barnhill previous to the charter of 1543, as it proceeded on his own resignation of the lands. He is the first known proprietor of these lands bearing the name of Colquhoun. We have not been able to ascertain his descent from the chief house of Colquhoun, nor is there any document known to exist which shows how he originally acquired Barnhill. But as John Colquhoun was in possession of these lands, which formed part of the barony of Colquhoun previous to the year 1543, it may be presumed that they were originally granted as the possession of a younger son of the house of Colquhoun. This is corroborated by the uniform tradition in the family, that they are descended from a younger son of Colquhoun of Luss. The present proprietor of Barnhill, Neil Colquhoun Campbell, Esq., Sheriff of Ayrshire, has been told by an aunt, who is now upwards of ninety years of age, that such was an old tradition in the family. He has heard the same statement from her mother, Margaret Colquhoun, who died more than thirty years ago, as well as from his father, the late Alexander Campbell, Esq., who succeeded to Barnhill in the year 1827, on the death of his uncle, Walter Colquhoun, who was the last male Colquhoun of Barnhill in the direct line. The property has been in the family for upwards of three centuries.

The territory which the earldom of Lennox embraced contained in it four clans—the Buchanans, who inhabited the south-eastern shores of Lochlomond and the adjacent valleys—the Macgregors, who, identified with no native soil, led a wandering and predatory life among the straths and glens of Perthshire—the Macfarlanes, who occupied the mountainous district of Arrochar, and the Colquhouns, who peopled the fertile vales of Luss.

Common interests, it might be supposed, would have united these clans together. Had they been confederated, they must, from their addiction to predatory warfare, have proved very formidable and dangerous to their lowland neighbours. But, so far from strengthening themselves by union, they were almost constantly distracted by mutual animosities, and were so

of Luss, against the clan Macgregor. The        Colquhoun of West Barnhill in the year
east half of Barnhill was acquired by James        1696.

much occupied in wasting their strength against each other as to have neither time nor means to disturb the low country. So little regard was then paid to authority, the rights of property, and even the sacredness of human life, that a powerful chieftain, with his clan, would often, under the capricious impulse of rapacity, revenge, or other malignant passions, commit theft, rapine, and murder upon the families of another clan with which they were at feud.

The origin of these feuds goes back beyond the period of authentic history. In contemporary records they become most conspicuous in the latter part of the sixteenth century. Some of the conflicts to which these feuds gave rise have been deemed worthy of being told by our historians, but a much greater number are commemorated in the ballads and legends of our Highland glens.

The lairds of Luss had their own share in these family feuds, and had experience of the ruthless violence, spoliation, and oppression of which they were productive. They suffered from the Macfarlanes, who in those times were chiefly known by the hostile incursions which they made upon their neighbours in the southern valleys. Surrounded by their mountains, and difficult of access from want of roads, they were cut off from the rest of the world, and their very existence might have been forgotten but for their predatory excursions, which were often accompanied by fire and blood, proving that—

> " Thair wes not in all Liddesdaill
> That kye mair craftelly could steil."

The Laird of Luss, of whom we are now writing, had, it would appear, in some way or other incurred the resentment of the Macfarlanes, to whom he was related by the marriage of his aunt, Katharine Colquhoun, with Duncan Macfarlane of that ilk, and of Arrochar. To retaliate some real or imagined wrong, or from the greed of plunder, large bodies of them repeatedly made hostile incursions into the lands of Luss.

In the month of February 1543, Robert Danzielston of Colgrain, Walter Makfarlane of Ardles, Andrew Macfarlane his son, and apparent heir, and others their accomplices, carried away from the Nether and Middle Mains

P

of Luss sixteen cows which belonged to John Colquhoun of Luss, the price of each being seven merks.

In less than a year after, these marauders, to the number of several hundreds, made a more terrible invasion on the lands of Luss, murdering several of the tenants in their beds, despoiling both them and the laird, plundering their houses, and carrying off their sheep and cattle, besides committing depredations on other lands. The outrages perpetrated on that occasion are thus described in a complaint and representation made to the Government by the Laird of Luss, as contained in letters under the signet of Queen Mary, 21st December 1544:—"That Duncan M'Ferlane of Arrochare, Andro M'Ferlane, Robert M'Ferlane, and Duncan M'Ferlane, his fader, brether, Vir [Ewer] Campbel of [Strachur], James Stewart, son to Walter Stewart in Buckquidder, and certane vtheris, grete thevis, lymmaris, robaris, commonn sornaris appoun our liegis, throtcuttaris, murthuraris, slaaris of men, willis, and bairnys, and thair complices to the nomver of six hundred men with the maire, come to the said John's landis and place of Rosdew, and landis and barony of Lus, and thare cruiellie slew and murdrest nyne of his pure tennentis in thair beddis, and hereit his hale cuntre, baith his self and his pure men, alswele of all insycht gudis within houss as of nolt and schepe, and vther bestiale, laithe in the moneth of December instant, and dailie perseueris in plane reiff and sornyng vpoun the pure liegis of our realme, and ar gaderand to thaim ma thevis and lymmaris tending to hery the hale cuntre to Glasgow and Striueling, and thai be not resistit, in high contemptioun of our auctorite and lawis."

But the judicial power of the Crown was then very feeble. By the combination of feudal lairds and their vassals, the administration of justice was greatly obstructed, and often rendered almost impracticable. So difficult was it to repress and punish these lawless banditti, that, as in the present instance, whole shires were summoned by the Government to unite and rise up to resist them, and bring them to condign punishment. This is only one of many other instances of the adoption of similar repressive measures to be found in the annals of our country at a period much more recent than that of which we now write.

The letters under the signet, above mentioned, are addressed to the

Sheriffs of Argyll, Dumbarton, Renfrew, and Stirling, commanding them
to summon all the lieges in these shires to muster and unite with John
Colquhoun of Luss, and others who might assist him in resisting, apprehending, and bringing to punishment the perpetrators of these outrages.
After narrating the facts already stated, the letters proceed :—"Our will is
herefor, and we charge zou straitlie and commandis, that incontinent thir
our lettrez sene ze pas to the mercat croces of our burrowis of the saidis
schiris, and vtheris places nedfull, and thair be oppin proclamatioun command and charge all and sindry our liegis within the boundis of our saidis
schirefdomes, to rys and cum togidder for resisting of the saidis thevis and
robaris to sik partis as thai salhappin to cum vpoun, and that thai tak
plane part with the saidis Johne, or ony vther gentilman that rysis for
resisting of the saidis thevis and lymmaris, and tak and apprehend thame,
and bring thame to our justice to be pvnist for thair demeritis conforme to
our lawis." Her Majesty's letters further provided that, should any of the
said thieves be slain in the attempts to apprehend them, no crime would
attach to the parties killing them, and that all persons who should fail
to obey the proclamation would be held as taking part with the said thieves
and robbers, and would be punished accordingly.[1]

In reference to the spoliation committed in February 1543, John Colquhoun of Luss, on 13th February 1550, obtained letters of diligence under
the signet of Queen Mary, in a process of spulzie against the depredators,
requiring them to compear before the Lords of Council at Edinburgh, on
the 16th of March following, to answer "for the wranguis, wiolent, and
maisterful spoliatioun be thame selfis, thair seruandis and complices in thair
names" and away taking from the Nether and Middle Mains of Luss,
"sixteen tydie kye," the property of Sir John, which they refused to restore
or to give him the value of in money.[2]

The feud between the M'Farlanes of Arrochar and the Colquhouns of
Luss appears to have been afterwards composed.  In the year 156—, Andrew
M'Farlane of Arrochar became cautioner for John Colquhoun of Luss for
such sums of money as the Lords of Session should modify, to be paid to
Humphrey Cunningham, in case the said John should not be able to disprove

¹ Original Letters of Summons at Rossdhu.     ² Original Letters of Summons at Rossdhu.

a pretended obligation produced or to be produced by the said Humphrey against him, alleged to have been made by his grandfather, Sir John Colquhoun of Luss.[1]

On 23d January 1547-8, John Colquhoun of Luss was infefted in the lands of Stukintebirt, Glenloning, and Tullichintaull, in the earldom of Lennox and shire of Dumbarton, his brother, Patrick Colquhoun, acting as his attorney.[2] Some of the property transactions of this laird of Luss with Archibald fourth Earl of Argyll about this time may be noticed. These transactions were, in consequence of the forfeiture of Mathew fourth Earl of Lennox in 1545, by the Parliament of Scotland, for having treasonably conspired with Henry the Eighth, King of England, for the subjugation of Scotland, and for having invaded it.[3] Upon that forfeiture the Earl of Argyll, who had firmly adhered to the Government, whilst others of the nobility had been guilty of repeated treasons, was rewarded with the largest share of the forfeited estates of the Earl of Lennox. He thus came to be connected with the lands of Colquhoun of Luss, of some of which the Earls of Lennox were the superiors, and in regard to many of which they had particular claims. John Colquhoun of Luss received from Archibald fourth Earl of Argyll a new charter and infeftment of the nine-merk lands of Mamore and Mambeg, which had formerly been held in chief of Mathew fourth Earl of Lennox, to be held of Argyll and his heirs. He granted to the same Earl of Argyll and his heirs several letters of reversion, all dated 8th December 1547, for the redemption of various lands, all in the earldom of Lennox and shire of Dumbarton, namely, the lands of Ballernick-mor, by payment of 380 merks ; the lands of Blairvaddan and Feorlingcarryt, by payment of 360 merks ; the lands of Auchingaicht, Auchenvennel-mor, Stuckiedow, and Blairhannan, by payment of 900 merks ; the mill of Auld Donald, with the multures and mill-lands, by payment of £100 ;[4] and the lands of Mamore and Mambeg, by payment of 400 merks. The Laird of Luss also granted to that Earl a reversion, dated 8th August 1549, for redemption of the five-merk land of Stroneratan, in the said earldom and shire, by payment of 700 merks.[5]

[1] Original Instrument at Rossdhu.
[2] Original Instrument of Sasine, ibid.
[3] Acts of the Parliament of Scotland, vol. ii. pp. 456-8.

[4] Inventar of Writs in Argyll Charter-chest.
[5] Original Letter of Reversion, ibid.

On 5th December in the same year, he was, upon a precept of sasine by the Earl of Argyll, infefted in the lands of Stroneratan. Among the witnesses were Patrick Colquhoun of Ardinconnal, Mr. Adam Colquhoun of Blairvaddoch, and Adam Colquhoun, clerk of the parish of Kilpatrick.[1]

During his possession of the estate of Luss, this laird had several opportunities of exercising his right as patron of the office of clerk of the parish church of Luss, in the diocese of Glasgow. That office having been vacant by the demission of Sir Thomas Henderson, chaplain, last clerk of the parish, the laird, having considered the merits, virtues, ability, and suitableness of Sir James Wright, chaplain, on 25th January 1551, elected him clerk of the parish of Luss (he being present and accepting the presentation), and invested him therein by the delivery of a vessel of hyssop, sprinkled with holy water, and other symbols of his election. This was done at the church of Luss at eight o'clock in the morning. Among the witnesses was Adam Colquhoun, brother-german of John Colquhoun of Luss.[2] On 8th February following, a precept was given by John Stewart, canon of the Metropolitan Church of Glasgow, and Commissary-General thereof, to the Dean of Lennox, and to all and sundry ecclesiastical persons, presbyters, whether curates or not, and notaries, throughout the diocese of Glasgow, commanding that one or more of them, being lawfully requested, should go to the church of Luss, and give Sir James Wright actual possession of the office of clerk of that parish, and the rights belonging thereto, by the delivering of a vessel sprinkled with holy water, as the custom was.[3]

This incumbent did not live to occupy this situation many years. In consequence of his death, the Laird of Luss, on 12th April 1556, presented a new clerk to the parish, the forms observed by him at this time being similar to those observed on the former occasion. On that day, in presence of a public notary and witnesses, he personally went to the altar of the Blessed Virgin Mary of Luss, situated in the south part of the parochial church, and there, as undoubted patron, presented and invested Sir Thomas Henderson as a suitable person for the said office, by delivering to him a missal book, a cup, and other vestments of the altar, according to the

1 Original Instrument of Sasine in Argyll Charter-chest.

2 Original Presentation at Rossdhu.
3 Original Precept, ibid.

118 SIR JOHN COLQUHOUN, KNIGHT,

form and tenor of the foundation thereof. This presentee, though bearing the same name as the chaplain who demitted in 1551, was probably a different person. Among the witnesses of this presentation were James Colquhoun, brother-german of John Colquhoun of Luss, Adam Colquhoun, rector of Kilpatrick-Juxta, and David Colquhoun of Drumfad.[1]

Mr. John Laing succeeded Mr. James Colquhoun, formerly noticed as rector of Luss. He is so designated in the Register of Ministers in 1560. In 1556 he mortified a house and garden in Glasgow as a manse for the prebends of Luss, to be held for six merks yearly, to be paid to the choir of the cathedral, who were to be bound to say weekly masses for his soul, and that of his patron, John Colquhoun of Luss, and to have the city bells tolled, and wax tapers burned on the anniversary of his decease.[2]

On 2d December 1552, a precept of clare constat was given by Robert, Commendator of Holyrood, for infefting John Colquhoun of Luss as heir of his grandfather, Sir John, in an annualrent of ten merks, out of a tenement in the Canongate of Edinburgh, which then belonged to William Cunninghame of Aikinbar. With this annualrent was conjoined a right of entertainment (jus hospitalitatis) in that house. The purport of this right may be learned from the precept, in which it is narrated " that the said William Cunningham of Aikinbar, his heirs and assignees, shall maintain and preserve the same tenement, before and behind, for the use and possession of John Colquhoun, his heirs and assignees, as it were for a lodging, in all time to come, and that the same William, his heirs and assignees, shall prepare, order, and procure for the said John, his heirs and assignees, three beds, with suitable clothes and ornaments, brazen and pewter vessels, table-cloths, towels, and other household articles, together with a stable, and whatever else is necessary to be had within the said tenement, at the cost of the said William, his heirs and assignees, whenever the said John Colquhoun and his heirs shall come to the said burgh of the Canongate, or stay there."[3]

[1] Original Notarial Instrument of Presentation at Rossdhu. In another notarial instrument the church is called the Church of Roisdow.

[2] Dennistoun's MSS. in Advocates' Library (Miscellaneous Charters), vol. vi.

[3] Original Precept, quoted in Dennistoun's MSS., vol. v. p. 83.

This laird of Luss next appears as purchasing the eight-merk lands of Finnard, Portincaple, and Ferlingbrek, in the earldom of Lennox and shire of Dumbarton, from Mathew Douglas of the Mains. A contract was entered into between them, dated 17th March 1553, whereby Mathew Douglas engaged to sell to John Colquhoun of Luss these lands, to be held of the Earl of Argyll, as superior thereof for the time, by whom, or by Mathew Earl of Lennox, in the event of his being restored to his lands and heritage of the Lennox,[1] heritable infeftment should be given to him ; and he further bound himself to deliver to the said John the reversion made by the late Sir John Colquhoun of Luss, Knight, to his (the seller's) father, for the redemption of the forenamed lands.[2]

John Colquhoun of Luss subsequently purchased from John Porterfield of that ilk his lands of Porterfield, in the barony and shire of Renfrew, of which he obtained a charter, dated 26th August 1554.[3] He also purchased from Robert Graham of Knokdolyane his lands of Auldmerrok, in the earldom of Lennox and shire of Dumbarton, of which he received a charter, dated 28th May 1555,[4] and another dated 3d March 1560.[5] These lands were sold to him, under reversion in favour of the seller, on his payment of 1200 merks Scots. He afterwards inhibited Robert Graham from redeeming them until the arrears of rents were paid with the reversion price. The tenants, from the date of the alienation of them for the space of two years or thereby, had paid the yearly rents and duties to the Laird of Luss. He refused, however, in respect of the above mentioned inhibition, to give them discharges ; but this he was decerned to do by the Sheriff Court of Dumbarton, on 28th April 1563.[6]

In the year 1559, the Laird of Luss acquired the lands of Strone and Letter, in the barony of Luss and shire of Dumbarton. On 18th December

---

[1] It was not till the year 1563 that the forfeiture of Mathew fourth Earl of Lennox was repealed by Act of Parliament.

[2] Copy Contract at Rossdhu. John Colquhoun of Luss obtained from Mathew Earl of Lennox a charter of these lands, dated 20th March 1553, and from Archibald Earl of Argyll a confirmation of this charter, dated 7th April 1554. Among the witnesses to the confirmation were David Colquhoun of Drumfad, James Colquhoun, and Adam Colquhoun.—[Original Confirmation at Rossdhu.]

[3] Original Charter at Rossdhu.

[4] Original Charter, ibid.

[5] Original Charter, ibid.

[6] Notarial Copy Decreet, ibid.

1558, he entered into a contract with Robert Colquhoun, son to the deceased Malcolm Colquhoun, by which the latter engaged to resign the five-pound lands of Stroue and Letter into the hands of John Colquhoun of Luss in favour of him and his heirs; and for this resignation the said John became bound that, on the occurrence of a vacancy in the clerkship of Luss, he and his heirs should cause the person who should be appointed to that situation to pay yearly to Robert Colquhoun during his lifetime the sum of twelve merks Scots out of that clerkship.[1] On the 29th of October 1559, Robert Colquhoun resigned the above-mentioned lands, in terms of the contract. In the instrument of resignation he is designed " Robart Culquhoun, the oy and air of vmquhill Wmfra Colquhoun of Letter ;" and in explaining the circumstances which led to this resignation, it narrates that he, " of his avin fre motive vill on compellit or coactit and for certen sowmes of mone, gratutudis and gud dedis gevin to the said Robart in his vrgent necessite and mister, and for vpholding of him in met, drink, and cloythis be the space of twelff zeris or thairby, and siclik for the completing, fulfilling, and ending of ane contract maid betuix the said Robert and Johne Colquhoun of Lus."[2]

On 14th June 1559, this laird of Luss received a charter of the third part of the five-pound lands of Garscadden, in the shire of Dumbarton ;[3] and, on 9th November 1561, a precept was given by John Colquhoun of Kilmardinny for infefting him in an annual rent of £10 from the lands of Garscadden.[4]

In the year 1559, John Colquhoun of Luss made other additions to his territorial possessions. His relative, John Colquhoun of Kilmardinny, having become involved in pecuniary difficulties, " takand respect of the said John Colquhoun off Killmerdonyis weill, rather nor his wter distructioun," he was willing to relieve him. With this view a contract, dated 5th August 1559, was entered into between John Colquhoun of Luss and Adam Colquhoun, parish clerk of Kilpatrick, his brother-german, on the one part, and John Colquhoun of Kilmardinny on the other. By this contract the latter engaged for himself and his heirs to pay out of his lands yearly an annual rent of

---

[1] Original Contract at Rossdhu.    [3] Original Charter at Rossdhu.
[2] Notarial Instrument of Resignation, ibid.    [4] Original Precept of Sasine, ibid.

seventy merks to Adam Colquhoun during his lifetime, and to infeft him therein; and, in consideration hereof, John Colquhoun of Luss, to whom John Colquhoun of Kilmardinny was owing the sum of five hundred merks, discharged the latter of that sum, whilst the latter engaged to renounce his right and title to the lands of Durling, Stroneratan, Stuckinduff, Blairvaddoch, Letterwald-mor, and Ballernick-mor, in the earldom of Lennox and shire of Dumbarton, to the said John Colquhoun of Luss.[1] On 5th September 1559, John Colquhoun of Kilmardinny resigned in favour of John Colquhoun of Luss these lands, which belonged to the deceased David Colquhoun, brother-german and heir to the deceased Mr. Adam Colquhoun.[2]

In 1564, the Laird of Luss purchased from Mathew fourth Earl of Lennox the reversion of the lands of Blairvaddoch and others,[3] all in the earldom of Lennox and shire of Dumbarton, which had been sold to his grandfather, Sir John Colquhoun, by Mathew, second Earl, and John third Earl of Lennox, under reversion. On 3d February 1563-4, Mathew fourth Earl of Lennox granted him a renunciation and discharge of the reversions and bonds made in favour of his grandfather and father by the grandfather of John Colquhoun of Luss.[4]

At the date of this writ that Earl was still under the sentence of forfeiture; but he was in high favour with Queen Mary; and his forfeiture was reversed, and his estates and honours restored, by an Act of the Parliament held at Edinburgh in 1564.

John Colquhoun of Luss was on the assize at the trial of Patrick Houston of that ilk, John Houston, elder, in Dumbarton, and others, for convocation of her Majesty's lieges, and invasion of Andrew Hamilton of Cochno, before the Justiciary Court at Edinburgh, 15th June 1564. The

---

[1] Original Contract at Rossdhu.

[2] Original Instrument of Renunciation, ibid.

[3] The other lands were Stuckinduff, Letterwald-mor, Ballernick-mor, Stroneratan, Durling, Auchingaich, with the Large, Auchenvennel, Stuckiedow, and the mill of Aldmill.

[4] Original Renunciation and Discharge at Rossdhu. In "Instructions by Mathew fourth Earl of Lennox as to the management of his affairs until his return from England," about the year 1563, is the following:—

"Touchand the landes that my lord of Argil hald syklyik in wedset and part of landes that the lard of Lwis hald, I trest that it pertenes to me be rason of ward, quhilk, or tha be entret, I wil that it be seyn clerly thar haldins, and geif the said landes pertenis to me.'—[Lennox Charters.]

Q

assize, by their verdict, convicted all the persons at the bar except John
Houston, elder, in Dumbarton, of coming upon Andrew Hamilton of Cochno,
within the burgh of Dumbarton, on the 18th day of March last, where they
beset him upon the Highgate thereof, and with drawn swords invaded
him, and compelled him to take suddenly a house for defence of his life.[1]

At the trial of John Henry, in Stirling, and others, for the slaughter
of John Rae, in Bukeburne, in the shire of Stirling, before the Justiciary
Court, 12th October 1564, the Laird of Luss was the proloquitor of the
pursuer, Janet Marshal, relict of the said deceased John Rae. A verdict
of acquittal, in this instance, was given in favour of the panels.[2]

In the summer of the year 1564, Christian Erskine, the wife of John
Colquhoun of Luss, to whom he had been united nearly thirty years, departed this life. By her he seems to have had no children. She made her
will on the 20th of May in the year in which she died.

In this deed, which contains an inventory of her "gudeis, geir, latter
will, and legacies," "gevin vp be hir awin mouth, with consent and assent
of hir said spous," on the day and year before mentioned ; the goods and
geir include 152 ky, 30 stirks, 36 oxen, 30 ewes, 21 lambs, 56 wedders,
200 bolls of oats sowen, estimated when reaped to extend to 600 bolls,
six bolls of bear sowen, estimated when reaped to extend to 18 bolls, 5
horse, 4 work horse, 13 mares, 6 year-old mares, 2 foals, and in the manor
4 chalders of meal, and the inside and outside pleuishing, together with
£400 money, the value of the whole amounting to £1618, 9s. 8d.  The large
number of cows included in this inventory is worthy of notice, as corrobo-
rating other proofs of the celebrity of the valleys of Luss at that period for
dairy produce.  The debts owing to the deceased were £363, 16s. ; and
after deducting the debts owing by her, which were £1007, 6s., there remained of free geir £925.

Among the debts which she owed, were—to Beatrix Coquhoune, Lady
Arthinglas, two years' annual rent, being 100 merks ; borrowed money, 100
merks ; and for salmond, £20 ; and to Dame Margaret Cunninghame £60.

The following are the legacies left by the dead :—

Item, the said Cristiane left the haill plenesing of the place, and victuellis

1 Pitcairn's Criminal Trials, vol. i. pp. 450*, 451*.          2 Ibid. vol. i. p. *453.

beand within the samin, to the Lairde of Lus, hir said spous, except tua furneist beddis. Item, she left to James Coquhoune and his spous, quhilk ar instantlie in his awin chalmer, and to Margarete Coquhoune the Lardis sister, ane furneist bed, quhen sho gais to hir awin hous. Item, to Peter Naper, Larde of Kilma-how, xl¹¹, to help him quhen he gangis to his first pleuesing. Item, to Elizabeth Cunninghame, hir sister dochter, xl merkis. Item, to Elizabeth Crowstoun, x¹¹ Item, to Schir Thomas Hendersoun, v merkis money, with an goun of blak claitht. Item, to Elizabeth Coquhoun, Patrick Coquhounis dochter, ten merkis. Item, to Katy Colquhoune, the Lady Arthinglas seruand, five merkis. Item, to Isobell Erskine, ane dames goun, with ane skirt dowblet of blak veluot, ane cloik of Pareis blak, begarnt with veluot, ane veluot hude. Item, to Margarete Coqu-houne, Lady Coldoun, ane goun of Pareis blak, with ane skirt of blak sating. Item, to Elizabeth Coquhoune, ane goun of lylis worsate furrit ; and all the rest of hir guddis and geir, pertenand to hir, or rychtuuslie may pertein, als weill nocht nominit as nominit, mouvable and inmouvable, scho leiffis to Adam Coqu-houne, broder germane to the said Jhonne Coquhoune of Lus, and to Isobell Erskin his spous, and to the bairnis gottin or to be gottin betuix thame quhat-sumeuir, the dettis being first payit. Item, to Margarete Coqhoune, Lady Cowdoun, ane chalder of aittis to hir first sawing. Item, to James Hammiltoun, hir foster, ane staig worth x¹¹ Item, to Jhonne Williamesoun, xl s. Item, the said Cristiane namit, maid, and constitute Alexander Erskin, broder to Jhonne Lorde Erskin, James Galbraith of Culcruich, Adame Coquhoun of Blairweddycht, hir executouris, and the said Jhonne Lorde Erskin to be ourisman. [1]

John Colquhoun of Luss did not remain long a widower. Within a few months apparently after the death of his first wife, Christian Erskine, he married, secondly, Agnes, daughter of Robert fourth Lord Boyd. Sir John and Agnes having been related to each other in the third and fourth degrees of consanguinity, a Papal dispensation was necessary, according to the canons of the Roman Catholic Church, to render their marriage lawful. This dispensation was, therefore, applied for from John Hamilton, Archbishop of St. Andrews, the Pope's legate a latere, who had the power of granting it, and it was readily obtained. This dispensation is dated 3d November 1564. The following is a translation from the original, which is in Latin :—

[1] Original Testament at Rossdhu. The testament was confirmed on the 23d of January following, by Mr. James Balfour, parson of Flisk, Robert Maitland, two of the Senators of the College of Justice, Edward Henderson, Doctor in the Laws, and Clement Litill, Commissars of Edinburgh.

John, by the Divine mercy Archbishop of St. Andrews, Primate of the Kingdom of Scotland, and, with the power of legate *a latere* of our most holy Lord the Pope, and legate of the holy Apostolic Seat, to the venerable men, Masters John Laing, John Houstoun, and David Gibsonne of Luss, Glasgow and Ayr respectively, prebendaries and canons of the Metropolitan Church of Glasgow, and to each of you, health in the Lord : The wise superintendence of the Apostolic Seat sometimes tempers the rigour of the law with gentleness, and with the grace of benignity indulges what the statutes of the sacred canons forbid, even as, the quality of the persons and times being considered, it acknowledges it to be salutary to expede such an indulgence in the Lord. Truly a petition presented to us on behalf of our known orators, John Colquhoun of Luss and Agnes Boyd, daughter of the noble Lord, Robert Lord Boyd, a woman of the diocese of Glasgow, contained, That desiring, from certain causes, to be joined together in marriage, but, because, knowing that they are related to each other in the third and fourth degrees of consanguinity, they cannot accomplish their desire in this respect without obtaining Apostolic dispensation hereupon, the said explainers have therefore caused that supplication may be humbly made to us, that they may be mercifully provided with the grace of a dispensation : We, therefore, earnestly wishing to take care for the salvation of their souls, and to remove this impediment, do, by the said apostolic authority granted to us, and which we exercise in this particular, commit to the wisdom of you and each of you, that if such is the case as to the said parties, you may mercifully give license, that notwithstanding the impediment of the third and fourth degrees of consanguinity, they may freely contract marriage with each other, and solemnize it in the face of the Church ; and after it has been contracted that they may lawfully remain therein, so that the said woman shall not, on account of this, be forcibly taken away : decerning the children perhaps born, if there is any, or to be born from that marriage, to be legitimate. Given at Paisley, of the diocese of Glasgow, in the year of the incarnation of the Lord one thousand five hundred and sixty-four, the third of the nones of November [3d November], in the fifth year of the Pontificate of our most holy Lord, Pope Pius the Fourth.

*Joannes Sanctandreus Legatus*[1]

[1] Original Dispensation at Rossdhu.

On the 15th of the same month effect was given to the apostolic letters of the Archbishop. Mr. David Gibson, rector of Ayr, and Thomas Colquhoun of Glen, procurators of John Colquhoun and Agnes Boyd, presented the letters to John Laing, prebendary of Luss, canon of the metropolitan church of Glasgow and Judge Commissary ; and he being asked to give speedy and effectual execution of the letters, according to the form delivered and directed therein, did, after having examined and learned from credible witnesses that the parties were related to each other in the third and fourth degrees of consanguinity, give dispensation for their being married, in terms of the Archbishop's letters.

A few months previous to the date of this dispensation, John Colquhoun of Luss sold, under reversion, to John Mackneil, Leith, his lands of Cowl-kippen, with a piece of land immediately adjacent thereto, in the barony of Luss and shire of Dumbarton. On 6th July 1564, he received from the said John Mackneil a letter of reversion, engaging to resign these lands in his favour, on his payment of £100.[1]

After this John Colquhoun of Luss acquired from Thomas Colquhoun of Glen the forty shilling land of Glen, in the earldom of Lennox and shire of Stirling. In an agreement between them, dated 1st January 1564-5, the latter bound himself to resign that land into the hands of the former, the immediate superior, *ad perpetuam remanentiam*, and to cause Dame Margaret Cunningham, his mother, renounce her right and infeftment in the same lands, and to deliver that renunciation to John Colquhoun of Luss, who, in consideration thereof, bound himself to grant to Thomas Colquhoun infeftment in an annual-rent of forty merks Scots from his forty-merk land of Colquhoun, in the earldom of Lennox and shire of Dumbarton.[2] The Laird of Luss also purchased from Patrick Colquhoun of Tullichintaull his lands of Kirkmichael-Buchanan, in the earldom of Lennox and shire of Dumbarton, of which he obtained from Patrick Colquhoun a charter, dated 4th September 1566, in which he is now designated John Colquhoun of Luss, knight. Patrick Colquhoun subscribed with his hand at the pen, led by a notary at his command, because he could not write.[3]

[1] Original Letter of Reversion at Ross-dhu.

[2] Original Agreement at Rossdhu.
[3] Original Charter, *ibid.*

On 10th February 1566-7, Sir John Colquhoun was infefted in the lands of Wester Kilbride, upon a precept of sasine by Archibald Galbraith of Portnellan.[1]

About two o'clock in the morning of the same 10th of February, Henry Stewart, Lord Darnley, son of Mathew, fourth Earl of Lennox, and consort of Mary, Queen of Scots, was murdered in the Kirk of Field, at Edinburgh, whither he had gone to sleep during the night. The circumstances attending this murder are matter of history, and are well known. Darnley held directly from the Crown certain lands in the earldom of Lennox. His death placed the ward of these lands at the disposal of the Crown. Sir John Colquhoun of Luss obtained a gift from Queen Mary of the ward of the lands of Lettrowald-mor, Finnart, Portincaple, Forlinbreck, Strongartan, Duirling, Stukedow, and Kilmardinny, dated 21st April 1567. This gift bears that these lands had fallen into the hands of the Queen, by reason of the ward through the decease of Henry King of Scots, Duke of Albany, Earl of Ross, and Levinax, etc., and most dear and beloved spouse to her Majesty, superior to Sir John Colquhoun of the lands, and the last lawful possessor and immediate tenant to her Majesty of the same.[2]

On 30th September in the same year, Sir John Colquhoun was, upon a precept from Chancery, infefted as heir of his paternal grandfather, Sir John Colquhoun, in annual-rents payable from various tenements, and in several parcels of land in the burgh of Dumbarton.[3] He also received from Robert Stewart, second son of James Stewart of Cardonald, a charter of sale of the one merk-lands of Kirkmichael-Buchanan, in the earldom of Lennox and shire of Dumbarton, dated 21st December 1567.[4]

Sir John favoured the cause of Queen Mary, in opposition to the nobles by whom she was opposed. Mary was married to Lord Darnley in the Abbey Church of Holyroodhouse on Sabbath the 29th of July 1565, and on the day after, by her command, he was, by the Lyon-King-of-Arms,

---

[1] Original Instrument of Sasine at Rossdhu.

[2] Registrum Secreti Sigilli, vol. xxxvi. fol. 36. A similar gift was made at the same time in favour of Sir John Colquhoun of Luss, and Patrick Napier, tutor of Kilma-

hew, of the ward of the lands of Kilmahew and Napierston, in the earldom of Lennox. [ *Ibid.* fol. 37.]

[3] Original Instrument of Sasine at Rossdhu.

[4] Original Charter, *ibid.*

proclaimed King.[1] A number of the most powerful of the nobility, headed by the Earl of Murray, and including the Earl of Argyll, opposed this marriage, and strongly condemned the Queen's conduct in commanding, without the consent of the Estates of Parliament, that Darnley should be proclaimed King. The Queen and these nobles were thus unhappily brought into collision. Acting on this occasion with great promptitude and decision, she mustered a strong force, and was everywhere successful against the rebel lords. It was at this time that the Laird of Luss charged the bailies of Dumbarton, in the King and Queen's name, to summon the whole town to come to the hill of Ardmore, where they were to remain four days for defence of the country, and, in case of Argyll's army making its appearance, to warn the towns of Dumbarton and Glasgow, and to adopt other defensive measures. The charge, which is subscribed by John Colquhoun of Luss, Knight, at Rossdhu on 15th October, the year not given, but probably 1565, is as follows :—

William Smollat and Wmphra Cwnighame, Ballies of Dunberten—Foresamekill as I chergit zow of befor in our souerane lord and ladeis name, that ze caus the haill toun of Dunberten to cum veill bodin in feir of veir to the hyll of Ardmoir, and thar to ramane wyth the gentill men of the cost syd, wyth four dayis furnesing for the releiff and veill of the cuntre and zourselffis ; and now, as I am informet that my Lord Argyllis armye is to cum vpon the cuntre for harschip tharof : Therfor zit as of befor, I charg zow that one all heast, pane and charg that ze and zour burgh, and the inhabitants duelland tharin, ma incur at our said Souerane lord and ladeis handis, that ze abyd and ramane at the said hyll of Ardmoir vith the cuntre folkis tharof, for suple and defens of the haill cuntre round about, wyth the said four dayis furnesing, as ze vill anser tharupon wpon zour lyff, landis, and gudis ; and gif the army of Argyll cumis fordwart to pas wyth boittis to the townes of Dunberten or Glasgow, I and the haill cuntre sall pas eftir thame for defens tharof, certefeand zow that gif ze and zour comburgess of Dunberten passis away hame, and vill nocht ramane vyth the rest of the cuntre, ze sall be callit and accusit tharfor, wyth all regor, as effeiris ; als ze sall aduertis the nychtboris of Glasgow and Ranfrew, and caus thame remane in the toun of Dunberten, quhill thar four dayis furnesing begane, and siclik caus the Capitane of Dunberten to be deligent and valkryf that na boittis

---

[1] Buchanan's History, Aikman's edition, vol. ii. pp. 471. See Proclamation in Keith's History, vol. i. p. 307.

128        SIR JOHN COLQUHOUN, KNIGHT,

nor veshell wyth folkis gang by, and caus the schippis quhilk ar in the revar to
schoit at thame in thar gangin by, quhilk may aduertis the haill cuntre round
about for thai intend to gang by in the nycht, and the Castell to schut efter
thar aduertisment siclik ; and this ze do as ze vill ansuer herupon : Subscribit
wyth my hand at Rosdew this xv. of October be

JHON COLQWHON OF LUSS, Knyt.[1]

It appears to have been shortly before the date of this charge that the
honour of knighthood was conferred upon this Laird of Luss, probably in
reward for the services he had rendered to his sovereign, Queen Mary.

Sir John Colquhoun is mentioned in the correspondence between Queen
Mary and the Earl of Bothwell, called the Casket Letters. The authenticity
of these letters has formed the subject of controversy. The letter which
mentions the Laird of Luss professes to have been written by the Queen
after she had gone to Glasgow to visit Darnley, who was seized there with
the small-pox. "The Laird of Lusse, Howstoun and Caldwellis sone,"
says the Queen, " with forty hors or thairabout, come and met me. The
Laird of Lusse said, he was chargeit to ane day of law be the Kingis father,
quhilk suld be this day aganis his awin handwrit, quhilk he hes. And zit,
notwithstanding, knawing of my cumming, it is delayit. He was inquyrit
to cum to him, quhilk he refusit, and sweris that he will indure nathing of
him." [2]

After the murder of Lord Darnley, and the marriage of Queen Mary
with his reputed murderer, James Earl of Bothwell, the greater part of
the nobility rose in arms against her; and having defeated her army,
and taken her prisoner at Carberry Hill on the 15th of June 1567, they
imprisoned her two days after in Lochleven Castle. Acting under con-
straint, Mary, on the 24th of July following, resigned the crown, transferred
the whole authority to her son James, who was then only thirteen months
old, and certain noblemen, and appointed James Stewart Earl of Murray
regent during the minority of the infant prince. To reduce such as were
refractory to the authority of the King, Murray, who held the reins of

[1] Original in the Charter-Chest of the
Duke of Montrose.
[2] Collections relating to the History of
Mary Queen of Scotland, by James Ander-
son, 4to, Edin. 1727, vol. ii. p. 132.

Government with a vigorous hand, raised an army on the 1st of September, and caused proclamation to be made that all males between sixteen and sixty years of age should be in readiness, upon the first warning, with twenty days' provision.[1] In October a rendezvous of the Regent's army took place at Maxwellheuch, near Kelso. Sir John Colquhoun of Luss was summoned to attend the army of the Regent, but from hostility to the new Government, he failed to be present at the place appointed, for which he was liable to be prosecuted as guilty of treason. He deemed it prudent, however, to submit to the authority of the Regent, and he obtained from him, early in the following year, a remission for his absence from the royal army on the occasion referred to, and for other crimes by which he may have rendered himself obnoxious to punishment. The special remission for non-attendance at Maxwellheuch is followed by a general one for many specified crimes, of some of which Sir John Colquhoun may have been guilty, but the greater number of which were probably added to the remission as mere words of form and style. A translation of the remission, which is in Latin, we here subjoin :—

James, by the grace of God King of the Scots, to our Chancellor, greeting : Because with the advice and consent of our dearest cousin James Earl of Murray, Lord of Abernethy, etc., regent of our kingdom, we have remitted to John Colquhoun of Luss, knight, dwelling within the shire of Dumbarton, our resentment, royal suit, and all action which we conceived, had, have, or in any way can have, for his treacherous remaining and being at home from the army convened and assembled at Maxwellheuch in the month of October, in the year of the Lord one thousand five hundred and fifty-seven, and for all action and crime which can follow, or in any way be imputed to the said John thereupon, and for all other actions, transgressions, crimes, and offences whatsoever, committed or in any way perpetrated by him at any time past, before the day of the date of the presents, by traitorous disloyalty against our own person, incendiarism, murder, homicide, mutilation, rape of women, common oppression by brigandage, magical art, theft, receipt of theft, common destruction of red fishes, mutual communication with and strengthening the clan Gregour, (the sorning and non-exhibition or presentation of certain persons before the justiciary to underlie the law, according to the tenor of the command of our said regent directed to him thereupon, alone excepted,) provided he

[1] Balfour's Annals, vol. i. p. 341.

R

130      SIR JOHN COLQUHOUN, KNIGHT,

entirely satisfy the parties complaining and suffering losses, that we may henceforth hear no just complaint in regard to this : We command and charge you
that you cause our letters of remission under our great seal to be made in due
form of our chancery to the said John upon the premises.—Given under our
Privy Seal, at the city of Glasgow, on the sixth of the month of April, in the
year of the Lord one thousand five hundred and sixty-eight, and in the first of
our reign.[1]

Having obtained this remission, and made his peace with the Regent
Murray, Sir John was obliged to lend his support to the cause of the
Regent against Queen Mary. When the Queen, on her escaping from
the Castle of Lochleven on the 2d of May 1568, assembled an army to
recover her crown and kingdom, Sir John Colquhoun fought against her
in the battle at Langside on the 15th of that month, at which her army
was completely routed, while his relative, Colquhoun of Balvie, was made
a prisoner when fighting for the Queen.

Several of Sir John's transactions connected with the purchase of lands
in the year 1569 were in favour of his wife, Agnes Boyd. Having purchased from Archibald Galbraith of Portnellan the lands of Easter and
Middle Kilbride, and the chapel of Middle Kilbride and the lands thereof,
in Glenfruin, in the earldom of Lennox and shire of Dumbarton, he
intended that the liferent of these lands should form a part of her jointure
in the event of her surviving him. A charter of them, dated 13th January
1569, was made to him and her in liferent, and to their son Humphrey
Colquhoun in fee; and they were infefted in them on the same day.[2] They
had also a charter dated 19th March following, from Robert Graham of
Knockdolean, of the lands of Wollastown and Ardochmore, which Sir John
had purchased from him.[3]

The baron court which Sir John, like other barons, held for trying
and determining causes, civil and criminal, within his own territories, was
held at the Port of Rossdhu, which is situated a little way to the west of
the old Castle of Rossdhu. Only two or three documents connected with
the jurisdiction which he exercised within the barony of Luss have, how-

[1] Original Precept of Remission at Rossdhu.
[2] Original Charter and Instrument of Sasine, ibid.
[3] Dennistoun's MSS., vol. iv. pp. 20, 24.

ever, been preserved in the archives of the House of Colquhoun. One of them is a precept, commanding his officers to warn certain tenants to remove out of his grounds, with the execution and citations indorsed. This precept may here be subjoined, as illustrating the customs of the times, and the manner of proceeding in the administration of the judicial power possessed by the barons within the bounds of their lands :--

Jhone Culquhoun of Lus, Knycht, to my louittis, James Makgybbun, Jhone Porter, my officiaris and seriandis in that part be me speciale constitut, coniunctlie and seuerale, greting : Forsamekle my vill is and als, I charg zou or ony ane of zou stratle, and commandis that incontinent thes my precept sene, ze pas to the landis of Ouir Kilbryd, liand in Glenfrone, wythin the erldome of Lennox and schirefdome of Dumberten, and thar in our soueran lordis name, the Kingis Maiestes and myne, lauchtfullie warne and charg Duncan Makknewar, Awlay Makcaulay, Vinfrais son, Perlen Makfarlen, and Andro Makkinne, for his entres, pretendit occupiaris and possessores of the saidis landis, to remuff and flit thame selffis, thar servandis, families and gudis furtht of the saidis landis aboue vrittin, at the nixt terme and feist of Vitsonday immediat following the dait herof, and to leiff the saidis landis woid and red to me, to be set, vsit, occupyit, manurit, and laborit be me at my plesour as my hereteg, and that ze or ony ane of zou deliuer attentik copyes herof to the sadis persones, and ilk ane of thaim respectiue for thair awin pairt, gif ze can apprehend thame personaly, and falzeing tharof, that ze affix the sadis copiis vpon the mast patent dur or zet of the dwellingis places respectiue within the saidis landis and vtheris places nedfull, and that ze or ony ane of zou pas, wpon ane Sonday, fourte dayis preceding the said feist and terme of Vitsonday, to thair paroch kyrk of Cardros, quhilk is the paroch kirk of the paroshoue wythin the quhilk the saidis landis lyis, and thar, in tyme of devyne seruic, quhen maist confluence of peple ar gaderit, caus reid thes precept oppinly in presens of the perrochinaris for the tyme, swa that the saidis personis pretend [nocht] ignorance, and that ze affix attentik copiis herof vpon the mast patent dur of the said kyrk, in takin of lauchtfull warnene makand publict intimation to the saidis personis and ilk ane of them respictiue, that gif thai or ony of thaime sittis, duellis, occupiis, manuris or laboris the saidis landis or ony pairt thairof our the said feist and terme of Vitsonday wythout tak or licience of me, that thai and ilk ane of thame respectiue salbe halding and reput as vyolent possessores, callit and accusit for the mast hie prophettis and awales that mycht haf bene had furtht of the sadis landis, according to the new Act of Parliament maid wpon violent possessoris ; and thes on nawys ze lef vndone, as ze vill ansuer to me wpon zour office. The quhilk to do I commit to zou coniunctle and scuerale my full powar be thes my precept be zou deulie execut and indorset agane to the barar. Gevin and subscriuit vith my hand at Rosdew, the xv day of Merch, the zer of God 1ᵐ vᶜ lxix zeris.

In another precept, dated 28th November 1570, Sir John commands his officers lawfully to summon two of the tenants of the lands of Kirkmichael-Buchanan to compear before him, or any of his bailies, in the Baron Court of Luss, to be held at the port of Rossdhu on the 15th of December following, in the hour of cause, to hear and see themselves decerned by decreet of that Court to pay the victuals and other duties due to him.[2]

On 14th August 1570, Sir John obtained from John Colquhoun of Kilmardinny a letter of reversion of an annual-rent of 120 merks, to be uplifted from the lands and barony of Colquhoun, engaging to resign that annual-rent on the payment of 1200 merks.[3]

When, in 1572, Alexander Master of Mar, was appointed guardian of the person of King James the Sixth, and keeper of the castle of Stirling during his Majesty's residence there, and when certain noblemen became cautioners for the Master of Mar that he would keep that castle for the use of the King, and preserve his Majesty's person in safety, Sir John Colquhoun of Luss was among the friends of the house of Erskine, who bound themselves to assist him in the performance of his duty, and to protect the persons of his cautioners. The bond is as follows :—

Be it kend till all men by thir present lettres, Ws, the freindis of the house of Erskin vndersubscrivand, that forsamekle as our Souerane Lordis present regent bering the cheif gouernament of his Hienes' persoun, and of his realme and liegis, and having like cair of his Majestie's sure preseruatioun and godlie

---

[1] Original Precept of Warning at Rossdhu.    [3] Original Letter of Reversion at Rossdhu.
[2] Original Precept of Warning, *ibid.*

and virtuus educatioun, with advise of the Lordis of his Hienes' secrete counsale,
hes thocht it convenieut that his Majestie's persoun zit still remane within his
Castell of Striuiling, aud for that effect Alexander, maister of Mar, as priucipall
taking and ressaneing vpoun him the chairge of the keping and governance of his
Maiesteis persoun and of his Castell of Striueling, during his Hienes being thairin,
and certain noblemen, cautionaris and souerteis with the said Alexander, ar
becum actit and oblist vpoun thair faythis, honouris, and allegence, that the said
Alexander be him self and the frieudis and seruaudis of the zoung erll of Mar,
his nepho, for quhilkis he may be ansuerable, shall keip the said Castell of
Striueling in name and to the vse and behuif of our Souerane Lord, and sall
alsua surelie and saulllie keip and obserue the maist noble persoun of his Hienes
within his said Castell, with certane vtheris conditionis, vnder the pane of thair
lyffis and heritages, as [in] ane act subscriuit thairanent mair largelie is conteuit,
and seing the said honorable chairge can not be surelie nor sufficientlie vsit without the erueist gudwill, assistence, and concurence of ws, the freindis of the hous,
Thairfoir to be bundin and oblist, and be the tennour heirof faithfulie bindis and
oblissis ws, vpoun our faythtis, honouris, and allegeuce, to concur and assist, with
the said Alexander maister of Mar, in the diligent performiug of his chairge
aboun specifiit, and that he and we sall freith, releif and keip his said cautioners
and souerteis skaythtles and blameles, as we will ansuer to our said Souerane
Lord his regent, and auctoritie, vpoun our honouris and vnder the pane of our
lyffis and heritages. Attour, we are content and consentis that this our obligatioun
be actit and registrat in the buikis of Privie Counsale *ad futuram rei memoriam*.
In witnes heirof we haue subscriuit thir presentis with our handis as followis, at
      the         day of
the zeir of I$^m$ v$^c$ threscoir tuelf zeiris.

JHONE ERSKYN of Inche.  
WILLIAM DOUGLAS of Lochleuin.  
ALEXANDER FORRESTER of Garden.  
GLENEGLES.  
JAMES ERSKYN.  
JAMES COLUILL of East Wemes.  
ROBERT DRUMMOND.  
ROBERT COLUILL of Cleische.  
JAMES GALBRAITH of Culcreuch.  
WALT. LECKIE of that llk.  
JHONE REID of Akynheid.

ALEX$^r$ ERSKYN.  
JHON COLQWHON of Lws, Knyt.  
WILLIAM M$^c$RAY of Tulibard.  
DRYBRUCH.  
TUCHT.  
CAMBUSKYNETH.  
ROSSYTH.  
DRUMQUHASSILL.  
ROBERT ERSKYN fier of Dun.  
JAMES KYNROSS off Kippanross.  
J. STERLING, Knyt.[1]

---

[1] Original in the Mar Charter-chest.

134        SIR JOHN COLQUHOUN, KNIGHT,

The Reformed minister of the parish of Luss at this time was Mr.
William Chirnside, whose wife, Gelis Colquhoun, was aunt of Sir John
Colquhoun, being a sister of Humphrey Colquhoun, his father.   On 10th
January 1572-3, a bond was entered into between Sir John and William
Chirnside, relative to the manse of the minister of Luss, in Glasgow.   Sir
John bound himself and his heirs that, though the minister had set in
feu-farm to Humphrey Colquhoun, Sir John's son and apparent heir, the
manse-place and yards in Glasgow, and the house contained therein, the
minister should have a right to occupy them whenever he chose, provided
that Sir John and his heirs should have thankful hospitality on their occasionally coming there, and that the minister should uphold the place and
yards, and the house water-tight whilst he occupied them.[1]   Sir John
also bound himself and his heirs to entertain in his house Mr. William
Chirnside as his familiar friend, with a man and a boy, his attendants,
whenever he should be pleased to come, in consideration of Mr. Chirnside's
having gratified him in sundry pleasures and good deeds, and having discharged him of ninety merks of his yearly duties of the parsonage of Luss.[2]

Sir John's subsequent transactions in reference to the acquisition of
new property, and the administration of his estates, are limited and unimportant.   On 28th December 1573, he was infefted in an orchard in the
King's gate, Dumbarton ; and on 11th January following, he was infefted
in three acres of land in the same burgh, which he had acquired from
John Smollet.[3]   Sometime after, he purchased from John Gibson, younger,
burgess of Glasgow, an annual-rent of £10 Scots, under reversion, to be
uplifted yearly from a tenement in the city of Glasgow.[4]

Sir John died in the month of January 1574-5, as appears from the
retour in which his son Humphrey was served heir to him.[5]

Sir John Colquhoun lived during the exciting events of the great revolution which overthrew the Roman Catholic religion, and established the
Reformed faith in Scotland.   He was the contemporary of John Knox,

[1] Original Bond at Rossdhu.

[2] Obligation narrated in Original Contract
between Alexander Colquhoun of Luss and
Mr. William Chirnside, dated 1st and 6th
November 1598, ibid.

[3] Dumbarton Sasine Records.

[4] Original Letter of Reversion, dated 11th
October 1574, at Rossdhu.

[5] Original Retour, ibid.

and survived the great Reformer only about three years. But he does not appear on the page of history as a prominent actor, either on the one side or on the other. It is, however, certain that for some years after the Reformed faith was established, he continued to adhere to the Roman Catholic faith in which he had been educated. When he asked and obtained, in 1564, from the Papal legate, a dispensation for his marriage with his second wife, Agnes Boyd, Scotland was a Protestant kingdom, and he was acting in violation of law. Four years previously, namely, in August 1560, not only was the Reformed faith ratified, and the jurisdiction and authority of the Pope in the kingdom of Scotland abolished by the Scottish Parliament, but by the Act abolishing the Papal jurisdiction, it was ordained "that nane of oure Soveranis subjectis sute or desyre in ony tyme heirefter, tytill or rycht be the Bischope of Rome or his sect, to ony thing within this realme, under the panis of barratrie, that is to say, proscriptioun, banishment, and never to bruik honour, office, nor dignitie within this realme : And the contraveaneris heirof to be callit befoir the Justice or his deputis, or befoir the Lordis of the Sessioun, and punist thairfoir according to the lawis of this realme. . . . . And that na Bischop nor uther Prelatt of this realme use ony jurisdictioun in tymes to cum be the said Bischope of Rome's authoritie under the paine foirsaid."[1] Sir John Colquhoun then, by asking this dispensation, showed that at the time when he did so, he not only continued attached to the old faith, but held it so firmly that he acted according to its canons, even at the risk of proscription and banishment; and the Archbishop of St. Andrews, in granting the dispensation, exposed himself to a similar penalty. But so numerous still were the adherents of the old religion, and so great were the confusions of those times of ecclesiastical and political convulsion, that no attempt was made to bring Sir John into trouble for this violation of the law. Whether he afterwards continued to live and die in the Roman Catholic faith, or joined the ranks of the Reformers, we have not discovered.

Agnes Boyd, Sir John's second wife, survived him about ten years. In February 1580 she received a discharge for the payment of teinds for the crop of the year 1579.[2] On 12th May 1581, as Sir John's relict, she was in-

---

[1] Knox's History, vol. i. p. 125.  [2] Original Discharge at Rossdhu.

fefted in an annual-rent of 20 merks from the forty-shilling lands of Wolton, in the barony of Cardross and shire of Dumbarton.[1] On 26th July 1583, she was infefted in an annual-rent of £40 Scots from the lands of Boquherrane in the parish of Kilpatrick, and from the Mains of Duntreath in the shire of Stirling, Adam Colquhoun, in Milton of Colquhoun, acting as the bailie of James Edmonstone of Duntreath in infefting her.[2] She died at Edinburgh on 18th July 1584. The testament-dative and inventar of her goods, gear, sums of money, and debts belonging to her at the time of her decease, were faithfully made and given up by Sir Humphrey Colquhoun of Luss, her lawful son and executor-dative. In this document, which is long, there is no will. The inventory of her own proper goods and gear consists chiefly of cattle pasturing on the lands of certain tenants, and of victual in the hands of tenants. The debts owing to her consisted mainly of rents due to her by the tenants of various lands. There remained of free gear, the debts being deducted, £2982, 13s. The inventory was confirmed 18th April 1588.[3] On 10th April 1590, Sir Humphrey, her son, compeared personally before the burgh court of Dumbarton as heir to her, and granted that an annual rent of £10 from a piece of land in Dumbarton was lawfully redeemed from him by Robert Sempill of Corruth.[4]

By this lady, Sir John had three sons and two daughters. The sons were—

1. Sir Humphrey, who succeeded him.

2. John.—John second son of Sir John Colquhoun of Luss, along with his father, granted a letter of reversion to Robert Colquhoun of Camstradden of the hill of Camstradden on 10th March 1573-4. On 3d February 1575-6, he was infefted in an annual-rent of £10 out of the twelve-merk lands of Milligs, which belonged to James Galbraith of Culcreuch, and another out of the lands of Kilmahew in 1584 ;[5] and he was infefted in an annual-rent of ten merks from the lands of Barris, 11th June 1584.[6] He had also an annual-rent out of the lands of Kirkmichael-Semple, to which his brother Alexander was served heir in 1607.

---

[1]  Dumbarton Sasine Records.

[2]  *Ibid.* fol. 70.

[3]  Original Testament at Rossdhu.

[4]  Dumbarton Sasine Records, fol. 150.

[5]  *Ibid.* fol. 53.

[6]  Original Instrument of Sasine at Rossdhu.

John obtained from Peter Napier of Kilmahew a charter dated 10th April 1588, of an annual-rent of ten merks, from the lands of Barris, in the dukedom of Lennox and shire of Dumbarton, for which the sum of a hundred merks was paid to the granter by James Colquhoun of Garscube, lawful tutor and administrator of the said John. On 11th April in the same year, he obtained from John Lindsay of Bolule (now called Bonhill) a charter of sale of an annual-rent of £8 from the £4 dominical lands of Bolule in the dukedom of Lennox and shire of Dumbarton. This annual-rent formerly belonged to James Colquhoun of Garscube, but he had resigned it into the hands of John Lindsay, the superior, in favour of the said John Colquhoun, for fulfilment of a contract dated 26th January 1587, made between him on the one part, and the said John Colquhoun and Alexander, his brother-german, with consent of James Crawfurde, fiar of Ferme, Walter Colquhoun of Kilmardinny and Adam Colquhoun in Hill, their curators, for their interest, and also with the consent of Robert Lord Boyd, John and Alexander Colquhouns, on the other part.[1]   On 29th April 1588, the said John Colquhoun was, upon a precept of sasine by John Lindsay of Bullull, infefted in an annual-rent of twelve merks, from the dominical lands of Bullull.[2]   On 17th May 1588, he obtained from George Buchanan of Buchanan a charter of an annual-rent of twenty merks, from the lands of Bordland, in the lordship of Buchanan and shire of Stirling, and he was infefted therein on the 22d of the same month.[3]   In all these writs he is designated " an ingenious youth, John Colquhoun, liberal son of the deceased John Colquhoun of Luss, knight."

John, it would appear, had acquired notoriety by his adventures in harassing and despoiling the tenants of neighbouring lands. He was charged with having in October 1590 spoilzeit John Dennistoun in Colgrain of a cart-horse, price £20, a grey horse, 20 merks, a dun grey mare, £10 ; Margaret Roger, relict of the deceased Patrick Lawrie in Colgrain, of a brown horse £20 ; Andrew Roger in Col-

[1] Original Charter at Rossdhu.
[2] Original Instrument of Sasine, ibid.
[3] Original Charter and Instrument of Sasine at Rossdhu.

grain of a lyart mare, £16 ; and Donald M'Kynnie in Little Camp-
seskin, of two ky, one of a black colour, and the other taggart, price of
each £10, and six sheep, price of each 25s. 8d.[1]  An account of the
subsequent melancholy fate of John Colquhoun is given under the
biographical sketch of his brother Sir Humphrey.

3. Alexander, who succeeded his brother Sir Humphrey.

Sir John's daughters by Agnes Boyd were—

1. Jean, who married Sir Mathew Stewart of Minto.  She was his
second wife, and they had a daughter, Annabel Stewart, who married
William Stewart of Finnich, which occasioned the notion that the
Stewarts of Finnich were a branch of Minto.  Sir Mathew Stewart's
male line failed with his descendant Sir John Stewart, last of Minto,
who, about the year 1699, went with the Scots expedition to Darien,
where he died.  He was reduced to such penury that he was maintained by his cousin, Lord Blantyre.  Sir Mathew Stewart, the husband of Jean Colquhoun, was buried in the choir of the cathedral
of Glasgow.  In the south wall there is a copper plate inserted near
the tomb of the Stewarts of Minto, with this inscription : " Heir ar
bvriet Sir Waltir, Sir Thomas, Sir Johne, Sir Robert, Sir Johne, and
Sir Mathiw, by lineal descent to vtheris, Barons, and Knichtis of the
hovs of Mynto, with thair vyfis, bairnis, and bretherein." Jean
Colquhoun was probably buried in the same place of sepulture, and
included in the above inscription as one of the wives of Sir Mathew,
the last named in the inscription.  The barons and knights who are
successively named are the same as in the more detailed histories of
the house, with the exception that in the latter Sir William, not Sir
Walter, as in the inscription, is generally stated as the father of Sir
Thomas, the second knight.[2]

2. Margaret, who married Sir James Edmonstone of Duntreath, knight.
From him she had a charter of the £8 lands of Mochomran and
Anchingree for herself in liferent, and for the heirs-male begotten,

[1]  These charges are brought against him
in a summons against his brother Humphrey's daughters, Margaret and Agnes,
dated at Edinburgh 11th August 1599, to

be afterwards quoted.  Original at Rossdhu.
[2]  Duncan  Stewart's  History  of  the
Stewarts, pp. 166-7 ; Collection of Epitaphs,
Glasgow, 1834, p. 175.

or to be begotten between them, in fee; and she was infefted there-
in on the 12th and 13th February 1585.   In this last transaction
Adam Colquhoun, in Miltoun of Colquhoun, acted as the bailie of
Sir James Edmonstone, and Gavin Colquhoun, son of the late John
Colquhoun of Luss, as the attorney of Margaret Colquhoun, sister of
Sir Humphrey Colquhoun.[1]   Margaret and her husband received a
crown-charter of the lands of Boquharan and Auchingree, 1st
December 1590;[2] and she also received a crown-charter of the
lands of Mochomran, Auchingree, and Gartkalton, in the shire of
Stirling, 3d January 1598.[3]   On 3d July 1591, William Edmonstone, lawful son and heir-apparent of Sir James Edmonstone of
Duntreath, knight, obtained from Sir Humphrey Colquhoun a charter
of sale of an annual-rent of 100 bolls of barley from the two-merk
lands of the Mains of Colquhoun.[4]   And on 23d August following
the said William was infefted in the said annual-rent.[5]

[1] Dumbarton Sasine Records, fol. 97.
[2] Reg. Mag. Sig., Lib. xxxvii. No. 294.
[3] Ibid. Lib. xli. No. 483.
[4] Original Charter at Rossdhu.
[5] Original Instrument of Sasine, ibid.

Besides these children, Sir John had a
natural son Gavin. This son was infefted in
1590 in an annual-rent of £40 out of Bou-
hill.   On 13th May 1590, Gavin Colquhoun, "natural son" of the deceased John
Colquhoun of Luss, was infefted, by Alexander Colquhoun, brother-german of Sir
Humphrey Colquhoun of Luss, knight, in
an annual-rent of 10 merks, to be raised
from the Mains of Bullull, in the earldom
of Lennox and shire of Dumbarton.—[Ori-
ginal Instrument of Sasine at Rossdhu.]

## XIV.—1. Sir HUMPHREY COLQUHOUN, Knight,

Fourteenth of Colquhoun and Sixteenth of Luss, 1574-1592.

Lady Jean Cunningham (of Glencairn), his first wife, 1583-1584.

Jean Hamilton, his second wife, 1585-1625.

Humphrey Colquhoun succeeded his father, Sir John, in the family estates in January 1574-5, when only about ten years of age. In the instrument of his infeftment in the lands of Kilbride, dated 13th January 1569, he is called a boy, son and apparent heir of John Colquhoun of Luss ; and in his revocation, on 2d November 1586, of certain deeds executed to his prejudice, during his minority, he is said to be " now approachand" to his age of twenty-one. It would thus appear that he was born in 1565, the year after the marriage of his father and mother.

After the death of Humphrey's father, Sir John Colquhoun, Robert fourth Lord Boyd, the maternal grandfather of Humphrey, obtained a gift from King James the Sixth, with the advice of James Earl of Morton, Regent, under the Privy Seal, dated 9th January 1574-5, of the ward and non-entries, mails and profits, of the lands and barony of Luss, and of all other lands, etc., which belonged to the deceased Sir John Colquhoun of Luss, Knight, till the lawful entry of the rightful heir or heirs thereto, being of lawful age, with the relief thereof, when it should happen, and also the maritage of Humphrey Colquhoun, son and heir of the said deceased Sir John.

On 16th August 1575 Humphrey Colquhoun was served heir to his father, Sir John, by a special service. The lands enumerated in the retour are Ballernick-mor, Lettrowald-mor [Letrualt-mor], and Stuckinduff, with the mill of Altdonalt in Letrualt, the lands of Kilmardinny, Blairvaddoch, Dureling, Stronratan, Auchingaich, Auchenveunel-mor, Stuckiedow, and Blairhangane, in the earldom of Lennox and shire of Dumbarton, which lands were held in chief of the Earl of Lennox. In the retour his father, Sir John, is said to have died in the month of January bypast.[1] Humphrey Colquhoun was infefted, on 7th November in the same year, in an annual

[1] Original Retour at Rossdhu.

rent of fifty-eight shillings and fourpence out of the lands of Dirtenclennan, in the earldom of Lennox and regality of Paisley, on a precept of sasine by John Hamilton of Dirtenclennan.[1] On the same day he was infefted in the lands of Kilmardinny, on a precept of sasine by Charles Earl of Lennox. To this infeftment, Matthew Colquhoun, son liberal of John Colquhoun of Kilmardinny, was a witness.[2] On the 8th of the same month Humphrey was infefted in the other lands mentioned in the retour, by which he was served heir to his father.[3] A precept of sasine was also given, on 27th January 1575-6, by Archibald Galbraith of Portnellan, as the superior, for infefting him as heir of his father in the lands of Easter Kilbride.[4]

After the abolition of the jurisdiction of the Pope and the establishment of the Reformed Faith in Scotland, various revenues, such as those derived from altarages, chaplainries, and other sources in the Roman Catholic Church, were, by several Acts of Parliament, granted to the magistrates of burghs, for the sustentation of the Reformed ministers, or for educational purposes within their respective jurisdictions. An instance of a transfer of this kind occurs in reference to a tenement in Rattoun Raw, Glasgow, which belonged to Humphrey Colquhoun of Luss. From this tenement £4 had been paid annually to the rectors of the quire of the kirk of Glasgow, conformably to the terms of his infeftment therein, 1st October 1573. But the masters of the College of Glasgow, it would seem, had been lawfully provided to this annual payment. Humphrey and his tutors, however, claimed it, and the College of Glasgow having asserted their right, the matter in dispute was brought before the Lords of Council at Edinburgh, on 3d February 1575, by letters, which had been raised at the instance of Mr. David Wemys, minister of Glasgow, against Humphrey Colquhoun and James Colquhoun, his tutor, on the one part, and Mr. Andrew Melville, Principal, and Mr. Peter Blackburn, Regent of the College of Glasgow, on the other part, making mention that the said Humphrey and his tutor had poinded and distrained his goods and geir for the mails of the house which he occupied for the terms of Whitsunday and Martinmas bypast, and that

---

[1] Dumbarton Sasine Records, fol. 52.
[2] Ibid. fol. 52. and Original Instrument of Sasine at Rossdhu.

[3] Dumbarton Sasine Records, fol. 53.
[4] Original Precept of Sasine at Rossdhu.

the said Principal and Regent had also caused charge him, by virtue of the King's letters, to pay to them the said sum; whereby he would be compelled to make double payment of the mails of his house. The Lords of Council decerned that Mr. David Wemys should pay the contested £4 to the said masters of the College of Glasgow, and the remanent mails of the tenement to Humphrey Colquhoun and his tutor.[1]

After this Humphrey received from John Earl of Mar a precept of *clare constat*, dated at Stirling, St. Andrews, and Edinburgh, 1st, 4th, and 8th June, respectively, 1577, for infefting him as heir of his father in an annual-rent of £40, to be raised from the Earl's dominical lands of Golden-house in the shire of Stirling.[2]

In 1582, Humphrey Colquhoun acquired the heritable office of coroner of the shire of Dumbarton. On 19th December that year he obtained from Robert Grahame of Knockdoliane a charter (which was confirmed 22d December by King James the Sixth,) to himself and his heirs, of that office, with the casualties and fees, to be held blench of the Crown; and on the 26th of February following he was infefted therein.[3]

About the year 1580 Humphrey's curators purchased for him, from Robert Colquhoun of Camstradden, an annual-rent of £20, to be raised from his lands of the hill of Camstradden, in the dukedom of Lennox and shire of Dumbarton. On 6th February 1582-3 he received a charter of this annual-rent from Robert Colquhoun, who granted it to his own spouse, Marjory Murray, in liferent, and after her decease to Humphrey Colquhoun. The purchase-money was paid by James Colquhoun of Garscube, one of his curators.[4]

Soon after, Humphrey Colquhoun, who had not yet reached his majority, married Lady Jean Cunningham, daughter of Alexander Earl of Glencairn, and widow of Archibald fifth Earl of Argyll. Their contract of marriage is dated at Glasgow, 15th May 1583. Humphrey, with consent of his curators, and of Robert Lord Boyd as donator of the ward and non-entries

---

[1] Munimenta Universitatis Glasguensis, vol. i. pp. 99, 100.

[2] Original Precept at Rossdhu.

[3] Original Charters and Instrument of Sasine, *ibid.*

[4] Original Charter at Rossdhu. Among the witnesses are Adam Colquhoun in Hill, and Patrick Colquhoun, natural son of the said James Colquhoun of Garscube.

of the lordship of Luss, with the relief and marriage thereof, engaged to marry and to take to his lawful wife, Lady Jean Cunningham, and to solemnize the band of matrimony with her in face of Holy Kirk, with all due solemnities, betwixt the date of the contract and the 24th day of June following ; and, before completing the marriage, to infeft her in liferent in the lands and barony of Colquhoun, the manor-place of Dunglas, the lands of Milton of Garscube, the lands of Sauchy (reserving the third of the whole of these lands to Dame Agnes Boyd, Lady Luss, his mother, during her lifetime), and other lands.  On the other hand, Lady Jean Cunningham bound herself to pay to Humphrey, in name of tocher, 12,000 merks, of which 2500 were to be paid to him before or at Martinmas following, and 2000 to be laid out in sufficient " pennyworths and plenishing" for the abulzement of her body at her first entry to household with him ; and the remainder, with his consent, she bound herself to pay to Robert Lord Boyd, in the manner following :—1000 merks before or at Whitsunday, 5000 merks in the shape of infefting him in various lands which belonged to her in wadset, and the remainder of the £5000, extending to £1000, before or at Martinmas following.[1]

In fulfilment of a part of this marriage-contract, Lord Boyd, on the 21st of May, in the same year, made an assignation to Lady Jean Cunningham and her heirs of the before-mentioned letter of gift of the ward and non-entries of the lands of Luss, with the relief and marriage thereof, beginning their entry thereto at the 15th of that month, the date of the marriage-contract.[2]

The sum of £5000, which, by her marriage-contract with Humphrey Colquhoun of Luss, Lady Jean became bound to pay to Robert fourth Lord Boyd, was duly paid by the time agreed upon.  On 10th November 1583, a discharge was granted to her by John Crawfurd, assignee of Lord Boyd, and Robert Boyd of Badinhath, commissioner of Lord Boyd, his father, acknowledging that they had received from her £1000, as the last payment

[1] Extract Registered Marriage-Contract at Rossdhu.  The contract is imperfect, but from other writs we learn that it contained other agreements and arrangements.  It was registered in the Commissary Books of Glasgow, 25th October 158[3].

[2] Original Assignation at Rossdhu.

of the whole sum of £5000, before Martinmas bypast; and they at the same time discharged Humphrey Colquhoun, her husband, and also William Cunningham of Caprintoun, as cautioner and surety for her.

On 18th August 1584, she personally compeared before the Burgh Court of Dumbarton, and, as assignee of Robert Lord Boyd, donator of the ward, non-entries, etc., of the lands and lordship of Luss, renounced and transferred to her husband, Humphrey, her whole right and title to the said ward, etc., which, in terms of her marriage-contract with him, she had bound herself to do after the completion of the marriage.[1]

By a precept of sasine from the Chancery of King James the Sixth, Humphrey Colquhoun was, 5th June 1583, infefted, as heir of his father, in the lands and barony of Luss, with the castle, tower, and fortalice of Rossdhu, the islands in Lochlomond, Inchlonaig, Incheconochan, and Inchefoeithillane, now called the island of Rossdhu, with the fishing in Lochlomond, and the advocation and donation of the rector of the parochial church of Luss, and of all other churches and chapels thereof; in the lands and barony of Colquhoun, with the manor of Dunglas, and the fishings in the water of Clyde; and in the lands of Garscube, Sauchie, Colquhounis Glen, with the mill and mill lands of Sauline. In the precept it is said that Humphrey is the nearest heir of his father, and that he is of lawful age, by virtue of the King's dispensation in respect of his minority, for entering into his ward lands, which were held of the Crown in chief. James Colquhoun of Garscube, brother-german of the late John Colquhoun of Luss, acted as Humphrey's attorney.[2]

In November 1583, Humphrey Colquhoun and Lady Jean Cunningham, his wife, granted a discharge to Robert Boyd of Badinhath, acknowledging that they had received from him the key of the Charter-room of Rossdhu, which contained the charters and other writs that belonged to the deceased Sir John Colquhoun of Luss, the key having been committed to the keeping

[1] Original Notarial Instrument at Rossdhu; Dumbarton Sasine Records. The witnesses are James Colquhoun of Garscube, uncle of the said Humphrey, John Colquhoun of Kilmardinuy, Walter Colquhoun, his son

and heir-apparent, Adam Colquhoun, in Hiltoun of Naperstoun, and Patrick Colquhoun, servant of the said Humphrey.

[2] Original Instrument of Sasine, *ibid.*

of Humphrey's grandfather, Robert Lord Boyd, who at his departure from this country had delivered it to the said Robert, his son.[1]

The wards, non-entries, mails, and duties of the lands of Finnart, Port-incaple, and Forlingbrek [Fairholmbreck], of all the years and terms during which they had been in the hands of Esme Duke of Lennox, or of his predecessors, by reason of non-entry, since the decease of the late Sir John Colquhoun of Luss, Knight, and also of all years and terms to come, until the entry of the righteous heir or heirs thereto, with relief thereof when it should happen, had been given to John Smollet of Kirktown, by the said Duke, by a gift and disposition, dated 30th October 1582. But, on 19th August 1584, they were transferred to Humphrey Colquhoun of Luss and his heirs, by Smollet, in consideration of "certane sowmes of money payit and vther gratitudes" done to him by Humphrey.[2]

Soon after, Humphrey Colquhoun lost his wife, Lady Jean Cunningham, to whom he had been united only about a year and a half. She died before the 6th of January 1584-5. Her brother, Alexander Cunningham, Com-mendator of Kilwinning, her heir and executor-dative, granted a discharge of that date to Humphrey Colquhoun of Luss, acknowledging that he had received from him, in fulfilment of a contract made between them, 24th December preceding, the heirship moveables which fell to him through his said sister's decease, with the ornaments and "abuilzementis" of her body, specially goldsmith work, jewels, etc., which she had and possessed at the time of her death.[3]

On 26th May 1585, Humphrey Colquhoun, on a precept by Patrick Denzelstoun of Auchindinanree, was infefted in an annual-rent out of the lands of Auchindinanree. Among the witnesses were Walter Colquhoun, son and apparent heir of John Colquhoun of Kilmardinny, and Gavin Colquhoun, natural son of the late John Colquhoun of Luss.[4]

About a year after the death of Lady Jean Cunningham, his wife, Sir Humphrey Colquhoun—for he had now become a knight,—who was still in his minority, married, secondly, Jean Hamilton, daughter of Lord John

---

[1] Original in the Boyd Charter-chest, Town-Clerk's Office, Kilmarnock.

[2] Original Assignation at Rossdhu.

[3] Original Discharge at Rossdhu.

[4] Dumbarton Sasine Records, fol. 93.

Hamilton, (second son of the Regent Arran, Duke of Châtelherault in France, and declared to be heir to the Scottish throne failing Queen Mary,) who was afterwards created Marquis of Hamilton.  Their contract of marriage is dated at Hamilton, 29th December 1585.  By it, Jean Hamilton, with consent of her father, and Sir Humphrey, with the advice of his curators, took each other as lawful spouses, and engaged to complete and solemnize the band of matrimony in face of Christ's Kirk and congregation, duly and visibly, with all solemnities requisite thereto, betwixt the date of the contract and the 26th of January following.  In contemplation of the marriage, Sir Humphrey bound himself to infeft his promised spouse, " now in her virginitie," before the marriage, in liferent, in the manor-house of Dunglas, the Mains of Col- quhoun, and the lands of Milton of Colquhoun and of Milton of Garscube, in the shire of Dumbarton and "dukrie" of Lennox, in the lands of Sauchy, in the shire of Stirling, and in the lands of Saulbine, in the shire of Fife, worth in all one thousand merks of yearly rent.  In the event of there being no male heirs, but only female children as the issue of the mar- riage, Sir Humphrey Colquhoun bound himself and his heirs, should there be only one, to pay to her ten thousand merks ; should there be two, to pay to each of them five thousand merks ; and should there be more than two, to divide ten thousand merks, equally among them, as their tochers or marriage provisions.  Lord John Hamilton bound himself and his heirs to pay to Sir Humphrey ten thousand merks, in name of tocher, with his said daughter.[1]

In implement of this marriage-contract, Dame Jean Hamilton was infefted, on 21st January 1585-6, in liferent, in the mansion-house of Dun- glas and in the various lands in which Sir Humphrey had become bound to infeft her.  On 19th September 1588 she was again infefted in the same manor-house and lands.  Among the witnesses to this second infeftment were Adam Colquhoun, in Milton of Colquhoun, and William Colquhoun, in Dunglas.[2]

Sir Humphrey had thus, at an early age, made matrimonial alliances with two families of the first rank.  The honour of knighthood he appears to

¹ Extract Registered Contract at Rossdhu.   It was registered in the Commissary Books of Glasgow, 14th April 1586.          ² Dumbarton Sasine Records, fol. 133.

have acquired between the time of his first and second marriage; for in the marriage-contract with his first wife he is designated simply Humphrey Colquhoun of Luss, but in that with his second wife he is designated Sir Humphrey Colquhoun of Luss, knight. From his relation to the head of the house of Hamilton, who rose high in favour with King James the Sixth, Sir Humphrey might naturally anticipate a successful career in the ambitious paths of courtly distinction; and these anticipations, but for his early death, might have been fulfilled.

In the year 1586, Sir Humphrey intended to visit the Continent, and before his departure he committed his servants, tenants, and dependants to the protection of his cousin, Ludovic second Duke of Lennox. The Duke granted them letters of protection in the following terms:—

We, Ludouick, Duke of Lennox, Erle of Dernelie, etc., vnderstanding that our cousing, Sir Vmphra Colquhoune of Luss, Knycht, is of mynd and purpose to depart furth of this realme to the partis of France and vtheris bezond sey, and that in this menetyme he hes expreslie ordanit, be his lettres subscryuit and deliuerit to ws, all his hous, men, tenantis, seruandis, vasselis, and dependaris, to depend, serue, and await vponn ws, and our tutour, Thairfoir, being weill myndit to the gud estait of our said cousing and his hous, we haif takeu, and, be the tenour heirof, takkis and ressauis him, his said hous, members thairof, men, tenentis, seruandis, vassellis and dependaris of the same, vnder our speciall protectioun, during the said space of his absence, promissing in this menetyme to protect, mainteue, and defend thame, in all thair honest actiones, as we do our awin men and dependaris, be these our lettres of protectioun, subscryuit with our hand, at Edinburgh, the xiiii day of Marche, the zeir of God j^r v^e lxxxvj zeiris, before thir witniss, Sir Patrik Houstoun of that ilk, Knycht, Johne Conynghaim of Drumquhassill, Aulay Makaulay of Ardingapill, Mr. Johne Skene, aduocatt, and Robert Chirnesyd, with wtheris diuers.

LENOX.
BLANTYRE.[1]

Whether Sir Humphrey carried into effect his intention of making a journey to the Continent we do not know, but if he did so he had returned to Scotland by the beginning of November in the same year.

When he had nearly reached his majority, conceiving that his tutors, in acting for him during his minority, had entered into many contracts and

[1] Dennistoun's MSS., Advocates' Library.

obligations which were injurious to his interests, Sir Humphrey took
measures for rendering these deeds null and void. At the Commissary
Court of Glasgow, 2d March 1586, Mr. William Chirnside, parson of
Luss, Commissar of Glasgow, sitting in judgment, Sir Humphrey, " now
approachand to his aige of twentie ane zeiris," personally compeared, and
understanding himself to be " havelie hurt and dampnifiet" by setting and
making of tacks and other contracts and obligations made to divers persons
in the time of his minority, he therefore revoked the same, and all other
things done by him during that period tending in any wise to his hurt,
protesting that the same should be held to be of no force in time coming.[1]

A dispute also arose between him and Mr. William Chirnside in reference to an obligation which this minister alleged Sir Humphrey's father
had come under to him. At Glasgow, 2d March 1586-7, David Chirnside, son
to the said Mr. William, passed to the personal presence of Sir Humphrey
Colquhoun of Luss, Knight, and required him, as son and heir to the
deceased Sir John Colquhoun of Luss, his father, to furnish to the said Mr.
William his boarding, with a gentleman and a boy, conform to the said obligation made by the deceased Sir John to the said Mr. William to that effect.
Sir Humphrey answered that he knew no such obligation, and therefore
refused to grant what was sought. David Chirnside, as procurator for his
father, instantly, in his name and behalf, asked instruments from a notary.
The premises were attested by Robert Blair, notary, and among the witnesses
were Walter Colquhoun, son to John Colquhoun of Kilmardinny.[2]

A commission was granted on 26th April 1588, by King James the
Sixth, for serving Sir Humphrey Colquhoun of Luss, knight, heir of his
father, in all the lands and annual-rents in which his father died vested
and seized within the shire of Fife.[3]

At Glasgow and at the Palace of Holyrood, on the 13th and 16th of
September 1588, Sir Humphrey received from Ludovic second Duke of
Lennox, with advice and consent of Walter Commendator of Blantyre, his
tutor and administrator, a gift and disposition of the mails, etc., of the nine-
merk land of old extent of Kilbride, with the chapel and chapel-lands

[1] Extract  Registered  Revocation  at        [2] Copy Notarial Requisition at Rossdhu.
Rossdhu.                                       [3] Original Commission, ibid.

thereof.  These lands had fallen into the hands of the Duke as superior
by reason of non-entries through the decease of the late Archibald Galbraith, last and immediate heritable possessor thereof.[1]

Sir Humphrey had failed to pay his part of the taxation of £40,000,
granted by the barons of the realm to King James the Sixth.  He was also
implicated in the slaughter of William Brisbane of Barnishill.  He thus
became obnoxious to the Government, and legal proceedings were instituted against him.  For his non-payment of his part of the said tax, and
for his non-compearance before the Lord-Justice or his deputies, to have
underlain his Majesty's laws for the said slaughter, and for the non-entry of
his person in ward within the Castle of Edinburgh, being charged thereto,
to have remained therein during his Majesty's pleasure, he was denounced
his Majesty's rebel, and put to the horn, and his goods forfeited to the
Crown.  This denunciation for non-payment of the tax, at the instance of
Thomas Master of Glamis, treasurer, and then captain of the guard, col
lector-depute in the shire of Dumbarton of the said taxation, was executed
against him on the 23d of November 1588.

Robert Chirnside of Over Possill obtained from the King, under the
Great Seal, 28th November 1589, a gift of the escheat of the liferent of
all the lands and heritages belonging to Sir Humphrey, held by him immediately of his Majesty, wherever lying within the realm.  And on the
1st of June 1591, he obtained a decreet of the Lords of Council, finding
and declaring that Sir Humphrey had been orderly denounced rebel, and
put to the horn, and had remained unrelaxed therefrom more than a year
and a day, and therefore decerning that Sir Humphrey had lost his liferent
of the £80 land of Luss, the £40 land of Colquhoun, in the shire of Lennox,
the £10 land of Garscube, in the shire of Renfrew, the £10 land of Sauchy,
and the £10 land of Glen, in the shire of Stirling, which were held by him
of the King; and that the liferent of these lands belonged to Robert
Chirnside, his Majesty's donator.

Not long after, namely, on the 14th of January 1591-92, Robert Chirnside, "for certane gratitudes, gude deidis, and pleasouris done to him be
Alexander Colquhoun, third lauchfull broder to Schir Vmphra Colquhoun

[1] Original Gift of Non-entries at Rossdhu.

of Luss," made an assignation to Alexander of the above-mentioned gift.[1]

On 8th October 1589, Sir Humphrey Colquhoun was infefted in the lands of Ardincannal, Finnart, Portincaple, Forlingbrek [Fairholmbreck], Tullichintaull, and others. Robert Colquhoun of Ballernick acted as his attorney on the occasion ; and among the witnesses was Gilchrist Macaulay, servant of Agnes Kelso in Ballernick-mor, mother of the said Robert Colquhoun.[2]

On 30th September 1590, Sir Humphrey Colquhoun resigned into the hands of Archibald Earl of Argyll, the superior, the lands of Bordland of Sauline, in the barony of Sauline and shire of Fife, for new charter and infeftment to be given in favour of himself and Jean Hamilton his spouse, and the longest liver of them in liferent, and his heirs-male. On the 30th of October following, instruments were taken thereupon, in the presence of a public notary and witnesses, by Sir Humphrey's procurator ; and on the same day Sir Humphrey and his wife, Jean, obtained a charter of these lands in liferent from the said Earl.[3]

With this last we close our notices of the property transactions in connexion with which the name of this laird of Luss appears on record. Those in which he was subsequently concerned must have been few and unimportant. During the time that he held the patrimonial estate, it seems to have been neither much increased nor diminished.

Some illustrations have already been given of the feuds which existed among the Highland clans. At this time, the disturbances caused by the hostilities of clanship rose to such a height, and proved so serious an obstruction to the settlement of the kingdom in peace, by constantly embroiling in confusion large districts, and rendering life and property insecure, as to call for the interference of the Government. In the Parliament which was held in July 1587, not fewer than nineteen Acts were passed " for the quieting and keeping in obedience of the disordered subjects, inhabitants of the Borders, Highlands, and Isles." In one of these Acts they are described in the preamble as " delyting in all mischeiffis, and maist vnnaturallie and cruellie waistand, slayand, heryand and distroyand

[1] Original Assignation at Rossdhu.
[2] Dumbarton Sasine Records, fol. 146.
[3] Original Notarial Instrument of Resignation and Charter at Rossdhu.

thair awin nychtbouris and natiue cuntrie people, takand occasioun of the leist truble that may occur in the [inner] pairtis of the realme, quhen thai think that cair and thocht of the repressing of thair insolence is ony-wayes forzett, to renew thair maist barbarous cruelties and godles oppres-sionis." In a " Roll of the names of the landlords and bailies of lands dwelling on the Borders and in the Highlands, where broken men have dwelt and presently dwell," to which one of these Acts refers, are the names of the Laird of Buchanan, the Laird of Macfarlane of the Arrochar, the Laird of Luss, the Laird M'Caulay of Ardincaple, and others. And in a " Roll of the clans that have captains, chiefs, and chieftains on whom they depend, oftimes against the wills of their landlords, as well on the Borders as Highlands, and of some special persons of branches of the said clans," ordained to be ratified and inserted in that Parliament, are the Buchanans, the Macfarlanes of the Arrochar, the clan Gregor, and others.[1]

Born in a district peculiarly liable to the aggressions of the Highland clans, and living in times when this turbulent spirit was at its height, Sir Humphrey Colquhoun suffered much from those who were at feud with his family. The outstanding family quarrel between the Colquhouns and the Macfarlanes, which in the time of his father had been so fatal to many of the dependants of the house of Colquhoun, was renewed in the closing years of the lifetime of Sir Humphrey. Prompted by resentment and by the love of plunder, which with the Highland clans as well as with the southern borderers rose to a passion, the Macfarlanes made marauding incursions into the glens of Luss, and carried off by force much property. In these fre-quent and destructive inroads they seem to have met with little opposition, though they must have created much discontent, and impaired industry and a sense of the security of property and life; effects so often produced by the disorders of the feudal system.

In a decreet-arbitral, pronounced betwixt Sir Humphrey Colquhoun of Luss for himself and his tenants on the one part, and Andrew Macfar-lane of Arrochar for himself, his sons, kin, and friends on the other part, dated Edinburgh, 10th August 1590, it was deemed that there should be paid to Sir Humphrey and his tenants, by Andrew Macfarlane of Arrochar,

---

[1] Acts of the Parliament of Scotland, vol. iii. pp. 461-467.

40 oxen, price of the piece £12; 60 kye, price of the piece £8; and 10 horse, price of the piece £13, 6s. 8d.[1] The depredations here referred to had evidently been committed previous to the year 1590.

From a paper containing a list of "the bestiall, and guidis, and geir spolzeit be the Macfarlanes fra the Lard of Lus his tennents, and profits, alswa the prices of the samyn, as thai ar reclamit in the zeires 1590-1594,[2] in the summonds of the Laird of Lus against the Macfarlanes," [in the year 1603,] an idea may be formed of the losses and harassments caused by these plundering expeditions. We here give the list under the first three of these years, not going beyond the year in which Sir Humphrey died.

| 1590. | | *lib.* | *s.* | *d.* |
|---|---|---|---|---|
| 5 horse, price . | . | 126 | 6 | 8 |
| 2 staiggis, . . | . | 20 | 0 | 0 |
| 21 meires and 11 fallowers, | . | 625 | 6 | 8 |
| 21 ky, . . | . | 248 | 0 | 0 |
| 5 oxen, . . | . | 62 | 0 | 0 |
| 20 sheep, . | . | 25 | 0 | 0 |
| 1591. | | | | |
| 8 horse, | | 148 | 0 | 0 |
| 2 staiggis, . . . | | 20 | 0 | 0 |
| 15 meires and 3 fallowers, . | . | 197 | 6 | 8 |
| 26 ky, . . . . | | 322 | 13 | 4 |
| 11 oxen, . . | | 138 | 0 | 0 |
| 68 sheep, | | 102 | 0 | 0 |
| 1592. | | | | |
| 7 horse, . | | 436 | 0 | 0 |
| 2 staiggis, . . | | 26 | 13 | 4 |
| 13 meires and 5 fallowers, . | | 262 | 0 | 0 |
| 34 ky, . | | 357 | 0 | 0 |
| 10 oxen, . . | | 140 | 0 | 0 |
| 44 sheep, | | 95 | 0 | 0 |
| | | £3351 | 6 | 8 |

---

[1] These facts are narrated in an assignation to Alexander Colquhoun of Luss by his tenants, dated 6th January 1602.     [2] List at Rossdhu.

As Sir Humphrey died about the middle of the year 1592, a part of the spoliation under that year may have taken place after his death; but enough remains to show the distress which he and his tenants experienced from this system of bold and successful brigandage. The above list is exclusive of the " spoliation of the insycht geir,"—that is, household furniture.

One of the last public transactions of this Laird of Luss was entering into a bond with George Earl of Huntlie, whereof he became bound to support the Earl in all his feuds, past, present, and to come, the sovereign's authority alone excepted. This bond, which is dated 16th March 1591-2, is as follows :—

Be it kend till all men be thir present lettres, me, Schir Umphrie Colquhoune of Luss, Knycht, to becum man, servand and dependar to ane nobill and potent Lord George Erlle of Huntlie, Lord Gordoun and Baidzenocht, etc., that I, and all that I may mak, of kin, freindis, servandis, suriuance, vassellis, and dependaries, sall at all timis heireftir, witht our haill forces, serve, concur and assist with the said nobill Lorde, in all and quhatsumeuir his actionis and caussis, contra quhatsumeuir persoun or persones, clan or clannis, within this realm, for quhatsumeuir causs he hes to do, in deidlie feidis, bypast, present, and to cum, and sall tak trew, plaine, and cafald pairt with, and sall entir in bluid witht his aduersar pairtie, and be reddy baith to perseu and defend, and wair our lyffis and heritages in his Lordschippis adois, as we salbe employit, aganis quhatsumeuir persones within this realme, the authorite only exceptit, etc. In witnes quhairof, I haue subscriuit this present band of seruice, witht my awin hand, at Blaknes, the sextein day of Marche, the yeir of God M.V⁰ four scoir alevin yeris, befor thir witness, Aulay Makcaulay of Artingaipill, Gorg Gordoun of Govlis, Thomas Gordoun of Drumbulg.

W͞MPHRA COLQUHONE off Luss, Knycht.[1]

This bond was connected with one of the most exciting and tragic events that took place in the reign of King James the Sixth, namely, the assassination of James third Earl of Murray by George sixth Earl of Huntly, though the circumstances are not mentioned in the deed. A feud existed between Huntly and that nobleman ; and previous to the date of this bond Huntly, to strengthen himself, had secured by bonds the assistance of

[1] The Miscellany of the Spalding Club, vol. iv. p. 247, referring to the Original at Gordon Castle.

powerful parties. For example, at Forres, on the 22d of November 1591, the barons of Murray entered into a bond with him, by which they bound themselves to fortify and assist him in all his quarrels, the King's Majesty's own person only excepted, "and speciallie in this querrell and deidlie feid, had and borne be his Lordschips aganis the Erll of Murraye, certane his confiderattis, and witheris within Murraye, etc."[1]

In prosecution of this "deadly feud," Huntly, with a considerable party, during the night of the 8th of February 1591-2, beset the Earl of Murray in his castle of Donibristle, in the parish of Dalgetty, on the banks of the Forth, and, setting the castle on fire, forced the Earl of Murray to come forth, who, being recognised by some sparks of fire on his head-piece, was cruelly murdered.[2] This tragedy created great excitement throughout the kingdom, and the popular belief was that King James was accessory to the crime. The King, it was surmised, hated the Earl of Murray, partly from his relation to the late Regent Murray, whose eldest daughter and co-heiress, Lady Elizabeth Stewart, he had married, partly from suspicions that he was a favourer of Bothwell, and more particularly from his jealousy of Murray, who, from his uncommon personal attractions, on account of which he obtained the popular name of the "Bonnie Earl of Murray," is said to have been a great favourite with Queen Anne. Various circumstances connected with this assassination are told by Robert Bowes, ambassador of Queen Elizabeth at the Court of Scotland, in a letter to Lord Burghley, dated Barnes, 17th February 1591-2. "By sundry letters," says Bowes, "received this day from divers of my friends in Scotland, I am advertised that the estate there is greatly changed and suddenly fallen into danger of hasty troubles, to arise as well to the peril of the King as also to the breach of the common quietness. For where this late and odious murder of Murray hath been laid to the charge only of Huntly and his complices, now some would gather and allege many circumstances (with what mind and truth I know not) that the King and the Lord Chancellor[3] should be blemished with the grant of the blank commission (by colour whereof Huntly attempted this fact,) and with

[1] The Miscellany of the Spalding Club, vol. iv. p. 247, referring to the Original at Gordon Castle.

[2] Calderwood's History, vol. v. p. 144.

[3] Chancellor Maitland, who, like King James, is said to have hated Murray because he was related to the Regent Murray, and was suspected to be a favourer of Bothwell.

privity and assent to the execution :   Wherein, albeit the King at first had so well persuaded many noblemen, the friends of Murray, and the ministry, of his own innocency and honourable part in the behalfs mentioned, as the hearers were satisfied, and the ministers published the same in their sermons, to the great comfort of the people, with promise given to them by the King, resolved to confirm his mind and actions herein by the expedition of the due punishment which he should lay on Huntly and all others found guilty of this outrage. . . . The picture of Murray's naked body and wounds are drawn, and intended to be showed at the Cross in Edinburgh. But the King liked not to look upon his corpse, which is thought shall be buried in St. Giles's Church, notwithstanding that the King hitherto is not pleased therewith.   When Murray found himself void of all hope of life, he committed his children and the revenge of his death to the Lord Ochiltree, praying his sister, then with him, and now saved, to make the same known to Ochiltree, who prepareth either to receive the like end to be given him by Huntly, or his means, or else that he shall yield the like reward to some of them.   In like manner, the mother of Murray, taking with her own hand three bullets out of her son's dead body, hath delivered them to the keeping of several and especial friends, who solemnly vowed to bestow the same bullets and others in the bodies of some principal executioners of this slaughter, for the taking of which revenge it appeareth that many of good quality will hazard themselves and lives, however their enterprise therein shall be afterwards punished." [1]

It was under these circumstances, when Huntly, from the bloody deed he had perpetrated, was exposed to the utmost peril from the powerful combinations which were likely to be formed for avenging the death of the Earl of Murray, and when he so greatly needed the assistance of his friends, that Sir Humphrey Colquhoun entered into the above bond for his assistance.

Besides suffering from the clan of the Macfarlanes, Sir Humphrey suffered much from the still more notable clan of the Macgregors.   To strengthen their hands both for attack and defence, that clan entered into bonds and alliances with various kindred families.   One of these bonds

[1] State Papers—Scotland, Elizabeth, MSS. in State Paper Office, London, vol. xlviii. No. 17.

was concluded 6th June 1571, between James Macgregor of that ilk and Lauchlan Mackinnon of Strathardill, and it narrates that these contracting parties were lawfully descended from " twa breather of auld descent." [1]   The Macgregors also made peace with their old enemies, the powerful Campbells of Argyll, enjoyed their protection, and were in close alliance with them. On the 24th of August 1573, Archibald fifth Earl of Argyll, Justice and Chancellor of Scotland, granted a protection, or bond of maintenance, to Duncan, Patrick, and Dowgall Macgregor, and others of their clan, to defend them in all their just and lawful matters against all men, the authority of Scotland excepted.[2]   Another bond was concluded between Alexander Macgregor of Glenstray and Awlay Macaulay of Ardincaple, on the 27th May 1591, when each of them, understanding themselves and their name to be MacAlpins of old, whereof they were all come, took burden upon himself, for his surname and friends, to fortify, maintain, and assist the other against whatsoever person or persons, his Majesty only excepted.[3]

From these connexions and alliances of the clan Gregor, it is easy to see how they might be brought into collision with the Colquhouns, and how the growing hatred between them might ripen into a standing feud. The Colquhouns were at enmity with the Earls of Argyll, as well as with the clan Gregor ; and it was the uniform policy of the Earls of Argyll to have the Macgregors always about them in such force as to enable them at will to annoy their neighbours, and to take summary vengeance on their personal enemies.   If Archibald fifth Earl of Argyll, the Chancellor, had any grudge against the Colquhouns, the Macgregors, having received the protection above mentioned, were at his service for giving effect to that antipathy.   That the Colquhouns and the Macgregors were in a manner constituted enemies to each other from the position in which the Macgregors were placed by these bonds and alliances, is confirmed by actual fact ; for in the very next year after the bond made between Macaulay of Ardincaple and the Macgregors, the latter, strengthened by the Macfarlanes, came into collision with the Colquhouns.   In July 1592, a body of the Macfarlanes and Macgregors, descending from the mountains, committed

[1] Douglas's Baronage, p. 497.                    [3] Copy Bond at Rossdhu.
[2] Original Bond at Rossdhu.

extensive depredations upon the fertile fields of Luss, which were now ripening for the harvest. To repel the aggressors, Sir Humphrey collected together a number of his vassals, and was joined by several neighbouring landed proprietors. The hostile parties met, and a sanguinary conflict, which lasted till nightfall, ensued. Sir Humphrey's assailants were more than a match for him, and he was forced to retreat. He betook himself to his castle of Bannachra, a stronghold which had been erected by the Colquhouns at the foot of the north side of the hill of Bennibuie, at the south end of the parish of Luss. But here the knight did not find the shelter he expected. A party of the Macfarlanes and Macgregors pursued him and laid siege to his castle. One of the servants who attended the knight was of the same surname as himself. He had been tampered with by the assailants of his master, and he treacherously made him their victim. The servant, while conducting his master to his room, up a winding stair of the castle, made him, by preconcert, a mark for the arrows of the clan who pursued him, by throwing the glare of a paper torch upon his person, when opposite a loophole. This afforded a ready aim to the besiegers, whose best bowmen watched for the opportunity. A winged arrow darted from its string with a steady aim, pierced the unhappy knight to the heart, and he fell dead on the spot. The fatal loophole is still pointed out, but the stair, like its unfortunate lord, has crumbled into dust.

Not content with the murder of the Lord of Bannachra, his merciless assailants also murdered three of his servants, Robert Colquhoun of Tullich-intaull, John Galloway, and Gavin Maclellan. And so little regard did these savage freebooters pay to the laws of chivalry that they brutally violated the person of Jean Colquhoun, the fair and helpless daughter of Sir Humphrey.

Having wreaked their vengeance on the inmates of the Castle of Bannachra, the assailants next set fire to the castle itself.

To the fatal battle of Bannachra Sir Walter Scott refers, in the Lady of the Lake, in the lines—

> " Proudly our pibroch has thrilled in Glen Fruin,
> And Banachra's groans to our slogan replied."

The main facts of this tragic scene are proved by two entries in the Records of the Privy Council, several years after the events. On 31st December

1608, Parlane Macwalter of Auchenvenell became surety for Dougall
Maccoull Macfarlane, sometime in Drunfad and now in Tullichintaull,
that he should compear on the third day of the next justice air of the
sheriffdom of Dumbarton, to underlie the law for the alleged crimes following; namely, for the alleged coming to the place of Bannachra, pertaining
to the deceased Sir Humphrey Colquhoun of Luss, in the month of July
1592, besieging of the said house of Bannachra, and raising of fire and
burning thereof, and for the slaughter of Sir Humphrey Colquhoun, and
ravishing of Jean Colquhoun, his eldest daughter.[1]

The other entry in the Records of the Privy Council, on 13th January
1614, shows that John Earl of Mar became surety for John Macfarlane
now of Arrochar, that he should compear and answer for the same crimes
as those specified in the preceding entry.[2]

A contract which was entered into between Alexander Colquhoun of
Luss and Malcolm Macfarlane, in 1603, also shows that the Macfarlanes
were accused of being art and part in the murder of Sir Humphrey
Colquhoun and his three servants, before mentioned.[3]

Traditions regarding these lawless proceedings still linger in the district
around the ruins of Bannachra. The memory of the traitor servant is still
held in odium, and his descendants are known to this day as the " Traitor
Colquhouns." Although the life of the chief of the Colquhouns was sacri-
ficed by the treachery of a servant, the descendants of that servant were
not banished from the barony of Luss, but, on the contrary, they have been
kindly treated and assisted by the Luss family. One of them, who was a
sergeant or corporal, and who lived at Dumfin, near Bannachra, had been
in the army, in the same regiment with the late Sir James Colquhoun of
Luss, who raised a company in Luss parish, and in that way got his commission. The old Corporal Colquhoun never liked any allusion to his
being one of the " Traitor Colquhouns."

There was another of that family, John Colquhoun, shoemaker at Muir-
land, about two miles from Rossdhu, who was nicknamed the Deacon of
the Shoemakers. This Deacon Colquhoun was well known, in three or
four of the surrounding parishes, as the lineal male descendant of the

---

[1] Records of the Privy Council.     [2] Ibid.     [3] Contemporary copy Contract at Rossdhu.

servant who betrayed his master at Bannachra, and probably derived his name John from his progenitor the traitor.

The Deacon and a neighbour, named Robert Machutcheon, at Dumfin, near Bannachra, had a quarrel when returning together from a collection of rents by the proprietor of the barony. From strong language, in the course of which the Deacon was called the traitor, they proceeded to heavy blows. One of the Deacon's legs was broken by a blow from Machutcheon, and he fell prostrate on the highroad. Unable to fight longer, the vanquished Deacon shouted defiant language to his victor as long as he was in sight. Although the fracture of his neighbour's limb was confessedly a very cruel deed, the old highlander who committed it related the circumstances with a peculiar satisfaction, and showed the greatest delight at having lamed his neighbour, the traitor Colquhoun, for life.

> "He talked of former victories,
> And former days he told." [1]

The circumstances attending the tragical death of Sir Humphrey Colquhoun, show that he and his adherents were overpowered by the combined forces of the Macfarlanes and Macgregors. While it is plain how Sir Humphrey was assassinated, it is unknown by whose hand the deadly arrow was actually shot. A contemporary chronicler has noted in a diary of events that happened in his time, which he recorded just as they occurred, that on "November 30 [1592,] Johnne Cachoune ves beheidit at the Crosse of Edinburghe for murthering of his auen brother, the Lairde of Lusse." [2] The painful charge against John Colquhoun, of imbruing his hand in his brother's blood, rests on the authority of Birrell alone. [3] The family papers afford no evidence of it. The retour of the service of Alexander Colquhoun, the younger brother of John, as heir to him in several annual-rents from the dominical lands of Bullull Lindsay and others, in the

---

[1] This was in 1861 and 1863. In the latter year he was in his 89th year. He was then very clear and distinct in his memory, and retained great bodily vigour. He died in 1864, aged 90 years.

[2] Diary of Robert Birrell, Burgess of Edinburgh, p. 29.

[3] The statement is repeated by Sir James Balfour in his Annals (vol. i. p. 392) ; but he obviously copies Birrell. Sir James lived too long after the event to be able to rank as a contemporary writer.

county of Dumbarton, which was expede on 11th February 1607, and which states that John died in December 1592,[1] seems to corroborate so far the statement of Birrell as to the time of the death of John, the slight discrepancy as to the month being unimportant. But then there is no documentary evidence among the family muniments that John was implicated in the death of his brother, and there is no tradition whatever on the subject. It is possible that the statement of Birrell is inaccurate to this extent, that he should have recorded that the John Colquhoun who was executed was the servant, instead of the brother, of the Laird of Luss, the brother having died in the following month, as we know that a servant of the name of Colquhoun was accessory to the murder; and it is certainly very improbable that, in a fierce feud between the family of Colquhoun and the Macfarlanes, the next brother of the chief of the Colquhouns would voluntarily take part with the enemies of his house against his own brother and chief, and actually shoot him dead with his own hand.

In the conflict which led to the death of Sir Humphrey, the Colquhouns were overpowered, and were entirely at the mercy of the victors. As they bribed the servant of the vanquished to accomplish the death of the chief, and also assaulted his innocent daughter, and burned the castle, it is also probable that they may have captured John Colquhoun the brother, and forced him to assist in the murder of his brother Sir Humphrey, in such a manner as to make him responsible for that crime, and save themselves, as there is no trace that any Macfarlane or Macgregor suffered at the same time with John Colquhoun.

Sir Humphrey, when he met with this tragical death, was only about twenty-seven years of age.

About a month after the assassination of Sir Humphrey Colquhoun, King James the Sixth granted to Walter Commendator of Blantyre the ward and nonentry duties of the lands and baronies which had belonged to Sir Humphrey. The grant is in these terms : —

JAMES, be the grace of God King of Scottis, to all and sindrie oure liegis and subdittis quhome it efferis, quhais knawlege thir oure lettres salcum, greting : Wit ze ws to haue gevin and grantit, and be thir our lettres gevis and grantis

_____
[1] Extract Retour at Rossdhu.

to our trustie and weilbelouit counsallour, Walter Commendatar of Blantyre,
Lord of our Privie Seill, his airis and assignais, ane or maa, the waird, nonentres,
maillis, fermes, proffitis, and dewiteis of all landis, baroneis, castellis, touris,
fortaliceis, manerplaces, mylnis, multouris, wodis, fischeingis, aduocatioun, doua-
tioun, and richt of patronage of kirkis, beneficis, and chaplanreis, annexis,
connexis, pairtis, pendiclis, tenuentis, tennandreis, seruice of fre tennentis of the
samin, and all thair pertinentis, alsweill propertie as tennandrie, quhairevir the
samin ly, or be within this our realme, quhilkis pertenit of befoir to vmquhil Sir
Vmphra Colquhoun of Luis, Knycht, or ony vtheris his predicessouris, last lauchfull immediat tennentis to ws or our predicessouris of the samin, off all zeiris
and termes bygane, that the samin lies bene in waird or nonentres sen the deceis
of the said vmquhile Sir Vmphra, or ony vtheris his predicessouris or successouris,
last lauchfull immediat teunentis, to ws or our predicessouris of the samin
lauchfullie enterit thairto, or throu reductioun of quhatsumevir retour or retouris,
infeftmentis, sessingis, or vther euidentis of the landis and vtheris foirsaidis
grantit to the said vmquhile Sir Vmphra, or ony vtheris his predicessouris of
the samin, or ony vtherwyis, and sielyke of all zeiris and termes to cum, during
the tyme of the said waird and nonentres, and ay and quhill the lauchfull entrie
of the richteous air or airis thairto being of lauchfull aige, togidder with the
releif thairof quhen it salhappin :   And als the mariage of the bairne, posthume
air maill or famell gottin betuix the said vmquhile Sir Vmphra and Deam Jeane
Hammiltoun his spous, and failzeing of that bairnie, air or airis maill or famell be
deceis vnmareit, or ony vtherwyis, the mariage of ony vther air or airis maill or
famell that salhappin to succeid to the said vmquhile Sir Vmphra in his landis
and heretage, with all proffittis of the said mariage :   To be haldin and to be had
the waird, nonentres, releif, and mariage abonespecifeit, and proffittis thairof,
during the space foirsaid, to our said trustie and weilbelouit counsallour, his
airis and assignais, ane or maa, with all and sindrie commoditeis, fredomes,
proffittis, and richteons pertinentis quhatsumevir pertenying, or that richteouslie
may pertene thairto, with power to the said Walter, his airis and assignais foirsaidis, to intromet with and tak vp the maillis, fermes, proffittis, and dewiteis
of the saidis landis, baroneis, and vtheris particularlie abonementionat, in quhais
handis or quhairevir the samin can be apprehendit of all zeiris and termes, baith
bygane and to cum foirsaidis, during the tyme of the said waird and nonentres,
and ay and quhill the lauchfull entrie of the richteous air or airis thairto being
of lauchfull aige, and thairvpoun, togidder with the releif thairof, quhen it salhappin, and als vpoun the said mariage and proffittis thairof, to dispone at thair
plesour, and gif neid beis, to call and persew thairfore as accordis of the law,
and to occupie the saidis landis and vtheris foirsaidis, with thair awin proper

X

guidis, or set the samin to tennentis as thai sall think expedient during the space foirsaid, with court plent, herezeld, bluidwite and mercheit, vnlawis, amerchiamentis, and escheitis of the saidis courtis, and with all commoditeis and fredomes, frelie, quietlie, weill, and in peace, but ony reuocatioun or aganecalling quhatsumevir : Quhairfore we charge straitlie and commandis zow all and sindrie our liegis and subditis forsaidis, that nane of zow tak vpoun hand to mak ony lat, stop, or disturblance to our said trustie and weilbelouit counsallour, his airis and assignais, in the peceabill brouking, joysing, vptaking, intrometting with, and disponyng vpoun the waird, nonentres, releif, and mariage abonespecifeit, and proffittis thairof, during the space foirsaid, efter the forme and tennour of thir our lettres, vnder all hieast pane, and charge that efter may follow. Gevin vnder oure Privie Seill, at Edinburgh, the ellevint day of August, the zeir of God j⁰ vᶜ fourescoir twelf zeiris, and of our rigime the twentie sex zeir.

Per signaturam manu S. D. N. Regis subscriptam.

Litera Walteri commendatarii de Blantyre, etc.[1]

A few days after, namely, on the 15th of August, Walter Commendator of Blantyre, for certain causes and considerations, disponed to Robert Chirnside of Over Possill and his heirs, the relief of the above-mentioned lands and baronies, with power to uptake it from the nearest and lawful heir of the deceased Sir Humphrey, when he should happen to be infefted in these lands and baronies.[2]

On the 18th of September 1592, a gift was made by King James the Sixth to Robert Chirnside of Over Possill, of the escheat of the goods, moveable and immoveable, debts, tacks, steadings, rooms, possessions, corns, cattle, inside plenishing, sums of money, jewels, gold, silver, and other goods and gear whatsoever which belonged to the deceased Sir Humphrey Colquhoun of Luss, Knight, and then belonging to his Majesty, into whose hands they had fallen by reason of escheat, in consequence of Sir Humphrey's having been denounced his Majesty's rebel, and put to the horn for non-payment of his part of the sum of 20,000 merks, the rest of the sum of £40,000 granted by the barons of this realm for their voices in Parliament and general councils, and for his non-compearance before the Lord Justice to answer for the slaughter of William Brisbane of Barnishill.[3]

---

[1] Original Royal Gift at Rossdhu.     [3] Original Royal Gift at Rossdhu.

[2] Original Assignation, ibid.

Dame Jean Hamilton, Lady Colquhoun, survived her husband many
years, and married, secondly, Sir John Campbell of Ardkinglas, whom she
also survived. On the 10th, 12th, and 16th of December 1612, she, with
consent of Sir John Campbell of Ardkinglas, knight, her second husband,
for certain sums of money paid to her and him, and for other considerations,
renounced and overgave the place of Dunglas, with the yards and orchards
thereof, and her terce of the lands and barony of Luss, in liferent, in favour
of Alexander Colquhoun of Luss.[1] On 22d December 1615, as relict of
Sir John Campbell of Ardkinglas, she, with the special advice of her
brother, Sir John Hamilton of Lettrik, knight, granted to Sir Alexander
Colquhoun of Luss, her first husband's brother, for a certain sum of money,
an assignation to 80 bolls of oats and 10 firlots of beir, steilbow, which
were upon the said Alexander's lands of Finlass, Middle Ross, within Ross
and Dumfin, in the barony of Rossdhu. Her signing her name is thus
described :—" The said dame Jeane Hammiltoune, led at the pen by the
tuay notars vndirwritin, at my comand, becaus I can nocht wreit my self."[2]
Her name appears as creditor for the crop of Milton of Colquhoun to
Catharine Lang, in the year 1618.

Dame Jean Hamilton, Lady Luss, relict of Sir John Campbell of Ardkinglas, knight, granted a discharge, dated at Dumbarton, 26th July 1625,
to William Stirling of Auchyle, in name and behalf of Archibald Earl of
Argyll, for £1000 Scots, for the maills and duties of the £10 lands of Mekile
Ross, Little Ross, and Portkile, and others, in the " Ile of Rosnaith and shire
of Dumbarton, for the Whitsunday and Martinmas terms of 1624, due to
her in virtue of a contract, dated 23d and 24th June and July 1610.[3]

Of the marriage of Sir Humphrey Colquhoun and Dame Jean Hamilton
there were three surviving daughters, but no sons.

1. Jean, who died in early life. Her uncle, Alexander Colquhoun,
was retoured nearest agnate to her on the father's side, 17th January
1592-3,[4] in order to qualify him to undertake the management of her
affairs. It would seem that she died not long after this ; and her

[1] Original Renunciation at Rossdhu.

[2] Original Assignation, *ibid.*

[3] Original Discharge in Argyll Charter-
Chest.

[4] Copy Retour at Rossdhu.

death, it is probable, was caused by the brutal treatment to which
she had been subjected at the death of her father and the burning
of the castle of Bannachra. Her name does not again appear in any
of the family writs subsequent to the date of that retour.

    2. Margaret Colquhoun.       3. Aunas Colquhoun.

Margaret and Annas Colquhoun were each served heir to their
father, Sir Humphrey, 30th July 1596, in three annual rents, one of
five merks Scots, from a tenement of land within the burgh of
Stirling, another of 6s. 8d., from a tenement in the same burgh, and a
third, of 13s. 4d., from a croft, with houses and stables built thereon.
In the retour it is said that Margaret and Annas were two of three of
the nearest heirs of their father, that they were of lawful age, and that
the said annual rents were then in the hands of the King, by reason
of the decease of their father, and had been so for the space of four
years past or thereby.[1]

Letters of summons, dated Edinburgh, 11th August 1599, were
issued, under the Royal Signet, against Margaret and Annas Colquhoun, commanding them to enter themselves heirs to the deceased
John Roy Colquhoun, their father's brother. These letters were
raised against them at the instance of Sir James Edmonstone of Duntreath, to whom the parties whom their uncle John had despoiled,
in October 1590, of a number of horses, cows, and sheep,[2] had made
an assignation, dated 29th September 1592, of the goods and gear
which had been thus taken from them. The object of Sir James
Edmonstone was to compel Margaret and Annas Colquhoun to enter
themselves heirs to their uncle, that he might pursue them for the
foresaid goods and gear, with the profits thereof. But the action
proceeded slowly. It was not till the 8th and 20th of February
1604 that the summons was executed by a messenger-at-arms.
From the execution it appears that Margaret was then residing in
Glasgow, and Annas in her mother's dwelling-house in Edinburgh.[3]

Annas and her sister Margaret were retoured co-heirs to their

---

[1] Extract of two Retours at Rossdhu.      [3] Original Summons at Rossdhu.
[2] *Vide supra*, p. 138.

father, and also to their ancestor, the Chamberlain ; but the estates,
being a male fee, devolved upon their uncle, Alexander Colquhoun, to
whom they renounced all their rights as heirs of line of their father,
in consideration of the sum of 5000 merks paid by him to each
of them.

In a renunciation subscribed at Edinburgh, Priestfield, Ardkinglas,
and Lanark, 4th, 6th, and 10th February and March 1609, Annas,
with the advice and consent of Sir Robert Hamilton of Siller-
tounhill, Knight, Thomas Hamilton of Priestfield, and Mr. James
Edmonstoun, Commissar of Lanark, her curators, renounced all
right and claim to be heir of line to her father, and specially renounced all lands, heritages, etc., that might fall to her as one of
his heirs of line, that Alexander Colquhoun of Luss, brother and
heir-male to her deceased father, might succeed thereto, and be
infefted therein.  In the renunciation, Annas is designed " youngest
of the lawful bairns and daughters of the deceased Sir Humphrey
Colquhoun of Luss." [1]

Alexander Colquhoun of Luss, by a bond dated 2d March 1609,
bound himself to pay to Annas Colquhoun and her heirs 5000
merks at the term of Whitsunday following.  But Annas, with the
advice and consent of her curators, on 23d May 1609, continued
the payment of that sum till the term of Martinmas, in respect that
her uncle Alexander had paid to her the annual interest thereof. [2]

Annas married, in 1610, Colin Campbell, younger of Carrick, son
and heir-apparent of Duncan Campbell of Carrick, in Roseneath.
On the 25th, 26th, and 27th of October 1610, she was, on a precept of sasine by Duncan Campbell of Carrick, infefted in the five-
merk lands of Kilbride, in the parish of Kilmodan, barony of
Glendarowall, and shire of Argyle, and in many others.  In the
instrument of sasine, she is designated " daughter of the late Sir
Humphrey Colquhoun of Luss," and Colin Campbell, eldest lawful
son of the said Duncan, is designated " her future spouse." [3]

---

[1] Original Renunciation at Rossdhu.          [3] Dumbarton Sasine Records, fol. 10.
[2] Original Obligation, ibid.

Annas' uncle, Alexander Colquhoun, paid to Annas, before 4th December 1615, the half of 10,000 merks provided to her in the contract of marriage betwixt her father and her mother. On that date, Colin Campbell, fear of Carrick, her husband, granted a discharge to her uncle Alexander for that sum, with the profit thereof. In the discharge he acknowledges that Alexander had done to him and his said spouse " many and divers other gratitudes, pleasures, and good deeds." He also bound himself to procure Annas' infeft- ment in all the unentailed lands, annual-rents, and feu-duties in which the late Sir Humphrey, her father, the late John Colquhoun, her father's brother, the late James Colquhoun of Garscube, her grandfather's brother, the late Sir John Colquhoun of Luss, her grandfather, and the late Sir John Colquhoun of Luss, her great great-grandfather had been vested ; and after her said infeftment, to move her to infeft her uncle Alexander in all the unentailed lands, annual-rents, and feu-duties in which her said relatives died invested. These properties are then enumerated. [Original Dis- charge and Obligation at Rossdhu.]

The following is a facsimile signature of Sir Humphrey Colquhoun in 1583, from the Boyd Writs :—

## XIV.—2. ALEXANDER COLQUHOUN,

Fifteenth of Colquhoun and Seventeenth of Luss, 1592-1617.

HELEN BUCHANAN, his wife—1595.

ALEXANDER COLQUHOUN succeeded his brother Sir Humphrey in the family estates in 1592. On 17th January 1592-3 he was served heir to him in the lands and barony of Luss, the castle, tower, and fortalice of Rossdhu, the islands of Lochlomond, Inchelonoche [Inchlonaig], Inchelonoquhan, and Inchefreithillane, called the island of Rossdhu, mills, woods, and fishings in Lochlomond, advocation of the rectory of the parish church of Luss, and of all other churches and chapels of the said lands, the lands and barony of Colquhoun, with the manor of Dunglas, mills, and fishings in the water of Clyde, the lands of Gartscube, in the shire of Dumbarton, the lands of Sauchie, the lands of Colquhoun Glen, in the shire of Stirling, the mill and mill lands of Sauline, in the shire of Fife, all which are united and incorporated into one entire and free barony, called the barony of Luss. The retour records that Sir Humphrey died in the month of July by-past.[1] A precept was granted by King James the Sixth, on the 3d of February 1594-5, for infefting Alexander as heir of his brother Sir Humphrey in these lands.[2]

The ward, non-entries, etc., of the lands and lordship of Luss, as we have seen before, had, by King James the Sixth, into whose hands they had fallen, by the decease of Sir Humphrey, been gifted to Walter Commendator of Blantyre, Lord of the Privy Seal. But Alexander Colquhoun purchased them for the sum of 5000 merks. An assignation of them was made to him by the Commendator, on 25th January 1592-3, for that sum;[3] and, on payment of the money, a discharge, on 13th November following, was granted to him, and Sir James Edmonstoun of Duntreath, knight, Aulay Macaulay of Ardincaple, and Walter Colquhoun of Kilmardinny, his cautioners.[4]

On the death of his brother, Sir Humphrey, the right and duty of

[1] Original Retour at Rossdhu.
[2] Original Precept of Sasine, ibid.
[3] Extract Registered Assignation at Rossdhu.
[4] Original Discharge, ibid.

acting as tutor to his three daughters naturally devolved on Alexander, who appears to have treated them with kindness and consideration.

He was retoured, 17th January 1592, as nearest agnate on the father's side, to Jean Colquhoun, lawful daughter to his deceased brother, Sir Humphrey, by Jean Hamilton, his spouse. The retour states that he is of lawful age, by virtue of a royal dispensation, granted on account of his minority; that he is provident of his own affairs, and able properly to attend to the administration of the affairs of another, and to the goods of Jean Colquhoun, his niece; that he is not immediately successive to her, should she happen to die, since she has two other lawful sisters surviving; and that he is her lawful tutor.[1]  On 25th December 1593, Alexander Colquhoun was constituted, by King James the Sixth, tutor to Margaret and Agnes[2] Colquhoun, lawful daughters of the deceased Sir Humphrey Colquhoun of Luss, knight, by Dame Jean Hamilton, his spouse, and administrator of their lands, heritages, etc., until they were of lawful age.[3]

In November 1594, Alexander Colquhoun granted a charter of sale to Thomas Lord Boyd of his lands of Chapelton, with the mill and mill lands of Colquhoun, under reversion, on payment of 1000 merks.[4]

Along with the landed estates of his brother Sir Humphrey there descended to Alexander, as an inheritance, the unhappy feuds that had long existed between the house of Colquhoun and several other neighbouring clans.  Among others with whom the Colquhouns were at feud were the Buchanans of that ilk and the Galbraiths of Culcreuch.

Robert Galbraith of Culcreuch, by the special counsel of George Buchanan of that ilk, had obtained, in 1593, a commission of justiciary for pursuing the clan Gregor, their resetters and assisters, with fire and sword, with power to convene the lieges for assisting him in its execution. Alexander Colquhoun, and his neighbour Aulay Macaulay of Ardincaple, with whom he was on a friendly footing, had, however, reason to believe that Galbraith had procured that commission, not with an intention to attempt

[1] Extract Retour at Rossdhu.

[2] In the family writs this daughter is sometimes designated Agnes, sometimes Annas. She subscribes Annas, which is an old form of Agnes.

[3] Original Gift of Tutory at Rossdhu.

[4] Original Letter of Reversion by Thomas Lord Boyd to Alexander Colquhoun of Luss, ibid.

anything against the clan Gregor, but under colour thereof to extend his malice against them, their kin and friends, with all extremity, and, under pretext of searching for that clan, to besiege and burn their houses. They, therefore, brought a complaint against Galbraith to that effect before the Privy Council, on the 3d of May 1593. They complained that Galbraith had already given sufficient proof that such was his object, by convening the Buchanans, for the most part armed, (with whom the said Aulay Macaulay stood under deadly feud,) by whose help he proceeded in all his actions. The complainers were not less willing than he was to pursue the clan Gregor with their whole force, yet they dared not rise and accompany him for that purpose, from fear of their lives. The deadly feud betwixt Alexander Colquhoun of Luss and him, by reason of the slaughter of the deceased Donald Macneill Macfarlane, household servant to Robert Galbraith of Culcreuch, committed by the said Alexander's late brother, still stood betwixt their houses unreconciled, and the Laird of Culcreuch was daily waiting for opportunities to revenge that slaughter. The feud betwixt the Laird of Ardincaple and the Buchanans had been lately renewed, and a bitter grudge and hatred existed between the Laird of Ardincaple and the Laird of Culcreuch, who having bereft his own mother, whom the Laird of Ardincaple had married, of her whole living, and having been compelled by law to make restitution to Ardincaple, vowed vengeance against him on that account. The King, with advice of the Lords of his Secret Council, therefore exempted Alexander Colquhoun of Luss and Aulay Macaulay, their kin and friends, etc., from rising, convening, or assisting the Laird of Culcreuch in putting the commission referred to in execution, and decerned that, in so far as it extended to the searching for the clan Gregor within their houses, it was suspended and discharged *simpliciter* in time coming.[1]

On the 8th of May 1593, Alexander Colquhoun bound himself, and all for whom he was answerable, in terms of the general bond (1587), not to reset any of the surname of Buchanan, Macgregor, and Macfarlane, under pain of £2000 Scots.[2]

[1] Records of Privy Council, quoted in Pitcairn's Criminal Trials, vol. i. pp. 289, 290.
[2] Records of Privy Council.

After the tragical death of Sir Humphrey Colquhoun, the Macfarlanes relentlessly continued to commit their depredations on the lands of Luss. A list of these depredations during the years 1590-1592 inclusive has already been given;[1] and here the list may be continued for the years 1593 and 1594, with the prices; all as reclaimed by the Laird of Luss, in his summons in the year 1603 against the Macfarlanes.

| 1593. | Price. | | | 1594. | Price. | | |
|---|---|---|---|---|---|---|---|
| One horse, | £20 | 0 | 0 | Four horse, | £96 | 13 | 4 |
| One staig, | 10 | 0 | 0 | One staig, | 6 | 13 | 4 |
| Three mares, | 36 | 13 | 4 | Twenty mares, | 197 | 13 | 4 |
| Four ky, | 46 | 0 | 0 | Thirty-seven ky, | 385 | 0 | 0 |
| Four oxen, | 56 | 0 | 0 | Ten oxen, | 132 | 0 | 0 |
| Eight sheep, | 12 | 0 | 0 | Fourteen sheep, | 21 | 0 | 0 |

Sum of both columns,   £1019  13   4

The same summons contains a statement of the profits of the horses, mares, staigs, cows, oxen, and sheep which had been stolen from 1590 to 1594, estimated from the time they were stolen to the time of the summons. The profit and the prices together, during the whole period, are calculated to amount to £155,501, 8s.

The disturbances caused by these clan contentions in the Highlands were a source of great uneasiness and anxiety to King James the Sixth and his Government. For the preservation of the peace, his Majesty and the Lords of the Privy Council issued letters to the sheriffs of those parts, requiring them to command the principal men within their jurisdiction to find sufficient sureties, to be registered in the Books of the Privy Council, that they themselves, and all for whom they were answerable by the laws of the realm, Acts of Parliament, and general band, should observe the peace and good rule in the country, and that they should satisfy and redress parties skaithed by themselves, or by those for whom they were answerable, under pecuniary pains, varying according to the rank and wealth of the parties.[2]

[1] Vide p. 152.
[2] These facts are stated in Extract Let-   ters of Horning against a great number of per-   sons, dated 27th December 1595, at Rossdhu.

In a paper without date, to Ludovick Duke of Lennox, containing offers made and given in by John Macfarlane, fiar of Arrochar, and Malcolm Macfarlane, fiar of Gartavartane, with special consent of Andrew Macfarlane of Arrochar and Andrew Dow Macfarlane of Gartavartane, their fathers, for themselves and their kin, friends, and surname, for whom they were answerable, they offer, first, to satisfy all parties skaithed by any of their deeds in time past, his Lordship assigning to them a reasonable day for that purpose; and, secondly, to find sufficient landed noblemen as cautioners and sureties for them in regard to the time to come, that they should compear before his Lordship, at his command, on a reasonable day, to answer for themselves and their friends foresaid, and to make satisfaction for any skaith that they might hereafter commit, and to deliver up the perpetrators, or else to banish them out of the bounds of Arrochar, and to give them no assistance, supply or entertainment, either directly or indirectly. The closing paragraph, however, leaves unsettled the feud that still existed between the Macfarlanes and the Colquhouns of Luss :—" Last, vnder protestatioun that thir offeris steck nocht aganes thame for ony particuler standing or committit in tymes bigane betuix thame and the house of Lus, in respect of the deidlie feid standing betuix thame vnrecoinseillit quhill the samyn be tane away, anent the quhilk thay offer all that thai may do onywyis thairanent, thair lywes and landis being exceptit, prayiug his Lordship to tak sum gude ordour thairwith."[1]

But the factious and turbulent spirit of these predatory banditti was not easily subdued. A more vigorous administration than that of James the Sixth would have found it no easy task to cope with the difficulties of such an enterprise. Disturbances of the peace were constantly occurring, defying and defeating the efforts of the civil magistrate to maintain order and tranquillity. The actions brought against those who had become sureties for some of the more unruly spirits of the clans, serve with other things to show the little success which attended the feeble endeavours of the Government to put an end to the confusions and disorders that prevailed in the Highlands.

On 13th September 1593, Robert Erskine of Sauchie had become

[1] Original Proposals in Montrose Charter-chest.

surety that Andrew Macfarlane of Arrochar, his men, tenants, and servants, for whom he was answerable, should satisfy parties skaithed. The Macfarlanes had, however, divers times committed reifes, stouthes, heirschippis, incursions, depredations, and oppressions upon the Laird of Luss, his men, tenants, servants, and friends. Alexander Colquhoun of Luss, therefore, obtained letters of inhibition, under the royal signet, 12th December 1593, addressed to the sheriffs of Stirling, charging them to inhibit the said Robert Erskine from selling, wadsetting, and disponing any of his lands, heritages, corns, cattle, goods or geir, and to inhibit by open proclamation at the market cross of Stirling and other places needful, the lieges from buying, receiving, or taking in wadset from the said Robert any of his lands, etc.[1]

Adam Colquhoun in Milton, in like manner, brought an action of contravention against William Cunningham, who had become cautioner for the Macfarlanes, before the Lords of Session; and on 1st March 1595 he obtained from them a decreet, decerning that the Macfarlanes had been guilty as charged by the complainer, and that William Cunningham had incurred the pains contained in the act of cautionary, and that therefore he should pay the one-half of these pains to his Majesty, and the other half to Adam Colquhoun, the party aggrieved.[2]

One of the modes of reconciling feuds in families was marriage. In or before the year 1595, the feud between the Colquhouns and Buchanans was settled, or arranged by the marriage of Alexander Colquhoun of Luss and Helen Buchanan, daughter of Sir George Buchanan of that Ilk, which took place in that year. The marriage-contract, entered into between him on the one part, and her father and herself on the other part, is dated Glasgow, 18th August 1595. By it Alexander the Laird of Luss bound himself, for divers sums of money paid to him by her father, Sir George, in the view of the marriage to be solemnized between him and her in her pure virginity, to infeft her in liferent in his five-merk dominical lands, called the Mains of Garscube, with the mill and mill lands thereof;

[1] Original Inhibition at Rossdhu.
[2] This information is contained in an Assignation by Adam Colquhoun, dated 23d September 1597, of his half of the foresaid pains, to Alexander Master of Elphinstoun. Original Assignation at Rossdhu.

his 40s. lands called Mylntoun of Garscube; his one-merk lands of Knap-poche, with a rent of 40 stones of cheese and four presents annually, to be raised from his lands of Glenmakerne ; his two-merk lands of Garcastoun, Long Inche and Green Inche ; and his 40s. lands of Woltoun, in the shire of Dumbarton ; but with the proviso that four chalders of victual were to be raised and received from the said lands by Dame Jeane Hamilton, relict of the deceased Sir Humphrey Colquhoun of Luss, knight, during her lifetime. A charter was accordingly granted by Alexander Laird of Luss to Helen Buchanan, as "his future spouse," of these lands, in liferent, on 15th October 1595.[1]    On the same day, in fulfilment of the marriage-contract, he also granted to her a charter in liferent of his five-pound lands of Wal-lacetoun, in the shire of Dumbarton, of which John Earl of Montrose was the lord superior.    Among the witnesses to these two charters were Walter Colquhoun of Kilmardinny, John Colquhoun, burgess of Edinburgh, and Adam Colquhoun in Hill.[2]

Alexander Colquhoun having granted by charter to Helen Buchanan, his spouse, the lands of Wallacetoun and Ardochmoir, in the parish of Cardross and shire of Dumbarton, in liferent, John Earl of Montrose, the superior, confirmed the charter, and on 25th October 1596, he bound himself that these lands should be free from all wards and non-entries during the lifetime of the said Alexander, and Helen his spouse, respec-tively.[3]    On 20th September 1598, Alexander, in fulfilment of the marriage-contract between him and Helen Buchanan, infefted her, *propriis manibus*, in the above-mentioned lands, Thomas Fallousdall acting as her attorney.[4]

By this auspicious marriage, a cordial union appears to have been effected between the house of Colquhoun of Luss and the house of Buchanan of that Ilk, which had previously been at feud with each other.    It had thus the happy effect of contributing in so far to secure the peace of the district, which had so often been the scene of strife, by converting one adversary into a friend.

On 23d December 1595, a charge was directed against a considerable

[1] Original Charter and Precept of Sasine at Rossdhu.

[2] Original Charter. *ibid.*

[3] Original Bond at Rossdhu.

[4] Original Instrument of Sasine, *ibid.*

number of persons under deadly feud, including nobles, knights, barons, and
others, to appear personally before the King and Council at Holyroodhouse, to underly such order as should be prescribed touching the removal
of these feuds. The name of Alexander Colquhoun of Luss was included.
He was commanded to appear on the 18th of February 1595-6. The
persons charged were to be accompanied with only a limited number of
their friends, proportioned to their rank—none of them with more than
sixty. The letters of charge concluded with certification, that if the parties
failed to appear, they should be reputed, and pursued with fire and sword,
with all rigour and extremity, as enemies to God, his Majesty, and the
common weal and quietness of their native country.[1]

The Laird of Luss was still exposed to the hostility of the sturdy clan
of the Macfarlanes, and various efforts were made to restore harmony between that clan and the Colquhouns.

In 1597 the Laird of Luss received from John Erskine, Earl of Mar, a
bond assuring him that he and his tenants would remain unmolested by the
Macfarlanes. The bond by which that Earl became surety that the Macfarlanes would keep the peace towards Alexander Colquhoun of Luss, his
friends, tenants, and dependants, is in the following terms :—

BE it kend till all men be thir presentis, we, Johnne Erill of Mar, Lord
Erskyne, for ourself, and takand the burdeing vpon ws for Andro M'Farlane of
Arroquhair, Johnne M'Farlane, his eldest sone, fear thairof, Andro M'Farlane
of Gartavirtane, Malcolme M'Farlane, his eldest sone, fear thairof, and remanent
surname of M'Farlane, our kin, freindis, men, tennentis, servandis, dependaris,
assistaris, partakaris, and all vtheris that, ore may guidlye let to haif assurit,
and, be the tennour heirof, speciallie and expreslie assuris Alexander Colquhoune
of Lus, his kin, freindis, men, tennentis, servandis, dependaris, assistaris, and partakaris, to be vnhurt, vnhairmit, vnmolestit, vntrublit, vninvadit, or in ony wayis
persewit criminallie or ciuilye, in the law, or by the law, be me or our foirsaidis, for quhatsumeuir caus, querrell, or occasioun bygane preceding the dait
heirof, vnto the ellevint day of Nouember nixt to cum, promitting to obserue,
and caus thir presentis be obseruit and kepit vnviolat in ony poynt, vnder the
pane of periurie, infamie, and tinsell of perpetuall credit, honour, and estima-
tioun, in tyme cuming. In witnes quhairof, we, for our help, and takand the

[1] Records of Privy Council, quoted in Pitcairn's Criminal Trials, vol. i. p. 352.

burdeng vpone ws, as said is, haif subscriuit thir presentis as followes, at Stirling Castell, the first day of Junij, the zeir of God j$^m$ v$^c$ fourscoir sevintene zeris, befoir thir witness, Harie Shaw, Thomas Hwme, Chairlis Panter, and Andro Buchannane, our seruitouris.

J. MAR.

A. Buchannan, witness.

Thomas Howme, witnes.[1]

On the 7th of November 1599, Alexander Colquhoun of Luss subscribed a bond, which was a sort of truce, binding himself that the Macfarlanes mentioned in the preceding bond, and their friends should remain unmolested by him and his friends to the end of that month. The bond is as follows :—

BE it kend till all men be thir present lettres, me, Alexander Colquhoun off Lus, for my selfe, and acceptand burdein vpon me for all my surname, kynd, freindes, followares, partie and partakares, be the tenor heirof, and be the fayth and truth of my body, to haif assuiret and speciallie assuires Androw M'Farlan of Arroquhair, Jhon M'Farlan, his son and appeirand air, Andro Dow M'Farlan off Gartartan, Malcum M'Farlan, his sone, the remanent of thair surname, kynd, freindes, partie and partakares to be vnhurt, vnharmet, vnpersewit, vnmolestit, and vntrublet in thair persones, landes, rentes, heritages, rowmes, stedings, takes, possessiounes, cornes, cattelle, gudes and geir, mowabill and vnmowabill quhatsumevir, derectlie or vnderectlie, vthervayes nor be onlour of law and justice vnto the last of November instant ; and heirto I bind and obleisshes me faythtfullie, vnder the pan off perjurie, defamatioun, dishonour, and tinsall of faytht, latey, and credeit forewir. In witnes quhairof this present letter of assuirance, wretten be Adam Colquhoun, I haif subscrywet with my hand as followes, at Rosdo, the sevint day of November, the zeir off God l$^m$ v$^c$ fourscoir nyntein zeires, befoir thir witnes, Wilzeam Stewart, capitan off the Castell of Dunbartan, Jhon Colquhoune, fiar of Camtostroddan, Adam Colquhoune, in Hill, and Thomas Fallesdaill, burges of Dunbartan.

William Stewart, witnes.                    ALEXANDER COLQUHOUN

Jhone Colquhoune, fiar of Camstrod-                              off Luss.

    dan, vitnes.

Thomas Fallusdaill, wittnes.[2]

For the punishing of theft, reif, and oppression committed by the various Highland clans upon each other, the Duke of Lennox was ap-

[1] Original Bond at Rossdhu.                    [2] Original in Montrose Charter-chest.

pointed by his Majesty Commissioner of Justiciary within the shire of Dumbarton, regality and dukedom of Lennox.

At Glasgow, on the 21st of November 1599, the Duke, with advice of certain of his honourable friends, gentlemen, and vassals, concluded that the chief masters and landlords after mentioned, for staunching of the said odious crimes, and punishing the committers thereof within their bounds, namely, the Lairds of Luss, Buchanan, Glengarnok, Culcreuch, Ardincaple, Colgraine, Glennegas, Merchistoun, Drumquhassall, Houstoun, younger, Duntraithe, and generally all others having broken men upon their lands and heritages within the said shire, should find sufficient cautioners and sureties to his Lordship that they, their men, tenants and servants, should be answerable to justice before his Lordship and his deputies, and give redress to parties who should be skaithed.[1]

In compliance with this order, Alexander Colquhoun of Luss found cautioners in Mungo Lindsay of Banull and Walter Colquhoun of Kilmardinny, who conjunctly and severally became bound for him on the same day under the pain of 5000 merks.[2]

The chiefs of the clan of Macfarlane declared that they were not able to find the said caution, but offered to make restitution of all bygone theft, reif, and oppression, so far as the parties that had sustained loss were able to make proof thereof. His Lordship, therefore, at the same meeting, in order to the settlement of such questions, ordained that the party who was skaithed should elect a number of honest men, not exceeding sixteen persons, dwelling within the shire of Dumbarton and regality of Lennox, or four halves about, and that the person accused of committing the crime should, out of this number, choose the one-half, as a jury by whose verdict he should either be exculpated or sentenced to refund the skaith that had been done. For refunding that loss, John Macfarlane, fiar of Arrochar, and Malcolm Dow Macfarlane of Gartavartane, as principals for themselves and their clan and surname of Macfarlane, were to find sufficient cautioners in so far as they had not been already found ; and that good order might be the better kept in future by the clan and surname of Macfarlane, it was ordained that the

---

[1] Original Order in Montrose Charter-chest.

[2] Bond of Cautionary in Montrose Charter-chest.

said John and Malcolm Macfarlane should be warded by the said noble lord until satisfaction should be made by them or their cautioners for the said bygone skaith, which should be done before the 1st of March following, and also until the said John and Malcolm found sufficient cautioners, under the pain of 5000 merks, that is to say, for the former 3000, and for the latter 2000, that they, their said clan and surname, should abstain *simpliciter* from all theft and oppression in time coming, and should refund the skaith that should happen to be committed by any of them to the persons damnified, upon its being proven. It was further ordained that the said John and Malcolm should enter the committers of the said crimes prisoners for trial by the said noble lord, or should banish them *simpliciter* from the bounds over which they had authority; and that should the principals, when they had opportunity, neglect to apprehend them before their banishment, or reset or maintain the fugitives when they re-entered within the said bounds, or suffer to pass through their bounds any other thieves, clans, or oppressors, whom it might be in their power to prevent, they should be held culpable of the said crimes.[1]

Soon after, John Macfarlane, fiar of Arrochar, and Malcolm Macfarlane, fiar of Gartavartane, compeared before Ludovic Duke of Lennox, for the purpose of giving the security required for themselves, their men, tenants and servants. Patrick Maxwell of Newark became cautioner for the former, and David Cunningham of Ibert, Walter Lekkie of Easter Poldar, William Grahame of Douchcall, became cautioners for the latter, binding themselves to present them before the Duke within the Castle of Edinburgh, upon the          day of November 1600, within the space of fifteen days after his Lordship's letters were delivered to the parties for whom they were cautioners, under the pain of 5000 merks, that the said persons might redress " ony enormities, reiffis, thiftis, or skaithis" that should be committed by them, or those for whom they were answerable.[2]

[1] Original Order in Montrose Charter-chest, *ut supra*.

[2] Original Bond in Montrose Charter-chest. The date of this bond is 1st November, which, from a comparison with the date of the preceding writ, appears to be a mistake for the 1st of December. The date of this bond, as is evident from the handwriting, was not inserted at the time when the bond was written.

z

Some of the property transactions of Alexander Colquhoun of Luss at this period may be briefly noticed.

On 28th September 1597, he sold the piece of land called the Torr, and an acre of his lands of Strone of Luss, in the barony of Luss and shire of Dumbarton, to Patrick Macturnour, in Edintagert, under reversion, and on the same day he granted him a charter thereof.[1]   On 9th November 1597, he entered into a contract with Andrew Wright, granting him in wadsett for nineteen years the house of Auldclye, and two acres of land and yard, with four "sowmes" of grass pasture, under reversion : and on 12th December following he granted him a charter of these properties.[2]   By a contract dated 12th December 1597, he granted the Isle of Inchlonaig in Lochlomond, in wadsett to Patrick Colquhoun of Inchlonaig, under reversion. But in the beginning of the next century he redeemed that Isle by paying to Patrick the redemption price, which was 500 merks, for which he received from him a discharge, dated 19th December 1600.[3]   On 4th February 1597-8, he obtained from King James the Sixth a charter of the lands of Woltoun and Auchidonanrie, in the parish of Cardross and shire of Dumbarton, which formerly belonged to Robert Campbell, son and heir of the deceased Donald Campbell of Auchinhowie, and which had been resigned by him into the hands of the King as the immediate superior.[4]   On 24th March following, a precept of sasine was issued from the chancery of King James for infefting Alexander in these lands.[5]

In the same year, the Laird of Luss and his nieces, Margaret and Agnes, became involved in a lawsuit with Ludovic second Duke of Lennox, Chamberlain of Scotland.   The Duke, who had been constituted by his Majesty assignee to all reversions granted by whatsoever persons to the deceased Earls of Lennox, wished to redeem various lands which his grandfather or father had sold under reversion to Alexander's grandfather.   But these lands Alexander wished to retain.   Hence the legal proceedings adopted by the Duke against him, and his deceased brother Sir Humphrey's daughters.

[1] Original Contract and Charter at Ross- dhu.

[2] Original Contract and Charter, ibid.

[3] Original Discharge at Rossdhu.

[4] Original Charter, ibid.

[5] Original Instrument of Sasine, ibid.

At the instance of the Duke, on 23d August 1597, they were summoned to compear before his Majesty, and the Lords of Council, at Edinburgh, on the 1st of January next, to resign and overgive in his favour the lands of Letterowald [Letrualt] and Stuknagart, which had been sold by Matthew Earl of Lennox, the pursuer's "foirgrandsyr" [great-grandfather] to John Colquhoun of Luss, Alexander's great-grandfather, under reversion, and the Mains of Inchinnan, which had been given in warrandice of these lands.[1]

In an action at the instance of the Duke against them in reference to the redemption of other lands, they were decerned and ordained by the Lords of Council, 10th March 1597-8, to renounce and overgive the mill of Altdonalt, the lands of Auchingaich, Auchenvennel-mor, Stuckiedow, Balchannan, Mamore, Mambeg, Blairvaddau, Feorlingcarry, the Stroue and Dureling, all which had been sold under reversion by Matthew and John, preceding Earls of Lennox, to the foresaid John Colquhoun of Luss.[2]

Alexander Colquhoun of Luss and his nieces, and the occupiers and possessors of the lands of Auchevache, Blair, Lettrualt-mor, and others, were again summoned, 24th May 1598, at the instance of the Duke, to compear before his Majesty and the Lords of Council at Edinburgh, on the 15th of June next, to hear and see themselves decerned by decreet of the Lords of Council to remove themselves, their wives, bairns, servants, subtenants, cottars, corns, cattle, goods, and gear, from the lands above mentioned.[3] But Alexander, his nieces, and his tenants, maintained that they ought not to be decerned to remove from these lands, because, by a contract made, 10th May 1593, betwixt Ludovic Duke of Lennox and him, it was specially agreed betwixt them that the Duke, after the decreet of redemption and renunciation of the said lands to be obtained by him, should set them in tack to Alexander, for the space of fifteen years following that decreet. When the case came again before the Lords of Council, 1st July 1598, they pleaded, by their procurators, that on this ground they should not be decerned by their Lordships to remove from these lands. But as, at the time of the making of the contract, the Duke was a minor, having curators, and as their consent had not been obtained in making it,

[1] Copy Summons at Rossdhu.   [2] Copy Decreet, ibid.   [3] Copy Summons, ibid.

the Lords of Council decerned that it was null, and repelled the plea founded thereon.[1]

On 23d February 1600, Alexander Colquhoun of Luss was infefted in the lands of Rosrewen, St. Sebastian, within the territory of the burgh of Dumbarton.[2]

On the death of Mr. William Chirnside, parson of Luss, Alexander Colquhoun, as patron, granted a presentation in favour of Duncan Arrall, then minister at Luss, giving to him the parsonage and vicarage of the parish kirk of Luss. The presentation, which is in the following terms, shows the form of presentation then in use :—

BE it kend till all men be thir present lettres, me, Alexander Colquhone of Luss, vndoutit patrone of the personage of Luss, to haif gevin, granted, and disponit, as be the tenour herof, gevis, grantis, and disponis, to my lovit Duncane Arrall, presentlie minister at Luss, the personage and vicarage of the paroche kirke of Luss, liand within the sheriffdome of Dunbertane, now vacand in my hand, as vndoutit laicall patrone thairof, be disceas of vmquhile Mr. Willeam Chirnesyde, last parsone and possessour of the samen, with all teyndis, fructes, emolumentis, glebis, mansis, and vther pertinentis quhatsumever, belanginge or perteyninge thairto, to be vptane, ressauit, intromittit withe and disponit vpone be the said Duncane Arrall, minister, his seruitouris and factours, in his name, duringe all the dayes of the said Duncane Arrallis lyfetime : Quhairfoir I, be the tennour of thir presentes, nominatis and presentis the said Duncane Arrall minister [at] Lwss (as person being able and qualefeit) in order to the personage, with all fructes and emolumentis thairof, to zow, the presbiterye of Dunbartane, or commissiones apoynted for the vest pairtis (giue ony be), and to all other officaris and membris of kirk, as efferis ; maist humblie requyringe zour visdomes, eftir sufficient tryall takinge of the said Duncane Arrallis doctrein, conuersatioune, lyfe, and qualificatioune, to admit and receave the said Duncane Arrall in and to the said personage of Luss, and to grant to him ordinarie collatione thairvpone, in dew forme efter the commone ordour, and to give him institutione laufull thairof, causinge hym to be thankfullie ansuerit and obeyit of all and sindrie teyndis, fructes, emolumentis, glebis, mansis, and quhatsumeuer vther pertinentis belangand to the said personage, duringe all the dayes of his lyfetime, and to do and exerce all vther thinges dew and requisit thairanent, that becum zow of zour

---

[1] Extract Interlocutor of Lords of Council at Rossdhu.   [2] Instrument of Sasine, ibid.

office and dewte, in sic cace. In vitnes herof to thir presentis subscryvit with
my hand, my seal is to hingin at            , the first day Marche, the
zeir of God 1ᵐ and sex hundreyt zeris, befoir thir witnes, Hew Crawford,
fear of Cloberhill, Adam Colquhoune in Hiltoun of Neperstoun, Arthour Colquhone of the Borrowfield, and Robert Colquhone, my seruitour, vrettar of
thir presentes, with vtheris diuers.

Hew Crawfurd of Cloberhill, witnes.     ALEXANDER COLQUHOUN off Lusse.
Ro. Colquhoun, vitness.
Arthur Colquhoune, witnes.[1]

On the 6th of January 1602, Alexander Colquhoun had an assignation
made to him by Walter Colquhoun in Miltoun of Colquhoun, James and
Adam Colquhouns there, and others, which illustrates the family feuds
so rife among the Highland clans in those times. This was an assignation, for divers great sums of money, other gratitudes, good deeds and
pleasures payed and done to them by him, to the horses, cows, oxen, and
other goods and gear wrongously taken away from them out of their rooms
and possessions by Andrew Macfarlane of Arrochar, John Macfarlane,
fiar of Arrochar, Humphrey Macfarlane, his brother, Malcolm Macfarlane
of Gartavartane, and their accomplices, in the month of February 1589 ;
and also to the decreet arbitral betwixt the deceased Sir Humphrey Colquhoun of Luss and his tenants on the one part, and Andrew Macfarlane
of Arrochar for himself and his sons, and friends, on the other part, dated
Edinburgh, 10th August 1590.[2]

On 12th March 1603, a large number of the friends and dependants [3]
of the Laird of Luss obtained a decreet of the Lords of Council and Session
against Andrew Macfarlane of Arrochar, John Macfarlane, fiar thereof, and
Humphrey Macfarlane, his second son, commanding them to make restitution to the pursuers of certain goods, geir, inside plenishing, abuilzeimentis,
and other property of which they had wrongously despoiled them, and to
make payment to them of the price and profits of the same, each to pay his
own proportion, as is particularly expressed in the decreet.

[1] Dennistoun's MSS., in Advocates' Library, Edinburgh, vol. v. p. 182.

[2] Original Assignation at Rossdhu.

[3] These included James Colquhoun of
Blairvaddoch, Robert Colquhoun, his brother,
John Colquhoun, parson of Kilpatrick,
Walter Colquhoun of Kilmardinny, John
Colquhoun, fiar of Camstradden, and John
Colquhoun in Hill.

A few months after, these parties made assignation to Alexander Colquhoun of Luss, whom they designate "our chief," each his own proportion,
of the said decreet, with all action and execution competent to them thereby
for fulfilment of the said decreet. The assignation is dated at Rossdhu,
28th June, 5th July, and 27th October 1603.[1]

Soon after, a reconciliation was effected between Alexander Colquhoun
of Luss and some of the Macfarlanes. A bond, dated 1603, day of the
month blank, by which their differences were composed, and by which
provision was made for preventing the recurrence of those unhappy
strifes, depredations, and murders which the hatreds and jealousies that
had hitherto existed between the two houses had occasioned, was entered
into between Alexander Colquhoun and Malcolm Macfarlane, apparent
heir of Gartavartane, for himself, and in name of his brothers, his father's
brothers, and the sons of his father's brothers. From this bond we learn
that the Macfarlanes were art and part in the slaughter of Alexander's
brother, Sir Humphrey, and of three of Sir Humphrey's servants, Robert
Colquhoun of Tullichintaull, John Galloway, and Gavin Maclelan. Alexander Colquhoun bound himself to stop proceedings against Malcolm
Macfarlane, and those whom he represented, on account of these slaughters,
and to grant them a remission for the spoliations and thefts which they
had committed at Colquhoun, Connaltoun, Tullychewen, the manor place
and fortalice of Rossdhu, on his brother Sir Humphrey, himself, and their
tenants. On the other hand, Malcolm became bound to grant a bond of
manrent and service to Alexander Colquhoun, himself, and his friends,
against all men except the Duke of Lennox; and engaged, should that bond
be contravened by himself personally, to pay to Alexander Colquhoun 5000
merks, and should it be contravened by others, to deliver up the contravener
to Alexander, and failing which, to pay to him for every contravener 1000
merks. It is further stipulated that this agreement should noways affect
the claims of the Laird of Luss against Andrew Macfarlane, Laird of
Arrochar, and his sons John and Humphrey, and their friends, for their
part in these crimes.[2]

[1] Original Assignation, narrating the above decreet, at Rossdhu.
[2] Contemporary Copy Bond, ibid.

If the Colquhouns suffered much from the Macfarlanes, they suffered still more from the Macgregors. As to the turbulence of the clan Gregor at this time, Chalmers, in his 'Caledonia,' says,—" While King James was thought-lessly employed in heaping estates and honours on his favourites, Dumbar-tonshire was suffering from the lawless depredations and barbarous murders committed by a ferocious banditti. The Macgregors, who inhabited some of the Highland glens on the north of Dumbartonshire, had long infested that country; and during the weak reign of King James the Sixth, their atroci-ties became intolerable." Previous to this, the Macgregors and Colquhouns, as has been already shown, were at open feud. The questions, how did the feud between them originate? and what was the special cause of its out-break in circumstances so atrocious, at the close of the year 1602, and at the beginning of the year 1603 ? are natural subjects of inquiry. Sir Walter Scott, in his introduction to Rob Roy, attributes the origin of this animosity to the summary vengeance taken by the Laird of Luss on two of the Mac-gregors, who having, when benighted, been denied shelter by a dependant of Colquhoun's, took a wedder from the tenant's fold, killed it, and supped on it, for which they offered payment to the owner, but whom the Laird of Luss, in the exercise of his ample powers as a feudal baron, seized, con-demned, and executed. In confirmation of the truth of this story, the Mac-gregors refer to the proverb current among them, execrating the hour (*mult dhu' an carbail ghil*) that the black wedder with the white tail was ever lambed. But it is difficult to trace the origin of these feuds, and this incident, if it did occur, which is doubtful, might be the evidence of a strife already existing, as well as constitute the ground or origin of one. These feuds often arose, not so much from one particular cause, as from a combination of causes, which produced mutual jealousies and resentments that gathered and grew with the course of time. The terrible outbursts of the fury of the Macgregors against the Colquhouns, which we are about to relate, and by which they seemed as if bent on their extermination, were the results of the standing hostility between the two families. The documents preserved relating to the feuds between the two parties exhibit the Macgregors as the aggressors, while the Colquhouns were the most inclined to cultivate habits of tranquillity, and had recourse to arms mainly in self-defence.

At this time it was the duty of Archibald seventh Earl of Argyll to keep the clan Gregor under restraint. In January 1593, he had obtained a commission investing him with power to charge "all and sundrie personis of the surname of Macgregour, thair assistaris and pairt-takaris, to find souirtie, or to enter plegeis as he sall think maist expedient for observatioun of his Hieness' peace, quietness, and guide reule in the countrey," and, if necessary, "to persew and assege their housis and strengthis, raise fyre and use all kynd of force and weirlyke ingyne" against that clan.[1]  On 5th March 1594, Argyll became bound that he himself and all for whom he was answerable, should observe his Majesty's peace and keep quietness and good rule in the country, under the pain of £20,000 : and further, that he and all for whom he was answerable should satisfy and redress all attempts committed by them in time bygone since the 1st of June 1592, and all attempts that should happen to be committed by them in time coming, under the same pains.[2]  In July 1596, he received, on paying a sum of money into the royal treasury, the commission of King's lieutenant in the bounds of the clan Gregor wherever situated.[3]  On 22d April 1601, Allaster Macgregor of Glenstra, as captain of the clan Gregor, gave him, as King's lieutenant over the Macgregors, a bail-bond for the whole clan ; one clause of which was, that any offence committed by any of the clan was to be understood as *ipso facto* a forfeiture of any lands they might possess.[4]

But if the declaration or confession made by Allaster Macgregor before his execution is true, Argyll, instead of repressing the clan Gregor, made use of the power which, as the King's lieutenant, he had acquired over them, to stimulate them to various acts of aggression against Colquhoun of Luss and others, who were his personal enemies.  Founding mainly on the dying declaration of the Laird of Macgregor, Pitcairn, in his Criminal Trials, says,—" It is to this crafty and perfidious system of the Earl, therefore, that

[1]  Records of Privy Council, Jan. 30, 1593.
[2]  Extract Bond from Books of Privy Council.
[3]  Records of Privy Council, 28th June 1602.

[4]  Argyll produced this bond to the Secret Council at Falkland, on 28th June 1602, and the Council engrossed it in their minutes.— Records of Privy Council.

we must solely trace the feud between the Colquhouns and the Macgregors, which proved in the end so hurtful to both; a result, no doubt, all along contemplated by this powerful but treacherous nobleman." [1]

We do not, however, agree with Pitcairn in founding so much on Macgregor's dying declaration. The feeling of Macgregor against Argyll must in the circumstances have been intensely strong, as his words plainly indicate, and though in the presence of death, the motive to speak only the truth was powerful, yet our knowledge of human nature suggests caution in giving implicit credit even to his dying declaration; and its main features are certainly not confirmed, as Pitcairn asserts, by the records of the Privy Council. The Laird of Macgregor's testimony, therefore, in the circumstances, unsupported by that of other credible witnesses, is not a sufficient ground on which to impeach Argyll.

Among the Luss Papers, there are lists of articles stolen by the Macgregors from the Colquhouns in the year 1594 and in other years previous to 1600, and these lists show how much the Colquhouns had suffered from the Macgregors. But in 1602, the Macgregors made more formidable inroads into the lands of Luss, spreading consternation among the inhabitants. Complaints were made against them by the Laird of Luss to King James, upon which his Majesty, dispensing with the provisions of an Act of Parliament, forbidding the carrying of arms, granted permission to him and his tenants to wear various kinds of offensive weapons. The royal letter granting him this liberty is in the following terms :—

REX.

WE, vnderstanding that sindrie of the disorderit thevis and lymmares of the Clangregour, with vtheris thair complices, dalie makis incursionis vpoun, and within the boundis and landis pertening to Alexander Colquhoun of Lus, steillis, reiffis, and awaytakis, diuers great heirschippis fra him and his tennentis ; lykas they tak greater hauldnes to continew in thair said stouth and reaff, becaus they ar enarmit with all kynd of prohibite and forbiddin wapynnis : Thairfoir, and for the better defence of the said Laird of Lus, and his saidis tennentis, guidis, and geir, fra the persute of the saidis thevis and broken men, to have gevin and grantit, and be the tennour heirof gevis and grantis licence and libertie to the said Alexander Colquhoun of Lus, his houshald men, and sernandis, and sic as sall accumpany him, not onlie to beir, weir, and schuitt with haghuittis and pistolettis, in the following and persute of the saidis thevis and lymmeris, quilk is lauchtfull be the Act of Parliament, bot also to beir and weir the same haghuittis and pistolettis in any pairt abone the water of Leavin, and at the said Lairdis place of Dunglas and lands of Colquhoun, for the watcheing and keiping of thair awne guidis, without any cryme, skayth, pane, or danger to be incurrit be thame thairthrou, in thair personis, landis, or guidis, be any maner of way, in tyme cuming, notwithstanding any our actis, statutis, or proclamationis maid in the contrair thairanent, and panis thairin contenit, we dispence be thir presentis.   Gevin vnder our signet and subscriuit with our hand, at Hamyltoun, the first day of September, and of our reigne the xxxvi zeir, 1602.

JAMES R.[1]

The right to carry arms thus granted to the Laird of Luss and his retainers, so far from inspiring the Macgregors with terror, seems rather to have inflamed their resentment against the Colquhouns, and proved, there is reason to fear, the immediate occasion of the disastrous conflicts at Glenfinlas and Glenfruin which followed.

The Laird of Luss made a complaint in November 1602, if not earlier, against the Earl of Argyll, as the King's lieutenant in the bounds of the Clangregour, for permitting them and others to commit outrages upon him and his tenants.[2]   The Lord High Treasurer and the King's Advocate had, before 30th November that year, prosecuted Argyll for certain alleged atrocities of that clan, of which the only one specified is said to have been committed "on the Lairds of Luss and Buchanan."   Argyll and his sureties in the bond, which, as King's lieutenant, he had given to the Government, not having appeared before the Council in obedience to the summons issued against them, were fined in terms of the bond; but he was assoilzied from the charge brought against him by Colquhoun, the latter having failed to prove it.[3]

The first of the raids referred to between the Macgregors and the Colquhouns took place on the 7th of December 1602, at Glenfinlas, a glen about two miles to the west of Rossdhu, and three to the north of Glenfruin, to which it runs parallel, namely, in a north-westerly or south-easterly direction.

[1] Original Royal Letter at Rossdhu.
[2] Records of Privy Council.          [3] Records of Privy Council.

This raid was headed by Duncan Mackewin Macgregour, tutor of Glenstra. Accompanied with about eighty persons, to quote from a contemporary Luss paper, by way of oppressions and reif, he came to the dwelling houses and steadings of many tenants, broke up their doors, and not only took their whole inside plenishing out of their houses, but also took and reft from them three hundred cows, one hundred horses and mares, four hundred sheep, and four hundred goats. Among the tenants despoiled were John Maccaslane of Caldenoth, and John Leich of Cullichippen, besides various tenants in Edintagert, Glenmacairne, Auchintullich, Finlas, Tomboy, Midros, etc. The houses plundered amounted to forty-five.[1]

Another of the Luss papers, entitled " Memorandum for Duncan Mackinturnour, elder in Lus," records that, in the month of December 1602 years, at the herschip of Glenfinlas, two mouths before the day of Glenfruin, Duncan Mackewin Macgregor and his accomplices, to the number of fourscore persons,[2] most cruelly reft, spoilzeit and away took from the said Duncane Mackinturnour, forth of his xxs. land of Glennakearne, twenty-five cows, and thirty sheep, the property of the said Duncan.

Various lists of the names of the accomplices of the Macgregors are preserved among the Luss papers. These accomplices were chiefly persons of the name of Macgregor, under the Earl of Argyll, and also under the lairds of Tullibardine and Strowan Robertson, etc.

The resetters of the plundered articles were chiefly about Lochgoylhead, Strachur, Ardkinlas, and Appin.

At the fray of Glenfinlas, besides the depredations committed, two of the Colquhoun people were killed, one of them a household servant of the Laird of Colquhoun, and the other a wobster. Under the date of 12th August 1603, Neill Macgregor was " delated and accused of being airt and pairt of the slauchter of umquhile Patrik Layng and of vmquhile John Reid, wobster, servandis to the Laird of Luss, committit in December last, and also of stealing,"[3] etc.

Sir Robert Gordon, who, in his History of the Earldom of Sutherland,

1 Luss Papers at Rossdhu.    3 Records of Privy Council.
2 Another Luss paper says " above fourscore."

writes strongly in favour of the Macgregors, represents the Colquhouns as
the aggressors.   " In Lent," says he, " in the yeir of God 1602, ther happened a great tumult and combustion in the west of Scotland, betuein
the Laird of Lus (chieff of the surname of Colquhoun) and Alexander
Mackgregor (cheiftane of the Clangregar).   Ther had been formerlie some
rancour among them, for divers mutuall harships and wrongs done on either
syd ; first by Luss his freinds, against some of the Clangregar, and then by
John Mackgregar (the brother of the forsaid Alexander Mackgregar) against
the Laird of Luss his dependers and tenuents."[1]

Alexander Colquhoun of Luss, as we have already seen, before this raid
complained to the Privy Council against the Earl of Argyll, for not repressing the clan Gregor.   Having then failed to obtain any redress from the
Council, he was advised by some of his friends, after the conflict at Glenfinlas, to appear before the King, who was at Stirling, to complain of
the depredations and cruel murders committed by the Macgregors, and
to give the greater effect to his complaint, to take along with him a
number of women, carrying the bloody shirts of their murdered or wounded
husbands and sons.   The idea of this tragical demonstration was suggested
to him by Semple of Fulwood and William Stewart, captain of Dumbarton
Castle, as we learn from the following letter, written to him by Thomas
Fallisdaill, burgess of Dumbarton, only a few days after the conflict :—

" Rycht honorable Sir, my dewtie wyth service remembrit, plas zour
ma[stership] the Lard of Fullewod and the Capitane thinkis best zour
ma[stership] adres to zour self, wyth als mony bludie sarks as ather ar deid
or hurt of zour men, togitter wyth als mony vemen, to present thame to
his Maistie in Stirling, and to zour ma[stership] to be thair vpone Tysday
nixt, for thai ar bayth to ryd thair vpone tysday, quha will asist zow at
thair power.   The meistest tyme is now, becauss of the French Imbais-
sadour that is wyth his Maistie.   The rest of thair opinioun I sall cum wpe
the morne vpone zour ma[stership] aduertisment.   I haif gottine fra Johne
Cunynghame of Rois zour hundrethe markis, vpone my obligatioune to gif
him his obligatiouns, and Donald Cunynghamis.   Sua aduertis me gif I sall

[1] History of the Earldom of Sutherland, by Sir Robert Gordon of Gordonstoun, folio :
Edinburgh, 1813, p. 246.

bring the same wyth me. Me Lord Duik is also in Stirling, quhome the Laird of Fullvad and the Capitane wald fain haif zow agreit wyth presentlie, and lat actionis of law rest ower. Sua I end, committing zour ma[stership] for ewer to the Lord. Dumbartane, this Sunday, the xix of December 1602.

> Zour ma[stership] awen for ewer,
>
> THOMAS FALLUSDAILL, Burges of Dunbertane."

" To the Rycht honorable Allexander Colquhoune off Luss, in haist, this vretting." [1]

Thus advised, Alexander Colquhoun of Luss went, on the 21st of the same month, to the King, at Stirling, accompanied by a number of females, the relatives of the parties who had been killed or wounded at Glenfinlas, each carrying the bloody shirt of her killed or wounded relative, to implore his Majesty to avenge the wrongs done them. The scene produced a strong sensation in the mind of the King, who was extremely susceptible to the impression of tragic spectacles. His sympathy was excited towards the sufferers ; and his resentment was roused against the Macgregors, on whom he vowed to take vengeance. As the speediest means of redress, he granted a commission of lieutenancy to Alexander Colquhoun of Luss, investing him with power to repress crimes of the description from which he had suffered, and to apprehend the perpetrators [2]

This commission granted to their enemy, appears to have roused the lawless rage of the Macgregors, who rose in strong force to defy the Laird of Luss ; and Glenfruin, with its disastrous and sanguinary defeat of the Colquhouns, and its ultimate terrible consequences to the victorious clan themselves, was the result.

Sir Robert Gordon, in his History of the Earls of Sutherland, mistakes the conflict of Glenfinlas for the more serious one of Glenfruin, which took place shortly after. " The report of this combat and victorie," says he, " came to the King's ears at Edinburgh [Stirling it should be], where elevin

---

[1] Original Letter at Rossdhu.
[2] Chalmers's Caledonia, vol. iii. p. 883. That Alexander Colquhoun had a royal commission to oppose the clan Gregor when he met them in arms at Glenfruin, about six weeks after this date, appears from the indictment of Allaster Macgregor, to be afterwards given.

score bloodie shirts (of these that were slain in that skirmish) were presented
to his Majestie, who was thervpon exceedinglie incensed against the Clangregor."[1]  Sir Walter Scott, founding on this account as his authority, im-
proves upon it by the addition of various circumstances which, however,
are purely fictitious.  "The widows of the slain," says he, "to the number
of eleven score, in deep mourning, riding upon white palfreys, and each
bearing her husband's bloody shirt on a spear, appeared at Stirling, in presence of a monarch peculiarly accessible to such sights of fear and sorrow,
to demand vengeance for the death of their husbands, upon those by whom
they had been made desolate."[2]  The bloody shirt scene was after the
raid at Glenfinlas, and as only a few were killed on that occasion,
though a greater number might be wounded, Sir Robert Gordon, and, after
him, Sir Walter Scott, exaggerates what actually took place.  The scene
was not repeated after the more sanguinary conflict at Glenfruin, though
then it would have been a spectacle much more impressive, from the far
greater number who were there killed and wounded.

It has been asserted by some writers that, in the beginning of the year
1603, the Macgregors and the Colquhouns made friendly propositions to
hold a conference with the view of terminating their animosities, while,
at the same time, each determined, should the result of a meeting be
unsuccessful, to have recourse to instant measures of hostility.  Sir Robert
Gordon, in his History of the Earldom of Sutherland, represents the
matter more favourably for the Macgregors.  "Alexander M'Gregar (being
accompanied with 200 of his kin and freinds) came from the Rannogh into
the Lennox, to the Laird of Luss his owne bounds, with a resolution to tak
away these dissentions and jarrs, by the mediation of freinds.  In this
meantyme the Laird of Luss doth assemble all his pertakers and dependers,
with the Buchannans and others, to the number of 300 horsemen and 500
foott, intending that iff the issue of their meitting did not ansuer his expectation, he might inclose the enemies within his cuntrey, and so overthrow
them.  Bot the Clangregar being vpon ther guard it happened otherwise ;
for presentlie after that the meitting dissolued, the Laird of Luss, thinking
to tak his enemies at vnawars, persued them hastylie and eagerlie at Glen-

[1] P. 247.                    [2] Introduction to Rob Roy.

Freon." [1]   Sir Robert Gordon was contemporary, but he is here incorrect in various of his statements, as can be proved from authentic documents of the period.   No evidence whatever exists of the conference referred to having been either held or intended.   From the position of the two parties, it is hardly possible that any such conference could then have been thought of, far less held.   The Macgregors were more in the position of rebels, whilst Colquhoun was invested with a commission from the King to apprehend and punish them for their crimes ; and the whole circumstances of the case, so far from affording any ground to believe that, at the close of the alleged conference, the Laird of Luss treacherously attacked the Macgregors, render it far more probable that he himself was entrapped by them while proceeding through the glen in the execution of his commission.

That the Macgregors were, in the present instance, the aggressors, is the conclusion to which we are led from the statements made in the indictment of Allaster Macgregor, in which he was accused of having deliberately planned the destruction of the Colquhouns and their allies, the extirpation of their name, and the plunder of their lands, and of having, for carrying out these plans, invaded Alexander Colquhoun's lands with numerous armed men ; all which was proved against him by a jury of most respectable gentlemen.   Similar statements are contained in the indictments of others who were tried for the same crime, and in many acts and proclamations against the clan.   If the correctness of the statement of the Government may be disputed, it is to be observed that its truthfulness is strongly confirmed by the declaration made by Allaster Macgregor before his execution.

That some desperate attack upon the Colquhouns was at this time contemplated by the Macgregors, appears to have been the feeling prevalent throughout the district of the Lennox.   The order issued by the Town-Council of Dumbarton, that the burgesses should be provided with armour, and be ready to present the same at muster, plainly indicates the apprehensions entertained in that burgh, that danger was impending, and that it was necessary to be prepared for resisting some dreaded foe, who was doubtless the clan Gregor.   " 1603. January 8.—It is ordained

[1] Gordon's History of the Earldom of Sutherland, p. 246.

that all burgesses within the burgh be sufficientlie furnissit with armor,
and that sik persones as the baillies and counsall think fitt sall be furnissit
with hagbuttis, that they haif the samyn with the furnitear thairto, utheris
quha sall be appointit to haif jak speir and steilbonnat, that thay be furnissit
with the samyn, and that the baillies and counsall, on the xxi of this instant, mak ane catholok of the saidis personis names with thair armor, and
thay be chargeit to haif the said armor redey, and to present thame with
the samyn at muster, and this to remaine in all tymes under the pane
of ten pundis, the ane half to the baillie, the uthir to the use of the burgh.
Item, that ilk merchand or craftisman, keipand baith haif ane halbart within
the samyn undir the pane of five pundis.  Item, that na burgess be maid
heirefter without production of his armor at his creatioun, and that he sweir
the samyn is his own."

How well founded these apprehensions were was proved by the event.
Allaster Macgregor of Glenstra, at the head of a large body of the clan
Gregor, with the addition of a considerable number of confederates from
the claus of Cameron and Anverich, armed with hagbuts, pistols, murrions,
mailcoats, pow-aixes, two-handed swords, bows, darlochs, and other weapons, advanced into the territory of Luss.  At that time there was no
turnpike on Lochlong side, the present Lochlong road having since been
made, it is supposed, by the Duke of Argyll, and therefore formerly called
" The Duke's Road."  There was, however, a tract or path of some kind
along the side of Lochlong, and this may have been the way by which the
Macgregors came to Glenfruin.  To repel the invader, the Laird of Luss
hastily collected together a considerable force of armed men, whom, under
a royal commission, he had raised for the protection of the district and
for the punishment of the Macgregors.

The statement made by Mr. Pitcairn, in his Criminal Trials,[1] that
the Macgregors and the Colquhouns at Glenfruin "were in a manner
equally armed with the royal authority," is quite unfounded.  The Laird
of Luss was indeed then acting under a commission from the King to
apprehend the clan Gregor,[2] but to speak of "the Laird of Macgregor as
marching to invade the Lennox under the paramount authority of the

---

[1] Vol. ii. p. 431.                    [2] Vide p. 189, ut supra.

King's lieutenant," Argyll, is a gratuitous assertion. Whatever the friends of the Macgregors may say as to Argyll's secretly encouraging the Macgregors to attack the Colquhouns, it is certain that he had no power to arm them with authority for that purpose, and there is no evidence that he formally did so. To place the two parties nearly on a footing of equality as to the right of meeting in hostile array for a trial of strength, is a view entirely erroneous. The Macgregors were rebels, and the Colquhouns were armed with royal authority to suppress their outrages.

The parties encountered each other on the 7th of February 1603, at Glenfruin, at a spot, according to tradition, situated upon the farm of Strone, or Auchengaich, near the source of the Fruin. The name Glenfruin, which means " the glen of sorrow," well accords with the sanguinary scene, which on this occasion it witnessed ; but it did not from thence derive its name. In charters of the lands of Luss, of a date previous to the battle, mention is made of Frevne. It forms a verdant valley, of considerable length, some of it under cultivation, with a deep loamy soil, nearly half a mile in breadth, between hills barren of trees and shrubs, with the exception of here and there a thorn or mountain ash, but whose sides, especially to the north of the glen, are covered with beautiful green pasturage for sheep, instead of the brown heather of the olden times. The spot on which the bloody conflict took place is still pointed out by tradition, which preserves fresh the memory of what has rendered it so memorable. In reference to the spot, the bard of the Macgregors, in commemorating their exploits, speaks in his native tongue, in words which may be thus translated :—

" At the gate of Rossdhu
Stood the armed party,
Sans fear, sans care, sans scar."[1]

What the numbers were on each side has not been exactly ascertained. The Macgregors have been estimated by some at 300 foot ; by others at

[1] " San aig geatabh Ros-duibh
A'sheasamh de Bhaidheann
Oun eagal ; gun amhail, gun leon."

2 B

400,[1] and there can be no doubt that this clan could, without difficulty, muster at least that number, when they had some great purpose to accomplish, as their taking vengeance on their enemy the Laird of Luss would doubtless be accounted. The forces of Colquhoun of Luss have been also variously estimated, some,[2] probably by exaggeration, making them 300 horse and 500 foot. That he would succeed in raising in his own district, including the town of Dumbarton, so large an army, is extremely doubtful. The ground on which the conflict took place was very unfavourable both for the horse and foot of the Colquhouns, especially for the former. Surprise has been expressed that the Laird of Luss should have risked a conflict with the enemy in such a position, but, having been entrapped, he was placed in circumstances which gave him no choice. The Macgregors assembled in Glenfruin in two divisions, one of them at the head of the glen, and the other in ambuscade near the farm of Strone, at a hollow or ravine called the Crate. The Colquhouns came into Glenfruin from the Luss side, through the glen of Auchengaich, which is opposite Strone, probably by Glen Luss and Glen Mackurin.[3] Alexander Colquhoun pushed on his forces, in order to get through the glen before encountering the Macgregors; but, aware of his approach, Allaster Macgregor, the captain of the clan, also pushed forward one division of his forces, and entered at the head of the glen, in time to prevent his enemy from emerging from the upper end of the glen, whilst his brother, John Macgregor, with the division of his clan which lay in ambuscade, by a detour, took the rear of the Colquhouns, which prevented their retreat down the glen without fighting their way through that section of the Macgregors who had got in their rear. The success of the stratagem by which the Colquhouns were thus placed between two fires seems to be the only way of accounting for the terrible slaughter of the Colquhouns and the much less loss of the Macgregors. Allaster Macgregor, at the head of his division, furiously charged the Laird of Luss and his men. For a time the Colquhouns bravely maintained the contest. An old weaver, resi-

---

[1] The indictment of Allaster Macgregor makes them 400 men or thereby.

[2] Sir Robert Gordon, in his History of the Earldom of Sutherland, p. 246.

[3] Tradition.

dent in Strone, who took part with the Colquhouns, is said to have been one of the best fighters on that day. He is said to have killed with his own hand a good many of the Macgregors, which confutes the story that they suffered so little at Glenfruin that though many of them were wounded, not more than two of them, during the whole battle, were killed, which was of course impossible in such a conflict.[1] But in the unfavourable circumstances in which they had to fight, the Colquhouns soon became unable to maintain their ground, and, falling into a moss at the farm of Auchengaich, they were thrown into disorder, and being now at the mercy of the Macgregors, who, taking advantage of the confusion, killed many of them, they made a hasty and disorderly retreat, which proved even more disastrous than the conflict : for they had to force their way through the men led by John Macgregor, whilst they were pursued behind by Allaster, who, reuniting the two divisions of his army, continued the pursuit. But even in the flight there were instances of intrepidity on the part of the Colquhouns. One of them, when pressed hard by some of the Macgregors as he fled from the scene of battle, on reaching the Coinach, a black, deep whirling pool or linn of the water of Finlas in Shantron Glen, with steep, almost perpendicular banks, on both sides, rising to a height of at least 120 feet above the pool at the bottom, where the rays of the sun never penetrate, and where the sky is scarcely visible overhead, by a desperate effort at once jumped over the frightful chasm. None of the Macgregors ventured to follow him by making the perilous leap. The Colquhoun immediately turned round, drew an arrow from his quiver, and shot the nearest of his pursuers as he stood perplexed and baffled on the opposite brink, and then made his escape without further molestation.[2] Whoever fell into the hands of the victors, even defenceless women and children, were remorselessly put to death. The chief of the Colquhouns was chased to the very door of the Castle of Rossdhu, whose loopholed walls, six feet in thickness, afforded a secure refuge, and his horse, while leaping over a fall or gully not far from Rossdhu, was killed under him by a Macgregor. The ruins of the castle are still to be seen near the present more modern mansion. In the flight the Laird of Bucklyvie was

[1] Tradition.                    [2] Family tradition.

killed by the Macgregors at the farm of Ballemenoch or Middle Kilbride, at the eastern entrance of Glenfruin ; and the small rivulet, which is a tributary to the Fruin, is called " Bucklyvie's Burn" to this day, from the Laird's having been killed there.   On that fatal day one hundred and forty of the Colquhouns were slaughtered, and many were wounded.

We here give the number of those slain, as stated by the Government. Some writers make them fewer.   Birrell in his Diary says, sixty honest men, besides women and children.   Calderwood says fourscore persons or thereby.[1]   This last writer informs us that the Laird of Luss himself escaped narrowly.   "It was reported," he adds, that the raid was made " at the instigation of the Duke of Lennox his lady, seeking the wrack of the Laird of Luce, who held of the King and not of the Duke."   This was probably one of the idle tales circulated in the time of Calderwood.   Such a report had no foundation whatever in truth.

Among the number of the killed, according to the indictment of Allaster Macgregor of Glenstra, to be afterwards more particularly referred to, were the following :—Peter Napier of Kilmahew; John Buchanan of Bucklyvie, who has been already referred to ; Tobias Smollet, bailie of Dumbarton ; David Fallusdaill, burgess there, with his sons Thomas and James ; Walter Colquhoun of Barnhill, and John his son and apparent heir ; Adam and John Colquhoun, sons of the Laird of Camstradden, and John Colquhoun of Dalmure.   When the pursuit ended, the work of spoliation and devastation commenced.   Six hundred cows and oxen, eight hundred sheep and goats, two hundred horses and mares, and much household plenishing were carried off as plunder, and fire was set to many of the houses and barnyards of the tenantry.

In a summons by Alexander Colquhoun of Luss against Sir Duncan Campbell of Glenurchy, as cautioner for certain of the aggressors at Glen fruin who dwelt upon his lands, viz., Gregour Macewne in Moinnche, Johnne and Duncane Macewnis, his brothers, 18th February 1603, the following narrative of the battle occurs :—

" Vpoun the aucht day of Februar instant [the persons named], with vtheris thair disorderit complices, thevis, sornaris, and lymmaris of thair clan, friendschip and assistance, all bodin in feir of weir, with halberschois, powaixis, tua handit suordis, bowis and arrowis, and vtharis wapounis, invasive, and with hagbutis and pistoletis, prohibite to be worne be the lawis of our realme and Actis of Parliament, come vpoun fair day licht, within the landis of the barony of Lus, Kilbryd and Fynnert, perteuing to the said complainer, and first cruelly and mercilessly murtherit and slew ane grit nowmer of gentilmen, the said compleneris freindis, and tenneutis, thair wyfis and bairnis, duelland vpoun the saidis landis, to the nommer of sevin scoir personis or thairby, and brunt and distroyit the said compleneris haill cornis, wictuellis, barnis and girnellis, cattell and guidis, being within the saidis houss, and herriet the saidis haill landis, and reft and away tuke furth thairof sax hundreth heid of ky, pryce of the pice ourheid xx merkis, ane thousand scheip, pryce of the pice ls, ane thousand gait, pryce of the pice xls., ane hundreth hors and meiris, pryce of the pice ourheid, xxx lib ; . . . . . . by and besydis diuers vtheris bluidschedis, reifis, rubries, and heirschipis committit be the saidis personis thairvpoun."[1]

One of many lists of the clan Gregor and their associates among the Luss papers divides those on whose heads a price was to be put into four classes, according to their rank. The first of these contained—Duncane Macewin Macgregour, tutor; Robert Aberoche Macgregour; Johnne Dow Macalester vick in Seouan ; Callum Macgregour V'Coulchear in Glengyill ; Duncan Macrobert V'Coule ; Dougal Chairche Macgregour, his brother ; Archibald Macondachie Macalister Macgregour, in Raynnache ; John Dow Macphadrik Macgregour in Cadzearnis.

The second class consisted of ten names, the third of twenty, and the fourth of thirty-five. The other lists are chiefly Macgregors, Maccondowies, Camerons, and Campbells, from Strowan, Glenurchy, Glenbucky, Strathfillan, Lawers, Glenlyon, Tullibardine, Rannoch, and Lochgoilhead.

On the memorable day of the conflict of Glenfruin, according to the traditions of the country, a number of youths who, from mere curiosity, had come from the grammar-school of Dumbarton to witness the battle that was expected to take place, were massacred in cold blood by one of the clan Macgregor. The boys came along the ridge of the high hills on the south side of the Fruin, called the Highland road; and they were shut up for safety in a hut or barn, to the west of the battle on Greenfield

---

[1] Summons at Rossdhu.

Moor, under the charge of a Highlander,[1] who, on seeing the Macgregors successful, stabbed them with his dirk, one by one, as they came out of this place of shelter. The site of the barn is still pointed out at a spot called Lach-na-faul Lagnagaul, "hollow of the Lowlander." The stone where the hapless youths are said to have been put to death was called the *Lec-ak-Mhinisteir*, the minister or clerk's flagstone; and the common report is that their blood could never be washed out of the stone. It is worthy of notice that this atrocious massacre forms no part of the charges in the indictment of any of the Macgregors who were tried before the High Court of Justiciary on account of the raid of Glenfruin, or "the field and murder of the Lennox," as that conflict is sometimes called. But some colour of truth seems to be given to the tradition by an Act of Privy Council, 5th January 1609, in which Allan Oig M'Intnach, in Glenco, is accused of having, while with the clan Gregor in Glenfruin, "with his awne hand murdered, without pity, the number of fourtie poor persons, who were naked and without armour."[2]   Nor do the Macgregors deny that the story is founded on fact; but they affirm that the clan as a body execrated the crime, and they impute it to the ferocity of one of their tribe, renowned for size and strength, called Dugald Ciar (Kiar) Mhor, or the Great Mouse-coloured Man, who was Allaster Macgregor's foster brother. Allaster, they say, committed the youths to his protection till the conflict was over. But whilst the Macgregors were hotly pursuing the Colquhouns, Ciar, in his savage fury, despatched them with his dirk, and, on being asked by Allaster, on his return, whether the youths were safe, he drew his bloody dirk, remorselessly exclaiming, in Gaelic, " Ask that, and God save me !" The Ciar was the ancestor of Rob Roy. He was buried at the Church of Farlingal, and his grave was covered with a large stone, which is still pointed out.

These accounts, given by Sir Walter Scott, in his Introduction to Rob

---

[1] Dennistoun says so in one place in his Notes. But in another place he says that they were, by Colquhoun's orders, shut up in a barn for safety.

[2] Records of Privy Council. "The barn of Blairvaddon, in the Dukedom of Lennox," was burnt by the Macgregors in February 1603, as appears from the Records of the Privy Seal, 28th July 1612 and 21st December 1613. In the Records there is no allusion to any person's having been killed or even injured on that occasion.

Roy, he found in a MS. history of the clan Macgregor, with the perusal of which he was indulged by Donald Macgregor, Esq., late Major of the 33d Regiment. But Sir Walter mentions an old and prevalent tradition, pre served in the country, and particularly among the clan of the Macfarlanes, to the effect that the massacre of these youths was perpetrated by one named Donald or Duncan Lean, who was assisted by one named Charliock, or Charlie. The perpetrators durst not again, it is said, join their clan, but resided as outlaws in an unfrequented part of the Macfarlane territory, where they remained undisturbed, till, having committed an act of brutal violence on two defenceless women, a mother and a daughter of the Mac-farlane clan, they were, in revenge of this atrocity, hunted down and shot by the Macfarlanes. Sir Walter is inclined to think that this is the true edition of the story, and that the name of Dugald Ciar Mohr had been substituted as being a person of higher position, or possibly because the perpetrators had only executed his orders.

Among the Macgregors who in the conflict at Glenfruin were killed was John Dhu Macgregor, the brother of Allaster who commanded in chief. John Dhu, who was surnamed nan Lurag (of the mail), fell by an arrow from one of the fugitive Colquhouns, whilst his party were pursuing them after the defeat. The natives of the district of Glenfruin still point out two large stones, called clachan Macgregor, "the stones of the Macgregor," as marking the spots at which fell the two Macgregors. The event is noted by the bard of the Colquhouns, whose Gaelic lines, eulogistic of the youth by whom the fatal arrow was thrown, may be literally translated thus :—

> " Quickly didst thou wheel,
> Stripling Mac Lintock,
> By thee was slain John of the Mail,
> Macgregor's victorious son." [1]

Sir Robert Gordon incorrectly says that John Dhu, brother of Glenstra,

---

[1] The original is—

> " Stapaidh thug th' un tronndath ort
> A' Mhic Illeanting Oig
> Thuit lein Dubh o'an Luragleat
> Mac ur Mhic Ghrigair Mhoir."

was killed at the raid of Glenfinlas in December 1602.[1]   That John Dhu was alive after that raid, and was at the conflict of Glenfruin, or the field of Lennox, appears from the Records of Justiciary, 5th July 1603, when his servant, Gillemichel Mackishok, was condemned to the gallows for having been there with his late master.[2]

The burial-place of those who fell in the battle of Glenfruin is near the head of the glen of that name where the battle commenced, on the farm of Auchengaich, directly opposite to the glen of Auchengaich, which conducts from Glen Mackurin and Glen Luss into Glenfruin.   It is marked by a green mound planted with six mountain fir trees and two mountain ashes.   This mound is about sixty-six paces in circumference.[3]   The field is perfectly level, consisting, as it is at present divided, of about fifty acres (though before being subdivided it consisted of several hundreds of acres), and it is bounded by the Fruin and Auchengaich burn on the south and west sides.

Near a large bare rock or stone on the banks of the Fruin, about half a mile below the source of the Fruin, and on the farm of Strone, a Macgregor, it is said, who had been killed in Glenfruin, was buried.   This was probably the grave of John Dhu Macgregor.   Formerly the grave was enclosed with a wall, which is now removed.   Mr. Macfarlane, the tenant of Strone, removed the stones to build walls on his farm.

Sir Walter Scott, in his Lady of the Lake, commemorates the battle of Glenfruin.   He introduces the boatsmen of the barges, laden with clansmen, as celebrating in wild cadence, in words and notes adapted for keeping time with the sweep of their oars, the victories achieved at Bannachra and Glenfruin by the Macgregors, under the name of Clan Alpine, from their having claimed a descent from Gregor, third son, it is said, of Alpin, King of Scots, who flourished towards the close of the eighth century.

[1] History of the Earldom of Sutherland, p. 247.

[2] Records of the High Court of Justiciary.

[3] Another spot, which is an old burial ground in the glen, and in which are occasionally interred illegitimate or still-born children, has been pointed out, but incorrectly, as the burial-place of the Colquhouns who were slain at Glenfruin.   This graveyard is two miles to the east of the proper burial-place of those who fell in that battle.

> " Proudly our pibroch[1] has thrilled in Glen Fruin,
>   And Bannachra's groans to our slogan replied ;
> Glen Luss and Ross-dhu they are smoking in ruin,
>   And the best of Loch Lomond lie dead on her side.
>       Widow and Saxon maid
>       Long shall lament our raid,
> Think of Clan-Alpine with fear and with woe ;
>       Lennox and Leven-glen
>       Shake when they hear agen,
> ' Roderigh Vich Alpine dhu, ho ! ieroe ! ' "

In a note to these lines, Sir Walter gives a somewhat confused account of the clan battle of Glenfruin. He mingles together the conflict of Bannachra, 1592, in which Sir Humphrey Colquhoun was killed, and the raids of Glenfinlas and Glenfruin, and the various circumstances attending them, as if they had been one battle. He represents Sir Humphrey Colquhoun as commanding the Colquhouns on that occasion, whereas it was Alexander who commanded them. He commits the same mistakes in his account of the battle of Glenfruin, in his Introduction to Rob Roy.

In a recent work on the battle of Glenfruin, it has been argued that there was only one conflict at this time—namely, that at Glenfruin in February 1603. But that there were two conflicts, one at Glenfinlas on the 17th of December 1602, and another at Glenfruin on the 7th or 8th of February 1603,[2] is placed beyond all doubt from the original records of the period. The letter of Fallusdaill to the Laird of Luss is alone sufficient proof of a conflict on the 17th of December 1602, though all other evidence had been wanting. Many of the Luss family papers, which are contemporary, not only establish the fact of the first encounter, but supply the exact date and locality. One of these papers is a list of the clans who assisted the Macgregors at Glenfinlas and Glenfruin,[3] which proves the two conflicts. Another of them is headed, " The names of the resseateris of the geir taine by the Clangregour

---

[1] The pibroch is a tune peculiar to the Highlands and Western Isles of Scotland, performed on the bagpipe, intended to represent by imitative sounds the march, conflict, flight, pursuit, and other circumstances of a battle.

[2] Both Chalmers in his Caledonia (vol. iii. p. 883), and Arnot in his Criminal Trials (p. 134), speak of two conflicts, one in December, another in February following.

[3] List at Rossdhu.

out of the Laird of Lwss his lands at the dayes of Glenfinles and Glenfrwne, given up by ——— Montgomerie, 8 June 1611."[1] The first entry is, " Item, resseat be Archibald Mac-clcriche in Glencrover of the geir, as said is, spwlzeit by the Macgregor, *at the day of Glenfinles, whilk was in December* 1602, twa kay." Another of the Luss papers, previously quoted, states that, " in the month of December 1602," took place " the herschip of Glenfynlayis, *twa moncthis befoir the day of Glenfrwne.*"[2] Another of them is an inventory of the goods taken by the clan Gregor from the lands of Luss, on the " 17th December 1602, the *day of Glenfinlas.*"[3]

These documents place the fact of the encounter at Glenfinlas on the 17th of December 1602 beyond all possibility of doubt; and, by establishing that point, they at the same time throw considerable light on the still more disastrous conflict of Glenfruin, which soon followed. It is thus rendered all but certain that it was after the raid of Glenfinlas and the exhibition of the bloody shirts at Stirling that Alexander Colquhoun was commissioned by the King to repress such crimes, and to apprehend the perpetrators.

Neill Macgregor, in the indictment against him formerly quoted, is charged with being art and part in the slaughter of two of the Laird of Luss's servants in December 1602 ;[4] and Dougall Macgregor, who was tried along with him, was accused of being art and part in the slaughter of four men-servants of the Laird of Luss on the field of the Lennox.[5] In the first of these indictments the encounter of December 1602 is expressly referred to, and in the second the subsequent raid at Glenfruin.

It is perfectly clear that no confounding of the old and new styles could have originated the mistake, even had it been one, that there were two raids, one in December 1602 and another in February 1603. It is manifest that any event happening in December 1602,

[1] List at Rossdhu.
[2] *Vide supra*, p. 187.
[3] Inventory at Rossdhu.
[4] *Vide supra*, p. 187.

[5] Pitcairn's Criminal Trials, vol. ii. p. 424. Both these persons were hanged at the Castle Hill of Edinburgh on 12th August 1603.

whether old or new style, would just be two months before an event happening on the corresponding day of February 1602 old style, or 1603 new style. Whatever style, therefore, is used, the distance of time between the given days of December and February remains the same ; and the conclusion that because one encounter was said to be in December 1602, and another in February 1603, there was therefore but one battle, is simply absurd.

With regard to the date of the conflict of Glenfruin, it may be remarked that in some of the original documents it is said that it occurred on the 7th of February 1603, and in others that it took place on the 8th of that month. Allaster Macgregor's indictment gives the 7th, whereas letters under the King's signet, dated 18th February 1603, give the 8th. But this discrepancy of a single day is quite unimportant.

The melancholy fate of the Colquhouns excited very general commiseration. But the results were more disastrous to the victors than to the vanquished. The resentment of the Government was intensely inflamed against the clan Gregor, whose lawless deeds, ruthless as they may have been before, had culminated in the terrific scenes enacted at Glenfruin. The measures of the Government against them were very severe, contemplating nothing less than the extermination of the clan.

To the Earl of Argyll, who was the King's lieutenant in the part of the country inhabited by the Macgregors, chiefly was committed the task of executing the severe enactments made against them. Indignant complaints were made against Aulay Macaulay of Ardincaple, who, though he had formally joined with the Laird of Luss against Galbraith of Culcreuch, was charged with having reset and intercommuned with, and with having been art and part with the Macgregors at Glenfruin, which certainly would have been only to act in conformity with the bond of clanship into which he had entered with Allaster Macgregor. Against Macaulay the Earl of Argyll now directed the weight of his official authority.

On 17th March 1603, John Stewart of Ardmolice, Sheriff of Bute, became surety for Aulay Macaulay of Ardincaple, that he would compear before his Majesty's justice, or his deputies, in the Tolbooth of Edinburgh, on the

17th day of May following, to underlie the law for reset and intercommuning with Ewin Macgregour,[1] [Allaster] Macgregour of Glenstra, the
deceased John Dow Macgregour, his brother, and others of the Macgregours,
and " for not rysing the fray and following the thre saidis Macgregours,
commoun thevis and soirnaris, in thair incumming in the cuntrey of the
Lennox, and steilling of leill menis guidis, and for inbringing of the saidis
thevis and rebells, and also for airt and pairt with them in the incumming
vpoune the Laird of Lussis lands, and for the slauchter of sewyn scoir of
persounis, and for airt and pairt with the saidis Macgregouris in steilling fra
the Laird of Luss, and his kyn and freindis and tennentis, of certane nolt,
scheip," etc.[2]

     But Macaulay escaped by a summary suppression of all investigation.
Shielded by the Duke of Lennox, and being in the Duke's train, which was
to accompany King James the Sixth on his way to England, to take possession of the English throne, vacant by the death of Queen Elizabeth,
his Majesty issued a warrant at Berwick, 7th April 1603, to the Justice-
General and his deputies, commanding them to " desert the dyet" against
Macaulay, as he was " altogedder frie and innocent of the allegit crymes
laid to his charge." The Justice, accordingly, on the 17th of May 1603,
when this warrant was presented in the Justiciary Court by a servant
of the Duke of Lennox, deserted the dict.[3] Many others were less mercifully dealt with.

     Before any judicial inquiry had been made, on the 3d of April 1603,
only two days before King James the Sixth left Scotland for England to
take possession of the English throne, an Act of Privy Council was passed,
by which the name of Gregor or Macgregour was for ever abolished. All
of this surname were commanded, under the penalty of death, to change it
for another, and the same penalty was denounced against those who should
give food or shelter to any of the clan. All who had been at the conflict

<hr>

[1] Misnomer, as is believed, for Gregor
Macewin Macgregor, whose father, late
tutor of Glenstra, had by this time been
deceased, as appears from the bond by
Allaster Macgregor of Glenstra, and others,
to the Earl of Argyll, as King's lieutenant, 22d April 1601, in which he is termed
" vmquhile."

[2] Records of Privy Council, quoted by
Dennistoun.

[3] Records of Privy Council, quoted in
Pitcairn's Criminal Trials, vol. ii. p. 414.

of Glenfruin, and at the spoliation and burning of the lands of the Laird of
Luss and other lands, were also prohibited, under the penalty of death, from
carrying any weapon except a pointless knife to eat their meat.[1]  Such a
commencement did not augur well for the impartial administration of
justice, much less for the exercise of clemency to this clan.  This was followed by the execution of many of those who had taken part in the sanguinary conflict of Glenfruin, some at the Burrowmure of Edinburgh, others
at the Castle Hill, and others at the public cross, and by other measures
which bore the impress rather of vengeance than of calm judicial procedure.
On the 28th of April 1603, Allaster Mackie, Gilchrist Kittoche, and Find-
lay Dow Maclean, were dilated, the first for certain points of theft, and the
others for being art and part in the murder and slaughter of divers of the
Laird of Luss's friends and servants, and for the harieing and spoiling of
the whole country thereabout in February last ; and the prisoners having
been found guilty by the assize, the judge sentenced them to be hanged at
the Burrowmure, Edinburgh, and all their moveable goods to be escheit.
Other four were, on the 20th of May following, tried for being art and part
in the same murder, slaughter, and reft, and sentenced to be hanged at the
Castle Hill of Edinburgh.  Other two on the 5th of July, one on the 14th
of that month, and one on the 12th of August thereafter, were for the same
crimes sentenced to be hanged at the Burrowmure.[2]  Thus cast beyond the
pale of the Royal mercy, except on the most dishonourable conditions, the
clan were driven to desperation, and thinking only of retaliation, broke
forth into new outrages.

After the conflict at Glenfruin, the Macgregors lost no time in selling
and distributing the plunder which they had then carried off, and this they
did chiefly in Argyllshire.  Some facts in reference to this subject we learn
from the depositions made, 20th July 1603, before Alexander Colquhoun
of Luss, in the presence of a public notary, by Donald Makglaschane in

---

[1] Acts of the Parliament of Scotland,
17th May and 28th June 1617, when the
Act of Council was confirmed by the Parliament.

[2] Pitcairn's Criminal Trials, vol. ii. pp.
413-415, 418, 419, 424.  In the indictment

of these parties, " the lait grit slauchter and
crewall murthour" in the Lennox, in February bypast, is said to have amounted to
" sevin scoir persones," and the " steilling
and reiffing" to " aucht hundreth oxin, ky,
and vther bestiall."

Baichybaine, officer, tenant, and servant to Sir John Campbell of Ardkinglas. He confessed that he himself had bought three cows, at the head of
Lochfine, from two of the most noted actors in these deeds of spoliation
and slaughter, three or four days after they were perpetrated. He also
confessed that he knew many of the tenants of the Laird of Ardkinglas,
for whom that Laird was responsible, who had bought from other of
Allaster Macgregor's men cows, horses, and other spoil, and who had
entertained some of the same party.[1]

Some of the Campbells who were said to have been the secret allies of
the Macgregors, having reset them after the battle of Glenfruin, and having
been receivers of their stolen property, the Government now resolved to
proceed against them. Duncan Campbell, Captain of Carrick, and Ewen
Campbell of Dargache, were charged with "the wilful and contemptuous
resetting, supplying, and furnishing with meat, drink, and herbrie of Allaster
Macgregor of Glenstra, or others of his unhappy race and associates, who
were lately at the cruel murder within the Lennox, committed upon the
8th day of February" last [1603]. They were also charged with "fostering
the said Allaster and the persons foresaid, divers and sundry times within
their houses, after the said barbarous murder, namely, in the months of
February, March, April, May, and June respective, or some days thereof,
and furnishing of the said persons in their necessities, and keeping with
them frequent trysting and meetings, as well by night and day." They
were further charged with receiving within their lands the goods and gear
that were reft and away-taken by the said thieves forth of the Lennox at the
time foresaid. On 12th July 1603, John Boyle of Kelburne, and Normand
Innes of Knokdarrie, became sureties for the parties that they should
compear on the third day of the next Justice Air of the shire of Argyll,
or sooner, upon fifteen days' warning, to underly the law for the said
charges, under the pains following,—for Duncan Campbell, captain of
Carrick, three thousand merks, and for Ewen Campbell, two thousand
merks, and also that they should not reset, nor keep trysting, with the
said persons, nor reset the goods and gear which were reft or taken away.[2]

---

[1] Original Notarial Instrument, dated 20th July 1603, at Rossdhu.
[2] Records of Privy Council.

Commissions had been given by the Government to "the gentlemen of the Lennox," empowering them to seize the property, as well as to pursue the persons of the clan Gregor. But this clan, as "the gentlemen of Lennox" describe them, "being in all their wicked actiounes maist subtel and craftie," with the view of defeating the object of these commissions, distributed by assignation and disposition their goods among some of their friends, and moved them to take action before the Lords of Secret Council against those invested with such commissions, for their wrongous intromissions with the said goods. "The gentlemen of the Lennox" therefore presented to the Lords of the Secret Council a supplication, praying that an Act of Council might be passed, freeing them from the danger of molestation from this cause. Their Lordships accordingly, on 25th August 1603, granted them a supersedere from all pursuit, criminal or civil, moved or to be moved against them, or any of them, for their intromissions with the goods and gear of the said clan Gregor, who were guilty of the attempt committed within the Lennox, during the time that the commission against that clan remained in force.[1]

Towards the end of the year 1603, Alexander Colquhoun and his men apprehended three of the clan Gregour,—Gregor Cruiginche Macgregor, John Dow Macrob Macgregour, and Allaster Macewne Macgregor. On 24th November that year, he compeared before the Lords of Secret Council at Stirling, presented these prisoners before them, and craved that he might be exonered and relieved of them. Their Lordships granted the prayer of his petition, and having taken them off his hands, delivered them to the magistrates of the burgh of Stirling.[2]

In the trials which took place from 20th May 1603 to 2d March 1604, thirty-five of the Macgregors were convicted, and only one acquitted. In most or in all of these instances, the sentence of death, as we learn from Birrell's Diary, was carried into effect.

Allaster Macgregor, the chief of the clan, did not fall into the hands of the Government till nearly a year after the battle of Glenfruin. He had been almost entrapped by Campbell of Ardkinglas, Sheriff of Argyllshire, who, with the intention of arresting him, and sending him to the Earl of Argyll, had invited him to a friendly banquet in his house, which was situated on a small island in a loch, and who there made him a prisoner, and put him into a boat, guarded by five men; but Macgregor, seeing that he was betrayed, made his escape by a deed of romantic daring, having leaped out of the boat into the water, and swum to the shore in safety. He was less successful in eluding Archibald Earl of Argyll.

One authority informs us that the Earl sent to him sundry messages desiring an interview with him, and promising that no infringement would be made on his liberty; that Macgregor complied with this request, and was well received by the Earl, who assured him that though he was commanded by the King to apprehend him, he had no doubt of obtaining for him a royal pardon, and that he would allow him to go to England, and would send with him two gentlemen, whilst he would himself follow without delay, it having been Macgregor's intention to proceed to the Court of King James the Sixth, to make offer of his service and obedience to his Majesty, in the hope of obtaining a pardon; and that, confiding in these assurances, Macgregor came with the Earl of Argyll to Edinburgh.[1] But Birrell represents Macgregor as having been taken by the Earl of Argyll, and brought to Edinburgh with eighteen of Macgregor's friends. He then describes him as conducted to Berwick by the guard, conformably to the Earl's promise that he would put him out of Scottish ground. " Swa," adds this author quaintly, " the Earle keipit ane Hielandmanis promes, in respect he sent the gaird to convoy him out of Scottis grund; but thai wer not directit to pairt with him, bot to fetche him bak agane."[2] The military escort conducted their prisoner only a short way beyond the bridge of Berwick-upon-Tweed, when, turning, they brought him back to Edinburgh, for the purpose of his being put on trial. He arrived in Edinburgh on the evening of the 18th of January 1604. Only two days after, his trial and that of four of his clan, Patrik Aldoche Mac-

---

[1] MS. History of Scotland, Anon., Advocates' Library (A. 4. 35), quoted in Pitcairn's Criminal Trials, vol. ii. p. 434.

[2] Birrell's Diary, quoted in Pitcairn's Criminal Trials, vol. ii. p. 434.

gregour, William Macneill, his servant, Duncan Pudrache Macgregour, and Allaster Macgregour Maccau, took place before the High Court of Justiciary, for the crime of treason, in their having attacked the Laird of Luss whilst armed with a royal commission to resist the " cruel enterprises " of the clan Gregor.

Among the jurors on the trial were the Laird of Grandtully, the chief of Menzies, and Donnach Dhu of Glenurchy.[1]

Having been found guilty, Allaster Macgregor and his four accomplices were sentenced to be hanged at the Cross of Edinburgh on the same day. They were executed in strict conformity with the sentence ; and the gibbet on which Allaster was hanged was, as Birrell informs us, " his awin hicht abone the rest of his freindis." Effect was also given to the forfeiture of their lands, heritages, etc.[2]

The heads of Allaster and of his associate, Patrick Aldoch Macgregour, were, by the orders of the Government, sent to Dumbarton, to be placed on the Tolbooth of that burgh, the chief town of the district where the crimes for which they were executed had been committed.    On 13th February 1604, the Town-Council of Dumbarton "concludit and ordanit that the Laird of Macgregor's heid, with Patrick Auldochy his heid, be put up on the Tollnuith, on the maist convenient place the Baillies and Counsall thinkis guid."[3]

On the 19th of January, the day before his execution, Allaster Macgregor made a declaration or confession, which, if entitled to credit, would throw light on the causes which led to the conflict of Glenfruin, as well as explain other matters connected with the family feuds of that

---

[1] Letter by Major Donald Macgregor to Sir William Drummond Stenart, Grandtully, dated 8th August 1842.—[Grandtully Charter-chest.]

[2] Gavin Colquhoun in Port obtained from King James the Sixth a gift, under the Privy Seal, dated 12th March 1614, of the escheat of all the goods, moveable and unmoveable, of one of them, Allaster Macgregour Macean. —[Original Gift at Rossdhu.]    Gavin summoned Elizabeth Campbell, relict of the de- ceased Allaster Macgregor Maccvan, John and Patrick, his sons, and his daughters, who are not named, to compear before the Lords of Council to hear and see a decreet given in his favour in regard to the said escheat. But the defenders having failed to compear, the Lords of Council, on 24th January 1615, granted a decreet in his favour.—[Copy Decreet at Rossdhu.]

[3] Dumbarton Town-Council Records.

period. In this confession he distinctly throws the whole blame of the outrages committed by the Macgregors against the Colquhouns upon the Earl of Argyll, and accuses that Earl of having instigated him to commit other slaughters and depredations. But, as observed before, declarations which so seriously criminated the Earl of Argyll are not entitled, in the circumstances, to implicit credit, for Allaster was doubtless much exasperated against the Earl, by whom he had been captured and delivered as a prisoner to the Government.

The execution of Allaster Macgregor was followed by the execution of eighteen others, at the Market-Cross of Edinburgh or at the Borrowmure, in February and March, in the same year, for being art and part in the slaughters, fire-raising, reif and herschippis, committed in the month of February 1603, against the Laird of Luss, his friends and partakers, or for intercommuning with the Laird of Macgregor, and reset of him and his friends.[1]

Among other measures adopted by the Government for the extermination of the clan Gregor was the offer of a free pardon to any who should arrest, put to death, and present to justice, any of that clan. Stimulated by the depredations and slaughters which these outlaws had committed upon those of his name, John Colquhoun, fiar of Camstradden, who probably had shared in the bloody conflict at Glenfruin, accompanied by an armed body of men, engaged in " many skirmishes and onsets with divers of them." On one of these occasions, " after a long and dangerous conflict had with them," he succeeded in apprehending two of them, whom he consigned to prison ; and one of them having committed suicide in prison, he presented to the Lords of Privy Council the head of the unhappy man, and he presented in person the other prisoner, who was soon after publicly executed. In these circumstances, he sent a petition to the Lords of Council, praying that they would pass an Act granting him a free pardon, in terms of the acts and proclamations which secured immunity to any one who should slaughter a Macgregor. These facts are detailed in his petition, as recorded in the proceedings of the Privy Council.[2]   That he succeeded in obtaining the object of his petition is highly probable ; but as

[1]  Pitcairn's Criminal Trials, vol. ii. pp. 436-440.        [2]  Act of Privy Council.

the records of the Privy Council at this period are imperfect, we are left without direct evidence to that effect.

While tracing the measures of severity adopted by the Government against the Macgregors, we may also advert to the terms on which the Government were disposed to exercise clemency towards the clan. These terms involved their renouncing their surnames and finding security for their future submission and obedience. With this object Archibald Earl of Argyll was appointed by an Act of the Secret Council, dated at Perth, 11th July 1606, to charge them by his own precept to compear before him when and where he should appoint, with power to grant respites and remissions in favour of such of them as would renounce their own surnames, and find caution to be answerable and obedient to his Majesty's laws in time coming. On the 10th of September 1606, a number of persons of the race and surname of Macgregor personally compeared before the Earl at Downe of Menteith. They took various surnames, such as those of Stewart, Dowgall, Grant, and Cunningham, and they swore that in all time coming they should call themselves and their children, born, or to be afterwards born, by the surnames which they had respectively assumed, under the pain of death. For these persons the Earl voluntarily became surety, under pecuniary penalties, varying from 200 to 500 merks for each, that they should behave themselves as dutiful and obedient subjects to the King, and that all for whom they were answerable, as well as themselves, should observe his Majesty's peace.[1]

In reward of the services of the Earl of Argyll on behalf of the Government against the Macgregors, King James the Sixth granted heritably to him and his heirs, in July 1607, as much of the lands and lordship of Kintyre as would yield a yearly rent of twenty chalders of victual, with the sum of 20,000 merks Scots. The following is the royal letter by which this grant was made, addressed to David Murray, Lord Scoone, his Majesty's Comptroller :—

JAMES R.

Dauid, Lord of Scoone, our Comptrollare, we great yow wele : Forsameikle as, in consideratioun and recompance of the goode and notable seruice done to

ws be our richt trusty and weilbeloued cousing and counsallour, Archibald
Erll of Argyle, Lord Campbell and Lorne, against that insolent and weikit race
of the Clangregour, notorious lymneris and malefactouris, specialie in the inbringing of the Larde of Macgregour, and a nowmer of the principallis of that
name, quhilkis wer worthilie executed for their transgressionis, and for reduce-
ing of a goode nowmer of vthers of that clan, and thair associattis, to our obedience, we ar gratiuslie pleased to bestow vpoun our said cousing sameikle of
our landis and lordship of Kintyre, as will anont in yearlie rent to twentie
chalder of victuall, heretabillie to him and his airis, togidder with the sowme of
twentie thowsand merkis Scottis money, to be payit to him at Martimes nixt.
It is thairfoir our plesour that yee designe sameikle of our said landis and lord-
schip of Kintyre as will affroode tuentie chalder of victuall yearlie, with the
kynd of victuall, and pas, and caus be past and expeid our infeftment thairvpoun in favouris of the said Erll and his airis, and for thair farder securitie, se
the same confirmit in our present Parliament. And heir withall it is lykuise
our pleasour that yee ansuer and mak payment to the said Erll off the said
sowme of tuentie thowsand merkis money foirsaid, at the said terme of Martimes
nixt, and the same salbe thankfullie allowit to yow vpoun compt, keipand this
present, with his discharge vpoun the ressait thairof, for your warrand. Gevin
at our Courte in Whytehall, the nyntein of July 1607.

                                                                DUMBARE.[1]

    Some transactions, though not important, by which Alexander Colqu-
houn of Luss about this time acquired property that had belonged to his
late brother John, may be recorded. These transactions also refer to the
daughters of his brother Sir Humphrey, the circumstances of whose unfortunate death throw around his history a melancholy interest. On 11th
February 1607, Alexander Colquhoun of Luss was retoured heir to his
brother John in an annual-rent of twenty merks from the lands of Kirkmichael-Semple, in the shire of Dumbarton, which was then in the hands
of Robert Semple of Fullwood, the superior, in respect of non-entry by
reason of the death of the said deceased James Colquhoun of Garscube,
possessor of that annual-rent, who died in the month of July 1604. He
was thus retoured, as nearest heir-male, to his brother John Colquhoun,
by reason of the renunciation made by Margaret and Annas Colquhouns,
his nieces, lawful daughters of the late Sir Humphrey Colquhoun of Luss,

                    [1] Original in Argyll Charter-chest.

eldest brother of the deceased John Colquhoun, of all right to be heirs
to the said John, their deceased father's brother, and to the deceased James
Colquhoun of Garscube, their grandfather's brother.[1]

From the chancellary of the Duke of Lennox's regality of Lennox,
Alexander Colquhoun received a precept of sasine, dated 9th May 1607,
for infefting him as nearest and lawful heir of his deceased brother John,
by reason of a renunciation made by his nieces, Margaret and Annas
Colquhouns, in an annual-rent of ten merks, to be yearly uplifted from the
lands of Barris. The precept was addressed to John Napier of Kilmahew,
the superior of the lands. But when required, on 23d May 1607, in the
presence of a notary public, to give Alexander Colquhoun infeftment in
this annual-rent, he refused, alleging that it was necessary for him to be
advised thereanent.[2] On the same day, Mungo Lindsay refused, in obedience to a similar precept, to infeft Alexander Colquhoun, as heir of his
brother John, in two annual-rents, one of five merks and another of £8,
to be uplifted yearly from the Mains of Bonyll Lindsay, in the dukedom
of Lennox and shire of Dumbarton.[3] In both these instances the procurator of Alexander Colquhoun protested in his name.

" Sir Alexander Colquhoun of Luss, knight," was one of the jury on
the trial of William Keith, lawful son to Alexander Keith of Auchquhirsk,
on 23d February 1608, for having killed, with his drawn sword, Thomas
Colstoun, an Englishman, beside the shore of the burgh of Burntisland, in
a quarrel that arose between them when they were drinking, and for which
he was sentenced to be beheaded at the Market-Cross of Edinburgh.[4]

Some of the Macfarlanes, it would appear, were present with the
Macgregors at the conflict of Glenfruin. Dougall Mac coull Macfarlane,
sometime in Drumfad, and afterwards in Tullichintaull, and John Macfarlane, afterwards of Arrochar, who, as we have seen before,[5] were implicated
in the scenes connected with the slaughter of Humphrey Colquhoun in

[1] Original Retour at Rossdhu.
[2] Original Notarial Instrument of Protest,
ibid.
    Original Notarial Instrument of Pro-
test, ibid.

[4] Pitcairn's Criminal Trials, vol. ii. p. 540.
The designation in this instance of Alexander
Colquhoun as a knight is a mistake, as he
did not receive the honour of knighthood.
[5] Vide p. 158.

July 1592, were accused of " being in companie with vmquhile Allaster Macgregour of Glenstra, his kyn and freindis, at the field of Glenfrune," and of being art and part in the slaughters and thefts there perpetrated.

On 31st December 1608, Parlane Macwalter of Auchenvennell became surety for Dougall Mac-coull Macfarlane, sometime in Drumfad and then in Tullichintaull, that he should compear on the 3d day of the next Justice Air of the shire of Dumbarton, where he dwelt, or sooner, upon fifteen days' warning, to underly the law for the above-mentioned crimes. There is also included in the indictment, " for steiling of lxx ky and oxin, pertaining to Alexander Colquhoun of Luss, Robert Macwattie, etc., furth of the lands of Glenmulloche, Innerotachin, and Drum Macnilling, in the moneth of Junii 1602. Item, for the steilling of six scoir ky and oxen in the moneth of July 1602, furth of the lands of Glenfinglas, etc., perteining to the said Alexander Colquhoun of Luss, John Layng, Thomas M'Gilfadrick, and Patrick Colquhoun." On 13th June 1614, John Earl of Mar became surety for Johnne Macfarlane, then of Arrochar, that he should compear, on the third day of the next Justice Air of the shire where he dwelt, to underlie the law for the same crimes as those charged against the others now mentioned.

By the severe laws which had been enacted against the Macgregors, and from the rigour with which these laws were executed, the proscribed clan were infuriated and driven to desperation. Placed beyond the pale of the protection of law, they often fiercely retaliated the wrongs which they believed had been done them, on those who were empowered to punish them, by fire and sword. Against the Laird of Luss, who was invested with such a commission, they were exasperated to the uttermost, and they continued to harass the inhabitants of the Lennox, keeping them in constant terror. In a letter to King James the Sixth, in the year 1609, Alexander Colquhoun renewed his complaints of the aggressions and spoliation which the Macgregors still committed on himself and his tenantry.

MOST GRACIOUS SOVERAIGNE,

May it pleis your most sacred Maiestie, I haif oftymes complained of the insolence and heavy oppressioun committit vpoun me and my tennentis and landis be the clangregour, and haif bene forced to be silent this tyme bygane, hoping that sometyme thair sould [have] bene ane end thairof, but now, finding myself disapoynted, and thay entred to thair former courssis, haif sein occasioun to acquaint zour sacred Maiestie thairwith, besechand zour Maiestie to haif pitie and compassioun vpoun ws, zour Maiestie's obedient subiectis, and remanent poor people quho sufferes, and to provyd tymus remeid thairin ; and, that zour Maiestie may be the better informed in the particulars, I haif acquainted zour Maiestie['s] Secritar thairin, to quhois sufficiency referring the rest, and creving pardoun for importuning zour Maiestie, I lif, in all humilitie, [in] zour Maiestie's most sacred handis.

Your sacred Maiestie's most humble and obedient subject,

ALEXANDER COLQUHOUN off Luss.

Rosdo, the 13th of November 1609.[1]

Influenced by these and similar complaints, the Privy Council continued to adopt other severe measures against the clan Gregor.

Formerly, this clan when pursued betook themselves to the Lochs of Lochlong, Lochegoyll, and Lochlomond, and having the means of transportation to and from these lochs, they found themselves secure, and defied the might of their enemies. The Lords of the Privy Council anticipated that, now when the means of punishing them were put into active operation, the Macgregors, according to their wonted manner, would seek shelter in these lochs, and would thus frustrate the measures of the Government against them. They therefore, on 6th September 1610, ordained that, by public proclamation, all his Majesty's subjects who were owners of the boats and skows upon these lochs, should be prohibited from carrying any of the clan Gregor, their wives, bairns, servants, or goods over them, upon any pretence whatsoever, under the pain of being reputed and punished with all rigour as favourers and assisters of the said clan in all their criminal enterprises.[2]

In the beginning of the following year, January 1611, an Act of the Privy Council was passed—one of the most odious and horrid acts that any Government could sanction,—by which it was attempted to bribe the Macgregors, by the offers of pardon and money, to assassinate each other. It was promised that any person of the name of Macgregor who should slay any person of the same name, of as good rank and quality as himself,

---

[1] Copy Letter at Rossdhu.       [2] Records of Privy Council.

and should prove that slaughter before the Lords of the Privy Council, should receive a free pardon for all his bygone faults, he finding security to be answerable and obedient to the laws in time coming ; and also that whoever should slay any of that race should have a reward in money instantly paid to him, according to the quality of the person slain, the least sum being 100 merks, and for each chieftain and ringleader of the Macgregors £1000.[1]

Despairing of mercy from the Government, the clan at this time mustered in the island of Loch Katrine, and fortified it with men, victual, powder, bullets, and other warlike materials, intending to keep that island as a place of defence against his Majesty's troops.   It was therefore neces - sary to the success of his Majesty's forces in the pursuit of these "woulffis and thevis," as they were called by the Lords of the Privy Council, that all the boats and birlingis which were upon Loch Lomond should be trans- ported from thence to Loch Katrine ; and accordingly the Lords of the Privy Council ordained that all his Majesty's subjects betwixt sixteen and sixty years of age, within the shire of Dumbarton, stewartry of Menteith, and six parishes of the Lennox, in the shire of Stirling, should be summoned, by open proclamation at the Market-Cross of Dumbarton, Stirling, Doune, and Menteith, to meet at the head of Lochlomond on the 12th of February next, for the purpose of carrying the boats and birlingis which were upon Loch Lomond to Loch Katrine.[2]

Whilst the Government were taking these active measures to stimulate the Macgregors to murder each other, and to prevent them from finding shelter in the western lochs, Alexander Colquhoun of Luss, exasperated not only by his great loss at the battle of Glenfruin, but by the additional injuries with which he and his tenants were threatened, or had actually suf- fered from the Macgregors, was prepared to carry into execution the deter- minations of the Government, by personally heading his vassals to fight the obnoxious clan.   On the 31st of January 1611, he appeared at Stirling, before the Lords of the Privy Council, in company with other distinguished personages, including John Earl of Tullibardine, William Lord Murray, his son, Henry Lord St. Colme, Sir Duncan Campbell of Glenurquhy, knight,

¹ Records of Privy Council.                    ² Records of Privy Council.

Sir George Buchanan of that Ilk, James Campbell of Lawers, and Andrew Macfarlane of Arrochar.   Each of them undertook " to go to the feildis, and to enter in actioun and bloode against" the clan Gregor betwixt that date and the 13th of February following, and to prosecute that service for a month at his own charges.   Thereafter the King was to defray the expenses of the maintenance of a hundred men to assist them, whilst they were to bear the cost of another hundred men till the service should be ended. At the same time, the Lords of Council ordained a missive to be written to Duncan Campbell, Captain of Carrick, requiring him to remove all boats out of Lochlong and Lochegoyll, that the clan Gregor might have no passage to these lochs.[1]

Here we may subjoin " Ane speciall Owertour for transplanting the bairnis of clangregour :"—

Item, First, the haill bairnis that is past xii zeir auld to be sent to Irland be zour Lordships warren, to sic settilmen as zour Lordships thinkis meitest that duellis thair, be quhais advysis thair namis to be chengit, and to be maid hirdis, and thair to remane vnder the paine of deid.

As amnent these that ar within tuell zeir auld, that thai be zour Lordships warren be transplantit be south the watteris of Forth and Clyd, conforme to his Majestie's will, to the Justices of Peace of these boundis, at thair nixt grate meitting, quhilk is the first Tuysday of Februar : And be thair advysis to be placeit, and sustenit in townis and parochines, and thair namis chengit, and thair to remane, vnder the pane of ded, with power to the saidis Justiceis of Peace to giff and allow ane fyne to evirilk ane of thame, for the help of thair sustentatioun, and quhen thai come to the age of xii zeris, that they be transplantit to Irland.[2]

Every means was thus used not only to subdue the unfortunate Macgregors, but to extinguish the name, if not to extirpate the race.   Hogg, like Sir Walter Scott, finds a theme for his muse in the tragic history of the clan Gregor, consequent on the battle of Glenfruin.   In his Queen's Wake he introduces a lady of wan visage of the Macgregor clan as bewailing to the bard of Lochlomond the fate of the Macgregors, upon whom, for their slaughter of the Colquhouns, the vengeance of the country was let loose.

[1] Records of Privy Council.            [2] Copy Overture at Rossdhu.

"She told me, and turned my chill'd heart to a stone,
The glory and name of Macgregor was gone :
That the pine[1] which for ages had shed a bright halo,
Afar on the mountains of Highland Glen-Falo,
Should wither and fall ere the turn of yon moon
Smit through by the canker of hated Colquhoun :
That a feast on Macgregors each day should be common,
For years to the eagles of Lennox and Lomond."

An account of some of the ecclesiastical affairs of the parish of Luss, in which Alexander Colquhoun of Luss was concerned, especially of the dispute in which he was involved with the Presbytery of Dumbarton, in regard to the presentation of a new minister to the parish on the death of Mr. Duncan Arrall, may here be introduced.

Mr. Arrall had been deprived, by an Act of the General Assembly in 1605, and the Synod of Clydesdale, 26th February 1606, ordained that the Presbytery of Dumbarton should put into execution against Mr. Arrall, minister at Luss, the Act made against him in the last Assembly, and that they should make provision, before his deposition from the ministry, for the maintenance of himself, his wife and bairns, during his lifetime, seeing he had served a long time in the ministry.[2]   But notwithstanding this deprivation, Mr. Arrall, supported, apparently, by the Laird of Luss and the parishioners, continued in the full possession of the Kirk of Luss until the time of his decease, administering the word and the sacraments, and uplifting the teind duties and teind sheaves thereof from the persons by whom they were payable.[3]

After the death of Mr. Arrall, Alexander Colquhoun of Luss, as lay patron of the kirk of Luss, presented Mr. Malcolm Colquhoun to that kirk, whilst the Presbytery of Dumbarton presented Mr. John Campbell, on the ground that Mr. Arrall, having been lawfully deprived thereof, and a successor not having been presented to that kirk in sufficient time thereafter by Alexander Colquhoun of Luss, laic patron, the right of presentation had *jure devoluto* fallen into their hands.

[1] The pine was the standard, and is still the crest, of the Macgregors.

[2] Extract Act of the Synod of Clydesdale, at Rossdhu.

[3] Information contained in letters of suspension at the instance of the parishioners of Luss against Mr. John Campbell, dated 7th April 1609.   Original at Rossdhu.

On the 15th of March 1609, Adam Colquhoun of Hill produced, before the Presbytery of Dumbarton, a presentation, subscribed by Alexander Colquhoun of Luss, as patron to the benefice of Luss, requiring the Presbytery to admit Mr. Malcolm Colquhoun to the benefice and cure thereof. The moderator, in name of his brethren, answered, that the presentation could not then be received, inasmuch as the patron, from his oversight and negligence, had, in the present instance, lost that right, which had fallen into the hands of the Presbytery. Duncan Arrall, last parson thereof, having been deprived long ago, and so civilly dead by the law, they had already taken some of Mr. John Campbell's trials, with a view to his induction.[1]

Two persons having been thus presented to the kirk of Luss, the payers of the teinds, understanding, or apprehending, that both presentees intended to exact from them the teinds and duties of their lands within that parish, and being willing to make payment thereof to any one of the said parties having best right thereto, letters of suspension, dated 7th April 1609, at the instance of Robert Colquhoun of Camstradden, John Colquhoun, fiar thereof, Gavin Colquhoun, in Inschevannock, and David Colquhoun of Port, for themselves, and in name of the other parishioners of Luss, were raised against both Mr. Campbell and Mr. Malcolm Colquhoun. By these letters the two presentees were summoned to compear before the Privy Council at Edinburgh, on the 16th of May following, bringing with them all their rights and titles whereby they made claim to the foresaid teinds, with the letters, if any, raised at their instance against the complainers thereupon, to be seen and considered by the Lords of Council, and to hear and see the same suspended *simpliciter* upon the said complainers in time coming.[2]

A considerable number of the parishioners of Luss opposed the admission of Mr. Campbell as minister of that parish. Their opposition did not, however, apparently arise from any objection to him personally, but from the circumstance that he had not received a presentation from Alexander Colquhoun of Luss, the patron of the parish kirk. In the following document, addressed to the Lords of the Privy Council and to the Presbytery of

[1] Extract Minute of the Presbytery of Dumbarton, subscribed by Mr. James Stirling, clerk to the Presbytery, at Rossdhu.

[2] Original Letters of Suspension at Rossdhu, *ut supra*.

Dumbarton, they dissent from his admission as minister of that parish until he had first received a presentation from the Laird of Luss :—

To all and sundrie quhom it effeiris, to quhais knawledge thir presentis sall cum, speciallie to the Lordis of his Maiestie's Secreit Counsell, Sessioun, Moderatour, and Brethrein of the Presbiterie off Dunbartane, We, certain of the gentillmen elderis, perrochineris off the perochin off Luss, and induellaris within the baronie thairoff, vnderscriveris, that is to say, Adame Lindsay of Stuckrodger, Mungo Buchannane, in Mydill Tullichewin [and 44 others], grant and confess us to haiff testifiet and declairit, lyke as we, the foirnamit personnes, perrochineris off Luss, and ilk ane of us, be the tenour heiroff, testifies and declairis that we gaiff nevir ony advyses, consentis and assentis, as zit, at ony tyme by past, nor zit sall giff our consentis and advyses in ony tyme to cum, to the admissioun, electioun, or ressaving of Maister Johne Campbell to be our pastour and minister at the said Kirk of Luss, unto the tyme that first he [be] qualifeit and tryit be the memberis of the kirk, and in especiall quhill he be lawfullie provydit and admittit to the service off the cuir thairat be the Richt Honorabill Alexander Colquhoun of Luss, as vndoubtit patroun thairoff, swa that we, and everie ane of ws, be thir presentis, dissassentis *simpliciter* fra the said Mr. Johne Campbell, his bruiking and joising off ony ministerie, at our said perroche kirk, without the said Alexander his admissioun, appoyntment, and consent being first had and obtenit thairto ; and thir presentis we ratifie and approve to be trew : The quhilk we mak notour, manifest and knawin, to all personnes haveing entres thairto. In witness quhairoff we haiff subscryvit this our testimoniall and testificatioun with our handis, as follows :—At the foirsaid Kirk of Luss, the elevint day of Februar, the zeir of God 1ᵐ sex hundreyth and ten zeiris.[1]

All objections were, however, overruled, and Mr. Campbell, the Presbytery's presentee, was admitted minister of the parish of Luss.

But his settlement in the parish, against the wish of the patron, who was also the principal heritor, and likewise against the wishes of many of the parishioners, was not likely to lead to a pacific incumbency.

Not long after the settlement of Mr. Campbell as minister of Luss, Alexander Colquhoun of Luss accused him of having taken part against

[1] Dennistoun's MSS. Dennistoun says that "the original of this paper and of the presentation to Mr. Arrall, given at p. 180, were bought in 1840 by W. B. D. D. Turn-bull, advocate, from Mr. Stillie, bookseller in Edinburgh, and copied by him (Mr. Dennistoun) April 1850."

him at the battle of Glenfruin ; and he brought a complaint against him on that ground before the Presbytery of Glasgow. The Laird of Luss, when examined before that court, admitted that though he could prove that Mr. Campbell was upon the field on that occasion, he could not prove that he was there as one of his enemies. He would have had the Presbytery by interrogation to make Mr. Campbell his own accuser. But this they very properly declined to do ; upon which the matter was dropped :—" Presbytery of Glasgow, May 16, 1610.—Quhilk day comperit Alexander Colquhoun of Lus, he lachtfullie summoned to this dyett be the synodall assemblie, to produce his witness aganst Mr. John Campbell, his minister, that he was ane pairtie aganst him with Clangregour at Glenfrune. The said laird bene enquyrit be the moderator, to wit, the Bischope of Glasgow, gif he could qualifie that Mr. John Campbell was present in the foirnamed day as a pairtie aganst him? Answerit, He could prove that he wes upon the field, bot he could not prove that he wes aganst him ; bot the said laird desyrit the brethren of the Presbyterie to demand sic interrogattar at the said Mr. John, quhilk wuld prove the said Mr. John to have been thair as a pairtie aganst him." Then follow the reasons for which the Presbytery declined to put any such question or questions to Mr. Campbell.[1]

Alexander Colquhoun of Luss became involved in another dispute with Mr. Campbell. Having been provided to the kirk of the parish of Luss, Mr. Campbell claimed the 20s. lands of Ross, in the barony of Luss and shire of Dumbarton, as his glebe, according to a designation made thereof in his favour ; and he obtained a decreet of the Lords of Council against Alexander Colquhoun of Luss and his son John Colquhoun, fiar thereof and their tenants, charging them to remove themselves, their goods and gear, from these lands within ten days after the charge, under the pain of rebellion and putting them to the horn.

Alexander Colquhoun of Luss and his son contested Mr. Campbell's right to these lands as his glebe. Accordingly, on 9th August 1616, they raised letters of suspension against him, and summoned him to compear before the Lords of Council and Session at Edinburgh, on the 1st of November, bringing with him the said designation, and the letters of horning which he had raised thereupon, with the execution thereof, to be seen and considered by their Lordships, and to hear and see the same suspended *simpliciter* upon the complainers in time coming, for the reasons assigned in the summons, and for others to be proposed by them, in their names and on their behalf.

In these letters of suspension they allege that, by an Act of Parliament anent the designation of ministers' glebes, it was specially provided that the designation of a glebe should be made with advice and consent of two of the parishioners, and not otherwise; but that the designation in favour of Mr. Campbell was made without advice and consent of the parishioners, at least without the advice of two of them; that, on the contrary, it was privily made by himself and certain of his brethren, the consent of the parishioners thereto having never been required, and was therefore, according to the said Act of Parliament, manifestly null; whence it was evident that no execution could follow thereupon to remove them from the lands of Ross. They further affirm that there was a glebe of land extending to four acres or thereby, which was designed of old to the ministers serving the cure of the kirk of Luss, and which the deceased ministers, Mr. James Colquhoun, Mr. William Chirnside, and Mr. Duncan Arrall, ministers of that kirk, and their predecessors, had by virtue thereof remained in possession of, during their lifetime, as their only glebe land, the greater part of which they had latterly converted into gardens and orchards for their greater profit. To this glebe, which lay partly on the north and partly on the south side of the kirk of Luss and water of Luss, Mr. Campbell had a right, but to nothing more. He could not take any new designation of the 20s. land of Ross, which was situated far distant from the kirk of Luss, whilst other lands intervened. If the present glebe was in any degree short of the four acres, it ought to be supplemented not from the lands of Ross, which were neither parsonage nor vicarage lands, but from others which lay betwixt them and the kirk of Luss. The lands of Ross contained more than twenty-six acres of land, including a wood of oak, extending to sixteen acres, and consisting of many thousands of trees, which Mr. Campbell daily cut down, destroyed, and sold in the country, and used at his pleasure, under pretence of the said designation, to the great damage of the complainers, the sole proprietors of the said lands, whom he excluded from them.[1]

The name of Alexander Colquhoun of Luss appears in the testament of his maternal uncle, Robert Boyd of Badinheath, a younger son of Robert fourth Lord Boyd. This relative died in 1611. In his testament, which was made at his dwelling-house of Badinheath, 14th July 1611, and in which he ordained his body to be buried in his predecessor's aisle, at the Kirk of Leinze, is the following clause:—" Item, I leif to the Laird of Lus, my sister['s] son, my ryding sword; and farder, I dischairge and levis the said Laird of Lus all debtis or sowmes of money that I or my saids execu-touris can ask or crave of him, either for himself or his vmquhile brother, for ony caus quhatsumevir, preceiding the date heirof; providing always that the said Laird of Lus exoner and dischairge me, my airis, execu-touris, and assignees of all sowmes of money that he can crave of me vtherwayis."[2]

The name of Alexander Colquhoun of Luss also occurs in the tes-tament of Elizabeth Hamilton, (sister-german to John Hamilton of Grange, beside Kilmarnock,) who died unmarried in June 1611. In the Inventar among the debts awand to her by others is—" Item, be Alexander Colquhoun of Lus, executour to vmquhile Dame Margaret Colquhone, relict of vmquhile Robert Lord Boyd, left in legacy be hir to the deid, the sowme of fourtie pundis."[3]

In 1612, Alexander Colquhoun of Luss and others, his friends and tenants, were involved in legal proceedings with the Provost, Bailies, and commu-nity of the burgh of Dumbarton. Certain burgesses and inhabitants of that burgh, it would appear, had surreptitiously procured from his Majesty a charter and pretended infeftment of sundry lands, tenements, annual-rents, etc., alleged to have belonged of old to the town of Dumbarton. In this pretended infeftment they had not only comprehended a great number of lands which were the property of sundry noblemen and gentlemen in that part of the country, but had also caused to insert therein sundry lands,

---

[1] Original Letters of Suspension at Ross-dhu.

[2] The Testament was confirmed 4th May 1612.—Commissariot of Glasgow.

[3] Records of the Commissariot of Glasgow.

moors, and commonties which belonged to Alexander Colquhoun of Luss, his tenants and servants, especially a great part of the moor of Colquhoun, in the shire of Dumbarton, which, as was well known to them, and to all the inhabitants of that part of the country, belonged to him, and had been held in peaceable possession by his predecessors, their tenants and servants, in all time bygone, past the memory of man. Proceeding further, the foresaid persons, their servants, complices, and others, in their names, of their causing, continually molested him, his tenants and servants, in the peaceable possession of all others their lands, heritages, woods, meadows, moors, commonties, and pasturages; cut and destroyed their wood plantations; cast down the dykes and hedges of their pastures; fed and herded their cattle therein, and upon all other their lands, commonties, meadows and pasturage; sheared and carried away the same; sold and disposed thereupon; made roads and passages through their lands, woods, etc., where none existed before; and committed other the like injuries. Accordingly Alexander Colquhoun of Luss, his friends and tenants, obtained against the Town Council and community of Dumbarton, on 15th May 1612, letters of lawborrows under the royal signet. By these letters the sheriffs, to whom they were addressed, were charged to take the complainers' oaths that they dreaded molestation from the foresaid persons; after which they were, in his Majesty's name, to command the same persons to find sufficient cautioners for them before the Lords of Council, to be recorded in the Books of Council, that the complainers, their wives, bairns, brothers, men, tenants, and servants, should not be harmed or molested in their bodies, lands, heritages, corns, cattle, etc., by them, nor by their men, tenants, servants, nor by any others of their causing or hounding out, nor by any others, whom it might be in their power to stop, under various penalties mentioned in the letters.[1]

Alexander Colquhoun of Luss had been appointed by Dame Margaret Colquhoun Lady Boyd, relict of the deceased Robert Lord Boyd, who died in August 1601, in her latter will and testament, her executor, by virtue whereof he had right to all the goods, gear, and debts that belonged to her at the time of her death. On 12th March 1613, he summoned Robert, then Lord Boyd, son and heir of the deceased Thomas

[1] Copy Letters of Lawborrows at Rossdhu.

Lord Boyd—who was summoned by open proclamation at the Market-Cross of Edinburgh and pier and shore of Leith, because he was then furth of the realm of Scotland—and many of her debtors, to compear before the Lords of Council at Edinburgh, 16th May following, to answer at the instance of the said complainer, and to hear and see themselves decerned, by decreet of the said Lords, to make payment to him of what they owed to the said deceased Lady Boyd.[1]

Since the raid of Glenfruin nothing had occurred to mitigate the animosity between the Colquhouns and the Macgregors : rather every circumstance had tended to embitter it on both sides.

Colin Campbell of Lundy had been appointed commissioner for pursuit of the clan Gregor in absence of Archibald Earl of Argyll, his brother, lieutenant over that clan. James Campbell of Lawers had a like commission from his Majesty and the Privy Council. By these two commissioners a petition was presented to the Lords of Secret Council to stop execution of a charge of horning, at the instance of Alexander Colquhoun of Luss, against some of the ill-fated clan. The petitioners set forth that Alexander Colquhoun of Luss, upon an old alleged grudge, had privily raised letters, whereby he had caused charge a certain number of the Clan Gregor, and some of the Clan Ean Devi Macallaster, and other alleged broken men of the towns, by open proclamation at the market crosses, where they were said to have residence, to find caution acted in the Books of Adjournal, for their compearance before the Justice-General and his deputies, in the Tolbooth of Edinburgh, at a certain day, to underly the law for the committing of certain slaughters at the field of Glenfruin, or thereafter, upon the said Alexander Colquhoun of Luss, his men, tenants, and servants, their lands and possessions. The petitioners further stated, that, as they had been informed, he had, most wrongously, considering that the said Macgregors were remitted, caused denounce the said clans his Majesty's rebels for not finding, as he affirmed, the said caution ; that some of them had done service, conformably to his Majesty's Acts and proclamations, and were in present service against the rest of that rebellious

[1] Original Summons at Rossdhu.

2 F

race; that some of the others who were charged were of the Clan Ean Devi Macallaster, who had done service and were remitted, had found caution, and were in present service; and that some of the others charged were at present in service with the petitioners. If, then, the said persons, they add, contrary to his Majesty's proclamations and special protection and remission granted in their favour, should be charged or denounced, the present service intrusted to the petitioners would not only result in disappointment, but the said persons would join and assist the said rebellious race, especially at that time, when the Laird of Luss had taken unlawful advantage against the Commissioners employed in that service, which they had almost finished. They therefore besought their Lordships that an Act might be expede in favour of the said persons; that letters should be published at the market crosses of the burghs where they were charged or denounced, relieving them from the process of horning; and also that command might be given to the Justice-Clerk and his deputies not to direct any such letters at the instance of the said Laird of Luss against the foresaid persons for the causes above mentioned.[1]

The Lords of Secret Council, 18th April 1613, ordained an officer to charge the Laird of Luss to compear personally before them upon the 18th of May next, to hear and see the desire of this petition granted, or else to show cause to the contrary; and, in the meantime, till that day they required the Laird of Luss to forbear the execution of the letters of horning.[2]

On the 15th of June the Laird of Lundie was, according to appointment, to give in to the Privy Council a report of his proceedings in the service against the clan Gregor. It being judged expedient that the noblemen, barons, and gentlemen, who were connected with the part of the country where that clan resided, and who were their landlords, should be present to hear that report and to give their judgment and advice to his Majesty, the following letter was addressed by the Secret Council to Alexander Colquhoun, desiring his attendance at the meeting of the Council on that day, for that purpose :—

TRAIST FREIND,—After oure hairtlie commendationis, the Laird of Lundy

[1] Petition at Rossdhu.
[2] Order of Privy Council endorsed on the foresaid Petition.

who hes the chairge and burdyne of the seruice aganis the Clangregour, now in the
absence of the Erll of Ergyle, his bruther, furth of this realme, being desyrous
to gif ane accompt of his procceidingis in that seruice, and what restis as zit
vnperfytit thairof, the counsale hes assignit vnto him the fyftene day of Junij
nixttocum, for making of this accompt, and whereas it is verie requisite and
expedient that suche noblemen, baronis and gentilmen as dwellis in the
cuntreyis ewest vnto the Clangregour, and ar landislordis vnto thame, be
present at this accompt-making, to the effect thay may informe his Maiestei's
Counsaill of all suche questionis as may result and be moved vpoun that
accompt : These ar, thairfore, to requeist and desyre yow to addresse your selff
heir agane the said day, to assist his Maieste's Counsaill be zour aduise, counsaill, and informatioun, in euerie suche thing as salbe proponned at the making
of that accompt. We looke that the Erll of Ergyle himselff wil be present at
the making of this accompt, and, thairfore, your presence and aduise thairin is
so mutche the more necessar and expedient; and so resting assured of zour
keiping of this dyet, as zou respect his Maiestei's obedience, the weill of that
seruice, and peace of the cuntrey, we commit zou to God. Frome Edinburgh,
the thrid day of May 1613.

Your verie good freindis,

AL. CANCELL'
To oure right traist freind, the Laird of Lus.[1]                      JO. PRESTOUN.

The landlords of the clan Gregor were, according to the proportion of
their lands, to take the children of that clan and bring them up till they
were eighteen years of age, when they were to present them to the Privy
Council, by whom their future fate was to be decided. At the meeting of
the Privy Council, on 8th July 1613, it was found that these landlords had
failed to take these children off the hands of the Laird of Lawers, for
which they were to be charged to make payment to him of twenty merks
out of every merkland pertaining to them and formerly possessed by the
clan Gregor. At their meeting, on 30th of November same year, the
Council relieved these landlords from this payment, provided they took
each his proportion of the clan Gregor's bairns and brought them up until
they were eighteen years of age. By the same Act it was ordained that,
should any of these children make their escape, they were, if under fourteen
years of age, to be scourged and burnt on the check for the first offence,

<hr>

[1] Original Letter at Rossdhu.

to be hanged for the second, and if above fourteen years of age they were to be hanged at once.[1]

The subsequent fate of the clan Gregor, around whom much interest has been thrown by their feuds and their misfortunes, which the genius of Sir Walter Scott has invested with additional attraction, may be briefly noticed. Though the clan assumed other surnames, and, finding caution for their future obedience, remained for a number of years in a great measure quiet, they still retained the memory of their descent and their attachment to each other. But a new generation of the clan grew up, which daily increased in number and strength. The Parliament, in 1617, formally ratified the Act of the Secret Council in 1603, by which the clan had been forbidden, under the penalty of death, to bear the name of Gregor or Macgregor. On 29th August 1621, the Privy Council complained that the clan were beginning to hold their meetings, and to go in troops over the country, armed with all offensive weapons, and that some of the ringleaders, who once gave obedience and found caution, had broken loose, and had committed sundry disorders in the country; and, therefore, they renewed their former Act made against such of the clan as had been at Glenfruin, forbidding them to wear any weapon but a pointless knife, with which to cut their food, under pain of death, the Act to be extended against the whole of that name. In the reign of Charles the First, the Parliament of 1633 re-established the former laws against the clan, by reason, as is stated in the preamble to the Act, of their having broken out in outrage on many of the surrounding counties. Notwithstanding these severe measures, the Macgregors maintained, during the civil war, their loyalty to the house of Stuart, whose banner they bravely supported with their claymores. For this unflinching loyalty, Charles the Second, upon his restoration, rescinded, in the first Scottish Parliament of his reign, in 1661, the various Acts that bristled on the Statute Book against the Macgregors, and restored them to all their rights and privileges as subjects. But in the year 1693 the penal laws against them were re-enacted by Parliament, in an Act of King William, entitled, An Act for the Justiciary in the Highlands. These laws were not, however, henceforth

[1] Records of Privy Council.

rigorously executed; but it was not till the reign of George the Third that they were finally repealed, and that the clan were allowed to resume their real name of Macgregor.

The escheat of Sir Humphrey Colquhoun of Luss, the eldest brother of Alexander Colquhoun, was gifted to Robert Chirnside of Over Possill. Having obtained an assignation of this gift, Alexander Colquhoun summoned Lord John Hamilton and his cautioners to appear before the Lords of the Privy Council, to hear and see a decreet of their Lordships ordaining Lord John Hamilton to make payment of 10,000 merks, promised by him as the tocher of his daughter Jean, in the marriage-contract between her and Sir Humphrey Colquhoun. But this summons having slept since 2d February 1597, when it was last called, and nothing having been done therein, to the complainer's great hurt, he, on 9th July 1613, summoned Andrew Hamilton of Lethame, (the only contracting party in that marriage-contract then in life, having been one of the cautioners of the deceased Lord John Hamilton,) Margaret and Annas Colquhoun, daughters and heirs of the deceased Sir Humphrey, and Jean Hamilton, his relict, and Sir John Campbell of Ardkinglas, then her spouse, to compear before the Lords of the Privy Council at Edinburgh, on the 22d day of July, to hear and see the said matter called anew and resumed.[1] How this matter ended we have not discovered.

In the year 1613,[2] Alexander Colquhoun of Luss obtained from Sir Aulay Macaulay of Ardincaple, knight, " for certain sums of money, commodities, pleasures and benefits paid and done" by him to the granter, a charter of the lands and isle of Inschvanik, with the houses, buildings, woods, fishings, and pertinents of the same, lying in Lochlomond, in the earldom of Lennox and shire of Dumbarton, without reversion.[3]

The year 1615 was notable for the trial of Patrick Earl of Orkney for treasonable rebellion committed by Robert Stewart, his illegitimate son, and his rebellious associates in Orkney, and specially caused, commanded, devised, and directed by the said Patrick Earl of Orkney, his father. For

[1] Original Summons at Rossdhu.
[2] The day of the month is left blank in the charter.
[3] Original Charter at Rossdhu.

that crime the Earl was tried on the 1st of February that year, and was sentenced to be beheaded at the Market-Cross of Edinburgh. Alexander Colquhoun of Luss was one of the assize appointed for the trial. Many of the assizors were absent on that important occasion, which may be partly accounted for from the "grit storme and seasone of the zeir," but Calderwood asserts that they "withdrew themselves from his [the Earl's] assise." The Laird of Luss was also absent, and he sent an excuse that he was unable to be present from sickness, which was admitted by the justice. "Compeirit the said day, Thomas Fallasdaill, Provoist of Dumbarten, *excusatorio nomine*, for Alexander Colquhoun of Luse, and declairit that he was visseit with ane grit seiknes, and nocht hable to travell to the keiping of this dyet, being summond to pas vpone the said Erle of Orknayis assise ; and thairupoune producet ane testimoniall, subscryvit be Mr. Walter Stewart, minister at Kilpatrik.   Quhilk the justice admittit," etc. [1]

Two years after this indisposition the death of Alexander Colquhoun of Luss occurred, namely, on the 23d of May 1617.   The testament, testamentar, and inventar of the goods, gear, debts, and sums of money which belonged to him at the time of his decease, were given up by himself, in so far as concerned the nomination of his executors and legacies, and by Humphrey Colquhoun for himself, and in name and behalf of Jean Colquhoun, Alexander, George, Walter, Adam, Nansy, Katharine, Helen, and Mary Colquhouns, executors nominated by the deceased, in so far as concerned the inventar of his goods and of the debts owing to him.   The sum of the inventar, which consisted of cattle, horses, oats, and bear, was £6052, 13s. 4d.   The debts owing to him, which form a lengthened enumeration, comprising chiefly rents due by tenants, were £27,666, 16s. 4d.   The sum of the inventar and debts was £33,719, 9s. 9d.

The testament is as follows :—

Att Rosdo, the sextein and sevintein dayes of Maij, the zeir of God j⁽ᵐ⁾ vj⁽ᶜ⁾ and sevintein zeiris, the quhilk day the said Allexander Colquhoun of Lus declairis out of his mouth that his bairnis, viz., Vmphra, Jeane, Allexander, Nans, Kathrein, Walter, Adame, Helein, Marie, and George Colquhounes, his lawfull sones and dochteris, [are] to be his executouris and intromettouris with his

[1] Pitcairn's Criminal Trials, vol. iii. p. 318.

gudis and geir ; and ordanes Jeane to haif quhatsumever silver and gold be in his kistis, by and attour quhatsumever is provydit to hir, with all the help hir brother may, swa be his will is, that he be first respectit in speciallie to advance her with the soume of ten thousand pundis, in name of tocher, for contentatioun of all, sche disponand all benefeit sche micht haif be hir father, in fauouris of Johne, quha is to pay the said soume. Lykas, he ordanes his eldest sone Johne, Mr. Andro Boyd, Bischop of Argyle, the Laird of Buchanan,[1] . . . . . . . . . . . . His will is, that notwithstanding quhatsumever provisioun is anent the Ireland landis, that Adame haif the same. Item, the said Allex-ander Colquhoun of Lus will is that his son Vmphra haif the comprysit landis, viz., the Camroun and Balveis land, and that Johne Colquhoun, portioner of Mylntoun, dispone his assignatioun of fourtie akeris land of Banachtane to the said Vmphra, and that Johne Colquhoun, fear of Lus, sone and air to the said Allexander, being helper and consenter to his said fatheris will, quhilk he promeiss. Witness day, zeir, and place foirsaid, John Colquhoun of Camstrodan, Mr. Archibald Camroun, persoun of Inchekalloch, John Colquhoun in Mylntoun, Parlan Macfarlane of Auchenvennel, Andro Colquhoun, and Johne Buntein of Ardoch, writer heirof. I, John Colquhoun, fear of Lus, obleiss me, be thir presentis, to performe and do my fatheris will in the haill premiss abonewritten, and farder to the weill of my brether and sisteris, sa far as I may, day and place, Witness foirsaidis : Sic subscribitur, Allexander Colquhoun of Lus, Johne Colquhoun, fear of Lus ; John Colquhoun of Camstrodan, witnes, Mr. Ard. Camroun, witnes, John Colquhoun, witnes, Johne Buntein, witnes. Item, to Thomas Falasdaill he willis to be gevin at Mertymes nixt ane thousand merkis. Item, to Johne Colquhoun of Camstrodane he willis to be gevin ane thousand merkis at Mertymes nixt. Item, to Robert Colquhoun of Ballarnik he willis to be gevin ane thousand merkis money, to be payit at the said terme. Item, to John Colquhoun of Mylnetoun he willis to be gevin fyve hundreth merkis money, and that in contentatioun of his pairt of the harschip of Col-quhoun, to be payit at the said terme. Item, to Patrik Colquhoun thair, he willis to be gevin fyve hundredth merkis at the said terme, for the foirsaid hairschip. Item, to Andro Colquhoun, his seruand, he willis to be gevin fyve hundreth merkis money at the said terme ; and to Beatrix Colquhoun, his ser-uand, ane hundreth pundis money at the said terme. Item, he ordanes and willis Mr. Archibald Camroun's band, conteining the soume of ane hundreth pundis, be deliuerit to him, without payment making of the said soume, in tackin of his guid will to discharge the said Mr. Archibald of the said soume. Item, to James Colquhoun he willis to be gevin fyve hundreth merkis money at

<hr>

[1] A portion is here evidently omitted.

the said terme. Item, he ordanes the haill thing that lyis vpoun Balveis landis to be onlie geviu to Vmphra, his secund sone, and the Cameroun to be sauld to the said Vmphrai's vse, and his bairnis pairt of guid that will fall him, to be maid in silvir. And ordanes Thomas Falasdaill to mak renunciatioun and resignatioun of his richt of vmquhile Mr. Johne Johnestoune's hous in Edinburgh, in fauoris of the said Vmphra, and thir haill thingis being maid in ane forme to be imployit vpoun the bying of the landis of Balvie, and that be the advyse of the Laird of Buchanan, the Bischop of Argyle, and his eldest sone Johne ; and, failzeing that the saidis thingis will extend to the soume that may by the saidis landis, ordanes the soume that sall happin be the price of the saidis landis to be fillit furth aff the haill heid of his geir. In witnessing of the premiss to be his will, he subscriuit thir presentis, writin be Mr. Archibald Cameroun, persoun of Inche Kalloch, with his hand, at Rosdo, the said day abonewrittin, befoir thir witness, Thomas Fallasdaill of Ardochbeg, Mr. Johne Campbell, minister at Lus, James Colquhoun at Port of Rosdo, and John Colquhoun, his eldest sone, and Duncane Macinturnour, in Tor. Sic subscribitur, Allexander Colquhoun of Lus ; Johne Colquhoun, witnes, Mr. Johne Campbell, witnes, James Colquhoun, witnes, Duncan Macinturnour, witnes.[1]

It does not appear that Alexander Colquhoun was ever knighted. Among the Luss writs there is none in which he is designated knight, although in some of the numerous official documents connected with the Macgregors he was so designated, apparently through mistake.

By his wife, Helen Buchanan, Alexander Colquhoun had six sons and five daughters. His sons were—

1. John, who succeeded him, and who was created a baronet.

2. Humphrey of Balvie, in the parish of East Kilpatrick and county of Dumbarton. By the will of his father, now quoted, a sum of money was left for the special purpose of purchasing for Humphrey, his second son, the estate of Balvie. When his elder brother, Sir John Colquhoun, was nearly ruined through the mismanagement of his affairs, Humphrey interposed and preserved the estates in the family. Having purchased the debts of the most urgent creditors, he acquired, by appraising, the lands and barouies of Luss and Colquhoun. Of these he obtained a charter under

[1] Contemporary Extract Testament confirmed by the Commissary of Glasgow, 7th September 1620.

the Great Seal, on 9th November 1633, and he also obtained, on 11th January 1644, a charter of the lands and barony of Luss.[1] Humphrey Colquhoun had the satisfaction of seeing his exertions for preserving the family estates crowned with success, and he reconveyed them, on 26th August 1647, to his nephew, John Colquhoun, younger of Luss, the legitimate heir. Humphrey Colquhoun of Balvic purchased from James Earl of Abercorn, by a contract, dated at Paisley, 12th July 1637, the teind-sheaves and parsonage teinds of his lands of Meikill Balvie, half lands of Forgiestoune, Ledcamroch, Bannachtane, and Coilheuche, in the parish of Kilpatrick and shire of Dumbarton. This sale and purchase were made in pursuance of a determination given out by his Majesty, ordaining that every heritor should have the teinds of his own lands upon the conditions expressed in that determination.[2]

On the restoration of King Charles the Second, in the year 1660, the Scottish Parliament, in demonstration of their loyalty, granted to the King, by an Act passed on 29th March 1661, a yearly subsidy of £40,000, " towards the entertainment of any such force as his Majesty should think proper to raise and support within the kingdom." Sir Humphrey Colquhoun of Balvie was one of the commissioners appointed for uplifting the proportion of the tax payable by the shire of Dumbarton.[3] The honour of knighthood was conferred upon Sir Humphrey previous to the year 1661. He was probably created a knight on the restoration of King Charles the Second. But the exact time when the honour was conferred has not been ascertained.

Sir Humphrey Colquhoun of Balvie married Dame Margaret Somerville, second daughter of Gilbert eighth Lord Somerville. No prenuptial contract had passed between them; but, in fulfilment of a promise made to her before their marriage, he made provision for her by a postnuptial contract, without date, by which he ratified all

[1] Reg. Mag. Sig., Lib. lvii. No. 398.
[2] Original Contract at Rossdhu.
[3] Acts of the Parliaments of Scotland, vol. vii. p. 92.

2 G

former provisions, rights, and infeftments, granted by him in her favour, and also became bound to infeft her in liferent in the lands of Garscube, Connaltoun of Colquhoun, and others.[1] Of the marriage of Sir Humphrey Colquhoun and Margaret Sommerville there was no issue.[2]

3. Alexander. Letters of resignation, by Gavin Colquhoun in Inchevauuogt and Elizabeth Colquhoun, spouses, of 20 merks from a tenement in the burgh of Dumbarton, in favour of Alexander's father in liferent, and of himself in fee, were produced at the Sheriff Court of Dumbarton, on 9th November 1602.[3] In 1607, Alexander Colquhoun of Luss purchased for his son Alexander, by contract, dated 4th September 1607, from James Dennistoun, in Boighous, an annual-rent of 600 merks, to be uplifted yearly from whatever lands or heritages belonged to him within the realm of Scotland, under reversion. In the contract the said James Dennistoun engaged to let his six pound lands of Tullychewen to the said Alexander Colquhoun, younger, until the redemption of that annual-rent.[4] Alexander obtained the half of the four pound land of Auchengaven from John Colquhoun of Camstraddcn, by contract, dated 15th May 1612. In this contract he is styled third son of Alexander Colquhoun of Luss. Robert Colquhoun, son of the said John, and Patrick Colquhoun of Auchintulloch, were witnesses.[5] Alexander was infefted, 29th December 1614, in an annual-rent of eight stones of cheese from the lands of Auchengaven, which his father had purchased for him.[6] Mr. Alexander Colquhoun, lawful son to the deceased Alexander Colquhoun of Luss, obtained from Mr. Alexander Seytoun of Culcreiche, for certain sums of money then paid to him, an assignation, dated 2d December 1626, of the mails, farms, and duties due to him by the tenants of Bannachries.[7]

Alexander Colquhoun married Marion Stirling before 18th June

[1] Original Contract at Rossdhu.
[2] Memorie of the Somervilles, vol. ii. p. 87
[3] Dumbarton Sasine Records, fol. 238.
[4] Original Contract at Rossdhu.

[5] Original Contract in Charter-Chest of Camstradden.
[6] Original Instrument of Sasine at Rossdhu.
[7] Original Assignation, ibid.

1632, on which date they had a daughter baptized Jean. In the registration of the baptism he is named and designated Alexander Colquhoun, brother-german to Sir John Colquhoun of Luss.[1] Alexander Colquhoun appears to have died without surviving issue.

4. Walter. For the furtherance of his business, and for his better outfit for foreign parts, he received certain sums of money from his brother, Sir John Colquhoun of Luss, for which he assigned to him, on 27th July 1629, all his right of bairns' portion of gear belonging to him by the death of his father, Alexander, and his mother, Helen Buchanan.[2] He died abroad, without issue.

5. Adam. In December 1634, Adam Colquhoun, brother to the Laird of Luss, was indebted to William Towart (Stewart) £42, 2s.[3]

6. George. He was matriculated a member of the University of Glasgow 1st March 1622.[4] His name appears in connection with one of the last of his father's transactions. Thomas Fallasdaill of Ardochbeg, on 31st January 1617, granted that he had borrowed and received from Alexander Colquhoun of Luss, and George, his son, 1100 merks Scots, and bound himself to repay that sum to the Laird, and, in the event of his death, to his son, George Colquhoun, at the term of Martinmas following.[5] This sum not having been paid, nor the annual-rent thereof for a number of years, George, on the 29th of March 1625, obtained in a court of appraising, held in the Burgh Court of Edinburgh, a decreet of appraising of the lands of Ardochbeg, Hoill, and Dalreoch, and several tenements, from the said Thomas Fallasdaill. This decreet was confirmed by the Court of Session, 30th September 1625.[6] George Colquhoun, on the 23d of May 1627, made an assignation of the above bond to his brother John, which proceeds on the narrative that " Johne, now of Lus, my eldest lawfull brother, in my necessitie hes contentit,

[1] Baptism Register of the Parish and City of Edinburgh.

[2] Original Assignation at Rossdhu.

[3] Dumbarton Records, loose slips, vol. i.

[4] Munimenta Universitatis Glasguensis, vol. iii. p. 76.

[5] Original Extract Obligation at Rossdhu. It was registered in the Books of Council and Session 18th August 1624.

[6] Original Decreet of Appraising at Rossdhu.

payit, and delyuerit to me ane certaine sowme of money imployit be me for outred of certaine my debtis and necessar effaires, and for my better outred and furnisching to my intendit voyage and jurney to wther forraine pairtes furth of this kingdome."[1] Like his brother Walter, he appears to have gone abroad, and died there, without issue.

The five daughters of Alexander Colquhoun, Laird of Luss, were—

1. Jean.  Her eldest brother, John, by his bond, subscribed with his hand at Glasgow, 22d August 1617, bound himself to pay to her, her heirs, executors, and assignees, the sum of £10,000 Scots, at the terms therein mentioned, and further, to pay to her and her foresaids 1000 merks yearly, at the term of Martinmas, until her lawful marriage, the first term to begin at the Martinmas following the date of the bond.  This bond he ratified by a new one, dated at Glasgow, 11th May 1625.  Jean was married first to Allan fifth Lord Cathcart.  Their contract of marriage, made with full advice and consent of John Colquhoun, then of Luss, her brother, is dated at Dunoon, 29th October 1626.  The parties " accept each of them the other to be their lawful sponses, and shall, God willing, complete and solemnize the band of matrimony betwixt them in face of the kirk, with all due solemnity requisite."  Lord Cathcart becomes bound to infeft her, his " future sponse," in liferent in the lands and barony of Dalmellington, and others; and Jean transfers to him the £10,000 which belonged to her by the preceding bond granted to her by her brother.[2]  On the 30th of June 1627, John paid her the £10,000, and gave her full satisfaction for the 1000 merks to be paid to her yearly, as contained in the said bonds.  On the same day when payment was thus made, Jean, with the special advice of her said husband, granted her brother John a discharge; and in fulfilment of an obligation she had come under to him, specified in his bonds, she made an assignation to him of her bairns' part of gear, which belonged to her by the

---

[1] Extract Registered Assignation at Rossdhu.  It was registered in the Books of Council, 2d May 1648.

[2] Original Marriage Contract at Rossdhu.

decease of her father, Alexander Colquhoun of Luss, and of her mother, Helen Buchanan.[1]

Lord Cathcart died in the following year. To him Jean Colquhoun had a son, Allan, who was born in 1628, and who succeeded his father as sixth Lord Cathcart. Jean married, secondly, Sir Duncan Campbell, Baronet, of Auchinbreck, in the county of Argyll. He distinguished himself as a gallant officer in the army of Argyll, in the wars with Montrose. In June 1640, when Argyll marched with an army of 4000 men against the Earl of Athole, Sir Duncan Campbell was with Argyll at Taymouth, an ancient seat of the Campbells of Glenorchy, and commanded his body-guard. The other chief captains in Argyll's army were Campbell of Glenorchy and Mungo Campbell, younger of Lawers. " No better captains," says Mr. Napier, " than these ever wielded the broadsword, or inspired the pibroch."[2] Sir Duncan Campbell was also one of the principal officers in Argyll's army at the battle of Inverlochy, fought between Montrose and Argyll on the 2d of February 1645.[3] In this sanguinary engagement, which proved so fatal to many of the clan of Campbell, Sir Duncan was among the slain. " In this battle," says Patrick Gordon, " the Laird of Auchinbreck was killed, with forty barons of the name of Campbell, two and twenty men of quality taken prisoners, and seventeen hundred killed of the army. In the Castle of Inverlochy, there were fifty of the Stirling regiment with their commanders that got their lives, but of two hundred Highlanders none escaped the Clan Donald fury."[4] Jean Colquhoun was the third wife of Sir Duncan. They had one son, Archibald Campbell, who carried on the line of the Campbells of Auchinbreck.

Jean married, thirdly, Sir William Hamilton, knight, third son of James first Earl of Abercorn. On 1st April 1656, for certain sums of money granted to him for expeding his urgent affairs, Sir William Hamilton sold and disponed to Sir John Colquhoun of

---

[1] Original Contract at Rossdhu.

[2] Memoirs of the Marquis of Montrose, vol. i. p. 257.

[3] Memoirs of the Marquis of Montrose, vol. ii. pp. 482-485.

[4] Patrick Gordon's Scots Affairs.

Luss the mails and duties of all lands, and all bonds, obligations, etc., belonging to Dame Jean Colquhoun, Lady Cathcart, his spouse, in conjunct fee, liferent, or otherwise, and these as belonging to him, her present spouse, *jure mariti*.[1]  Sir William Hamilton was long Resident at Rome, from Henrietta-Maria, Queen-Dowager of England.  To him Jean Colquhoun had no children.

2. Nancy.

3. Katharine, who married Sir John Mure of Auchindraine, Knight, in the parish of Maybole and county of Ayr.  In a disposition by them, dated 2d December 1642, she is styled sister of John Col quhoun of Luss.[2]

4. Helen.

5. Mary.

The five daughters of Alexander Colquhoun are all mentioned in his will, dated 16th and 17th May 1617.  It has not been ascertained whether Nancy, Helen, and Mary Colquhoun had ever married, although it is understood that one of them became the wife of William Cunninghame of Laigland, in the parish and county of Ayr.

[1] Original Disposition at Rossdhu.    [2] Original Disposition at Rossdhu.

The following is a facsimile signature of Alexander Colquhoun, 7th November 1599, from bond, printed p. 175, *supra*.

## XV.—Sir JOHN COLQUHOUN, Sixteenth of Colquhoun and Eighteenth of Luss, First Baronet, 1617-1647.

### Lady Lilias Graham, his wife.

Sir John Colquhoun, the next proprietor of Luss, was the eldest son of a large family of eleven children. He was probably born about the year 1596, his parents having been married in the previous year. At the early age of about six years, he was, for some family reason not now apparent, put in possession of the fee of the baronies of Colquhoun and Luss by his father, Alexander Colquhoun, who merely reserved his liferent. On the resignation of his father, a charter was granted by King James the Sixth, and passed under the Great Seal on 1st December 1602, to John Colquhoun, as the eldest son and heir apparent of his father, of the baronies of Colquhoun and Luss.[1] In these properties the youth was infefted on a precept from the King on the 17th of February 1603. In the instrument of sasine in favour of John Colquhoun, the notary styles him " *nobilis puer*"—a noble boy.[2]

The young Laird of Luss had previously received from his father special grants of several of his heritages. On the 3d of January 1602, his father gave him a liferent disposition of the altarages within the Kirk of Luss, and the chaplainry of Rossdhu, with all the lands, houses, yards, and rents belonging thereto, with full power to intromit with the fruits, profits, and emoluments of the same. In this disposition it is stated that the chaplainry was vacant through the decease of John Colquhoun, the last chaplain, indweller in Edinburgh.[3] As the first-born son of Alexander Colquhoun of Luss, John Colquhoun received, on the 20th of February 1602, from King James the Sixth, a charter of the lands of Auchintorly and Dunnerbuck, which were then in the hands of the Crown, as superior, by recognition of Robert Lord Boyd, who had alienated the greater part of them without the confirmation of the superior.[4] By a subsequent arrange-

[1] Original Charter at Rossdhu ; Registrum Magni Sigilli, Lib. xliii. No. 267.

[2] Extract Instrument of Sasine at Ross-

dhu ; Dumbarton Sasine Records, folio 248.

[3] Original Disposition at Rossdhu.

[4] Registrum Magni Sigilli, Lib. xliii. No. 81.

ment with Lord Boyd, Sir John Colquhoun acquired his right to these lands.[1]

Like his father, John Colquhoun became involved in disputes with Mr. John Campbell, minister of the parish of Luss.  At the Parliament held at Edinburgh on the 28th of June 1617, by an Act " Anent the Plantation of Kirks," Commissioners, consisting of bishops, noblemen, barons and burgesses, were appointed to assign out of the teinds of the parishes a perpetual local stipend to such ministers in the church as were not provided for at all, or whose stipends were less than 500 merks, or five chalders of victual yearly, besides manse and glebe ; but from this commission were excepted those cases in which the stipend of the minister was already of that amount.

The Commissioners, on the 13th of December that year, took into consideration the estate and stipend of the Kirk of Luss, with the annual value of the teinds of that parish, and heard the representation made by the minister, Mr. Campbell.   They found that three chalders of meal, and one chalder of bear, with the sum of fourteen score merks (one score of that sum being for furnishing the elements for the celebration of the Communion) yearly, should henceforth be the local stipend of the Kirk of Luss, to be paid out of the remanent teinds of that parish, the first yearly payment of the increased stipend to begin with the crop of the year 1618.[2]

This decree the Laird of Luss refused to implement, and, on the 21st of January 1620, he raised letters of suspension against Mr. Campbell. He complained that Mr. Campbell had wrongously procured the decreet of the Commissioners for the additional stipend.   That decreet, he argued, was given by the Commissioners against him in his absence, he being at that time in France, and not having been lawfully summoned.   His plea was that the minister already enjoyed as much stipend as could be legally awarded to him.[3]

Soon after the death of his father, the young Laird of Luss went abroad on his travels.   This appears from the legal proceedings with

---

[1] Original Contract of Sale, dated 27th March 1622, at Rossdhu.

[2] Original Summons, *ibid.*

[3] Original Letters of Suspension at Rossdhu.

the minister of Luss just quoted, which show that he was in France in
the end of the year 1617; and the following letter from his maternal
uncle, Sir John Buchanan of that ilk, shows that Luss was at Heidelberg
in June 1619 : —

LOWING nephew, iff zow knew how I am rejoised be zouir letteris,
quhairby I knaw zouir hailthe, I am assured zow wald wret ofter. Thairfore,
iff my ernest intreatj mey hawe swae muche force withe zow as to mowe
zow [to] vret of zouir hailthe, I will again and again most ernestlj reqweist zow
to imbrace all occasionis that offeris, and to seik quhair the occasionis
offeris nocht, and let zouir letteris be direct to Mr. Robert Hayes, gentilman off his Majesteis robis at the Cowrt of Ingland.    Be this adress zouir
letteris will ewer come to my handis, and zow will ewer find commoditj to this
Cowrt off Ingland.    As to zouir painis be zouir trawelis and scharges in zouir
trawelis, swa being God off his merej send zow home to me again, I am
indifferent off all vther thingis.    Thairfore, altho' I hawe said alreddie als muche
as I hop sall suffeis for mowing zow to vret, I am zit forced to sey that as zow
vald geiwe my mynd contentment let me heir from zow, for, withowt the sam,
feare off the worst sall doo me more harm then anj thing els can do me contentment.    And iff it pleis God to viseit zow withe anie seiknes, iff zow regaird
my forsaid intreatj, and meak me advertised, zow sal be in no pairt off Ewrop
bot I sall, wil God, sie zow.    As to zouir bissines at home, I hawe vretin home,
and I sall zit wret, and sall geiwe testimonie that at home and frome home my
eair off zouir turnis sal be greater nor my eair off my awin.    For I protest to
God I heir nocht as zit bot all is in qwyetnes and guid ordoure, and iff I heir
eather the contrair or apparens of the contrair quhilk sall reqwyir my presens
thair, it sall be sein that nothing heir sall hawld me frome them, altho' I meak
nocht swae great heast to my awin seruing that zouir turnis ar weall.    I hawe
hard no new occurrentis in owr cuntrj quhairof I can vret to zow, bot that my
Ladie Semple is dead, and that zouir cowsen, my Lord Boid, has ane sone withe
his ladie.    In this cuntrj of Ingland we hawe no newis heir for the present, bot
sic as cumis from my Lord Imbassador, quhilk newis zow hawe before they cum
to us.    His Majestie beginis his progres the 19 off Julj, and continowis to the
28 of Agust, and gois northe within sex mylis to Duncaster.    As to zouir post-
script anent that matier quhairof I spok last to zow, I will neather dowt zouir
favor nor mistrust zouir lowe, altho' that, for the walor off ten tymes swae muche,
I wald nocht that vtheris, owt off thair splein to me, sowld hawe haid caws of
contentment by mowing ane alteratioun be thair credeit withe zow.    Let me knaw
thair credeit hes nocht that force, and that zow continow in hailthe, quhairvithe

I must end my letter as I hawe begun, and dois remain as I sall ewer continow,

                   Zouir werie loving wncle alwayes assured,
                                           J. BUCHANAN of that Ilk.
Lundoun, the penult of Jun 1619.
To the honourabill his lowing nephew, the Laird of Luss, at Hedleberg.[1]

The Laird of Luss returned to Scotland previous to the summer of the following year, when a matrimonial alliance was arranged between him and the eldest sister of the great Montrose. This was Lady Lilias Graham, eldest daughter of John fourth Earl of Montrose. Luss was then, probably, about twenty-four years of age. Their contract of marriage is dated at the Earl's ancient Castle of Mugdock, in Strathblane, in the Lennox, on 30th June and 6th July 1620. This was one of the residences of the gallant Grahams before they acquired Buchanan, opposite to Rossdhu, and on the other side of Loch Lomond. The marriage was arranged to be completed in the face of the kirk, with all due solemnity, betwixt the date of the contract and the 20th of July thereafter. The Laird of Luss became bound to infeft Lady Lilias in liferent in the barony of Colquhoun, the lands of Sauchy, and bordlands of Sawling and others; and her father bound himself to pay £10,000 of tocher.[2]

In fulfilment of his part of the marriage-contract, the Laird of Luss, on 30th June same year, granted to Lady Lilias, his "future spouse," a charter of his five pound lands of Wallastoun and Ardochmoir, in the parish of Cardross and shire of Dumbarton, in liferent, to be held of the Earl of Montrose and his heirs.[3]

In the same year this Laird acquired by purchase, from John Logane of Balvey, the four merk lands of Balvey, commonly called Balvey Logan, with the tower, fortalice, and manor-place thereof, and the lands of Gartconnell, Fergnstoun Logane, Ledcamroch Logane, and Bannachtane Logane, in the dukedom and regality of Lennox and shire of Dumbarton. The contract of sale between the parties is dated at Glasgow, 27th July and

---

[1] Original Letter at Rossdhu.

[2] The Contract was registered in the

Books of Council and Session, 7th November 1628.

[3] Original Charter at Rossdhu.

11th August 1620,[1] and the charter of sale following thereon is dated 1st December same year.[2] Sir John afterwards sold Balvey to his brother Humphrey, to whom he gave a charter of them, dated at Rossdhu, 11th June 1629.[3]

The Laird of Luss was a Member of the Parliament opened at Edinburgh 1st June 1621, by which the Five Articles of the General Assembly of the Kirk, held at Perth in August 1618, were ratified—kneeling at the celebration of the sacrament, private communicating, private baptism, confirmation, and the observance of certain holidays, namely, those in commemoration of the birth, passion, resurrection, and ascension of our Lord, and the descent of the Holy Ghost.[4]

A variety of friendly transactions had taken place at different times between the house of Luss and the house of Lennox. Misunderstandings had, however, arisen between them, and they became involved, as we have seen, in litigation before the Civil Courts. In reference to these misunderstandings, John Colquhoun of Luss received from Ludovic second Duke of Lennox the following letter, expressing his strong desire that friendly relations should exist between the two houses :—

AFTER my hartly commendationes, I receaued your letter, and I haue vnderstood by Sir George Elphinston and Sir Robert Stewart of your affectione and respect to mee, which I will bee willing ase kyndly to acknowledge ase any of my predecessors or myself haue done to any of yours. As for any questione that may be betweine yow and mee, yow may expect at my hands ase good satisfactione ase any man ; and particularly concerning the lands of Glenfruine I ame content to referre myself to the arbitriment of frends, and if at any time I doe parte from them yow shall haue the offer of them before all men. And wherein els I can doe yow pleasure, yow may assure yourself alwayes to find mee.

Your very loueing frende,

Greenwiche, the 8 of June 1622.                                    LENOX.

To my loueing frende the Laird of Lusse,—These.[5]

---

[1] Original Contract at Rossdhu.

[2] Original Charter, ibid.

[3] This Charter is engrossed in a charter of confirmation by commissioners of James Duke of Lennox, as lord superior, in favour of Humphrey Colquhoun of Balvey, dated 29th June 1629. Original at Rossdhu.

[4] Acts of the Parliaments of Scotland, vol. iv. pp. 593, 595.

[5] Original Letter at Rossdhu.

But notwithstanding the friendly tone of this letter a good understanding between the houses of Lennox and Colquhoun was not maintained, as we shall shortly see.

The Laird of Luss was desirous to acquire the tenement called the *Parson of Luss's Manse* in the city of Glasgow, at the head of the Vennell called the Rottenrow, on the south side. His uncle, Sir Humphrey, obtained it in feu from Mr. William Chirnsyde, formerly parson of Luss. It was probably occupied as a residence by the Colquhoun family during their stay in Glasgow. To acquire this manse the Laird of Luss, on the 20th of March 1624, entered into a contract with Mr. John Campbell, minister of Luss. By this contract Mr. Campbell, for the sum of £100 Scots, bound himself to infeft Luss as nearest heir-male to his deceased uncle, Sir Humphrey, in this tenement. He further bound himself, after John Colquhoun of Luss was infefted in that tenement, and had again resigned it, to infeft him and Dame Lilias Graham, his spouse, therein and the heirs-male of their marriage, whom failing, his heirs-male whomsoever, and that by his charter of feu-farm, to be subscribed by him, and by the Archbishop of Glasgow and the Dean and Chapter of the Metropolitan Kirk thereof, whose signatures he became bound to procure.[1]

In the year 1625, this Laird of Luss shared in the honours and in the gifts of property conferred by King Charles the First in connection with the colony of Nova Scotia in America, which Sir William Alexander of Menstrie, afterwards Earl of Stirling, had projected and settled at his own expense, and of which King James the Sixth had made a grant to him, dated 21st December 1621. Charles the First, with consent of the Lords of the Privy Council of Scotland, for the advantage and good government of that plantation, and also for the good and gratuitous service rendered to him by John Colquhoun of Luss, and for divers other great and weighty considerations moving him thereto, granted, disponed, and confirmed to him, and his heirs-male and assignees whomsoever, heritably, that part of the region of Nova Scotia beginning at the meridional point of the east side of the port or river called La Heave, extending three miles towards the east by the sea-shore, and thence going northward *in terram firmam*,

[1] Original Contract at Rossdhu.

the breadth to be three miles in every way from the said meridional
point upon the sea-shore northward, with the castles, towers, and manor-
places, built or to be built thereupon, gardens, orchards, planted or to
be planted, fishings, red and white, of salmon and other fishes, great
and small, in salt water and in fresh, the rights of patronage of bene-
fices, chaplainries and churches, all mineral veins, including the royal
metals, silver and gold, as well as iron, steel, brass, copper, and other
minerals whatsoever, and all precious stones, gems, pearls, crystal, alum,
corals, and others within the said boundaries. This charter also granted
to Sir John Colquhoun, and his heirs-male and assignees, the power
and privilege of free regality within the said bounds and lands, of
digging and searching the ground thereof for minerals, precious stones,
gems, pearls, and others above mentioned, and of adopting all means
for extracting and purifying them, and of applying them to their own use,
reserving to his Majesty and his successors only a tenth part of the royal
metals, commonly called the ore of gold and silver, in all time coming, to
be extracted from the said lands; all other metals, minerals, and precious
stones to be the property of the said John Colquhoun and his heirs-male.
By the same charter, containing numerous other rights, powers, and privileges besides those already mentioned, his Majesty erected the foresaid
lands and bounds into one full and free barony, to be called the BARONY OF
COLQUHOUN, to be held of the Crown of Scotland for an annual payment of
one penny Scots upon the ground of the said lands, or any part thereof, in
name of blench farm, at the Feast of the Nativity of our Saviour, only if
asked ; and created and preferred the said John and his heirs-male
whomsoever to the hereditary RANK and DIGNITY of BARONET. The
charter is dated at Edinburgh, the 30th of August 1625.[1]  As will be
afterwards shown, the dignity of Baronet thus conferred was surrendered
by Sir Humphrey Colquhoun, the fourth Baronet, who obtained a regrant of the title to a new series of heirs—a practice which was not
uncommon in regard to dignities in Scotland previous to the Union with
England.

[1] Original Charter at Rossdhu.   This   parchment, which measures 3 feet 4 inches
charter is engrossed on a large skin of   by 3 feet 1 inch.

On the death of Alexander Colquhoun, the last Laird of Luss, King James the Sixth granted to Andrew Lord Avendale the ward, relief and non-entries of the lands of Mamore and Mambeg, Ballernic-mor, Letrualt, Stuckinduff, and Blairvaddoch, and others. But arrangements having been made by Sir John Colquhoun, now Laird of Luss, for the recovery of this gift, Lord Avendale, by a letter of procuratory, dated 6th April 1628, appointed procurators to resign into the hands of the King the ward, relief, and non-entries of the said lands in favour of Sir John Colquhoun of Luss.[1]

Lady Lilias Graham, the spouse of Sir John, was, as formerly mentioned, the sister of James Graham, afterwards the celebrated Marquis of Montrose. At the time of the marriage of his sister he was only eight years of age. While a student at St. Andrews in 1628 and 1629, when sixteen years of age, he made frequent visits to his sister and brother-in-law at Rossdhu. In an account of his personal expenditure, when a student at that University in these years, are the following entries :—" Item, crossing Leven, to ferrie-man, 6$^{sh}$; given to the keeper of Inchmirran, 30$^{sh}$; crossing Leven again, 6$^{sh}$; to the porter in the Castell of Dumbartane, 58$^{sh}$; to the poor of the Kirk of Dumbartane, 6$^{sh}$; in Garscube, given to the servant in drink silver, 5$^{lib}$ 16$^{sh}$; to the nurrice ther, 58$^{sh}$; at the cards in Cumernald, 30$^{sh}$." From the same source of information we discover that young Montrose, on Monday, 9th November 1629, purchased at Montrose golf-balls, in order to play a match with his brother-in-law, Sir John Colquhoun of Luss, who had come from the west to be present at the marriage of Montrose with Magdalene Carnegie, youngest daughter of David first Earl of Southesk, which was solemnised on the following day, 10th November, in the parish kirk of Kinnaird.[2]

This Laird of Luss took considerable interest in the district and town of Dumbarton. On the 19th of September 1628 the Provost, Magistrates, and Council of that burgh, in court assembled, resolved to desire the Laird of Luss to visit the water-works, as Lord Ross had done, and to give his opinion concerning them in writing, which opinion was to be sent to the

[1] Original Letter of Procuratory at Ross-    [2] Memorials of Montrose printed for the
dhu.                                        Maitland Club.

Lords of Secret Council on the 24th of next month.[1]   The Laird also took part in the management of the affairs of his friends and neighbours.  On 31st December 1629 he was chosen by Duncan Campbell, then of Carrick, during his minority, as his curator, and, having accepted this office, he gave his oath for the faithful administration thereof.[2]

In the year 1630 a commission was granted by the curators of James Duke of Lennox for the redemption of the four pound lands of Easter Tullychewen, in the dukedom of Lennox and shire of Dumbarton, at the parish kirk of Luss, for the sum of 600 merks Scots, from Sir John Colquhoun of Luss and Margaret and Annas, daughters of the deceased Sir Humphrey Colquhoun of Luss, Knight, heirs of the deceased James Colquhoun of Garscube, their " goodschir's brother," granter of the reversion of these lands.[3]   The commission is dated 31st March 1630.   On the same day Daniel Clerk, servant to James Duke of Lennox, in name of the said commissioners, warned and required Sir John Colquhoun of Luss, personally within his dwelling-house of Garscube, and on the 1st of April Margaret Colquhoun, personally within the mains of Colquhoun, and Annas Colquhoun, relict of the deceased Colin Campbell, fiar of Carrick, at her dwelling place of Camsayle, within the Isle of Roseneath, (by affixing a copy to that effect on the gate, and delivering another copy to Robert Macmainis, her servant, in Camsayle, to be given to her, because she could not be found personally,) to compear upon Whitsunday eve next, within the parish kirk of Luss, betwixt sun-rising and sun-setting, to receive from his Majesty, as heir of blood to the deceased Matthew Earl of Lennox, his Majesty's grandschir on the father's side, or from James Duke of Lennox, or from their procurators for redemption of the said lands, the sum of six hundred merks, with a sufficient letter of tack of the four pound land of Easter Tullychewen for five years next after the redemption foresaid, for the yearly payment of twenty merks, and to grant the same land to be lawfully redeemed from them.   This land had been wadset to the said James Colquhoun of Garscube and his heirs by the deceased Esme Duke of Lennox.

---

[1] Dumbarton Records, vol. i.
[2] Dumbarton Records, ibid.
[3] Original Commission in Montrose Charter-chest.

"and gudschyr to the said James," then Duke of Lennox, under reversion, for the sum above mentioned.[1]

In the year 1630, Sir John Colquhoun added to his estates by new purchases of lands. At Glasgow, on 13th May of that year, he purchased from John Colquhoun of Kilmardinny, "for great sums of money," the lands of Auchingaich, Larg, Auchenvennel-mor, Stuckiedow and Blairhangen, in the dukedom of Lennox and shire of Dumbarton. The disposition of these lands in his favour states that they were first disponed by Sir John Colquhoun of Luss, Knight, "foir grandschir to John Colquhoun, now of Luss," to Walter Colquhoun, lawful son of the granter, and "grandschir" of the said John Colquhoun of Kilmardinny.[2]

The latter will of Alexander Colquhoun of Luss has already been noticed. John Colquhoun, as the eldest son of his father, was thereby brought under various obligations with respect to his brothers and sisters, and Andrew Bishop of Argyll was constituted one of the principal overseers of Alexander's children, with power to settle various matters in regard to the provision which Sir John should make for them. By the advice of the Bishop, Sir John agreed upon a sufficient provision for his brother Adam. Having made this arrangement, he bound himself, by a bond dated 29th June 1631, to provide his other brothers and his sisters to such sums of money as the Bishop should determine, under the penalty of 20,000 merks.

The Bishop by his decreet, dated 27th June 1632, decerned that John should pay to his sister Catherine, the eldest, who was then of the age of twenty-one years, and so marriageable, the sum of 7000 merks, and to his brothers and sisters specified the particular other sums of money mentioned therein; that he should do so between the date of that decreet and the 11th of November following; and that in case the payment should be deferred, he should pay to his brothers and sisters a yearly annual-rent of ten merks for each hundred of the said sums; and that, notwithstanding the payment of that annual-rent, it should be lawful for them to make suit for the payment of their respective sums at any time after the said term.

Although Sir John Colquhoun was nominally in possession of the

[1] Original Instrument of Warning in Montrose Charter-chest.
[2] Original Disposition at Rossdhu.

family estates for upwards of forty years, he was not successful in his
management of them. This arose from various misfortunes, to which it is
unnecessary here particularly to allude, further than that they required his
residing abroad for a considerable time during the period of his ownership
of the estates. His father had a large family of eleven children, and Sir
John had to make considerable provisions for his brothers and sisters. He
had thus to begin with large provisions, which burdened the estate; and
his absence from Scotland was unfavourable to the proper management of
large Highland domains. This accounts to some extent for the pecuniary embarrassments of Sir John. The splendid heritages which had been
transmitted to him—the constantly accumulating possessions of his ancestors for many generations—were nearly ruined. He borrowed large sums
of money from many parties, for the payment of which several of his friends
became cautioners.

In this embarrassment of Sir John's affairs, his brother, Sir Humphrey,
interposed, for the purpose of saving the estates to the family. He made
large advances to creditors, and obtained an appraising of the barony of
Luss in his favour. Sir Humphrey obtained from King Charles the First
a charter of appraising, dated 9th November 1633, and, on a precept from
Chancery of the same date, he was infefted in the family estates on the
20th of the same month.[1]

In consideration of the large sums of money which Humphrey had
advanced to Sir John, and to others in his name, " for outredding of sundry
his urgent affairs, and for payment of his debts," Sir John granted Humphrey
a disposition, dated at Rossdhu, 31st August 1634, of the barony of Luss
and the remainder of the estates of Colquhoun, including the office of
coroner within the bounds of the shire of Dumbarton, and within the
bounds of those seven kirks and parishes which then were within the jurisdiction of the shire of Stirling.[2] In these transactions Sir Humphrey
Colquhoun acted very honourably; and he reconveyed the barony of Luss
to his nephew, the second Baronet.

[1] Original Charter, Precept of Sasine, and Instrument of Sasine at Rossdhu.
Books of Session, 23d October 1634, at Rossdhu.
[2] Extract Disposition, registered in the

On the 16th of September 1639, a supplication, given in to the Parliament by Lady Luss (Lady Lilias Graham), craving that the Laird of Balvie,
who had intromitted with the estate, should maintain all her children, was
brought under the consideration of the Parliament. The result was that,
on 23d September 1639, the Lords of Articles, after hearing the report of
the matter in dispute betwixt the Lady Luss and Balvie, made by the
Earls of Lauderdale and Southesk, who had been appointed to peruse the
defences and answers given in by the parties, found that the aliment
ought presently to be modified to stand until the defender should conde-
scend and instruct the true rental and burdens of the lands; and they
modified 2000 merks yearly for payment, whereof they ordained the
supplicant to have both personal execution against Balvie and real against
the land.[1]

The exact date of the death of Sir John Colquhoun has not been
ascertained.

He was alive on 8th November 1647, when a resignation of that date
of the barony of Luss was made in favour of his son John, "with consent
of John Colquhoun, sometime of Luss, brother to Sir Humphrey Colquhoun,"
by whom the resignation was made. In the Crown Charter of the barony
of Luss, following on the resignation of the same date, his son is designated
simply "John Colquhoun now of Luss."[2]   In other writs, for a short time
after, and in an Act of Parliament passed on 15th February 1649, he is
designated " John Colquhoun of Luss."[3]   But in a contract, dated 8th and
9th of May 1650, between him and the Commissioners of James Duke of
Lennox, whereby they granted him a lease of the lands of Letrualt and
Blairvaddoch and others, he is designated " Sir John Colquhoun of Luss,
Knight."[4]   From this it may be inferred that Sir John, the first baronet,
died between 15th February 1649 and 8th May 1650, assuming that the
designation of Knight, which was applied to the son on that date, was
equivalent to the title of Baronet which he inherited from his father.

[1] Acts of the Parliaments of Scotland,
vol. v. pp. 260-263.
[2] Original Resignation and Charter at
Rossdhu.
[3] Acts of the Parliaments of Scotland,
vol. vi. p. 374.
[4] Original Contract at Rossdhu.

The issue of the marriage of Sir John Colquhoun and Lady Lilias Graham was three sons and three daughters. The sons were—

1. John, who succeeded his father as second Baronet.
2. James, who succeeded the son of his brother John as the fourth Baronet.
3. Alexander of Tullychewen or Tillyquhoun, in the parish of Bonhill and county of Dumbarton. An account of Alexander Colquhoun of Tullychewen and his descendants is given in the Appendix.

The three daughters were—

1. Jean. She married Mr. Walter Stewart in 1647. Their banns of marriage were proclaimed once on Thursday and twice on the Sabbath day thereafter, and then they were married by Mr. Archibald M'Lachlan, minister of Luss. This was an irregularity, the laws of the Church then requiring that parties to be united in marriage should be duly proclaimed in the parochial church on three successive Sabbaths previous to their marriage. For the violation of the laws of the Church in this matter, and also, as was surmised, for celebrating the marriage without the consent of the lady's father, Mr M'Lachlan was brought before the Presbytery of Dumbarton. In self-defence, he affirmed that he had received her father's consent, through Robert Colquhoun of Ballernick. The Presbytery continued the case till their return from the Synod, and in the meantime ordered Mr. M'Lachlan to be publicly rebuked before his congregation. He had been previously suspended for celebrating irregular marriages in 1641, but was restored a month after.[1] He was ultimately deposed, as we shall afterwards see.

2. Lilias. She married John Napier, eldest son and apparent heir of Robert Napier of Kilmahew, in the county of Dumbarton. Their marriage-contract is dated at the place of Kilmahew and of Rossdhu, 10th and 12th February respectively, 1649. In the contract, in which Lilias is designated second sister of John Colquhoun of Luss.

[1] Dumbarton Presbytery Records.

they engaged to solemnize and complete the band of matrimony
betwixt them in face of God's holy kirk and congregation, as the
word of God prescribed and allowed, before the last day of May
following. Robert Napier of Kilmahew, in consideration and contemplation of this marriage, became bound to infeft his son, John
Napier, and Lilias Colquhoun, his future spouse, in her pure virginity, in liferent and conjunct fee, and the heirs-male of their
marriage, whom failing, the said John Napier's nearest heirs-male
whomsoever, in the lands of Maynes and Little Balvie, otherwise
called Balvie-Douglas, with tower, place, and fortalice thereof, mill,
mill-lands, multures, sequels, and whole pertinents belonging thereto,
and in his lands of Kilmahew, with the tower and fortalice thereof,
etc., in the dukedom and regality of Lennox, and shire of Dumbarton,
held by him of James Duke of Lennox. Robert Napier reserved to
himself the liferent of the lands of Kilmahew, excepting those
parts thereof called Achiusayll and Barres of Kilmahew, which were
to be a part of the conjunct fee lands of Lilias Colquhoun. These
last-mentioned lands were estimated to amount, in all the duties
thereof, to a yearly rent of 400 merks Scots. The lands of
Maynes and Little Balvie were estimated, in all the duties thereof,
to be worth in yearly rent the sum of 1100 merks. The lands
thus provided to Lilias Colquhoun in conjunct fee and liferent
yielded £1000 of yearly rent. And, because the lands of Maynes
and Little Balvie belonged in liferent to Margaret Napier, relict of
the deceased John Napier of Kilmahew, during her lifetime, which
prevented John and Lilias Colquhoun from then entering thereto,
and uplifting the rents thereof, the said Robert Napier bound himself
to infeft them in the lands of Ledcamroch, in the regality and shire
foresaid, in special warrandice and security of the foresaid lands of
Maynes and Little Balvie, during the lifetime of the said Margaret
Napier, his stepmother.[1]

In 1653, John Napier, husband of Lilias Colquhoun, acquired the
lands of Walton and Wallacetoun from his brother-in-law, the Laird

[1] Original Marriage-Contract at Rossdhu.

of Luss. He was one of the Commissioners appointed to uplift from the shire of Dumbarton its proportion of the yearly subsidy of £40,000 sterling, granted by the Parliament of Scotland to King Charles the Second on his restoration, for the maintenance of a military force within the kingdom.[1] He represented the county of Dumbarton in Parliament in the years 1661 and 1669. His nonconforming principles seem to have rendered him obnoxious to the Government. He and his spouse, Lilias Colquhoun, with many others, were summoned to appear to answer for Nonconformity before a Court held at Dumbarton on the 19th of February 1685, by Commissioners of the Privy Council and Justiciary, consisting of William Hamilton of Orbiston, Sheriff-Principal; Humphrey Colquhoun, fiar of Luss; Major George Arnot, Lieutenant-Governor of Dumbarton Castle; and Archibald Macaulay of Ardincaple. The libel was found relevant, and for non-compearance John Napier was held as confessed, and fined in the sum of £2000 for himself and his lady.[2]

Of the marriage of John Napier of Kilmahew and Lilias Colquhoun there were two daughters, Margaret and Catharine. Having no male children, the father executed an entail of his lands, 6th July 1689, in favour of the heirs-male of the bodies of these two daughters successively, and the heirs of the bodies of such heirs-male, whom failing, the heirs-female of these daughters.[3] Margaret, the eldest, married, first, Patrick Maxwell of Newark; and her eldest son, George, by this marriage, carried on the line of the family of the Napiers of Kilmahew, assuming, in fulfilment of the conditions of the entail, the name and arms of Napier of Kilmahew. She married, secondly, John eleventh Earl of Glencairn. The other daughter, Catharine, became the wife of Robert Campbell of Netherwoodside.

3. Catharine. She married John Drummond, ninth Laird of Pitkellonie, in the county of Perth. Their contract of marriage is dated 19th

---

[1] Acts of the Parliaments of Scotland, vol. vii. pp. 4, 92, 549.
[2] Wodrow's History, vol. iv. p. 188.
[3] Kilmahew Writs.

October 1659. On the same date he granted a bond to Catharine Colquhoun for securing her jointure in terms of the marriage-contract.[1] They had two sons, John and Laurence Drummond, and two daughters, Margaret and Beatrix. John Drummond survived Catharine Colquhoun, and married, secondly, Jean Rollo, daughter of Andrew first Lord Rollo, and widow of Rollo of Powes.[2]

[1] Original Obligation at Rossdhu.     [2] Genealogy of the Drummonds, 4to, 1831, p. 59.

The following is a facsimile of the signature of Sir John Colquhoun, first baronet, at a letter by him to his "loving uncle the Laird of Buchannane," dated 22d October 1619. [Original in Montrose Charter Chest.]

THE BLACK COCK OF THE WEST.

MARGARET BAILLIE HEIRESS OF LOCHEND
LADY LUSS.

## XVI.—1. Sir JOHN COLQUHOUN, Seventeenth of Colquhoun and Nineteenth of Luss, Second Baronet,—1647-1676.

MARGARET BAILLIE, Heiress of Lochend, his wife.

SIR John Colquhoun of Luss, second Baronet, was educated at the University of Glasgow. He was matriculated a member of that University on 15th March 1642. He is designated "eldest son of the Laird of Luss," and is marked as among the "novitii" of the fifth class.[1] He was then probably about twenty years of age, his parents having been married in the year 1620. This Laird was put in possession of the family estates during his father's lifetime. His uncle, Sir Humphrey, as we have seen before,[2] having acquired the Luss estates in the year 1634, conveyed them to his nephew, the second Baronet, in the year 1647. This arrangement was carried into effect by Sir Humphrey Colquhoun and his wife, Dame Margaret Somerville, and other parties interested, who granted a disposition, dated 26th August 1647, in favour of John Colquhoun of Luss, his nephew, and his heirs-male whomsoever, of the lands and barony of Luss, the islands in Loch Lomond, called Inschlonnochie, Inscheonnaquhan, and Inchfreithillane, called the Isle of Rosdo, the right of patronage of the kirk of Luss, and of all other kirks and chaplainries of the same, the lands and barony of Colquhoun, with the manor-place of Dunglas, the lands of Garscube, all in the shire of Dumbarton ; the lands of Sauchie, in the shire of Stirling ; the mill of Sawling, with the mill-lands thereof, in the shire of Fife ; the office of crownarie within the bounds of the shire of Dumbarton, with all fees and casualties belonging thereto ; all united with certain other lands, into a whole and free barony, called the barony of Luss, conformably to the charter granted thereupon by King James the Sixth, under the Great Seal, to John Colquhoun, sometime of Luss, dated 1st December 1602 ; and the lands of Waltoun, Wallacetoun, and Ardochbeg, in the parish of Cardross and shire of Dumbarton. The resignation was formally made on the 8th of November 1647, by Sir Humphrey's procurator, in presence of

[1] Munimenta Universitatis Glasguensis, vol. iii. p. 97.  [2] Vide p. 249.

a public notary, into the hands of the Lords of his Majesty's Exchequer, Commissioners appointed for receiving resignations in his Majesty's name. This resignation was made " with consent of John Colquhoun, sometime of Luss, brother to the said Sir Humphrey."[1]

On the same 8th of November, a charter was granted by King Charles the First, under the Great Seal, to John Colquhoun and his heirs-male whomsoever of the said lands and baronies, erecting the whole anew into a whole and free barony, to be called in all time coming the barony of Luss, and ordaining the manor-place of Rossdhu to be the principal messuage thereof;[2] and he was infefted therein on the 26th of February 1648.[3] Both in the charter and sasine he is designated John Colquhoun of Luss.

In the same year John Colquhoun of Luss married Margaret Baillie, daughter of Sir Gideon Baillie of Lochend,[4] in the county of Haddington, by his wife, Magdalene Carnegie, the second daughter of David Lord Carnegie, eldest son of David first Earl of Southesk. The marriage-contract between Sir Gideon and Magdalene Carnegie is dated at Edinburgh, 17th February 1636, and registered in the Books of Council and Session 20th August 1640.[5] Sir Gideon was served heir to his father, Sir James Baillie of Lochend, Knight, on 26th November 1635.[6] He received from King Charles the First a charter, dated 21st November 1636, giving and disponing to him and his heirs-male, and assignees whomsoever, a portion of land in Nova Scotia, in America, and creating him and his heirs-male whomsoever knights-baronets for ever, with all the prerogatives and privileges of that rank. This portion of land was bounded as follows :—Beginning at the

[1] Original Instrument of Resignation at Rossdhu.

[2] Original Charter, ibid.

[3] Original Instrument of Sasine, ibid.

[4] King James the Fifth granted Lochend to John Boig, his Majesty's servitour, by a charter dated 20th February 1540. John Boig was succeeded in Lochend by his son, Nicol Boig, who, in 1588, conveyed Lochend to his grandson, John Boig. Sir James Baillie, one of the receivers of the Crown rents in Scotland, purchased Lochend in the year 1614 from Robert, son of Nicol Boig, and John Boig, for seventeen thousand merks Scots. Lochend continued in the family of Baillie from that date till the year 1676, when Margaret Baillie, granddaughter of Sir James Baillie, with consent of her husband, Sir John Colquhoun, sold Lochend to Sir Robert Sinclair of Longformacus.

[5] Extract Registered Marriage-Contract at Rossdhu.

[6] Inquis. Retor. Abbrev. Haddington, No. 162.

west side of the lands and barony of Wrothame, heritably belonging to Sir
John Rany of Wrothame, alias Rothame, in the county of Kanrie, Knight-
Baronet, lying on the north side of the river, called the Great Schiboun, in
Capbriton, and extending westward from the said barony three miles up
the said river, keeping always the river for the boundary of it to the south,
and therefrom northwards six miles in length, and three miles in breadth,
the said barony being its boundary towards the east.    The land thus
bounded was to be called in all time coming the barony of Lochend.[1]  The
charter was granted upon a resignation made of that portion of land in
Nova Scotia, by the procurator of William Earl of Stirling, Viscount of
Canada, into the hands of the Lords of Exchequer, in special favour of Sir
Gideon Baillie of Lochend.[2]

The death of Sir Gideon Baillie was tragical.   When in the Castle of
Dunglas, in East Lothian, with the Covenanters' army, he and the Earl of
Haddington, and many others, knights, barons, and gentlemen, were killed
by an explosion which took place about midday on the 30th of August
1640.[3]  This terrible disaster, according to tradition, was the flagitious deed
of an English page of the Earl's, who, in a transport of rage at the Scots for
having sneered at his countrymen for running away at the battle of New-
burn, thrust a red-hot iron into the powder magazine, himself perishing in
the catastrophe.

Sir Gideon Baillie was succeeded by his son Sir James ; and an Act of
Parliament was passed on 11th August 1641, authorizing him, in conformity with previous Acts of Parliament, to enter himself heir to the lands
of his father without composition, since his father had fallen in the service
of his country.

Sir James having died without issue before 1618, his two sisters, Jean
and Margaret, were heirs-portioners of his estates.

Thus, Margaret Baillie, in the year 1648, when a romantic attachment
was formed between John Colquhoun of Luss and her, was a rich heiress.
The circumstances connected with the commencement of his acquaintance

[1] Original Charter at Rossdhu.                [3] Spalding's Troubles, vol. i. p. 337 ;
                                             Bishop Guthrie's Memoirs, Glasgow, 1747.
[2] Original Instrument of Resignation, ibid.    p. 84 ; Sir Thomas Hope's Diary, p. 119.

with this lady, it is said, were these : Several gentlemen of family and position were dining at Lochend with the Laird.  Margaret, who was then a very young lady, being present, her father jocularly asked her, " Well, Maggie, which of these gentlemen will you have for a husband ?"  Without a moment's pause, to the surprise of all, she answered, " The Black Cock of the West," a hint, as shown by the sequel, not thrown away on the very handsome baronet, Sir John Colquhoun,[1] who often received the sobriquet she applied to him from his dark appearance, a description corresponding with a portrait of him by Sir Peter Lely, preserved at Rossdhu, which represents a handsome man with black hair and olive complexion.[2]

The first recorded information we obtain on this subject is contained in a letter from Margaret's mother and her second husband, Sir John Crawford of Kilbirnie, Knight, to the Laird of Luss, younger, expressing their warm approval of his prospective marriage with their daughter, on whom they evidently doated with no common affection :—

" HONORABILL AND DEIRE SONNE,—We haue sent youe the richest jewell belonging to us in this wordill, our deireste dochter, Mistresse Margaratte Baillie, heretrix of Lochend, quhom we desyre you may espousse to be your deireste wyffe.  Sume things I haue committed to the beirer, Capitane Walter Stirling, quhilk I desire youe will obey to the full, as youe ar about to honor God, quho hes caste this precius jewell and ritcheste earthy blissing into youre hands.  And as youe ar about to honor and obey us, the only instruments of all youre happines in this particular greet blising, evine so sall youe be blised of God, as we the father and mother do blisse you bothe with all the blisings that ever he missoured out to husband and wyffe upon earthe ; quhilk sall be the continuell prayers to God of your most deirly loveing parents and servants to our death,

J. C. KILBIRNY.

Edinburgh, the 12th May 1648.    M. CARNEGY.

For the richt honorabill the Laird of Lusse, younger."[3]

---

[1] Tradition communicated by John Colquhoun, Esq.

[2] In the wall of the old castle of Rossdhu a stone was formerly to be seen bearing the names of Sir John Colquhoun and Dame Margaret Baillie.  It was removed from the ruins of the castle, and lay for some time near the old stables, but it is now lost.

[3] Original Letter at Garden.

By the marriage-contract between Margaret Baillie's parents, it was provided that, in case there should be no heirs-male of their marriage, their eldest daughter should succeed to her father's estates, and that she should marry a person bearing the name and arms of Baillie, and that with the advice of four nearest of kin of her father and mother. But whether this latter provision could be carried out, when the event anticipated—her succession to her father's estates—was realized, would depend upon the affections of the lady after she could choose for herself. Margaret's affections refused to be restrained by such trammels. The object of her choice was John Colquhoun, the young Laird of Luss.

The marriage between the Laird of Luss and Margaret Baillie was celebrated with great haste, without any previous proclamation of banns in the parish church. This probably gave rise to the report that they had made an elopement. The lady, it is said, was conducted to Rossdhu, the family seat of John, in such a way as to show that she had run off with him, not he with her, for he rode behind her on the same horse, and thus she actually arrived at Rossdhu before him. The reason assigned for this was, that the heiress of Lochend being a ward of Chancery, John Colquhoun wished to avoid the consequences of running away with her. As both her mother and her stepfather were friendly to the marriage, this report of an elopement is probably unfounded. It is, however, certain that these hasty nuptials were regarded as a scandal at that period, when the ecclesiastical laws required that the proclamation of banns should be made in the parish church three successive Sabbaths before the celebration of a marriage; and so rigid were the presbyteries in enforcing the regulations of the church in this matter, that the uniting of this couple in marriage " without any proclamatioue of the bandis of thair mariage,"[1] was one of the grounds on which Mr. Archibald M'Lauchlan, minister of the parish of Luss, was deposed by the Presbytery of Dumbarton.

Mr. M'Lauchlan, as we have seen before, had been formerly censured more than once by the Presbytery of Dumbarton for offences of the same kind. On the 16th of May 1648, he appeared before the Presbytery to answer for the repetition of his old offence by this irregular marriage. He

[1] Records of the Presbytery of Dumbarton, 16th May 1648.

admitted that he had married the parties, though their banns of marriage had not been publicly proclaimed, as required by the laws of the church. He alleged in self-defence that he had the authority of the lady's mother and stepfather for what he had done. Another accusation connected with this marriage was brought against him. To provide against the risk of deposition, should he solemnize the marriage, he had obtained from the Laird of Luss, on the day before its celebration, a bond for 1000 merks, which would make up for the loss of his stipend should he be visited by the Presbytery with that sentence. That report having reached the Presbytery, they interrogated him whether it was true, and whether the bond contained a clause prejudicial to the kirk. He admitted that he had received the bond, and promised to produce it to the Presbytery at their next meeting. But at several of their subsequent meetings he evaded the production of the bond, and at the meeting held on 26th December 1648, he acknowledged that it was destroyed. The result was, that for irregular marriages and various other irregularities, including his going to "the leaguer of James Graham at Bodwell," where he delivered up his son apparently to serve in Graham's army, and for drinking healths, he was deposed from the office of the holy ministry. About a year and a half after, he applied to the Presbytery for restoration to the communion of the church ; and having satisfied them, he obtained from them, on 25th May 1652, a testimonial to the Presbytery of Argyll, to whose bounds he intended to remove.[1]

But on the same 26th December 1648 on which Mr. M'Lauchlan was deposed, the Presbytery of Dumbarton was more lenient to the young couple. "Anent the Laird of Lus his mariage, the Presbyterie hes searched and hes fund the lait General Assembly hes referit a generall questioune to ane committee, and no censur is put vpon the parties, only it is reported by the Commissioners to the Assembly that the committee thought the mother of the young ladie sould confes her fault in her awn paroch kirk."[2]

It may here be noted that shortly after this the Covenant was renewed in the parish kirk of Luss. The following is an extract from the minutes of the Presbytery of Dumbarton on this subject :—

[1] Dumbarton Presbytery Records.          [2] Dumbarton Presbytery Records.

Januari 23, 1649.

ANENT the vacant Kirk of Lus, and renuing of the Covenant thair, Mr. David Elphinstoune, Mr. Archibald M'Leane, and Mr. Johne Stewart ar appontit to repair to the said kirk on Wedinsday com eight dayes for keeping of the fast, and the said Mr. David to preach befoir noune, and Mr. Archibald M'Leane afternoon, in the Irish language, and betuixt the sermones the said Mr. David and Mr. Johne Stewart are to go on, on the tryall of the paroch, conform to ordour, and Mr. Johne Stewart to read the solemn ingadgment and Covenant after the first sermon, and Mr. Archibald M'Lean to renue the Covenant on the Sabbath thairafter, and Gillish M'Arthur, Clerk to the Session, is ordained to haue the parishioners dwely advertised to keep the fast at the said kirk, and especiallie to advertise the Lard of M'Farlan to haue his people of the Aroqhair present, and the said Mr. David to intimat the vacancie of the place.[1]

At the next meeting of the Presbytery of Dumbarton, 23d February, the Moderator reported that the Covenant had been renewed in the Kirk of Luss, according to appointment.   On the same day on which the Covenant was renewed, the deposition of Mr. Archibald M'Lauchlan and the vacancy of the parish were publicly intimated.[2]

At the time of her marriage with John Colquhoun of Luss, Margaret Baillie was only about nineteen years of age.   Having attained her majority, she was retoured heir to her father, Sir Gideon, on 24th May 1650, in the lands of Woodhall, Knockindunce, Tripslaw, Falslie, and others in the constabulary of Haddington ; and in the lands of Ellem and Wynesheillis, Ellemsyde, Felcleuche, Dyishauche, Easter and Wester Skairshill in the county of Berwick.   On the same day she was retoured heir to her sister Jean Baillie in the half of the barony of Lochend, comprehending the lands of Lochend, the lands and bounds of the Great Loch of Dunbar, the lands of Bromepark, Westbarnes, Easter and Wester Bromehouse, and others, united into the barony of Lochend ; in the half of the lands of Standartis ; in the half of the Templar lands in the town of Spott ; and in Easter and Wester Broomhouse, within the constabulary of Haddington.[3]

The marriage between John Colquhoun and Margaret Baillie had been too hasty, it would appear, to permit of the preliminary step of a marriage-

[1] Records of the Presbytery of Dumbarton.          [3] Inquis. Retor. Abbrev. Berwick, No.
[2] Ibid.                                                        287 ; Haddington, Nos. 223, 224.

contract being entered into between them. But about two years after that
event they made a postnuptial contract of marriage, which is dated the
13th of May and the 17th and 20th of June 1650. It narrates that as there
was no contract matrimonial passed and subscribed between them before
their marriage, Sir John considered himself bound in honour and duty to
provide his spouse in a suitable liferent out of his own estate, having
special reference to the means and estate which pertained to her, and which
before pertained to her late sister Jean, her late brother, Sir James Baillie
of Lochend, her late father, Sir Gideon Baillie of Lochend, Knight, and her
late grandfather, Sir James Baillie of Lochend, Knight, and in which Sir
John Colquhoun, her husband, was now to be secured. Sir John, therefore, bound himself and his heirs to infeft Margaret, his spouse, in liferent
in the lands of Garscube, with the manor-place and others, in the Mains of
Colquhoun, in the lands of Connoltoun and Dunglas, and also in the lands
of Dunnerbuck and Auchintorlie, all in the shire of Dumbarton. Margaret
Baillie, on the other hand, became bound to infeft Sir John, her husband, in all the lands of Lochend pertaining to her as one of the two
heirs of her sister, brother, father, and grandfather above named. Both
parties further bound themselves to make suitable provision for the heirs-
female of their marriage. Should there be no heir-male, but only daughters of the marriage, John Colquhoun and his spouse, Margaret Baillie,
bound themselves equally between them to educate and maintain their
daughters honourably, according to their rank, until they were married,
and thereafter to pay equally betwixt them to their daughter, if only one,
2000 merks yearly, and if two or more daughters, 3000 yearly, to be divided
equally among them. And Margaret, as one of the two heirs-portioners of
her deceased brother, father, and grandfather, bound herself to resign her equal
half of the lands and barony of Lochend, and other lands before mentioned,
into the hands of the King, as the immediate superior thereof, in favour of
and for new infeftment of the same to be granted to John Colquhoun of
Luss and the heirs lawfully begotten or to be begotten betwixt him and
her ; whom failing, to any other lawful heirs of her body in any other
lawful marriage ; whom failing, to the said John Colquhoun of Luss, and
his heirs-male and assignees whomsoever, reserving to her the liferent

thereof, and to Dame Magdalene Carnegie, Lady Kilbirnie, her liferent of so many of the said lands as were provided to her.[1]

In fulfilment of this postnuptial contract, Margaret Baillie, in 1663, as one of the two heirs-portioners to her deceased brother, father, and grand father, and also as heir to the deceased Jean Baillie, her sister, who was the other heir-portioner, being then in her majority and perfect age of twenty-one years complete, resigned the lands mentioned in the said contract, to and in favour of the said Sir John, her spouse.[2]

The marriage of Sir John Colquhoun with Margaret Baillie thus added greatly to the extent and value of his family estates.

Lady Luss's charter-chest of the estate of Lochend was in the hands of Dame Margaret Hamilton, Countess of Hartfell, her grandmother, and of James Earl of Hartfell, her spouse, or of William Baillie of Lethan, or of Sir Patrick Hamilton of Little Preston, her tutors-testamentars then in life. She and her spouse required of course access to the charter-chest, yet these parties refused to deliver it to them unless compelled. A supplication was accordingly given in to the Estates of Parliament by Dame Margaret Baillie, Lady Luss, and Sir John Colquhoun of Luss, Knight, her spouse, for his interest, humbly beseeching the Estates of Parliament to give warrant to cite the foresaid persons to compear before them to hear and see them decerned to deliver to the supplicant her charter-chest, at the least to her said spouse, upon inventar and his discharge granting that he had received the same, and binding himself to make it forthcoming to all parties interested. This supplication having been taken into consideration by the Parliament on 25th June 1650, Sir John Colquhoun of Luss, Knight, for himself and his lady, having compeared personally, and the Earl of Hartfell, for himself, his lady, and the remanent defenders, having been present also personally, the Parliament ordained that the said charter-chest with the whole evidents it contained should be inventoried, and then delivered to Sir John Colquhoun of Luss for himself and his lady, upon his discharge to be granted to the Earl of Hartfell, and his lady, and remanent tutors, Sir John bind-

---

[1] Copy Postnuptial Contract at Rossdhu.

[2] Original Resignation at Rossdhu. In this writ the day of the month is left blank.

ing himself to make the writs forthcoming to all parties having interest therein.[1]

A dispute having arisen between the Provost and bailies of Dumbarton and Sir John Colquhoun of Luss, Knight, and others, the Provost and bailies of that burgh obtained in 1656 letters of lawborrows, by which the parties complained against were required to find caution for their observing the peace in regard to them.   The letters are in the name of Oliver, Lord Protector, and bear—

"OLIVER, Lord Protector of the Commonwealth of Scotland, England, and Ireland, and the dominions thereto belonging, to messingeris," regarding the complaint of the Provost and bailies of Dumbarton, "npon Sir John Colquhoun of Luss, Knight, Sherrif-principal of the Sherrifdom of Dumbartane, Alexander and James Colquhouns, his bretheren german, and John Colquhoun of Kilmardonie, his deputt of the said Sheriffdom, Sir Humphray Colquhoun of Balvey, Knight, John Colquhoun, elder of Kilmardonie . . . Humphray Colquhoun of Balernik,          Colquhoun of Camstrodden,          Colquhoun, fear thereof, his sone . . . Archibald Colquhoun, portioner of Wester Kilpatrik . . . David Colquhoun in Mylnetoun of Colquhoun, Walter Colquhoun of Barnhill, Walter Colquhoun in Connelltoun, James          and          Colquhouns in Mylnetoun, and Robert Colquhoun in Gairlocheid," and others, who had " conceavet ane deidlie hatred, evill will and malice causeless" against the above complainers, so as to disturb them in the enjoyment of those rights and privileges which, as inhabitants of that royal burgh, they had possessed " for many yeres bygaine past memorie of man."

The Lord Protector favoured the complainers, and gave a decree to the following effect :—

"We will, therefore, and we charge you straittlie and command that incontinent these our letters sein, ye pas and take the saide compleiners oathes that they dread the forenamed persons abone complenit upon their trouble and mollestatioun ; and therefore that ye, in our name and authoritie, command and charge them personally, if they can be apprehendit, and faillieing thereof, at their dwelling places, and be oppin proclamatioun at the mercat croce of the heid burghe of the Sherelldome, or vther jurisdictiouns where they dwell, to cum and find sufficient cautioun, sovertie, and lawborrowes actit in the books of the Court of Justice, etc., that the said complainers, their wyffes, bairnes, families, customers, taksmen, officers, etc., shall be harmeles and skaithles in

[1] Acts of the Parliaments of Scotland, vol. vi. p. 528.

their bodies, and in the peaceable possession, bruiking, and joyeing of their said rights and priviledges, and uther particularlie and generallie abone specifyit, and nowayis to be troubled nor mollested therein by the forenamet persons abone complenit upon, nor nane of them, their wyffes, bairnes, families," etc., under severe penalties. "Given under our signet, att Edinburghe, the twentie-fourt day of July, in the year of our Lord 1656.

By warrand of the Commissioners for Administration of Justice to the people in Scotland.

"28 July 1656."                                              "JA. ALLANE."[1]

From the great extent of the parish of Luss, it had long been considered desirable that the lands of Arrochar, which were the most northerly part of it, should be separated and formed into a distinct parish. The Presbytery of Dumbarton brought the matter before the Council of Estate in Scotland, and, on a petition and recommendation from the Presbytery, the Council of Estate, by an order dated Holyrood House, 24th December 1658, appointed Robert Hamilton of Barnes and others their Commissioners, to call before them all parties interested in the dismembering of the lands of Arrochar from the parish of Luss, and in the erection of a new church at Tarbet, with a manse and the provision of a glebe for the minister, and if they found a general concurrence, that all parties concerned should forthwith proceed to the building of a church and manse, and to the providing of a glebe, conformably to the Act of Parliament.

To this proposal Sir John Colquhoun had always been favourable, and he had frequently expressed his readiness to concur in the furtherance of so good a work. To carry out the views of the Presbytery of Dumbarton and the Government, he, on 25th January 1659, subscribed a bond to denude himself of the sum of 400 merks yearly, payable by the Laird of Macfarlane for the tithes of his lands of Arrochar, and 15 bolls teind meall, payable forth of the lands in Arrochar, belonging to Walter Macfarlane of Gartardane, in favour of the minister of Tarbet and his successors in all time coming, and to be uplifted by the first minister after his entry to the ministry at Tarbet.[2]

John Macfarlane, fiar of Arrochar, was also favourable to the division of the parish of Luss. He granted a bond, dated 25th January 1659,

¹ Dumbarton Records.                    ² Original Obligation at Rossdhu.

2 L

binding himself to cause begin, finish, and perfect the building of a new kirk, with a manse for the minister of Tarbet, and also to give and mortify a competent glebe, under the pain of 3000 merks Scots, to be uplifted by the Presbytery of Dumbarton, and employed by them for pious uses, within the said lands of Arrochar, "seriously entreating the said Commissioners and all parties concerned forthwith to proceed in all points, conform to the said order" of the Council of Estate in Scotland.[1]

Some differences had arisen between Sir John Colquhoun and Archibald Marquis of Argyll with regard to the holding of various lands, such as Auchintorlie, Dunnerbuck, and others. A letter of the Marquis to him on this subject has been preserved, expressing the Marquis's earnest desire to have everything settled in an amicable way. The letter is as follows :—

Inveraray, 7 Maij 1652.

LOVEING FREIND,—I receaveit your lettre by Mr. James Campbell, and, as I told zour selffe, I am still willing to doe the bussines, swa that quhat I doe may be wpone certaine knowledge. I doubt not bot ze remember that the questione was anent the haldeing, and that ther was nothing produceit to cleir it, except quhat was done be my father in his minoritie, partlie without consent of a quorum of his couratouris, and partlie without consent of any of thame at all. And, as I remember, it was promeist at that tyme to cleir the halding by ane chartour granted be some other of my predicessouris to zouris. Tharfore I desyre that this may be done without delay, and zour bussines shal be perfytted ; and albeit zow be not hable to cleir this, zitt, wpone the knowledge thairof, I wil be verie willing to satle with zow in a freindlie way without any heiring at all.

Ze may also remember of the note gevine zow anent my right to Achintwerlie and Dunerbock, and anent the reversionis of landis in the Lennox, and that ze promeist to sie how thes thinges could be cleired ; quhilk I desyire zitt may be done. Iff zow can shawe any thing that may elcid thes rightes, ther shal be no more of it. And iff otherwayes, zitt I shal be moist willing to satle in a faire and freindlie way, for I am so fare frome desyreing to have any questiouns with zow at all, that it is my desyre still to remaine,

Zour moist affectionate freind to serve zow,

For the Laird of Luss.                                        A. M. ARGYLL.[2]

During the civil wars in Scotland and England, Sir John Colquhoun

[1] Original Obligation at Rossdhu.                [2] Original Letter at Rossdhu.

was a firm adherent of the royalist party, and he suffered considerably for the royal cause. When the Estates of Parliament passed an Act, 15th February 1649, for putting the kingdom in a posture of defence against the evil practices of such as laboured to subvert religion and government, and, for the better and more speedy effectuating thereof, nominated and appointed commissioners and committees of war within the several shires of the kingdom, John Colquhoun of Luss, the Marquis of Argyll, and the Provost and bailies of Dumbarton, were appointed Commissioners and a Committee of War for the shire of Dumbarton, the Laird of Luss to be convener.[1]    It is not, however, probable that the Laird of Luss, from the opinions he held, took any active part in supporting the measures adopted by the Estates of Parliament in opposition to the Sovereign.

In the year 1654 Cromwell's forces and those of the royalists contended for the possession of the Castle of Rossdhu, belonging to Sir John Colquhoun.    At the beginning of that year the castle was defended by John Dennistoun of Colgrain, who had obtained, from William Earl of Glencairn, Commander-in-Chief of the royalist troops in Scotland, commissions in November and December 1653.    But when Dennistoun marched northward from Rossdhu with the Lennox fencibles, the castle fell into the hands of a party of Cromwell's soldiers from Glasgow, under the command of Lieutenant-Colonel Cottrel.    Soon after, it was recovered by the royalists under the command of the Laird of Macnaughton and the eldest son of Sir George Maxwell of Newark.    They were again forced to abandon it by a troop of Cromwell's horse under Colonel Cooper.[2]

In the same year General Middleton, after having been appointed by Charles the Second, on the resignation of the Earl of Glencairn, General and Commander-in-Chief of the royalist forces in Scotland, visited Rossdhu, when proceeding with the main body of the army, which was then in Sutherland, through the Highlands southward for the purpose of strengthening it by new recruits.    His army was refreshed at Rossdhu and increased in number; but he was, notwithstanding, defeated by Cromwell's troops at Lochgair on the 26th of July following.[3]

---

[1] Acts of the Parliaments of Scotland, vol. vi. p. 374.    [2] Dennistoun's MSS.    [3] Ibid.

When Cromwell had conquered Scotland, and proclaimed himself Protector of that kingdom, Sir John Colquhoun, like other royalists, was forced
to yield to the new Government. He was included in Cromwell's Act of
Grace to the people of Scotland granted in 1654 ; but by it he was fined in
the sum of £2000 sterling. This fine, however, was modified to £666,
13s. 4d., by an ordinance, dated 6th April 1655, and by a subsequent order in
the same month it was ordained, as a further mitigation, that three months
should elapse between the payment of the first half and that of the second.
The following is a discharge for the payment of the first half of the modified
fine by Sir John :—

Leith, 25 June 1655.

WHEREAS, by an ordinance of his Highness the Lord Protector, by and with
the consent of his Councill, intituled, An Ordinance of Pardon and Grace to the
people in Scotland, it is ordained that severall persons therein named should
pay unto me the several and respective sums therein mentioned, as a fine and
fines, for and in respect of his and their estate and estates, to be paid in such
manner as is therein mentioned : And in particular, Sir John Colquhoun of Luz
is to pay the sum of two thousand pounds sterling : And whereas, upon severall
addresses made by the persons upon whom the said fines were imposed, his
Highness, by and with the consent of his Councill, by order dated the sixth of
April 1655, hath ordered that the fines imposed upon some persons by the said
ordinance should be wholly suspended, and that others should pay in such sum
or sums of money as part of their fines at two payments, viz., one moiety
thereof on or before the 21 day of May then next ensuing, and the other moiety
thereof on or before the second day of July following, and the remainder of the said
fines to be forborn : by which order the said Sir John Colquhoun of Luz is
ordered to pay the sum of six hundred sixty-six pounds thirteene shillings and
fower pence at the said times : Notwithstanding, his Highness and Councill, by
their order, dated the 19 of April 1655, have given further time to the said
persons for paiment of the sums charged upon them in the said order, viz., one
moiety thereof on or by the 25 of June then next coming, and the other
moiety on or by the 29 of September following.   Now I do hereby certifie that
the said Sir John Colquhoun of Luz hath, according to the above-recited orders,
paid in to me, the day and year above written, the sum of three hundred thirty-
three pounds six shillings and eight pence sterling, being the first moiety of the
fine charged on him : the receipt whereof I do hereby acknowledge.

GEO. BILTON.[1]

[1] Original Discharge at Rossdhu.

From the benefit of Cromwell's general indemnity to the Scots, numbers of the more formidable royalists were expressly excluded. Among these was Archibald Lord Lorne, eldest son of Archibald eighth Earl and first Marquis of Argyll, who had adhered so steadfastly to the interests of King Charles the Second during the Protectorate, and had resisted with such effect the forces of the Parliament, as to excite the special resentment of Cromwell. Nor though he was made a prisoner would he submit to the Usurper till he received his Majesty's permission, which is dated 31st December 1655. The new Government, on his submission, required from him sureties, bound jointly in the sum of £5000, that he would act neither directly nor indirectly against Cromwell and the Commonwealth of England.

Sir John Colquhoun of Luss was one of the sureties for the good behaviour of Lord Lorne. In connexion with this bond of suretyship his Lordship granted to Sir John, as his cautioner, a bond of relief without date, which is in the following terms :—

BE it knowen to all men be these present lettres, Me, Archibald Lord Lorne, Forsameikle as, att my earnest requeist and desire, Charles Earle of Dumfermling, Williame Earle of Selkrig, James Maister of Rollo, Sir James Dowglas, brother to the deceast Earle off Mortoune,        Menzies off Weines, Allexander Bruce, brother to my Lord Kincairdein, and Sir Johne Colquhonne off Lus, Knycht, are become bound and obliged, ewery one of thame severallie, in each of thair proportiounes of the soume of fyve thowsand poundis sterling, to be payed in to the publict receipt of the Lord Protector, in case att any tyme heirafter I shall act, directlie or indirectlie, against the said Lord Protector and the commounewealthe off Ingland, or his successouris, as the band and securitie maid and subscryved thairanent at more lenth beares : and I, being most willing (as reasoune and equitie wold) that the said Sir Johne Colquhoune off Lus, Knicht, be sufficientlie fred and liberat of his obligement foirsaid, and of all inconvenient he may incurre thairthrow : Therfore, witt zea me to be bound and obliged, lykeas I be the tenour heiroff faithfullie bind and oblige me, my aires, executouris, successouris quhatsomever, to warrand, frieth, releive, and skaithles keip the said Sir Johne Colquhoune of Lus, Knycht, his aires, executouris, and successouris of his obligement abovewritten, and of all coist, skaithe, dammage, expenses, danger, and inconvenient quhilk he or his foirsaidis shall happine to susteane or incure thairthrow be quhatsomever maner off way ; consenting thir

presentis be insert and registrat in the bookes off any judicatorie established, or
to be established, to have the strenth off ane decreitt of ony off the juges
thairoff respectiue interponit heirto, that lettres of horneing and others necessar
on six dayes may pas heirvpon, and constituitis                     my procura-
touris :  in witnes whereoff, written be Gillies M'Arthoure, notare in Duchlashe,
I haue subscrivit thir presentis with my hand at

                                                            LORNE.

    W. Douglas, witnes.
    Hugh Schaw, witnes.
    Ja. Campbell, witnes.[1]

Whilst thus concerned in political matters, this second baronet of Luss
appears much on record both as giving and as receiving various charters, and
otherwise transacting property and family business to the close of his life; 
but these transactions it is unnecessary minutely to record.  Only a few
of them may here be mentioned.  In 1652 he purchased the lands of
Balloch and others from James fourth Duke of Lennox.  The disposition
made to him of these lands by the Duke is dated 7th October that year.
In the year 1653 he sold in feu-farm the lands of Easter Tullychewen to
Patrick Lyndsay in Dalquherne.  The contract by which this sale was
made, is dated Edinburgh, 14th January that year.[2]

On the 27th, 28th, and 29th of the same month, Sir John was infefted, on a precept of sasine contained in a charter from James Duke of
Lennox, in Blairvaddoch, Stuckiedow, Letrualt-mor, Faslane, Garelochhead,
Mamore, Mambeg, Ferlincary, Dureling, Auchenveunel-mor, Auchingaich,
three Tullychewens, Craigroston, Balloch, and other lands.[3]

By his letters of disposition, dated 20th May 1653, Sir John sold to
Robert Napier of Kilmahew in liferent, and to John Napier, fiar thereof,
and his heirs-male in fee, the lands of Waltoun and Wallastoun, in the
parish of Cardross and shire of Dumbarton.[4]

On the 3d of March 1655, he received a charter from the burgh of
Dumbarton of subjects appraised at his instance from Adam Colquhoun, as

[1] Original Bond of Relief at Rossdhu.

[2] Original Contract, ibid.

[3] Original Charter and Instrument of
Sasine, ibid.

[4] This is stated in an original contract
between Sir John and Robert Napier of
Kilmahew, of the above date, at Rossdhu.

heir to the deceased William Colquhoun, his father, or Adam Colquhoun, his uncle.  For this charter, the Council, on the 10th of the same month, found the composition due to be £70 Scots, but for certain good deeds done by the Laird to the burgh, they reduced it to one-half.[1]

Sir John afterwards became involved in a contest with the burgh of Dumbarton, in reference to the salmon and other fishings on the Water of Leven, under Balloch, to which both parties claimed a right.  The point in dispute was brought before the Court of Session.  A deputation of bailies, commissioned by the Council for themselves, and in name of the community of Dumbarton, met and conferred with the Laird of Luss anent the differences between him and the burgh, who charged him with violently usurping, intruding, and taking possession of salmon and other fishings on the Water of Leven, under Balloch, which they alleged belonged heritably to the said burgh ; but the Laird of Luss would in noways desist from the said fishings, nor from the pursuit of the fishers in the said Water of Leven before his own court.  The bailies having reported to the Town Council, on the 22d of July 1657, the unsatisfactory result of their conference with the Laird of Luss, the Town Council on that day appointed Mr. Donald Macalpine, with the clerk, and Walter Watson, younger, to compear as procurators for the said fishers, to defend them in this action.[2]

Sir John Colquhoun was a man of ability and learning, and took a prominent part in the educational and political affairs of his time.  In the year 1651, he was recommended as one of the Commissioners for the Visitation of the University of Glasgow ; and he was again appointed Commissioner for Lennox for the same purpose in 1661.[3]  He is mentioned as occupying the position of patron in connection with the ceremony of conferring degrees in that University, in the year 1672, by an English student, Josiah Chorley, from Preston in Lancashire, in an account which he gives of his laureation in that year.  Writing on the 1st of April, he says, " My tutor would not excuse my journey to Edinburgh to invite the grandees there to our Laureation ; so that I went, furnished with gloves

[1] Dumbarton Sasine Records, vol. iii.
[2] Dumbarton Records, vol. ii.
[3] Baillie's Letters and Journals, vol. iii. pp. 136, 456.

and theses, which I first presented to the patron, the Laird of Colquhoun, upon white satin."[1]

Sir John was a member of the first Parliament of Charles the Second, after his restoration, which was opened with great pomp and splendour on the 1st of January 1661, and was very numerously attended.[2] He granted a receipt, dated 20th November 1660, to his uncle, Sir Humphrey Colquhoun of Balvie, for a black velvet foot mantle, and corresponding furniture, which he bound himself to return, when the ensuing Parliament was ended, under the penalty of 500 merks.[3] He was one of the Commission appointed by the Parliament, 8th January 1651, for the more speedy despatch of business in the Parliament, to prepare overtures for advancing trade, navigation, and manufactories, and for that end to call for the advice and assistance of intelligent merchants, or any who could give the best information in these matters, with power to receive and hear all such complaints and petitions of private parties as should be given in to them, upon which they were to report.[4] He was also one of the Commissioners appointed by the Parliament to uplift from the shire of Dumbarton its proportion of the annual tax of £40,000 sterling, which they granted to their restored sovereign for the support of a military force in the Kingdom of Scotland.[5]

The tragical fate of Sir John's uncle, the celebrated James Marquis of Montrose, is well known. He was hanged in the market-place of Edinburgh, near the Cross, on 21st May 1650, after which his head was placed on the Tolbooth of that city, whilst his arms and legs were exposed to public view in the four principal towns of the kingdom, and his body, being put into a chest, was buried among malefactors in the Burrow Muir of Edinburgh.

[1] Munimenta Universitatis Glasguensis, Preface, p. xxvi.
[2] Acts of the Parliaments of Scotland, vol. vii. pp. 4, 369, 447.
[3] The foot mantle was a covering, often gorgeously ornamented, for horses in State processions, such as the coronation of the sovereign, and the riding of Parliament. At the coronation of King Charles the First in 1633, the nobility rode from the Castle of Edinburgh to Holyrood House, "on great horses, with rich foot clothes and caparisons;" the King, "on a riche foote clothe, all embrodred with siluer and pearle;" and the Marquis of Hamilton, following him, on "a gennett of Spaine, and a werey riche foote clothe, and leding an wther in hes hand, the richest of all."—[Balfour's Annals, vol. iv. pp. 386, 388.]
[4] Acts of the Parliaments of Scotland, vol. vii. p. 9.
[5] Ibid. vol. vii. p. 92.

In the ceremony of collecting the remains of Montrose, and taking down his head from the Tolbooth of Edinburgh, on Monday the 7th of June 1661, in obedience to an order of the Parliament on the 4th of that month, to the effect that his body, head, and scattered members should be gathered together and interred with all honour imaginable, Sir John Colquhoun of Luss took an active part. In an account of the ceremony, published in the *Mercurius Caledonius* at the time, it is said that the Lord Marquis of Montrose, with his friends of the name of Graham, the whole nobility and gentry, with the Provost, Bailies and Council of Edinburgh, together with four companies of the trained bands of the city, went to the place where the coffin containing the trunk of Montrose's body had been buried, and found it. It is then added :—

"The noble Lord Marquis and his friends took care that these remains were decently wrapt in the finest linen; so did likewise the friends of the other—[Sir William Hay of Dalgetty, whose remains were similarly honoured]; and so incoffined suitable to their respective dignities.

"The trunk of his Excellency, thus coffined, was covered with a large and rich black velvet cloth, taken up, and from thence carried by the noble Earls of Mar, Athole, Linlithgow, Seaforth, Hartfell, and others of these honourable families ; the Lord Marquis himself, his brother, Lord Robert, and Sir John Colquhoun, nephew to the deceased Lord Marquis, supporting the head of the coffin ; and all under a very large pall or canopy, supported by the noble Viscount Stormont, the Lords Strathnaver, Fleming, Drumlanrig, Ramsay, Maderty, and Rollo.

"Being accompanied with a body of horse, of nobility and gentry, to the number of two hundred, rallied in decent order by the Viscount of Kenmure, they came to the place where the head stood, under which they set the coffin of the trunk, on a scaffold made for that purpose, till the Lord Napier, the Barons of Morphie, Inchbrakie, Orchill, and Gorthie, and several other noble gentlemen placed on a scaffold next to the head—and that on the top of the town's tolbooth, six stories high—with sound of trumpet, discharge of many cannon from the Castle, and the honest people's loud and joyful acclamation, all was joined, and crowned with the crown of a Marquis, conveyed with all honours befitting such an action, to the

Abbey Church of Holyrood House, a place of burial frequent to our Kings, there to continue in state, until the noble Lord his son be ready for the more magnificent solemnization of his funerals."

The collected remains of Montrose lay in state in the Abbey Church of Holyrood House from Monday 7th January to Saturday 11th May 1661, the day on which his public funeral was performed with a splendour and heraldic pomp rarely equalled, by carrying his remains from the Abbey Church of Holyrood House to that of St. Giles. The corpse was carried by fourteen Earls, and the pall above the corpse was likewise sustained by twelve noblemen. Among the gentlemen appointed for relieving those who carried the coffin under the pall was "Colquhoun."

"Next to the corps went the Marquis of Montrose and his brother, as chief mourners, in hoods and long robes carried up by two pages, with a gentleman bare-headed on every side.

"Next to them followed nine of the nearest in blood, three and three, in hoods and long robes, carried up by pages, viz.,—

"The Marquis of Douglas ; the Earls of Marischal, Wigton, Southesk ; Lords of Drummond, Maderty, Napier, Rollo, and Baron of Luss, nephew to the defunct."[1]

Sir John Colquhoun of Luss was again elected Commissioner for Dumbartonshire to the Convention of Estates in the year 1665.[2]  He was elected to represent the same shire in the Parliament of 1667 ; and when that Parliament, on the 23d of January that year made a voluntary offer to his Majesty of seventy-two thousand pounds Scots monthly, for the space of twelve months, to be paid by the several shires and burghs of the kingdom, according to the valuations, he was one of the Commissioners appointed to uplift from the shire of Dumbarton its proportion, which was seven hundred and sixty-four pounds ten shillings Scots.[3]  He also represented, along with John Napier of Kilmahew, the same shire in the second Parliament

---

[1] "A Relation of the True Funerals of the Great Lord Marquesse of Montrose, his Majesty's Lord High Commissioner, and Captain General of his Forces in Scotland : with that of the renowned Knight, Sir William Hay of Dalgetty." This pamphlet was written at the time by Thomas Sydserf, (son of Thomas Sydserf, Bishop of Galloway,) editor of the *Mercurius Caledonius*.
[2] Acts of the Parliaments of Scotland, vol. vii. p. 527.
[3] *Ibid*. vol. vii. pp. 536, 540, 544.

of Charles the Second, in 1669 ;[1] and in that year he was made Lieutenant-Colonel of Argyll's Regiment of Militia, of the shires of Argyll, Dumbarton and Bute.    He appears as still representing the shire of Dumbarton in the third session of the second Parliament of Charles the Second in 1672.[2]

Sir John Colquhoun was infefted in the office of Crownarie within the shire of Dumbarton, and seven parishes in the shire of Stirling.    On 26th April 1671, in the Tolbooth of Stirling, his brother Alexander, in presence of the public clerk to the West and South Circuits, and other witnesses, compeared before Alexander Lord Halkerstoun and Sir John Baird of New-byth, two of the Lords Commissioners of Justiciary sitting in judgment, and declared that his brother, the said Sir John, was infefted in the said office of Crownarie, and produced his infeftments for verification thereof.    He there-fore protested that the establishment of the said Justice Court, and the power and authority exercised by the several Sheriffs relating thereto, should in no ways be prejudicial to the said Sir John's said office, but that all the privileges, immunities, and freedoms competent to him as holding that office should be reserved to him.[3]

For the punishment of theft, riefe, oppression, and sorning, in conse-quence of the barbarous cruelties and daily thefts committed by various clans, inhabiting the Highlands and Islands, the Parliament passed an Act in 1594, ordaining that all landlords should be charged to find surety to make their men, tenants and servants, answerable to justice, and to re-dress parties skaithed.[4]    In the year 1672, Sir John Colquhoun, from various circumstances, gave a bond with cautioners to the Privy Council, that his vassals, tenants, and their tenants and sub-tenants, of his name and clan in the Kingdom of Scotland, should live peaceably and obey the laws, wherein if they failed, by perpetrating slaughter, raising fire, committing theft, depredation, robbery, or other crimes, he and his said cautioners were bound not only to produce the persons, but also to pay the loss and mischief thereby sustained, under certain pecuniary penalties.

In the month of May that year, the tenants of his various lands, in

[1] Acts of the Parliaments of Scotland, vol. vii. p. 549, and vol. viii. p. 4.
[2] Ibid. vol. viii. pp. 56, 209.
[3] Original Instrument of Sasine at Rossdhu.
[4] Acts of the Parliaments of Scotland, vol. iv. p. 71.

obedience to an Act of the Privy Council, gave to Sir John bonds for their good behaviour and due observance of the laws. This they did for his better relief as to the bond which he had granted to the Privy Council. They also bound themselves, in case any of them, or any other sub-tenants or possessors of the said lands, should commit the crimes mentioned, or any others contrary to the laws, to produce all such persons to underly the laws.[1]

In 1673, Sir John purchased from George Easdell the five pound land of old extent of Cameron, with the spittell of land called Darleith's Spittell, with the teinds in the parish of Bonhill and shire of Dumbarton, of which Sir John was the immediate superior. He obtained from the said George a disposition of them, dated the 3d and 4th of December that year. The disposition narrates that the said lands were wadset and disponed to John Colquhoun of Glinns by the said George, for 5000 merks, under reversion for payment of that sum, which Sir John was to pay to the said John Colquhoun of Glinns.[2]

Sir John obtained, 13th April 1675, from the Commissioners of Frances Duchess of Lennox, a gift of the ward, non-entry, mails, farms, profits, and duties of the five pound land of Bannachra, with mill, woods, fishings, and pertinents of the same, by reason of ward and non-entry of the said lands through the decease of Robert Colquhoun of Ballernick. This gift thereof was of all years bygone since the death of the said Robert, and in time coming, until the entry of the next lawful heir thereto, being of lawful age, with the relief of the said ward when the same should happen, with the marriage of Robert Colquhoun of Bannachra, son and apparent heir of the said deceased Robert, and failing of him by death unmarried, with the marriage of any other heir or heirs, male or female, that should happen to succeed. On the same day Sir John caused notarial intimation to be made to the tenants of Bannachra that the said gift had been made to him, and that they should make payment of the rents of the land to no other person, but to him as donator.[3]  Of this gift Sir John made an assignation to Alexander Colquhoun of Tullychewen on 1st February 1676.[4]

[1] Original Bond at Rossdhu.

[2] Original Disposition, *ibid.*

[3] Original Instrument, *ibid.*

[4] This fact is stated in a disposition of the same gift by the said Alexander to Sir James Colquhoun of Balvie, dated 6th April 1682. at Rossdhu.

Shortly before the death of Sir John Colquhoun, he and Lady Luss sold her patrimonial estate of Lochend to Sir Robert Sinclair of Longformacus. The disposition of sale by them in favour of Sir Robert is dated 1st March 1676. At this time Sir John appears to have been in bad health. In order to give validity to the sale of Lochend, according to the practice of the law of Scotland, he, on Sabbath the 5th of March same year, between one and four o'clock in the afternoon, went from a lodging in the Canongate to the Abbey Kirk of Holyrood House, without any support, remained there during the whole time of divine service, and at the close returned without any support to the chamber from which he came. All this he did in the presence of a notary-public and witnesses. The notarial instrument which contains these particulars is curious, from the minuteness with which they are recorded. It is as follows :—

At Canongaitt, the fyfth day of Merch sixteen [hundred] and seaventie sex yeares, and of our Soveraigne Lord's reigne the twentie eight year,—
The quhilk day, in presence of me, notar publict, vnder subscryveand, and witness efter specifeit, as effeires, compeired personallie within the lodging belonging to James Deanes, bailzie of the Canongaitt, Sir John Colquhoune of Luss, knight and barronet, and came without any help, support, or assistance, walking vigorouselie fra his chamber at the head of the turnpyke of the said lodging belonging and possest be the said James Deanes, downe the wholl staires, and through the closs and entrie to the foirstreit, and thair did take coatch with his Ladie, and goe to the Abbay Kirk of Halyrudhous, and before the entrie of the said kirk the said Sir John came out of the said coatch, and walked as before to the said kirk be the foirgate or principall entrie thairof downe thrie or four steps, and through the said kirk to ane dask or piew thairin belonging to                    , and thair did stay and heir psalmes, prayer, and sermone, preached be Mr.                    Hepburne, minister thairat, with prayers and psalmes efter sermone ; and efter the close of publict worship and baptizieing of some childern, and at the dissolving of the said kirk, the said Sir John Colquhoune did, without any support, help, or assistance, walk vigorouslie through the said kirk, vp the saids stepps, and out of the said kirk, and take coatch with his Lady, as before, to the Hie Streit, foiranent the said James Deanes, and thair came out of the said coatch, and walked through and doune the said closs and entrie to the said lodging, and up the wholl staires to his chamber, fra quhich he came, and that without any help, support, or assistance,

as afoirsaid : Quhervpon, and vpon all and sundrie the haill premiss, the said
Sir John Colquhoun askit and took instruments in the hands of me, notar
publict vnder subscryveand. Thir things were done at the places respective
foirsaid, betuixt the hour of ane and four in the efternoone, day, moneth, year
of God and King's reigne respective foirsaid, in presens of Walter Stirling of
Ballagane, Michaell Malcolme of Nethill, Mr. Hairie Olyphant, wryter in Edinburgh, Robert Deanes, sone to the said Bailzie James Deanes, Ferquhard
Macculloch, wryter in Edinburgh, David Gowand, merchant there, John Mac-
cairtor, and Jon Maclean, servitors to the said Sir Jon Colquhoune, and
                        , officer in the Canongait, with diverse vther witness to
the premiss speciallie desyred and requyred.

Ita est Joannes Macfarlane, notarius publicus, in premissis specialiter requi-
situs testante manu signoque subscribendo.[1]

After the date of this notarial instrument Sir John lived only a short
time. He died about the 11th of April 1676. This we learn from the retour of the service of his son James as heir to him, dated 11th August 1676,
which narrates that he had died about four months previously. In a
declaration made by Thomas Walker, town-clerk of Dumbarton, dated 9th
June 1676, to Dame Margaret Baillie, Lady Luss, James Colquhoun of
Balvie, and Alexander Colquhoun of Tullychewen, the said Margaret is
styled " relict " of the deceased Sir John Colquhoun of Luss, Knight.[2]

Sir John by his testament nominated his eldest son James his sole
executor and intromitter with his goods, gear, and debts, reserving to
Dame Margaret Baillie, his spouse, the third of the insight plenishing and
domicils, conform to a right and assignation thereof made by him to her
of the same, dated the          day of          167 .  In the same deed
Sir John appointed, as tutors to his son James, Dame Margaret Baillie,
Patrick Lindsay of Kilbirnie, Sir John Stirling of Keir, Sir Archibald
Stewart of Blackhall, James Colquhoun of Balvie, John Napier of Kilmahew,
and Alexander Colquhoun of Tullychewen. This testament was duly confirmed by the Commissar of Glasgow on the 27th of February 1677.[3]

---

[1] Original Instrument at Rossdhu.

[2] Original Declaration, ibid.

[3] The information contained in this paragraph is taken from a summons at the instance of Sir James Colquhoun of Luss against
his mother, Margaret Baillie, dated 20th
February 1679, at Rossdhu ; and from a factory dated 13th September 1677. The date
of the testament is not given.

Sir John Colquhoun, having only one son surviving, and having a large family of daughters, made an alteration in the destination of the Luss estates, which would have included the daughters of his son and of himself, and their descendants, preferably to his brother and his male descendants.

A bond of tailzie, it was alleged, was made and granted by Sir John on 1st March 1676, of his estate of Luss in favour of the heirs of tailzie therein mentioned, whom failing, to the heirs of tailzie nominated in a nomination of the same date, alleged to have been subscribed by him, whereby he nominated (failing heirs-male of the body of James Colquhoun, his son, and of his own body) the eldest daughter or lawful heir-female of the body of his said son successive, without division, and the heirs-male of her body; whom failing, her eldest daughter or heir-female, without division, and the heirs-male of her body; failing whom, her eldest daughter or heir-female successive, likewise without division, and so forth successive, so long as there should be son or daughter in the line descending from the body of his said son, or from the sons or daughters of the line of his body; whom all failing, Christian, his sixth daughter by Dame Margaret Baillie, his spouse, and the heirs-male of her body; whom failing, her eldest daughter or heir-female successive, likewise without division, in the manner above mentioned; whom failing, Helen, his youngest daughter, and the heirs of her body, in like manner; whom failing, Anna, his fourth daughter, and the heirs of her body, in like manner; whom failing, Magdalene, his fifth daughter, and the heirs of her body, in like manner. This pretended nomination, it was said, was blank as to the date and witnesses for several years after the death of Sir John, and was thereafter unwarrantably filled up, and the date made the 1st of March 1676, the same with the alleged bond of tailzie, when only one of the two witnesses said to have subscribed it was alive, rendering it impossible to prove the date. This alleged bond of tailzie and pretended nomination were afterwards renounced by the daughters of Sir John, who were favoured by it.[1]

Margaret Baillie, Lady Luss, survived Sir John. But she did not long

---

[1] This information is contained in a ratification by Christian Colquhoun, sixth daughter of Sir John, in favour of her uncle, Sir James Colquhoun, dated 11th August 1688, to be afterwards more fully quoted.

remain a widow, having married, secondly, Archibald Stirling of Garden. The marriage was solemnized on the 1st of April 1677, only about a year, or less than a year, after the death of her first husband. Whether the banns in this instance had been duly proclaimed we are not informed, but her second marriage, after so short a period of widowhood, took her friends by surprise, and some of them doubted whether she had acted with discretion, though they admitted that the gentleman of her second choice was worthy of her affections. The Honourable Patrick Lindsay of Kilbirnie, the husband of Margaret Crawford, younger daughter of Sir John Crawford and Magdalene Carnegie, wrote to her on the occasion to that effect in answer to a letter from her :—

Kilbirny, April 24, [16]77.

DEARE SISTER,—I was just taking horse for Achaus when your letter arrived to my hands. I shall not say but the newes of your mariage surprised me, neither shall I dissemble my thoughts so farre as not to confesse I had rather wished you had continued unmarried for the advantage of your sonne's affairs ; but since the caise is otherwayes, I shall not condemne your choice, since the gentleman is very deserving. If your sonn's bussinesse go weel on, it is that which I shall looke upon as the light of my ambition ; the family of Lusse being on of the familys on earth I wish most happinesse to. I am your husband's most humble servant. I wish you both much joy togither, for 1 shall ever endevour to approve myselfe to be,

Deare sister,[1] your affectionat brother and most humble servant,

P. LINDSAY of Kilbirny.[2]

For the Lady Lusse.

Another of Margaret Baillie's friends, Sir Archibald Stewart of Blackhall and Ardgowan, to whom she had communicated the intelligence of her second marriage, apologizing for her haste, thus writes to her, 24th April 1677 :—"MADAM,—God give you joy. Ye have made good hast indead, and I shall conclude charitable of all ye have done, in regard thos that ar wise knoweth best where ther oune shooe binds them. Your Ladyship might have spared your trouble in makeing ane appollogie to me

---

[1] Margaret Crawford, the wife of the writer of this letter, was sister uterine to Lady Luss, and accordingly the husband of

Margaret Crawford addresses Lady Luss as sister.

[2] Original Letter at Garden.

for your speidie dispatch. The ward of your mariadge was not in my hand; and if ye have manadged your business to your owne satisfaction, and your sonn's advantage, I shall not be ill to please. . . . I think you have maried a very fyne gentleman, and whatever good oppinion I have of him, I wish you may have ane hundreth tymes more, and continue so till the end."[1]

To her second husband Margaret Baillie had only one son, Archibald Stirling of Garden; but after this marriage she lived only about two years and three and a half months, having died on 20th July 1679.[2] In an account of the intromissions of John Colquhoun, younger of Camstradden, with the Laird of Luss's rents of the barony of Luss, etc., for the year 1679, is the following item :—" Givin to Mistris Kirke for mournceing cloakis that was sent to Rosdoc to the Ladie Gardenne's buriall, conforme to her receipt, £5."[3]   Although some of her friends blamed her for her extraordinary speedy despatch in her second marriage, she gained for herself a high reputation among all who knew her for the sedulous and faithful discharge of her duties as a wife and mother.   Law describes her in his Memorials as "a pattern for temperance and modesty, and an exact instructor of her children."[4]   Another writer, whose name has not been preserved, but who evidently knew and highly esteemed her, has drawn her portrait in the following lines : —

> " As verteue, prudence, wisdome, goodness, grace
> Are treue characters of this Gracious Guyd,
> So meekness, loue, illustrating her place
> To be suprem, includeth all besyd.
>         So wee perceaue no splendor one can haue
>         Will free them from fatalite of graue,
> Iff ought could plead exemption from that strok,
> Hir immence mynd adorned with sacred store
> Off select scantion, might the heauens provok
> To pittie people that can plead no more ; '
> Bot since nor grace nor vertene this can moue,
> We most submit vnto the God of Loue.
> Wee sie her losse may weal compared bee

---

[1] Original Letter at Garden.   This letter is printed entire in "The Stirlings of Keir," p. 511.

[2] There is an Original Portrait of her at Garden.

[3] Original Account at Rossdhu.

[4] P. 89.

Vnto the fall of sum great fabrick fair,
Which guylted ore shyn'd with excellencie
Non to be seen that with it could compair,
Bot now decayed : So shee whil hear below
Had no compair for any thing wee know.
Itt is most sure she lived all her lyffe
A most kynd mother, widow, and a wyffe. [1]

Sir John Colquhoun, the second Baronet of Luss, had by his wife, Margaret Baillie, a family of nine children, two sons and seven daughters. The sons were—

1. John, the eldest son and apparent heir, who was a youth of much promise, predeceased his father, unmarried.

2. James, who succeeded his father as third Baronet.

The seven daughters were :—

1. Lilias, the eldest, who was born on the 21st of March 1654, and was obviously named after her grandmother, Lady Lilias Graham. Lilias Colquhoun, when about twenty-one years of age, was wooed by two widowers at the same time; the one the Laird of Buchanan, who was advanced in years; and the other Sir John Stirling of Keir, who was in the prime of life. The father of Lilias, it appears, was favourable to the addresses of the Laird of Buchanan, between whose family and that of the house of Luss there had formerly been frequent alliances and the interchange of mutual good offices. But the young lady herself and her mother and sisters gave the preference to Sir John Stirling of Keir. Mr. Walter Stirling, minister of Baldernock, and his father, of the same name, were both active in promoting the success of the courtship of the Laird of Keir, and various particulars respecting it are detailed in their correspondence. The former, in a letter to the Laird of Keir, on 8th October 1675, thus writes :—"I went to Rosdo, wher I fownd the Laird of Buchannan (a most passionet lover) the second time in play. . . . I consulted my father hou to carie in the dischairg of that trust, who was most unwilling that I should speak to the young

<hr>

[1] Original Lines at Garden.

lealie first, though opportunatey then offered (as it did not, shee was
so well attended,) bot to her father, which I did. . . . The reson
whey I was not permited to make known your Honnor's suit to
the young ladie and hir mother, was lest it should alltogether heave
brock wp Buchannan's busines (non of them being cordial for it,)
which was not desaired til your Honnor's further pleasour was
known; and if I should be blaimed for not doing of it, I most say my
commission did not reatch so farr, for her berther told me that your
Honnor said that if Buchannan was in the play, ye wold not meddle
in it. So, Sir, if ye and my father accord, I doubt nothing, bot
Buchannan wil be permitted to go his jurney to the anttipods, which
he sayes (as I am informed) shall not termenat it." The father
of this correspondent, in a letter to the Laird of Keir, dated Rosdo,
19th October 1675, writing on the same subject, says,—" I thocht
fit, acording to my promis, to acquent you that Buchannen's bussines heir is fullie and fairlie giffen vpe wpon the gentill womane's
declearing hir possitife avertiouue from that bussines, which she
ever did from begining, together with hir mother [and] sisteres
dysascent from the maitter, which hes giffen the effinell strok to
that affeare ; so, Sir, Buchanannen went from this this day, with
ane resolution not to sie this pleac no more, nor to be ane Scotis
man, so that he sayes he will live the cuntrie shortlie. I find
Buchannen passiovn to be very great."[1] The Laird of Buchanau
had goue to London to get a new charter of his estate in the prospect
of his marriage with Lilias, which he fully anticipated would take
place ; but his design was defeated by the opposition of the lady
and her mother. "This disappointment had such effects upon the
Laird of Buchannan's high spirit as in a little time threw him
into a palsie, and prejudiced him in his judgment, in which unhappy circumstances he continued till his death."[2]

---

[1] " The Stirlings of Keir," by William
Fraser, 1858, pp. 66, 67, 508, 509. There
is at Keir an original portrait of Lilias
Colquhoun, with her granddaughter, Lilias
Stirling, daughter of her eldest son, James

Stirling. A lithograph of that portrait is
given in the same work, p. 579.

[2] Buchanan of Auchmar's History of the
Buchanans, p. 37.

The marriage between Lilias Colquhoun and Sir John Stirling of
Keir was celebrated on 2d December 1675, at the Abbey of Holyrood
House, by Mr. Walter Stirling, minister of Baldernock.  On the day
of the marriage, and previous to its celebration at the Canongate
foot, a minute of contract matrimonial was entered into between
Sir John Stirling of Keir and Sir John Colquhoun of Luss, for
himself, and as taking burden for Lilias, his eldest daughter.  Sir
John Stirling became bound to infeft her in his manor-place of
Cawder, and in so many of his lands of his barony of Cawder
as would extend to 4000 merks of yearly rent, to be enjoyed
by her during her lifetime.  Her father bound himself to pay
with her, in name of tocher, 20,000 merks.  This minute of contract was extended into a formal contract of marriage on 2d
March 1676.[1]  Lady Lilias and her sisters, as heirs of line to their
father, were charged by some of his creditors to enter themselves as heirs to him, that they might take action for the payment
of certain debts.  Considering that no benefit would accrue to her
by entering herself heir to her father or her deceased brother Sir
James, Lilias, with advice and consent of her husband, Sir John
Stirling of Keir, on 13th February 1682, renounced her right to
enter herself as heir to them, in favour of their respective
creditors.[2]

Lilias Colquhoun had issue to Sir John Stirling, five sons and
two daughters.  From James Stirling, the third son, who succeeded
to Keir, the present Sir William Stirling Maxwell of Keir and
Pollok, Baronet, is lineally descended, and he thus represents the
eldest co-heiress of Sir James Colquhoun, the third Baronet of Luss.
Under the will of her husband, dated 12th June 1682, Lilias Colquhoun, as his well-beloved spouse, is appointed tutrix, *sine qua
non*, to their children during her widowhood.  Lilias Colquhoun
became a widow in March 1684, and she married, secondly, in
1701, the Honourable Charles Maitland, third son of Charles
third Earl of Lauderdale, by whom she had one daughter, who

[1] " The Stirlings of Keir," p. 469.        [2] Original Renunciation at Rossdhu.

died in childhood. Mr. Maitland died at Cawder, in June 1716. Lilias survived him upwards of ten years, having died at her jointure house of Cawder, on the 31st of December 1726,[1] in her seventy-third year. She was buried at Cawder, on 5th January 1727.[2] Her Bible, a quarto volume, imperfect, " London : printed by John Field, *Anno Dom*. 1648," was recently found at Preston-field, near Edinburgh, the residence of Sir William Dick Cunyng-ham, Baronet. On the back of the title-page of the New Testament is inscribed—"This Bible did belong to Dame Lilias Collquhoune, daughter to Sir John Collquhoune of Luss, Lady Keir, who was borne March the 21st, in the year 1654, and died upon Thursday, 29th December 1726." By whom this inscription was written is unknown.

2. Margaret. On 25th February 1682, Margaret and Magdalene Col-quhoun, lawful daughters to the deceased Sir John Colquhoun of Luss, made a renunciation of their right to enter themselves as heirs to their deceased father and brother similar to what had been made by their sister Lilias.[3] On 20th August 1686, Margaret Col-quhoun granted a discharge of a bond of provision to Sir James Colquhoun of Luss and Humphrey his son. No other trace of Margaret Colquhoun has been found amongst the family papers, and it is presumed that she died unmarried. An account of the expenses of her funeral is among the Luss papers, but it is undated.

COMPT OF THE EXPENSS OF MRS. MARGARET COLQUHOUN'S BURIALL.

| | *lib.* | *s.* | *d.* |
|---|---|---|---|
| Imprimis, payd for 5 men that brought doun the boat, and took up the furnishing for the buriall, | 5 | 12 | 0 |
| Payd for salt and candle, | 2 | 02 | 0 |
| Payd for 5 pynts of claret wyn to the house at Balvie, | 5 | 00 | 0 |
| Payd for 32 pynts of claret wyne, and a barrel to put it in, | 30 | 00 | 0 |
| Payd for 19 pynts of seck, and ane barrell to put it in, | 30 | 00 | 0 |

[1] Register of Deaths, etc., printed in "The Stirlings of Keir," p. 475.

[2] Cawder Parish Records.

[3] Original Renunciation at Rossdhu.

*lib.*  *s.*  *d.*

Payd for the moart cloath six pound,  .  06 00  0
Payd for the coffin fourtie aught pound,  .  .  .  48 00  0
Payd for tuo men and tuo horse that carried the corps to
   Rosedoe,  .  .  .  .  12 00  0

Summa,  138 14  0[1]

3. Beatrice.  She was sent to Dumbarton for her education, and
while residing there she died, in the year 1679.  Her remains were
carried from Dumbarton to Rossdhu, where they were interred in
the family burying-place, within the chapel of Rossdhu.  Various
particulars respecting her last illness and funeral are given in an
account by John Colquhoun, younger of Camstradden, factor on
the barony of Luss, for the year 1679 :—

Item, payed for necessaris the tyme of Mistris Beatrix
   Colquhowne her sicknes at Dumbritan to the women
   that attended her, and to a man that attended her
   corps thrie nights befor they wer taken of Dum-  *lib.*  *s.*  *d.*
   britane, conforme to accompt,  .  .  .  .  011 : 03 : 10
Item, to Katreine Buchanan for drinke and super to some
   gentillmen the night the corps wer taken out of
   Dumbritane, and tobacco and pyps,  .  .  .  013 : 00 :  6
Item, payed out for necessaris to the funerall, conform to
   particular recepts,  .  .  .  .  .  .  244 : 07 :  2
Item, payed to William Colquhowne for the said Mistris
   Beatrix her boarding, conforme to a discharge,  .  116 : 13 :  4
Item, payed to the said William Colquhown for dressing
   the said Mistris Beatrix her cloathes and furnitor
   therto, conforme to accompt and ane discharge,  .  018 : 19 :  4
Item, givin to John Colquhowne, wright, for Mistris
   Beatrix coffine,  .  .  .  .  .  .  032 : 00 :  0
And to the lads of drink money,  .  .  .  000 : 18 :  0
Item, givin to John Craufurd to buy naills and tackets,
   and his charges in bringing home necessaris to the
   said funerall for himself and vthers from Glasgow,  .  006 : 00 :  6
Item, givin for the mortcloath for ten dayes' space, .  .  008 : 00 :  0

¹ Original Account at Rossdhu.

Item, of drinke money to the boy that tooke away the *lib. s. d.*
mortcloath, . . . . . . . . 001 : 09 : 0
Item, to William Colquhowne in Dumbritane for some
necessaris, . . . . . . . . 000 : 13 : 4
Item, givin to a man that went to Glasgow with money to
be sent to Edinburgh to William Bonteine at Killma-
hewes directione, . . . . . . 000 : 12 : 0
Item, to boyes that went to Keire, Kilburney, Argowane,
Glasgow, and elsquhair with the funerall lettres to
Mistris Beatrix buriall, . . . . . 004 : 00 : 0
Item, the compter was in charges in goeing to Glasgow
to buy necessaris to the buriall, attending the corps
in Dumbritane and homecomeing, and ordoreing the
affairis of the buriall at severall tymes, . . . 012 : 00 : 0
Item, at John M'Lintockis the night the corps came home,
the tyme the litter was chargeing and ferricing, for
aell, being six pyntis, and a pynte of brandj, . . 002 : 00 : 0
Item, payed to the officer's wyfe for nyne gallowns of aell
and a pynte of brandj to Mistris Beatrix buriall,
inde, . . . 007 : 06 : 8

4. Anna, the fourth daughter. She died before 11th August 1688, as
Christian, her sister, mentions her as deceased in a ratification of
that date by her to the Laird of Luss. In that ratification, Anna
is called the fourth daughter of Sir John Colquhoun of Luss. She
appears to have died unmarried.

5. Magdalene. Only a few notices concerning Magdalene have been
found in the family papers. One of these refers to her and five
of her sisters as the representatives of their father Sir John and
their brother Sir James. Action was taken at the instance of John
Darleith, only lawful son to the deceased Mr. John Darleith, indweller in Dumbarton, and others, before the Lords of Council and
Session, against Margaret, Anna, Christian, Helen, Magdalene and
Madam Lilias Colquhoun, sisters-german, and apparent heirs-portioners to the deceased Sir James Colquhoun of Luss, their brother,
and daughters and heirs-portioners to the deceased Sir John Col

quhoun, their father, and against James Colquhoun of Balvie, their
uncle, heir of tailzie, for compelling them to enter themselves heirs
of line, tailzie, male and provision respective; and a decreet in
favour of the pursuers was granted by the Lords of Council and
Session on the 20th July 1681.[1] On the 20th of August 1686,
Magdalene, having then reached her majority—twenty-one years
complete—granted a discharge to Sir James Colquhoun of Luss, and
Humphrey, his eldest son, of all former bonds of provision made by
her deceased father to her.[2] There is no trace of Magdalene having
ever been married.

6. Christian, the sixth daughter. She married William Cunninghame
of Craigends, in the county of Renfrew, who represented that
county in several Parliaments prior to the Union.[3] She is mentioned as spouse to him in a ratification by her sister Helen to
Sir Humphrey Colquhoun of Luss, dated 3d July 1693. Christian
granted a discharge of a bond of provision to Sir James Colquhoun
of Luss and Humphrey his son, dated 11th August 1688. In
this discharge she says that she had now reached her majority, and
was past the age of twenty-one years complete.[4] She also granted
to them a ratification of their title to the barony of Luss, etc., of the
same date, in which she is called the sixth daughter of Sir John.[5]
Christian Colquhoun and William Cunninghame had a family of
three sons, Alexander, William, and James. Alexander succeeded
his father in Craigends.

7. Helen, the youngest daughter. She married Robert Dickson of
Sornbeg, in the county of Ayr. The contract of their marriage is
dated 31st January 1693. With advice of her husband, Robert
Dickson of Sornbeg, she granted to Sir Humphrey Colquhoun of
Luss, 3d July 1693, a ratification and renunciation, whereby she
fully and absolutely secured Sir Humphrey Colquhoun, then of

[1] Extract Decreet at Rossdhu.

[2] Original Discharge, ibid.

[3] In an Act of Privy Council, 12th February 1695, Christian is mentioned as a
daughter of Sir John Colquhoun of Luss,
and William Cunningham of Craigend as her
husband.

[4] Original Discharge at Rossdhu.

[5] Original Renunciation, ibid.

Luss, from any trouble, damage, and expense he and his heirs could incur through any pursuit at her instance against them, in regard to the foresaid alleged bond and pretended nomination. By her disposition, dated 23d September 1693, in implement of her obligation contained in the said marriage-contract, and for other onerous causes, she granted an assignation to an heritable bond of provision made in her favour by Sir Humphrey Colquhoun, younger of Luss, dated 20th and 26th August 1686, of 10,000 merks Scots, with £1000 Scots of penalty in case of failure of payment, and the annual-rent of the said principal sum resting unpaid since the term of Whitsunday 1692, and in time coming during the non-payment thereof. Sir Humphrey having paid to her said husband the foresaid 10,000 merks principal, and to herself £1097, the annual-rent thereof, from the term of Whitsunday 1692 to the term of Candlemas past, she granted a discharge to Sir Humphrey, dated at Edinburgh, 31st January 1695.[1]

[1] Original Discharge at Rosedhu.

The following are the facsimiles of the signatures of Sir John Colquhoun and Margaret Baillie, as at their marriage-contract in 1650.

## XVII.—Sir JAMES COLQUHOUN, Eighteenth of Colquhoun and Twentieth of Luss, Third Baronet,—1676-1680.

On the death of Sir John Colquhoun, the second Baronet, on 11th April 1676, his title and estates devolved on his only surviving son, who then became Sir James Colquhoun, third Baronet. Having been in possession for four years only, during his minority, this Baronet has been omitted in the published histories of the family by Sir Robert Douglas, and all subsequent writers. His existence, however, is fully instructed. He was served heir to his father on 11th August 1676.[1] In the retour he is designated "James Colquhoun of Luss, knight and baronet;" and his father, "the deceased John Colquhoun of Luss, knight and baronet." He was infefted in the barony of Luss on 6th November following.[2] At the date of his succession to the estates the third Baronet was a minor, and as the greater number of his tutors lived at a distance, and could not conveniently give the personal attention necessary for the proper superintendence of his affairs, they appointed, on 13th September 1677, James Colquhoun of Balvie, the uncle of Sir James, who was one of his tutors, to act as chamberlain on the estates, and John Colquhoun, younger of Camstradden, was appointed to collect the rents and to pay the accounts.[3]

Sir James obtained, on 11th March 1679, from the Commissioners of Frances Duchess of Lennox, a gift of the ward and non-entries of the lands which belonged to his deceased father, namely the lands of Fergustoun Logan, Bannachtan, Little Ledcamroch-Logan, and Ardconnel, in the regality of Lennox and shire of Dumbarton, and of all other his said father's lands, heritages, etc., which were held by his father immediately of the Duchess and of her late husband, Charles Duke of Lennox.[4] On the same date he received from them a charter of the Mains of Balvie-Logan, the lands of Drumfad, Tullichintaull, Cameron, Finnart, Craigerostan, Balloch, etc., all in the same county.[5] In these lands he was infefted on 9th, 10th, 11th, 12th, and 14th April following.[6]

[1] Original Retour at Rossdhu.
[2] Original Instrument of Sasine, ibid.
[3] Original Factory, ibid.
[4] Original Gift at Rossdhu.
[5] Original Charter, ibid.
[6] Original Instrument of Sasine, ibid.

After the marriage of Dame Margaret Baillie, Lady Luss, to her second husband, the Laird of Garden, a misunderstanding arose between her and the curators of her son. Their complaint against her was that though by the latter will of her former husband, Sir John Colquhoun, which appointed his son the sole executor of his personal estate, and reserved to Dame Margaret Baillie the third of the " inside plenishing," or household furniture, yet after his father's decease she did intromit with the other two parts of the moveable goods, sums of money, debts, etc., which belonged to him, at the least that she ought to have intromitted with them and applied them for the behoof of Sir James, and that she had wrongfully refused to do so unless compelled. A summons was therefore raised, on 20th February 1679, at the instance of Sir James against his mother, charging her and her second husband, the Laird of Garden, to compear before the Lords of Session at Edinburgh, the        to hear and see the premises proven, and herself and her husband decerned to deliver to the pursuer the said moveable goods, etc.[1] This dispute appears, however, to have been amicably composed, as no further trace of it is to be found in the family papers.

In the year 1679, the Macdonalds threatened to march with fire and sword against the Western Highlands, actuated either simply by the love of plunder, or by a desire to retaliate some real or imagined wrong. To protect the country from their ravages, a number of men were despatched from the territory of Luss, at the expense of Sir James Colquhoun, to the head of Lochlong. This we learn from an account of the intromissions of John Colquhoun, younger of Camstradden, with the Laird of Luss's rents of the barony of Luss for the year 1679, containing the following entries :—

" Item, to allow to the compter his expenss in goeing with
    a number of men to the heid of Lochloug to protect
    the country, the tyme of the Macdonalds, at the Laird's    lib.    s.    d.
    speciall command,    .    .    .    .    .    .    040 : 00 : 0
Item, payed to John Colquhowne, officer at the Laird's com-
    mande, for his owne and tuo men's charges at the heid
    of Lochlong, ten dayes tyme keeping the country,    .    010 : 00 : 0"[2]
The Macdonalds were a powerful clan. They had extensive possessions

on the mainland of Scotland. But their principal strength lay in the isles, where it was difficult to attack them; and it was in Islay, the most southerly of these isles, that they chiefly resided. At the close of the fifteenth century, when the last of the Lords of the Isles died without heirs, his estate fell into the possession of different parties, but a great proportion descended to the principal branches of the family, the Macdonalds of Slate and Lords Macdonald, or, as they were called in Gaelic, " Maconnell." The Macdonalds had frequent feuds with rival clans.

This is the first instance in which their name and forays appear in connexion with the Colquhouns. But this threatened encroachment on peace, property, and life, so frequent in those turbulent times, passed away without any serious consequences.

Sir James Colquhoun was educated, it would appear, at the University of Glasgow, but whether he completed his course at that University before his death is uncertain. While in Glasgow he was boarded in the house of a Mrs. Montgomery, and had for his tutor Mr. John Herriot. In an account of the intromissions of John Colquhoun, younger of Camstradden, with the Laird of Luss's rents of the barony of Luss for the year 1679, are the following entries with respect to this Laird :—

> " Item, pay'd be the compter to Mistris Montgomrj in Glasgow, for the boording of the late Laird of Luss, from the 5th of November 1679 to the 5th of May 1680, 0240$^{lib}$ 00$^s$ 00$^d$. Item to Mr. John Herriot, pedagogue to the Laird of Luss, 0065$^{lib}$ 16$^s$ 0$^{d}$."[1]

Sir James died at Glasgow, in April 1680. The date of his death we learn from the retour of his uncle as heir to him. Immediately on his death a special messenger was despatched to Ireland to communicate the mournful tidings to his uncle, James Colquhoun of Balvie, who had gone to that country in the month of October 1679. The remains of Sir James, it is probable, were conveyed from Glasgow to Rossdhu, and interred in the chapel there, which has long been used as a mausoleum by the family. The magistrates of Dumbarton, with thirty-one persons mounted, attended the funeral. In an account for "painting the Laird of Luss's funeral," as it is headed, the following among other items are included :—For painting 34

---

[1] Original Account at Rossdhu.

small escutcheons at 16? a piece ; for six mort heads at 16? a piece ; for mending and gilding a helmet, £4 ; for mending the Lochend arms, £1, 10?, etc. In the account of John Colquhoun of Camstradden are the following particulars respecting the death and funeral of Sir James :—

| | lib. | s. | d. |
|---|---|---|---|
| Item, givine to John Colquhowne for goeing to Ireland to Balvey efter Luss' death, . . . . . . . . | 009 | : 00 | : 0 |
| Item, given to the boyes that went to Glasgow for wynes and necessaris to Luss' buriall, . . . . . . | 005 | : 16 | : 0 |
| Item, given to William Johnstowne when he went for fresh meat to Glasgow for the buriall, . . . . . | 002 | : 18 | : 0 |
| Item, to John Glen, wright, when he was setting up the towre staire, | 003 | : 00 | : 0 |
| Item, to Duncan M'Owne to buy chickens to the buriall, . . | 004 | : 04 | : 0 |
| Item, to the men that went to Glasgow to bring home the furnitor of the Laird's chamber, . . . . . . | 004 | : 00 | : 0 |
| Item, to buy cocks, pales for wyne, aell, and brandj, calke and glew, | 002 | : 18 | : 0 |
| Item, to the boy that went from Rosdoe to Ineraray to my Lord Arguyll, and to Cowall to the Captaine of Dunnoone with funerall lettres, . . . . . . . . | 002 | : 10 | : 0 |
| Item, for a chappine of secke to the footmen the day the corps wes lifted at Glasgow, . . . . . . | 000 | : 16 | : 0[1] |

As Sir James Colquhoun was only four years in possession of the Luss estates, namely, from April 1676 to April 1680, and as he died while he was a minor and unmarried, there is little to record of his personal history. The intended new entail of the estates on female heirs not having been effectual, Sir James Colquhoun was succeeded in his title of Baronet and in the Barony of Luss by his uncle, James Colquhoun, then of Balvie.

[1] Original Account at Rossdhu.

## XVI. 2.—Sir JAMES COLQUHOUN, Nineteenth of Colquhoun and Twenty-first of Luss, Fourth Baronet,—1680-1688.

### Penuel Cunningham, his wife.

Sir James Colquhoun, the second son of Sir John Colquhoun and Lady Lilias Graham, succeeded his nephew in the title of Baronet, and also in the barony of Luss, in the month of April 1680. He was previously designated of Balvie.

Less is known respecting him than about his brother Sir John. A protection was granted to him by General Monck in 1655 for going to England and again returning to Scotland. The protection is in the following terms :—

" Permitt the bearer heerof, Mr. James Colquhoun, with his servant, horses, and necessaries, to passe with his travayling armes to London or other pairts of England, and to repasse into Scotland without molestation, hee doing nothing prejudiciall to his Highnesse. Given vnder my hand and seale att Dalkeith the 22th day of September 1655.

" GEORGE MONCK.
" To all officers and soldiours and others whome these may concerne."[1]

On 28th July 1674, James Colquhoun of Balvie, along with Humphrey Colquhoun, fiar thereof, James Marquis of Montrose, and others, was made a burgess of Dumbarton.[2]

On 19th April 1679 he was infefted in the lands of Balvie and others.

James Colquhoun of Balvie married, about the year 1670, Penuel, one of the four daughters and co-heiresses of William Cunningham of Ballichen, in Ireland, son of Sir James Cunningham of Glengarnock, in the county of Ayr, by Lady Catherine Cunningham his wife, daughter of James Earl of Glencairn.[3]

Penuel Cunningham, Lady Balvie, died previous to the month of October in the year 1679. After her death, Sir James went in that month to

---

[1] Original Letter of Protection at Rossdhu.

[2] Dumbarton Records, vol. i.

[3] The Cunninghams of Glengarnock were an ancient branch of the Glencairn family, having acquired the barony of Glengarnock by marriage in the thirteenth century. Glengarnock Castle was built on a precipitous ridge overhanging the Garnock Water. The castle is now in ruins.

Ireland to visit her friends, with whom he remained for some time. These facts are ascertained from an account of the intromissions of John Colqu houn, younger of Camstradden, with the Laird of Luss's rents of the barony of Luss, etc., for the year 1679, in which the following entries occur with respect to the funeral of Lady Balvie :—

" Item, given to Mr. Wmphray Colquhowne for the vse of his decest mother, the Lady Balvey, in her lyftyme, to be exspended on her funerall, with 30 lib. for his owne vse, since his father went to Ireland in October last, to the 9th September 1680, conforme to ane particular accompt,

lib. 0208 : 18 : 8

" Item, allowed to Dugald and Patrick M'Causlaines in Kilbryde for four wedders to the Ladie Balveye's buriall, . . . . . . . 008 : 00 : 0"[1]

An order by Sir James Colquhoun of Luss and others in September 1681 to the soldiers quartered on the lands of Kilmahew has been preserved, and is as follows :—

THESE are to will and requyr all officeris and sojouris who are presentlie quartered upon Achindinnanine belonging to Killmahew, imediatlie efter sight heirof to remove off the saidis landis belonging to Killmahew, as they will answer at Dumbartan, the nynt day of September 1681.

S. J. COLQUHOUNE of Luss.<br>J. ARDINGAPLE.<br>BALWY.[2]

In the following month of October, James Duke of York, having made a progress through the west of Scotland, visited Dumbarton, and on the 4th of that month he was made a burgess and guild-brother of the burgh along with many gentlemen of his suite. Within a week of the visit of the Duke of York, the Provost, Bailies, and Councillors, to testify their loyalty, and their gratification at the honour done them by this royal visit, swore the test oath. The part which Sir James Colquhoun of Balvie acted on this occasion does not appear. But his name has no place among the signatures—twenty-four in number—of the Commissioners for the county of Dumbarton who took the test oath on the 12th July 1683.[3]

[1] Original Account at Rossdhu.       [2] Original at Dumbarton.       [3] Supply Records.

Sir James Colquhoun of Balvie for some time after the death of his nephew, Sir James Colquhoun of Luss, declined to enter himself as his heir. He and his sons Humphrey and James Colquhouns, with his advice and consent as tutor and administrator to them, and Alexander Colquhoun of Tullychewen, the said deceased Sir John's brother-german, and John and James Colquhouns his sons, with advice and consent of their father, renounced their right to enter themselves heirs to the said deceased Sir John and James Colquhouns of Luss, in consequence of which they were charged by Matthew Colquhoun in Erskine to enter themselves heirs to them that, as their heirs, he might pursue them for the payment of certain debts. The renunciation is dated at Bonhill 17th and at Balvie 18th January 1682.[1]

It was afterwards arranged that Sir James Colquhoun should enter himself heir both to his brother Sir John and his nephew Sir James.

In the year 1682, James Colquhoun of Balvie purchased from Alexander Colquhoun of Tullychewen, the ward, non-entry, and maritage of the lands of Bannachra, which had been disponed to him by Sir John Colquhoun of Luss, to whom they had been gifted by the Commissioners of Frances Duchess of Lennox, 3d April 1675; and he obtained a disposition thereof from the said Alexander, dated 6th April 1682.[2]

On the 17th of February 1685, a commission was granted for serving Sir James Colquhoun of Balvie heir of the late Sir James Colquhoun of Luss, his brother's son, and also heir of his brother, the late Sir John Colquhoun, in all the lands and hereditary offices held by them. On the 18th March of the same year Sir James was served heir-male of his nephew Sir James Colquhoun of Luss in all his lands as particularly specified in the retour, in which it is stated that Sir James, the nephew, died in the month of April 1680.[3] On the 21st of May following he was infefted in the lands and baronies of Luss and Colquhoun on a precept from Chancery.[4]

Sir James Colquhoun was in possession of the Luss estates for eight years—from 1680 to 1688. During that period his name appears only in a few instances in connection with the public transactions of his time. Being

[1] Original Renunciation at Rossdhu.      [3] Original Retour at Rossdhu.
[2] Original Disposition, ibid.      [4] Original Instrument of Sasine, ibid.

one of the barons of the kingdom, he was appointed by the Government to perform in that part of the country where he resided certain services for giving effect to the measures which they adopted. When the Parliament, on the 10th of July 1678, offered to his Majesty the sum of eighteen hundred thousand pounds Scots, to be uplifted from the shires and burghs of the kingdom in the space of five years, according to the valuations at that time, for the defence of the kingdom, " in a time when these dangerous field conventicles, declared by law rendezvouses of rebellion, do still grow in their numbers and insolencies," against all which intestine commotions, as well as foreign invasions, the present forces were insufficient, James Colquhoun of Balvie was one of the Commissioners appointed to raise from the shire of Dumbarton its proportion.[1] In the commission given to Colonel James Douglas, 27th March 1685, in the southern and western shires, for trying Renwick's followers, and such as harboured them in what Lauderdale used to call that "woeful west," and empowering him to call to his assistance all magistrates, heritors, officers, and soldiers of the standing forces and the militia, Sir James Colquhoun of Luss, in the shire of Dumbarton, was included in a long list of landed proprietors and others who were commanded to concur with him in giving effect to that commission.[2] Sir James Colquhoun was also appointed one of the Commissioners for ordering and uplifting from the shire of Dumbarton its proportion of the amount of eight months' cess offered to his Majesty by the Parliament, 13th May 1685. The object for which this money was to be raised was the suppression of the "rebellious insurrections and designs of fanatical traitors, from whom they could expect no less than confusion in religion, oppression in their estates, and cruelty against their persons and families, . . . considering that not only these enemies continue their inveterate hatred against King and people, but that their frequent disappointments have heightened their malice to despair, and that the present forces may be too few to undergo all the fatigue which his Majesty's service for the protection of the country doth require."[3]

---

[1] Acts of the Parliaments of Scotland, vol. viii. p. 225.

[2] Wodrow's History, vol. iv. p. 207.

[3] Acts of the Parliaments of Scotland, vol. viii. p. 466.

Sir James Colquhoun of Luss and Humphrey Colquhoun, his eldest son, instituted a process before the Lords of Council and Session against John Napier of Kilmahew for payment of £20,000 Scots. For this sum the deceased Sir John Colquhoun had become cautioner for Napier to several persons his creditors, and for the payment of it Sir James and Humphrey Colquhouns were charged and distressed, at least might be distressed. They therefore raised letters of inhibition, dated 3d September 1685, inhibiting and discharging John Napier from selling or letting any of his lands, heritages, etc., and any of his Majesty's lieges from buying or taking in wadset any of them.[1]

A precept of clare constat, dated 20th March 1687, was given by the Commissioners of Frances Duchess of Lennox for infefting Sir James Colquhoun of Luss in the lands of the Mains of Balvie-Logan, and in numerous other lands, and he was infefted therein on the 14th, 15th, 16th, 19th, and 24th of September that year.[2] On 24th and 25th October that year he was also, on a precept of clare constat, by the Commissioners of the said Duchess, infefted in the ten pound lands of Craigrostan.[3]

It has been stated before that a bond of tailzie and a nomination as to the succession to the estates of Luss were said to have been executed by Sir John Colquhoun of Luss, second Baronet, dated 1st March 1676. These deeds, if genuine and legal, would have excluded Sir James Colquhoun of Balvie from succeeding to the estates of Luss, as they would have secured the succession to the daughters of Sir John.

Endeavours were made to reduce these deeds. A summons of reduction and improbation of them was raised at the instance of Mr. William Hamilton, advocate, as creditor to Sir James Colquhoun, brother of the said Sir John, against Christian, Helen, Anna, and Magdalene Colquhoun, daughters of the said Sir John ; and certification was obtained against them on the 23d of January 1685. Another summons of reduction and improbation of the same deeds was raised at the instance of Sir James Colquhoun as heir-male and of tailzie to his deceased brother Sir John of

---

[1] Original Letters of Inhibition at Rossdhu.
[2] Original Precept and Instrument of Sasine, ibid.
[3] Original Instrument of Sasine at Rossdhu.

Luss, second Baronet, and to his nephew, Sir James of Luss, third Baronet, in the lands of Luss, against his nieces above named, upon which he obtained certification against them on 6th February 1686.

After this Sir James obtained from his niece, Christian Colquhoun, on 11th August 1688, a ratification of the foresaid decreets, whereby she bound herself and her heirs never to impugn them; declared the alleged bond of tailzie and pretended nomination to be improven (disproved) by the certification, and to be of no strength or effect; renounced all action competent to her for reducing the said certifications; and consented that the said Sir James and Humphrey Colquhoun, elder and younger of Luss, should cancel and destroy the foresaid alleged bond of tailzie and pretended nomination wherever they could find them, as being papers already improven by the foresaid certifications. In the narrative of this renunciation it is stated that,—" Seeing I nor my freinds had no will to produce the forsaid allegeit bond of talzie and pretendit nominatione abone writtin, knowing that albeit the samen had bein treulie subscrived be my said deceast father, yet it would have been reduced *ex capite leeti*, as a bond of twentie thousand merks granted be my father to the Laird of Blackhall of the same date was reduced on that ground *in foro contentioso*, beside that the filling vp of the date might have bein improven be famous witnesses, who saw the samin blank for severall years after my father's deceas, and that the vnwarrantable filling vp thereof would then have appeared by ocular inspectione by the newnes of the ink, and that therfor I and my saidis freindis rather suffered certificatione to pass then to have the said bond of talzie and nomination reduced and improven be positive probatione."[1]

The Revolution of 1688 was now imminent. James the Seventh by his arbitrary measures had created widespread disaffection to his person and government in England as well as in Scotland. He was threatened with an invasion by William Prince of Orange, who in his manifesto

[1] Original Ratification at Rossdhu. A similar Ratification was afterwards granted to Sir Humphrey Colquhoun of Luss on 3d July 1693 by Helen Colquhoun, the youngest daughter of Sir John Colquhoun and Margaret Baillie, with consent of her husband Robert Dickson of Sornbeg. [Original Ratification, *ibid.*]

designated himself "Protector of the Protestant religion and defender of the liberties of England." In this emergency, among other measures adopted by the friends of James, the Privy Council on 3d October issued a proclamation, commanding all heritors and others to convene with their best horses and arms at the places mentioned, for the defence of the kingdom.

On the 31st of October 1688, with the same object a letter was written by the Earl of Perth, Chancellor of Scotland, to Sir James Colquhoun of Luss, requiring him, among other things, to send to Stirling thirty Highlanders sufficiently armed and clothed. The letter is as follows :—

SIR,—His Majestie's service requiring that some Highlanders should be brought down to Stirling, and there to continue in armes and receaue such commands as the Councill upon this emergent shall think fitt, you are therefore hereby required and authorised with all convenient diligence to send down to Stirling thretty Highlanders, sufficient men, well armed and cloathed, of your tennents. And you, or such as you appoint, are to receave ten men to be sent thither by the tutoris of the Laird of Keir, and other ten to be sent to that place by the Laird of Leny, all which you are to forme in a company. And you are to name, or be Captain thereof, and Leny is to name the Lievtennant, and the tutoris of Keir are to appoint some fit person to be Ensigne, which officeris is to be payed out of his Majestie's thesaury at the rate of the officeris of the militia. Att their arrival at Stirling the Council will take care to provide them with amunition and provisionis for their subsistance during the time they are to be imployed in his Majestie's service. And therefore you would take good care that they observe good discipline and do no skaithe in the country since his Majesty is to be at the charge of their mantinance. Your cheerfull complyance in this is expected by the Councill, in whose name and by whose warrant this is signified to you by, Sir, your assured friend,

Edinburgh, last October 1688.                    PERTH, Cancell. I.P.D.

For the Laird of Luss.   For his Majestie's service.

But the cause of King James the Seventh was hopeless, and he soon abdicated the throne of England and retired to France. Only a few days after this letter was written, on the 5th of November, William Prince of Orange landed at Torbay, and in a few weeks the Earl of Perth was a prisoner in the Castle of Stirling, where he attempted to concentrate a force to support the Government of King James.

Sir James Colquhoun died about the end of the year 1688. His death must have taken place between the 11th of August 1688, when in a ratification of that date by Christian Colquhoun, in his favour, she designates him "Sir James Colquhoun now elder of Luss, my uncle,"[1] and the 1st of December 1688, when "Sir Humphrey Colquhoun of Luss, Knight and Baronet," granted a bond to Archibald Stirling of Garden for the payment of £889, 12s. Scots.[2] As the precise date of his death is uncertain, it may be doubtful whether the preceding letter from the Earl of Perth was addressed to him or to his son and successor Humphrey.

Of the marriage of Sir James Colquhoun, the fourth Baronet, and his wife Penuel Cunningham there were two sons and a daughter :—

1. Humphrey, who became fifth Baronet.

2. James, who is mentioned as the second son of Sir James Colquhoun in the renunciation dated in 1682. There is no later trace of James among the family papers.

3. Elizabeth, who married Alexander Falconer of Kipps, advocate, second son of Sir James Falconer of Phesdo, one of the Senators of the College of Justice, under the title of Lord Phesdo, and had issue. Lord Phesdo was a nephew of Alexander, the first Lord Falconer of Halkerston.

[1] Original Ratification at Rossdhu.      [2] Original Bond at Rossdhu.

The following is a facsimile of the signature of Sir James Colquhoun of Balvie, afterwards of Luss, appended to a renunciation by him, dated 17th and 18th January 1682, narrated at p. 296, *supra*.

## XVIII.—Sir HUMPHREY COLQUHOUN,

### TWENTIETH OF COLQUHOUN AND TWENTY-SECOND OF LUSS, FIFTH BARONET,—1688-1718.

#### MARGARET HOUSTOUN, his wife.

SIR HUMPHREY COLQUHOUN succeeded his father, Sir James, in the year 1688. He was educated at the University of Glasgow. In the catalogue of the students of the fourth class, he is enrolled, on 2d February 1676, as "Humphridus Colquhoune filius Balvie."[1] His father, Sir James, was then proprietor of the estate of Balvie.

Eight years after his enrolment as a student, Humphrey Colquhoun married Margaret, eldest daughter of Sir Patrick Houstoun of that Ilk, Baronet, in the county of Renfrew.

The marriage-contract between Humphrey Colquhoun and Margaret Houstoun is dated at Edinburgh and Houstoun the 1st and 4th of April 1684. By this contract Sir James Colquhoun of Luss disponed to his son Humphrey, and the heirs-male of his marriage with Margaret Houstoun, whom failing, to the heirs-male of Humphrey in any other marriage, whom failing, to return to Sir James Colquhoun's own heirs-male, the lands and baronies of Luss and Colquhoun, the lands of Dunnerbuck and Auchintorlie, reserving to himself the liferent of the lands of Colquhoun, Dunnerbuck, and Auchintorlie, and burdening Humphrey with the payment of debts to the extent of 160,000 merks. Sir James afterwards, by a contract between him and his son Humphrey in 1686, renounced his liferent of the reserved lands in consideration of his getting the debts owing to him in the kingdom of Ireland, that he might uplift and employ them for provision of his other children, James and Elizabeth.[2]

Towards the close of the reign of Charles the Second, when Commissioners of the Privy Council, invested with justiciary powers, were appointed to hold courts in various parts of the country for the suppression of nonconformity,

---

[1] Munimenta Universitatis Glasguensis, tom. iii. p. 131.

[2] Original Contract at Rossdhu. This contract narrates the contract of marriage between Humphrey and Margaret Houstoun.

Humphrey Colquhoun, then younger of Luss, was one of the Commissioners appointed for the shire of Dumbarton. He was present in that capacity at a court held at Dumbarton on 19th February 1685. Among others who were summoned to answer to the charge of nonconformity, were his paternal aunt, Lilias Colquhoun, and her husband, John Napier of Kilmahew, who, not having compeared, which was interpreted as amounting to a confession, were heavily fined, as we have seen before.[1]

Humphrey Colquhoun and Margaret Houstoun, his spouse, obtained from King James the Seventh a charter, dated 5th August 1685, of the lands and baronies of Luss and Colquhoun, and others. That charter proceeded upon the procuratory of resignation by Sir James Colquhoun, contained in the contract of marriage between Humphrey and Margaret Houstoun ; and the limitation to heirs in the charter was similar to that contained in the marriage-contract. Humphrey Colquhoun and his spouse were infefted in the lands and baronies on the 28th of the same month.[2]

Humphrey Colquhoun next appears as granting an heritable bond of provision, dated 20th August 1686, whereby, with consent of Sir James Colquhoun of Luss, his father, he bound himself to make payment to his cousins, Magdalene, Christian, and Helen Colquhoun, daughters of his uncle Sir John, the second Baronet, of 30,000 merks Scots, equally and proportionally among them, that is, 10,000 merks to each at the expiry of a year and a day after their respective marriages. The bond, however, contained this condition, that should any of them die unmarried, or within a year and a day after their marriage, without lawful children, the deceased's part should fall to Humphrey. He also became bound to infeft them in an annualrent of 1800 merks Scots, equally among them, being 600 merks to each, to be uplifted yearly from his lands and baronies of Luss and Colquhoun. It was also agreed—and this was the cause why the bond of provision was granted—that Sir James and Humphrey Colquhoun should be fully discharged by the nieces of Sir James, on their attaining their majority, of all that they could ask of him in any manner of way since they had accepted the foresaid bond of provi-

[1] Wodrow's History, vol. iv. p. 188.
[2] Original Charter and Instrument of Sasine at Rossdhu.

SIR HUMPHREY COLQUHOUN, FIFTH BARONET, 1688-1718.

sion. In terms of this agreement, Magdalene Colquhoun, on 20th August 1686, being then past the age of twenty-one years complete, exonered Sir James and Humphrey Colquhoun of all former bonds of provision granted by her deceased father to her, and of all provisions contained in her father and mother's contract of marriage, and in any other contract passed between them.[1] Christian Colquhoun, sister of Magdalene Colquhoun, granted to Humphrey Colquhoun, younger of Luss, a similar discharge, dated 11th August 1688.[2] A few years after, Humphrey having paid to Robert Dickson of Sornbeg, the husband of Helen Colquhoun, the proportion due to her by the said bond of provision, and the annual rent thereof for several terms, she granted him a discharge, dated at Edinburgh, 31st January 1695.[3]

Humphrey Colquhoun received from the commissioners of Frances Duchess of Lennox, as superior, a charter, dated 29th March 1687, of the lands of Mains of Balvie-Logan, and others,[4] and on the 24th and 25th October in the same year, the said commissioners also infefted Humphrey Colquhoun in the ten-pound lands of old extent of Craigrostan, and in four acres of land, commonly called the meadow of Auchinhowie, in the regality of Lennox and shire of Stirling.[5] These reinvestitures proceeded on the resignation of Sir James Colquhoun, the previous proprietor.

Some of the subsequent property transactions of Humphrey Colquhoun may here be noted.

He sold the lands of Balvie to Captain Robert Sanderson of Castle Sanderson, in the county of Cavan in Ireland, who, by a bond, dated 13th January 1688, became bound to pay to Humphrey's creditors, therein specified, the sum of £3066, 13s. 4d. Scots, as part of the price of the lands of Balvie.[6]

Towards the close of the year 1688, on the death of his father, Humphrey Colquhoun succeeded to the title of Baronet, and to the full possession of the family estates of Luss and Colquhoun, of which he had previously obtained the fee.

Sir Humphrey's time and attention were not exclusively devoted to his

<hr>

[1] Original Discharge at Rossdhu.
[2] Original Discharge, ibid.
[3] Original Discharge, ibid.
[4] Original Charter at Rossdhu.
[5] Original Instrument of Sasine, ibid.
[6] Original Bond, ibid.

own private affairs. He was a warm adherent of the revolution government, and he took an active part in the public transactions of his time. Being one of the leading barons in the west of Scotland, he was called upon by the Government to employ himself in its service by maintaining the public tranquillity and defending the kingdom. He was Lieutenant-Colonel of the militia regiment of the shires of Argyll, Dumbarton, and Bute, the Earl of Argyll being Colonel. In that capacity he appeared when, on the 30th of March 1689, the Estates of Parliament, taking into their consideration that the Protestant religion and the public peace of the kingdom were in imminent danger, the Papists being in arms in great numbers in the kingdom of Ireland, and that there was just ground to apprehend, in case they prevailed, that, in conjunction with other enemies to the religion and peace of the kingdom, they might attempt to invade the kingdom, issued a proclamation for calling together the militia on this side of the Tay, and the fencible men in some shires, for resisting any foreign invasion and suppressing any intestine commotion that might arise.[1]

Sir Humphrey was appointed one of the Commissioners for uplifting from the shire of Dumbarton its proportion of the sum of two hundred and eighty-eight thousand pounds Scots ordained by the Parliament, 27th April 1689, to be raised from the shires and the burghs of this kingdom, according to the proportions imposed upon each shire and burgh by the Act of Convention of Estates in the year 1667.[2] He was again appointed one of the Commissioners for bringing in the shire of Dumbarton's proportion of the sum of two millions nineteen thousand seven hundred and thirty-three pounds six shillings eight pennies Scots, extending in whole to twenty-eight months' cess, to be raised out of the land rent of the kingdom of Scotland from the several shires and burghs. This sum the Parliament, on the 7th of June 1690, offered to their Majesties, King William and Queen Mary. The shire of Dumbarton's proportion was seven hundred and sixty-four pounds ten shillings Scots monthly.[3] When again, on the 25th of September 1696, the Parliament offered to King William the supply of eighteen

[1] Acts of the Parliaments of Scotland, vol. ix. p. 26.

[2] Ibid. vol. ix. p. 71.

[3] Acts of the Parliaments of Scotland, vol. ix. p. 140.

months' cess upon the land rent, amounting to twelve hundred fourscore sixteen thousand pounds Scots, the Laird of Luss was one of the Commissioners appointed to raise the proportion of supply payable by the shire of Dumbarton, which was the same as before mentioned.[1]

At Rossdhu, 11th January 1692, Sir Humphrey Colquhoun let in feufarm and disponed by contract, without reversion, to John MacEanvuy in Easter Aldochlay, the lands of Craigintuy, lying upon the side of Lochlomond, in the barony and parish of Luss, and shire of Dumbarton.[2]

The lands of Portincaple and Forlingbrek were feued by Sir Humphrey Colquhoun in the same year to John Glen, from whose grand-daughter they returned to Luss. By a disposition, dated at Edinburgh 11th February 1693, Sir Humphrey Colquhoun purchased from Archibald Macaulay of Ardincaple, for 3250 merks, without reversion, the three merk and half merk lands of Letrault-mor and the fourth part of the lands of Stroue, in the parish of Row, and shire of Dumbarton.[3] After being infefted in these lands, on the 18th of March following, Archibald Macaulay, by his procurator, immediately resigned them in favour of Sir Humphrey Colquhoun.[4]

Sir Humphrey granted a charter of the lands of Easter and Wester Bannachras to James Donaldson of Moorhauch, who was infefted therein on 2d April 1694.[5]

On 13th November 1695, Sir Humphrey Colquhoun, with consent of Lady Luss, as liferenter, sold for £9808 Scots, to John Colquhoun of Garshake, the lands of Chapleton and Chaplecroft, Middleton and Meikle and Little Overtouns of Colquhoun, as parts of the lands and barony of Colquhoun, in the parish of Kilpatrick and shire of Dumbarton.[6]

By a contract, dated 2d February 1697, Sir Humphrey also sold under reversion to John Macfarlane, in Luss, for 2000 merks, the lands of Glemolachan, Inverbeg, and the said John Macfarlane's dwelling-house in the clachan of Luss.[7]

[1] Acts of the Parliaments of Scotland, vol. x. p. 29.

[2] Original Contract at Rossdhu.

[3] Original Disposition, ibid.

[4] Original Instrument of Sasine and Resignation at Rossdhu.

[5] Original Instrument of Sasine, ibid.

[6] Original Contract, ibid.

[7] Original Contract, ibid.

By a contract, dated at Auchindenan, 21st December 1697, Sir Humphrey Colquhoun sold to John Colquhoun of Middleton of Colquhoun, the fourth part of the lands of Milnetoun of Colquhoun, and Carcastoun, in the barony of Colquhoun, parish of Kilpatrick and shire of Dumbarton, with the teinds of all these lands, reserving the fishings of Lochlomond, and coble fishings in the water of Clyde.[1]

On the 17th of July 1695, Sir Humphrey obtained, by Act of Parliament, for himself and his heirs, the liberty and privilege of holding four annual free fairs and a weekly market at the town of Luss, which was most commodiously situated for holding the same. One of these free fairs was to be held upon the 24th of May, to be called          fair, another upon the 11th of August, to be called          fair, a third upon the 14th of October, to be called          fair, and a fourth upon the 7th of November, each of the said fairs to continue three days; and the weekly market was to be held upon Tuesday. To Sir Humphrey and his heirs were granted the tolls, customs, and duties, which, by the laws and daily practice of the realm, were known to belong thereto, to be collected by them or such as they should employ.[2]

Part of Auchintorlie, sometimes called Silver Banks, and the contiguous lands of Dunnerbuck, were of old incorporated with the estate of Erskine, on the opposite side of the river Clyde. They were subsequently added to the barony of Colquhoun, and were feued by Sir Humphrey Colquhoun of Luss in 1695 to John Colquhoun, whose daughter Elizabeth, wife of Captain James Colquhoun, sold both, in 1709, to Mungo Buchanan, Writer to the Signet.

Sir Humphrey, by his heritable bond, dated 15th February 1698, bound himself to pay to Robert Colquhoun, only lawful son of Robert Colquhoun of Ballernick, 2300 merks Scots, as the remainder of the price of the lands of Meikle Ballernick and Bannachra.[3] This bond, as we shall afterwards see, was subsequently redeemed by the Luss family.

John Colquhoun of Camstradden having been under the necessity of

[1] Original Contract at Rossdhu.
[2] Extract Act of Parliament, ibid.
[3] Contained in a Disposition, dated 5th

December 1726. Original Instrument of Sasine at Rossdhu.

selling his lands in consequence of the debts with which they were burdened, Sir Humphrey Colquhoun, in the year 1698, purchased from him the lands of Camstradden, Aldochlay, Hill of Camstradden, and the Slate Crag, excepting Auchingaviu, one of the farms, on which the said John Colquhoun was in the meantime to live. Sir Humphrey, by his backbond of the same date to Camstradden, became bound that, upon his receiving payment of £5640 Scots, and the annual rent thereof, he would denude himself of the lands disponed to him, except the Slate Crag in the said lands, with a servitude for gates and roads.[1]

Sir Humphrey Colquhoun of Luss represented the shire of Dumbarton in the Parliament which was opened at Edinburgh on 6th May 1703, in the reign of Queen Anne. William Cochrane of Kilmaronock was the other representative of that shire.[2]

In the Parliament, 13th September 1703, Sir Humphrey, with many of the lords, barons, and burgesses, adhered to the protestation of the Marquis of Lothian against the Act for allowing the importation of all sorts of wines and other foreign liquors. The protestation states that "this Act, allowing the importation of French wines and brandy, ought not to pass, as being dishonourable to her Majesty, inconsistent with the grand alliance wherein she is engaged, and prejudicial to the honour, safety, interest, and trade of this kingdom."[3]

Sir Humphrey appears in his place in Parliament as representing the shire of Dumbarton in the second and third sessions of the first Parliament of Queen Anne, in the years 1704 and 1705.[4] He was one of the Commissioners of Supply, appointed by an Act of Parliament in 1704, for uplifting from the shire of Dumbarton its proportion of the supply of £132,000 Scots, extending to six months' cess, to be raised out of the landrent of the kingdom.[5]

[1] Both these writs have been lost, but they are narrated in the Disposition granted by Sir Humphrey Colquhoun and his son-in-law, James Grant of Pluscardine, to John Colquhoun, 1713, mentioned in a subsequent paragraph.

[2] Acts of the Parliaments of Scotland, vol. xi. pp. 30, 43, 44.

[3] Ibid. vol. xi. p. 102.

[4] Ibid. vol. xi. pp. 114, 207.

[5] Ibid. vol. xi. pp. 138, 143.

RESIGNATION and REGRANT of the COLQUHOUN BARONETCY of Nova Scotia in the year 1704.

IN the Memoir of Sir John Colquhoun, the grandfather of Sir Humphrey, it has been shown that, in the year 1625, he was created a Baronet of Nova Scotia by King Charles the First, with a limitation of the dignity to his heirs-male whomsoever.  Sir Humphrey, the fifth baronet in succession from Sir John, the original patentee, having no sons but an only daughter, Anne, resolved, after her marriage with James Grant of Pluscardine, second son of Ludovick Grant of that Ilk, to settle the barony of Luss, and his other estates, in a line of heirs that would prevent the two families of Colquhoun of Luss and Grant of Grant from becoming merged into one house.  It was within the power of Sir Humphrey to make such a settlement of his territorial barony.  He resolved also to settle his title of honour and dignity of Baronet on the same series of heirs as those to whom he had destined his barony of Luss.  To accomplish this arrangement, however, Sir Humphrey required the consent of the Crown, as the title stood limited to heirs-male.

It was a peculiarity in the law of Scotland, that titles of honour of all grades in that kingdom, including that of a Duke, which was the highest, could be surrendered by the holder of the title for the time, with the consent of the Crown, for a new patent with an altered limitation of heirs.  A new limitation might be more extended than the original one, or it might be narrower and more restricted, according to the circumstances of the family at the time of the surrender.  The most common cases of surrenders of patents of peerages were those which were first limited to males.  The holder of a title limited to males, having no sons but daughters only, and being desirous to provide his dignity in the direct line of his family, surrendered his patent for a regrant of the dignity in favour of female heirs.

In the family of Lord Gray of Gray, the title of Lord Gray was on two separate occasions resigned by the holders of the dignity for the time, and regranted by the Crown to their sons-in-law, and the descendants of their marriages with the daughters of the respective Lords Gray.  These regrants became the regulating patents of the title ; and the dignity of Gray is now held by the present Lady Gray in virtue of them, without reference to the original patent of creation of the title.    In other noble families similar instances of resignations and regrants of dignities occurred, changing the original limitation of heirs from male to female.

Following these examples, Sir Humphrey Colquhoun, having settled his barony of Luss on his only daughter and heiress and her husband, and the heirs of their marriage, was desirous that his title of Baronet should also be provided in the same way, that the title and estates might continue to descend together in the same series of heirs.

Sir Humphrey, by a procuratory of resignation made by him on the 20th March 1704, resigned into the hands of Queen Anne, as the fountain of all honour and dignity, his title of Baronet, with the whole precedencies and others belonging thereto, as contained in the original patent thereof. Her Majesty was graciously pleased to accept of that resignation and demission ; and her Majesty also, by a regrant and new patent, dated at her Palace of St. James, the 29th of April 1704, for the causes therein expressed, granted, renewed, and conferred upon Sir Humphrey, and his sons to be born ; whom failing, upon James Grant of Pluscardine, and the heirs-male of his marriage with Anne Colquhoun, only daughter of Sir Humphrey; whom failing, upon the other heirs therein specified, with a remainder over to the other heirs of taillie whomsoever of the said Sir Humphrey, the hereditary rank, dignity, and designation of Knight-Baronet, with all precedencies belonging thereto, in the same manner as if Sir Humphrey had existed at the date of the original patent of 1625, and had been specially named and designated therein.[1]

The surrender of the title by Sir Humphrey, the acceptance of the same by the Crown, and the regrant and investiture to him and the new series of heirs, completely altered the limitation to heirs-male in the original patent of 1625 ; and, upon the death of Sir Humphrey, in 1718, his title descended to his son-in-law, James Grant, who was designated Sir James Colquhoun of Luss, Baronet.  The title of Baronet has ever since been held by the successive inheritors of the barony and estates of Luss.

It has been deemed necessary to explain fully the entire surrender of the original patent of baronetcy as granted in 1625, because the family of

---

[1] Registrum Magni Sigilli, Lib. lxxxiv. No. 130.

Colquhoun of Tillyquhoun, who claimed to be the heirs-male collateral of Sir Humphrey Colquhoun of Luss, also claimed the title of Baronet under the original patent, as if it had never been surrendered.  At first the Colquhouns of Tillyquhoun appear to have acquiesced in the surrender of the baronetcy, as after the death of Sir Humphrey Colquhoun, in the year 1718, no claim was made by the then Laird of Tillyquhoun.  But they afterwards assumed the title without any right.  The last male representative of the Colquhouns of Tillyquhoun died without issue in the year 1838, when the male line of Tillyquhoun became extinct.  It was only by a great abuse of such titles that the family of Tillyquhoun assumed the baronetcy.  They had no right whatever to it as a surrendered dignity, and their assumption of it could have been quashed by a court of law in a suit at the instance of the Crown, or of any person interested.  In the case of the dormant baronetcy of Sibbald of Rankeillour, a common sailor, named William Sibbald, assumed the title of Sir William Sibbald, Baronet of Rankeillour, without having any right to the title.  In that case, the Crown very properly came forward with an action of reduction, and quashed his claim after a full discussion in the Court of Session in the year 1846.

Previous to the surrender of his baronetcy, Sir Humphrey Colquhoun, as already stated, provided in the contract of marriage, dated 10th January 1702, between his only daughter, Anne, and James Grant of Pluscardine, that they and the children of their marriage should succeed to the barony of Luss and to the title of Baronet.  The resignation and regrant of the title, as now explained, secured the succession in regard to it.  To carry out more fully his intentions of succession to the territorial barony, Sir Humphrey made a bond of tailzie of his landed estates, which bears date the 4th and 27th December 1706.  This bond of tailzie, which was recorded in the Register of Tailzies on the 26th February 1707, contains, besides the whole lands and barony of Luss, with the castle, tower, fortalice, and manorplace of Rossdhu, the fishings of salmon and other fish in Lochlomond, and the fishings of salmon and other fish in the river Leven, *usque ad mare salsum*, that is, to where the tide from the sea comes up the Leven at Dalquhurn; also the fishings of salmon and other fish in the Gareloch.  The Office of Coroner within the sheriffdom of Dumbarton is included in the entail. The superiorities of the following lands are also in the entail, namely, Ardenconnel, Blairvadock, the three Tillyquhouns, the lands of Balloch, the mill of Balloch, the ferry of Balloch, with the hail privileges belonging thereto, and Cameron, extending to a five-pound land, of old extent. In east Kilpatrick the superiorities of the following lands are included in the entail, namely, Balvie-Logan, Gartconell, Ferguston-Logan, Bannachtown, Ledcameroch, and Kilmardinny. By the deed of entail, which was granted by Sir Humphrey Colquhoun, with the consent of Dame Margaret Houstoun, his spouse, he bound himself and his heirs to resign his lands and barony of Luss, and his numerous other lands, into the hands of his immediate lawful superior of the same in favour of Anne Colquhoun, his daughter, and James Grant, her husband, for his liferent. After them, the destination was to Humphrey, the eldest son of their marriage, and the heirs-male of the body of the said Humphrey, and the heirs-male of their bodies; whom failing, to the other heirs-male of the marriage between the said James Grant and Anne Colquhoun ; whom failing, to the heirs-female of the body of the said Humphrey, and to the heirs-male of the bodies of the said heirs-female, the eldest always to exclude the rest, and to succeed without division ; whom failing, to the eldest heir-female of the marriage between the said James Grant and Anne Colquhoun, and the descendants from the body of the eldest heir-female without division, the eldest heir-female and the descendants of her body to exclude all other heirs-portioners, and always to succeed without division ; whom failing, to the heirs-male of the foresaid Anne Colquhoun of any other marriage, and to the heirs of their bodies ; whom failing, to the heirs-female of the said Anne Colquhoun, in any other lawful marriage, and their descendants ; whom failing, to the heirs-male of the body of the said Sir Humphrey Colquhoun ; whom failing, to the heirs-female of his body ; whom failing, to his other heirs-male ; whom failing, to his heirs-female ; whom failing, to his heirs and assignees whomsoever ; reserving to him and to the said Margaret Houstoun, his spouse, their liferent of the lands, etc., therein mentioned.

This bond of tailzie contained the provision that it should not be in the power of the said James Grant and Anne Colquhoun, nor any of the heirs of tailzie above mentioned, to sell, alienate, and dispone the said lands, etc., or any part thereof, or to grant securities, redeemable or irredeemable, by infeftments or otherwise, nor to contract debts thereupon, except in so far as they had power in the manner therein mentioned, nor to violate or change in any way the order of succession above mentioned.

That the estate of Luss should never be absorbed in that of Grant, the bond of tailzie expressly provided that it should never be held by the Laird of Grant. Should the estate of Grant fall to the said James Grant or to Humphrey, his son, or to any other heir-male of the same marriage, then the next son of the same marriage should succeed to the estate of Luss; and, failing a son, the eldest heir-female of the same marriage, without division; whom failing, the heirs-male who should be lairds of Grant of that Ilk, descending from the said Anne Colquhoun, until a second son should exist, to whom the estate of Luss should belong; and such a son failing, the estate should descend to the eldest heir-female of the body of the said Anne Colquhoun, without division; whom failing, to the other heirs of entail of the said Sir Humphrey Colquhoun, in the order foresaid.

It was the wish of Sir Humphrey that the possessor of the estate of Luss should bear and perpetuate the name of Colquhoun. It was therefore provided by this bond of tailzie that the said James Grant, and his son Humphrey, and the other heirs-male and female specified, who should succeed to the said estate of Luss, etc., or the children of the said Anne Colquhoun of any other marriage, should, upon their succession, change their own surname, and assume and bear the surname, designation, and arms of Colquhoun of Luss, and that all their descendants should assume the surname of Colquhoun.[1]

Various transactions took place between Sir Humphrey and his cousin, Captain James Colquhoun of Silver Bank, who was the second son of Alexander Colquhoun, the first of Tillyquhoun.

Sir Humphrey granted a precept of clare constat, dated at Rossdhu, 30th September 1704, for infefting Captain James Colquhoun of Silver Bank and

---

[1] This Bond of Tailzie was recorded in the Register of Tailzies, at Edinburgh, 26th February 1707.

Elizabeth Colquhoun, his spouse, in the lands of Dunnerbuck, Auchintorly, and Conneltoun.  Yet the said James acknowledged that he had not paid to him the bygone feu-duty, but was accountable to him for it, in so far as it remained unpaid, either by the deceased John Colquhoun of Auchintorly, or, since his death, by James Williamson of Chapeltoun, or others, in name of his said spouse.[1]

Captain James Colquhoun of Auchintorly, in an obligation, dated at Rossdhu, 14th May 1706, bound himself to deliver up to Sir Humphrey a bond of £800 granted to him by Sir Humphrey.  In this obligation reference is made to a bond for £266, 13s. 4d., granted by John Colquhoun of Camstradden to the deceased John Colquhoun of Auchintorly, or Mathew Colquhoun, his father, and to Elizabeth Colquhoun, spouse of the said James Colquhoun, as representing either the said deceased John Colquhoun of Auchintorly, or Mathew Colquhoun, his father.[2]

Sir Humphrey Colquhoun of Luss took an active part against the Treaty of Union between Scotland and England.  This Treaty, however desirable, as what, if accomplished, would put an end to the ancient feuds that had existed between the two Kingdoms, and however beneficial it has been in its results—which, however, did not become so apparent till a considerable time after the Union—was very unpopular in Scotland.  A formidable conjunction of opposite and discordant parties in that kingdom arrayed themselves against it.  It was opposed by the Jacobites, as what would effectually fix the succession, to the exclusion of the family to which they adhered.  It was opposed by the Episcopalians, as what would render the settlement of the Presbyterian Church more secure, and destroy all hope of their recovering the government of the Church in Scotland.  It was opposed by the Presbyterians from an apprehension that it would be followed by a successful effort on the part of the Government to assimilate the government of the Church of Scotland to that of the Church of England.  To the last of these parties Sir Humphrey Colquhoun belonged.  He persistently opposed the Treaty at every stage of its progress through the Parliament, adhering for the most part to those who protested against the various articles, and voting against their approval.

[1] Original Declaration and Obligation at Rossdhu.    [2] Original Obligation, ibid.

On the 1st of September 1706, a draft of the Act for a Treaty of Union between the two Kingdoms was read before the Estates of Parliament. This being done, the Duke of Athole proposed that a clause should be added to the Act for a treaty with England to the effect that the Scottish Commissioners should not go out of the kingdom to enter into any treaty with those to be appointed for England until an Act recently passed by the English Parliament, by which the subjects of the Kingdom of Scotland were to be adjudged aliens born out of the allegiance of the Queen, as Queen of England, after the 25th December 1705, was rescinded by that Parliament. But the Parliament of Scotland, notwithstanding their disapproval of that Act, decided that this clause should not be added to the Act for a treaty with England, but should be put into a separate resolution. Sir Humphrey Colquhoun was of the same opinion with the Duke of Athole, and he adhered, along with many noblemen, barons, and burgesses, to the protest given in before the taking of the vote by that Duke. The protest was, " That for saving the honour and interest of her Majesty as Queen of this kingdom, and maintaining and preserving the undoubted rights and privileges of her subjects, no Act for a treaty with England ought to pass in this House unless a clause be added thereto prohibiting and discharging the Commissioners that may be nominated and appointed for carrying on the said treaty to depart the kingdom in order thereto, until the said clause be repealed and rescinded by the Parliament of England."[1]

On the 4th of November 1706, the first Article of Union, namely " That the two Kingdoms of Scotland and England shall, upon the first day of May next ensuing the date hereof, and for ever after, be united into one Kingdom by the name of Great Britain," was passed by the Parliament by a large majority. But Sir Humphrey Colquhoun of Luss, with a considerable number of noblemen, barons, and burgesses voted against it, and they adhered to a protest given in before the taking of the vote by the Duke of Athole[2] in the following terms :—" That an incorporating Union of the Crown and Kingdom of Scotland with the Crown and Kingdom of England,

[1] Acts of the Parliaments of Scotland, vol. xi. p. 236.

[2] John first Duke of Athole vigorously opposed the Union with England. He did not make such set speeches as the Duke of Hamilton and Lord Belhaven, but the oppo-

and that both nations should be represented by one and the same Parliament, as contained in the Articles of the Treaty of Union, is contrary to
the honour, interest, fundamental laws, and constitution of this Kingdom,
the birthright of the peers, the rights and privileges of the barons and
burghs, and is contrary to the claim of right, property, and liberty of the
subjects, and third Act of her Majesty's Parliament 1703, by which it is
declared High Treason in any of the subjects of this kingdom to quarrel or
endeavour by writing, malicious and advised speaking, or other open act or
deed, to alter or innovate the claim of right, or any article thereof."[1]

One of the principal causes of the unpopularity of the Union between
Scotland and England was an apprehension that the Presbyterian Church
established in Scotland at the Revolution would be overthrown after the
Union, and the Church of Scotland assimilated to that of England. This
objection was strongly urged by the Church Courts and by many of the
people in Scotland. It was argued that the bishops in a Parliament of
which they were members, might, if they chose, easily obtain a majority in
Parliament to vote for the establishment of Episcopacy in Scotland; that thus
the Presbyterian Church of Scotland, as established, would be overthrown;
that the most it could expect to obtain was a precarious and uncertain toler-
ation, and that for even this it would have to become the humble petitioner
of the bishops. With these views Sir Humphrey Colquhoun entirely sym-
pathized. He regarded the "Act for security of the true Protestant religion
and government of the Church of Scotland as by law established," engrossed
in the Articles of Union, though expressed in very clear and strong terms,
as inadequate to secure to the Church of Scotland her ecclesiastical government in the event of an incorporating Union between the two Kingdoms.
On 12th November 1706, the Act of Security was finally read and approved
by a large majority. Sir Humphrey adhered to the protestation given in
by Lord Belhaven, before the vote was taken, in the following terms :—
"That he did protest in his own name, and in name of all those who shall

sition of His Grace of Athole was very formidable. He was the brother-in-law of the
Duke of Hamilton, having married his eldest
sister, Lady Katherine Hamilton. Their fifth
son was Lord George Murray, who was so
celebrated for his services to Prince Charles
in the Rebellion of 1745.

[1] Acts of the Parliaments of Scotland,
vol. xi. pp. 313, 315.

adhere to him, that this Act is no valid security to the Church of Scotland as it is now established by law in case of an incorporating Union, and that the Church of Scotland can have no real and solid security by any manner of Union by which the claim of right is unhinged, our Parliament incorporated, and our distinct sovereignty and independency entirely abolished." Sir Humphrey also voted against the approval of the Act of Security. Forty noblemen, forty-one barons, and thirty-one burgesses gave their votes in favour of the Act, and eighteen noblemen, fifteen barons, and five burgesses voted against it.[1] It was during the keen and animated discussions in Parliament on the Union Treaty that Lord Belhaven made his famous anti-union speeches. After the Act of Union was passed, he erected a tablet at his residence of Beil, in East Lothian, lamenting the ruin of his country, in the following brief but expressive terms :—

"TRADITIONIS SCO: ANNO PRIMO, 1707."

On 14th November 1706, after the reading of the second Article of Union, a motion was made that the House should proceed to the consideration of that Article. A counter-motion was made that the House should proceed to the consideration of the fourth and other Articles in the Treaty which related to trade and taxes before any of the other Articles. Sir Humphrey voted for the latter motion, but the former was carried by a large majority. On the following day, when the motion to approve of the second Article of Union was carried, also by a large majority, Sir Humphrey Colquhoun, with a considerable number of the nobility, barons, and burgesses, voted against its being approved.[2]

Sir Humphrey also adhered to the protest given in by Lord Belhaven on 7th December 1706, that the voting for the first clause of the fifteenth Article of the Treaty of Union does not infer consent or agreement in any respect that Scotland shall be liable for the English debt in general, but that it may be lawful to object against any branch of the said debt not already determined, and he voted against the approving of that Article.[3]

[1] Acts of the Parliaments of Scotland, vol. xi. pp. 320, 322.

[2] Acts of the Parliaments of Scotland. vol. xi. pp. 322, 324, 327.

[3] Ibid. vol. xi. pp. 350, 353.

Sir Humphrey was one of those who voted in favour of an overture proposed on the 31st of December 1706, in the Parliament, to be added to the eighteenth Article of Union, in these terms :—"That all Scotchmen be exeemed from the English sacramental test, not only in Scotland but in all places of the United Kingdom, and dominions thereunto belonging, and that they be declared capable of offices throughout the whole, without being obliged to take the said test." It having been carried by a majority that this clause should not be added, he voted against the approval of the eighteenth Article of the Union.[1]

He also voted against the first paragraph of the twenty-second Article of Union, by which only sixteen of the Peers of Scotland were to sit, and vote in the House of Lords, and only forty-five members were to represent Scotland in the House of Commons of the Parliament of Great Britain. This paragraph was opposed by Sir Humphrey and other opponents of the Union, on various grounds. He regarded it as subversive of the rights of the Peers of Scotland, whose number then was 160, and each of whom was a hereditary member of the Sovereign's Great Council and Parliament, and as subversive of the rights of the shires and burghs of the Kingdom, who sent to the estates of the Parliament of Scotland 150 representatives. It did not give to Scotland, he maintained, an equal share in the representation of the British Parliament, either in the House of Lords, of which the English members then were 180, or in the House of Commons, of which the English members then were 513. He argued that the Scottish members could have no influence in the Houses of Parliament by reason of such a vast disproportion in their numbers.[2]

On 10th January 1707, Sir Humphrey voted in favour of an overture for adding to the twenty-second Article of the Treaty a clause to the effect that as long as that part of the 2d Act, anno 25 Charles II., appointing a sacramental test, should continue in force in England, all persons in public trust, civil or military, within the limits of Scotland, should swear and sign the following formula :—"I, A. B., do sincerely and solemnly declare, in the presence of God, that I own the Presbyterian

[1] Acts of the Parliaments of Scotland, vol. xi. pp. 378, 380.
[2] Ibid. vol. xi. pp. 386, 389.

government of the Church, as by law established in Scotland, to be a lawful government of the Church, and that I shall never, directly nor indirectly, endeavour the subversion thereof, nor any alteration in the worship, discipline, or government of the said Church, as by law established.    So help me God." The overture was, however, rejected.    Thirty-nine lords, thirty barons, and twenty-nine burgesses voted against it ; and twenty lords, twenty-five barons, and eighteen burgesses voted for its being added.[1]

Sir Humphrey also voted, 13th January 1707, for a proposed addition to the twenty-third Article of Union of a clause in these terms :—" That all the Peers of that part of Great Britain, now called Scotland, qualified according to law, shall, after the Union, have right to sit covered in the House of Peers of Great Britain, notwithstanding that the right to give vote therein belongs only to the said sixteen Peers who are to be summoned in the manner appointed in the preceding Article." Thirty of the nobility, thirty-three of the barons, and twenty-eight of the burgesses voted against it ; seventeen of the nobility, nineteen of the barons, and fourteen of the burgesses voted for its being added.[2]

The Act ratifying the Treaty of Union was passed on the 16th of January 1707.    Sir Humphrey Colquhoun voted against it.    Forty-two of the nobility, thirty-eight barons, and thirty burgesses voted for it ; and nineteen of the nobility, thirty of the barons, and twenty of the burgesses, voted against it.    The Act was thereafter touched with the Royal Sceptre by the Duke of Queensberry, her Majesty's High Commissioner, in the usual manner.[3]

The Duke of Queensberry, for his successful accomplishment of the Union betwixt Scotland and England, was much applauded in England, while he was execrated in Scotland, so unpopular was the measure in his own country.

Sir Humphrey adhered to a protest given in to the Parliament 21st January 1707, by James Duke of Hamilton,[4] against the electing, by this

[1] Acts of the Parliaments of Scotland, vol. xi. pp. 397, 398.
[2] Ibid. vol. xi. pp. 399-401.
[3] Ibid. vol. xi. pp. 404-406.
[4] The Duke of Hamilton, like his cadet of

Belhaven, also made very vigorous speeches against the Union.   One of his speeches, in which he forcibly referred to the restoration of Scotland by King Robert the Bruce, drew tears from many of his auditors.

present Parliament, of the sixteen Peers and forty-five barons and boroughs
who were to represent Scotland in the first Parliament of Great Britain, as
inconsistent with the whole tenour of the twenty-second Article of the
Treaty of Union, and contrary to the express words thereof, whereby it is
provided that after the time and place of the meeting of the said Parliament is appointed by her Majesty's proclamation, which time shall not be
less than fifty days after the proclamation, a writ shall be immediately
issued under the Great Seal of Great Britain, directed to the Privy Council
of Scotland, for summoning the sixteen Peers, and for electing forty-five
members, by whom Scotland is to be represented in the Parliament of
Great Britain ; and further, as utterly subversive of the right of election
competent to the barons and boroughs of this kingdom.   Sir Humphrey also
adhered to a protest given in to the Parliament on the same day by Mr.
William Cochrane, his fellow-representative for the shire of Dumbarton,—
that the electing of members to represent this part of the United Kingdom
in the Parliament of Great Britain out of this present Parliament by the
members of this House, is contrary to, and inconsistent with, the birth-right
and privileges of the barons and boroughs of Scotland; that it is contrary to
the principles of common law and divers Acts of Parliament, and directly
opposite and contradictory to the express words and meaning of two several
paragraphs of the twenty-second Article of the Treaty of Union betwixt
Scotland and England so lately ratified in this House.[1]

The following letters were written by Captain James Colquhoun of
Silver Bank to Sir Humphrey, in reference to business and other
matters :—

Roseburn, October 18th 1708.

DEAR SIR,—Yow may think it strange ye have not heard from me so long
considering the business ye intrusted me with, butt I'le presume to give yow a
full narrative of my expeditione in order to exculpate my self.   Primo, upon
the receipt of your letter, quhich was Sunday afternoon, I repaired to Edinburgh
from Roseburn on Tuesday, in order to goe for Carcady along with Mr. David
Campbell, who was the only man could assist me in the affair, being Grant's
agent and ours both.   I went accordingly on Wednesday morning from Leith,

---

[1] Acts of the Parliaments of Scotland, vol. xi. pp. 415, 417.

having stayed there Tuesday afternoon and all night there with contrary winds. I mett with Grant, who was very kind, and desyred me to wrytte to yow that he expected to have seen Sanders Gordon in the north. I was for four dayes almost drunk deed, for he just received his orders for marching to Newcastle in order to be shiped there for Ostend, and Straithnaver, who marched both last week, and will be there be this comes to yowr hand. Grant was so kind he gave me a bill upon Mr. Campbell, butt sadly grudged the price of the horse. My nixt difficulty was with Mr. Campbell anent the tyme of payment, quhich he could not grant for six moneths by reason it was advance, and the arrears not payed, and he going for London. I thought it more fitt to make it sure, and was forced to whidle and drink him in to a more ready payment, quhich I fear ye'll grudge the expences of. Ye allowed me on[e] guinea; butt I assure yow it cost me two, besydes a compliment of a pair of new bootes I had butt two houres on my leggs he challenged, and I readiley granted upon account of my business: they coast me a guinea. I also was oblidged to bribe his clerk for ready payment. The expences is dear, butt I hope ye wont grudge it, for I am willing to joyne with yow in the expence. As for your money, I must say, dear Sir, it was most seasonable; for quhen yow wrotte anent my cautionery for yow I was under diligence by Joseph Young, who ye know is assigney to Mr. Muir, the minister, to whom I am cautioner for Kenmure, and I presumed to putt six hundered merkis in his hand to save me from the tolbooth, and I hope ye'le think it secure enuff, for I could not gett it to borrow att the tyme. So I desyre to know how ye will order your security, for if I had my papers from Mr. Adam Willson Hilltoun, and I will end our business, and that of Joseph Young's is amongst the debts he is to clear imediatly of myne. Hilltoune hes wrotte to yow this post, and if ye think fitt he'll send yow ane ample disscharge of six hunder merkis in pairt of quhatt is betwixt yow and him, and I'le give him securcity for the money; butt this as yow think fitt. I shall wait your return, quhich I desyre may be *per* first. I hope ye'll pardon the freedom I have used with yow; but belive yowr money is secure, and the horse well sold. I had another stop in not wrytting, for on Munday last, att four in the morning, it pleased God my wife was safly brought to bed of a brave son at Roseburn, to our great surprise, for she designed to goe in to Edinburgh the Tuesday following, and had sent all things in for her inlying, butt had misreckoned herself two dayes; but (blessed be God) she is mending very well, and on Saturday last the child was christed here, quhair my Lord Dallhoussie, the godfather, Colonel Hamilltoun, Ensign Hammilltoun, your cussin, Captain Drumond, with some others, were all very merry, where we drank yowr health. The Lady Roseburn and severall other ladyes were present, and very blyth. I thought to have had yowr sister,

Mistris Falconer, butt she durst not venter a coach, being pritty bigg herself. My sister and the sick wife gives yow, yowr lady, and familly, Pluss[cardine] and his lady, their hearty respects, and so docth, dear Sir, your most affectionatt cussin and humble servant,

JA. COLQUHOUNE.

There is no newes here, but expecting dayly to hear from Lisle, quhich is not yett taken. Pray let me hear from yow with the first, and hast my brother home, who is mightily long'd for here. The Lady Roseburn, I hope, will lett fall our concern for William Colquhoun, for she was very merry here at our christening. Adieu. Be so kind as deliver the inclosed to my brother.

After wrytting of this I went to enquire for Hilltounc's letter, who I understood was gone to Dalkeith, and will not return untill Saturday : so expect his letter on his return.[1]

The son whose birth is announced in the above letter was probably George Colquhoun, who appears to have been the only son of Captain James Colquhoun. Another letter written by the Captain to Sir Humphrey is as follows :—

Edinburgh, November 1st, 1708.

SIR,—I am sorry to understand by yowrs the huffe ye are in for my dissposing of yowr money without yowr consent, and, in the nixt place, to belive I would wrytte yow a lye, thatt yowr money was in my hands. As for mentioning of Hilltoune, I proposed nothing without yowr consent. As to the scrouple of my boots, I had no business with Mr. Campbell as being agent to the Guards, butt what I payed him, as all our officers and grants did in allowing him a shilling sterling *per* pound, beside exchange, quhich I have not charged yow with. All I had from him was about ten or eleven pound of arrears, quhich I payed the same for. He declared publickly thatt my compliment of the boots would oblidge him to pay yowr bill, butt I hope the value of a guinea will not cast us out. As for yowr credit, I tender it as my own, and for quhatt strait ye have occasioned to yowrself by restricting to a liferent is your own fault, and in my aplying yowr money to save me from the tolbooth was a fault in me, butt putting me to such straits, quhen no man could registrat my bond, how occasion'd thatt I leave to yow. However, dear Sir, yowr money is secure ; only be so kind as use yowr interest with Mr. Adam Willson as send me that contract of few, or send me ane new one, and the rest of my papers, quhich ye will have for calling for att Milltoune, and I shall pay

<hr>

[1] Original Letter at Rossdhu.

the postage (quhich hinders Hilltoun and me from concluding our bargain), and ye shall have yowr money quhat way yow pleas.  Pray be so kind as know Mr. Willsone's last answer anent my papers, for I have another lay for him in caice he'l refuse them, quhich will trouble him and bold aunty also.  So pray, dear Sir, belive I'le be guillty of no ill thing to any, particularly to my best frind.  As for yowr grandchild's saddle, there is none of that sort ready here, butt my brother and I went this day and bespoke it.  So expect it with Tullich.  Pardon quhatt I have been guilty of, and belive me still, dear Sir,

Your most affectionatt cussin and humble servantt,

JA. COLQUHOUNE.

I have sent yow inclosed our last print of newes.[1]

Sir Humphrey sold, in 1710, to James Colquhoun of Barnhill the meadowland, consisting of four acres, called the "old milndam of Colquhoun."  The price was 1200 merks.[2]

On the 9th of November 1710, Sir Humphrey sold his lands of Stronrattan, Garelochhead, and Tombuye, in the shire of Dumbarton, to Dougall Macfarlane, younger of Tullichintaull.[3]

In the year 1713, Sir Humphrey and his son-in-law, James Grant of Pluscardine, redisponed to John Colquhoun of Camstradden—on his having paid to them the redemption-money—the lands of Camstradden, hill thereof, and Aldochlay, with the pertinents.  This disposition excepted the Slate Crag in the town of Camstradden, with a servitude of gates and roads for leading and boating the slates taken therefrom, in terms of a disposition and backbond in 1698, and of a disposition containing a procuratory of resignation of the Slate Crag, granted by the said John Colquhoun in 1710 to the said Sir James Grant of Pluscardine, his superior, in order to consolidate the property of the Slate Crag, with the superiority, as it was not thought that the deeds of a prior date above mentioned, or reservations in them, were a proper title for holding so valuable a subject as the Slate Crag.  By this disposition and resignation, in like manner as by the foresaid disposition in 1713, and the disposition and back-bond in 1698, while the estate of Camstradden, disponed to the family of Luss, was redeemable for a certain

---

[1] Original Letter at Rossdhu.
[2] Original Disposition, dated 27th January 1710, at Barnhill.
[3] Original Contract of Sale at Rossdhu.

sum, a reservation was made as to the Slate Crag in the town and lands of Camstradden, which was not to be redeemable, together with a servitude of gates and roads for leading and boating the slates, for which a separate sum was then paid, as the said back-bond likewise bears. This reservation was afterwards keenly litigated.[1]

In 1715, when the Jacobites raised the standard of the Pretender in opposition to the Hanoverian succession, Sir Humphrey Colquhoun strenuously defended the revolution settlement.

At that time the Macgregors caused great annoyance and alarm to Sir Humphrey's tenants, and to that part of the country where he resided. Inspired, it is said, by the Earl of Mar, with the hope of having the penal laws against them repealed, and their name restored, they mustered, and hastened, under the command of Gregor Macgregor of Glengyle, nephew to Rob Roy Macgregor, to join the Earl of Mar at Braemar. At the same time they committed depredations on many of the people in Dumbartonshire, whom they robbed of arms, horses, and whatever might be serviceable to them in this military enterprise. Having made themselves master of the boats on the water of Enrick, Lochlomond, they occupied Inchmurrin, a large island in that loch, and, rowing towards the head of the loch, took with them all the boats they could find. These boats they drew upon the land at Inversnaid, about eighteen miles up from the mouth of the loch, that their enemies might not be able to pursue them, and that they might make a descent whenever they chose upon any part of the surrounding country. They thus kept in terror the people, who did not know where they might make their descent. The whole shire of Dumbarton being thus exposed to danger, or to constant apprehension from the Macgregors, Sir Humphrey and others consulted what was to be done; and it was concluded that to retake from them the boats upon Lochlomond would be a great security against their hostile incursions and violence, and would relieve the minds of the people. This led to what was called the Lochlomond Expedition, the object of which was to take possession of these boats.

[1] From additional Petition and Answers for Major James Colquhoun of Luss to the    Petition of Robert Colquhoun of Camstradden, dated 10th February 1747, pp. 5-7.

With this intention a considerable body of armed men put off, on the morning of the 12th of October 1715, from the quay of Dumbarton in several pinnaces and boats, which were drawn by horses three miles up the river Leven. These armed men, on their arriving at Luss, were to be joined by Sir Humphrey Colquhoun, with a body of his friends and tenants. Their journey on their way to Luss is thus described in a contemporary account of this adventure, evidently written by one of the party :—" When they were got to the mouth of the loch, the Paisley men, and as many more as the boats could conveniently stow, went on board ; and at the same time the Dumbarton men, the men of Easter and Wester Kilpatrick, Roseneath, Row, and Cardross marched up on foot along the north-west side of the loch ; and after them, on horseback, the Honourable Master John Campbell of Mamore, uncle to his Grace the Duke of Argyll, attended by a fine train of gentlemen of the shire, viz., Archibald Macaulay of Ardencaple, Aulay Macaulay, his eldest son, George Naper of Kilmahew, Walter Graham of Kilmardeny, John Colquhoun of Craigton, John Stirling of Law, James Hamilton of Barnes, with many others, all very richly mounted and well armed."

The same writer thus describes the accession made to their numbers on their arriving at Luss, where they met with a cordial reception from Sir Humphrey Colquhoun, and where they remained all night, and the courage displayed by the whole of this body of volunteers, notwithstanding the reports they heard as to the formidable resistance which the Macgregors intended to make :—" Against evening they got to Luss, where they came ashore, and were met and joined by Sir Humphrey Colquhoun of Luss, Baronet, and chief of that name, and James Grant of Pluscarden, his son-in-law, and brother-german to Brigadier Grant, followed by forty or fifty stately fellows, in their short hose and belted plaids, armed each of them with a well fixed gun on his shoulder, a strong, handsome target, with a sharp-pointed steel of above an ell in length screwed into the navel of it, on his left arm, a sturdy claymore by his side, and a pistol or two, with a dirk and knife, in his belt. Here the whole company rested all night. In the meantime, many reports reached them, contrived, or at least magnified by the Jacobites, in order to discourage them from the attempt, such as that M'Donald of Glengarry, who was indeed lying with his men about

Strathfillan, sixteen miles from the head of the loch, had reinforced the Macgregors, so that they at least amounted to 1500 men, whereas there were not fully 400 on the expedition against them; that the loch being narrow at Inversnaid, where the rebels were lying, they might pepper the boats with their shot from the shore without any danger to themselves, being shaded by the rocks and woods; in a word, that this was a desperate project, and would be a throwing away of all their lives. But all could not dishearten these brave men. They knew that the Macgregors and the devil are to be dealt with after the same manner, and that if they be resisted they will flee. Wherefore, on the morrow morning, being Thursday the 13th, they went on in their expedition, and about noon came to Inversnaid, the place of extreme danger. In order to rouse those thieves out of their dens, Captain Clark loaded one of his great guns, and drove a ball through the roof of a house on the face of the mountain, whereupon an auld wife or two came crawling out and scrambled up the hill, but otherwise there was no appearance of any body of men on the mountains, only a few standing far out of reach on the craggy rocks looking at them."

The enterprise was completely successful. The companies alighted on the shore, and met with no enemy to oppose them. Without much difficulty, they found the boats of which they were in search drawn up a good way on the land. They hurled them down into the loch, and carried off with them such as were fit for use, whilst they cut in pieces such as were damaged.

"That same night," to quote from the said contemporary record, "they returned to Luss, and thence next day (without the loss or hurt of so much as one man) to Dumbarton, from whence they had set out altogether, bringing along with them the whole boats they found on their way on either side of the loch, and also in the several creeks of the islands and moored them all under the cannon of Dumbarton Castle; and thus, in a very short time, and with little expense, were the clan of the Macgregors cowed, and a way pointed out how the Government may in future easily keep them in awe."

"There are two or three things," adds the same writer, "may be remarked on this expedition :

"First, That, though the Macgregors deserved extremities, and our men were in a sufficient capacity to have destroyed and burned their whole goods and housing, yet they did not take from them the value of a shoe-latchet, save one fork, which might have been used as weapon.

"Secondly, The providence of God was very observable in that though, for three days before, it had blown a prodigious storm, yet in the morning, when our men were to go on board from Dumbarton, it calmed, and they got a fair wind in their poop, the whole way up the loch. When they had done their business, it kindly veered about, and brought them safely and speedily down the loch, immediately after which, on the Friday evening, it began to blow boisterously as before.

"Thirdly, The cheerfulness of the men who went on this expedition deserves to be noticed and applauded. They were not forced to it, as the clans are by their masters and chiefs, who hack and butcher such as refuse to go along with them : witness Duncan Macfarlane in Rowardennin. But they offered themselves voluntarily to do it. No wonder, for men begin now to be convinced that all is at stake."[1]

After this expedition, Sir Humphrey Colquhoun lived only between two and three years. He died in the year 1718, having been in possession of the Luss estates about twenty years, and was buried in the chapel at Rossdhu.

By his wife, Margaret Houstoun, he had only one child, a daughter, ANNE COLQUHOUN, HEIRESS OF LUSS.

[1] "The Lochlomond Expedition ; with some short Reflections on the Perth Manifesto. Glasgow, 1715." This tract was reprinted from a copy discovered among the Wodrow Manuscripts, by James Dennistoun of Dennistoun in 1834.

XVIII.—1. ANNE COLQUHOUN, HEIRESS OF LUSS, TWENTY-FIRST OF COLQUHOUN, AND TWENTY-THIRD OF LUSS,—1718-1724.

JAMES GRANT of Pluscardine, afterwards Sir JAMES COLQUHOUN, her husband, sixth Baronet, 1718-1719.

ON the death of Sir Humphrey Colquhoun of Luss, his daughter, Anne, succeeded him in the family estates. She was born on the 11th of August 1685, and she married James Grant of Pluscardine, second son of Ludovick Grant of that Ilk, on the 29th of January 1702. In terms of the regrant of the title, and of the entail of the Luss estates, made by her father, Sir Humphrey Colquhoun, her husband, James Grant, first designated of Pluscardine, succeeded his father-in-law, in 1718, in his title of Baronet, and in a liferent interest in the lands and barony of Luss, under the designation of Sir James Colquhoun of Luss. Sir James was born on the 28th July 1679.

His father, Ludovick Grant of that Ilk, possessed large estates in the shires of Inverness, Elgin, and Forres, and his wealth and abilities procured for him much influence in the country. Opposed to the measures adopted in the reigns of Charles the Second and James the Seventh, he early attached himself to the Revolution of 1688, and was much esteemed by King William, by whom he was appointed, in 1689, colonel of a regiment, and also principal Sheriff of Inverness, an office which had been held by many of his ancestors. In support of the Revolution Government, he raised, in 1690, a regiment of 600 of his own clan, and joined Colonel Livingston, with whom he encountered the Highlanders, who had risen on behalf of the abdicated monarch, at Cromdale, on the 1st of May that year, and reduced them to the necessity of laying down their arms.

The family of Grant of that Ilk is of great antiquity. It was powerful in the reign of Alexander the Second, King of Scotland, who succeeded to the crown in 1214, and died in 1249, when authentic records of their history are first to be met with. Many of this family have signalized themselves for the distinguished part they have acted in the civil, diplomatic,

ANNE COLQUHOUN HEIRESS OF LUSS

SIR JAMES (GRANT COLQUHOUN,
( HUSBAND OF THE HEIRESS OF LUSS.)
ÆTATIS 64. DIED 1747.

and military transactions of their country; and they often intermarried with noble and opulent families.  One of them, Radulphus de Grant, second son of Sir Laurence de Grant, was a steadfast adherent of Robert Bruce, in opposition to Baliol, and fell into the hands of Edward the First, King of England, by whom he was carried a prisoner to London about the year 1296.  Sir John de Grant, eldest son of Sir Laurence, supported the standard of Sir William Wallace for the maintenance of the independence of his country, and he also was made a prisoner, and carried to London, with his brother, by the English monarch, but they were liberated upon bail in 1297.[1]  John Grant of that Ilk joined the ranks of the Reformers in the sixteenth century, and he was a member of the Convention of Estates in 1560, by which the Papal jurisdiction was abolished, and the Protestant religion established in the Kingdom of Scotland.

Thus had James Grant of Pluscardine, the husband of the heiress of Luss, the honour to be descended from a distinguished ancestry.

He, however, held the estates of Luss only about one year.  His eldest brother, Alexander, who made choice of the military profession, and who rose to the rank of a brigadier-general, succeeded, on his father's death in 1717, to the estates of Grant.  The general was twice married; first, to Elizabeth Stewart, eldest daughter of James Lord Doun, son and apparent heir of Alexander sixth Earl of Moray; and secondly, to Anne, daughter of John Smith, Speaker of the House of Commons, and one of Queen Anne's maids of honour.  But he had no surviving children by either of these marriages.  General Grant died at Edinburgh, in 1719, and was buried in the Abbey Church.

The estates of Grant, accordingly, then devolved on Sir James Colquhoun, as the second born, but now the eldest surviving son of Ludovick Grant of Grant, and Sir James resumed his paternal surname of Grant, and dropped the surname and arms of Colquhoun of Luss; whilst Ludovick, the second son of his marriage with the heiress of Luss, became the representative and possessor of the estate of Luss, bearing the name and arms of Colquhoun of Luss, according to the deed of entail, his elder brother Humphrey being considered the heir-apparent of the Grant estate.

[1] Rymer's Fœdera.

2 T

Though Sir James Grant held the Colquhoun estates only for a very short period, and then became the representative of the family of Grant of that Ilk, yet, as the ancestor of the present house of Colquhoun of Luss, we may here glance at his subsequent history. Following the example of his father, he was a strenuous supporter of the principles on which the Revolution of 1688 was founded, and steadfast in his loyalty to the House of Hanover. For many years he was a Member of the British Parliament, and represented during the greater part of that time the county of Inverness, which the Lairds of Grant had, almost without interruption, represented since the Union. On the death of his spouse, Anna Colquhoun, in the year 1724, and especially on the death of his eldest son, Humphrey, in the year 1732, he, to a great extent, retired from public business, and lived in a private manner, though he continued to retain his seat as a Member of Parliament. His election for the county of Inverness generally involved him in much expense and harassment. Ultimately attempts were made to deprive him of his seat as representative of that county. These attempts were headed by Duncan Forbes of Culloden, afterwards Lord President of the Court of Session, and supported by various Highland chiefs, barons, and others. On one of these occasions so vehemently excited were his opponents that it was threatened that his election would be resisted by violence. For his protection, several hundreds of gentlemen with their servants entered the town of Inverness in his retinue, and took possession of the Town-house. By their promptitude the measures of his opponents were disconcerted, and his election became unanimous, nor did any disturbance of the public peace take place, great as was the crowd that had assembled, and intense as was the excitement both of his friends and of his opponents.

At the first general election that took place after the suppression of the rebellion in 1745, Lord President Forbes threw the weight of his influence, which, from his official position, and from the trust with which the Government had invested him during the rebellion, was great, into the scale for securing the return of the Laird of M'Leod as member for the county of Inverness, in opposition to Sir James Grant of Grant. In contesting the election this formidable opposition, it was evident, would largely increase

Sir James's expenses and the other difficulties which, in former contests, had pressed so heavily upon him, and therefore, with the advice of his friends, he withdrew from the field, and became a candidate for the burghs of Cullen, Banff, etc., for which he was elected. His son was chosen member for the county of Moray, in the room of Alexander Brodie of Brodie, who had been repeatedly returned a member for that county, chiefly by the influence of the family of Grant.

Sir James did not live long after his election. He had been much afflicted with gout in the stomach, and of this illness he died at London, on 16th January 1747.[1] He was succeeded in the estate of Grant by his second son, Ludovick, who possessed the estate of Luss from 1719 till 1732, when, his elder brother, Humphrey, having died unmarried, he took the place of heir-apparent of the estate of Grant, and his younger brother, James, succeeded to the estate and honours of Colquhoun of Luss.

The following character of Sir James Grant has been given by one who obviously knew him intimately :—" He was a gentleman of a very amiable character, justly esteemed and honoured by all ranks of men ; his natural temper was peculiarly mild, his behaviour grave, composed, and equal ; and his social conduct was full of benevolence and goodness. To his clan he was indulgent, almost to a fault ; to his tenants just and kind ; and did not very narrowly look into things himself, but committed the management of his fortune to his factors and favourites. To sum up his character, he was a most affectionate husband, a most dutiful and kind parent, sober, temperate, just, peaceable, an encourager of religion and learning, a lover of all virtue and good men ; he was very solicitous for the welfare and support of the families, both of Grant and Luss ; and when, upon the death of his eldest son, Humphrey, and the resignation of the second son, Ludovick, of the estate of Luss in favour of his third son, James, he was put into the possession of it, it gave Sir James the highest satisfaction. He was very happy in his children, and they in him."

By his wife, Anne Colquhoun, who died at Castle Grant on 25th June 1724, Sir James Grant had fourteen children, six sons and eight daughters.

---

[1] Scots Magazine, vol. ix. p. 50.

The sons were—

1. Humphrey, who was born on Wednesday, 2d December 1702,[1] and who died, unmarried, in 1732.

2. Ludovick, who was born on Monday, 13th January 1707, and who succeeded to the estates of Luss and afterwards to those of Grant.

3. Alexander, who was born on Saturday, 8th September 1709, and died 12th March 1712.

4. James, who was born on Monday, 22d February 1714, and was baptized on the 24th of that month.[2]    He succeeded to the Luss estates, and carried on the line of the family of Colquhoun of Luss.

5. Francis, who was born on Saturday, 10th August 1717, and who became a lieutenant-colonel of the Royal Scotch Highlanders, and afterwards a general in the army.    He married Miss Cox, by whom he had a large family.

6. Charles Cathcart, who was born 3d April 1723, and who became a captain in the Royal Navy.

The daughters were—

1. Janet, who was born 31st May 1704, and died on the 5th of October in the same year.

2. Jean, who was born on Friday, 28th September 1705.    She married, in 1722, William Duff, who was raised to the Peerage of Ireland by the Queen Regent Caroline, under the title of Baron Braco of Kilbryde, in the county of Cavan, on 28th July 1735, and who, on 26th April 1759, was advanced to the rank of Viscount Macduff and Earl of Fife.    She was his second wife, and had to him seven sons and seven daughters.    From the eldest son the present Earl of Fife is descended.

3. Margaret, who was born on Monday, 19th January 1708, and died on Wednesday, 7th September 1709.

---

[1] From a leaf pasted into an old Bible at Rossdhu.  The entry is holograph of Sir James Colquhoun, husband of Lady Helen Sutherland.  The dates of the births of the other children are taken from the same authority, supplemented from another family list.

[2] Luss Register of Baptisms.

4. Anne Drummond, who was born 2d May 1711, and who married, in 1727, Sir Henry Innes of Innes, ancestor of the present Duke of Roxburghe.

5. Elizabeth, who was born 22d January 1713, and died on 1st February thereafter.

6. Sophia, who was born 12th January 1716, and died unmarried.

7. Penuel, who was born on Thursday, 12th August 1719, and who married, in 1739, Captain Alexander Grant of Balindalloch.

8. Clementina, who was born at Castle Grant 12th April 1721, and who married Sir William Dunbar of Durn, in the county of Banff.

The following facsimile signature of Anne Colquhoun is from an order, dated at Rosdoe, 27th September 1715; and that of her husband, James Grant, from a letter to his son James, printed at p. 358.

# XIX.—1. Sir LUDOVICK COLQUHOUN,

TWENTY-SECOND OF COLQUHOUN, AND TWENTY-FOURTH OF LUSS,
SEVENTH BARONET OF NOVA SCOTIA, 1719-1732.

MARIAN DALRYMPLE (of North Berwick), his first wife.

LADY MARGARET OGILVIE (of Findlater), his second wife.

SIR LUDOVICK COLQUHOUN, as has been already stated, as second son of
Sir James by his wife Anne Colquhoun, heiress of Luss, succeeded to the
Luss estates in 1719, when his father succeeded to those of Grant. By the
deed of entail, executed on the 4th and 27th of December 1706 by Sir
Humphrey Colquhoun of Luss, Baronet, Ludovick's grandfather, formerly
described, it was provided that if the estate of Grant should fall to James
Grant, the son-in-law of Sir Humphrey, or to Humphrey Colquhoun, his
eldest son, or to any other heir of the marriage with Anne Colquhoun,
then, and in that case, the next son of the marriage should succeed to the
estates of Luss. But Sir James Grant's elder brother, Brigadier-General
Alexander Grant, last Laird of Grant, having died without leaving children,
Sir James was retoured heir to him in the estate of Grant by a special
service before the bailie of the regality of Grant on the 24th of October
1720, and was infefted therein on the 10th of November following. Ludovick Colquhoun, as being the second son of Sir James Grant and Anne
Colquhoun, was now nearest heir-male of tailzie and provision of his
mother in the lands and barony of Luss.[1]

At the time of his succession, Ludovick Colquhoun was only about
twelve years of age. He afterwards studied law, and made choice of the
profession of an advocate, into which he was admitted in the year 1728.
His mother having died in 1724, he was, on the 27th of March 1729,
retoured as nearest heir-male of tailzie and provision to her in the lands
and barony of Luss and others.

Under the designation of " Luddovick Colquhoun of Luss, Advocate,"
he obtained a charter, dated 14th and 18th December 1730, from the Com-

[1] Copy Retour at Rossdhu.

missioners of James Duke of Montrose, to himself and the heirs of his body, in terms of the deed of entail executed by his grandfather, Sir Humphrey Colquhoun, formerly quoted, of the four merk lands of the dominical lands of Balvie-Logan and others.   In these lands he was, on a precept of sasine contained in the said charter, infefted on the 24th, 25th, and 26th December 1730.[1]

On the 22d of June 1732, under the designation of Mr. Ludovick Colquhoun of Luss, Advocate, he resigned the lands and barony of Luss, etc., into the hands of the Commissioners of Frederick Prince of Great Britain and Wales, for new infeftments of the same to be made and granted to him and to the other heirs of tailzie in the deed of entail executed by his deceased grandfather, Sir Humphrey Colquhoun of Luss, Baronet, before quoted.[2]   On the same day he obtained from Frederick Prince of Great Britain, etc., with consent of the Barons of the Exchequer, his Commissioners, for himself and the heirs of his body, as contained in the foresaid bond of tailzie, a charter of the lands and barony of Luss ; and on the 2d of August following he was infefted therein.[3]

Ludovick retained possession of the lands and barony of Luss till 1732 when, Humphrey, his elder brother, having died unmarried, he succeeded him as heir-apparent to the Grant estates, upon which the estates and honours of Colquhoun of Luss, according to the deed of entail, devolved on his younger brother, James, who became Sir James Colquhoun of Luss.

Ludovick Grant now withdrew from the practice of the profession of law, and applied himself chiefly to the management of the estates of Grant, with which his father now wholly intrusted him.   He was a Member of Parliament for the county of Moray, from the year 1741 to the year 1761, when his son Sir James was elected in his stead.

During the Rebellion of 1745, Ludovick patriotically exerted himself in support of the House of Hanover.   He was ready zealously to support George the Second and his Government, in opposition to Prince Charles, with the whole of his clan, who were brave, loyal, united under their chief

[1] Original Charter and Instrument of Sasine at Rossdhu.
[2] Original Instrument of Resignation, *ibid.*
[3] Original Charter and Instrument of Sasine at Rossdhu.

and among themselves, and attached to the then established Government.
But he was prevented from rendering assistance to the extent which he
desired, mainly by Lord President Forbes, who, chagrined at his defeat
in opposing the election of Ludovick's father as Member of Parliament for
the county of Inverness, as before narrated, threw obstructions in Ludovick's path.

From his powerful interest in the north, the President was engaged by
the Government to exert his influence to gain over some of the Highland
chiefs to the side of the Government, and to divert others of them from
joining in the rebellion. In furtherance of this object he was instructed
to raise twenty companies of one hundred each. But in the distribution
of these companies he assigned four to his favourite, the Laird of M'Leod,
whilst, apparently to deprive the Grants of an opportunity of distinguishing
themselves in the suppression of the rebellion, he offered only one to
Ludovick Grant, who was acting in his father's absence in London as the
representative of the clan of the Grants. To put it out of the power of
Lord President Forbes to represent him as disaffected to the Government,
Ludovick Grant accepted the one company which the President offered to
him. But his clan, who, had they been called in a body to support the
Government on this occasion, would at once have mustered strongly,
showed great reluctance to form this company, regarding it as an insult to
the clan that they were called to raise only one company, as if they could
not be trusted. Other circumstances served to aggravate their irritation of
feeling. The territory which they occupied was surrounded almost on
every side with rebels—by the Duke of Gordon's people in Strathbogie,
Glenlivet, Strathaven, and Badenoch. Urquhart, which was peopled
with Grants, was completely surrounded by the Macdonalds, Camerons,
Frasers, Chisholms, and Mackenzies—all hostile clans to the Grants. The
situation of the clan of the Grants thus afforded a favourable opportunity
to the emissaries of the rebels to mingle with them, and to do mischief by
the circulation of all kinds of reports injurious to the Government; and
though these reports failed to seduce the Grants into the service of Prince
Charles, they somewhat cooled their loyalty and rendered them luke-
warm in the service of their country.

When Prince Charles landed in Lochaber, and set up his standard at Glenfinnin, General Sir John Cope, Commander of the Royal Forces, was ordered to march against him and give him battle. With this intention he hastened northward with about 1500 men until he came to Carvriarick, a pass between Badenoch and Lochaber. Ludovick Grant was desirous, without receiving any orders from those in power, to raise his men and join General Cope. His clan, however, was so backward, that, instead of assembling eight hundred or nine hundred, as he purposed to do, he had to rest contented with sending forty or fifty gentlemen with their friends to meet and welcome Sir John into the country. But they had ridden only a little way on this errand when unhappily new counsels prevailed. "This," it was said, " is acting officiously, going to war without any regular call, arming ourselves contrary to law, throwing away our lives, and exposing our fortunes to our rebel neighbours : in a word, it is doing what no other gentlemen or noblemen in Scotland have done at this time, not even the Duke of Argyll, though he is one of the Governors of Scotland, and has Prince Charles and his adherents in his neighbourhood, and whom, no doubt, he has it in his power to crush, if he choose to volunteer himself in the service of the Government." This reasoning had little effect upon Ludovick Grant, but to the bulk of these gentlemen it was very plausible, and they stopped short in their journey. The consequence was that it was resolved that only one gentleman or two should be sent with compliments to General Cope, and to assure him that whenever they were properly called they would cheerfully take up arms in defence of the Government.

General Cope, either from the nature of the intelligence he received concerning the insurgents, or from the difficulty of providing for the supply of his troops in that country, where everything was scarce and costly, marched to Inverness. This movement on his part led the rebels to fall down upon the low country, and from Perth by Stirling they marched to Edinburgh, where they took possession of Holyroodhouse. In the meantime the Camerons, Macdonalds, and others, emboldened by the reported success of the insurgents, invaded Glenmoriston and Urquhart, the country of the family of Grant, and were maltreating the inhabitants in order to compel them to join in the rebellion.  For the protection of his people, Ludovick Grant resolved to despatch immediately a number of men, and, the alarm having been given for a general rendezvous, a great many assembled, all ready to stand in their defence against the enemies of the Government.  That he might act in concert with Lord President Forbes, Ludovick Grant communicated to him this resolution.  But the answer of the Lord President, who did not desire that the Grants should perform any conspicuous part, was that it would be rather premature for him to take the step he proposed, and he desired him to raise his company, which with great difficulty was done, and in a few days it was sent to Inverness.  Not receiving from the clans that were reputed to be well affected to his Majesty and his Government the reinforcements which he expected, General Cope determined on returning to the south, and he marched from Inverness to Aberdeen, and from thence passed by sea to East Lothian. This was followed by the battle of Prestonpans, in which the royal General sustained a defeat.

Lord Lewis Gordon, youngest brother of the Duke of Gordon, having joined the rebellion, was appointed by Prince Charles Lord Lieutenant of the counties of Aberdeen and Banff.  When, in this capacity, he was collecting about Keith, on Lord Findlater's estate, the contributions appointed by the insurgents to be raised in all the disaffected counties where they had any interest, much dissatisfaction was produced.  Heavy complaints were made to Lord Findlater, who at the time was at Castle Grant with his son Lord Deskford, Lord Braco, and others, who regarded that castle as a place of refuge from the insults that might have been offered to them by the rebels. In these circumstances Ludovick Grant marched his men from Strathspey to Mulben, a district which formed part of the estate of Grant, and which was in the neighbourhood of Lord Findlater's property.  He sent a detachment of his men to be a garrison to his Lordship's house at Cullen.  Whilst in this part of the country, with about 700 men, Ludovick Grant was informed that Lord Lewis Gordon's men, though scarcely amounting to 300, yet calculating on the protection of the river Spey, and on the favourable disposition of the inhabitants, had marched from Keith to Spey-side to prevent the Laird of M'Leod and his four companies from crossing the

river, should they attempt it. On receiving this intelligence, Ludovick
Grant despatched two gentlemen to inform M'Leod that, without coming
into collision with the rebels, he could command for him the passage of the
river Spey at Boat of Bridge, in the country of Mulben, and to conduct him
on the road. But before these messengers reached him, M'Leod was far
advanced on the road from Elgin to Fochabers. On his arrival, however,
at Fochabers, he did not meet with the slightest opposition in crossing the
river, Lord Lewis Gordon's men, on understanding that Ludovick Grant
with his followers were in the neighbourhood, having retreated during the
night ; for had they waited to oppose M'Leod's party on their coming up,
they would have been exposed to two fires, M'Leod's men in the front and
Ludovick Grant's in the rear.

On the night on which the Laird of M'Leod was at Fochabers, Ludovick
Grant was with his men at Keith. On the following day, attended by only
two or three gentlemen, he rode from Keith to Cullen, a distance of about
eight miles, to wait on M'Leod, and he entertained him and his friends at
the seat of the Earl of Findlater, Ludovick's father-in-law. About this time
Ludovick, through Lord Deskford and Sir Archibald Grant, offered to Lord
President Forbes that he would gladly lead his men for the relief of the
city of Aberdeen, which was laid under heavy contributions, and for the
relief of the whole surrounding country, which was greatly oppressed, provided the Government would supply them with proper arms ; and, in the
hope that his proposal would be favourably regarded, he proceeded with
his men as far as Strathbogie. But the Lord President answered that he
had no authority to arm the clan of the Grants, and that therefore he
hoped that Mr Grant would not interfere with the King's troops. Offended
at this repulse, Ludovick Grant informed the Laird of M'Leod that it was
his intention to return home, and this intention he speedily carried into
effect.

Scarcely had he arrived at Castle Grant, when he received intelligence
that the M'Leods were routed by the forces of Prince Charles, at Inverury,
on the 27th of December 1745. Shortly after, the insurgents, having obtained a victory over the royal troops at Falkirk, set out for their homes,
loaded with the spoils obtained at that battle, marching northward in two

columns, one by Aberdeen and the coast road, and the other by the Highland road, through Badenoch, Strathspey, and Inverness. Whilst they marched through Strathspey, accompanied by Prince Charles, who stopped a night at Saverlardner, Ludovick Grant, who was then at Castle Grant, distant from them about six miles, put his men under arms, placed outposts, and made such other preparations as were necessary for defence; but the rebel army passed through the country without inflicting any damage whatever on any individual.

They were not, however, long in their quarters at Inverness, when it is said they threatened with military execution such as would not rise and join the Prince, and they demanded hostages of the country. At this time Ludovick Grant, with his friends, retired from Castle Grant, and went to wait upon the Duke of Cumberland, to whom he proffered his services. The Duke, though—in consequence of certain misrepresentations  he did not at first receive Ludovick Grant so warmly as he might otherwise have done, yet assured him that his men would be thankfully welcomed, and would be supplied with proper arms and entered upon pay. Ludovick was strenuous in his efforts to collect together as many of his clan as possible, but he could bring together only about 200 men, who, having joined the Duke's army, were immediately placed upon the advanced guards at Inverury and Old Rain.

Four of the most respected gentlemen of Strathspey, of the name of Grant,—Rothiemurchus, Tullochgorum, Dellachaple, and Whitecraw,—their chief being from home, thought it expedient, from the threats of the rebels that they would put to the sword whoever did not join their standard, or were constrained to agree, to observe a strict neutrality while the war continued. A deed to that effect was drawn up and signed by them, and they remained with the rebels as hostages, in security for the fulfilment of the treaty. When this deed of neutrality was devised and executed, Ludovick Grant was either with the Duke of Cumberland at Aberdeen, or with a part of the army, and such of his own men as he had prevailed with to attend him, who lay about Old Rain, Strathbogie, etc. During his absence Lord Nairn, with a battalion of Athole Highlanders, took possession of Castle Grant.

The agreement of neutrality interposed a powerful barrier against Ludovick's further success in levying men for the Duke of Cumberland's army.
He returned repeatedly to the country for that purpose, but recruits were
not forthcoming.  In several instances his efforts were attended with
considerable personal danger, both to himself and his friends, particularly
at Castle Forbes, and Balveny, where he narrowly made his escape from a
detachment of the rebel army who were watching his motions.

Upon the defeat of Prince Charles's army at Culloden by the Royalist
troops, on the 7th of April 1746, Ludovick's hostages became the prisoners
of the King's forces.  The Grants captured Lord Balmerino, and he was
delivered up to the Duke of Cumberland.  The subsequent fate of the
brave Balmerino is well known.  As the rebels might rally again, Ludovick
Grant continued to employ every means to muster his clan for the Duke's
assistance.  He was now more successful, for when they understood the
situation of their friends, the hostages,[1] 700 or 800 were assembled about
the 20th of April, and marched to Inverness.  This body of men was first
sent up to Strathearn, among the Macintoshes, and then despatched to
Urquhart and Glenmoriston.  Nearly 100 who had taken part in the
rebellion were, though with difficulty, prevailed upon to surrender themselves, in the hope that they would obtain protection, and be allowed
to return to their own homes.  Such also was the expectation of Ludovick
Grant, who had no desire that they should be ill-used.  But, unfortunately,
from some misunderstanding, they were treated, not as persons who had
surrendered, but as prisoners of war.  They were sent on board the King's
ships, where for some weeks they greatly suffered, and, soon after, they were
carried to Tilbury Fort, where they were kept under close confinement.
Had they been brought to a legal trial, they might have obtained some
justice in the end, but though attempts were made to do this, it was never

[1] The four gentlemen of the name of
Grant, who had entered into a deed of
neutrality with the rebels, and became hostages in their hands for the fulfilment of the
treaty, were found at Inverness with them,
when the King's army arrived there, after
the battle of Culloden.  As the step which
these gentlemen had taken was illegal, they
were ordered up to Edinburgh, at which they
arrived on the 29th of May 1746, and they
remained prisoners at large there till November following, when they were set at
liberty.—[Scots Magazine, vol. viii. pp. 237,
545.]

done. The most of them were transported to America, many of them died in prison, and a few ultimately returned from America to their native country.

Ludovick Grant, on the death of his father, Sir James Grant of Grant, in 1747, succeeded to the estates of Grant, and became Sir Ludovick Grant of Grant. After having possessed the estates of Grant nearly twenty-four years, he died at Castle Grant, 18th March 1773, and was interred in the family burying-place at Duthil. He was an affectionate husband and father, a steady friend, benevolent and warm-hearted, of great hospitality, and an excellent chief of a clan, respected for his talents and beloved for his virtues, both public and private.

After his death, the following tribute to his memory, commemorating these and his other virtues, appeared in the Scots Magazine :—

Like shadowy forms that flee the solar ray,
On Time's swift pinions, Mankind soon decay,
Unmark'd the place where erst they flaunting play'd
Along the plain, or darken'd in the glade.
But while the mean thus share a vulgar fate,
Must dull oblivion shroud in night the great ?
Must those bright souls, who living glorious shone,
Fall unlamented, and to fame unknown ?
Involv'd in darkness, circumscrib'd their lot,
Must all their virtues sleep in dust forgot ?
They must not : fragrant as the gales that blow
From vernal flowers, beyond the tomb they glow ;
Impartial Time its plausive voice shall raise,
And deck their virtues with unenvy'd praise.
Thee too, lov'd Chieftain, shall await that meed,
These grateful honours that embalm the dead :
Grav'd on the heart, thy virtues long shall live,
Thro' years and ages undecay'd survive.
For thine each winning, each endearing art,
That or attracted or engag'd the heart,
Charm'd sense of pain, could anxious thought beguile,
Bid festive mirth and pleasure round thee smile ;
Bid rising comfort glad the pensive brow ;
And joy illume the languid face of woe.
How didst thou shine, view'd in that milder light,
Where no false glare deceives the dazzl'd sight,
But where, unveil'd, the native soul appears,
And every feature bright or gloomy wears !
There thou wert all that cheers or softens life ;
The fondest husband of the loveliest wife ;
The tend'rest parent, past a parent's name,
Whose breast e'er kindled with that sacred flame ;
The kindest master, and the friend most true,
By time unmov'd, chang'd by no partial view ;

The frankest landlord, gave the gen'rous bowl,
The best companion, breath'd a social soul.
    Nor here alone beam'd thy diffusive mind,
But, raying wide, embrac'd the human kind ;
For others bliss that joying learn'd to glow,
For others sorrows bade the tear to flow.
    Cheer'd from thy table, from thy lib'ral door,
Rejoicing hie'd the stranger and the poor :
Oft were they heard along the road prefer,
With grateful hearts, for thee the ardent prayer,
That on thine house Heaven's blessings might descend,
And guardian angels still thy race attend.
    Let others boast assume the borrow'd name,
Here rest, nor feel the energetic flame ;
But thine was Virtue's sacred pow'r confest,
The active flame that kindles in the breast ;
Above th' applause paid by the giddy crowd,
Content in secret to be truly good.
    Benign, in death, the heav'nly form was seen ;
Light the fix'd eye-ball, and serene the mien ;
Faith, Love, and Hope, that in her train attend,
There beam'd expressive, and their smiles did blend :
Bless'd harbingers of that eternal day,
That now is thine, secur'd beyond decay.
Strathspey.                                   J. G.[1]

Sir Ludovick Grant of Grant was twice married. First to Marion,
daughter of Sir Hew Dalrymple of North Berwick, Lord President of
the Court of Session, by whom he had one daughter, Anna, who died
unmarried, at the age of nineteen ; and secondly, to Lady Margaret
Ogilvie, daughter of James fifth Earl of Findlater and Seafield, by Lady
Elizabeth Hay, his wife, daughter of Thomas Earl of Kinnoul. By
this lady, who died in January 1757, he had issue one son, James,
born in May 1738, who succeeded him in the title and estates of Grant,
and eleven daughters, of whom six survived their father. Sir James
Grant of Grant was the grandfather of the present Earl of Seafield. The
six daughters who survived their father were—1. Marian ; 2. Anna-Hope,
who married, 3d April 1781, Robert-Darly Waddilove, D.D., Dean of
Ripon ;[2] 3. Pennel, who married Henry Mackenzie, of the Exchequer in
Scotland, author of the Man of Feeling and other popular works, and had
issue ; 4. Mary ; 5. Helen, who married, 9th September 1773, Sir Alexander Penrose-Cumming Gordon of Albyn and Gordonstoun, Baronet, of
the 13th Regiment of Foot ;[3] 6. Elizabeth.

[1] Scots Magazine, vol. xxxv. p. 154.      [2] Ibid. vol. xliii. p. 222.      [3] Ibid. vol. xxxv. p. 500.

344

## XIX.—2. Sir JAMES COLQUHOUN, Twenty-third of Colquhoun and Twenty-fifth of Luss, Eighth Baronet of Nova Scotia, created Baronet of Great Britain, 1732-1786.

### Lady Helen Sutherland, his wife, 1740-1791.

James Colquhoun, the fourth born, but the second surviving son of Anne Colquhoun, the heiress of Luss, by her husband, Sir James Colquhoun, afterwards, Grant of Grant, succeeded his brother, Sir Ludovick Colquhoun, in the Luss estates in 1732, on Ludovick's having then become heir-apparent to the estates of Grant, by the death of his eldest brother, unmarried. James Colquhoun now assumed the surname and arms of Colquhoun of Luss.

In a letter from Colonel John Campbell of Mammore, who, in 1761, became fourth Duke of Argyll, to Andrew Fletcher, Lord Milton, written at the end of the year 1733, there is a somewhat obscure allusion to James Colquhoun, then Laird of Luss. From it we also learn that his father, Sir James Grant of Grant, was regarded at the Court of England as a man of great merit, and that had he taken advantage of the very favourable opinion formed respecting him, he might have obtained promotion in the service of the State. " My dear Milton," says the Colonel, " the Peer arriv'd last night in town. I attempted to talk to him of the affairs below, but he had not a stomach for them, so I was snub'd ; but yet we eat up a barrell of oysters and drank a cuple of bottles of claret, and parted good friends. I have had Mr. Colquhoun's confession of faith in the bosom of on[e] of Lovat's letters, and I have return'd the favour full as strong in the same manner. I really think Grant a very considerable commoner, and if he did but know how to make the most of his interest he would be courted. The Peer is well disposed towards him, and seems prepaired to do what is right." This letter is dated at Somerset House, Thursday, December 6, 1733.[1]

James Colquhoun did not succeed to the lands and barony of Luss without opposition. His brother Ludovick, notwithstanding he had now become apparent heir to the estates of Grant, was unwilling to give up to

[1] Original Letter in Salton Charter-chest.

SIR JAMES COLQUHOUN, FIRST BRITISH BARONET
(HUSBAND OF LADY HELEN SUTHERLAND)
DIED 1786.

LADY   HELEN   SUTHERLAND
(WIFE OF SIR JAMES COLQUHOUN OF LUSS
DIED 7TH JANUARY 1791, AETAT 73

his younger brother the lands and barony of Luss during his father's lifetime. He refused to do so even after his father had, in the year 1735,
settled the estates of Grant in fee upon him, reserving to himself only a
liferent interest therein. The occasion of this settlement on the part of
his father was the marriage of Ludovick with a daughter of the Earl of
Findlater, when it was necessary to make some arrangement in the marriage
contract in favour of the lady and the heirs and children of the marriage in
connexion with the estate of Grant, to which Ludovick, as apparent heir,
would succeed on his father's death. But by that settlement Ludovick,
according to the terms of the tailzie of the estate of Luss, relinquished the
name of Colquhoun, and with it a right and title to that estate, and assumed
the name of Ludovick Grant younger of that Ilk.

Ludovick's style of reasoning for retaining the barony of Luss was that
he had not as yet succeeded to the estate of Grant, and could not do so during
his father's lifetime, and that therefore he could not be obliged to part with
the estate of Luss in favour of either his brother James or of his own daughter
Anne; that in the event of his succeeding to the estate of Grant by surviving his father, he might have a second son of his own body, who should be
entitled to succeed to the estate of Luss in preference either to the said James
and Anne, or to any heir pretending right by the tailzie to the estate of
Luss; and that therefore he was entitled to hold that estate in his father's
lifetime in expectation of such second son of his own body to succeed to
it, when he might succeed to the estate of Grant.

But Ludovick was not permitted to possess the lands and barony of Luss
after having thus become apparent heir to the estates of Grant, and after
having got a disposition of them from his father, by virtue whereof he was
infefted in them.

His brother James and his own daughter, Anne Colquhoun, claimed each
a right to the succession, and the case was brought before the Lords of the
Court of Session.

At the instance of James a summons of declarator was pursued before
that Court for having it found and declared, by decreet of their Lordships,
that he was entitled to succeed to the estate of Luss, and that Ludovick Colquhoun should be decerned and ordained to denude himself of the said estate

2 x

and to dispone it in favour of the pursuer. Another summons of declarator was pursued at the instance of James Colquhoun against Ludovick and Anne his daughter, and only child in life, by Marion Dalrymple his deceased wife, for having it found that the said Anne had no right or title to the estate of Luss, and that the pursuer had the only undoubted right to it.

A third summons of declarator was pursued, at the instance of Anne Colquhoun, daughter of Ludovick, against Ludovick and his brother James, who had assumed the name of James Colquhoun of Luss, for having it found and declared that her father, having now become fiar of Grant, the right of succession to the estate of Luss devolved on the next heir of entail that would have succeeded if her father had been dead, and that the pursuer was the person on whom the said succession devolved according to the entail of the estate of Luss.

A fourth summons of declarator was pursued, at the instance of Ludovick, against his brother James and his own daughter Anne, for having it found and declared, on the grounds already stated, that by his becoming eldest son or apparent heir of the estate of Grant, he was under no obligation by the said entail to denude himself of the estate of Luss, since he could not possess the former during his father's lifetime, and that therefore he could not be obliged, during his father's lifetime, to part with the estate of Luss in favour either of his brother James or of his own daughter Anne.

All the parties having compeared by their advocates, and the rights, reasons, and allegations of each having been read, heard, and considered, the Lords of Session, by their decreet, dated 27th January 1737, found " that the right of the estate of Grant being then in the said Ludovick Grant, by virtue of disposition from his father, Sir James Grant of Grant, upon which he stands infeft by charter under the Great Seal, and he being in possession of that estate, with the exception of a part of the said lands reserved to his father in liferent, the devolving clause in the taillie of the estate of Luss takes place, and that therefore he, the said Ludovick Grant, younger of Grant, is obliged now to denude himself of the estate of Luss, lands, and others expressed in the foresaid taillie in favours of the pursuer, James Colquhoun, his brother, who is now the next son of the marriage betwixt their father, Sir James Grant, and Mrs. Anne Colquhoun, and decern and ordain the said Ludovick Grant, younger of Grant, to denude himself of the said estate of Luss and others above specified, and to dispone the samin, *habili modo*, in favours of the said James Colquhoun."[1]

In obedience to this decreet, Ludovick, then designated Ludovick Grant, younger of Grant, by a disposition, made with consent of his father, dated 25th and 30th January, and 9th day of February 1738, disponed to the said James Colquhoun, and the heirs of entail, the lands and heritages which composed the estate of Luss.

On the 13th of February 1738, James Colquhoun of Luss obtained from Frederick Prince of Wales, with consent of the Barons of the Exchequer, his Commissioners, a charter of the lands and barony of Luss, which Ludovick, with consent of his father, Sir James Grant, had resigned into the hands of the Barons of the Exchequer for new infeftment of the same to be made and granted to the said James Colquhoun.[2] And, on 29th August 1739, he was infefted in the lands and barony of Luss.[3]

James Colquhoun of Luss adopted the military profession, and he is often designated captain and major in the family writs.

In the year 1739, there was granted in his favour a resignation by Robert Colquhoun of Camstradden, proceeding upon a general narrative of the old rights of the family of Luss, to "all and haill the Slate Crag, lying in the town of Camstradden, parish and barony of Luss, and shire of Dumbarton, with a servitude of roads upon his said lands of Camstradden for gates and roads, for leading and boating the slates."[4]

This Laird of Luss married on 12th April 1740, Lady Helen Sutherland, eldest daughter of William Lord Strathnaver (eldest son of John nineteenth Earl of Sutherland), who died in 1720. Their contract of marriage is dated at Edinburgh and Castle Grant, the 3d, 5th, and 10th of April and 4th of June 1740. "Captain James Colquhoun of Luss," as he is designated in the contract, with consent of Sir James Grant of Grant, his father, and Ludovick Grant, younger of Grant, his eldest brother, Lachlan Grant, writer in Edinburgh, and Francis Grant, third son of the said Sir James

---

[1] Extract Decreet Declarator at Rossdhu.

[2] Original Charter, *ibid.*

[3] Original Instrument of Sasine, *ibid.*

[4] From Petition and Answers for Major James Colquhoun of Luss to the Petition of Robert Colquhoun of Camstradden, 10th February 1747.

Grant, as expectant heir of entail of the estate of Luss, became bound to resign the lands and barony of Luss in favour of himself and the heirs-male of his marriage with Lady Helen, whom failing, to the heirs of entail and provision contained in the procuratory and right of entail made by Sir Humphrey Colquhoun, with consent of Margaret Houston, his wife, to Anne Colquhoun, their daughter, and James Grant, her husband, dated 4th and 27th December 1706. He also bound himself to provide and secure Lady Helen in a liferent or jointure of £4000 Scots yearly, to be restricted, in case there should be heirs-male of the marriage betwixt her and him, to a life-rent of £3000 Scots yearly; and to infeft her in certain parts of the estate of Luss computed to amount to £1600 Scots of yearly rent, as being the third part of the free rent of that estate, to which he was empowered to provide her by the said entail. He further bound himself, in case there should be no male heir, to provide the daughters of the said marriage, according to their number, to the several sums and provisions mentioned in the contract, viz., if there be but one daughter, £2000 sterling to her, if there be two daughters, £3000 sterling to them, and if there be three or more daughters, £3500 sterling to them. The tocher which Lady Helen brought to Captain James Colquhoun was £3400 sterling, with the annual rent thereof after Whitsunday 1740, a sum due to her by her brother William, then Earl of Sutherland, which he became bound to pay conformably to the rights and securities mentioned in the marriage contract.

By the deed of entail before mentioned, Captain James Colquhoun was disabled from making effectual the whole of the liferent provision pro-mised to Lady Helen, and from making any provision to the daughters of their marriage so as to affect the estate of Luss. But it was agreed in the marriage contract that the annual rent of the sum of £24,599 19s. Scots, with which, by the terms of the deed of entail, the estate of Luss might be burdened, should be applied to make up the deficiency, and that the sum of £3400 sterling, Lady Helen's tocher, should be settled and vested in trustees. Accordingly Lady Helen assigned the sum of £3400 sterling and annual rents thereof to and in favour of the following trustees : Duncan Forbes of Culloden, Lord President of the College of Justice ; Robert Dundas of Arniston, Esq., one of the Senators, and afterwards Lord President of

the College of Justice ; Sir James Ferguson of Killkerran, also one of the
Senators of the College of Justice ; Mr. Patrick Boyle of Shewalton, and Mr.
Alexander Boswell of Auchinleck, Advocates, and afterwards Senators of
the College of Justice, and the said Captain James Colquhoun, and the sur-
vivors or survivor of them : by whom the annual rent of the two sums before
mentioned—£3400 sterling and £24,599, 19s. Scots—should be appropriated
to the said Sir James Colquhoun during his lifetime, and after his decease,
in case Lady Helen should survive him, for supplementing the deficiency
of her foresaid liferent of £4000 Scots.  The fee of the said two sums was
to be secured and assigned to the heir-male of the marriage, whom failing,
it was to be applied for providing the respective provisions of the daughters
of the said marriage, after the liferent provisions in favour of Lady Helen
were completely paid.  But should there be an heir-male and also younger
children of the marriage, it should be competent to Captain James Colquhoun to provide for these younger children out of the said two principal
sums, yet without prejudice of the liferent provision of Lady Helen.  Failing
issue of the marriage, and upon her decease, these two principal sums
were to be applied to such purposes as should be appointed by Captain
James Colquhoun, whom failing, they were to go to his heirs and assignees
whomsoever.[1]

At the time of her marriage, Lady Helen was in the twenty-third year
of her age, having been born 8th April 1717.[2]  Her brother William, Earl
of Sutherland, having died at Montauban, in France, his son William, who
succeeded him, made payment by the hands of John Mackenzie of Delvine,
Writer to the Signet, to Sir James Colquhoun of Luss and the said Lady
Helen, his spouse, of the whole bygone annual rents due at and preceding
the terms of Candlemas last, of the sum of £1150 sterling, as the balance
remaining unpaid of the said sum of £3400 sterling, as also of the said
balance of £1150 sterling itself, being the full payment of the said debt due
to her by the said William Earl of Sutherland in manner foresaid.[3]

The disposition made to him by his brother Ludovick of the lands of
Luss, in January and February 1738, Captain James conveyed in favour of

[1] Extract Marriage Contract at Rossdhu.   extracted from a Bible at Dunrobin Castle.
[2] From Luss Bible at Rossdhu, edit. 1663,   [3] Extract Marriage Contract at Rossdhu.

himself and the heirs-male of the marriage between him and Lady Helen Sutherland, his spouse; whom failing, in favour of the other heirs of entail and provision before mentioned in their marriage contract.  And the lands and other heritages thus disponed were resigned into the hands of the commissioners of William Duke of Montrose, who was the superior, for new infeftment to be granted to Captain James Colquhoun and the heirs of entail before mentioned.

A charter, dated at Edinburgh 19th March 1755, was granted by the commissioners of William Duke of Montrose of the four merk land of old extent of the Mains of Balvie-Logan, etc., in favour of Sir James Colquhoun of Luss, and the heirs-male of the marriage between him and Lady Helen Sutherland, his wife; whom failing, in favour of his heirs-male in any subsequent marriage; whom failing, in favour of the other younger sons of the marriage between the deceased Sir James Grant and dame Anne Colquhoun, and their heirs-male successively, as specified in the deed of entail executed by Sir Humphrey Colquhoun.[1]  In these lands he was infefted on 2d, 4th, 5th, 6th, and 8th September same year.[2]

In his military capacity, Captain James Colquhoun was for some time in Flanders.  When the Government of Great Britain, in order to maintain the balance of power in Europe, undertook to assist the Queen of Hungary in the war carried on against her by France, and despatched into the Low Countries a force which might join the Austrians, Hessians, and Hanoverians in supporting her, Captain James Colquhoun and his regiment were sent on this enterprise.  He was at the battle of Dettingen, fought on the 27th of June 1743, in which the British and the Austrians, amounting to 18,000 troops, gained a victory over the French, who numbered 28,000, after an obstinate engagement, which lasted upwards of four hours, during which time the French were constantly reinforced.[3]  Soon after this battle, Captain James Colquhoun was promoted to the rank of major of Lord Sempill's Highland Regiment, in the room of Major Campbell, deceased.  This was the famous "Black Watch," now the 42d Regiment.[4]  But the climate of Flanders, and

[1] Original Charter at Rossdhu.
[2] Extract Registered Instrument of Sasine at Rossdhu.
[3] Scots Magazine, vol. v. pp. 284-290.
[4] Ibid. vol. v. p. 387.

the fatigues of the campaign, pressed so heavily on the constitution of Sir James, that he contracted an illness so severe and dangerous, that his friends, both at home and abroad, despaired of his life.[1] He was unable to take part in the battle of Fontenoy fought in the same cause. For the benefit of his health he returned to Scotland, previous to the Rebellion of 1745.

In that year, when Prince Charles, encouraged by his friends in England and Scotland, made a last effort to recover the throne of his ancestors, Sir James Colquhoun warmly supported the house of Hanover. The Prince appeared in the north of Scotland in the month of August, his standard was erected, and a considerable army was collected. At first fortune seemed to smile on his adventure. On the 21st of September, he totally routed the King's troops under Sir John Cope at Prestonpans, and he gained a similar victory over them at Falkirk on 17th January 1746. For both these victories the Prince was mainly indebted to Lord George Murray, his lieutenant-general. The Government, which had been disposed to treat the insurrection with contempt, now became seriously alarmed; and soon after, the Duke of Cumberland, who was commander of the British army in Flanders, having been invested with the command of the royal troops in Scotland, arrived in that kingdom. Having speedily secured the important posts of Stirling and Perth, he advanced with his army to Aberdeen, where he was joined by various noblemen and barons, including the Laird of Grant, father of Major Colquhoun.

The bad health of Major Colquhoun prevented him from joining the army of the Duke of Cumberland, but he took the deepest interest in whatever might contribute to the suppression of the rebellion.

Major Colquhoun was an intimate friend and a frequent correspondent of Andrew Fletcher, Lord Milton, Lord Justice-Clerk. Both were sincere and warm friends of the Revolution Settlement and of the House of Hanover. Lord Milton signalized himself by his activity in restoring order and tranquillity after the suppression of the rebellion in 1745; and for this purpose he was in constant correspondence with the Secretary of State, with the sheriffs of counties, with the magistrates of

[1] This is stated in Additional Petition and Answers to the Petition of Robert Colquhoun of Camstradden, addressed to the Lords of Council and Session, dated February 10, 1747.

burghs, and with the various military commanders. He had great influence in the management of public affairs at that time, and this influence he
uniformly exerted in pressing upon the Government the adoption of merci-
ful measures, as what promised to be most successful in allaying the animosities of the friends of the exiled Stuarts, and in gaining them over
to loyalty to the reigning family. Major Colquhoun of Luss was emi-
nently zealous and successful in his efforts to put down an insurrectionary
spirit, and to restore peace and order, in the north-west of Scotland, where
he resided, and, like Lord Milton, he was a strenuous advocate for the lenient treatment of those who had taken part in the rebellion. Many of the
letters which he wrote on this subject to Lord Milton bear testimony to his
assiduous exertions in the cause of order; for even after the rebels had
been defeated, there remained the rancour of much disaffection to the
Government.

In the spring of the year 1746, by the assistance of his tenants, he
apprehended a lieutenant in the service of Prince Charles, and lodged him
in Dumbarton Castle. This adventure he relates in a letter to Lord Milton,
dated 10th March that year; and he expresses his readiness to make other
rebels prisoners, should he obtain the approval of the Government. The
letter is as follows :—

Rosedoe, 10th March 1746.

MY LORD,—I beg leave to trouble your Lordship with a few lines to
acquaint you that, having information of one Duncan MacLachlan, a lieutenant
in the Pretender's service, being in my neighbourhood, I thought, for the service
of the Government, I could doe no less then use my endeavours to apprehend
him, and accordinglie, upon Friday last, I went with a party of my own tenants,
and first of all took possession of the boats upon the severall ferrys of Lochlomond, and was then preparing to make an attack upon the house of the above
person, who lives about four miles above me, in a possession belonging to Mr.
M'Alpine, minister of Arrochar, M'Farlane's parish. As I was just goeing to
land my men, I observed a boat crossing over from the opposite shoars, and in a
very little time one of my people discovered that the person I wanted was in
her, upon which I gave imediate orders to make all haste towards him. How
soon he observed us he turn'd back again, and jump'd out of his boat before he
got near the shoar; but my men being as nimble as him followed his example,
and when he found two of them were up with him he presented his pistle and

luckily it snapt. I call'd to them not to fire at him unless absolutely neces-sary. One of them did fire, but mised; upon which he took to his heels and endeavour'd to get through the water of Douglass to gain the hills. However, one man got up with him in the water, and being a sturdy, able fellow seised him and tuisted the dirk, which he had also drawen, out of his hand. I have sent him to Dumbarton Castle, where he is safely lodged. As I have no orders or warrant for apprehending of any body, yet I hope, as what I have done pro-ceeds from my firm attachment to the present Government, that I shall have your Lordship's approbation, and as very probably more of those rebellious people may come in my way, if your Lordship thinks proper to authorise me to seise them, I doe assure you none will be more ready to act in every respect for the service of his Majesty and our present happy constitution; but unless your Lordship gives me powers I will medle no further. My wife desires me make offer of her kind compliments to your Lordship, Lady Justice-Clark, and the young ladys, in which I sincerely joyne, who am, my Lord,

Your Lordship's most obedient humble servant,

JA. COLQUHOUN.

*P.S.*—I seised the boats by General Campbell's orders.[1]

Soon after the date of this letter, namely, on the 16th of April, was fought the battle of Culloden, at which the victory gained by the royal troops over the insurgents was so complete as utterly to extinguish the hopes of Prince Charles and the Jacobites, who for more than half a century had anticipated that propitious circumstances would arise under which their efforts for the restoration of the exiled family might be crowned with success.

Sir James's next letter in connexion with the rebellion was written to Mr. John Grant, Advocate, Edinburgh, requesting him to solicit Lord Milton's interposition in behalf of a young man of the name of Colquhoun, who had been apprehended under the mistaken belief that he was a rebel, and imprisoned in Dumbarton Castle :—

Rosedoe, 27 May 1746.

DEAR SIR,—I beg to know if you have as yet spoke to the Justice-Clark about the young lad, my namesake, who has been confin'd in Dumbarton Castle ever since September. I will answer for his appearance when called for, and will baill him in whatever sum is demanded, for I can assure you that his being

---

[1] From Original in Salton Charter-chest.

present when Glengyle carried of the soldiers was entirely accidentall. Neither had the boy any such principalls as that of Jacobitism. So I beg you'll apply imediately to get him liberate, that he may be able to assist his poor father and mother, who have nine or ten children besides himself. I send your waistcoate by Mr. Smollet, who will be in toun sometime nixt week. Lady Strathnaver and my wife offer their kindest compliments to Lord and Lady Elchies, yourself, and the young ladys, in which I sincerely joyne, who am, dear Sir,

Your most obedient humble servant,

JA. COLQUHOUN.

To Mr. John Grant, Advocate, at the Lord Elchie's House, in Edinburgh.[1]

The Duke of Cumberland, when on his way from the south to Aberdeen, by virtue of a plenary power with which he had been invested for the suppression of the rebellion, had issued a proclamation at Montrose, dated February 24, 1746, requiring all persons who had been with Prince Charles to deliver up their arms, and give in their names to the nearest magistrate or minister, on pain of being treated as rebels and traitors. After the defeat of the rebels at Culloden, he issued a proclamation requiring all the sheriffs, magistrates, and justices of the peace to search for such persons as had been in arms against his Majesty who had not submitted to mercy, and to seize and secure their arms.[2] And an Act of Attainder was passed, by which it was enacted that the persons therein named should be held guilty of high treason, and stand attainted if they did not surrender themselves to justice before the 12th of July.

The clan Macgregor, or the most of that clan, then despairing of the cause of Prince Charles, were willing to surrender themselves and their arms, and to submit to the Government. They made known their wishes and intentions to Sir James Colquhoun of Luss, and expressed their readiness to surrender to him. Averse to the adoption of severe measures against the misguided and unfortunate rebels, Sir James was desirous that they should obtain the benefit of the indemnity; but doubtful whether the Government would consider them suitable objects of the royal clemency, he wrote a letter to Lachlan Grant, writer in Edinburgh, to be communicated to Lord

---

[1] From Original in Salton Charter-chest.
[2] Aikman's History of Scotland, vol. vi. p. 542.

Milton, informing him of these particulars, and requesting instructions as to the course which he should take. The letter is as follows :—

13 July 1746.

SIR,—I beg you'l wait of the Justice-Clerk directly upon receipt hereof, and acquaint his Lordship that yesterday I had a message from some of the M'Grigors, acquainting me they inclined to surrender themselves and arms to me, and submit to his Majesty's mercy. I would give no answer to them untill I knew from his Lordship whether or not I might receive them, and give them certificates of their having taken the benefite of his Royall Highnes the Duke of Cumberland's proclamation. I believe the whole clan design to surrender. Only I believe Glengyle, Glencarnoch, and James, Rob Roy's son, can't expect the benefite of the proclamation ; neither has the two first given any hint of their inclination that way, but as to the clan, they are fully determined to do it, if accepted off.[1]

Lord Milton, to whose disinclination to the adoption of severe measures against the rebels we have already adverted, made a reply to Sir James's letter favourable to the Macgregors. Many on their surrender and submission to the Government were to be admitted to share the benefit of his Majesty's indemnity.

For the purpose of obtaining recruits for the service of Prince Charles, commissions had been promised and given to any person in arms who should bring a few men to join their ranks. Several of this class of officers offered to Sir James to surrender themselves and their arms to him. His opinion was that they were not included among the officers of the rebels, whom the Duke of Cumberland's proclamation excluded from the benefit of the indemnity ; but, doubtful whether the Government would consider them as included or not, he wrote a letter to Lord Milton, desiring to be instructed whether or not he should accept of their surrender. He at the same time informs his Lordship of the surrender of three of the Macgregors, and again solicits the liberation of the young man of the name of Colquhoun, on whose behalf he had formerly interposed :—

MY LORD,—I had the honour of your Lordship's letter of the 19th, with a coppy of Brigadier Mordaunt's sent me express from Stirling upon Monday last. I wrote him that very day, that as there was several people amongst those con-

[1] Copy Letter in Salton Charter-chest.

cern'd in the rebellion who were neither gentlemen nor men of estates, but were
nominal officers, I therefore desired to know if they were intituled to his Royal
Highness' proclamation in case they delivered up their arms, and submitted
themselves to his Majesty's royal mercy, for I am inform'd that any fellow who
cou'd bring a man or two with him was directly promised a commission, and
from that time had his title, so that I imagine such persons can't be comprehended amongst those secluded by the Brigadier's letter.  However, I would not
accept of the surrender of such untill I have his answer.  Upon Satterday last
three of the M'Grigors came and deliver'd up their arms, and submitted themselves to his Majesty's mercy, and I gave them certificates accordingly, and
acquainted the Brigadier thereof.  I would take it as a very particular favour
if your Lordship would be so good as order Robert Colquhoun, a young lad
prisoner in Dumbarton Castle, to be set at liberty.  He was very innocently
brought into the scrape which occasioned his confinement, and was brought up
with quite other principalls then that of Jacobiteism, as will appear by the
minister's certificate.  I will bail him (if needful) for any summ.  His father's
numerous family is really starving for want of his assistance.  I am, my Lord,
Your Lordship's most faithfull and obedient servant,
JA : COLQUHOUN.
Rosedoe, 29th July 1746.
To the Right Honourable the Lord Justice-Clerk, at Edinburgh.[1]

Many of the Macgregors surrendered to Sir James, and many of them
to Brigadier-General Mordaunt, and others.  Those who did so were indeed so numerous, that Sir James was hopeful that the most of that clan,
whose loyalty to the exiled family had hitherto been so unflinching, would
surrender and submit to the Government.  He thus wrote to his Lordship
on the subject :—

MY LORD,—According to your Lordship's directions, I sent a list of the
MacGrigors, from time to time, as they surrendered to Brigadier-General Mordaunt at Perth, and when General Campbell returned to Inveraray, I went there
to wait of him, and showed him also the names of such as had then submitted,
and have since that time acquainted him of every person who surrenders to
me.  I hope, considering the number who have come in to me, as well as to
others, that very few of that clan remain in the hills, and possibly in a very
short time the principal people of the name will surrender also to Major-General
Campbel ; at least I have good reason to think so, from messages sent me by

[1] Original Letter in Salton Charter-chest.

them.  If there is such a person as one Ogilvie, who is master of [a] ship at Leith, and soon to sail, by the information I lately received, Mr. Buchanan, who came from Rome with the Pretender's son (and has some employment about that family), is to endeavour to get of in that ship, being disappointed of a vessel from Clyde.  I have sent your Lordship, by the bearer hereof, a buck.  I am affraid he is not so good as I cou'd wish, being rather too young, but hopes to send soon a better one.  My wife desires me make offer of her best respects to your Lordship, Lady Miltoun, and the young ladys, and in which I beg leave to joyne, who am, upon all occasions, my Lord,

Your Lordship's most faithfull and obedient humble servant,

JA : COLQUHOUN.

Rosedoe, 24 September 1746.[1]

After the overthrow of Prince Charles's army at Culloden, the most energetic measures were adopted by the Government to extinguish the remains of the rebellion, and the cause of the Prince seemed now to be utterly hopeless.  But still in the central and west Highlands, the stronghold of the Highland clans, secret conspiracies might exist, to the harassment of the Government, and the disturbance of the public tranquillity.  Sir James, in a letter to Lord Milton, dated Rossdhu, 3d February 1747, informs him that James Drummond, Rob Roy's son, had important revelations to make, apparently respecting matters of this kind, should the Government be disposed to receive his depositions :—

My LORD,—I had yesternight a message sent me from James Drummond, Rob Roy's son, acquainting me that he had lately been in Rannoch and Badenoch, where he got a great deal of newes, the imparting of which, he says and affirms, wou'd be of great service to the Government, and that he wants nothing so much as to show his sincerity by divulgeing of it, and beged I wou'd, by express, acquaint your Lordship therewith, that in case you wou'd allow him, or procure him a pass, to come and wait of you, that he would devulge matters of the greatest consequence to your Lordship, and beged no time might be lost. I therefor think it proper to acquaint your Lordship herewith, and if you incline to have him open his breast, please send me the needfull, which I shall forward to Craigroyston to his friends, who will find him out.  I am fully persuaded that there are emissarys in the Highlands, and if they cou'd be found out and

[1] Original Letter in Saltou Charter-chest.

apprehended, I doe think such rascles deserve the gallows.    I am, with great truth, my Lord,

> Your Lordship's most faithful and obedient humble servant,
>
> JA : COLQUHOUN.[1]

Of the favourable disposition of Sir James to such of the rebels as were disposed honestly to submit to the Government, Rob Roy's son James had probably special information.  Rob Roy had, at one time, an interview with Sir James on the island of Inch-lonaig in Lochlomond.  What passed at that meeting was never allowed to transpire, but it appears to have been of a friendly character, as they were ever after on the best terms.  This, which it may be presumed was known to the son of the freebooter, encouraged him to apply to Sir James to make overtures to the Government on his behalf, and may account for the readiness with which Sir James was inclined to promote the success of his application.

Sir James's next letter to Lord Milton relates to some rebel prisoners who had been taken in the north, and whom he had met at Glasgow on their way to Edinburgh.  He prays his Lordship that they might be allowed to continue upon their parole of honour till their trial or liberation.  The letter is as follows :—

> Glasgow, 4 March 1747.

MY LORD,—I met with the Inveraray prisoners this morning, going for Edinburgh, and, as I told your Lordship, it had been much better for them to have continued here untill their tryall or releasement, but in any event, in case they are not allowed to return to this place, I beg your Lordship may be so good as allow them to continue as usuall upon parole of honours, and I think I may safely answer for their behaviour in every respect, but could wish them out of your cursed city.    I am, my Lord,

> Your Lordship's most faithfull and obliged humble servant,
>
> JA : COLQUHOUN.

To the Right Honourable the Lord Justice-Clark, Edinburgh.[2]

For some time after the battle of Culloden active search was made in different parts of the kingdom for rebels, and the prisons were filled with these unhappy captives.  The following letter shows the diligence and vigour with which Sir James and others served the Government in his part

---

[1] Original Letter in Salton Charter-chest.    [2] Original Letter, *ibid.*

of the country, by searching for and apprehending rebels who were concealing themselves and cluding pursuit as they best could :—

Rosedoe, 6 April 1747.

MY LORD,—Enclosed I send your Lordship a coppy of J. D. his letter in answer to the one I wrote him about Mr. Bayne. It seems Captain Campbell of Inveraw's company has frighted these gentlemen who were lurking in Raunoch, and I am apt to believe what J. D. says is very true ; for the account he gives of the miscarriage in apprehending those who were concealed in the house of Ductroa, was really so, for it's most certain they were in the house at the very time the party was searching it. How soon he returns from his present expedition he is to send me an express ; but I am affraid all of these folks will be now much upon their guard, and not be quite so easily taken as they might have been. Had it not been for Richie the messenger, the party from Bocklivie had miscarried in takeing Drunkie.[1] If Campbell gives you any intelligence about Bayne, please acquaint me, that J. D. may be inform'd how to proceed. My wife makes offer of her best respects to your Lordship, Lady Milton, and the young ladys, in which I sincerely joyne, who am, my Lord,

Your Lordship's most faithfull and obedient servant,

JA. COLQUHOUN.

To the Right Honourable the Lord Justice-Clark, at Edinburgh.[2]

At this time a misunderstanding arose between Major James Colquhoun of Luss and Robert Colquhoun of Camstradden respecting certain property rights and other matters. Reference is made to these in the following letter written to the major by his father, Sir James Grant of Grant :—

DEAR JAMIE,—Yours of the 3d, which I had last night, gives me noe litle surprise to see the unaccountable behaviour of your nieghbour Camstrodan, both in regard to you and the minister, Mr. Robertson. I make noe doubt but at last he will deny that he is your vassall, ore holds any thing of you. As for the minister, I make noe doubt of the Lords giving him speedy justice ; and as to your affaire with him, I think you should, without loss of time, take the best advice how to proceed in it. I believe he must be charged to produce his rights, in which I can take on me to say that there is noe mention made either of the houses in Luss ore any acres there, and that in the charters of the family of Luss the whole is contained. I believe Camstroden will finde that possession for as many years as he pleases to name without any title at all (quhich I take to be his case) will never make a right, tho' I own it might establish a bad and

---

[1] Graham of Drunkie.　　　[2] Original Letter in Salton Charter-chest.

lame one. I wont take on me to say who you should imploy as your agent in this affaire, but 1 think he should be such as will be very carefull, and prosecute it with vigour. I can give no newes from this. Lord Lovat's letter is in print here. Lewie and I doe goe to-day the length of Hatfield to take the air and see his horses, which he left there at grass. He joins with me in humble compliments to Lady Strathnaver and Lady Helen. Lord Sutherland came here two dayes ago, but as yet I have nott gott waiting of him. I am, dear Jamie,
                                           Your very affectionate father,
     London, 12 July 1746.                                    JA. GRANT.
To Major Colquhoun.[1]

     The dispute between Major James Colquhoun of Luss and Robert Colquhoun of Camstradden, referred to in the preceding letter, is probably that which arose at this time between them respecting the slate crag in the ten pound land of Camstradden. This crag was very valuable, on account of the good quality of the slate, the largeness of the vein, and its convenient situation, being by the side of a large loch —Lochlomond, which made the demand great, from the easy transport of the slates by water to the remote parts of the country, where there were few or no slate quarries. That Major James Colquhoun of Luss had right to the slate crag in the ten pound land of Camstradden, which had then for a long time been wrought, was admitted. The only point in dispute between the parties was whether the Major, as he maintained, had a right to the whole crag, or whole vein of slate in these lands, or whether, as the Laird of Camstradden maintained, it should be limited to a part of it, namely,— to the quarry already opened in the farm of Camstradden, so that he would be at liberty to work slates in any other part thereof.

     Some time before, as Robert Colquhoun of Camstradden "had been so lucky," he says, "to discover another slate crag within the tenement known by the name of the Hill of Camstradden," which he opened and began to work. In this attempt he was met by a suspension at the instance of the Laird of Luss, his superior, whose plea was that all the slate within these lands, which were wadset to his predecessor by John Colquhoun of Camstradden, was his property, as having been reserved in the year 1713, when the lands were redeemed.

_____
     [1] Original Letter at Rossdhu.

The matter in dispute having been debated before Lord Tinwald, Ordinary, his Lordship, 18th November 1746, " having considered the memorials for either party, and writs produced, Finds that Major James Colquhoun of Luss has the sole privilege of working slates in that part of the ten pound land of Camstradden called the four merk land of Camstradden, comprehending therein the lands called the Half Town of Camstradden : And that Robert Colquhoun of Camstradden has the sole privilege of working slates in the haill other parts of the said ten pound land of Camstradden, and decerns and declares accordingly." To this decision, upon mutual representation and answers, his Lordship adhered, by interlocutor, 15th January 1747. This interlocutor of his Lordship, which amounted to a compromising of the matter in dispute, satisfied neither of the parties. Both conceiving themselves aggrieved by this deliverance, applied to the Lords of Session, by petition, for redress. Major James Colquhoun objected to the last part of the interlocutor, by which he was excluded from the privilege of working slates in any other part of the ten pound land of Camstradden, except what was specially called the four merk land thereof. Robert Colquhoun of Camstradden acknowledged the justice of the interlocutor, in so far as it confined Major James within the four merk land of Camstradden, but he could not acquiesce in the other part of it which found that Luss had the exclusive privilege of working slate in the four merk land of Camstradden, comprehending therein the half town of Camstradden.

Both parties having thus complained to the Lords of Session, their Lordships, 14th June 1748, adhered to the interlocutor of Lord Tinwald, Ordinary, and the prayer of both petitions was refused.

Major James Colquhoun reclaimed, and presented another petition to the Lords of Council and Session, dated 23d June 1748, praying them to alter so much of the interlocutor as was complained of in the petition, and to find that he had right to the whole slate crag in those parts of the ten pound land of Camstradden that were disponed to Sir Humphrey Colquhoun in the year 1698, and which lands were redisponed to the Laird of Camstradden in the year 1713, with reservation of the slate crag in the said lands. In this petition he says, " Camstradden gave your Lordships

2 z

such a geographical description of the ground as might induce your Lordships to believe that these were different crags, lying at a considerable
distance from one another, separated and divided by glens, rivulets, and
oak woods; a description which your petitioner takes the liberty to say,
and, if need be, offers to prove, is altogether fictitious and imaginary. What
influence this averment, on the part of Camstradden, may have had with
your Lordships in determining the point of right, is to your petitioner
unknown."

Their Lordships, on 15th July 1748, having considered this petition,
with the answers made thereto, found that the reservation of the slate
crags in the disposition by Luss to Camstradden, in the year 1713, was
equally broad and extensive with the disposition of the slate crags in the
year 1698, and therefore found that the pursuer, Major James, had right
not only to the slate crags in the town and lands of Camstradden,
properly so called, comprehending the Half Town of Camstradden, but also
to the slate crags in the lands of Aldochlay and Hill of Camstradden, and
remit to the Lord Ordinary to proceed accordingly.

Mention has already been made of the heritable bond, dated 15th February 1698, which Sir Humphrey Colquhoun gave to Robert Colquhoun,
only lawful son of Robert Colquhoun of Ballernick, for the sum of 2300
merks Scots, with an annual rent of 115 merks from the lands of Ballernick
during the non-payment thereof. This heritable bond, after passing
through various hands, was acquired by Helen Countess of Glasgow.
About this time it was redeemed by Sir James Colquhoun. Out of the
sum of £1150 sterling, the balance of Lady Helen his spouse's tocher,
before referred to as paid to him and her by her nephew, William Earl of
Sutherland, he made payment to Helen Countess of Glasgow of the sum
of 2300 merks, the principal contained in the said heritable bond. He
paid her another sum of 3000 merks Scots contained in another bond.
And he paid her the whole bygone annual rents of these two principal
sums. She therefore, on 19th February 1755, granted a disposition and
assignation of these various principal sums to Sir James Colquhoun and
others, the surviving trustees, before mentioned, in his marriage-contract,
for securing and making up to Lady Helen, his spouse, the full jointure

and liferent provided to her by it, and for securing to the daughters of the marriage the respective provisions made in their favour by the contract.[1]

In the year 1748, Sir James Colquhoun finally retired from the army, as appears from a list of the original officers of the Black Watch.[2]

Lord Milton, from his friendship with Archibald third Duke of Argyll, to whom the chief management of Scottish affairs was intrusted, had it largely in his power to obtain for persons whom he recommended situations of trust and emolument in every department in the State. Sir James Colquhoun, from the friendly terms on which he stood with Lord Milton, frequently solicited, on behalf of parties in whom he was interested, his Lordship's patronage. An Act having been made by the Parliament for the encouragement of fishing in Scotland, according to which two persons were to be appointed by the Commissioners and Trustees as judges, or kind of admirals to attend the fishing fleets, and determine differences that might arise among them, or between the fishers and others, one for the Orkneys and Lochs, and the other for the Firth of Clyde, he wrote a letter to Lord Milton, dated Rossdhu, 5th July 1756, praying his Lordship to use his influence for the appointment of Robert Colquhoun of Camstradden to be judge or admiral for the fisheries of the Clyde :—" I beg leave to recommend the bearer, Mr. Colquhoun of Camstradden, as a very fit person to act in that capacity, and, in case your Lordship has not alreadie some other body in view, I beg earnestly you 'll use your interest with the rest of the Trustees to get him appointed admiral for Clyde."[3]

In another letter to Lord Milton, Sir James requests his Lordship to use his endeavours for the appointment of Mr. William Panton, schoolmaster of Dumbarton, to be Latin teacher in the Canongate New Academy, Edinburgh. The letter is as follows :—

" MY LORD,—Being informed that some time nixt week, or very soon thereafter, the affair with regard to a schoolmaster (that teaches Lattin) for the Canongate New Academy is to be settled, might I, in that event, beg the favour of your Lordship's interest for Mr. William Panton, schoolmaster at Dumbarton, to be appointed teacher of the Lattin in the Canongate. He is a very worthy

[1] Extract Registered Disposition at Rossdhu.
[2] Major-General Stewart's Sketches of the Highlanders, p. 253.
[3] Original Letter in Saltoun Charter-chest.

man, and I doe believe one of the fittest persons in Scotland for such an under-
taking.    Mr. Bennet, at Duddistoun, where he was formerly schoolmaster, I
dare say, will likewise recommend him.    I have been here for some time drinking the salt water, and this day my wife and I are goeing to visit Lady Carrick,
and from thence the Castle of Roseneath.    Wee both joyn in the offer of our
most humble respects to your Lordship, Lady Milton, and family, and I am, my
Lord,
            Your Lordship's most obedient humble servant,
                                                        JA : COLQUHOUN.
Faslane, 11th August 1756.[1]

Mr. Panton was a competitor worthy of the situation to which he
aspired, and Lord Milton, who was always anxious to secure for vacant
situations in the Church and State such individuals as he judged to be
best qualified to fill them, threw, in compliance with the request of this
letter, the weight of his influence on the side of Mr. Panton, whose election by this means was without difficulty secured.    Sir James, on receiving
intelligence to that effect from Edinburgh, wrote the following letter of
thanks to his Lordship :—

MY LORD,—By last post I had letters from Edinburgh, acquainting me that
your Lordship has now got the Cannongate affair with regard to the schoolmaster entirely settled, and that the election of Mr. Panton is fixed for the 26th
curt.    I therefore take this opportunity of returning your Lordship my most
hearty thanks, which I hope to doe personally when the Assembly of the Kirk
meets.    I rejoice to see by the newes that Colonel Campbell is now free of
Gibraltar, and mounted upon an Irish regiment of dragoons.    I hope his abode
in that country wont be of any long duration either.    My wife desires the offer
of her respectfull compliments to your Lordship, Lady Milton, and the young
ladys, in which I beg leave to joyn.    I have the honour to be, my Lord,
            Your Lordship's most obedient humble servant,
                                                        JA : COLQUHOUN.
Rosedoe, 15th Aprile 1757.
P.S.—At last we have fine weather, and never was there greater need of it.[2]

Another of Sir James's letters to Lord Milton, in which he begs his
Lordship to promote the appointment of Mr. Flint, father of his surgeon,
and father-in-law to Mr. Panton, to be governor in Heriot's Hospital,

[1] Original Letter in Salton Charter-chest.    [2] Original Letter, ibid.

though the application was not successful, may here be given, as illustrating the readiness with which his friendly offices were employed on behalf of those whom he regarded as deserving :—

My Lord,—I am asshamed to be so often troublesome to your Lordship in asking favours, but I am greatly press'd at present to sollicit your Lordship's interest (if not alreddie otherways engaged) in favours of Mr. Flint, father to our surgeon, and father-in-law to Mr. Panton, who, it seems, is a candidate for the governorship in Herriott's Hospitall. He is a burgher in Edinburgh, and bore arms and acted as a lieutenant in the time of the late rebellion, and will be very well recommended as a sober, well-qualified man to Church and State, and therefore hopes, providing your Lordship's interest be for him, that he will be successfull, if otherwise, I dare say he will not attempt it. My wife joyns me in the offer of respectfull compliments to your Lordship, Lady Milton, and the young ladys ; and in hopes of having the honour now of seeing your Lordship soon in this country, I am, my Lord, your Lordship's most obedient humble servant,                                                         JA : COLQUHOUN.[1]
Rosedoe, 16 July 1757.

On the 5th of October 1761, Sir James purchased from Robert Colquhoun of Camstradden the lands of Cragentuy, upon Sir James making over to him his slate quarry in the four merk land of Camstradden, comprehending the half town thereof (now called Halftown), a property about which there had been so keen a litigation between them.[2]

Following in the footsteps of his ancestors, the Grants of Grant, Sir James was, in his political sentiments, a Whig, and he associated himself with the Duke of Argyll in supporting that policy in the affairs of State which it was the object of the Whigs of his day to carry out. This created a coldness and a misunderstanding between him and his neighbour the Duke of Montrose, whose family had in former times been good friends of the Colquhouns of Luss, with whom they had been connected by intermarriage. The house of Montrose took the opposite side in politics, and these political differences did not conduce to the promotion of a mutual friendly feeling between the Duke and Sir James.

About the end of the year 1778, Sir James executed a summons for setting aside the liferent rights granted by Lord Graham over such of

[1] Original Letter in Salton Charter-chest.       [2] Extract Registered Disposition at Rossdhu.

Sir James's lands as were held of the family of Montrose. The Duke of Montrose and Lord Graham were, of course, prepared to adopt counter measures to defeat this attempt on his part. This led to a correspondence between David Erskine, Writer to the Signet, who acted on behalf of the family of Montrose, and Sir James on the subject. Mr. Erskine, in order to defend the Duke of Montrose and Lord Graham, and to weaken Sir James's power of attack, purposed to take legal action against him with respect to some of his own transactions. Sir James, as is alleged, had granted different rights over the estate of Luss, in opposition to the deed of entail; and Mr. Erskine, as one of the heirs of entail under Sir Humphrey Colquhoun of Luss's settlement, had entered an action against him for a reduction of these rights. Unwilling to proceed further, Mr. Erskine would have him to get the liferent rights and other encumbrances on the entailed estate properly renounced and discharged. On these points Mr. Erskine writes to him as follows :—

Edinburgh, 3 January 1779.

DEAR SIR,—When your son, Mr. Colquhoun, acquainted me that you was about to execute, or rather had executed, a summons for setting aside the liferent rights granted by Lord Graham over the lands held by you of the family of Montrose, he told me that he hoped it would be no breach of the friendship which had subsisted between the families, and that nothing but the obligations which you lay under to the family of Argyle could have induced you to have taken so decided a step.

I answered Mr. Colquhoun, that however unexpected such procedure might be from you, who well knew that neither the Duke of Montrose nor Lord Grahame meant to hurt your interest in the least degree, yet, since you considered yourself under so great obligations to the Argyle family, I was persuaded they would most readily admit your apology, but that since you had stated yourself as aggressor, I hoped that, on the other hand, you would as readily take in good part whatever steps they, or their friends, should be advised to take against you. Mr. Colquhoun assured me you would cheerfully submit to every thing of that kind.

I believe you are no stranger to the many favours conferred on me by the family of Montrose from my early years, and sure I am you would think them most undeservedly bestowed were I not to acknowledge them whenever an opportunity offers.

The same motives, therefore, which induced you to challenge a deed of Lord Graham's that cannot possibly hurt you, have led me to challenge some deeds of yours, which may, however, be attended with very serious consequences to my prejudice, were they allowed to subsist.

In short, as one of the heirs of taillie under Sir Humphrey Colquhoun's entail of the estate of Luss, I have directed a reduction to be brought of the different rights which you have been advised to grant over that estate, in direct opposition to the entail. These deeds, if allowed to remain, would soon put an end to the settlement under which alone you have right to that estate. My own interest, therefore, and my ardent desire to preserve the estate of Luss in the line chalked out by Sir Humphrey, as well as my wish to support the interest of the family of Montrose, the old friends and relations of the Colquhoun's, prompt me to take this step, in which, I believe, I shall have the good wishes equally of the heir-male and heir of line of the Luss family. And as my motives are the same with yours, I assure myself not merely of your forgiveness but of your approbation.

I need not tell you that this very case has already received the determination of the Court in the question between our cousin Colonel Ralph Dundas and Mr. Murray of Touchadam.

As it would be matter of regret to have my name called in Court in a question with you, even when, as in this case, we understand each other perfectly, it would give me infinite pleasure to be freed from that necessity by your getting the liferent rights and other incumbrances on the entailed estate properly renounced and discharged, and your titles brought back to the neat complete state in which they ought to be. And, therefore, tho' I have directed the summons immediately to be executed against such of the incumbrancers as are abroad, I shall delay executing it against you and the other defenders in Scotland for some days, that I may have an opportunity of learning from yourself your resolutions on the subject.

I shall only add that I have adopted this measure without the knowledge of the Duke of Montrose or Lord Graham, neither of whom have hitherto been apprised of the situation of parties.

I beg leave to offer most respectful compliments to Lady Helen ; and have the honour to be, with esteem, dear Sir,

Your most obedient humble servant,

DAVID ERSKINE.

Sir James Colquhoun, Bart.[1]

---

[1] Original Letter at Rossdhu.

At the close of the year 1779, Francis seventh Lord Napier, whose ancestors had acquired right to a share of the ancient Earldom of Lennox, through marriage with one of the co-heiresses of the old Earl of Lennox, contested the rights of Colquhoun of Luss to the islands in Lochlomond. The Duke of Montrose had been making inquiries respecting them, and Lord Napier therefore intimated to Mr. James Colquhoun, eldest son and heir of Sir James Colquhoun of Luss, that unless he made a composition with him in regard to them there was a danger of their falling into the possession of the family of Montrose. Lord Napier's letter to him on this subject is as follows :—

Edinburgh, 13th December 1779.

Sir,—Mr. Buchan informs me that the Duke of Montrose has been enquiring about the islands in Lochlomond. I acquaint you with this circumstance that you may have an opportunity of declaring whether you are inclined to make a composition with me or not. My connections with the Montrose family are such as will oblige me to assist the Duke as far in that matter as may be in my power. His Grace has not yet applied to me personally. If he should, it will be impossible for me to refuse him. I am, Sir,

Your most obedient servant,

NAPIER.

James Colquhoun, Esq.[1]

Lord Napier founded his claim to these islands on original charters from Queen Mary to his family, which he said were in his possession, and made his right to these islands appear exceedingly clear. He wished to settle the matter amicably with Sir James Colquhoun of Luss. His ancestors had granted a long lease of these islands to the Napiers of Kilmahew. Though the family of Colquhoun had got these islands inserted in their titles, yet it would not be difficult, he asserted, to prove that the right was vested in his family, not in that of Colquhoun. But the possession of them being desirable from their situation to the family of Colquhoun of Luss, he would confirm them to that family for a small gratuity. On these points he writes to Mr. Colquhoun in the following terms :—

Edinburgh, 18 November 1780.

Sir,—I directed Mr. Buchan yesterday to mention to you my desire of having some conversation with you about the islands in Lochlomond. I for-

---

[1] Original Letter at Rossdhu.

merly told you that the original charters from Queen Mary to my family are now in my possession, from which my right to those islands appears exceedingly clear. It is my wish to settle this matter in an amicable way, and if you will favour me with half an hour's conversation at any time this evening which may be most convenient for you, I make no doubt of our coming to a proper agreement about them. My ancestors had granted a long lease of those islands to the Napiers of Kilmahew. This lease expired about 26 or 27 years ago; and though your family have got those islands inserted in their titles, it will be found no difficult matter to prove that the right is vested in my family, and not in yours. However, as from their situation they become desirable objects for you to possess, a very small gratuity will prevail upon me to confirm your right to them, and render it indisputable. I am, Sir,

Your most obedient servant,

NAPIER.

*P.S.*—I am desirous of seeing you this evening, as I set out for England at five o'clock on Monday morning.

James Colquhoun, Esq.[1]

The difference in political sentiment between Sir James and the house of Montrose is more fully referred to in another letter from Mr. Erskine to Sir James. With the view of promoting his interests, apparently by obtaining seats in Parliament for his son and his two sons-in-law, Sir James had intended to create votes upon his estate. Mr. Erskine gives it as his opinion that it was unwise and perilous to his own interests for Sir James to act in this manner. He also blames him for having included in his Crown charter passed in 1774 part of those lands which were unquestionably held of the Duke of Montrose, and informs him that he had been instructed by the Duke to raise a process for reducing that charter, and for having it found that by this repudiation of him as Lord Superior the lands had reverted to him. The letter is as follows :—

Edinburgh, 24th January 1780.

DEAR SIR,—Your favour of the 6th instant reached me in the south country, where I remained for some days, and I then delayed answering it till I should have the pleasure of seeing your son, Mr. Colquhoun, to whom you refer me. Since my return I have met with him twice or thrice, but as he did not enter

[1] Original Letter at Rossdhu.

upon the subject, I thought I could no longer delay acknowledging the receipt of yours.

I am firmly persuaded that the different political views presently entertained by the families of Montrose and Luss will be no breach of the mutual friendship and intercourse which has so long subsisted between them. Both may have good reasons for their conduct, and neither are influenced by motives of disgust or resentment towards each other. In general their interest in the country must lye the same way, and tho' adverse at present, they will in all probability co-operate soon together. In the meantime, however, as you are not only supporting your own family interest, but attacking that of Montrose, surely the same liberty may be indulged to that family and its friends.

For my own part I have ever been surprised how any proprietor of an entailed estate, for the sole view of increasing his political interest, could think of putting it in the breasts of any set of men, however respectable, to determine whether his estate was his own. For this reason I have uniformly dissuaded the measure where my opinion was asked, and have even declined to take charge of executing the deeds. In conformity with this are the measures I now take with you. Certainly, if your entailed estate was to be mangled, and votes to be created upon it, no persons were less exceptionable than your son and your two sons-in-law. But it is the measure, not the men, to which I object. And I do not despair of having your thanks for showing you the imprudence and danger of meddling with so ticklish a matter as an entail.

I and every other heir are, I am persuaded, fully sensible of the very great advantage the estate of Luss has reaped from your care and attention ; and I trust your family will long enjoy the sweets of it. The steps I am taking evidently tend to perpetuate and secure their interest in it instead of impairing or weakening their title.

I am desired by the Duke of Montrose to acquaint you that as you included in your Crown charter past in 1774 part of the lands unquestionably held by you of his Grace, he has directed me to raise a process for reducing that charter, and for having it found that by your disclamation of him the lands held by you of him have reverted to him. The Duke assures himself that when you challenge him for doing what cannot hurt you, you will readily excuse him for challenging what might in the course of years carry off part of his property, and that no apology is necessary for founding on a well known casuality of superiority laid down by our writers for centuries past, when you found on a feudal nicety, which, if to be found at all in our writers, is but slightly hinted at. I have accordingly raised and executed a summons against Colonel Campbell, who, I observe, is infeft in the lands of Tullichantaul, as held of the Prince, tho' in fact you held them of the Duke, and I shall give directions for executing it against you and Mr. James.

I beg to be respectfully remembered to Lady Helen. I sincerely hope you have got the better of your complaints; and have the honour to be, with esteem and regard, dear Sir,

Your most obedient humble servant,

DAVID ERSKINE.

Sir James Colquhoun.[1]

In the year 1780 the representation for the county of Dumbarton in the British Parliament was contested with great keenness. The candidates were Lord Frederick Campbell, brother of John fifth Duke of Argyll, and the Honourable George Keith Elphinstone, a captain in the navy, afterwards Lord Keith and Chamberlain of Scotland. The former was supported by the Duke of Argyll and Sir James Colquhoun of Luss, the latter by the Duke of Montrose and the family of Smollett. Both parties freely availed themselves of electioneering arts, in which they proved themselves well skilled. Lord Frederick was supported by a majority of the old freeholders, but a number of new electors had been created for the occasion by his opponents, and these, it was expected, would turn the scale in favour of Captain Elphinstone. In order to their being entitled to vote, it was, however, necessary that they should have been in possession of that right a full twelve months before the day of election. To turn to account this provision of the law, Sir James Colquhoun of Luss, who was Sheriff, and who acted as returning-officer for Lord Frederick, whom he supported, fixed the day of election twenty-four hours before the expiry of the time when the new freeholders could legally give their vote. Another objection, made to not less than thirteen of Captain Elphinstone's supporters, was that the Lennox retour as to the value of their lands was not sufficient evidence of their right to be enrolled as voters. Not to be outwitted by the device of the Sheriff, Captain Elphinstone's party met it by a counter stratagem. They secured as speakers at the election the celebrated Henry Erskine, and other lawyers from Edinburgh, and, on the day of election, by the lengthened speeches of these learned gentlemen, and other means, they protracted the proceedings till the clock struck twelve, when the twelvemonth's possession of right to vote, required by the Statute,

[1] Original Letter at Rossdhu.

having now expired, they demanded that the votes of the new freeholders
should be immediately taken. But by this ruse the agents of Lord Frederick were not to be outmanœuvred. They urged that the election ought,
according to the law, to have terminated on the day on which it had commenced. The dispute was prolonged till about five o'clock of the morning
of the day following. When the votes were taken, the preses, Archibald
Edmonstone of Duntreath, declared that his friend, Lord Frederick, was the
successful candidate by a majority of nine. The votes for Lord Frederick
Campbell were twenty-seven in all, and those for Captain Elphinstone
nineteen in all. But each new freeholder having protested against the
rejection of his vote, Captain Elphinstone himself, and certain freeholders
of the county also, presented petitions to the House of Commons against
the return,[1] and numerous cases connected with it were also raised in the
Court of Session. But the contest was terminated by the withdrawing
of Lord Frederick. Captain Elphinstone accordingly took his seat in Parliament as Member for Dumbartonshire, and continued to represent that
county till 1790.

About five months before his death, Sir James Colquhoun was created
a baronet of Great Britain by patent of King George the Third, dated at
Westminster, the 15th of June, in the 26th year of his reign [1786]. The
patent narrates that Sir James was a man eminent for family, inheritance,
estate, and integrity of manners, who generously and freely gave and
furnished to the King an aid and supply large enough to maintain and
support thirty men in his Majesty's foot companies in the kingdom of
Ireland, to continue for three whole years, for the defence of that kingdom,
and especially for the security of the plantation of the province of Ulster.
The limitation of the dignity was to the grantee and the lawful heirs-male
of his body.

During his possession of the Luss estate, which extended over the long
period of about half a century, Sir James Colquhoun added largely to the
estate by purchase of other lands. In the year 1751 he purchased from
Dougall Buchanan of Gartencaber, for 12,270 merks Scots, or £681, 13s. 4d.
sterling, the towns and lands of Little Balernick on Gareloch, in the parish

[1] Scots Magazine, vol. xlii. p. 637.

of Row, and Inverutachan, Corriehenagan in Glen Douglas, and Inverbeg, all in the parish of Luss, with the teinds. In the same year he purchased from Aulay Macaulay of Ardincaple and others, for £1250 sterling, the lands of Faslane, in the parish of Row.

In the year 1757, Sir James Colquhoun purchased from Charles Lord Cathcart, for £6500, the barony of Malligs, including the three merk land of Kirkmichael marching with Colgrain; the five merk land of Drumfad, in the moor above Malligs; the £8 land of Malligs and miln of the same, with the teinds; the £1, 6s. 8d. land of Stuckleckie, and the easter town of Ardincaple, with the teinds and the fishings; a pendicle of the mains of Ardincaple, extending to about half an acre; the two merk land of Little Drumfad or Drumfad-Leckie, in the moor above Malligs, with the teinds, all in the parish of Row; and the lands or Meallin of Auchintaal, on the east side of the Garvil Glen, in the parish of Cardross.

In the year 1760, Sir James purchased from John Sydeserf of Chappell, for £600, the lands of Auchintullich-na-moine, with Poffle, called the Spittle, in the parish of Luss, with the teinds, and a proportion of the moor called Laichlaran.

In the year 1763, Sir James purchased from John MacFarlane of Auchinvenallmore, for £1000, the £3 land of old extent of Auchinvenallmore, in Glenfruin, with the teinds and fishings, and a servitude of casting peats on the hill of Stuckiedow, all in the parish of Row.

In the year 1776, Sir James purchased from John Crawford of Inverlaren, price not known, the lands of Upper Inverlaren, at the entrance of Glenfruin, with the teinds, and a right of common pasturage upon the moor of Laichlaran, in the parish of Luss.

Among the preceding purchases of land made by Sir James, one of the most important was that of the barony of Malligs from Lord Cathcart. Sir John Shaw of Greenock, the previous proprietor of Malligs, died in the year 1752, leaving an only child, a daughter, Margaret, who married Charles eighth Lord Cathcart. Sir John was succeeded in the entailed estate of Greenock by his grand-nephew, Sir John Shaw Stewart of Blackhall and Ardgowan, but the Malligs being unentailed, was left to his widow, Lady Shaw, and then to his daughter and her husband, and by them it was sold to Sir James Colquhoun. In a memorandum-book kept by Sir James, there is an entry in his own handwriting stating that the last instalment of the price of the Malligs was paid to Lord Cathcart on the 5th of June 1756.

At the time of the purchase, a considerable part of that property was covered with whins and broom, but it has since been improved and cultivated, and it is now good arable land. Sir James purposed to have a burgh of barony on the lower part of it next to the Clyde, and commenced it by feuing different portions of the ground. He was somewhat perplexed with respect to the name by which the intended burgh might be designated, not approving of any of the names suggested to him. At last, having mentioned his difficulty to a gentleman, one of his friends, and asked his advice, his friend replied that he saw no difficulty in the matter, as Sir James could not find a better name than in calling it after his good Lady, Helen's Burgh. The appropriateness of the name struck Sir James, and the suggestion was at once adopted.

The Act constituting Helensburgh a burgh of barony was not, however, obtained till the year 1802, after the death of Sir James. The progress of the burgh was at first very slow. In the year 1794 there were only seventeen feuars in Helensburgh, as appears from a list of the Malligs feu-duties of that date. But the natural advantages of Helensburgh as a coast residence gradually became more obvious, and after the invention of steam navigation, the facility of communication and intercourse with other localities was greatly increased. Henry Bell, who established the Baths Inn in Helensburgh, where he resided for thirty years, was the first who introduced its practical application, having in 1812 launched his little steamboat, "The Comet," on the Clyde, and had thus the honour of being the founder of steam navigation in this country. He was the first Provost of Helensburgh. More recently the railroad has completely opened up the communication with every part of the country. From these advantages the population of Helensburgh has continued more and more rapidly to increase. It is now a prosperous and populous town, and one of the first watering-places on the west coast. There was a mill upon the lands, which, at that time, was driven by water, and there is still a mill upon the same spot, but it is now driven by steam. In the year 1867 the old mill-

dam was enlarged, and it now forms the reservoir that supplies Helensburgh with water. This mill and the lands attached to it seem to indicate
the derivation of the original name Malligs, the name Muillag in Gaelic
signifying a corn milling.

About the year 1774, Sir James commenced to build the present
mansion-house of Rossdhu, with the exception of the portico and wings,
which were added by the late Sir James Colquhoun, but he died before it
was completed.

After the new house was built, the old castle of Rossdhu was deserted
as a residence. The late Sir James Colquhoun took down part of the castle
and used the materials for building purposes; a use to which the stones
of old castles were formerly not unfrequently applied. The south wall
only now remains. It is from six to seven feet thick; and this solid
masonry has preserved it still pretty entire against many a blast from lake
and land.

In leaving the old castle for the new mansion of Rossdhu, Lady Helen,
who survived her husband, was much affected, and her grandson, the late
Sir James Colquhoun, who was then seven years old, remembered that she
shed tears, saying in her quaint way, in reference to the castle, it was a
" lucky hole."

In person, Sir James Colquhoun was stout and well made, and had a
very aristocratic appearance, preserving a military bearing from his early
training in the army. According to the fashion of his time, he wore a
powdered wig. In his old age he frequently walked from Rossdhu to the
foot of Shemore road, where there was a smithy. As a resting place, he
occasionally sat down on the smith's bench, and not unfrequently went
asleep. During his repose, the smith could not ply his hammer, as
it would have disturbed his master, and he had to wait till Sir James
awoke.

Sir James kept hounds for coursing hares, and in the season there was
always coursing over the Luss estate. This was the chief sport in which
Sir James latterly engaged.

In the days of double and heavily-constructed family carriages, Sir
James had always four horses with which to drive to Dumbarton, Helens

burgh, and even to the church of Luss on the Sundays, although the distance from Rossdhu was only three miles.

Sir James was much esteemed and honoured for his personal worth, and he exerted in many ways a salutary influence on the habits and manners of the parishioners of Luss, who are described at that time as being sober and industrious, humane and charitable. The late Dr. Stewart, minister of Luss, the eminent botanist, who knew him well, bears testimony to his high character. Speaking of the excellent modern house of Rossdhu, he says, " It was built by the late Sir James Colquhoun, who resided in the parish for many years, and the influence of whose authority and example in checking all tendency to disorder, and in promoting the interests of virtue and religion, is still sensibly felt, and his memory, therefore, much and justly respected." As a proof of his liberality, and of his attention to the spiritual well-being of the parishioners, it may be mentioned, that in 1771 he built the church of Luss, then represented as " uncommonly good," entirely at his own expense, laying no part of the burden upon the other heritors.[1]

Sir James died at his family seat of Rossdhu, on the 16th of November 1786, aged seventy-two years.[2]

Lady Helen Sutherland, Lady Colquhoun, survived Sir James only a few years, having died 7th January 1791, aged seventy-three years.[3]

The mortal remains of Sir James Colquhoun and Lady Helen Sutherland, his spouse, were interred in the family burying-place, the old Chapel of Rossdhu.

Lady Helen Sutherland was reserved but dignified in her manners, and much respected by the people in the neighbourhood of Rossdhu. As her portrait shews, she was handsome, slender in form, and very ladylike, and she was anxious about the carriage and appearance of her children. Besides the careful personal attention she devoted to her large family, she performed many of the duties of a notable housewife, as well as superintended some of the outdoor agricultural arrangements. In former times, and the custom

---

[1] First Statistical Account of Scotland, vol. xvii. pp. 263, 265.

[2] Luss Bible at Rossdhu, edit. 1663. Ex-

tracted from a Bible at Dunrobin Castle.—
Scots Magazine, vol. xlviii. p. 571.

[3] Luss Bible at Rossdhu, *ut supra*.

prevails to some extent even in the present day, the tenant-farmers paid rents to their landlords partly in kind, such as kane fowls, eggs, meal, or other farm produce. Lady Helen kept an iron ring for gauging the eggs, and if they went through the ring they were rejected as too small, and others of a larger size had to be substituted. She had also a marking-iron for marking sheep or cattle. An iron of this description, bearing the initials "L. H. S." (Lady Helen Sutherland), was found in 1830, on removing the foundations and *débris* of the old farm, stables, and offices, situated at no great distance from the mansion-house of Rossdhu, and it is preserved as a family relic. During the harvest season, each tenant and cottager on the Luss estate had to provide a certain number of reapers to cut their landlord's crops, the number varying according to the size of the farms or crofts, sometimes as many as 80 or 100 being assembled. Dinner was provided for them, consisting of oatmeal cakes or bannocks, cheese, and milk. This custom prevailed on the Luss estate till a very recent period, and it was of some advantage to the proprietor at a time when it was difficult to procure labourers. It was only put a stop to by the present proprietor, Sir James Colquhoun, on the introduction of reaping machines. Like the other ladies of the Colquhoun family, Lady Helen took an interest in these operations, and superintended them, the most of the reapers being the sons and daughters of the tenantry and cottagers on the estate.

Lady Helen Colquhoun was very particular in having the house kept in the neatest order, and everything properly arranged. A curious anecdote is told of this peculiar quality in her character. When Dr. Johnson made his celebrated tour to the Hebrides, he paid a visit to the Baronet of Luss at the Castle of Rossdhu. Having got himself drenched with water in some boating expedition on Lochlomond, he came into the drawing-room with the water splashing out of his boots. Lady Helen could no longer restrain her displeasure, muttering "What a bear!" "Yes," replied one of the company, "he is no doubt a bear, but it is Ursus Major."

Lady Strathnaver, mother of Lady Helen, latterly resided with her daughter at Rossdhu. The tradition of the district of Luss is that her Ladyship was rather haughty and imperious to those with whom she was connected. She was daughter of William Morrison of Prestongrange, in the county of Haddington. She died at Edinburgh, on 21st March 1765.[1]

Two papers, which Lady Helen Sutherland wrote with her own hand, relating to the legacies which she intended to leave to her children in the event of her death, may be here introduced. The first is a disposition, dated 5th December 1777, made in their favour, expressly setting forth her intentions on that subject. It is as follows :—

" I, Lady Helen Colquhoun *alias* Sutherland, spouse of Sir James Colquhoun of Luss, Baronet, for the love, favour, and affection which I have and bear to my children after named, do, by these presents, give, grant, and dispone to and in favour of the said Sir James Colquhoun and myself, in conjunct fee and life-rent for the said Sir James Colquhoun, his liferent use allenarly, the sum of £5000 sterling, due to me by Sir James Colquhoun and my eldest son James; and I order the said sum to be divided, at my death, in the following manner :—I leave to my eldest son James the sum of £500 sterling only, as the family have got already by me the sum of £3500, what was my portion ; as also to my second daughter, Janet, spouse to Colonel Campbell of Barbreck, the sum of £500 sterling, provided only if she has children by this or any other marriage, £250 sterling from her brother William, and £250 sterling from her brother Ludovick, and if she has no children, I only leave her £50 to buy mournings, to be paid her by her brother William : As also to my third daughter, Margaret, spouse to William Baillie of Polkemmet, advocate, the sum of £500 sterling : Also to my fourth daughter, Helen, spouse to William Colquhoun of Garscadden, the sum of £500 sterling, provided only she has children by this or any other marriage, £250 sterling by her brother William, £250 by her brother Ludovick, and if she has no children, I only leave her £50 to buy mournings, to be paid her by her brother William : Also to my fifth daughter, Jean, £500 sterling, if married and having children, and if unmarried, I leave the £500 sterling to my eldest son James, to pay her double interest for the above sum of £500 sterling until married ; and if she has no children, I leave the said £500 to my eldest son James : Also to my second son, William, the sum of £2000 sterling, with the burden of £50 sterling to buy mournings to both Janet and Helen : Also to my third son, Ludovick, the sum of £1500

---

[1] Lady Helen Sutherland—younger sister of William Lord Strathnaver, and aunt of Lady Helen Sutherland, Lady Colquhoun— died, unmarried, at Rossdhu, on 19th September 1749.

sterling: All which make the sum of £5000 sterling. And in case I succeed, by the death of any of my relations, to any lands or sums of money, particularly the lands of Assint, or others, I leave and bequeath them to any of my sons that represent the family of Luss; and failing all of my sons and their sons, to my daughters, equally among them that have children, always declaring that I reserve the liferent of all to myself and my said husband, whichever of us is the longest liver; and also order, that in case my second son, William, dies before me, having no children, that Ludovick shall succeed to his money, he having no children: And also that in case my third son, Ludovick, dies before William, that William shall succeed to his money, if he has no children. And I hereby reserve full power to myself to revoke or alter these presents, in whole or in part, any time in my life, and declare the same a valid evident to my said children, albeit it be found lying by me at the time of my death. And I consent to the registration hereof in the Books of Council and Session, or other Judges books competent, therein to remain for preservation, and thereto constitute my procurators. In witness whereof I have subscribed these presents, wrote upon this and the two preceding pages of stamped paper, by myself, at Rosedochouse, the 5th day of December 1777, before these witnesses, Robert Colquhoun and James M'Millan, both my servants.

Robert Colquhoun, witness.[1]                HELEN COLQUHOUN.
James M'Millan, witness.[2]

The other paper is what she calls "a codicil to my former disposition, dated the 5th day of December 1777." It was written towards the close of the year 1790, only about two months before her death, when she was probably anticipating that event, and is as follows:—

I, Lady Helen Colquhoun, widow of the deceased Sir James Colquhoun of Luss, Baronet, having, on the 5th day of December 1777 years, made a deed and disposition, reserving full power to myself any time in my life to revock or alter the whole or any part of it, and also make over to my eldest son, Sir James, the estate of Assint, if I should succeed thereto,—I have since that period acquired certain sums, which for the love and favour I bear my children herein named, for which purpose I dispone and make over to my second son,

[1] This witness, Robert Colquhoun, who was formerly gamekeeper, and afterwards deer-forester in Inch Lonach, died in that island, where he was born, nearly a century before, in May 1843, in the ninety-second year of his age.

[2] Copy Disposition at Rossdhu.

William Colquhoun, of the Guards, all the different sums, heretable or moveable, which I have or may have at the time of my death, and to any claim I have to the estate of        Morrison, Esq., my uncle-in-law,[1] with full power to him to uplift or discharge all sums due to me, and recover whatever I may claim or have right to, and to do every other thing, as any executor, administrator, or assignee and residuary legatee, with full power to him to uplift or discharge all sums due to me, and recover whatever I may have claim or have right to, and to do every other thing as any other executor, administrator, or assignee and residuary legatee, with the following burdens :—In the first place, to pay my funeral charges in a decent way and manner, and to pay Major Ludovick Col-quhoun, my third son, the sum of hunder pounds, and to Jane, my fifth daughter, the sum of five hunder pounds, and to Ketherine M'Kenzie, my eldest daughter, four hund. ; to Helen M'Kenzie, my name daughter, a hunder pounds each ; to Sutherland and Helen, my grandchildren, Sir James's children, five [hund]er, and to Helen Baillie, my name daughter, a hunder ; and for the regard I bear the following persons, I leave them the following sums to buy mournings, first to Mrs. Colquhoun, Barnhill, ten pounds ; the Revd. Mr. John Robertson, at Dumblane, £10 sterling ; to Helen, his sister, ten ; and to the Rev. Mr. Drummond, at Roseneath, the sum of ten pounds each, to buy mournings ; and to Agnes Campbell, my own maid servant, if she is living with me at my death, the sum of ten pounds sterling to buy mournings.    This is my meaning and in-tention ; perhaps it may not be form or law, but it is to be considered as my own act and deed as much so as if a delivered deed or settlement.    This is my codicil to my former disposition ; and I consent to the registration hereof in whatever books is necessary, and therefore constitute and appoint my son William Colquhoun            my procurators, etc.    In witness whereof I have both written and subscribed these presents at Rosedoe House, the twenty-third day of November 1790 years, before these witnesses,

                                                        HELEN COLQUHOUN.

William M'Gregor, *witness.*
Robert Colquhoun, *witness.*
Thomas M'Kay.[2]

Sir James Colquhoun, eighth Baronet of Luss, had by Lady Helen Sutherland three sons and six daughters.    The sons were—

1. James, the eldest, who succeeded his father.

---

[1] Lady Strathnaver, mother of Lady Helen Sutherland, was a Morrison of Prestongrange.
[2] Copy Codicil to Disposition at Rossdhu.

2. William, who was born on the 20th of January 1750. Having made choice of the military profession, he entered the army at an early period of life. He was promoted by purchase, on 2d March 1772, to be Ensign in the 36th Regiment of Foot.[1] On 3d August 1773 he was transferred from the 36th Regiment of Foot to the 1st Regiment of Foot Guards, in which he also held the rank of Ensign.[2] On 12th March 1776 he was appointed quarter-master in the same regiment.[3] On 18th March 1782 he was made Captain-Lieutenant in that regiment, then commanded by His Royal Highness William Duke of Gloucester, General of the Forces, and brother of King George the Third. On the 16th of May following Captain Colquhoun was advanced to be captain of a company.[4] He was afterwards a colonel of the First Regiment of Guards, and he died at London in March 1803.[5] By his marriage with Elizabeth Hillersdon, a lady who was descended from an ancient family in England, he had one child, William James Hillersdon Colquhoun, who died at Elstow, in the county of Bedford, on 22d September 1861, unmarried.

3. Ludovic, who was born 25th July 1757, and was baptized on the following day. Like his brother William, he entered the army.[6] On the 14th of May 1776 he was promoted to the rank of Lieutenant of the 2d battalion of the 71st Regiment of Foot.[7] On 9th May 1778 he was appointed Captain of that regiment.[8] On 11th November 1783 he was transferred from the 74th Regiment of Foot to the 4th battalion of the 60th Foot, in which he was raised to the rank of Major.[9] He was afterwards Lieutenant-Colonel Colquhoun. When residing at Ross Lodge, in the parish of Luss, Colonel Colquhoun married Barbara Camilla, daughter of the Reverend Doctor Joseph Macintyre, minister of the parish of Glenorchy, in the county of Argyll. The proclamation of their marriage was

[1] Scots Magazine, vol. xxxiv. p. 167.
[2] Ibid. vol. xxxv. p. 447.
[3] Ibid. vol. xxxviii. p. 166.
[4] Ibid. vol. xliv. pp. 224, 391.
[5] Ibid. vol. lxv. p. 220.
[6] Scots Magazine, vol. xii. p. 54.
[7] Ibid. vol. xxxviii. p. 342.
[8] Ibid. vol. xlv. p. 279.
[9] Ibid. vol. xlv. p. 616.

made in the church of Luss on 19th December 1801.[1]    Lieutenant-
Colonel Ludovic Colquhoun served for several years in America,
during the first American war, under Sir Henry Clinton.    He held
the office of *His Majesty's Falconer for Scotland.*  The Colonel died
at Edinburgh, on 5th January 1835.    Of this marriage there were
six sons and one daughter :—

1. James Andrew, now of No. 26 Broughton Place, Edinburgh, who
   was born on 1st October 1803.  He married, first, Elizabeth,
   daughter of the Rev. Dr. Traill, minister of Panbride, county
   of Forfar, and had one son, James Traill Colquhoun, who died
   on 6th April 1835, eight days after his birth.  He married,
   secondly, on 10th October 1838, Sophia, daughter of William
   Cantis, Esq., late of Old Park, Kent, by whom he has a son,
   Ludovic, who was born on 29th July 1842, and resides in Edinburgh, and a daughter, still-born.

2. Joseph William, who was born on 3d March 1805, and entered
   the military service of the East India Company, in India, in
   which he held the rank of Lieutenant at the time of his death,
   which occurred on 6th July 1827, unmarried.

3. Ludovic, who was born on 18th May 1807, was an Advocate at
   the Scottish Bar, and latterly held the office of Secretary to the
   Prison Board for Scotland.    He died at Edinburgh on 29th
   June 1854, unmarried.

4. Sutherland Grant, who was born on 25th November 1809, and
   died on 4th January 1832, unmarried.

5. Archibald Campbell, who was born on 27th March 1811, went to
   the West Indies, where he married, and had issue, a son, Ludovic.
   Archibald Campbell Colquhoun died about the year 1842.

6. Ebenezer Marshall Gardiner, born at Glenorchy Manse on 22d
   April 1815, now of Glasgow, unmarried.

7. Helen Sutherland, the only daughter of Colonel Ludovic Colquhoun, born at Belleville, Edinburgh, 12th December 1812,
   married, on 30th April 1837, Dugald, son of John Campbell of
   Achurossan, who in 1840 succeeded his uncle, Captain John
   Campbell of Drimnamuckloch and Carse, in the county of Argyll,
   and has issue three sons and three daughters.    Dugald Campbell

---

[1] Luss Parish Records.

died on 19th March 1852, and was succeeded by his eldest son, John Breadalbane Campbell. The youngest son, Dugald, died on 17th November 1863 of fever, on board the "Ontario," off Cuba.

The six daughters of Sir James Colquhoun and Lady Helen Sutherland were—

1. Katharine, the eldest, who was born 6th September 1742, and was baptized 6th November 1742.[1] She married Sir Roderick Mackenzie, Baronet, of Scatwell, in the county of Ross, by whom she had two sons and two daughters. She died on 11th March 1804, aged sixty-one years.[2]

2. Anne Sutherland Colquhoun, who was born 26th December 1746, and who died on the 9th of April 1748.

3. Janet, who was born 7th April 1748, and was baptized on the 18th of the same month.[3] She married at Rossdhu, on the 5th of March 1766, General John Campbell of Barbreck, in the county of Argyll. They had one son, Archibald, who died in childhood. General Campbell was uncle of Mr. Campbell of Lochnell. He predeceased his wife, who died at Edinburgh on 7th July 1806.[4]

4. Margaret, who was born 1st March 1751, and was baptized on the same day.[5] She married at Edinburgh, on 3d December 1768,[6] William Baillie, younger of Polkemmet, afterwards a Lord of Session, under the title of Lord Polkemmet. By him she had a large family, of whom the eldest was Sir William Baillie, Baronet. She predeceased her husband, and after her death he married Miss Janet Sinclair, a sister of Sir John Sinclair, Baronet, and cousin-german to his first wife; but by her he had no children.[7] He died in March 1816. His death is thus recorded by Lady Colquhoun, in her Diary:—"March

---

[1] Register of Baptisms in the Parish of Luss.

[2] Luss Bible at Rossdhu, Edition 1663, on blank leaf between the Old and New Testaments, written by her brother, Sir James Colquhoun, Clerk of the Court of Session.

[3] Register of Baptisms in the Parish of Luss.

[4] Scots Magazine, vol. xxviii. p. 222.

[5] Register of Baptisms in the Parish of Luss.

[6] Scots Magazine, vol. xxx. p. 613.

[7] Kay's Original Portraits, vol. ii. p. 217.

17, [1816.]--Another striking event among our connexions happened last week, in the sudden death of Lord Polkemmet. He had been long complaining, but was much in his usual way when he dropped down and expired." [1]

5. Helen, who was born 11th February, N.S., 1753. She married William Colquhoun of Garscadden, in the county of Dumbarton. Their names were given up for proclamation 25th December 1773, and the marriage was celebrated at Rossdhu on the 6th of January 1774.[2] She died, without issue, 27th May 1834.

6. Jane, who was born 18th January 1761, and was baptized on the day following.[3] In her mother's settlement, dated at Rossdhu, 23d November 1790, she is provided to a legacy of £500. She married Ebenezer Marshall Gardiner of Hillcairney, in the county of Fife. They had two sons and one daughter. The eldest son was Thomas Marshall Gardiner, who died, unmarried, on 17th November 1864, and the younger, James, who died in infancy. Their sister Helen married Mr. Scott, a writer in Edinburgh, but had no issue.

The dates of the births of the children of Sir James and Lady Helen Colquhoun are taken from a Bible at Rossdhu, edition 1663, the entries in which were extracted from a Bible at Dunrobin Castle.

[1] The Rev. Dr. James Hamilton's Life of Lady Colquhoun, p. 49.
[2] Luss Register of Marriages ; also Scots Magazine, vol. xxxvi. p. 54.
[3] Luss Parish Register of Baptisms.

Sir

Rosdoe House Jan.r 5.th
1745

I Received yours this moment; we had
an alarm last night that the Macgregors had
Crossed Lochlomond and were at Inverbeg, but the
thing turned out to be intirely groundless, otherwa,
ys you may deppend upon it I had been all Dum,
barton Castle Ere now; I verey much approve
of General Campbelles orders to Secure all the
Boat's & for an Exemple to all the Countrey I
sent to Dumbarton some days ago, two of ours
I can Command as mane Men as the Generall
Can need for the above purposs but for Armes
thay have next to none.; I shall derectly
gave orders to our folkes to gave all the assis
tance thay can to your party, I shall make
the Commanding Officer verey wellcom hear
& I am

P S
please See that
Mr Colquhouns trunk
that Came with Generall
Campbells be in the Castle.

Your Humble Servant Sir

385

## XX.—Sir JAMES COLQUHOUN, Twenty-fourth of Colqu- houn, and Twenty-sixth of Luss, Second British Baronet, 1786-1805.

Mary Falconer of Monktown, Lady Colquhoun, 1773-1833.

Sir James Colquhoun of Luss, second British Baronet, was born on 28th July 1741.[1] He received a liberal education, and having made choice of the law as a profession, he was admitted a member of the Faculty of Advocates, at Edinburgh, in the year 1765.

Out of compliment to the Colquhoun family, the young Laird of Luss was, on 16th December 1763, admitted a burgess and guild brother of the City of Glasgow, in presence of the Lord Provost and Magistrates.[2]

When he had nearly completed the thirty-second year of his age, he married, at Edinburgh, on 22d July 1773, Mary, younger daughter and co-heiress of James Falconer of Monktown, in the parish of Inveresk and county of Edinburgh, and of Miltonhaven and Laurieston in the county of Kincardine. The contract of marriage between Mr. Colquhoun and Miss Falconer is dated at Edinburgh, 12th July 1773.[3] She was then about sixteen years of age. Sir James Colquhoun's town-house in Edinburgh was the large mansion now occupied as the Douglas Hotel, on the east side of St. Andrew Square, the only square at that time in the new town of Edinburgh. He was the first owner of the house, which was then newly built.

[1] Luss Bible at Rossdhu. Scots Magazine, vol. iii. p. 331.
[2] Burgess Ticket at Rossdhu.
[3] Scots Magazine, vol. xxxv. p. 390. As some obscurity exists as to this branch of the Falconer family, it may here be noted that Mr. Falconer of Monktown, the father of Lady Colquhoun, was son of Patrick Falconer, who was son of Sir James Falconer, a Lord of Session, as Lord Phesdo, and

Dame Elizabeth Trent, his spouse. Lord Phesdo was a son of Sir John Falconer, Master of the Mint to King Charles the Second. Sir John was a younger brother of the first Lord Falconer of Haulkerton. The mother of Lady Colquhoun was also of the same family as her father, being the Hon- ourable Jean Falconer, eldest daughter of David Lord Falconer of Haulkerton.— [Monktown Papers at Rossdhu.]

3 C

Mr. Colquhoun, before succeeding to the baronetcy, was made Sheriff-depute of Dumbartonshire, in the end of the year 1775, in room of James Smollett of Bonhill.[1] In the year 1779, he was also appointed by his Majesty George the Third, one of the six principal Clerks of Session in Scotland, in the room of Mr. Thomas Gibson, deceased.[2] Sir James held both these offices, but resigned the latter shortly before his death.

In the year 1774, during his father's lifetime, Mr. Colquhoun purchased from John Macfarlane, son of Robert Macfarlane, in Meikle Drumfad, for £450, the half of the 40s. land of old extent of Meikle Kilbryde, in Glenfruin, that piece of land called the Chapel of Glenfruin, and the Acre, called Mackenzie's Acre, and those parts called Laggachapel being excepted; the one merk land of old extent of Blairvryan, also in Glenfruin, with the fishings, all in the parish of Row. In the same year Mr. Colquhoun also purchased from Peter MacAdam, saddler in Glasgow, price not known, the lands of Garelochhead, with the teinds, in the same parish. In the year 1780, he purchased from Allan Bogle, merchant in Glasgow, and his spouse, Mrs. Janet Glen or Bogle, only child of the deceased James Glen of Portincaple, for £3000, the 40s. land of Durling, which is situated at the entrance to Glenfruin, near the chapel, in the parish of Row, formerly in the parish of Cardross; the half of the 40s. land of Meikle Kilbryde; the two merk land of old extent of Portincaple, on Loch Long, with the fishings and ferryboat of Portincaple; the two merk land of old extent of Feorlinbreck, all in the parish of Row, reserving to Sir James Colquhoun the mill of Feorlinbreck, and excepting the poffle of land called the Chapel of Glenfruin, Mackenzie's Acre, and those parts of the lands disponed by James Glen of Portincaple to the Presbytery of Dumbarton, on 13th May 1755, for the purpose of endowing a school in Glenfruin, in the parish of Row, the right to nominate the schoolmasters being vested in Sir James Colquhoun of Luss, Bart., and his heirs, Walter M'Farlane of M'Farlane, and the heirs succeeding to him in the estate of Arrochar, and Mr. John Allan, minister of Row, and his successors in office.

In the year 1785, whilst his father was still living, some transactions took place between Mr. Colquhoun, younger of Luss, and Robert Colquhoun

[1] Scots Magazine, vol. xxxvii. p. 696.          [2] Scots Magazine, vol. xli. p. 222.

of Camstradden, in reference to the purchase of the estate of Camstradden by the former. The latter was desirous to sell part of that estate, or the whole, in order to make up the provision which he had destined for his daughters at his death. Mr. Colquhoun, younger of Luss, intending to purchase from him some of his lands, or even the whole, had offered, for three crofts on the north side of the Water of Luss, £1000, provided another small possession at Luss was added. This other croft Mr. Colquhoun of Camstradden, however, declined to add; and in a letter to James Dennistoun of Colgrain, he desired him to inform the Sheriff (Mr. Colquhoun) of his intentions on the subject :—

MY DEAR SIR,—Your letter of the 25th instant came in course. In answer to which, please know that when Mr. Rouet was last here our conversation turned upon the sale and value of lands, etc., and particularly upon ane offer the Sheriff had made me some time agoe, for three maillings of mine upon the north side of the Water of Luss, of £1000, provideing I threw into the bargain the possession of Alexander M'Naughtan at Luss. I told Mr. Rouet that I could well conceive the advantages that would accrue to the family of Luss from the first three maillings, but there could be none from Alexander M'Naughtan's, and that while I retained a single acre of property, I would never part with that, which I had positively told the Sherriff of at our last communeing on that subject ; but that Mr. Rouet (if he pleased) might tell the Sherriff, that when he should frankly offer me the £1000 for the first three maillings, I would then resume a conversation with him on the subject ; or if he offerred me the price given John Craufurd for Inverlaran for all my property (which surely in proportion is deserving of as good a price), even for that I would treat with him.

It surprises me how the Sherriff comes to believe and say that the rent of the first three maillings is only £25, and that there is a chance of their falling. Strange ! that they should fall, and all the lands in the neighbourhood riseing to near double. The reverse is the truth ; for there has been a small rise upon these maillings since his offer ; and were I to live but few years, I would expect a large rise in proportion to their rent.

In short, the Sherriff's ideas and mine are so very different with respect to the value and purchase of land, that I am convinced we shall never settle a point of that kind, great or small. As to my makeing a demand for the whole of my property, he must excuse me. Without I am tempted with a better price than I think he will give, I have resolved to keep my small estate, if I can.

When I determine myself otherwise, he will know by publick intimation; for I am more and more confirmed in opinion that a public sale is the best; and when that does happen, I hope he, and some Nabob who will cast up, will lend a good lift. These particulars I beg you'll take the trouble to inform the Sherriff of. In hopes of seeing you here soon, according to promise, I ever am, my dear Sir,

Your very affectionate and much obliged servant,

Cam., 28th January 1785.                                        RO. COLQUHOUN.

James Dennistoun, Esq., Junior, of Colgrain.[1]

Mr. Colquhoun, younger of Luss, then offered to Mr. Colquhoun of Camstradden, for the three crofts, a sum equivalent to twenty-five years' purchase. This offer the Laird of Camstradden declined to accept in the following letter :—

DEAR SIR,—The offer you made me last night in your card, for my mail-lings of Cullichippan, Toir, and Tomglass, amounts, according to calculation, to 25 years' purchase of the present rent, without anything like payment for my woods and standing timber. This I cannot think of accepting, as my family and friends might very reasonably reflect on me for selling lower than any lands whatever (that I know of) have been sold in any part of the county of Dunbartane for 40 years back; and why these lands should be the lowest, I cannot figure to myself.

One, and, indeed, my principal view of selling at present, was to find part of the price to answer demands which my daughters might have at, or after, my death, for part of the provisions I destined for them; and if I cannot get ane adequate price for these lands in my lifetime, they must take their chance, and I must keep the subject.

That you and your family may long enjoy happiness and prosperity is my sincere wish. I offer my very respectfull compliments to all the family at Rose-doe House; and wishing particularly to know how Sir James and Lady Helen are, I am, dear Sir,

Your most obedient and most humble servant,

Cam., 3d May 1785.                                        RO. COLQUHOUN.

James Colquhoun, Esq. of Luss.[2]

Sir James Colquhoun was in the forty-fifth year of his age when, in 1786, he succeeded his father in the title of Baronet, and in the lands and barony of Luss. He was served heir-male of taillie and provision to his

---

[1] Original Letter at Rossdhu.                    [2] Original Letter at Rossdhu.

father in the lands and barony of Luss, etc., on the 16th of August 1787, and heir in general to him on the 24th of September following.[1]

On the 29th of October 1787 he was infefted in those parts of the barony of Luss that were held of the Prince, and on the same day in the lands of Ardochbeg, which were held of the Crown.[2]

Sir James Colquhoun claimed the patronage of the parish of Cardross in opposition to the Crown. He contested this right in 1790. In that year Mr. Alexander Macaulay was presented by the Crown and Mr. Abraham Forrest, who had been tutor to Sir James Colquhoun's sons, was presented by Sir James. After a litigation in the Court of Session, it was decided that the patronage of that parish belonged to the Crown, and Mr. Macaulay's presentation was accordingly preferred. In reference to this claim by Sir James Colquhoun, it may be stated that the patronage of the church and parish of Cardross formerly belonged to the Colquhoun family, but the father of Sir James Colquhoun having failed to issue presentations when vacancies occurred within the prescribed period, the right of patronage of this parish was thus lost, and lapsed to the Crown.

On the 26th of September 1794, Sir James made a disposition and assignation to himself in liferent, and to his eldest son, James, and the heirs-male of his body in fee, of part of the lands and barony of Luss, and they were infefted therein on the same day.[3]

Sir James Colquhoun was a friend and correspondent of the famous Horace Walpole, who, in early life, was successively a Member of Parliament for Callington, in Cornwall, Castle Rising, and King's Lynn, but who, in 1786, retired from public life, and occupied himself in the improvement of his villa, called Strawberry Hill, near Twickenham. Walpole, whose "Castle of Otranto," "Catalogue of Royal and Noble Authors," and Papers in the "World," gained him celebrity, presented to Sir James Colquhoun of Luss a copy of some of his works. Gratified with this token of friendship, Sir James, who admired his literary abilities, sent to him the present of a beautiful goat's horn snuff-box, bearing the following inscription on the

[1] Extract Retours of Special and General Service at Rossdhu.

[2] Original Instrument of Sasine, ibid.

[3] Original Disposition and Instrument of Sasine at Rossdhu.

silver plate round the brim :—" This trifle, given by Sir James Colquhoun of Luss, Bart., to the Honourable Horace Walpole, as a mark of respect." Below is a silver plate, on which are engraved the armorial bearings of Mr. Walpole.[1]    Walpole acknowledged the gift in the following letter :—

Berkeley Square, March 31, 1791.

SIR,—I yesterday received the beautiful goat's horn, which you have been so good as to send me, with the inscription with which you have been pleased to overhonour me.    Indeed, Sir, I am ashamed that you should think that such a trifle as any writing of mine, that was of no value to me, should deserve so curious a reward.    The horn is a great rarity, and will be doubly valuable to me from the donor.    I shall preserve it in my little collection, with great care ; and have the honour of being, with the utmost gratitude and respect, Sir,

Your most obedient and most obliged humble servant,

HOR. WALPOLE.[2]

[Address wanting.]

Horace Walpole, in 1791, the year in which the preceding letter was written, succeeded his nephew as Earl of Orford.    In the year 1796, Sir James Colquhoun sent to him a present of two books and two engravings. This gift the Earl of Orford, who was now about seventy-nine years old, and suffering from the infirmities of age, acknowledged in the following note :—

Berkeley Square, May 3, 1796.

LORD ORFORD should be ashamed of not having sooner acknowledged the agreeable present of two books and two engravings from Sir James Colquhoun if he had not been dangerously ill, in consequence of a long fit of the gout, which fell upon one of his legs and produced an abscess, for which he is still under the surgeon's hands, and which has reduced him to a state of extreme weakness, and he hopes will apologise for thanking Sir James so superficially at present.

To Sir James Colquhoun,

In St. Andrew's Square, Edinburgh.[3]

[1] This horn returned to Rossdhu.    It was purchased at the sale of the Honourable Horace Walpole's effects, at Strawberry Hill, in 1842, by a London dealer in curiosities and antique relics, and the present Sir James Colquhoun being informed of this by a friend who had seen it in the shop, purchased it, and it is now in his possession.

At the time when this present was made, there were goats in Inchlonaig with horns of a very large size, as well as deer, and the horn was probably one of these goats' horns.

[2] Bound up in a volume of curious Tracts, in the possession of Sir James Colquhoun.

[3] Ibid.

Sympathizing with Lord Orford under his sufferings, Sir James gave expression, in a letter to him, to his feelings of sympathy, and to his anxious desire to be particularly informed concerning the state of his health. Lord Orford was now so infirm that it was necessary for him to employ the hand of another in writing the following answer:—

Berkeley Square, June 20th, 1796.

I am infinitely obliged to you, Sir, for your very kind enquiries after a poor old cripple, who is the more unfortunate at not being able to thank you with his own hand.

I have been laid up for four months by a severe fit of the gout, and it was scarce going off when the venom fell on one of my legs, and produced two very dangerous abscesses, yet the two closed in nine weeks, and I am assured that I am getting well, though at near seventy-nine. I am not so weak as to expect more than a partial recovery for some short time. During such a period, if it does happen, I shall not forget how very kind you have been, Sir, to one, who has the honour to be, with great respect and gratitude,

Your most obliged and obedient humble servant,

ORFORD.

To Sir James Colquhoun, at Edinburgh.[1]

The Earl of Orford died on the 2d of March 1797.

Having resigned the lands and estate of Milligs and others, Sir James Colquhoun obtained a charter of novodamus erecting them into a barony, to be called the barony of Milligs, and at the same time erecting the town of Helensburgh into a burgh of barony.[2] Upon his resignation of the barony of Milligs, he obtained a charter of that barony on the 5th of July 1806.[3]

After he had succeeded his father, he purchased, in 1801, from John Campbell of Auchenvenalmoulin, son of the deceased Jean Macwalter, daughter of the deceased Parlane Macwalter, price not known, one-third part of the lands of Auchvenalmoulin, near Auchenvenal, in Glenfruin, extending to a five merk land of old extent, with the teinds, in the parish of Row.

In the year 1802, Sir James purchased the lands of Laigh or Little Kilbryde, for £1800, from the Commissioners of John Innes Crawford of

[1] Bound up in a volume of curious Tracts, in the possession of Sir James Colquhoun.
[2] Copy Charter at Rossdhu.
[3] Extract Charter, ibid.

Bellfield, in the island of Jamaica, who had shortly before succeeded as nearest heir of his grandfather, Charles Crawford, in these lands. A disposition of them was made to Sir James 23d November that year; and he was infefted in them on the 11th of January 1803.[1]

Sir James Colquhoun made a large collection of paintings, landscapes, engravings, etc., and the rooms at Rossdhu still contain some fine specimens of the taste and discrimination displayed by Sir James in his patronage of this branch of the fine arts. He also collected many ancient coins, and other articles of antiquity, for which he had a very considerable taste, and in the acquisition of which he spent much time and money. His collection of rare old china was also very superior, and the Chinese having now lost the art of making it, this renders it the more valuable.

Sir James died at Edinburgh, on the 23d of April 1805,[2] in the sixty-fourth year of his age, and his mortal remains were interred beside those of his ancestors in the ancient chapel of Rossdhu.

By all who knew him, this baronet was loved and respected as a man of a generous, kind, and benevolent character. He was educated as a Presbyterian in religion, and he adhered to that system throughout life. He took a warm interest in the Society for the Propagation of Christian Knowledge, and was a member of the Board of Directors for about ten years. He was most punctual in his attendance at the meetings of the Board for the transaction of the business of the Society. Sir James was for some time one of the Vice-presidents of the Society of Antiquaries when the Duke of Montrose was the President.

As a landlord, Sir James was very indulgent to his tenantry. When the leases of his farms had expired, he generally renewed them to the former tenants, and he was averse to the system of high or rack-renting. So considerate was he in his transactions with his tenantry, that if on trial it was found that any tenant had undertaken to pay too much rent, not only was he readily disposed to modify the rent, but he seemed to be as uneasy as the tenant himself until it was properly adjusted.

After Sir James's death, his house in St. Andrew Square was sold to

---

[1] Extract Registered Disposition and Instrument of Sasine at Rossdhu.
[2] Scots Magazine, vol. lxvii. p. 327.

Mr. Dumbreck, hotel-keeper, who sold it to Mr. Douglas, by whom it was converted into a first-class hotel, and patronized by the most distinguished visitors to Edinburgh. It is now The Douglas Hotel.

Lady Colquhoun survived her husband for twenty-eight years. After the death of her husband Lady Colquhoun resided for some time at St. John's Hill, Edinburgh. She died at Annfield House, in the parish of Kettle, Fifeshire, where she resided for many years, on 12th of April 1833.

Of the marriage of Sir James and Lady Colquhoun there were seven sons and four daughters.

The sons were—

1. James, who succeeded his father.
2. William, who died in infancy.
3. Patrick, who became an advocate at the Scottish Bar, and died unmarried, aged about twenty-three years. His death occurred before 25th November 1803, as appears from its being alluded to in a letter from his mother of that date.
4. Ludovic, who died in infancy.
5. John Campbell, of whom a notice is given at the end of the present Memoir of his father.
6. Sutherland Morrison, who entered the Royal Navy, in which he became a captain. He caught the yellow fever at Jamaica, where his ship was at the time stationed, and died there in February 1827, unmarried.
7. Roderick, who also entered the Royal Navy, and afterwards engaged in the service of the Honourable the East India Company. He died unmarried, at Edinburgh, in 1834, and was buried in the Greyfriars Churchyard there.

The four daughters were—

1. Jane Falconer, who married, at Edinburgh, on 8th of September 1803,[1] David Kemp of Balsusney Lodge, in the county of Fife. They had three sons and eight daughters.
2. Helen Sutherland, now of No. 10 Melville Street, Edinburgh.

[1] Scots Magazine, vol. lxv. p. 737.

3. Wilhelmina, who married, at Rossdhu, on 15th July 1808, John Campbell of Stonefield, in the county of Argyll, and had issue two sons and three daughters. The eldest son, Colin George Campbell, is now of Stonefield, and the younger son, James Colquhoun Campbell, is the present Lord Bishop of Bangor. Mrs. Campbell died at Pau, on 22d December 1833. The event is thus noted by Lady Colquhoun in her Diary: "Jan. 12, 1834.—Have heard of the death of my dear Christian sister-in-law, Mrs. Campbell of Stonefield. She died at Pau, full of peace and hope. She will be an irreparable loss to her family, and a real loss to me."[1]

4. Catharine Falconer, who married, on 25th July 1815, Alexander Millar of Earnock, in the county of Lanark, and of Dalnair,[2] in the county of Stirling, but had no issue. He predeceased his wife, who survived him several years, and died at Edinburgh, on 22d November 1862, and was buried in the Canongate Churchyard there. Her nephew, the Right Reverend James Colquhoun Campbell, Lord Bishop of Bangor, was her executor.

[1] Dr. Hamilton's Memoir of Lady Colquhoun, p. 173.
[2] Register of Marriages for Luss Parish.

# JOHN CAMPBELL COLQUHOUN, Advocate, Sheriff of Dumbartonshire, Fifth Son of Sir James Colquhoun of Luss, Second British Baronet.

John Campbell Colquhoun was born at Edinburgh, on 31st January 1785;[1] and he was named after General John Campbell of Barbreck, the husband of his aunt Janet. He made choice of the profession of law, and, having passed through a course of studies with that object, went to Germany, where he might be more fully equipped for his profession. At the University of Göttingen he studied Roman Law under the celebrated jurists Waldeck and Hugo. During his residence in Germany, while attentive to his legal studies, he assiduously applied himself to the cultivation of metaphysics and literature in general. He there became acquainted with Herbart, a young man of high promise, who, as a lecturer, was then commencing his illustrious philosophical career, and who afterwards successively adorned the Universities of Königsberg and Göttingen. He also formed an intimate friendship with Ludwig, then the Crown-Prince of Bavaria, who was a fellow-student in the University of Göttingen. Having remained in Hanover several years, during which he acquired a complete command of the German language, and an extensive knowledge of German literature, he returned to Scotland, and became an advocate at the Scottish Bar in the year 1806. Much of his time was, however, devoted to literary pursuits, and he was the author of several important articles in different literary works. But the subject to which he seems to have been specially partial was the investigation of what has been called animal magnetism. This predominant taste he had acquired in Germany, where many philosophical and literary inquirers were strongly attracted to this curious and mysterious science. When the French Academy of Medicine, after diversified experiments and observations, formally pronounced in favour of the science, Mr. Colquhoun translated into English the Report of the Academy, with numerous additions of his own, such as his extensive knowledge of the subject enabled him to supply. This work he afterwards enlarged, and

---

[1] Scots Magazine, vol. xlvii. p. 51.

published, in two volumes, under the title of "Isis Revelata." In the second edition he enlarged still more on his favourite subject, and the work in that extended form exhibits the most ample collection of facts and testimonies on the subject to be found in our language. " The principles established in the ' Isis,' " says Sir William Hamilton, " enabled Mr. Colquhoun also to explain by natural causes the facts of *magic* and *witchcraft*,—facts which he expounded in a most entertaining and instructive history."

Mr. Colquhoun was long the intimate friend of Sir William Hamilton, Professor of Logic and Metaphysics in the University of Edinburgh. Their community of study and, generally, of sentiment on the subjects now referred to, contributed to foster the constant and affectionate intimacy which subsisted between them. Sir William, while opposed to phrenology, was much interested in animal magnetism, and disposed apparently to believe in the more general facts on which it is founded,—at least to regard them as matter for careful scientific investigation. To one who was indisposed to accept the apparent phenomena of mesmerism, he remarked, " Before you set aside the science of the mesmerist, you ought to read the evidence in its favour, given by all the greatest medical authorities in Germany." " Sir William had no doubt," says a friend, " of the power of mesmerism in nervous temperaments to produce sleep and other cognate phenomena; but he utterly disbelieved *clairvoyance*, and when Mr. Colquhoun used to bring forward instances to that effect, he would remind him of the story of the £1000 bank-note, which had been lying sealed up for years, ready to be delivered to any *clairvoyant* who, without opening the envelope, could read its contents."

Sir William Hamilton had frequent experiments at his house in mesmerism, along with his friend Mr. Colquhoun.

An extract from the Reminiscences of a Literary Veteran, published in 1851, throws light on Mr. Colquhoun's habits, as well as on those of his friend Sir William Hamilton. " Among impressions of this epoch (1823-1825) few are more pleasant in retrospection than those of long pedestrian excursions in company with two near neighbours, numbered still among the few surviving friends who have not changed their conduct towards me during the chance and change to which I have been subjected,—I mean

Sir William Hamilton and Mr. J. C. Colquhoun. Dissimilar as were the members of this *petit comité*, there was at all events one point on which we quite agreed, namely, in a hearty liking for long walks out of town, reckless whether the season was that of wintry storms or summer sunshine. Numberless were the subjects broached in these rambles, and numberless as the changes in Dr. Brewster's kaleidoscope the lights and shades which they assumed under our desultory discussions." [1]

As Mr. Colquhoun resided in the immediate neighbourhood of Manor Place, where Sir William Hamilton resided, he was much with him, and a walk together on Sunday afternoons was their regular practice for many years. [2]

Mr. Colquhoun was one of a small club that was formed for procuring and circulating German periodicals. Sir William Hamilton and Dr., afterwards Sir David, Brewster, were also members of this club. [3]

In 1815, Mr. Colquhoun was appointed Sheriff-depute of the shire of Dumbarton, and he continued to discharge with fidelity the duties of that office for more than forty years. In consequence of failing health he resigned that office only a few months before his death. He died at Edinburgh, on 21st August 1854, unmarried, in the sixty-ninth year of his age, and his remains were interred in the Dean Cemetery, Edinburgh. Sir William Hamilton wrote an obituary notice of Mr. Colquhoun, which appeared in the Edinburgh Courant 31st August 1854. It was probably written by Sir William at Cordale, on the banks of the Leven, Dumbartonshire, where he resided from June to September that year, for the benefit of his health.

[1] "Memoirs of a Literary Veteran," published by Gillies, quoted in Memoir of Sir William Hamilton, Baronet, by John Veitch, M.A., Professor of Logic and Rhetoric in the University of Glasgow. Edinburgh and London, 1869, pp. 117, 118.

[2] *Ibid.* p. 140.

[3] *Ibid.* p. 92.

## XXI.—Sir JAMES COLQUHOUN, Twenty-fifth of Colquhoun and Twenty-seventh of Luss, Third British Baronet, 1805-1836.

### Janet Sinclair (of Ulbster), Lady Colquhoun, 1799-1846.

Sir James Colquhoun of Luss, third British Baronet, was born at Edinburgh, on the 28th, and baptized on the 30th, of September 1774.[1]

In early life, when he was James Colquhoun, younger of Luss, he served in the army. Having raised a company in his neighbourhood, as was customary at the time by such as held his position in life, he was appointed its captain, and at the age of eighteen joined the 97th or Inverness-shire Regiment of Foot. There is a portrait of him at Rossdhu in his uniform, painted by Raeburn, soon after he was gazetted. His cousin, Colonel Grant of Grant, afterwards Earl of Seafield, who was about the same age, joined the same regiment as captain, and the friendship which thus originated between them continued throughout their lives. As Mr. Colquhoun, younger of Luss, he also raised a corps of volunteers on the family estate, called the Luss and Row Volunteers, and was appointed Major of the Dumbartonshire Battalion of Volunteers, in 1804, by Lord Elphinstone, then Lord Lieutenant of Dumbartonshire, and his knowledge of military affairs was of great advantage to him as commanding officer, enabling him to train the volunteers thoroughly, who consequently became very efficient. Sir James had a very powerful voice, and was better heard in giving the word of command than any other officer in the regiments where he served.

In these days the numbers of the volunteers were greater, and the service even more popular, than at the present time, for Napoleon Bonaparte was then at the height of his power and threatening the country with invasion. In the army Sir James rose to the rank of major.

In June 1799 he married Janet Sinclair, younger daughter of the Right Honourable Sir John Sinclair of Ulbster, Baronet, by his first wife, Sarah

---

[1] Scots Magazine, vol. xxxvi. p. 502, and Edinburgh Record of Baptisms.

Maitland, only child and heiress of Alexander Maitland, Esquire, of Stoke-Newington, in the county of Middlesex. Their contract of marriage is dated at Edinburgh, 11th June 1799. Sir John Sinclair thereby provided the sum of £7500 with his daughter.

In the year 1801 Major Colquhoun was elected Member of Parliament for the county of Dumbarton. He was then designated " Major James Colquhoun, younger of Luss." He was re-elected to represent the same county in Parliament in the year 1802, and sat till the year 1806.

Sir James was in the thirty-first year of his age when he succeeded his father, in the year 1805. He was served heir-male of taillie and provision to him in the lands and barony of Luss, Ardochbeg, etc., on the 21st of June 1806 ; and heir in general to him on the 3d of March 1807.[1] On the 25th of the same month he was infefted in the lands and barony of Luss, with the exception of those parts in which he had been infefted on the 26th of September 1794, as before mentioned.[2] Some years after his succession significant testimony was given that the ancient feud between his family and that of the Macgregors, which had frequently led to such disastrous results to both, had given place to feelings of hearty good-will and friendship. On an invitation from Sir James and Lady Colquhoun, Sir John Murray Macgregor and Lady Macgregor came on a visit to Rossdhu. The two baronets visited Glenfruin. They were accompanied by Lady Colquhoun and Misses Helen and Catherine Colquhoun. After the battle-field had been carefully inspected by the descendants of the combatants, Sir John Murray Macgregor insisted on shaking hands with Sir James Colquhoun and the whole party on the spot where it was supposed that the battle had been hottest. On the occasion of the same visit to Rossdhu, the party ascended Benlomond, which dominates so grandly over Lochlomond. On the summit of this lofty mountain, Sir John Murray Macgregor danced a highland reel with Miss Catherine Colquhoun, afterwards Mrs. Millar of Earnoch. Sir John was then fully eighty years of age.

When he returned from that excursion to Rossdhu Sir John's activity was unabated. He insisted on walking the ladies at a speedy pace up

[1] Original Retours of Special and General Service at Rossdhu.
[2] Original Instrument of Sasine, ibid.

and down the large drawing-room, having one lady on each arm. The reason which he assigned for this indoor exercise, after so much exertion out of doors, was to prevent the ladies from becoming stiff.

Subsequently to this visit to Rossdhu, Sir James and Lady Colquhoun, whilst staying with some friends in Perthshire, met with Sir John Murray Macgregor. He courteously invited them to visit him at Lanrick, afterwards called Clangregor Castle. But this visit, if made out, seems to have been tame and uninteresting compared with the first friendly meeting of the representatives of the old antagonistic clans of Colquhoun and Macgregor on the scene of former strife.

On his succession to the Luss estates in 1805, Sir James Colquhoun withdrew from the army, and resided for the most part at Rossdhu, occupying himself with the superintendence and improvement of his estate, and spent large sums of money in embellishing the grounds and policies of Rossdhu. Formerly the only entrance to the old castle was what was called the Port Avenue. This avenue was quite straight, with a row of old lime, beech, and elm trees on each side of it.

The north avenue, with two lodges, was formed by Sir James Colquhoun's father. This was a great improvement, and almost indispensable in travelling between Luss and Rossdhu. Sir James Colquhoun, however, made other two approaches to Rossdhu. The first was the middle avenue, with one lodge, near the bridge of Finlas, and the second the south avenue, two miles and a half in length, which extends along the shores of the lake ; and he built two lodges, with a beautiful archway, at the entrance. He also enclosed the policies by a park wall, with a stone cope, extending to about three miles and a half in length. The Ross Finlays, which was an arable farm of 120 acres, was now included in the policy, and the fences which divided it removed. The moss, which now forms part of the deer-park, and was upwards of 70 acres in extent, and covered with long heather, was drained and topdressed with six or eight inches of gravelly soil, and now yields most excellent pasturage. It was no doubt from this black moss that the demesne derived the name of Rossdhu, or the black promontory.

By his tenants and dependants among whom he lived Sir James Colquhoun was much beloved ; and, well acquainted with their character and circumstances, he was friendly, considerate, and kind in all his transactions and intercourse with them. In him the widow and the orphan always found a friend.

Drumfork was the first purchase of land made by this baronet, when he was a very young man. It marched with the estate of Colgrain, and was afterwards exchanged with Mr. Dennistoun for a farm he possessed in Glenfruin.

On the 23d of November 1818, Sir James obtained a disposition from the trustees of Sir John Sinclair of Ulbster, Baronet, with consent of Sir John himself, of the right of patronage of the parishes and parish churches of Bower, Latheron, Olrig, Dunnet, Watten, and the united parishes of Halkirk and Skinnan, in the lordship and barony of Berriedale and shire of Caithness.[1] In the right of patronage of the last three of these parishes he was infefted on the 6th of July 1819, and in the patronage of the first three on the 8th of the same month and year.[2] The purchase price of these patronages was £2200.

Sir James Colquhoun added very much to the size of his estate, and made still larger purchases than his grandfather had done, having invested altogether about £180,000 in the purchase of land.

The purchase of the estate of Arrochar, which had been possessed by the Macfarlanes for five centuries and a half, was made by Sir James in the year 1821 from Robert Ferguson of Raith, for £78,000. The disposition made to him of the lands and barony of Arrochar by Mr. Ferguson is dated 21st May 1821;[3] and he was infefted in them on the 11th of November 1833.[4] The last laird of the name of Macfarlane who possessed them was William. He sold them in the year 1785 to William Ferguson of Raith for £28,000, the rental being then under £600 a year. But in the course of a few years the valuable woods were sufficient to pay the purchase-money; and the lands had tripled in value when Robert Ferguson, the son of William, who had purchased them from the Macfarlane family, sold them to Sir James Colquhoun.

---

[1] Original Disposition at Rossdhu.

[2] Original Instruments of Sasine, ibid.

[3] Original Disposition and Assignation, at Rossdhu.

[4] Original Instrument of Sasine, ibid.

3 E

On the 9th of February 1824, Sir James made a disposition of part of the lands and barony of Luss in favour of himself in liferent, and Mr. James Colquhoun his eldest son in fee, whom failing, to the other heirs of entail therein mentioned;[1] and they were infefted therein on the 12th of the same month.[2]

There were two farms in Glenfruin, called Ballievoulin and Ballienock, known in the feudal titles by the name of Auchinvenalmoulin, which had been left to three sisters called Macwalter. The eldest sister, Jean Macwalter, had the half of Ballienock, with the house, mill, and garden of Ballievoulin, and her husband's name was Dougald Campbell. Another sister, Ann Macwalter, had the farm of Ballievoulin, less the house, mill, and garden, and her husband's name was Cunningham. The third sister, Janet, had the other half of Ballienock, and was twice married, to men of the same name, M'Auslan. The eldest sister's portion of Ballienock, with the house, mill, and garden of Ballievoulin, extending to a third part of the whole, was purchased by Sir James Colquhoun, the second British Baronet, in the year 1801, from John Campbell, eldest son of Jean Macwalter, deceased. Mr. Dennistoun of Colgrain bought Ballievoulin and the other half of Ballienock, and in the year 1825 his son, then Mr. Dennistoun of Colgrain, exchanged with Sir James Colquhoun these lands of Ballievoulin and half of Ballienock for the lands of Drumfork, which was the first purchase of land made by Sir James.

During the lifetime of Sir James's father, as previously stated, negotiations, which resulted in nothing, had taken place between Sir James, then younger of Luss, and the Laird of Camstradden, with reference to the purchase of the estate of Camstradden by the former. But, in the year 1826, Sir James purchased these lands from Robert Colquhoun, the proprietor, for £32,500. The minute of sale of the whole of the lands of Camstradden, Aldochlay, Auchengaven, Hill of Camstradden, and Slate Crag, the lands of Collichippen, Tomglass, Torr, and High Shandons, all in the parish of Luss, by Robert Colquhoun to Sir James Colquhoun of Luss, Baronet, is dated 21st March, and 3d and 6th days of April 1826.[3] Sir James was

[1] Original Disposition at Rossdhu.          [3] Original Minute at Rossdhu.
[2] Original Instrument of Sasine, *ibid.*

iufefted in these lands on 29th May following.[1] The estate of Camstradden was thus reacquired by the Colquhouns of Luss after it had been possessed by a branch of the Colquhoun family as a separate property for nearly four centuries and a half.

In the year 1827, Sir James purchased from the trustees and commissioners on the sequestrated estate of James Buchanan, merchant, Glasgow, for £50,400, the estate of Ardenconnel, comprehending the lands of Laggarie and Blairvuthan, with the croft and pendicle of Feoline, the ferry of the Row with the fishings, the town and lands of Ardenconnel, property and superiority, and the piece of ground called Ferry Acre, excepting four and a half acres ; also a part of the common muir, with the privilege of wreck upon the shore of the Laggarie, all in the parish of Row, with the teinds and fishings ; the lands of Letteruelbeg, alias Letteruel-mouline, extending to a four merk land, with the teinds, fishings, and part of the common muir, and privilege of wreck ; the lands of Wester Kilbride and Blairvaddock, with the teinds ; the lands of Stuckiehoich, extending to a three merk land, and a part of the common muir, with the teinds and fishings ; and the lands of Stucknaduff and Pofile, called Chappelvarroch. Sir James Colquhoun also purchased, in the year 1829, from James Oswald of Shieldhall, for £2990, the lands of Gortan, on Lochlong, extending to a 40s. land of old extent, with the fishings. The last purchase of land made by Sir James was in the year 1834, from William Dick Macfarlane, Captain in the Ninety-Second Regiment of Foot, for £4000, of the lands of Easter and Wester Blairnairns in Glenfruin. extending to a four merk six shilling and eight penny land of old extent. These acquisitions are all situated in the parish of Row, with the exception of Gortan, which is in the parish of Arrochar.

It may be interesting to mention, in connection with this family, that the son of Mrs. Macfarlane, by her marriage with Mr. Nolan,—for she was twice married,—was Captain Nolan, who was killed in the Crimea while gallantly advancing with the Light Cavalry Brigade to charge a Russian battery, in the famous cavalry charge at Balaklava.

The three baronets of Luss, before the present Sir James, purchased up no less than fourteen lairdships, but some of them were small.

[1] Original Instrument of Sasine, *ibid.*

Among the eminent foreigners who shared in the hospitality of Sir James Colquhoun at Rossdhu was Cæsar Malan, of Geneva. When in 1825 Monsieur Malan, with whom Mr. James Colquhoun, younger of Luss, had resided for a year at Geneva, was staying at Rossdhu for a few days, Sir James, in July of that year, obtained for him the degree of Doctor of Divinity from the University of Glasgow. Monsieur Malan had, nine years before, separated from the National Church of Geneva on account of its Socinianism, and opened a place of worship in his own garden outside the city. But the hostility displayed against him by the magistrates was such as to give reason to fear that he would be compelled to serve as a soldier. To prevent his enlistment by securing his ecclesiastical status, the theological degree was conferred; and under its protection he was saved from being forced into the army.[1]

In the summer of the year 1833 Sir James's health became seriously affected, and from that time to his death frequent reference is made to that subject by Lady Colquhoun in her journal. On 2d June 1833, she writes, " I have been in Edinburgh with Sir James. His medical attendant there (Dr. Wood) has prescribed various remedies, but evidently thinks seriously of his complaints."[2]

Sir James's health somewhat improved, and in the spring of the following year, after he had returned from Edinburgh to Rossdhu, the same affectionate hand thus writes :—" April 20, 1834. Once more settled in our beautiful abode, where nature, or rather nature's God, has done so much to charm the eye. I have much reason for gratitude that my dear husband has been so much benefited by medical advice while in Edinburgh."[3] But this improvement was not permanent. Writing on 13th September 1835, Lady Colquhoun says,—" Have been in Edinburgh, where my dear husband's health called me. He consulted Dr. Abercrombie and Dr. Wood. The opinion of both seems to be that his complaints are alarming. I have long thought so."

Sir James having been worse than usual on 20th of September, he and Lady Colquhoun fixed on going to Edinburgh to reside. Sir James died there on 3d February 1836, in the sixty-second year of his age, and his remains

---

[1] Dr. Hamilton's Memoir of Lady Colquhoun, p. 150.    [2] Ibid. p. 172.    [3] Ibid. p. 174.

were interred in the old chapel of Rossdhu.[1] His funeral is thus described by Dr. Hamilton :—" In a few weeks some of the mourners who encircled the grave of Sir John Sinclair [Sir James's father-in-law, who died December 21, 1835, aged eighty-one years] in Holyrood Chapel, were called to join the sable procession which, up the vale of Leven and through the solemnized hamlets, conveyed to the ancestral cemetery the dust of his son-in-law. As it passed, one aged clansman was propped up in bed, and when he saw the hearse containing the lifeless form of his much-loved landlord the old man fainted away, and everywhere was manifested the emotion of a people reverential to old lineage, and grateful to the proprietor whom constant residence had converted into their friend and protector. It was a fine winter's day, and the sunshine had suspended the frost, when round the old 'chapel' were congregated the tenantry of Luss, Row, and Arrochar, as well as many friends, and the gentlemen of the county, and borne on the shoulders of three Grants and three Colquhouns, the coffin was lowered into its appropriate resting-place."[2] This usage has obtained since the time of Sir James Grant.

Another account states that, in addition to the county gentlemen and the tenantry of the estates, and the relatives of the deceased Sir James Colquhoun, there were present to pay this last tribute of respect to his memory some of the old retainers of the family, whose heads had become blanched in the successive service of three or four generations, but who still retained undiminished that feeling of clanship and family attachment which, although now fast fading away, constituted a distinguishing characteristic of the feudalism of a former age.

## JANET LADY COLQUHOUN.

Lady Colquhoun survived Sir James more than ten years, and a memoir of her by James Hamilton, D.D., was published in 1849, and has passed through four editions.

---

[1] The old chapel, which is now in ruins, is believed to have been built about the beginning of the twelfth century, or perhaps earlier. The remains of it still standing are used as the burying-place of the family.

[2] Dr. Hamilton's Memoir of Lady Colquhoun, pp. 182, 183.

A brief sketch of her cannot here be omitted.

Janet Sinclair, who was born in London on the 17th April 1781, was, as already stated, the younger daughter of the Right Honourable Sir John Sinclair of Ulbster, Baronet, by his first wife, Sarah Maitland, only child and heiress of Alexander Maitland, Esquire of Stoke-Newington.

Sir John Sinclair is so well known as having been a man of distinguished abilities, and for his indefatigable endeavours to promote the improvement of agriculture, having founded the Board of Agriculture in 1793, and also for his literary labours, including his Statistical Account of Scotland, that any extended notice of him here is not required.

Lady Colquhoun lost her mother when four years old. Of the marriage of Sir John Sinclair with Miss Maitland, there was only another child, a daughter, called Hannah, and the sisters were much attached to each other. Their childhood was passed at Thurso Castle, under the care of their paternal grandmother, Lady Janet Sinclair, who was a daughter of William Lord Strathnaver, and sister to Lady Helen Colquhoun. They were then sent to school at Stoke-Newington, near London, where their mother had been educated. At the respective ages of fifteen and sixteen they returned to Edinburgh, and were introduced into society there, which at that period was much frequented by the nobility and gentry of Scotland.

In 1799, as already stated, Janet Sinclair, when in the nineteenth year of her age, married Major James Colquhoun, eldest son of Sir James Colquhoun of Luss, and she became Lady Colquhoun in 1805, when her father-in-law died, and her husband succeeded to his title and estates. Lady Colquhoun occupied herself in superintending the education of her two daughters, whom she taught herself, with the exception of some branches of education, for which she obtained masters when in Edinburgh during the winter months.

She and Sir James resided chiefly at Rossdhu, where her sister Hannah paid lengthened visits, but in 1818, Hannah was seized with an illness of which she died on the 26th May of that year. A memoir of her was afterwards published by the Rev. Legh Richmond. Her death was much deplored and regretted by Lady Colquhoun.

On the 29th of June, same year, a Bible Society was formed at Luss,

called "the Luss and Arrochar Bible Society." Though not the originator
of this Society, Lady Colquhoun was very useful in putting it into operation ; and it flourished beyond her expectations.

Lady Colquhoun was a frequent visitant of the dwellings of the poor in
the neighbourhood. On these occasions she regretted to observe a sad
want of neatness and good housekeeping in their domestic arrangements,
and convinced of the necessity of the establishment of a school for girls,
in which they might be taught needlework, and other industrial arts particularly suitable to their sex and condition of life, she obtained and fitted
up a school-house, near Rossdhu, at her own expense, and appointed and
paid for a qualified female teacher. When the school was opened, she
visited it almost daily, and taught the elder class of girls at the Sunday-
school, which was held in the school-room. Soon the effects became percep-
tible to every observer, in the improved manners and happier appearance
of the children of the district. Their parents were gratified to find that
their daughters, from what they learned in the school, were able to do
many things which largely conduced to domestic economy and comfort.

When Lady Colquhoun came to reside at Rossdhu, and for many years
after, the minister of the parish of Luss was Dr. John Stuart,[1] who, though
not popular as a preacher, was famed as a scholar and as a botanist.
Under the sanction of the Church of Scotland he translated the Scriptures
into Gaelic. His manse-garden at Luss contained many rare and valuable
flowers and shrubs. During the summer months Dr. Stuart was often
visited by men of science and others, who were attracted by his reputation
as a naturalist, and they were treated by the doctor with much hospitality.
This, it would appear, was so conspicuous, that it caused considerable
annoyance to the innkeeper at Luss, as we learn from reminiscences of
early life by a writer in Blackwood's Magazine.

"I well remember," says he, "in my boyhood the picturesque manse of
Luss, filled with guests all the summer. Indeed, no strangers of distinction would have missed the opportunity of inspecting the rare botanical
collection contained in the manse-garden, or of becoming acquainted with

[1] Dr. John Stuart, who had been suc-     was admitted minister of Luss in 1777, and
cessively minister of Arrochar and Weems,   died 24th May 1821.

its scholarly and scientific possessor. The hospitalities of the manse were, however, a perpetual source of irritation to the drunken innkeeper, who fancied himself robbed of his annual harvest; and one night, when the manse was very full, and the inn very empty, he slyly took down his sign-post and stuck it over the minister's parlour window. Dr. Stuart's first intimation that he had set up in the public line was the fiery visage of Boniface glaring in upon the breakfast-table with the ominous words, ' Since ye 've ta'en awa a' the company, ye must just tak' the sign tae.' "

In the year 1820 or 1821, Lady Colquhoun suffered from enfeebled health, and she continued long in this condition. It was now that she occupied herself in preparing for the press those excellent religious works, which acquired considerable popularity from the refined and elegant taste, the matured judgment, the graceful ease, and natural truthfulness with which they are written.

On 21st November 1824 she and Sir James went to Edinburgh to witness the marriage of her sister Julia with George fourth Earl of Glasgow.[1] One of Lady Colquhoun's favourite ideas was the erection of a chapel at Helensburgh, a much frequented watering-place on the estuary of the Clyde, and upon the Luss estate. This was the first of several church-extension movements to which she largely contributed.

For many years Lady Colquhoun was the patroness and an influential director of various benevolent societies in Edinburgh, such as the Ladies' Association for Promoting Female Education in India, in connection with the Scottish Missions there ; the Ladies' Society in Scotland in Aid of the Home Mission of the Presbyterian Church in Ireland ; and the Ladies' Auxiliary Association in connexion with the Gaelic School Society.

Whilst resident in Edinburgh, she undertook, in co-operation with some other benevolent ladies, the visitation of the poor, each having a certain

[1] Lady Glasgow survived her husband from 1843 till 19th February 1868, when she died at Edinburgh. She was interred on Tuesday, 25th of that month, in the family vault attached to the church at Renfrew. On the coffin was placed, previous to the reading of the funeral service at the vault, a very beautiful wreath of camellias, etc., sent by friends from Cumbrae as a last token of affection for one whom they all deeply mourned. Lady Glasgow's jointure-house was in the island of Cumbrae. In the winter season her ladyship resided chiefly in Edinburgh ; but went to London in spring, where she had a house in Chesham Place.

district, and she occupied a considerable portion of her time in this bene-
ficent ministry.

At the Disruption of the Church of Scotland, 18th May 1843, Lady
Colquhoun attached herself to the Free Church, and was a munificent
contributor to the various schemes of that Church.

In the year 1846, Lady Colquhoun was in an enfeebled state of health,
and in the winter of that year she was recommended to remove to England.
In a letter to her daughter-in-law, Mrs. John Colquhoun, dated Rossdhu,
21st September 1846, she thus writes:—" You may perhaps be surprised
to hear that Dr. Simpson has ordered me to England for the winter, pressing it much. I felt it a duty to accede, although not very willingly, and
Helen and Mr. Reade have promised to meet me wherever I may go.
James has agreed to my taking little man with me, so he and I are to set
off on our travels in November. No place is yet decided upon, and I feel
like Abraham, 'going out, not knowing whither I go.' I am continuing
better and feel stronger. We are all returned here now for good."

When this letter was written, which was only three weeks before the
death of Lady Colquhoun, no apprehensions were entertained that she was
so near the close of her life. Her last illness was brought on by a cold,
contracted in consequence of her having been overtaken, on 29th September
1846, in a shower. Next morning she complained of sore throat and fever,
and before the 4th of October she had taken to that bed from which she
was never again to arise. She died full of faith and hope, on Wednesday,
the 21st of that month, in the sixty-sixth year of her age. Her funeral,
which was private, took place on the 27th. She was interred in the
chapel, which ten years before had received the remains of her husband,
wearing, in compliance with her own request, her wedding-ring and a
mourning-ring containing Sir James's hair.

Lady Colquhoun was the author of the following works :—

1. Despair and Hope : Exemplified in a Narrative founded on Fact, 1822.
2. Thoughts on the Religious Profession, and Defective Practice of the
   Higher Classes of Society, 1823.
3. Impressions of the Heart, relative to the Nature and Excellence of
   Genuine Religion, 1825.

3 F

4. The Kingdom of God : containing a Brief Account of its Properties, Trials, Privileges, and Duration, 1836.

5. The World's Religion as contrasted with Genuine Christianity, 1839.

These works have been collected and published in one volume.

Sir James and Lady Colquhoun had three sons and two daughters. The sons were—

1. James, present Baronet.

2. John, who was born at the house of his maternal grandfather, in Charlotte Square, Edinburgh, on 7th February 1805. The first part of his education was received at Rossdhu from a tutor. Mr. Colquhoun afterwards attended classes in the High School of Edinburgh for a short time, and then went to a private school in Lincolnshire, and concluded his education at the University of Edinburgh. He entered the army as an officer in the 33d Regiment, and in the course of a year or two he exchanged into the 4th Dragoon Guards. He sold his commission before his marriage, and retired from the service. Mr. Colquhoun is the author of " The Moor and the Loch," " Rocks and Rivers," " Salmon Casts and Stray Shots," " Sporting Days," and other works on kindred subjects. These publications are all very popular, and have gone through several editions. Mr. Colquhoun married, on 29th January 1834, Frances Sarah, fourth daughter of Ebenezer Fuller-Maitland, Esquire, of Park Place, Henley-on-Thames, in the county of Berks, and has issue, four sons and five daughters, viz.-—

1. James, born on 3d March 1835 ; an officer in the army. 2. Alan John, born on 19th September 1838 ; he is also an officer in the army. 3. Roderick William, born on 29th August 1847. 4. Sutherland Grant, born on 20th March 1850.—1. Frances Mary. 2. Helen Augusta, married, on 8th September 1863, the Rev. Norman Macleod, now minister of Blair-Athole. 3. Flora Maitland. 4. Jessie St. Clair. 5. Lucy Bethia, married at St. John's Episcopal Church, Edinburgh, on 23d June 1869, Alfred Saunders Walford, son of Alfred Walford, Esq., Belington, Cheshire.

3. William, who was born at Rossdhu, 1st October 1806. Along

with his brothers, he was educated by a tutor at Rossdhu for some years. He afterwards attended private English schools, first in Lincolnshire and subsequently in Buckinghamshire. From the years 1828 to 1830 he was an under-graduate of Trinity College, Cambridge, and he took his degree of Master of Arts in 1831.

In the year 1843, Mr. Colquhoun purchased from the late Colonel William Mure of Caldwell the lands of Auchendennan-Lindsay, in the parish of Bonhill. The price was £12,200. Mr. Colquhoun only retained this éstate for about a year, having sold it to a neighbouring proprietor, Mr. William Campbell of Tilliechewan. As an instance of the great demand for property on the banks of Lochlomond, it may be mentioned that although the rental was very little, if at all, increased, Mr. Campbell's son, Mr. James Campbell, now of Tilliechewan, sold the lands of Auchendennan, within the last few years, for £23,000, to Mr. George Martin, of Glasgow, who has erected a large mansion-house on the property. The price of the lands had thus more than doubled in the course of twenty years. There are three adjoining properties named Auchendennan, which are described in an old local verse as —

> " Auchendennan-Dennistoun,
> Auchendennan-Ree,
> Auchendennan-Lindsay,
> The best of all the Three."

The rapid increase in the value of Auchendennan Lindsay may well warrant the opinion expressed in these lines.

The daughters were—

1. Sarah Maitland, who was born 8th August 1802. Miss Colquhoun died, unmarried, at Rossdhu, on the 28th of January 1865; and her mortal remains were interred in the old chapel at Rossdhu. Along with her mother, Lady Colquhoun, Miss Colquhoun became a member of the Free Church at its formation in 1843, and she continued in that communion till her death. Her mother, Lady Colquhoun, by her last will and testament, dated on 14th July 1846, bequeathed to her the copyrights of whatever books she had

written, with whatever sums might be raised from them, should they go through any more editions.[1]

2. Helen, who was born 7th November 1807. She married John Page-Reade of Sutton House, near Ipswich, in the county of Suffolk, a Deputy-Lieutenant and Justice of the Peace for that county. The marriage was celebrated at Edinburgh, on the 9th of April 1829. Her mother has the following entry in her Diary respecting their marriage :—" 18, Circus, Edinburgh, April 5, 1829.—This is the last Sabbath previous to my beloved Helen's leaving me. I feel strangely in the prospect of her being removed from my care, and sorrowfully when I think of the days that are past, her infant years, as well as those when she has been my sweet and cheerful companion. This marriage is the subject of my ardent prayer; therefore it is well, it is right." After having been long in a declining state of health, she died at Florence, on the 17th of October 1852, leaving behind her an affectionate husband and an only son. She was interred in the Protestant burying-ground at Florence, and her grave is marked by a marble tablet, with a short inscription, and the text, " Blessed are the dead who die in the Lord."[2]   Of this marriage there is an only child, James Colquhoun Revell Reade, who was born in May 1839, in Harley Street, London.   He was educated at Harrow and Christ Church, Oxford, and was called to the English Bar in 1868.

---

[1] Original Holograph Will at Rossdhu.
[2] Dr. Hamilton's Memoir of Lady Colquhoun, pp. 157, 158.

## XXII.—Sir JAMES COLQUHOUN,

### Twenty-sixth of Colquhoun, and Twenty-eighth of Luss, Fourth and Present British Baronet.

Jane Abercromby [of Birkenbog], Lady Colquhoun.

Sir James Colquhoun, the fourth and present British Baronet, was born at the house of his maternal grandfather, in Charlotte Square, Edinburgh, on 7th February 1804.   He was educated at Rossdhu, by a private tutor, for some years; he then passed a short time at the High School of Edinburgh; and after attending a private school in Lincolnshire, in England, he became a student in the University of Edinburgh.   Thence he went to Geneva, and prosecuted his studies in various branches of learning with the Rev. Cæsar Malan.   This was followed by a grand tour which he made through Switzerland, Germany, Italy, and other foreign parts.

On the death of his father, which, as already stated, took place on the 3d of February 1836, Mr. Colquhoun succeeded to the title and estates of the family.   It is unnecessary to enumerate all the numerous feudal titles that were made up by Sir James on his succession to his father, which, of course, were all in accordance with the forms of feudal investiture in landed estates then in use.   Since that time these forms have been greatly simplified by several beneficial Acts of the Legislature.   It may however be mentioned, in reference to some of the leading lands and baronies, that, on the 1st of September 1836, Sir James was served heir-male of tailzie and provision to his father in the lands and barony of Luss; and on a precept from Chancery he was infefted in these lands on the 2d of November following.   On the 2d of September that year Sir James Colquhoun also expeded a general service as eldest lawful son and nearest lawful heir to his father.   He was infefted in the lands of Camstradden on 2d November thereafter, on a precept of *clare constat* by himself, as the feudal superior.   On a precept from Chancery following on another service as heir to his father, he was infefted in the barony of Arrochar on 22d of that month, same year.   He was also infefted, on a precept of *clare constat* by himself, as the feudal superior, in the lands of Gorton, in the barony of Luss, on 10th November 1837.

On the 13th of January 1840, Sir James was served heir of tailzie by the bailies of the Canongate of Edinburgh to Sir Humphrey Colquhoun, fifth baronet of Nova Scotia, his great-great great-grandfather, who died in the year 1718, and, in virtue of the entail and diploma of reinvestiture, resumed the original title of 1625.

Since his succession to the Luss estates, Sir James has rebuilt almost every farm-steading on the property, and many of the cottages. The new farm-houses are ornamental and substantial buildings, in a style of simple architectural taste, and the appearance of them bespeaks the attention paid to provide every convenience and comfort for the possessors. Sir James also greatly embellished the lower grounds by the transplantation of trees, which has been effected by the use of the ingenious machine of which Sir Henry Stewart was the inventor. By this means the large area of ground reclaimed by his father, called the Moss, has been covered with trees of from fifty to sixty years' growth, as well as the Rossfinlas Park, and other parts of the grounds. So extensively has this process of transplantation been carried out by Sir James that he has done more in this way than even the inventor, Sir Henry Stewart, himself. The process has been very successful, all the transplanted trees being in the most thriving state, and many of them are double the size they were when transplanted.

Besides improving his property in this and other respects, Sir James has made an important addition to it by the purchase of lands. In the year 1862 he purchased from her Grace, Ann Colquhoun Cunningham, Duchess Dowager of Argyll, for £50,000, the estate of Ardincaple, in the parish of Row, comprehending the lands of Wester, Easter, and Middle Ardincaple, and feus appertaining thereto. As Helensburgh is bounded on the west by these lands, they are a very important acquisition to the proprietor of that flourishing watering-place. Ardincaple was originally the inheritance of the family of Ardincaple of that Ilk, who were succeeded in it about the middle of the sixteenth century by the Macaulays, who held Ardincaple for about two centuries. The Macfarlanes, Ardincaples, and the Macaulays were for centuries the neighbouring clans to the Colquhouns, by whom, amidst the ever-recurring feuds and forays of clanship in former times they were most effectually kept in check. The properties once possessed by these three clans have gradually and peacefully come by purchase to swell the broad acres of their old enemies the Colquhouns of Luss. In the numerous acquisitions which the Colquhoun family have made of the territories of their neighbours, as recorded in this work, it may be noticed that they have always given the most ample prices to the previous proprietors. Ardincaple is an instance of this—the price paid by Sir James being considered very high, and far above any former prices realized for the same lands. Arrochar, already mentioned, is a still more remarkable instance of the high and handsome prices paid by the Colquhoun family for their territorial acquisitions.

In the same year in which Sir James Colquhoun purchased Ardincaple, he acquired from the burgh of Dumbarton, for £2500, the salmon-fishings in the rivers Leven and Clyde, as possessed by that burgh. The salmon-fishings in the upper half of the Leven, next to Lochlomond, had previously been in the possession of the Colquhouns of Luss for many generations, having been purchased by Sir John Colquhoun of Luss along with the salmon-fishings in Lochlomond, etc., from James Duke of Lennox in 1652.

In the year 1837, Sir James was elected Member of Parliament for the county of Dumbarton, and he continued to represent that county till the year 1842. In the year 1837 he was appointed Lord-Lieutenant of the county of Dumbarton, and he still holds that office.

Sir James married, on 14th June 1843, Jane, second daughter of Sir Robert Abercromby of Birkenbog, Baronet. Lady Colquhoun died on 3d May 1844, leaving one son—James Colquhoun, younger of Colquhoun and Luss.

## XXIII.—JAMES COLQUHOUN, Younger of Colquhoun and Luss.

He was born in George Street, Edinburgh, on 30th March 1844. When ten years of age he was sent to a private school in England, taught by the Rev. Mr. Faithfull, Rector of Hatfield, Hertfordshire; and four years afterwards he became a student at Harrow, under Dr. Vaughan, now Master of the Temple. Mr. Colquhoun continued at Harrow for three years and a half. He afterwards, in October 1863, went to Trinity College, Cambridge. Having completed the usual course of study, he took his degree of B.A. in March 1867. In the following year he travelled in Germany, Austria, and Holland.

In the year 1868, Mr. Colquhoun was made a Justice of the Peace for the county of Dumbarton, and in the following year he was appointed a Deputy-Lieutenant of the same county.

### Armorial Bearings.

*Shield:* *Argent*, a saltier ingrailed, *sable*.

*Supporters:* Two ratch-hounds *argent*, collared *sable*.

*Crest:* A hart's head couped *gules*, attired *argent*.

*Motto:* *Si je puis.*

*Badge:* The sauch-tree.

*Slogan* or *War-Cry:* Cnoc Elachan.—[The knoll of the sauch or sallow, a species of willow.]

*Principal Seat:* Rossdhu House, Luss. The other seats are, Arroquhar House, on Loch Long; Ardlui, at the head of Lochlomond; and Ardincaple Castle, Helensburgh; all in Dumbartonshire.

Colquhoune of Lees

www.ingramcontent.com/pod-product-compliance
Lightning Source LLC
Chambersburg PA
CBHW022016110726

47901CB00006B/1554